PHASES OF THE MOON

STORIES OF SIX DECADES

ROBERT SILVERBERG

ibooks

new york

www.ibooks.net

DISTRIBUTED BY SIMON & SCHUSTER, INC.

phases of the moon

contents

For Peter Hamilton and Harry Harrison
who bought the first one

INTRODUCTION

All through my adolescence there was very little I wanted as badly as to see a story bearing my name appear in one of the science-fiction magazines. I was not the happiest of boys—younger and for a long time smaller than most of my classmates, too bright and much too smart alecky for my own good, and—an only child—not very well equipped for the give-and-take of ordinary daily dealings with ordinary people. By no coincidence, I also was a passionate sf-f fan, a devoted reader since discovering H.G. Wells' *The Time Machine* and Jules Verne's *Twenty Thousand Leagues Under the Sea* when I was ten. When I discovered the science-fiction magazines of the day—*Astounding Science Fiction, Amazing Stories, Startling Stories,* and the rest of that gaudy group—I began devouring them voraciously and collected all the back issues I could find.

In those days the magazines were the center of the sf world; any member of the small cult-group that called itself "fandom" who sold a story to one of the professional magazines attained an increment of instant fame and prestige that can barely be comprehended today. (Among the writers who emerged from fandom in the 1940s via those gaudy-looking magazines were such people as Ray Bradbury, Isaac Asimov, Frederik Pohl, and Arthur C. Clarke.) If I could manage somehow to sell a story, I told myself—just one story!—it would in a single stroke free me from every aspect of teenage insecurity and admit me to the adult world of achievement and community respect. Or so I believed.

And to some degree I was right, since my debut as a professional writer coincided with my transition from awkward, uncertain, maladjusted adolescent to poised and confident adult. But it didn't happen overnight. I began writing stories when I was barely into my teens—the first, "The Last Days of Saturn," written in collaboration with my schoolmate (and lifelong friend) Saul Diskin, must surely be one of the worst science-fiction stories ever spawned—and went on writing and submitting them to the sf magazines all through my high-school years, without the slightest success. Eventually, of course, success did come, but there were a few ironic complications along the way.

For one thing, my first sale (barring a couple of semiprofessional things) was a novel that was to be published in hard covers. You might argue that selling a book to a major New York publisher was a bigger achievement than selling a short story to a pulp magazine, and you would be correct. But I didn't see it that way. All I saw was that the book, since it wouldn't be sold on newsstands and thus easily available to impecunious young men, would be far less visible and impressive to my friends in fandom than, say, a short story printed in the awesomely prestigious magazine *Astounding Science Fiction*, which everybody read. So that book sale, significant though it was to my career, failed to transform my self-image in the way I had hoped.

But just a few weeks after the sale of that novel I *did* sell a story to one of the professional science-fiction magazines — in January, 1954, during my second year of college. My skills had progressed considerably by then from my "Last Days of Saturn" period. I was, in fact, at work that month on what would become the very ambitious "Road to Nightfall," which is reprinted here to demonstrate the level of proficiency I had reached by the time I was nineteen. But it would take me another four years to find a publisher for that story. The story I did sell, there in the first month of 1954, was a much less ambitious item indeed, a slender thing called "Gorgon Planet," which is not included here because its only value to modern readers would be, alas, as a sort of historical curiosity.

Minor tale though it was, I did manage to get not one but *two* editors to express a willingness to publish it. I wrote it in September, 1953 for the first sf editor I had come to know personally: Harry Harrison, who had just taken over the editorship of three magazines. That summer he had asked me to write a short article explaining sf fandom for one of his magazines — my first real professional sale, though because it was nonfiction it didn't really count in my eyes. A few weeks later I brought him "Gorgon Planet," which he said wasn't quite good enough for his top-of-the-line magazine, *Science Fiction Adventures*, but which he was willing to publish in one of its lesser companions, *Rocket Stories* or *Space Science Fiction*. But this was not quite the long-dreamed-of first story sale, because *Rocket* and *Space* paid only on publication. A sale wasn't a sale until the check came in; a mere editorial acceptance wasn't enough to allow me to think of myself as having made the grade at one of the professional sf magazines.

Since Harry had said he was going to buy only North American rights, I was free to submit my story overseas — and immediately did, to *Nebula Science Fiction*, a pleasant, somewhat old-fashioned magazine that had begun operations in Scotland the year before. Reasoning correctly that *Nebula*'s youthful editor, Peter Hamilton, might be having difficulties getting stories from the better-known writers, I had begun sending him mine as soon as I learned of his magazine's existence. He replied with rejection letters containing friendly encouragement: "If you'd like to go on trying," he told me in July of 1953, "I'll be only too happy to continue to advise you. If you become a big name through *Nebula* it will be as big a thing for me (nearly) as it will be for you." And on January 11, 1954, he wrote to me to say, "You will be pleased to hear that I have accepted 'Gorgon Planet,' and it will appear in the 7th issue of *Nebula*." Through Hamilton's American agent I duly received my payment—$12.60—and, a few weeks later, a copy of the published story itself.

So I had made a story sale, a *real* sale, to one of the magazines at last! But where was my instant fame, where was my sudden prestige? Nowhere, as a matter of fact, because *Nebula* was virtually unknown in the United States and gained me no awe whatever from my friends in fandom. I would have to wait until the story appeared in *Rocket Stories* or *Space Science Fiction* for that. And *Rocket* and *Space* went out of business almost at once, neither publishing my story nor paying me for it. To Peter Hamilton of *Nebula* went the glory, such as it was, of bringing Robert Silverberg's first professionally published science fiction story into print.

All that happened half a century ago. I continued to write stories all through my college years, sold two or three more in 1954 and then broke through in 1955 with a great many acceptances all at once, and from then on have supported myself entirely as a freelance writer, concentrating primarily on science fiction and fantasy. My indefatigable bibliographer, Phil Stephensen-Payne, credits me with something like 550 published stories, though the number keeps creeping up as he and I discover still more in the archives of ephemeral magazines of the 1950s, and I suspect the real total is closer to 750. For someone whose original goal was to sell just *one* story, that's a considerable overfulfillment of quota.

But even after making those 550 sales—or 650, or 750, or however many it was—I still have not lost touch with the adolescent boy within me, the one who bought those issues of *Astounding Science Fiction* and *Thrilling Wonder Stories* in the far-off 1940s and dreamed of being a writer some day, by which he meant selling a story or two to one of those magazines. Whenever I see my name on a magazine cover, *he* reacts with astonishment and delight. So now, looking back over my long career, bringing together a representative sampling of stories from each of the six decades—so far—in which my work has found publication, I shake my head in wonder at the way it all turned out, and give silent thanks to all (and there were plenty of them, very few of them still alive) who helped me on my way.

Robert Silverberg

ONE

The 1950s

THE 1950s

The Eisenhower years: in hindsight, bland and safe. But they were also the period of the Cold War, the development of the hydrogen bomb, of the Egyptian seizure of the Suez Canal, of the Soviet crushing of the Hungarian uprising, of the launching of Sputnik, the first space satellite. I made my first story sales in 1954. Two years later I received my Bachelors degree from Columbia University, married, moved into a handsome apartment in uptown Manhattan, and was awarded a Hugo as the year's most promising new science-fiction writer. It was, for me, a time of vast evolutionary change — a time of entry into adult life and the beginning of my writing career.

ROAD TO NIGHTFALL (1954)

INTRODUCTION

I was in my late teens, a sophomore at Columbia University, when I began sketching this story in the fall of 1953. I had, I recall, been reading "Crossing Paris," a story by the French writer Marcel Ayme, in an old issue of *Partisan Review* — a literary magazine that I followed avidly in those days. It opened this way:

"The victim, already dismembered, lay in a corner of the cellar under wrappings of stained canvas. Jamblier, a little man with graying hair, a sharp profile, and feverish eyes, his belly girdled with a kitchen apron which came down to his feet, was shuffling across the concrete floor. At times he stopped short in his tracks to gaze with faintly flushed cheeks and uneasy eyes at the latch of the door. To relieve the tension of waiting, he took a mop which was soaking in an enameled bucket, and for the third time he washed the damp surface of the concrete to efface from it any last traces of blood which his butchery might have left there...."

It sounds like the beginning of a murder mystery, or a horror story. But in fact "Crossing Paris" is about the task of transporting black-market pork by suitcase through the Nazi-occupied city. The grim, bleak atmosphere and the situational-ethics anguish of the characters affected me profoundly, and almost at once I found myself translating the story's mood into science-fictional terms. What if I were to take Ayme's trick opening paragraph literally? That is, assume that the "victim" is not a pig but a man, as I had thought until the story's second page, and have the city suffering privations far more intense even than those of the war, so that cannibalism is being practiced and the illicit meat being smuggled by night through the streets is the most illicit meat of all.

I wrote the story in odd moments stolen from classwork over the next couple of months, intending to submit it to a contest one of the science-fiction magazines was running that year. A thousand-dollar prize (roughly ten thousand in modern purchasing power) was being offered for the best story of life in twenty-first century America written by a college undergraduate. For some reason I never entered the contest — missed the deadline, perhaps — but in the spring of 1954 I started sending my manuscript around to the science-fiction magazines. I was nobody at all then, an unpublished writer (although, somewhat to my own amazement, I had just had my first novel, *Revolt on Alpha C,* accepted and scheduled for publication in the summer of 1955.) Back the story came with great speed, just as all the fifteen or twenty other stories I had sent out over the previous six years had done. (I was about thirteen when I began submitting my stories to magazines.) When it had been to all seven or eight of the magazines that existed then, and every editor had told me how depressing, morbid, negative, and impossible to publish it was, I put it aside and wrote it off as a mistake.

A couple of years passed. I started selling my stories at a rapid clip and became, before I turned twenty-one, a well-known science-fiction writer. I was earning a nice living from my writing while still an undergraduate at Columbia.

Meanwhile, a young would-be writer from Cleveland had come to New York and moved in next door to me. His name was Harlan Ellison, and I have maintained a warm, turbulent, and indissoluble friendship with him ever since, despite enormous differences of opinion on almost everything on which it's possible to have differing opinions. One day in 1956 I mentioned to him that I had managed to sell every story I had written except one, which no editor would touch, and he demanded to see it. Harlan read it on the spot. "Brilliant!" he said, "Magnificent!" Or words to that effect. He was indignant that such a dark masterpiece should meet with universal rejection, and he vowed to find a publisher for it. Around that time, the gentle and unworldly Hans Stefan Santesson took over the editorship of a struggling magazine called *Fantastic Universe,* and Harlan, telling him I had written a story too daring for any of his rivals, essentially defied him not to buy it. Hans asked for the manuscript, commented in his mild way that the story was pretty strong stuff, and, after some hesitation, ran it in the July 1958 issue of his magazine.

After all these years I find it hard to see what was so hot to handle about "Road to Nightfall." Its theme — that the stress of life in a post-nuclear society could lead even to cannibalism — seemed to upset many of the editors who turned it down, but there was no taboo *per se* on the theme. (*Cf.* Damon Knight's 1950 classic, "To Serve Man," just to name one.) Most likely the protagonist's moral collapse at the end was the problem, for most sf editors of the time preferred stories in which the central figure transcends all challenges and arrives at a triumphant conclusion to his travail. That I had never published anything at the time was a further drawback. Theodore Sturgeon or Fritz Leiber, say, might have persuaded an editor to buy a story about cannibalism, or one with a downbeat ending — but a long downbeat cannibal story by an unknown author simply had too much going against it, and even after my name had become established it still required the full force of the Ellison juggernaut to win it a home.

To me it still seems like a pretty good job, especially for a writer who was a considerable distance short of his twentieth birthday. It moves along, it creates character and action and something of a plot, it gets its not-extremely-original point across effectively. If I had been an editor looking at this manuscript back then, I would certainly have thought its writer showed some promise.

The dog snarled, and ran on. Katterson watched the two lean, fiery-eyed men speeding in pursuit, while a mounting horror grew in him and rooted him to the spot. The dog suddenly bounded over a heap of rubble and was gone; its pursuers sank limply down, leaning on their clubs, and tried to catch their breath.

"It's going to get much worse than this," said a small, grubby-looking man who appeared from nowhere next to Katterson. "I've heard the official announcement's coming today, but the rumor's been around for a long time."

"So they say," answered Katterson slowly. The chase he had just witnessed still held him paralyzed. "We're all pretty hungry."

The two men who had chased the dog got up, still winded, and wandered off. Katterson and the little man watched their slow retreat.

"That's the first time I've ever seen people doing that," said Katterson. "Out in the open like that—"

"It won't be the last time," said the grubby man. "Better get used to it, now that the food's gone."

Katterson's stomach twinged. It was empty, and would stay that way till the evening's food dole. Without the doles, he would have no idea of where his next bite of food would come from. He and the small man walked on through the quiet street, stepping over the rubble, walking aimlessly with no particular goal in mind. "My name's Paul Katterson," he said finally. "I live on 47th Street. I was discharged from the Army last year."

"Oh, one of those," said the little man. They turned down 15th Street. It was a street of complete desolation; not one prewar house was standing, and a few shabby tents were pitched at the far end of the street. "Have you had any work since your discharge?"

Katterson laughed. "Good joke. Try another."

"I know. Things are tough. My name is Malory; I'm a merchandiser."

"What do you merchandise?"

"Oh…useful products." Katterson nodded. Obviously Malory didn't want him to pursue the topic, and he dropped it. They walked on silently, the big man and the little one, and Katterson could think of nothing but the emptiness in his stomach. Then his thoughts drifted to the scene of a few minutes before, the two hungry men chasing a dog. Had it come to that so soon? Katterson asked himself. What was going to happen, he wondered, as food became scarcer and scarcer and finally there was none at all?

But the little man was pointing ahead. "Look," he said. "Meeting at Union Square."

Katterson squinted and saw a crowd starting to form around the platform reserved for public announcements. He quickened his pace, forcing Malory to struggle to keep up with him.

A young man in military uniform had mounted the platform and was impassively facing the crowd. Katterson looked at the jeep nearby, automatically noting it was the 2036 model, the most recent one, eighteen years old. After a minute or so the soldier raised his hand for silence, and spoke in a quiet, restrained voice.

"Fellow New Yorkers, I have an official announcement from the Government. Word has just been received from Trenton Oasis—"

The crowd began to murmur. They seemed to know what was coming.

"Word has just been received from Trenton Oasis that, due to recent emergency conditions there, all food supplies for New York City and environs will be temporarily cut off. Repeat: due to recent emergency in the Trenton Oasis, all food supplies for New York and environs will temporarily be cut off."

The murmuring in the crowd grew to an angry, biting whisper as each man discussed this latest turn of events with the man next to him. This was hardly unexpected news; Trenton had long protested the burden of feeding helpless, bombed-out New York, and the recent flood there had given them ample opportunity to squirm out of their responsibility. Katterson stood silent, towering over the people around him, finding himself unable to believe what he was hearing. He seemed aloof, almost detached, objectively criticizing the posture of the soldier on the platform, counting his insignia, thinking of everything but the implications of the announcement, and trying to fight back the growing hunger.

The uniformed man was speaking again. "I also have this message from the Governor of New York, General Holloway: he says that attempts at restoring New York's food supply are being made, and that messengers have been dispatched to the Baltimore Oasis to request food supplies. In the meantime the Government food doles are to be discontinued effective tonight, until further notice. That is all."

The soldier gingerly dismounted from the platform and made his way through the crowd to his jeep. He climbed quickly in and drove off. Obviously he was an important man, Katterson decided, because jeeps and fuel were scarce items, not used lightly by anyone and everyone.

Katterson remained where he was and turned his head slowly, looking at the people round him — thin, half-starved little skeletons, most of them, who secretly begrudged him his giant frame. An emaciated man with burning eyes and a beak of a nose had gathered a small group around himself and was shouting some sort of harangue. Katterson knew of him — his name was Emerich, and he was the leader of the colony living in the abandoned subway at 14th Street. Katterson instinctively moved closer to hear him, and Malory followed.

"It's all a plot!" the emaciated man was shouting. "They talk of an emergency in Trenton. What emergency? I ask you, what emergency? That flood didn't hurt them. They just want to get us off their necks by starving us out, that's all! And what can we do about it? Nothing. Trenton knows we'll never be able to rebuild New York, and they want to get rid of us, so they cut off our food."

By now the crowd had gathered round him. Emerich was popular; people were shouting their agreement, punctuating his speech with applause.

"But will we starve to death? We will not!"

"That's right, Emerich!" yelled a burly man with a beard.

"No," Emerich continued, "we'll show them what we can do. We'll scrape up every bit of food we can find, every blade of grass, every wild animal, every bit of shoe-leather. And we'll survive, just the way we survived the blockade and the famine of '47 and everything else. And one of these days we'll go out to Trenton and — and — roast them alive!"

Roars of approval filled the air. Katterson turned and shouldered his way through the crowd, thinking of the two men and the dog, and walked away without looking back. He headed down Fourth Avenue, until he could no longer hear the sounds of the meeting at Union Square, and sat down wearily on a pile of crushed girders that had once been the Garden Monument.

He put his head in his hands and sat there. The afternoon's events had numbed him. Food had been scarce as far back as he could remember — the twenty-four years of war with the Spherists had just about used up every resource of the country. The war had dragged on and on. After the first rash of preliminary bombings, it had become a war of attrition, slowly grinding the opposing spheres to rubble.

Somehow Katterson had grown big and powerful on hardly any food, and he stood out wherever he went. The generation of Americans to which he belonged was not one of size or strength — the children were born undernourished old men, weak and wrinkled. But he had been big, and he had been one of the lucky ones chosen for the Army. At least there he had been fed regularly.

Katterson kicked away a twisted bit of slag, and saw little Malory coming down Fourth Avenue in his direction. Katterson laughed to himself, remembering his Army days. His whole adult life had been spent in a uniform, with soldier's privileges. But it had been too good to last; two years before, in 2052, the war had finally dragged to a complete standstill, with the competing hemispheres both worn to shreds, and almost the entire Army had suddenly been mustered out into the cold civilian world. He had been dumped into New York, lost and alone.

"Let's go for a dog-hunt," Malory said, smiling, as he drew near.

"Watch your tongue, little man. I might just eat you if I get hungry enough."

"Eh? I thought you were so shocked by two men trying to catch a dog."

Katterson looked up. "I was," he said. "Sit down, or get moving, but don't play games," he growled. Malory flung himself down on the wreckage near Katterson.

"Looks pretty bad," Malory said.

"Check," said Katterson. "I haven't eaten anything all day."

"Why not? There was a regular dole last night, and there'll be one tonight."

"You hope," said Katterson. The day was drawing to a close, he saw, and evening shadows were falling fast. Ruined New York looked weird in twilight; the gnarled girders and fallen buildings seemed ghosts of long-dead giants.

"You'll be even hungrier tomorrow," Malory said. "There isn't going to be any dole, any more."

"Don't remind me, little man."

"I'm in the food-supplying business, myself," said Malory, as a weak smile rippled over his lips.

Katterson picked up his head in a hurry.

"Playing games again?"

"No," Malory said hastily. He scribbled his address on a piece of paper and handed it to Katterson. "Here. Drop in on me any time you get really hungry. And—say, you're a pretty strong fellow, aren't you? I might even have some work for you, since you say you're unattached."

The shadow of an idea began to strike Katterson. He turned so he faced the little man, and stared at him.

"What kind of work?"

Malory paled. "Oh, I need some strong men to obtain food for me. *You* know," he whispered.

Katterson reached over and grasped the small man's thin shoulders. Malory winced. "Yes, I know," Katterson repeated slowly. "Tell me, Malory," he said carefully. "What sort of food do you sell?"

Malory squirmed. "Why—why—now look, I just wanted to help you, and—"

"Don't give me any of that." Slowly Katterson stood up, not releasing his grip on the small man. Malory found himself being dragged willy-nilly to his feet. "You're in the meat business, aren't you, Malory? *What kind of meat do you sell?*"

Malory tried to break away. Katterson shoved him with a contemptuous half-open fist and sent him sprawling back into the rubble-heap. Malory twisted away, his eyes wild with fear, and dashed off down 13th Street into the gloom. Katterson stood for a long time watching him retreat, breathing hard and not daring to think. Then he folded the paper with Malory's address on it and put it in his pocket, and walked numbly away.

***

Barbara was waiting for him when he pressed his thumb against the doorplate of his apartment on 47th Street an hour later.

"I suppose you've heard the news," she said as he entered. "Some spic-and-span lieutenant came by and announced it down below. I've already picked up our dole for tonight, and that's the last one. Hey—anything the matter?" She looked at him anxiously as he sank wordlessly into a chair.

"Nothing, kid. I'm just hungry—and a little sick to my stomach."

"Where'd you go today? The Square again?"

"Yeah. My usual Thursday afternoon stroll, and a pleasant picnic that turned out to be. First I saw two men hunting a dog—they couldn't have been much hungrier than I am, but they were chasing this poor scrawny thing. Then your lieutenant made his announcement about the food. And then a filthy meat peddler tried to sell me some 'merchandise' and give me a job."

The girl caught her breath. "A job? Meat? What happened? Oh, Paul—"

"Stow it," Katterson told her. "I knocked him sprawling and he ran away with his tail between his legs. You know what he was selling? You know what kind of meat he wanted me to eat?"

She lowered her eyes. "Yes, Paul."

"And the job he had for me—he saw I'm strong, so he would have made me his supplier. I would have gone out hunting in the evenings. Looking for stragglers to be knocked off and turned into tomorrow's steaks."

"But we're so hungry, Paul—when you're hungry that's the most important thing."

"What?" His voice was the bellow of an outraged bull. "What? You don't know what you're saying, woman. Eat before you go out of your mind completely. I'll find some other way of getting food, but I'm not going to turn into a bloody cannibal. No longpork for Paul Katterson."

She said nothing. The single light-glow in the ceiling flickered twice.

"Getting near shut-off time. Get the candles out, unless you're sleepy," he said. He had no chronometer, but the flickering was the signal that eight-thirty was approaching. At eight-thirty every night electricity was cut off in all residence apartments except those with permission to exceed normal quota.

Barbara lit a candle. "Paul, Father Kennon was back here again today."

"I've told him not to show up here again," Katterson said from the darkness of his corner of the room.

"He thinks we ought to get married, Paul."

"I know. I don't."

"Paul, why are you—"

"Let's not go over that again. I've told you often enough that I don't want the responsibility of two mouths to feed when I can't even manage keeping my own belly full. This is the best—each of us on our own."

"But children, Paul—"

"Are you crazy tonight?" he retorted. "Would you dare to bring a child into this world? Especially now that we've even lost the food from Trenton Oasis? Would you enjoy watching him slowly starve to death in all this filth and rubble, or maybe growing up into a hollow-cheeked little skeleton? Maybe you would. I don't think I'd care to."

He was silent. She sat watching him, sobbing quietly.

"We're dead, you and I," she finally said. "We won't admit it, but we're dead. This whole world is dead—we've spent the last thirty years committing suicide. I don't remember as far back as you do, but I've read some of the old books, about how clean and new and shiny this city was before the war. The war! All my life, we've been at war, never knowing who we were fighting and why. Just eating the world apart for no reason at all."

"Cut it, Barbara," Katterson said. But she went on in a dead monotone. "They tell me America once went from coast to coast, instead of being cut up into little strips bordered by radioactive no-man's-lands. And there were farms, and food, and lakes and rivers, and men flew from place to place. Why did this have to happen? Why are we all dead? Where do we go now, Paul?"

"I don't know, Barbara. I don't think anyone does." Wearily, he snuffed out the candle, and the darkness flooded in and filled the room.

***

Somehow he had wandered back to Union Square again, and he stood on 14th Street, rocking gently back and forth on his feet and feeling the lightheadedness which is the first sign of starvation. There were just a few people in the streets, morosely heading for whatever destinations claimed them. The sun was high overhead, and bright.

His reverie was interrupted by the sound of yells and an unaccustomed noise of running feet. His Army training stood him in good stead as he dove into a gaping trench and hid there, wondering what was happening.

After a moment he peeked out. Four men, each as big as Katterson himself, were roaming up and down the now deserted streets. One was carrying a sack.

"There's one," Katterson heard the man with the sack yell harshly. He watched without believing as the four men located a girl cowering near a fallen building.

She was a pale, thin, ragged-looking girl, perhaps twenty at the most, who might have been pretty in some other world. But her cheeks were sunken and coarse, her eyes dull and glassy, her arms bony and angular.

As they drew near she huddled back, cursing defiantly, and prepared to defend herself. *She doesn't understand,* Katterson thought. *She thinks she's going to be attacked.*

Perspiration streamed down his body, and he forced himself to watch, kept himself from leaping out of hiding. The four marauders closed in on the girl. She spat, struck out with her clawlike hand.

They chuckled and grabbed her clutching arm. Her scream was suddenly ear-piercing as they dragged her out into the open. A knife flashed; Katterson ground his teeth together, wincing, as the blade struck home.

"In the sack with her, Charlie," a rough voice said.

Katterson's eyes steamed with rage. It was his first view of Malory's butchers — at least, he suspected it was Malory's gang. Feeling the knife at his side, in its familiar sheath, he half-rose to attack the four meat-raiders, and then, regaining his sense, he sank back into the trench.

So soon? Katterson knew that cannibalism had been spreading slowly through starving New York for many years, and that few bodies of the dead ever reached their graves intact — but this was the first time, so far as he knew, that raiders had dragged a living human being from the streets and killed her for food. He shuddered. The race for life was on, then.

The four raiders disappeared in the direction of Third Avenue, and Katterson cautiously eased himself from the trench, cast a wary eye in all directions, and edged into the open. He knew he would have to be careful; a man his size carried meat for many mouths.

Other people were coming out of the buildings now, all with much the same expression of horror on their faces. Katterson watched the marching skeletons walking dazedly, a few sobbing, most of them past the stage of tears. He clenched and unclenched his fists, angry, burning to stamp out this spreading sickness and knowing hopelessly that it could not be done.

A tall thin man with chiseled features was on the speaker's platform now. His voice was choked with anger.

"Brothers, it's out in the open now. Men have turned from the ways of God, and Satan has led them to destruction. Just now you witnessed four of His creatures destroy a fellow mortal for food — the most terrible sin of all.

"Brothers, our time on Earth is almost done. I'm an old man — I remember the days before the war, and, while some of you won't believe it, I remember the days when there was food for all, when everyone had a job, when these crumpled buildings were tall and shiny and streamlined, and the skies teemed with jets. In my youth I traveled all across this country, clear to the Pacific. But the war has ended all that, and it's God's hand upon us. Our day is done, and soon we'll all meet our reckoning.

"Go to God without blood on your hands, brothers. Those four men you saw today will burn forever for their crime. Whoever eats the unholy meat they butchered today will join them in Hell. But listen a moment, brothers, listen! Those of you who aren't lost yet, I beg you: save yourselves! Better to go without food at all, as with this kind of new food, the most precious meat of all."

Katterson stared at the people around him. He wanted to end all this; he had a vision of a crusade for food, a campaign against cannibalism, banners waving, drums beating, himself leading the fight. Some of the people had stopped listening to the old preacher, and some had wandered off. A few were smiling and hurtling derisive remarks at the old man, but he ignored them.

"Hear me! Hear me, before you go. We're all doomed anyway; the Lord has made that clear. But think, people — this world will shortly pass away, and there is the greater world to come. Don't sign away your chance for eternal life, brothers! Don't trade your immortal soul for a bite of tainted meat!"

The crowd was melting away, Katterson noted. It was dispersing hastily, people quickly edging away and disappearing. The preacher continued talking. Katterson stood on tip-toes and craned his neck past the crowd and stared down toward the east. His eyes searched for a moment, and then he paled. Four ominous figures were coming with deliberate tread down the deserted street.

Almost everyone had seen them now. They were walking four abreast down the center of the street, the tallest holding an empty sack. People were heading hastily in all directions, and as the four figures came to the corner of 14th Street and Fourth Avenue only Katterson and the preacher still stood at the platform.

"I see you're the only one left, young man. Have you defiled yourself, or are you still of the Kingdom of Heaven?"

Katterson ignored the question. "Old man, get down from there!" he snapped. "The raiders are coming back. Come on, let's get out of here before they come."

"No. I intend to talk to them when they come. But save yourself, young man, save yourself while you can."

"They'll kill you, you old fool," Katterson whispered harshly.

"We're all doomed anyway, son. If my day has come, I'm ready."

"You're crazy," Katterson said. The four men were within speaking distance now. Katterson looked at the old man for one last time and then dashed across the street and into a building. He glanced back and saw he was not being followed.

The four raiders were standing under the platform, listening to the old man. Katterson couldn't hear what the preacher was saying, but he was waving his arms as he spoke. They seemed to be listening intently. Katterson stared. He saw one of the raiders say something to the old man, and then the tall one with the sack climbed up on the platform. One of the others tossed him an unsheathed knife.

The shriek was loud and piercing. When Katterson dared to look out again, the tall man was stuffing the preacher's body into the sack. Katterson bowed his head. The trumpets began to fade; he realized that resistance was impossible. Unstoppable currents were flowing.

***

Katterson plodded uptown to his apartment. The blocks flew past as he methodically pulled one foot after another, walking the two miles through the rubble and deserted, ruined buildings. He kept one hand on his knife and darted glances from right to left, noting the furtive scurryings in the sidestreets, the shadowy people who were not quite visible behind the ashes and the rubble. Those four figures, one with the sack, seemed to lurk behind every lamppost, waiting hungrily.

He cut into Broadway, taking a shortcut through the stump of the Parker Building. Fifty years before, the Parker Building had been the tallest in the Western world; its truncated stump was all that remained. Katterson passed what had once been the most majestic lobby in the world, and stared in. A small boy sat on the step outside, gnawing a piece of meat. He was eight or ten; his stomach was drawn tight over his ribs, which showed through like a basket. Choking down his revulsion, Katterson wondered what sort of meat the boy was eating.

He continued on. As he passed 44th Street, a bony cat skittered past him and disappeared behind a pile of ashes. Katterson thought of the stories he had heard of the Great Plains, where giant cats were said to roam unmolested, and his mouth watered.

The sun was sinking low again, and New York was turning dull gray and black. The sun never really shone in late afternoon any more; it snaked its way through the piles of rubble and cast a ghostly glow on the ruins of New York. Katterson crossed 47th Street and turned down toward his building.

He made the long climb to his room—the elevator's shaft was still there, and the frozen elevator, but such luxuries were beyond dream—and stood outside for just a moment, searching in the darkness for the doorplate. There was the sound of laughter from within, a strange sound for ears not accustomed to it, and a food-smell crept out through the door and hit him squarely. His throat began to work convulsively, and he remembered the dull ball of pain that was his stomach.

Katterson opened the door. The food-odor filled the little room completely. He saw Barbara look up suddenly, white-faced, as he entered. In his chair was a man he had met once or twice, a scraggly-haired, heavily bearded man named Heydahl.

"What's going on?" Katterson demanded.

Barbara's voice was strangely hushed. "Paul, you know Olaf Heydahl, don't you? Olaf, Paul?"

"What's going on?" Katterson repeated.

"Barbara and I have just been having a little meal, Mr. Katterson," Heydahl said, in a rich voice. "We thought you'd be hungry, so we saved a little for you."

The smell was overpowering, and Katterson felt it was all he could do to keep from foaming at the lips. Barbara was wiping her face over and over again with the napkin; Heydahl sat contentedly in Katterson's chair.

In three quick steps Katterson crossed to the other side of the room and threw open the doors to the little enclosed kitchenette. On the stove a small piece of meat sizzled softly. Katterson looked at the meat, then at Barbara.

"Where did you get this?" he asked. "We have no money."

"I—I—"

"I bought it," Heydahl said quietly. "Barbara told me how little food you had, and since I had more than I wanted I brought over a little gift."

"I see. A gift. No strings attached?"

"Why, Mr. Katterson! Remember I'm Barbara's guest."

"Yes, but please remember this is my apartment, not hers. Tell me, Heydahl—what kind of payment do you expect for this—this gift? And how much payment have you had already?"

Heydahl half-rose in his chair. "Please, Paul," Barbara said hurriedly. "No trouble, Paul. Olaf was just trying to be friendly."

"Barbara's right, Mr. Katterson," Heydahl said, subsiding. "Go ahead, help yourself. You'll do yourself some good, and you'll make me happy too."

Katterson stared at him for a moment. The half-light from below trickled in over Heydahl's shoulder, illuminating his nearly bald head and his flowing beard. Katterson wondered just how Heydahl's cheeks managed to be quite so plump.

"Go ahead," Heydahl repeated. "We've had our fill."

Katterson turned back to the meat. He pulled a plate from the shelf and plopped the piece of meat on it, and unsheathed his knife. He was about to start carving when he turned to look at the two others.

Barbara was leaning forward in her chair. Her eyes were staring wide, and fear was shining deep in them. Heydahl, on the other hand, sat comfortably in Katterson's chair, with a complacent look on his face that Katterson had not seen on anyone's features since leaving the Army.

A thought hit him suddenly and turned him icy-cold. "Barbara," he said, controlling his voice, "what kind of meat is this? Roast beef or lamb?"

"I don't know, Paul," she said uncertainly. "Olaf didn't say what—"

"Maybe roast dog, perhaps? Filet of alley cat? Why didn't you ask Olaf what was on the menu. *Why don't you ask him now?*"

Barbara looked at Heydahl, then back at Katterson.

"Eat it, Paul. It's good, believe me—and I know how hungry you are."

"I don't eat unlabeled goods, Barbara. Ask Mr. Heydahl what kind of meat it is, first."

She turned to Heydahl. "Olaf—"

"I don't think you should be so fussy these days, Mr. Katterson," Heydahl said. "After all, there are no more food doles, and you don't know when meat will be available again."

"I like to be fussy, Heydahl. What kind of meat is this?"

"Why are you so curious? You know what they say about looking gift-horses in the mouth, heh heh."

"I can't even be sure this is horse, Heydahl. What kind of meat is it?" Katterson's voice, usually carefully modulated, became a snarl. "A choice slice of fat little boy? Maybe a steak from some poor devil who was in the wrong neighborhood one evening?"

Heydahl turned white.

Katterson took the meat from the plate and hefted it for a moment in his hand. "You can't even spit the words out, either of you. They choke in your mouths. Here—cannibals!"

He hurled the meat hard at Barbara; it glanced off the side of her cheek and fell to the floor. His face was flaming with rage. He flung open the door, turned, and slammed it again, rushing blindly away. The last thing he saw before slamming the door was Barbara on her knees, scurrying to pick up the piece of meat.

***

Night was dropping fast, and Katterson knew the streets were unsafe. His apartment, he felt, was polluted; he could not go back to it. The problem was to get food. He hadn't eaten in almost two days. He thrust his hands in his pocket and felt the folded slip of paper with Malory's address on it, and, with a wry grimace, realized that this was his only source of food and money. But not yet—not so long as he could hold up his head.

Without thinking he wandered toward the river, toward the huge crater where, Katterson had been told, there once had been the United Nations buildings. The crater was almost a thousand feet deep; the United Nations had been obliterated in the first bombing, back in 2028. Katterson had been just one year old then, the year the War began. The actual fighting and bombing had continued for the next five or six years, until both hemispheres were scarred and burned from combat, and then the long war of attrition had begun. Katterson had turned eighteen in 2045—nine long years ago, he reflected—and his giant frame made him a natural choice for a soft Army post. In the course of his Army career he had been all over the section of the world he considered his country—the patch of land bounded by the Appalachian radioactive belt on one side, by the Atlantic on the other. The enemy had carefully constructed walls of fire partitioning America into a dozen strips, each completely isolated from the next. An airplane could cross from one to another, if there were any left. But science, industry, technology, were dead, Katterson thought wearily, as he stared without seeing at the river. He sat down on the edge of the crater and dangled his feet.

What had happened to the brave new world that had entered the twenty-first century with such proud hopes? Here he was, Paul Katterson, probably one of the strongest and tallest men in the country, swinging his legs over a great devastated area, with a gnawing pain in the pit of his stomach. The world was dead, the shiny streamlined world of chrome plating and jet planes. Someday, perhaps, there would be new life. Someday.

Katterson stared at the waters beyond the crater. Somewhere across the seas there were other countries, broken like the rest. And somewhere in the other direction were rolling plains, grass, wheat, wild animals, fenced off by hundreds of miles of radioactive mountains. The War had eaten up the fields and pastures and livestock, had ground all mankind under.

He got up and started to walk back through the lonely street. It was dark now, and the few gaslights cast a ghostly light, like little eclipsed moons. The fields were dead, and what was left of mankind huddled in the blasted cities, except for the lucky ones in the few Oases scattered by chance through the country. New York was a city of skeletons, each one scrabbling for food, cutting corners and hoping for tomorrow's bread.

A small man bumped into Katterson as he wandered unseeing. Katterson looked down at him and caught him by the arm. A family man, he guessed, hurrying home to his hungry children.

"Excuse me, sir," the little man said, nervously, straining to break Katterson's grip. The fear was obvious on his face; Katterson wondered if the worried little man thought this giant was going to roast him on the spot.

"I won't hurt you," Katterson said. "I'm just looking for food, Citizen."
"I have none."

"But I'm starving," Katterson said. "You look like you have a job, some money. Give me some food and I'll be your bodyguard, your slave, anything you want."

"Look, fellow, I have no food to spare. Ouch! Let go of my arm!"

Katterson let go, and watched the little man go dashing away down the street. People always ran away from other people these days, he thought. Malory had made a similar escape.

The streets were dark and empty. Katterson wondered if he would be someone's steak by morning, and he didn't really care. His chest itched suddenly, and he thrust a grimy hand inside his shirt to scratch. The flesh over his pectoral muscles had almost completely been absorbed, and his chest was bony to the touch. He felt his stubbly cheeks, noting how tight they were over his jaws.

He turned and headed uptown, skirting around the craters, climbing over the piles of rubble. At 50th Street a Government jeep came coasting by and drew to a stop. Two soldiers with guns got out.

"Pretty late for you to be strolling, Citizen," one soldier said.
"Looking for some fresh air."
"That all?"
"What's it to you?" Katterson said.
"Not hunting some game too, maybe?"
Katterson lunged at the soldier. "Why, you little punk—"

"Easy, big boy," the other soldier said, pulling him back. "We were just joking."

"Fine joke," Katterson said. "You can afford to joke—all you have to do to get food is wear a monkey suit. I know how it is with you Army guys."

"Not any more," the second soldier said.

"Who are you kidding?" Katterson said. "I was a Regular Army man for seven years until they broke up our outfit in '52. I know what's happening."

"Hey—what regiment?"

"306th Exploratory, soldier."

"You're not Katterson, Paul Katterson?"

"Maybe I am," Katterson said slowly. He moved closer to the two soldiers. "What of it?"

"You know Mark Leswick?"

"Damned well I do," Katterson said. "But how do you know him?"

"My brother. Used to talk of you all the time—Katterson's the biggest man alive, he'd say. Appetite like an ox."

Katterson smiled. "What's he doing now?"

The other coughed. "Nothing. He and some friends built a raft and tried to float to South America. They were sunk by the Shore Patrol just outside the New York Harbor."

"Oh. Too bad. Fine man, Mark. But he was right about that appetite. I'm hungry."

"So are we, fellow," the soldier said. "They cut off the soldier's dole yesterday."

Katterson laughed, and the echoes rang in the silent street. "Damn them anyway! Good thing they didn't pull that when I was in the service; I'd have told them off."

"You can come with us, if you'd like. We'll be off duty when this patrol is over, and we'll be heading downtown."

"Pretty late, isn't it? What time is it? Where are you going?"

"It's quarter to three," the soldier said, looking at his chronometer. "We're looking for a fellow named Malory; there's a story he has some food for sale, and we just got paid yesterday." He patted his pocket smugly.

Katterson blinked. "You know what kind of stuff Malory's selling?"

"Yeah," the other said. "So what? When you're hungry, you're hungry, and it's better to eat than starve. I've seen some guys like you—too stubborn to go that low for a meal. But you'll give in, sooner or later, I suppose. I don't know—you look stubborn."

"Yeah," Katterson said, breathing a little harder than usual. "I guess I am stubborn. Or maybe I'm not hungry enough yet. Thanks for the lift, but I'm afraid I'm going uptown."

And he turned and trudged off into the darkness.

***

There was only one friendly place to go.

Hal North was a quiet, bookish man who had come in contact with Katterson fairly often, even though North lived almost four miles uptown, on 114th Street.

Katterson had a standing invitation to come to North at any time of day or night, and, having no place else to go, he headed there. North was one of the few scholars who still tried to pursue knowledge at Columbia, once a citadel of learning. They huddled together in the crumbling wreck of one of the halls, treasuring moldering books and exchanging ideas. North had a tiny apartment in an undamaged building on 114th Street, and he lived surrounded by books and a tiny circle of acquaintances.

Quarter to three, the soldier said. Katterson walked swiftly and easily, hardly noticing the blocks as they flew past. He reached North's apartment just as the sun was beginning to come up, and he knocked cautiously on the door. One knock, two, then another a little harder.

Footsteps within. "Who's there?" in a tired, high-pitched voice.

"Paul Katterson," Katterson whispered. "You awake?"

North slid the door open. "Katterson! Come on in. What brings you up here?"

"You said I could come whenever I needed to. I need to." Katterson sat down on the edge of North's bed. "I haven't eaten in two days, pretty near."

North chuckled. "You came to the right place, then. Wait—I'll fix you some bread and oleo. We still have some left."

"You sure you can spare it, Hal?"

North opened a cupboard and took out a loaf of bread, and Katterson's mouth began to water. "Of course, Paul. I don't eat much anyway, and I've been storing most of my food doles. You're welcome to whatever's here."

A sudden feeling of love swept through Katterson, a strange, consuming emotion which seemed to enfold all mankind for a moment, then withered and died away. "Thanks, Hal. Thanks."

He turned and looked at the tattered, thumb-stained book lying open on North's bed. Katterson let his eye wander down the tiny print and read softly aloud.

"The emperor of the sorrowful realm was there,
Out of the girding ice he stood breast-high
And to his arm alone the giants were
Less comparable than to a giant I."

North brought a little plate of food over to where Katterson was sitting. "I was reading that all night," he said. "Somehow I thought of browsing through it again, and I started it last night and read till you came."

"Dante's *Inferno*," Katterson said. "Very appropriate. Someday I'd like to look through it again too. I've read so little, you know; soldiers don't get much education."

"Whenever you want to read, Paul, the books are still here." North smiled, a pale smile on his wan face. He pointed to the bookcase, where grubby, frayed books leaned at all angles. "Look, Paul: Rabelais, Joyce, Dante, Enright, Voltaire, Aeschylus, Homer, Shakespeare. They're all here, Paul, the most precious things of all. They're my old friends; those books have been my breakfasts and my lunches and my suppers many times when no food was to be had for any price."

"We may be depending on them alone, Hal. Have you been out much these days?"

"No," North said. "I haven't been outdoors in over a week. Henriks has been picking up my food doles and bringing them here, and borrowing books. He came by yesterday—no, two days ago—to get my volume of Greek tragedies. He's writing a new opera, based on a play of Aeschylus."

"Poor crazy Henriks," Katterson said. "Why does he keep on writing music when there's no orchestras, no records, no concerts? He can't even hear the stuff he writes."

North opened the window and the morning air edged in. "Oh, but he does, Paul. He hears the music in his mind, and that satisfies him. It doesn't really matter; he'll never live to hear it played."

"The doles have been cut off," Katterson said.

"I know."

"The people out there are eating each other. I saw a woman killed for food yesterday—butchered just like a cow."

North shook his head and straightened a tangled, whitened lock. "So soon? I thought it would take longer than that, once the food ran out."

"They're hungry, Hal."

"Yes, they're hungry. So are you. In a day or so my supply up here will be gone, and I'll be hungry too. But it takes more than hunger to break down the taboo against eating flesh. Those people out there have given up their last shred of humanity now; they've suffered every degradation there is, and they can't sink any lower. Sooner or later we'll come to realize that, you and I, and then we'll be out there hunting for meat too."

"Hal!"

"Don't look so shocked, Paul." North smiled patiently. "Wait a couple of days, till we've eaten the bindings of my books, till we're finished chewing our shoes. The thought turns my stomach, too, but it's inevitable. Society's doomed; the last restraints are breaking now. We're more stubborn than the rest, or maybe we're just fussier about our meals. But our day will come too."

"I don't believe it," Katterson said, rising.

"Sit down. You're tired, and you're just a skeleton yourself now. What happened to my big, muscular friend Katterson? Where are his muscles now?" North reached up and squeezed the big man's biceps. "Skin, bones, what else? You're burning down, Paul, and when the spark is finally out you'll give in too."

"Maybe you're right, Hal. As soon as I stop thinking of myself as human, as soon as I get hungry enough and dead enough, I'll be out there hunting like the rest. But I'll hold out as long as I can."

He sank back on the bed and slowly turned the yellowing pages of Dante.

***

Henriks came back the next day, wild-eyed and haggard, to return the book of Greek plays, saying the times were not ripe for Aeschylus. He borrowed a slim volume of poems by Ezra Pound. North forced some food on Henriks, who took it gratefully and without any show of diffidence. Then he left, staring oddly at Katterson.

Others came during the day—Komar, Goldman, de Metz—all men who, like Henriks and North, remembered the old days before the long war. They were pitiful skeletons, but the flame of knowledge burned brightly in each of them. North introduced Katterson to them, and they looked wonderingly at his still-powerful frame before pouncing avidly on the books.

But soon they stopped coming. Katterson would stand at the window and watch below for hours, and the empty streets remained empty. It was now four days since the last food had arrived from Trenton Oasis. Time was running out.

A light snowfall began the next day, and continued throughout the long afternoon. At the evening meal North pulled his chair over to the cupboard, balanced precariously on its arm, and searched around in the cupboard for a few moments. Then he turned to Katterson.

"I'm even worse off than Mother Hubbard," he said. "At least she had a dog."

"Huh?"

"I was referring to an incident in a children's book," North said. "What I meant was we have no more food."

"None?" Katterson asked dully.

"Nothing at all." North smiled faintly. Katterson felt the emptiness stirring in his stomach, and leaned back, closing his eyes.

***

Neither of them ate at all the next day. The snow continued to filter lightly down. Katterson spent most of the time staring out the little window, and he saw a light, clean blanket of snow covering everything in sight. The snow was unbroken.

The next morning Katterson arose and found North busily tearing the binding from his copy of the Greek plays. With a sort of amazement Katterson watched North put the soiled red binding into a pot of boiling water.

"Oh, you're up? I'm just preparing breakfast."

The binding was hardly palatable, but they chewed it to a soft pulp anyway, and swallowed the pulp just to give their tortured stomachs something to work on. Katterson retched as he swallowed his final mouthful.

One day of eating bookbindings.

"The city is dead," Katterson said from the window without turning around. "I haven't seen anyone come down this street yet. The snow is everywhere."

North said nothing.

"This is crazy, Hal," Katterson said suddenly. "I'm going out to get some food."

"Where?"

"I'll walk down Broadway and see what I can find. Maybe there'll be a stray dog. I'll look. We can't hold out forever up here."

"Don't go, Paul."

Katterson turned savagely. "Why? Is it better to starve up here without trying than to go down and hunt? You're a little man; you don't need food as much as I do. I'll go down to Broadway; maybe there'll be something. At least we can't be any worse off than now."

North smiled. "Go ahead, then."

"I'm going."

He buckled on his knife, put on all the warm clothes he could find, and made his way down the stairs. He seemed to float down, so lightheaded was he from hunger. His stomach was a tight hard knot.

The streets were deserted. A light blanket of snow lay everywhere, mantling the twisted ruins of the city. Katterson headed for Broadway, leaving tracks in the unbroken snow, and began to walk downtown.

At 96th Street and Broadway he saw his first sign of life, some people at the following corner. With mounting excitement he headed for 95th Street, but pulled up short.

There was a body sprawled over the snow, newly dead. And two boys of about twelve were having a duel to the death for its possession, while a third circled warily around them. Katterson watched them for a moment, and then crossed the street and walked on.

He no longer minded the snow and the solitude of the empty city. He maintained a steady, even pace, almost the tread of a machine. The world was crumbling fast around him, and his recourse lay in his solitary trek.

He turned back for a moment and looked behind him. There were his footsteps, the long trail stretching back and out of sight, the only marks breaking the even whiteness. He ticked off the empty blocks.

90th. 87th. 85th. At 84th he saw a blotch of color on the next block, and quickened his pace. When he got to close range, he saw it was a man lying on the snow. Katterson trotted lightly to him and stood over him.

He was lying face-down. Katterson bent and carefully rolled him over. His cheeks were still red; evidently he had rounded the corner and died just a few minutes before. Katterson stood up and looked around. In the window of the house nearest him, two pale faces were pressed against the pane, watching greedily.

He whirled suddenly to face a small, swarthy man standing on the other side of the corpse. They stared for a moment, the little man and the giant. Katterson noted dimly the other's burning eyes and set expression. Two more people appeared, a ragged woman and a boy of eight or nine. Katterson moved closer to the corpse and made a show of examining it for identification, keeping a wary eye on the little tableau facing him.

Another man joined the group, and another. Now there were five, all standing silently in a semi-circle. The first man beckoned, and from the nearest house came two women and still another man. Katterson frowned; something unpleasant was going to happen.

A trickle of snow fluttered down. The hunger bit into Katterson like a red-hot knife as he stood there uneasily waiting for something to happen. The body lay fencelike between them.

The tableau dissolved into action in an instant. The small swarthy man made a gesture and reached for the corpse; Katterson quickly bent and scooped the dead man up. Then they were all around him, screaming and pulling at the body.

The swarthy man grabbed the corpse's arm and started to tug, and a woman reached up for Katterson's hair. Katterson drew up his arm and swung as hard as he could, and the small man left the ground and flew a few feet, collapsing into a huddled heap in the snow.

All of them were around him now, snatching at the corpse and at Katterson. He fought them off with his one free hand, with his feet, with his shoulders. Weak as he was and outnumbered, his size remained as a powerful factor. His fist connected with someone's jaw and there was a rewarding crack; at the same time he lashed back with his foot and felt contact with breaking ribs.

"Get away!" he shouted. "Get away! This is mine! Away!" The first woman leaped at him, and he kicked at her and sent her reeling into the snowdrifts. "Mine! This is mine!"

They were even more weakened by hunger than he was. In a few moments all of them were scattered in the snow except the little boy, who came at Katterson determinedly, made a sudden dash, and leaped on Katterson's back.

He hung there, unable to do anything more than cling. Katterson ignored him and took a few steps, carrying both the corpse and the boy, while the heat of battle slowly cooled inside him. He would take the corpse back uptown to North; they could cut it in pieces without much trouble. They would live on it for days, he thought. They would—

He realized what had happened. He dropped the corpse and staggered a few steps away, and sank down into the snow, bowing his head. The boy slipped off his back, and the little knot of people timidly converged on the corpse and bore it off triumphantly, leaving Katterson alone.

"Forgive me," he muttered hoarsely. He licked his lips nervously, shaking his head. He remained there kneeling for a long time, unable to get up.

"No, no forgiveness. I can't fool myself; I'm one of them now," he said. He arose and stared at his hands, and then began to walk. Slowly, methodically, he trudged along, fumbling with the folded piece of paper in his pocket, knowing now that he had lost everything.

The snow had frozen in his hair, and he knew his head was white from snow—the head of an old man. His face was white too. He followed Broadway for a while, then cut to Central Park West. The snow was unbroken before him. It lay covering everything, a sign of the long winter setting in.

"North was right," he said quietly to the ocean of white that was Central Park. He looked at the heaps of rubble seeking cover beneath the snow. "I can't hold out any longer." He looked at the address—Malory, 218 West 42nd Street—and continued onward, almost numb with the cold.

His eyes were narrowed to slits, and lashes and head were frosted and white. Katterson's throat throbbed in his mouth, and his lips were clamped together by hunger. 70th Street, 65th. He zigzagged and wandered, following Columbus Avenue, Amsterdam Avenue for a while.

Columbus, Amsterdam — the names were echoes from a past that had never been.

What must have been an hour passed, and another. The streets were empty. Those who were left stayed safe and starving inside, and watched from their windows the strange giant stalking alone through the snow. The sun had almost dropped from the sky as he reached 50th Street. His hunger had all but abated now; he felt nothing, knew just that his goal lay ahead. He faced forward, unable to go anywhere but ahead.

Finally 42nd Street, and he turned down toward where he knew Malory was to be found. He came to the building. Up the stairs, now, as the darkness of night came to flood the streets. Up the stairs, up another flight, another. Each step was a mountain, but he pulled himself higher and higher.

At the fifth floor Katterson reeled and sat down on the edge of the steps, gasping. A liveried footman passed, his nose in the air, his green coat shimmering in the half-light. He was carrying a roasted pig with an apple in its mouth on a silver tray. Katterson lurched forward to seize the pig. His groping hands passed through it, and pig and footman exploded like bubbles and drifted off through the silent halls.

Just one more flight. Sizzling meat on a stove, hot, juicy, tender meat filling the hole where his stomach had once been. He picked up his legs carefully and set them down, and came to the top at last. He balanced for a moment at the top of the stairs, nearly toppled backwards but seized the banister at the last second, and then pressed forward.

There was the door. He saw it, heard loud noises coming from behind it. A feast was going on, a banquet, and he ached to join in. Down the hall, turn left, pound on the door.

Noise growing louder.

"Malory! Malory! It's me, Katterson, big Katterson! I've come to you! Open up, Malory!"

The handle began to turn.

"Malory! Malory!"

Katterson sank to his knees in the hall and fell forward on his face when the door opened at last.

THE MACAULEY CIRCUIT (1955)

INTRODUCTION

This one was written in June of 1955, right on the eve of the real beginning of my career as a professional science-fiction writer. I was still a Columbia undergraduate then, having just finished my junior year, but I had managed to meet most of the magazine editors and had received considerable encouragement from them, and in just another few weeks would be making my first flurry of consistent story sales, enough to convince me that I would be able to sustain a career as a full-time writer.

Like most of my stories at that time this one made its modest way from editor to editor, descending from the top-paying markets to those further down the pecking order, and early in 1956 was bought, for a glorious $40, by Leo Margulies, the publisher of *Fantastic Universe*, who was beginning to accept my work with some regularity. He ran it in the August 1956 issue. It's not a masterpiece, no: I wasn't really up to turning out a lot of masterpieces when I was twenty years old. But it stands up pretty well, I think—an intelligent consideration of some of the problems that the still virtually unborn computer age was likely to bring. When you read it, please bear in mind that computers, in 1955, were still considered experimental technology—"thinking machines" or "electronic brains" is what they were generally called then—and musical synthesizers existed only in the pages of science fiction.

There's a nice irony—one of the many pleasures of having had a long career—in this story's later history. I have survived to see the cumbersome "electronic brains" of 1955 evolve into the ubiquitous personal computers of our own era, and to see the publishing industry begin to migrate from the print media to the various electronic formats. In 1997, one of the pioneering electronic-publishing companies asked me for the rights to some of my stories for Internet distribution. I included "The Macauley Circuit" in the package, not without some misgivings about how today's computer-savvy readers, most of whom had not even been born when I wrote the story, would react to its quaintly archaic view of how computers and synthesizers would work. Evidently the story wasn't as quaint as I thought. Through all the years since it first became available to on-line readers, it has been one of the top three bestselling stories on that web site.

The Macauley Circuit

I don't deny I destroyed Macauley's diagram; I never did deny it, gentlemen. Of course I destroyed it, and for fine, substantial reasons. My big mistake was in not thinking the thing through at the beginning. When Macauley first brought me the circuit, I didn't pay much attention to it — certainly not as much as it deserved. That was a mistake, but I couldn't help myself. I was too busy coddling old Kolfmann to stop and think what the Macauley circuit really meant.

If Kolfmann hadn't shown up just when he did, I would have been able to make a careful study of the circuit and, once I had seen all the implications, I would have put the diagram in the incinerator and Macauley right after it. This is nothing against Macauley, you understand; he's a nice, clever boy, one of the finest minds in our whole research department. That's his trouble.

He came in one morning while I was outlining my graph for the Beethoven *Seventh* that we were going to do the following week. I was adding some ultrasonics that would have delighted old Ludwig — not that he would have heard them, of course, but he would have *felt* them — and I was very pleased about my interpretation. Unlike some synthesizer-interpreters, I don't believe in changing the score. I figure Beethoven knew what he was doing, and it's not my business to patch up his symphony. All I was doing was *strengthening* it by adding the ultrasonics. They wouldn't change the actual notes any, but there'd be that feeling in the air which is the great artistic triumph of synthesizing.

So I was working on my graph. When Macauley came in I was choosing the frequencies for the second movement, which is difficult because the movement is solemn but not *too* solemn. Just so. He had a sheaf of paper in his hand, and I knew immediately that he'd hit on something important, because no one interrupts an interpreter for something trivial.

"I've developed a new circuit, sir," he said. "It's based on the imperfect Kennedy Circuit of 2261."

I remembered Kennedy — a brilliant boy, much like Macauley here. He had worked out a circuit which almost would have made synthesizing a symphony as easy as playing a harmonica. But it hadn't quite worked — something in the process fouled up the ultrasonics and what came out was hellish to hear—and we never found out how to straighten things out. Kennedy disappeared about a year later and was never heard from again. All the young technicians used to tinker with his circuit for diversion, each one hoping he'd find the secret. And now Macauley had.

I looked at what he had drawn, and then up at him. He was standing there calmly, with a blank expression on his handsome, intelligent face, waiting for me to quiz him.

"This circuit controls the interpretative aspects of music, am I right?"

"Yes, sir. You can set the synthesizer for whatever aesthetic you have in mind, and it'll follow your instructions. You merely have to establish the aesthetic coordinates—the work of a moment—and the synthesizer will handle the rest of the interpretation for you. But that's not exactly the goal of my circuit, sir," he said gently, as if to hide from me the fact that he was telling me I had missed his point. "With minor modifications—"

He didn't get a chance to tell me, because at that moment Kolfmann came dashing into my studio. I never lock my door, because for one thing no one would dare come in without good and sufficient reason, and for another my analyst pointed out to me that working behind locked doors has a bad effect on my sensibilities, and reduces the aesthetic potentialities of my interpretations. So I always work with my door unlocked and that's how Kolfmann got in. And that's what saved Macauley's life, because if he had gone on to tell me what was on the tip of his tongue I would have regretfully incinerated him and his circuit right then and there.

Kolfmann was a famous name to those who loved music. He was perhaps eighty now, maybe ninety, if he had a good gerontologist, and he had been a great concert pianist many years ago. Those of us who knew something about presynthesizer musical history knew his name as we would that of Paganini or Horowitz or any other virtuoso of the past, and regarded him almost with awe.

Only all I saw now was a tall, terribly gaunt old man in ragged clothes who burst through my door and headed straight for the synthesizer, which covered the whole north wall with its gleaming complicated bulk. He had a club in his hand thicker than his arm, and he was about to bash it down on a million credits' worth of cybernetics when Macauley effortlessly walked over and took it away from him. I was still too flabbergasted to do much more than stand behind my desk in shock.

Macauley brought him over to me and I looked at him as if he were Judas.

"You old reactionary," I said. "What's the idea? You can get fined for wrecking a cyber—or didn't you know that?"

"My life is ended anyway," he said in a thick, deep, guttural voice. "It ended when your machines took over music."

He took off his battered cap and revealed a full head of white hair. He hadn't shaved in a couple of days, and his face was speckled with stiff-looking white stubble.

"My name is Gregor Kolfmann," he said. "I'm sure you have heard of me."

"Kolfmann, the pianist?"

He nodded, pleased despite everything. "Yes, Kolfmann, the *former* pianist. You and your machine have taken away my life."

Suddenly all the hate that had been piling up in me since he burst in—the hate any normal man feels for a cyberwrecker—melted, and I felt guilty and very humble before this old man. As he continued to speak, I realized that I—as a musical artist—had a responsibility to old Kolfmann. I still think that what I did was the right thing, whatever you say.

"Even after synthesizing became the dominant method of presenting music," he said, "I continued my concert career for years. There were always some people who would rather see a man play a piano than a technician feed a tape through a machine. But I couldn't compete forever." He sighed. "After a while anyone who went to live concerts was called a reactionary, and I stopped getting bookings. I took up teaching for my living. But no one wanted to learn to play the piano. A few have studied with me for antiquarian reasons, but they are not artists, just curiosity-seekers. They have no artistic drive. You and your machine have killed art."

I looked at Macauley's circuit and at Kolfmann, and felt as if everything were dropping on me at once. I put away my graph for the Beethoven, partly because all the excitement would make it impossible for me to get anywhere with it today and partly because it would only make things worse if Kolfmann saw it. Macauley was still standing there, waiting to explain his circuit to me. I knew it was important, but I felt a debt to old Kolfmann, and I decided I'd take care of him before I let Macauley do any more talking.

"Come back later," I told Macauley. "I'd like to discuss the implications of your circuit, as soon as I'm through talking to Mr. Kolfmann."

"Yes, sir," Macauley said, like the obedient puppet a technician turns into when confronted by a superior, and left. I gathered up the papers he had given me and put them neatly at a corner of my desk. I didn't want Kolfmann to see *them*, either, though I knew they wouldn't mean anything to him except as symbols of the machine he hated.

When Macauley had gone I gestured Kolfmann to a plush pneumo-chair, into which he settled with the distaste for excess comfort that is characteristic of his generation. I saw my duty plainly—to make things better for the old man.

"We'd be glad to have you come to work for us, Mr. Kolfmann," I began, smiling. "A man of your great gift—"

He was up out of that chair in a second, eyes blazing. "Work for you? I'd sooner see you and your machines dead and crumbling! You, you scientists—you've killed art, and now you're trying to bribe me!"

"I was just trying to help you," I said. "Since, in a manner of speaking, we've affected your livelihood, I thought I'd make things up to you."

He said nothing, but stared at me coldly, with the anger of half a century burning in him.

"Look," I said. "Let me show you what a great musical instrument the synthesizer itself is." I rummaged in my cabinet and withdrew the tape of the Hohenstein *Viola Concerto,* which we had performed in '69—a rigorous twelve-tone work which is probably the most demanding, unplayable bit of music ever written. It was no harder for the synthesizer to counterfeit its notes than those of a Strauss waltz, of course, but a human violist would have needed three hands and prehensile nose to convey any measure of Hohenstein's musical thought. I activated the playback of the synthesizer and fed the tape in.

The music burst forth. Kolfmann watched the machine suspiciously. The pseudo-viola danced up and down the tone row while the old pianist struggled to place the work.

"Hohenstein?" he finally asked timidly. I nodded.

I saw a conflict going on within him. For more years than he could remember he had hated us because we had made his art obsolete. But here I was showing him a use for the synthesizer that gave it a valid existence—it was synthesizing a work impossible for a human to play. He was unable to reconcile all the factors in his mind, and the struggle hurt. He got up uneasily and started for the door.

"Where are you going?"

"Away from here," he said. "You are a devil."

He tottered weakly through the door, and I let him go. The old man was badly confused, but I had a trick or two up my cybernetic sleeve to settle some of his problems and perhaps salvage him for the world of music. For, whatever else you say about me, particularly after this Macauley business, you can't deny that my deepest allegiance is to music.

***

I stopped work on my Beethoven's *Seventh,* and also put away Macauley's diagram, and called in a couple of technicians. I told them what I was planning. The first line of inquiry, I decided, was to find out who Kolfmann's piano teacher had been. They had the reference books out in a flash and we found out who—Gotthard Kellerman, who had died nearly sixty years ago. Here luck was with us. Central was able to locate and supply us with an old tape of the International Music Congress held at Stockholm in 2187, at which Kellerman had spoken briefly on 'The Development of the Pedal Technique;' nothing very exciting, but it wasn't what he was saying that interested us. We split his speech up into phonemes, analyzed, rearranged, evaluated, and finally went to the synthesizer and began feeding in tapes.

What we got back was a new speech in Kellerman's voice, or a reasonable facsimile thereof. Certainly it would be good enough to fool Kolfmann, who hadn't heard his old teacher's voice in more than half a century. When we had everything ready I sent for Kolfmann, and a couple of hours later they brought him in, looking even older and more worn.

"Why do you bother me?" he asked. "Why do you not let me die in peace?"

I ignored his questions. "Listen to this, Mr. Kolfmann." I flipped on the playback, and the voice of Kellerman came out of the speaker.

"Hello, Gregor," it said. Kolfmann was visibly startled. I took advantage of the prearranged pause in the recording to ask him if he recognized the voice. He nodded. I could see that he was frightened and suspicious, and I hoped the whole thing wouldn't backfire.

"Gregor, one of the things I tried most earnestly to teach you — and you were my most attentive pupil — was that you must always be flexible. Techniques must constantly change, though art itself remains changeless. But have you listened to me? No."

Kolfmann was starting to realize what we had done, I saw. His pallor was ghastly now.

"Gregor, the piano is an outmoded instrument. But there is a newer, a greater instrument available for you, and you deny its greatness. This wonderful new synthesizer can do all that the piano could do, and much more. It is a tremendous step forward."

"All right," Kolfmann said. His eyes were gleaming strangely. "Turn that machine off."

I reached over and flipped off the playback.

"You are very clever," he told me. "I take it you used your synthesizer to prepare this little speech for me."

I nodded.

He was silent an endless moment. A muscle flickered in his cheek. I watched him, not daring to speak.

At length he said, "Well, you have been successful, in your silly, theatrical way. You've shaken me."

"I don't understand."

Again he was silent, communing with who knew what internal force. I sensed a powerful conflict raging within him. He scarcely seemed to see me at all as he stared into nothingness. I heard him mutter something in another language; I saw him pause and shake his great old head. And in the end he looked down at me and said, "Perhaps it is worth trying. Perhaps the words you put in Kellerman's mouth were true. Perhaps. You are foolish, but I have been even more foolish than you. I have stubbornly resisted, when I should have joined forces with you. Instead of denouncing you, I should have been the first to learn how to create music with this strange new instrument. Idiot! Moron!"

I think he was speaking of himself in those last two words, but I am not sure. In any case, I had seen a demonstration of the measure of his greatness — the willingness to admit error and begin all over.

I had not expected his cooperation; all I had wanted was an end to his hostility. But he had yielded. He had admitted error and was ready to rechart his entire career.

"It's not too late to learn," I said. "We could teach you." Kolfmann looked at me fiercely for a moment, and I felt a shiver go through me. But my elation knew no bounds. I had won a great battle for music, and I had won it with ridiculous ease.

***

He went away for a while to master the technique of the synthesizer. I gave him my best man, one whom I had been grooming to take over my place someday. In the meantime I finished my Beethoven, and the performance was a great success. And then I got back to Macauley and his circuit.

Once again things conspired to keep me from full realization of the threat represented by the Macauley circuit. I did manage to grasp that it could easily be refined to eliminate almost completely the human element in music interpretation. But it's many years since I worked in the labs, and I had fallen out of my old habit of studying any sort of diagram and mentally tinkering with it and juggling it to see what greater use could be made of it.

While I examined the Macauley circuit, reflecting idly that when it was perfected it might very well put me out of a job (since anyone would be able to create a musical interpretation, and artistry would no longer be an operative factor), Kolfmann came in with some tapes. He looked twenty years younger; his face was bright and clean, his eyes were shining, and his impressive mane of hair waved grandly.

"I will say it again," he told me as he put the tapes on my desk. "I have been a fool. I have wasted my life. Instead of tapping away at a silly little instrument, I might have created wonders with this machine. Look: I began with Chopin. Put this on."

I slipped the tape into the synthesizer and the *F Minor Fantasy* of Chopin came rolling into the room. I had heard the tired old warhorse a thousand times, but never like this.

"This machine is the noblest instrument I have ever played," he said.

I looked at the graph he had drawn up for the piece, in his painstaking crabbed handwriting. The ultrasonics were literally incredible. In just a few weeks he had mastered subtleties I had spent fifteen years learning. He had discovered that skillfully chosen ultrasonics, beyond the range of human hearing but not beyond perception, could expand the horizons of music to a point the presynthesizer composers, limited by their crude instruments and faulty knowledge of sonics, would have found inconceivable.

The Chopin almost made me cry. It wasn't so much the actual notes Chopin had written, which I had heard so often, as it was the unheard notes the synthesizer was striking, up in the ultrasonic range. The old man had chosen his ultrasonics with the skill of a craftsman—no, with the hand of a genius. I saw Kolfmann in the middle of the room, standing proudly while the piano rang out in a glorious tapestry of sound.

I felt that this was my greatest artistic triumph. My Beethoven symphonies and all my other interpretations were of no value beside this one achievement of putting the synthesizer in the hands of Kolfmann.

He handed me another tape and I put it on. It was the Bach *Toccata and Fugue in D Minor;* evidently he had worked first on the pieces most familiar to him. The sound of a super-organ roared forth from the synthesizer. We were buffeted by the violence of the music. And Kolfmann stood there while the Bach piece raged on. I looked at him and tried to relate him to the seedy old man who had tried to wreck the synthesizer not long ago, and I couldn't.

As the Bach drew to its close I thought of the Macauley circuit again, and of the whole beehive of blank-faced handsome technicians striving to perfect the synthesizer by eliminating the one imperfect element—man. And I woke up.

My first decision was to suppress the Macauley circuit until after Kolfmann's death, which couldn't be too far off. I made this decision out of sheer kindness; you have to recognize that as my motive. Kolfmann, after all these years, was having a moment of supreme triumph, and if I let him know that no matter what he was doing with the synthesizer the new circuit could do it better, it would ruin everything. He would not survive the blow.

He fed the third tape in himself. It was the Mozart *Requiem Mass,* and I was astonished by the way he had mastered the difficult technique of synthesizing voices. Still, with the Macauley circuit, the machine could handle all these details by itself.

As Mozart's sublime music swelled and rose, I took out the diagram Macauley had given me and stared at it grimly. I decided to pigeonhole it until the old man died. Then I would reveal it to the world and, having been made useless myself (for interpreters like me would be a credit a hundred), I would sink into peaceful obscurity, with at least the assurance that Kolfmann had died happy.

That was sheer kindheartedness, gentlemen. Nothing malicious or reactionary about it. I didn't intend to stop the progress of cybernetics, at least not at that point.

No, I didn't decide to do that until I got a better look at what Macauley had done. Maybe he didn't even realize it himself, but I used to be pretty shrewd about such things. Mentally, I added a wire or two here, altered a contact there, and suddenly the whole thing hit me.

A synthesizer hooked up with a Macauley circuit not only didn't need a human being to provide an aesthetic guide to its interpretation of music, which is all Macauley claimed. Up to now, the synthesizer could imitate the pitch of any sound in or out of nature, but we had to control the volume, the timbre, all the things that made up interpretation of music. Macauley had fixed it so that the synthesizer could handle this, too. But also, I now saw that it could create its own music, from scratch, with no human help. Not only the conductor but the composer would be unnecessary. The synthesizer would be able to function independently of any human being. And art is a function of human beings.

That was when I ripped up Macauley's diagram and heaved the paperweight into the gizzard of my beloved synthesizer, cutting off the Mozart in the middle of a high C. Kolfmann turned around in horror, but I was the one who was really horrified.

I know. Macauley has redrawn his diagram and I haven't stopped the wheels of science. I feel pretty futile about it all. But before you label me reactionary and stick me away, consider this:

Art is a function of intelligent beings. Once you create a machine capable of composing original music, capable of an artistic act, you've created an intelligent being. And one that's a lot stronger and smarter than we are. We've synthesized our successor.

Gentlemen, we are all obsolete.

SUNRISE ON MERCURY (1956)

INTRODUCTION

That curious ancient custom—now extinct, I think—of having writers construct stories around cover paintings, rather than having covers painted to illustrate scenes in stories that had already been written—brought "Sunrise on Mercury" into existence in the hyperactive November of 1956, when I was beginning to enter my most prolific years as a writer. In that vanished era, the pulp-magazine chains liked to print their covers in batches of four, which meant that there was usually no time to go through the process of buying a story, sending it out to an artist to be illustrated, making plates from the artist's painting, etc. Instead the artists thought up ideas for illustrations—a scene conceived for its qualities of vivid and dramatic visual excitement, but not necessarily embodying any sort of plausibility—and it went to press right away, while some reliable writer was hired to work it, by hook or by crook, into a story that could be published to accompany it. It's a measure of how quickly thing had changed for me at this point that I was already being given such assignments, here in the second year of my career. But the editors had come to see that I could be depended on to utilize the illustration in some relatively plausible way and to turn my cover story in on time.

So Bob Lowndes, the editor of *Science Fiction Stories* and *Future Science Fiction,* would hand me two or three covers at once, and I would go home and write stories of five or six thousand words to accompany each one. The money wasn't much—a cent or maybe a cent and a half a word, cut-rate stuff even in those days—but it was a guaranteed sale, and so speedy was I at turning out the stories that even at $60 for 6000 words, which is what I was paid for "Sunrise on Mercury," I did all right. (I could write a short story in a day, four a week with the fifth day reserved for visiting editors, back then. $60 for a day's pay was nothing contemptible in 1956, when annual salaries in the mid-four-figure range were the norm.)

The cover that inspired this one, by Ed Emshwiller, showed the bleak landscape of Mercury with the sun rising ominously in the upper left-hand corner, a transparent plastic dome melting in Daliesque fashion in the upper right, and two harassed-looking men in spacesuits running for their lives below. Obviously something unexpected was going on, like sunrise happening a week ahead of schedule; so all I had to do was figure out a reason why that might occur, and I had my sixty bucks. The result, all things considered, wasn't half bad; and the story, which Lowndes used in the May, 1957 *Science Fiction Stories,* has been frequently anthologized over the past forty years.

Sunrise on Mercury

Nine million miles to the sunward of Mercury, with the *Leverrier* swinging into the series of spirals that would bring it down on the solar system's smallest world, Second Astrogator Lon Curtis decided to end his life.

Curtis had been lounging in a webfoam cradle waiting for the landing to be effected; his job in the operation was over, at least until the *Leverrier's* landing-jacks touched Mercury's blistered surface. The ship's efficient sodium-coolant system negated the efforts of the swollen sun visible through the rear screen. For Curtis and his seven shipmates, no problems presented themselves; they had only to wait while the autopilot brought the ship down for man's second landing on Mercury.

Flight Commander Harry Ross was sitting near Curtis when he noticed the sudden momentary stiffening of the astrogator's jaws—Curtis abruptly reached for the control nozzle. From the spinnerets that had spun the webfoam came a quick green burst of dissolving fluorochrene; the cradle vanished. Curtis stood up.

"Going somewhere?" Ross asked.

Curtis' voice was harsh. "Just—just taking a walk."

Ross returned his attention to his microbook for a moment as Curtis walked away. There was the rachety sound of a bulkhead dog being manipulated, and Ross felt a momentary chill as the cooler air of the super-refrigerated reactor compartment drifted in.

He punched a stud, turning the page. Then—

What the hell is he doing in the reactor compartment?

The autopilot would be controlling the fuel flow, handling it down to the milligram, in a way no human system could. The reactor was primed for the landing, the fuel was stoked, the compartment was dogged shut. No one—least of all a second astrogator—had any business going back there.

Ross had the foam cradle dissolved in an instant, and was on his feet in another. He dashed down the companionway and through the open bulkhead door into the coolness of the reactor compartment.

Curtis was standing by the converter door, toying with the release-tripper. As Ross approached, he saw the astrogator get the door open and put one foot to the chute that led downship to the nuclear pile.

"Curtis, you idiot! Get away from there! You'll kill us all!"

The astrogator turned, looked blankly at Ross for an instant, and drew up his other foot. Ross leaped.

He caught Curtis' booted foot in his hands, and despite a barrage of kicks from the astrogator's free boot, managed to drag Curtis off the chute. The astrogator tugged and pulled, attempting to break free. Ross saw the man's pale cheeks quivering; Curtis had cracked, but thoroughly.

Grunting, Ross yanked Curtis away from the yawning reactor chute and slammed the door shut. He dragged him out into the main section again and slapped him, hard.

"Why'd you want to do that? Don't you know what your mass would do to the ship if it got into the converter? You know the fuel intake's been calibrated already; 180 extra pounds and we'd arc right into the sun. What's wrong with you, Curtis?"

The astrogator fixed unshaking, unexpressive eyes on Ross. "I want to die," he said simply. "Why couldn't you let me die?"

He wanted to die. Ross shrugged, feeling a cold tremor run down his back. There was no guarding against this disease.

Just as aqualungers beneath the sea's surface suffered from l'ivresse des grandes profondeurs — rapture of the deeps — and knew no cure for the strange, depth-induced drunkenness that induced them to remove their breathing tubes fifty fathoms below, so did spacemen run the risk of this nameless malady, this inexplicable urge to self-destruction.

It struck anywhere. A repairman wielding a torch on a recalcitrant strut of an orbiting wheel might abruptly rip open his face mask and drink vacuum; a radioman rigging an antenna on the skin of his ship might suddenly cut his line, fire his directional pistol, and send himself drifting away sunward. Or a second astrogator might decide to climb into the converter.

Psych Officer Spangler appeared, an expression of concern fixed on his smooth pink face. "Trouble?"

Ross nodded. "Curtis. Tried to jump into the fuel chute. He's got it, Doc."

Spangler rubbed his cheek and said: "They always pick the best times, dammit. It's swell having a psycho on a Mercury run."

"That's the way it is," Ross said wearily. "Better put him in stasis till we get home. I'd hate to have him running loose, looking for different ways of doing himself in."

"Why can't you let me die?" Curtis asked. His face was bleak. "Why'd you have to stop me?"

"Because, you lunatic, you'd have killed all the rest of us by your fool dive into the converter. Go walk out the airlock if you want to die—but don't take us with you."

Spangler glared warningly at him. "Harry—"

"Okay," Ross said. "Take him away."

The psychman led Curtis within. The astrogator would be given a tranquilizing injection and locked in an insoluble webfoam jacket for the rest of the journey. There was a chance he could be restored to sanity, once they returned to earth, but Ross knew that the astrogator would make a beeline for the nearest method of suicide the moment he was let loose in space.

Scowling, Ross turned away. A man spends his boyhood dreaming about space, he thought, spends four years at the Academy, and two more making dummy runs. Then he finally gets up where it counts and he cracks up. Curtis was an astrogation machine, not a normal human being; and he had just disqualified himself permanently from the only job he knew how to do.

Ross shivered, feeling chill despite the bloated bulk of the sun filling the rear screen. It could happen to anyone...him. He thought of Curtis, lying in a foam cradle somewhere in the back of the ship, blackly thinking over and over again, *I want to die,* while Doc Spangler muttered soothing things at him. A human being was really a frail form of life.

Death seemed to hang over the ship; the gloomy aura of Curtis' suicide wish polluted the atmosphere.

Ross shook his head and punched down savagely on the signal to prepare for deceleration. The unspinning globe that was Mercury bobbed up ahead. He spotted it through the front screen.

***

They were approaching the tiny planet middle-on. He could see the neat division now: the brightness of Sunside, the unapproachable inferno where zinc ran in rivers, and the icy blackness of Darkside, dull with its unlit plains of frozen CO_2.

Down the heart of the planet ran the Twilight Belt, that narrow area of not-cold and not-heat where Sunside and Darkside met to provide a thin band of barely tolerable territory, a ring nine thousand miles in circumference and ten or twenty miles wide.

The *Leverrier* plunged downward. "Downward" was actually a misnomer—space has no ups or downs—but it was the simplest way for Ross to visualize the approach. He allowed his jangled nerves to calm. The ship was in the hands of the autopilot; the orbit was precomputed, and the analog banks in the drive were happily following the taped program, bringing the ship to rest smack in the middle of — My *God!*

Ross went cold from head to toe. The precomputed tape had been fed to the analog banks — had been prepared by — had been the work of —

Curtis.

A suicidal madman had worked out the *Leverrier's* landing program.

Ross's hands began to shake. How easy it would have been, he thought, for death-bent Curtis to work out an orbit that would plant the *Leverrier* in a smoking river of molten lead — or in the mortuary chill of Darkside.

His false security vanished. There was no trusting the automatic pilot; they'd have to risk a manual landing.

Ross jabbed down on the communicator button. "I want Brainerd," he said hoarsely.

The first astrogator appeared a few seconds later, peering in curiously. "What goes, Captain?"

"We've just carted your assistant Curtis off to the pokey. He tried to jump into the converter."

"He — ?"

Ross nodded. "Attempted suicide. I nabbed him in time. But in view of the circumstances, I think we'd better discard the tape you had him prepare and bring the ship down manually, yes?"

The first astrogator moistened his lips. "Maybe that's a good idea."

"Damn right it is," Ross said, glowering.

***

As the ship touched down, Ross thought, *Mercury is two hells in one.* It was the cold, ice-bound kingdom of Dante's deepest pit — and it was also the brimstone empire of another conception. The two met, ice and fire, each hemisphere its own kind of hell.

He lifted his head and flicked a quick glance at the instrument panel above his deceleration cradle. The dials all checked: weight placement was proper, stability 100 percent, external temperature a manageable 108°F, indicating they had made their landing a little to the sunward of the Twilight Belt's exact middle. It had been a sound landing.

He snapped on the communicator. "Brainerd?"

"All OK, Captain."

"How was the landing? You used manual, didn't you?"

"I had to," the astrogator said. "I ran a quick check on Curtis' tape, and it was all cockeyed. We'd have grazed Mercury's orbit by a whisker and kept going — straight for the sun. Nice?"

"Sweet," Ross said. "But don't be too hard on the kid; it's not his fault he went psycho. Good landing, anyway. We seem to be pretty close to the center of the Twilight Belt, give or take a mile or two."

He broke the contact and unwebbed himself. "We're here," he announced over the shipwide circuit. "All hands to fore double pronto."

The men got there quickly enough—Brainerd first, then Doc Spangler, followed by Accumulator Tech Krinsky and the three crewmen. Ross waited until the entire group had assembled.

They were looking around curiously for Curtis, all but Brainerd and Spangler. Crisply, Ross said, "Astrogator Curtis won't be with us. He's aft in the psycho bin; luckily, we can shift without him on this tour."

He waited till the implications of that statement had sunk in. The men adjusted to it well, he thought, judging from the swiftness with which the horror faded from their faces.

"All right," he said. "Schedule calls for us to spend a maximum of thirty-two hours on Mercury before departure. Brainerd, how does that check with our location?"

The astrogator frowned and made some mental calculations. "Current position is a trifle to the sunward edge of the Twilight Belt; but as I figure it, the sun won't be high enough to put the Fahrenheit much above 120 for at least a week. Our suits can handle that sort of temperature with ease."

"Good. Llewellyn, you and Falbridge break out the radar inflaters and get the tower set up as far to the east as you can go without roasting. Take the crawler, but be sure to keep an eye on the thermometer. We've only got one heatsuit, and that's for Krinsky."

Llewellyn, a thin, sunken-eyed spaceman, shifted uneasily. "How far to the east do you suggest, sir?"

"The Twilight Belt covers about a quarter of Mercury's surface," Ross said. "You've got a strip forty-seven degrees wide to move around in— but I don't suggest you go much more than twenty-five miles or so. It starts getting hot after that, and keeps going up."

Ross turned to Krinsky. The accumulator tech was the key man of the expedition; it was his job to check the readings on the pair of solar accumulators that had been left here by the first expedition. He was to measure the amount of stress created by solar energies here, so close to the source of radiation, study force lines operating in the strange magnetic field of the little world, and reprime the accumulators for further testing at a later date.

Krinsky was a tall, powerfully built man, the sort of man who could stand up to the crushing weight of a heatsuit almost cheerfully. The heatsuit was necessary for prolonged work in the Sunside zone, where the accumulators were—and even a giant like Krinsky could stand the strain only for a few hours at a time.

"When Llewellyn and Falbridge have the radar tower set up, Krinsky, get into your heatsuit and be ready to move. As soon as we've got the accumulator station located, Dominic will drive you as far east as possible and drop you off. The rest is up to you. We'll be telemetering your readings, but we'd like to have you back alive."

"Yes, sir."

"That's about it," Ross said. "Let's get rolling."

***

Ross's own job was purely administrative—and as the men of his crew moved busily about their allotted tasks, he realized unhappily that he himself was condemned to temporary idleness. His function was that of overseer; like the conductor of a symphony orchestra, he played no instrument himself and was on hand mostly to keep the group moving in harmony toward the finish.

Now, he had only to wait.

Llewellyn and Falbridge departed, riding the segmented, thermo-resistant crawler carried in the belly of the *Leverrier*. Their job was simple: they were to erect the inflatable plastic radar tower far to sunward. The tower that had been left by the first expedition had long since librated into a Sunside zone and been liquefied; the plastic base and parabola, covered with a light reflective surface of aluminum, could hardly withstand the searing heat of Sunside.

Out there, it got up to 700° when the sun was at its closest. The eccentricities of Mercury's orbit accounted for considerable Sunside temperature variations; but the thermometer never showed lower than 300° on Sunside, even during aphelion. On Darkside, there was little variation; temperature hung down near absolute zero, and frozen drifts of heavy gases covered the surface of the land.

From where he stood, Ross could see neither Sunside nor Darkside. The Twilight Belt was nearly a thousand miles broad, and as the planet dipped in its orbit the sun would first slide above the horizon, then dip back. For a twenty-mile strip through the heart of the Belt, the heat of Sunside and the cold of Darkside canceled out into a fairly stable temperate climate; for five hundred miles on either side, the Twilight Belt gradually trickled toward the areas of cold and raging heat.

It was a strange and forbidding planet. Humans could endure it only for short times; the sort of life that *would* be able to exist permanently on Mercury was beyond his conception. Standing outside the *Leverrier* in his spacesuit, Ross nudged the chin control that lowered a pane of optical glass. He peered first toward Darkside, where he thought he saw a thin line of encroaching black—only illusion, he knew—and then toward Sunside.

In the distance, Llewellyn and Falbridge were erecting the spidery parabola that was the radar tower. He could see the clumsy shape outlined against the sky now—and behind it? A faint line of brightness rimming the bordering peaks? Illusion also, he knew. Brainerd had calculated that the sun's radiance would not be visible here for a week. And in a week's time they'd be back on Earth.

He turned to Krinsky. "The tower's nearly up. They'll be back with the crawler any minute. You'd better get ready to make your trip."

As the technician swung up the handholds and into the ship, Ross's thoughts turned to Curtis. The young astrogator had prattled of seeing Mercury all the way out—and now that they were actually here, Curtis lay in a web of foam deep within the ship, moodily demanding the right to die.

Krinsky returned, now wearing the insulating bulk of the heatsuit over his standard rebreathing outfit. He looked like a small tank rather than a man. "Is the crawler approaching, sir?"

"I'll take a look."

Ross adjusted the lensplate in his mask and narrowed his eyes. It seemed to him that the temperature had risen somewhat. Another illusion, he thought, as he squinted into the distance. His eyes picked out the radar tower far off toward Sunside. His mouth sagged open.

"Something the matter, sir?"

"I'll say!" Ross squeezed his eyes tight shut and looked again. And—yes—the newly erected radar tower was drooping soggily and beginning to melt. He saw two tiny figures racing madly over the flat, pumice-covered ground to the silvery oblong that was the crawler. And—impossibly—the first glow of an unmistakable brightness was beginning to shimmer on the mountains behind the tower.

The sun was rising—a week ahead of schedule!

Ross gasped and ran back into the ship, followed by the lumbering Krinsky. In the airlock, mechanical hands descended to help him out of his spacesuit; he signaled to Krinsky to remain in the heatsuit, and dashed through into the main cabin.

"Brainerd! Brainerd! Where in hell are you?"

The senior astrogator appeared, looking puzzled. "Yes, Captain?"

"Look out the screen," Ross said in a strangled voice. "Look at the radar tower!"

"It's—*melting*," Brainerd said, astonished. "But that's—that's—"

"I know. It's impossible." Ross glanced at the instrument panel. External temperature had risen to 112—a jump of four degrees. And as he watched it clicked up to 114.

It would take a heat of at least 500° to melt the radar tower that way. Ross squinted at the screen and saw the crawler come swinging dizzily toward them: Llewellyn and Falbridge were still alive, then—though they probably had had a good cooking out there. The temperature outside the ship was up to 116. It would probably be near 200 by the time the two men returned.

Angrily, Ross faced the astrogator. "I thought you were bringing us down in the safety strip," he snapped. "Check your figures again and find out where the hell we *really* are. Then work out a blasting orbit. That's the *sun* coming up over those hills."

***

The temperature reached 120. The ship's cooling system would be able to keep things under control and comfortable until about 250; beyond that, there was danger of an overload. The crawler continued to draw near; it was probably hellish in the little land car, Ross thought.

His mind weighed alternatives. If the external temperature went much over 250, he would run the risk of wrecking the ship's cooling system by waiting for the two in the crawler to arrive. He decided he'd give them until it hit 275 to get back and then clear out. It was foolish to try to save two lives at a cost of six. External temperature had hit 130. Its rate of increase was jumping rapidly.

The ship's crew knew what was going on now. Without direct orders from Ross, they were readying the *Leverrier* for an emergency blast-off.

The crawler inched forward. The two men weren't much more than ten miles away now; and at an average speed of forty miles an hour they'd be back within fifteen minutes. Outside it was 133. Long fingers of shimmering sunlight stretched toward them from the horizon.

Brainerd looked up from his calculation. "I can't work it. The damned figures don't come out."

"Huh?"

"I'm computing our location—and I can't do the arithmetic. My head's all foggy."

What the hell, Ross thought. This was when a captain earned his pay. "Get out of the way," he snapped. "Let me do it."

He sat down at the desk and started figuring. He saw Brainerd's hasty notations scratched out everywhere. It was as if the astrogator had totally forgotten how to do his job.

Let's see, now. If we're—

His pencil flew over the pad—but as he worked he saw that it was all wrong. His mind felt bleary, strange; he couldn't seem to handle the computations. Looking up, he said, "Tell Krinsky to get down there and be ready to help those men out of the crawler when it gets here. They're probably half-cooked."

Temperature 146. He looked back at the pad. Damn; it shouldn't be that hard to do simple trig, he thought.

Doc Spangler appeared. "I cut Curtis free," he announced. "He isn't safe during takeoff in that cradle."

From within came a steady mutter. "Just let me die...just let me die..."

"Tell him he's likely to have his wish," Ross murmured. "If I can't work out a blastoff orbit we'll all roast here."

"How come *you're* doing it? What's the matter with Brainerd?"

"Choked up. Couldn't do the figures. And come to think of it, I feel funny myself."

Fingers of fog seemed to wrap around his mind. He glanced at the dial. Temperature 152 outside. That gave the boys in the crawler 123 degrees to get back here...or was it 321? He was confused, utterly bewildered.

Doc Spangler looked strange too. The psych officer was frowning curiously. "I feel very lethargic suddenly," Spangler declared. "I know I really should get back to Curtis, but—"

The madman was keeping up a steady babble inside. The part of Ross's mind that could still think clearly realized that if left unattended Curtis was capable of almost anything.

Temperature 158. The crawler seemed nearer. On the horizon, the radar tower was becoming a crazy shambles.

There was a shriek. "It's Curtis!" Ross yelled, his mind returning to awareness hurriedly, and peeled out from behind the desk. He ran aft, followed by Spanger, but it was too late.

Curtis lay on the floor in a bloody puddle. He had found a pair of shears somewhere.

Spangler bent. "He's dead."

"Of course. He's dead," Ross echoed. His brain felt totally clear now; at the moment of Curtis' death, the fog had lifted. Leaving Spangler to attend to the body, he returned to the desk and glanced at the computations.

With icy clarity he determined their location. They had come down better than three hundred miles to sunward of where they thought they had been. The instruments hadn't lied—but someone's eyes had. The orbit that Brainerd had so solemnly assured him was a "safe" one was actually almost as deadly as the one Curtis had computed.

He looked outside. The crawler was almost there; temperature was 167. There was plenty of time. They would make it with a few minutes to spare, thanks to the warning they had received from the melting radar tower.

But why had it happened? There was no answer to that.

***

Gigantic in his heatsuit, Krinsky brought Llewellyn and Falbridge aboard. They peeled out of their spacesuits and wobbled unsteadily, then collapsed. They looked like a pair of just-boiled lobsters.

"Heat prostration," Ross said. "Krinsky, get them into takeoff cradles. Dominic, you in your suit yet?"

The spaceman appeared at the airlock entrance and nodded.

"Good. Get down there and drive the crawler into the hold. We can't afford to leave it here. Double-quick, and then we'll blast off. Brainerd, that new orbit ready?"

"Yes, sir."

The thermometer grazed 200. The cooling system was beginning to suffer—but its agonies were to be short-lived. Within minutes, the *Leverrier* had lifted from Mercury's surface—minutes ahead of the relentless advance of the sun—and swung into a temporary planet-circling orbit.

As they hung there, virtually catching their breaths, just one question rose in Ross's mind: *why?* Why did Brainerd's orbit bring them down in a danger zone instead of the safety strip? Why had both Brainerd and Ross been unable to compute a blasting pattern, the simplest of elementary astrogation techniques? And why had Spangler's wits utterly failed him— just long enough to let the unhappy Curtis kill himself?

Ross could see the same question reflected on everyone's face: why?

He felt an itchy feeling at the base of his skull. And suddenly, an image forced its way across his mind in answer.

It was a great pool of molten zinc, lying shimmering between two jagged crests somewhere on Sunside. It had been there thousands of years; it would be there thousands, perhaps millions of years from now.

Its surface quivered. The sun's brightness upon the pool was intolerable even to the mind's eye.

Radiation beat down on the zinc pool—the sun's radiation, hard and unending, and then a new radiation, an electromagnetic emanation with a meaningful message:

I want to die.

The pool of zinc stirred fretfully with sudden impulses of helpfulness.

The vision passed as quickly as it came. Stunned, Ross looked up hesitantly. The expressions on the six faces surrounding him told him what he wanted to know.

"You felt it too," he said.

Spangler nodded, then Krinsky and the rest of them.

"Yes," Krinsky said. "What the devil was it?"

Brainerd turned to Spangler. "Are we all nuts, Doc?"

The psych officer shrugged. "Mass hallucination…collective hypnosis…"

"No, Doc." Ross leaned forward. "You know it as well as I do. That thing was real; it's down there, out on Sunside."

"What do you mean?"

"I mean that wasn't any hallucination we had. That's *life* – or as close to it as Mercury can come." Ross's hands shook; he forced them to subside. "We've stumbled over something very big," he said.

Spangler stirred uneasily. "Harry –"

"No, I'm not out of my head! Don't you see – that thing down there, whatever it is, is sensitive to our thoughts! It picked up Curtis' godawful caterwauling the way a radar set grabs electromagnetic waves. His were the strongest thoughts coming through; so it acted on them and did its damnedest to help Curtis' wish come true."

"You mean by fogging our minds and deluding us into thinking we were in safe territory, when actually we were right near sunrise territory?"

"But why would it go to all that trouble?" Krinsky objected. "If it wanted to help poor Curtis kill himself, why didn't it just fix it so we came down right *in* Sunside? We'd cook a lot quicker that way."

Ross shook his head. "It knew that the rest of us *didn't* want to die. The thing down there must be a multivalued thinker. It took the conflicting emanations of Curtis and the rest of us, and fixed things so that he'd die and we wouldn't." He shivered. "Once Curtis was out of the way, it acted to help the surviving crew members get off to safety. If you'll remember, we all thought and moved a lot quicker the instant Curtis was dead."

"Damned if that's not so," Spangler said. "But –"

"What I want to know is, do we go back down?" Krinsky asked. "If that thing is what you say it is, I'm not so sure I want to go within reach of it again. Who knows what it might make us do *this* time?"

"It wants to help us," Ross said stubbornly. "It's not hostile. You're not afraid, are you? I was counting on you to go out and scout for it in the heatsuit."

"Not me!" Krinsky said hastily.

Ross scowled. "But this is the first intelligent life form we've hit in the solar system yet. We can't simply run away and hide!" To Brainerd he said, "Set up an orbit that'll take us back down again – and this time put us down where we won't melt."

"I can't do it, sir," Brainerd said flatly. "I believe the safety of the crew will be best served by returning to Earth at once."

Facing the group of them, Ross glanced quickly from one to the next. There was fear evident on the faces of all of them. He knew what each of them was thinking: *I don't want to go back to Mercury.*

Six of them; one of him. And the helpful thing below.

They had outnumbered Curtis seven to one—but Curtis' mind had radiated an unmixed deathwish. Ross knew he could never generate enough strength of thought to counteract the fear-ridden thoughts of the other six.

This is mutiny, he thought, but somehow he did not care to speak the thought aloud. Here was a case where a superior officer might legitimately be removed from command for the common good, and he knew it.

The creature below was ready to offer its services. But, multivalued as it might be, there was still only one spaceship, and one of the two parties— either he or the rest of them—would have to be denied its wishes.

Yet, he thought, the pool had contrived to satisfy both the man who wished to die and those who wished to stay alive. Now, six wanted to return—but could the voice of the seventh be ignored? *You're not being fair to me,* Ross thought, directing his angry outburst toward the planet below. *I want to see you. I want to study you. Don't let them drag me back to Earth.*

When the *Leverrier* returned to Earth, a week later, the six survivors of the Second Mercury Expedition could all describe in detail how a fierce death wish had overtaken Second Astrogator Curtis and caused his suicide. But not one of them could recall what had happened to Flight Commander Ross, or why the heatsuit had been left behind on Mercury.

WARM MAN (1957)

INTRODUCTION

We arrive now at January, 1957. My ledger entry for that month shows business as usual for those days — seventeen stories, 85,000 words, and I was still just warming up for the *really* productive times a couple of years ahead. How I did it, God only knows. By the time we reach the 1990s I will be happy to manage three or four stories a *year*; that was a week's work for me in 1957.

A phenomenon, I was. And one who took notice was Anthony Boucher, the urbane, sophisticated editor of *Fantasy & Science Fiction.* He was a collector at heart, who wanted one of everything for his superb magazine — including a story by this hypermanic kid from New York who seemed able to turn one out every hour. (If he could have discovered giants, infants, Siamese twins, Martians, or cats who wrote science fiction, I think he would have solicited their work, too.) But Boucher's desire to add me to his roster of contributors did not mean he would relax his high standards simply for the sake of putting my name on his contents page, and so, though he let me know he'd be delighted to publish something of mine, he turned down the first few stories I sent him, offering great regrets and hope for the future. What I had to do in order to sell one to him, I saw, was to break free of the pulp-magazine formulas that I had taken such trouble to master, and write something about and for adults. (Not so easy, when I was only twenty-two myself!)

The specific genesis of "Warm Man" came at the famous Milford Writers' Conference of September, 1956, where I was the youngest author, surrounded by some of the most illustrious people in the sf field. During one workshop session Cyril Kornbluth had some sort of epiphany about his writing, and suddenly cried out in a very loud voice, "Cold!" Or so it seemed to me, though my colleague Algis Budrys, who was also there, tells me that what Cyril actually said was "Gold!", the name of an important editor of the time. What his outburst signified to him, be it "Cold!" or "Gold!", I never knew, but it seemed to me that his sudden insight must certainly have been a very powerful one. It set something working in me which must not have had anything at all to do with whatever had passed through Cyril's mind — "if 'Cold,'" I thought, "then why not 'Warm!?'" and out came, a few months later, this tale of psychic vampirism. I sent it to Boucher (who had been present at Milford also, I think) and by return mail across the continent came his expression of delight that I had broken the ice at last with him. It was an exciting moment for me, bringing me the sense of having qualified for a very exclusive club. He ran the story a few months later—May 1957—and put my name on the cover, a signal honor. Boucher was the best kind of editor—a demanding one, yes, but also the kind who is as pleased as you are that you have produced something he wants to publish. He (and a few others back then) helped to teach me the difficult lesson that quantity isn't as effective, in the long run, as quality. Which is demonstrated by this story's frequent reappearance in print over the span of more than four decades since it was written.

Warm Man

No one was ever quite sure just when Mr. Hallinan came to live in New Brewster. Lonny Dewitt, who ought to know, testified that Mr. Hallinan died on December 3, at 3:30 in the afternoon, but as for the day of his arrival no one could be nearly so precise.

It was simply that one day there was no one living in the unoccupied split-level on Melon Hill, and then the next *he* was there, seemingly having grown out of the woodwork during the night, ready and willing to spread his cheer and warmth throughout the whole of the small suburban community.

Daisy Moncrieff, New Brewster's ineffable hostess, was responsible for making the first overtures toward Mr. Hallinan. It was two days after she had first observed lights on in the Melon Hill place that she decided the time had come to scrutinize the newcomers, to determine their place in New Brewster society. Donning a light wrap, for it was a coolish October day, she left her house in the early forenoon and went on foot down Copperbeech Road to the Melon Hill turnoff, and then climbed the sloping hill till she reached the split-level.

The name was already on the mailbox: DAVIS HALLINAN. That probably meant they'd been living there a good deal longer than just two days, thought Mrs. Moncrieff; perhaps they'd be insulted by the tardiness of the invitation? She shrugged and used the doorknocker.

A tall man in early middle age appeared, smiling benignly. Mrs. Moncrieff was thus the first recipient of the uncanny warmth that Davis Hallinan was to radiate throughout New Brewster before his strange death. His eyes were deep and solemn, with warm lights shining in them; his hair was a dignified gray-white mane.

"Good morning," he said. His voice was deep, mellow.

"Good morning. I'm Mrs. Moncrieff—*Daisy* Moncrieff, from the big house on Copperbeech Road. You must be Mr. Hallinan. May I come in?"

"Ah—please, no, Mrs. Moncrieff. The place is still a chaos. Would you mind staying on the porch?"

He closed the door behind him—Mrs. Moncrieff later claimed that she had a fleeting view of the interior and saw unpainted walls and dust-covered bare floors—and drew one of the rusty porch chairs for her.

"Is your wife at home, Mr. Hallinan?"

"There's just me, I'm afraid. I live alone."

"Oh." Mrs. Moncrieff, discomforted, managed a grin nonetheless. In New Brewster *everyone* was married; the idea of a bachelor or a widower coming to settle there was strange, disconcerting…and just a little pleasant, she added, surprised at herself.

"My purpose in coming was to invite you to meet some of your new neighbors tonight—if you're free, that is. I'm having a cocktail party at my place about six, with dinner at seven. We'd be so happy if you came!"

His eyes twinkled gaily. "Certainly, Mrs. Moncrieff. I'm looking forward to it already."

***

The *ne plus ultra* of New Brewster society was impatiently assembled at the Moncrieff home shortly after 6, waiting to meet Mr. Hallinan, but it was not until 6:15 that he arrived. By then, thanks to Daisy Moncrieff's fearsome skill as a hostess, everyone present was equipped with a drink and a set of speculations about the mysterious bachelor on the hill.

"I'm sure he must be a writer," said Martha Weede to liverish Dudley Heyer. "Daisy says he's tall and distinguished and just *radiates* personality. He's probably here only for a few months—just long enough to get to know us all, and then he'll write a novel about us."

"Hmm. Yes," Heyer said. He was an advertising executive who commuted to Madison Avenue every morning; he had an ulcer, and was acutely aware of his role as a stereotype. "Yes, then he'll write a sizzling novel exposing suburban decadence, or a series of acid sketches for *The New Yorker*. I know the type."

Lys Erwin, looking desirable and just a bit disheveled after her third martini in thirty minutes, drifted by in time to overhear that. "You're *always* conscious of *types*, aren't you, darling? You and your gray flannel suit?"

Heyer fixed her with a baleful stare but found himself, as usual, unable to make an appropriate retort. He turned away, smiled hello at quiet little Harold and Jane Dewitt, whom he pitied somewhat (their son Lonny, age nine, was a shy, sensitive child, a total misfit among his playmates), and confronted the bar, weighing the probability of a night of acute agony against the immediate desirability of a Manhattan.

But at that moment Daisy Moncrieff reappeared with Mr. Hallinan in tow, and conversation ceased abruptly throughout the parlor while the assembled guests stared at the newcomer. An instant later, conscious of their collective *faux pas*, the group began to chat again, and Daisy moved among her guests, introducing her prize.

"Dudley, this is Mr. Davis Hallinan. Mr. Hallinan, I want you to meet Dudley Heyer, one of the most talented men in New Brewster."

"Indeed? What do you do, Mr. Heyer?"

"I'm in advertising. But don't let them fool you; it doesn't take any talent at all. Just brass, nothing else. The desire to delude the public, and delude 'em good. But how about you? What line are you in?"

Mr. Hallinan ignored the question. "I've always thought advertising was a richly creative field, Mr. Heyer. But, of course, I've never really known at first hand—"

"Well, I have. And it's everything they say it is." Heyer felt his face reddening, as if he had had a drink or two. He was becoming talkative, and found Hallinan's presence oddly soothing. Leaning close to the newcomer, Heyer said, "Just between you and me, Hallinan, I'd give my whole bank account for a chance to stay home and *write*. Just write. I want to do a novel. But I don't have the guts; that's my trouble. I know that come Friday there's a $350 check waiting on my desk, and I don't dare give that up. So I keep writing my novel up here in my head, and it keeps eating me away down here in my gut. *Eating*." He paused, conscious that he had said too much and that his eyes were glittering beadily.

Hallinan wore a benign smile. "It's always sad to see talent hidden, Mr. Heyer. I wish you well."

Daisy Moncrieff appeared then, hooked an arm through Hallinan's, and led him away. Heyer, alone, stared down at the textured gray broadloom.

Now why did I tell him all that? he wondered. A minute after meeting Hallinan, he had unburdened his deepest woe to him—something he had not confided in anyone else in New Brewster, including his wife.

And yet—it had been a sort of catharsis, Heyer thought. Hallinan had calmly soaked up all his grief and inner agony, and left Heyer feeling drained and purified and warm.

Catharsis? Or a bloodletting? Heyer shrugged, then grinned and made his way to the bar to pour himself a Manhattan

***

As usual, Lys and Leslie Erwin were at opposite ends of the parlor. Mrs. Moncrieff found Lys more easily, and introduced her to Mr. Hallinan.

Lys faced him unsteadily, and on a sudden impulse hitched her neckline higher. "Pleased to meet you, Mr. Hallinan. I'd like you to meet my husband Leslie. *Leslie!* Come here, please?"

Leslie Erwin approached. He was twenty years older than his wife, and was generally known to wear the finest pair of horns in New

Brewster—a magnificent spread of antlers that grew a new point or two almost every week.

"Les, this is Mr. Hallinan. Mr. Hallinan, meet my husband, Leslie."

Mr. Hallinan bowed courteously to both of them. "Happy to make your acquaintance."

"The same," Erwin said. "If you'll excuse me, now—"

"The louse," said Lys Erwin, when her husband had returned to his station at the bar. "He'd sooner cut his throat than spend two minutes next to me in public." She glared bitterly at Hallinan. "I don't deserve that kind of thing, do I?"

Mr. Hallinan frowned sympathetically. "Have you any children, Mrs. Erwin?"

"Hah! He'd never give me any—not with *my* reputation! You'll have to pardon me; I'm a little drunk."

"I understand, Mrs. Erwin."

"I know. Funny, but I hardly know you and I like you. You seem to *understand*. Really, I mean." She took his cuff hesitantly. "Just from looking at you, I can tell you're not judging me like all the others. I'm not really *bad*, am I? It's just that I get so *bored*, Mr. Hallinan."

"Boredom is a great curse," Mr. Hallinan observed.

"Damn right it is! And Leslie's no help—always reading his newspapers and talking to his brokers! But I can't help myself, believe me." She looked around wildly. "They're going to start talking about us in a minute, Mr. Hallinan. Every time I talk to someone new they start whispering. But promise me something—"

"If I can."

"Someday—someday soon—let's get together? I want to *talk* to you. God, I want to talk to someone—someone who understands why I'm the way I am. Will you?"

"Of course, Mrs. Erwin. Soon." Gently he detached her hand from his sleeve, held it tenderly for a moment, and released it. She smiled hopefully at him. He nodded.

"And now I must meet some of the other guests. A pleasure, Mrs. Erwin."

He drifted away, leaving Lys weaving shakily in the middle of the parlor. She drew in a deep breath and lowered her décolletage again.

At least there's one decent man in this town now, she thought. There was something *good* about Hallinan—good, and kind, and understanding.

Understanding. That's what I need. She wondered if she could manage to pay a visit to the house on Melon Hill tomorrow afternoon without arousing too much scandal.

Lys turned and saw thin-faced Aiken Muir staring at her slyly, with a clear-cut invitation on his face. She met his glance with a frigid, wordless *go to hell*.

Mr. Hallinan moved on, on through the party. And, gradually, the pattern of the party began to form. It took shape like a fine mosaic. By the time the cocktail hour was over and dinner was ready, an intricate, complex structure of interacting thoughts and responses had been built.

Mr. Hallinan, always drinkless, glided deftly from one New Brewsterite to the next, engaging each in conversation, drawing a few basic facts about the other's personality, smiling politely, moving on. Not until after he moved on did the person come to a dual realization: that Mr. Hallinan had said quite little, really, and that he had instilled a feeling of warmth and security in the other during their brief talk.

And thus while Mr. Hallinan learned from Martha Weede of her paralyzing envy of her husband's intelligence and of her fear of his scorn, Lys Erwin was able to remark to Dudley Heyer that Mr. Hallinan was a remarkably kind and understanding person. And Heyer, who had never been known to speak a kind word of anyone, for once agreed.

And later, while Mr. Hallinan was extracting from Leslie Erwin some of the pain his wife's manifold infidelities caused him, Martha Weede could tell Lys Erwin, "He's so gentle—why, he's almost like a saint!"

And while little Harold Dewitt poured out his fear that his silent nine-year-old son Lonny was in some way subnormal, Leslie Erwin, with a jaunty grin, remarked to Daisy Moncrieff, "That man must be a psychiatrist. Lord, he knows how to talk to a person. Inside of two minutes he had me telling him all my troubles. I feel better for it, too."

Mrs. Moncrieff nodded. "I know what you mean. This morning, when I went up to his place to invite him here, we talked a little while on his porch.

"Well," Erwin said, "if he's a psychiatrist he'll find plenty of business here. There isn't a person here riding around without a private monkey on his back. Take Heyer, over there—he didn't get that ulcer from happiness. That scatterbrain Martha Weede, too—married to a Columbia professor who can't imagine what to talk to her about. And my wife Lys is a very confused person too, of course."

"We all have our problems," Mrs. Moncrieff sighed. "But I feel much better since I spoke with Mr. Hallinan. Yes: *much* better."

Mr. Hallinan was now talking with Paul Jambell, the architect. Jambell, whose pretty young wife was in Springfield Hospital slowly dying of cancer. Mrs. Moncrieff could well imagine what Jambell and Mr. Hallinan were talking about.

Or rather, what Jambell was talking about—for Mr. Hallinan, she realized, did very little talking himself. But he was such a *wonderful* listener!

She felt a pleasant glow, not entirely due to the cocktails. It was good to have someone like Mr. Hallinan in New Brewster, she thought. A man of his tact and dignity and warmth would be a definite asset.

***

When Lys Erwin woke — alone, for a change — the following morning, some of the past night's curious calmness had deserted her.

I have to talk to Mr. Hallinan, she thought.

She had resisted two implied, and one overt, attempts at seduction the night before, had come home, had managed even to be polite to her husband. And Leslie had been polite to her. It was most unusual.

"That Hallinan," he had said. "He's quite a guy."

"You talked to him too?"

"Yeah. Told him a lot. Too much, maybe. But I feel better for it."

"Odd," she had said. "So do I. He's a strange one, isn't he? Wandering around that party, soaking up everyone's aches. He must have had half the neuroses in New Brewster unloaded on his back last night."

"Didn't seem to depress him, though. More he talked to people, more cheerful and affable he got. And us, too. You look more relaxed than you've been in a month, Lys."

"I *feel* more relaxed. As if all the roughness and ugliness in me was drawn out."

And that was how it felt the next morning, too. Lys woke, blinked, looked at the empty bed across the room. Leslie was long since gone, on his way to the city. She knew she had to talk to Hallinan again. She hadn't got rid of it all. There was still some poison left inside her, something cold and chunky that would melt before Mr. Hallinan's warmth.

She dressed, impatiently brewed some coffee, and left the house. Down Copperbeech Road, past the Moncrieff house where Daisy and her stuffy husband Fred were busily emptying the ashtrays of the night before, down to Melon Hill and up the gentle slope to the split-level at the top.

Mr. Hallinan came to the door in a blue checked dressing gown. He looked slightly seedy, almost overhung, Lys thought. His dark eyes had puffy lids and a light stubble sprinkled his cheeks.

"Yes, Mrs. Erwin?"

"Oh — good morning, Mr. Hallinan. I — I came to see you. I hope I didn't disturb you — that is — "

"Quite all right, Mrs. Erwin." Instantly she was at ease. "But I'm afraid I'm really extremely tired after last night, and I fear I shouldn't be very good company just now."

"But you said you'd talk to me alone today. And — oh, there's so much more I want to tell you!"

A shadow of feeling—*pain? fear?* Lys wondered—crossed his face. "No," he said hastily. "No more—not just yet. I'll have to rest today. Would you mind coming back—well, say Wednesday?"

"Certainly, Mr. Hallinan. I wouldn't want to disturb you."

She turned away and started down the hill, thinking: *he had too much of our troubles last night. He soaked them all up like a sponge, and today he's going to digest them—*

Oh, what am I thinking?

She reached the foot of the hill, brushed a couple of tears from her eyes, and walked home rapidly, feeling the October chill whistling around her.

***

And so the pattern of life in New Brewster developed. For the six weeks before his death, Mr. Hallinan was a fixture at any important community gathering, always dressed impeccably, always ready with his cheerful smile, always uncannily able to draw forth whatever secret hungers and terrors lurked in his neighbors' souls.

And invariably Mr. Hallinan would be unapproachable the day after these gatherings, would mildly but firmly turn away any callers. What he did, alone in the house on Melon Hill, no one knew. As the days passed, it occurred to all that no one knew much of anything about Mr. Hallinan. He knew *them* all right, knew the one night of adultery twenty years before that still racked Daisy Moncrieff, knew the acid pain that seared Dudley Heyer, the cold envy glittering in Martha Weede, the frustration and loneliness of Lys Erwin, her husband's shy anger at his own cuckoldry— he knew these things and many more, but none of them knew more of him than his name.

Still, he warmed their lives and took from them the burden of their griefs. If he chose to keep his own life hidden, they said, that was his privilege.

He took walks every day, through still-wooded New Brewster, and would wave and smile to the children, who would wave and smile back. Occasionally he would stop, chat with a sulking child, then move on, tall, erect, walking with a jaunty stride.

He was never known to set foot in either of New Brewster's two churches. Once Lora Marker, a mainstay of the New Brewster Presbyterian Church, took him to task for this at a dull dinner party given by the Weedes.

But Mr. Hallinan smiled mildly and said, "Some of us feel the need. Others do not."

And that ended the discussion.

Toward the end of November a few members of the community experienced an abrupt reversal of their feelings about Mr. Hallinan—weary, perhaps, of his constant empathy for their woes. The change in spirit was spearheaded by Dudley Heyer, Carl Weede, and several of the other men.

"I'm getting not to trust that guy," Heyer said. He knocked dottle vehemently from his pipe. "Always hanging around soaking up gossip, pulling out dirt—and what the hell for? What does *he* get out of it?"

"Maybe he's practicing to be a saint," Carl Weede remarked quietly. "Self-abnegation. The Buddhist Eight-fold Path."

"The women all swear by him," said Leslie Erwin. "Lys hasn't been the same since he came here."

"*I'll* say she hasn't," said Aiken Muir wryly, and all of the men, even Erwin, laughed, getting the sharp thrust.

"All I know is I'm tired of having a father-confessor in our midst," Heyer said. "I think he's got a motive back of all his goody-goody warmness. When he's through pumping us he's going to write a book that'll put New Brewster on the map but good."

"You always suspect people of writing books," Muir said. "*Oh, that mine enemy would write a book…!*"

"Well, whatever his motives I'm getting annoyed. And that's why he hasn't been invited to the party we're giving on Monday night." Heyer glared at Fred Moncrieff as if expecting some dispute. "I've spoken to my wife about it, and she agrees. Just this once, dear Mr. Hallinan stays home."

It was strangely cold at the Heyers' party that Monday night. The usual people were there, all but Mr. Hallinan. The party was not a success. Some, unaware that Mr. Hallinan had not been invited, waited expectantly for the chance to talk to him, and managed to leave early when they discovered he was not to be there.

"We should have invited him," Ruth Heyer said after the last guest had left.

Heyer shook his head. "No. I'm glad we didn't."

"But that poor man, all alone on the hill while the bunch of us were here, cut off from us. You don't think he'll get insulted, do you? I mean, and cut us from now on?"

"I don't care," Heyer said, scowling.

His attitude of mistrust toward Mr. Hallinan spread through the community. First the Muirs, then the Harkers, failed to invite him to gatherings of theirs. He still took his usual afternoon walks, and those who met him observed a slightly strained expression on his face, though he still smiled gently and chatted easily enough, and made no bitter comments.

And on December 3, a Wednesday, Roy Heyer, age ten, and Philip Moncrieff, age nine, set upon Lonny Dewitt, age nine, just outside the

New Brewster Public School, just before Mr. Hallinan turned down the
school lane on his stroll.

Lonny was a strange, silent boy, the despair of his parents and the
bane of his classmates. He kept to himself, said little, nudged into corners
and stayed there. People clucked their tongues when they saw him in the
street.

Roy Heyer and Philip Moncrieff made up their minds they were going
to make Lonny Dewitt say something, or else.

It was *or else.* They pummeled him and kicked him for a few minutes;
then, seeing Mr. Hallinan approaching, they ran, leaving Lonny weeping
silently on the flagstone steps outside the empty school. Lonny looked up
as the tall man drew near. "They've been hitting you, haven't they? I see
them running away now."

Lonny continued to cry. He was thinking, *There's something funny about
this man. But he wants to help me. He wants to be kind to me.*

"You're Lonny Dewitt, I think. Why are you crying? Come, Lonny,
stop crying! They didn't hurt you that much."

They didn't, Lonny said silently. *I like to cry.*

Mr. Hallinan was smiling cheerfully. "Tell me all about it. Something's
bothering you, isn't it? Something big, that makes you feel all lumpy and
sad inside. Tell me about it, Lonny, and maybe it'll go away." He took the
boy's small cold hands in his own, and squeezed them.

"Don't want to talk," Lonny said.

"But I'm a friend. I want to help you."

Lonny peered close and saw suddenly that the tall man told the truth.
He wanted to help Lonny. More than that: he *had* to help Lonny.
Desperately. He was pleading. "Tell me what's troubling you," Mr. Hallinan
said again.

OK, Lonny thought. *I'll tell you.*

And he lifted the floodgates. Nine years of repression and torment
came rolling out in one roaring burst.

*I'm alone and they hate me because I do things in my head and they never
understood and they think I'm queer and they hate me I see them looking funny
at me and they think funny things about me because I want to talk to them with
my mind and they can only hear words and I hate them hate them hate hate
hate —*

Lonny stopped suddenly. He had let it all out, and now he felt better,
cleansed of the poison he'd been carrying in him for years. But Mr. Hallinan
looked funny. He was pale and white-faced, and he was staggering.

In alarm, Lonny extended his mind to the tall man. And got:

*Too much. Much too much. Should never have gone near the boy. But the
older ones wouldn't let me.*

Irony: the compulsive empath overloaded and burned out by a compulsive sender who'd been bottled up.

...like grabbing a high-voltage wire...

...he was a sender, I was a receiver, but he was too strong...

And four last bitter words: *I...was...a...leech....*

"Please, Mr. Hallinan," Lonny said out loud. "Don't get sick. I want to tell you some more. Please, Mr. Hallinan."

Silence.

Lonny picked up a final lingering wordlessness, and knew he had found and lost the first one like himself. Mr. Hallinan's eyes closed and he fell forward on his face in the street. Lonny realized that it was over, that he and the people of New Brewster would never talk to Mr. Hallinan again. But just to make sure he bent and took Mr. Hallinan's limp wrist.

He let go quickly. The wrist was like a lump of ice. *Cold* – burningly cold. Lonny stared at the dead man for a moment or two.

"Why, it's dear Mr. Hallinan," a female voice said. "Is he – "

And feeling the loneliness return, Lonny began to cry softly again.

TWO

The 1960s

THE 1960s

Y̶ou know what a crazy time it was — either because you were there and still able to remember some of what went on, or because you've been told. I was there. I can even remember a lot of what went on.

But it's important to bear in mind that the period we call "the Sixties" actually began in the middle of the decade, somewhere around the time of the advent of the Beatles in England and the San Francisco drug/rock culture in the States, and finally fizzled out, in a final burst of druggy stupor and sexual capers, eight or nine years later. But first we had to live through the first half of the *chronological* decade, which was marked not by flamboyant clothing, extravagant sexual behavior, the ingestion of strange chemical substances, and a landing on the Moon, but by such dark and troublesome events as the Eichmann trial in Israel, the failed Bay of Pigs invasion in Cuba, the Cuban missile crisis that followed it, the Kennedy assassination, the strife over civil rights, and the beginning of America's costly and inherently doomed struggle to wage war in Vietnam.

Those early-Sixties events were the direct cause of the bizarre circus that the later Sixties became. Science fiction, which (am I revealing a secret here?) is really about the present rather than the future, reflected the same evolution, becoming stranger, more radical, from 1965 on. My own life grew increasingly strange as the decade proceeded, too. In 1961 I had bought a glorious house, a magnificent mansion, at the northern end of New York City; seven years later I was driven from it in the middle of the night by a fire that created damage to the structure that required fourteen months of repair and damage to my psyche that has, I think, never fully healed. I was experiencing marital troubles, as well, that were destabilizing my existence at every level. And also my attitude toward my career as a science-fiction writer was going through changes, too. At the beginning of the decade the science-fiction publishing world, afflicted by distribution problems that jeopardized the existence of even the best magazines, turned into such a dreary, pallid, limited place that I left it entirely, and divided my time between writing serious books on archaeological subjects and highly unserious soft-core erotic novels. Gradually, as the world grew weirder and talented new writers like Roger Zelazny, Ursula K. Le Guin, Samuel R. Delany, Thomas

Disch, and R. A. Lafferty entered science fiction, bringing with them liberating new ways of writing the stuff, I found myself being drawn back in. The section ahead shows the step-by-step unfolding of the process by which that happened.

TO SEE THE INVISIBLE MAN (1962)

INTRODUCTION

There is a big break in the continuity of the record here. Between 1955 and 1958, most of what I wrote, and I wrote quite a lot in those years, was science fiction. In the following five years I wrote hardly any science fiction at all.

I have never made any secret of the fact that my primary (though not only) concern as a writer in the 1950s was to earn money. I was out of college and on my own in the adult world; I had an apartment to furnish, rent to pay, and all sorts of other new real-world expenses to meet. But after 1958, my fourth year as a full-time writer, making money began to be very difficult to do, if your specialty happened to be science fiction. Midway through that year the American News Company, the vast, omnipotent, and (I think) mob-controlled distribution company that was responsible for getting most of the nation's fiction magazines to the newsstands, abruptly went under as a result of some miscarried financial manipulation, and its collapse brought down dozens of small publishers who depended on advance payments from American News to stay afloat. Among them were most of the science fiction magazines to which I was a regular contributor.

The best ones — John Campbell's *Astounding,* Horace Gold's *Galaxy,* Tony Boucher's *Fantasy & Science Fiction* — were able to survive the debacle. But selling stories to those editors was always an iffy business for any writer this side of Heinlein or Asimov. Most of my mainstays, the risk-free ones who cheerfully bought all the copy I could provide at a cent or two a word, vanished right away or else entered a stage of obvious terminal decline. Larry Shaw's *Infinity* and its companion *Science Fiction Adventures* disappeared, W. W. Scott's *Super Science Fiction* (for which I wrote 36 of the 120 stories it published in four years) did likewise, Bob Lowndes' *Future* and *Science Fiction Stories* began to totter toward their doom, and so forth. I was still free to take my chances with the demanding Boucher, Campbell, and Gold, of course, but the salvage markets that I depended on to accept the stories which those three editors rejected were no longer there, and with the same number of writers competing for space in ever fewer magazines I was faced with the prospect of writing material that would find no publisher whatever. And in any case the magazines that remained had become cautious,

85

bland, unadventurous, their editors preoccupied with the problem of surviving rather than looking for new horizons to explore. So by late 1958 I began to disappear from science fiction myself — the first of several such withdrawals from the field that I would stage.

I was accustomed by now to a pretty good standard of living, and so, fast on my feet as ever, I found a bunch of new markets outside the science-fiction sphere for whom I wrote just about anything and everything. Some typical examples from my ledger: a piece called "Stalin's Slave Barracks" for a magazine called *Sir* in March, 1959, "Cures for Sleepless Nights" in the January, 1960 issue of *Living For Young Homemakers*, "Wolf Children of India" written for *Exotic Adventures* in May, 1959, and so on and on in a really astonishing fashion, reams of stuff that I have completely forgotten doing. I did continue to appear regularly in the science-fiction magazines all through 1959, but these were mostly stories that I had written the year before, or even earlier. 1960 saw just four short sf stories of mine published — what would have been a week's work a couple of years before — and the little novel for young readers, *Lost Race of Mars*, which proved very popular and remained in print for decades. In 1961 I wrote just *one* sf story, and expanded an old magazine novella into a hardcover book for a lending-library publisher. In 1962, no sf short stories of mine appeared, just the novel *The Seed of Earth*, another expansion, based on a story from 1957.

But the veteran writer and editor Frederik Pohl had taken over the editorship of *Galaxy* and its companion magazine *If* from Horace Gold in June of 1961, and he was the one who brought me back into science fiction. So a word about Fred Pohl is necessary here:

As I write this in the summer of 2002, he and I have maintained a close and warm friendship for more than forty years. It has been, as many friendships and a good many marriages tend to be, often a turbulent relationship, in which each of us has done things displeasing to the other, and sharp words have been exchanged, after which we go right back to being friends. We have disagreed over politics, over story themes, over matters of professional responsibility, and any number of other things, including the nature and purpose of science fiction itself. In the beginning, when I was a brash and seemingly incorrigible young writer and Fred (who had made many of the same early mistakes I was then making) felt obliged to show me the error of my ways, he was something of a Dutch uncle tome. Later on, when I entered into the maturity of my career and Fred himself tumbled into difficult personal circumstances, it was I who lectured him, once or twice quite angrily. These days, now that I'm a senior citizen and Fred is an even more senior one, there's no lecturing at all between us, only the occasional halfhearted tossing of a barbed quip. (Usually over political matters, since we're farther apart than ever there.)

In the late 1950s Fred had been vexed with me for my willingness to churn out all that lucrative junk, and he believed (rightly, as time would prove) that a top-rank sf writer was hidden behind the pyramid of literary garbage that I had cheerfully been producing over the past few years. So he made me an offer shrewdly calculated to appeal to my risk-abhorring nature. He agreed to buy any story I cared to send him—a guaranteed sale—*provided* I undertook to write it with all my heart, no quick-buck hackwork. If he wanted revisions, I would pledge to do one rewrite for him, after which he would be bound to buy the story without asking anything more of me. If I turned in a story he didn't like, he would buy it anyway, but that would be the end of the deal. I was, of course, to say nothing about these terms to any of my fellow writers, and I kept the secret until long after Fred had left the magazine.

It was an irresistible arrangement, as he damned well knew. I would get three cents a word—the top rate at the time—without the slightest risk, and without any necessity whatever to slant my work to meet the imagined prejudices of a dictatorial editor. All I had to do was write what I believed to be good science fiction, and Fred would buy it. I had never had an arrangement like that with a first-class sf magazine before, and I lost no time in writing "To See the Invisible Man," the first of what would be a great many stories for Fred Pohl's *Galaxy*.

That story, written in June of 1962, marks the beginning of my real career as a science-fiction writer, I think. The 1953-58 stories collected in the first section of this book are, as you have seen, respectable professional work, some better than others but all of them at least minimally acceptable— but most of them could have been written by just about anyone. They were designed to slip unobtrusively into the magazines of their time, efficiently providing me with regular paychecks. By freeing me from the need to calculate my way around the risk of rejection, Fred Pohl allowed—indeed, *required*— me to reach as deep into my literary resources as I was capable of doing. I would reach deeper and deeper, in the years ahead, until I had moved so far away from my youthful career as a hack writer that latecomers would find it hard to believe that I had been emotionally capable of writing all that junk, let alone willing to do it. In "To See the Invisible Man" the distinctive Silverberg fictional voice is on display for just about the first time.

(The voice of another and greater writer can be heard in the background, though. I found the idea for my story in the opening paragraph of Jorge Luis Borges' "The Babylon Lottery," where he says, "Like all men in Babylon I have been a proconsul; like all, a slave... During one lunar year, I have been declared invisible; I shrieked and was not heard, I stole my bread and was not decapitated." Borges chose to do no more with the theme of statutory invisibility in that story—it was, for him, nothing more than an embellishment in a story about something else entirely. So I fell upon the notion and developed it to explore its practical implications, thus doing the job Borges had left undone.)

Oddly, the story didn't appear in *Galaxy* despite my arrangement with Fred. Soon after taking over the editorial post, he created a new magazine, *Worlds of Tomorrow*, and shifted some stories out of the *Galaxy* inventory to fill its first issue, dated April, 1963. "To See the Invisible Man" was among them. To those readers who quite rightly thought of me as a heartless manufacturer of mass-produced fiction, the story was something of a revelation — and there would be more such surprises to come.

Many years later, by the way, it was adapted for television's *Twilight Zone* program, with a superb screenplay by Steve Barnes.

To See the Invisible Man

And then they found me guilty, and then they pronounced me invisible, for a span of one year beginning on the eleventh of May in the year of Grace 2104, and they took me to a dark room beneath the courthouse to affix the mark to my forehead before turning me loose.

Two municipally paid ruffians did the job. One flung me into a chair and the other lifted the brand.

"This won't hurt a bit," the slab-jawed ape said, and thrust the brand against my forehead, and there was a moment of coolness, and that was all.

But there was no answer, and they turned away from me and left the room without a word. The door remained open. I was free to leave, or to stay and rot, as I chose. No one would speak to me, or look at me more than once, long enough to see the sign on my forehead. I was invisible.

You must understand that my invisibility was strictly metaphorical. I still had corporal solidity. People *could* see me — but they *would not* see me.

An absurd punishment? Perhaps. But then, the crime was absurd too. The crime of coldness. Refusal to unburden myself for my fellow man. I was a four-time offender. The penalty for that was a year's invisibility. The complaint had been duly sworn, the trial held, the brand duly affixed.

I was invisible.

I went out, out into the world of warmth.

They had already had the afternoon rain. The streets of the city were drying, and there was the smell of growth in the Hanging Gardens. Men and women went about their business. I walked among them, but they took no notice of me.

The penalty for speaking to an invisible man is invisibility, a month to a year or more, depending on the seriousness of the offense. On this the whole concept depends. I wondered how rigidly the rule was observed.

I soon found out.

I stepped into a liftshaft and let myself be spiraled up toward the nearest of the Hanging Gardens. It was Eleven, the cactus garden, and those gnarled, bizarre shapes suited my mood. I emerged on the landing stage and advanced toward the admissions counter to buy my token. A pasty-faced, empty-eyed woman sat back of the counter.

I laid down my coin. Something like fright entered her eyes, quickly faded.

"One admission," I said.

No answer. People were queuing up behind me. I repeated my demand. The woman looked up helplessly, then stared over my left shoulder. A hand extended itself, another coin was placed down. She took it, and handed the man his token. He dropped it in the slot and went in.

"Let me have a token," I said crisply.

Others were jostling me out of the way. Not a word of apology. I began to sense some of the meaning of my invisibility. They were literally treating me as though they could not see me.

There are countervailing advantages. I walked around behind the counter and helped myself to a token without paying for it. Since I was invisible, I could not be stopped. I thrust the token in the slot and entered the garden.

But the cacti bored me. An inexpressible malaise slipped over me, and I felt no desire to stay. On my way out I pressed my finger against a jutting thorn and drew blood. The cactus, at least, still recognized my existence. But only to draw blood.

I returned to my apartment. My books awaited me, but I felt no interest in them. I sprawled out on my narrow bed and activated the energizer to combat the strange lassitude that was afflicting me. I thought about my invisibility.

It would not be such a hardship, I told myself. I had never depended overly on other human beings. Indeed, had I not been sentenced in the first place for my coldness toward my fellow creatures? So what need did I have of them now? *Let* them ignore me!

It would be restful. I had a year's respite from work, after all. Invisible men did not work. How could they? Who would go to an invisible doctor for a consultation, or hire an invisible lawyer to represent him, or give a document to an invisible clerk to file? No work, then. No income, of course, either. But landlords did not take rent from invisible men. Invisible men went where they pleased, at no cost. I had just demonstrated that at the Hanging Gardens.

Invisibility would be a great joke on society, I felt. They had sentenced me to nothing more dreadful than a year's rest cure. I was certain I would enjoy it.

But there were certain practical disadvantages. On the first night of my invisibility I went to the city's finest restaurant. I would order their most lavish dishes, a hundred-unit meal, and then conveniently vanish at the presentation of the bill.

My thinking was muddy. I never got seated. I stood in the entrance half an hour, bypassed again and again by a maitre d'hotel who had clearly been through all this many times before. Walking to a seat, I realized, would gain me nothing. No waiter would take my order.

I could go into the kitchen. I could help myself to anything I pleased. I could disrupt the workings of the restaurant. But I decided against it. Society had its ways of protecting itself against the invisible ones. There could be no direct retaliation, of course, no intentional defense. But who could say no to a chef's claim that he had seen no one in the way when he hurled a pot of scalding water toward the wall? Invisibility was invisibility, a two-edged sword.

I left the restaurant.

I ate at an automated restaurant nearby. Then I took an autocab home. Machines, like cacti, did not discriminate against my sort. I sensed that they would make poor companions for a year, though.

I slept poorly.

***

The second day of my invisibility was a day of further testing and discovery.

I went for a long walk, careful to stay on the pedestrian paths. I had heard all about the boys who enjoy running down those who carry the mark of invisibility on their foreheads. Again, there is no recourse, no punishment for them. My condition has its little hazards by intention.

I walked the streets, seeing how the throngs parted for me. I cut through them like a microtome passing between cells. They were well trained. At midday I saw my first fellow Invisible. He was a tall man of middle years, stocky and dignified, bearing the mark of shame on a domelike forehead. His eyes met mine only for a moment. Then he passed on. An invisible man, naturally, cannot see another of his kind.

I was amused, nothing more. I was still savoring the novelty of this way of life. No slight could hurt me. Not yet.

Late in the day I came to one of those bathhouses where working girls can cleanse themselves for a couple of small coins. I smiled wickedly and went up the steps. The attendant at the door gave me the flicker of a startled look—it was a small triumph for me—but did not dare to stop me.

I went in.

An overpowering smell of soap and sweat struck me. I persevered inward. I passed cloakrooms where long rows of gray smocks were hanging, and it occurred to me that I could rifle those smocks of every unit they contained, but I did not. Theft loses meaning when it becomes too easy, as the clever ones who devised invisibility were aware.

I passed on, into the bath chambers themselves.

Hundreds of women were there. Nubile girls, weary wenches, old crones. Some blushed. A few smiled. Many turned their backs on me. But they were careful not to show any real reaction to my presence. Supervisory matrons stood guard, and who knew but that she might be reported for taking undue cognizance of the existence of an Invisible?

So I watched them bathe, watched five hundred pairs of bobbing breasts, watched naked bodies glistening under the spray, watched this vast mass of bare feminine flesh. My reaction was a mixed one, a sense of wicked achievement at having penetrated this sanctum sanctorum unhalted, and then, welling up slowly within me, a sensation of—was it sorrow? Boredom? Revulsion?

I was unable to analyze it. But it felt as though a clammy hand had seized my throat. I left quickly. The smell of soapy water stung my nostrils for hours afterward, and the sight of pink flesh haunted my dreams that night. I ate alone, in one of the automatics. I began to see that the novelty of this punishment was soon lost.

***

In the third week I fell ill. It began with a high fever, then pains of the stomach, vomiting, the rest of the ugly symptomatology. By midnight I was certain I was dying. The cramps were intolerable, and when I dragged myself to the toilet cubicle I caught sight of myself in the mirror, distorted, greenish, beaded with sweat. The mark of invisibility stood out like a beacon in my pale forehead.

For a long time I lay on the tiled floor, limply absorbing the coolness of it. Then I thought: What if it's my appendix? That ridiculous, obsolete, obscure prehistoric survival? Inflamed, ready to burst?

I needed a doctor.

The phone was covered with dust. They had not bothered to disconnect it, but I had not called anyone since my arrest, and no one had dared call me. The penalty for knowingly telephoning an invisible man is invisibility. My friends, such as they were, had stayed far away.

I grasped the phone, thumbed the panel. It lit up and the directory robot said, "With whom do you wish to speak, sir?"

"Doctor," I gasped.

"Certainly, sir." Bland, smug mechanical words! No way to pronounce a robot invisible, so it was free to talk to me!

The screen glowed. A doctorly voice said, "What seems to be the trouble?"

"Stomach pains. Maybe appendicitis."

"We'll have a man over in—" He stopped. I had made the mistake of upturning my agonized face. His eyes lit on my forehead mark. The screen winked into blackness as rapidly as though I had extended a leprous hand for him to kiss.

"Doctor," I groaned.

He was gone. I buried my face in my hands. This was carrying things too far, I thought. Did the Hippocratic Oath allow things like this? Could a doctor ignore a sick man's plea for help?

Hippocrates had not known anything about invisible men. A doctor was not required to minister to an invisible man. To society at large I simply was not there. Doctors could not diagnose diseases in nonexistent individuals.

I was left to suffer.

It was one of invisibility's less attractive features. You enter a bathhouse unhindered, if that pleases you — but you writhe on a bed of pain equally unhindered. The one with the other, and if your appendix happens to rupture, why, it is all the greater deterrent to others who might perhaps have gone your lawless way!

My appendix did not rupture. I survived, though badly shaken. A man can survive without human conversation for a year. He can travel on automated cars and eat at automated restaurants. But there are no automated doctors. For the first time, I felt truly beyond the pale. A convict in a prison is given a doctor when he falls ill. My crime had not been serious enough to merit prison, and so no doctor would treat me if I suffered. It was unfair. I cursed the devils who had invented my punishment. I faced each bleak dawn alone, as alone as Crusoe on his island, here in the midst of a city of twelve million souls.

***

How can I describe my shifts of mood, my many tacks before the changing winds of the passing months?

There were times when invisibility was a joy, a delight, a treasure. In those paranoid moments I gloried in my exemption from the rules that bound ordinary men.

I stole. I entered small stores and seized the receipts while the cowering merchant feared to stop me, lest in crying out he make himself liable to my invisibility. If I had known that the State reimbursed all such losses, I might have taken less pleasure in it. But I stole.

I invaded. The bathhouse never tempted me again, but I breached other sanctuaries. I entered hotels and walked down the corridors, opening doors at random. Most rooms were empty. Some were not.

Godlike, I observed all. I toughened. My disdain for society — the crime that had earned me invisibility in the first place — heightened.

I stood in the empty streets during the periods of rain, and railed at the gleaming faces of the towering buildings on every side. "Who needs you?" I roared. "Not I! Who needs you in the slightest?"

I jeered and mocked and railed. It was a kind of insanity, brought on, I suppose, by the loneliness. I entered theaters—where the happy lotus-eaters sat slumped in their massage chairs, transfixed by the glowing tridim images—and capered down the aisles. No one grumbled at me. The luminescence of my forehead told them to keep their complaints to themselves, and they did.

Those were the mad moments, the good moments, the moments when I towered twenty feet high and strode among the visible clods with contempt oozing from every pore. Those were insane moments—I admit that freely. A man who has been in a condition of involuntary invisibility for several months is not likely to be well balanced.

Did I call them paranoid moments? Manic depressive might be more to the point. The pendulum swung dizzily. The days when I felt only contempt for the visible fools all around me were balanced by days when the isolation pressed in tangibly on me. I would walk the endless streets, pass through the gleaming arcades, stare down at the highways with their streaking bullets of gay colors. Not even a beggar would come up to me. Did you know we had beggars, in our shining century? Not till I was pronounced invisible did I know it, for then my long walks took me to the slums, where the shine has worn thin, and where shuffling stubble-faced old men beg for small coins.

No one begged for coins from me. Once a blind man came up to me.

"For the love of God," he wheezed, "help me to buy new eyes from the eye bank."

They were the first direct words any human being had spoken to me in months. I started to reach into my tunic for money, planning to give him every unit on me in gratitude. Why not? I could get more simply by taking it. But before I could draw the money out, a nightmare figure hobbled on crutches between us. I caught the whispered word, "Invisible," and then the two of them scuttled away like frightened crabs. I stood there stupidly holding my money.

Not even the beggars. Devils, to have invented this torment!

So I softened again. My arrogance ebbed away. I was lonely, now. Who could accuse me of coldness? I was spongy soft, pathetically eager for a word, a smile, a clasping hand. It was the sixth month of my invisibility.

I loathed it entirely, now. Its pleasures were hollow ones and its torment was unbearable. I wondered how I would survive the remaining six months. Believe me, suicide was not far from my mind in those dark hours.

And finally I committed an act of foolishness. On one of my endless walks I encountered another Invisible, no more than the third or the fourth such creature I had seen in my six months. As in the previous encounters, our eyes met, warily, only for a moment. Then he dropped his to the pavement, and he sidestepped me and walked on. He was a slim young man, no more than forty, with tousled brown hair and a narrow, pinched face. He had a look of scholarship about him, and I wondered what he might have done to merit his punishment, and I was seized with the desire to run after him and ask him, and to learn his name, and to talk to him, and embrace him.

All these things are forbidden to mankind. No one shall have any contact whatsoever with an Invisible—not even a fellow Invisible. Especially not a fellow Invisible. There is no wish on society's part to foster a secret bond of fellowship among its pariahs.

I knew all this.

I turned and followed him, all the same.

For three blocks I moved along behind him, remaining twenty to fifty paces to the rear. Security robots seemed to be everywhere, their scanners quick to detect an infraction, and I did not dare make my move. Then he turned down a sidestreet, a gray, dusty street five centuries old, and began to stroll, with the ambling, going-nowhere gait of the Invisible. I came up behind him.

"Please," I said softly. "No one will see us here. We can talk. My name is—"

He whirled on me, horror in his eyes. His face was pale. He looked at me in amazement for a moment, then darted forward as though to go around me.

I blocked him.

"Wait," I said. "Don't be afraid. Please—"

He burst past me. I put my hand on his shoulder, and he wriggled free.

"Just a word," I begged.

Not even a word. Not even a hoarsely uttered, "Leave me alone!" He sidestepped me and ran down the empty street, his steps diminishing from a clatter to a murmur as he reached the corner and rounded it. I looked after him, feeling a great loneliness well up in me.

And then a fear. *He* hadn't breached the rules of Invisibility, but I had. I had seen him. That left me subject to punishment, an extension of my term of invisibility, perhaps. I looked around anxiously, but there were no security robots in sight, no one at all.

I was alone.

Turning, calming myself, I continued down the street. Gradually I regained control over myself. I saw that I had done something unpardonably foolish. The stupidity of my action troubled me, but even more the sentimentality of it. To reach out in that panicky way to another

Invisible—to admit openly my loneliness, my need—no. It meant that society was winning. I couldn't have that.

I found that I was near the cactus garden once again. I rode the liftshaft, grabbed a token from the attendant, and bought my way in. I searched for a moment, then found a twisted, elaborately ornate cactus eight feet high, a spiny monster. I wrenched it from its pot and broke the angular limbs to fragments, filling my hands with a thousand needles. People pretended not to watch. I plucked the spines from my hands and, palms bleeding, rode the liftshaft down, once again sublimely aloof in my invisibility.

***

The eighth month passed, the ninth, the tenth. The seasonal round had made nearly a complete turn. Spring had given way to a mild summer, summer to a crisp autumn, autumn to winter with its fortnightly snowfalls, still permitted for aesthetic reasons. Winter had ended, now. In the parks, the trees sprouted green buds. The weather control people stepped up the rainfall to thrice daily.

My term was drawing to its end.

In the final months of my invisibility I had slipped into a kind of torpor. My mind, forced back on its own resources, no longer cared to consider the implications of my condition, and I slid in a blurred haze from day to day. I read compulsively but unselectively. Aristotle one day, the Bible the next, a handbook of mechanics the next. I retained nothing; as I turned a fresh page, its predecessor slipped from my memory.

I no longer bothered to enjoy the few advantages of invisibility, the voyeuristic thrills, the minute throb of power that comes from being able to commit any act with only limited fears of retaliation. I say *limited* because the passage of the Invisibility Act had not been accompanied by an act repealing human nature; few men would not risk invisibility to protect their wives or children from an invisible one's molestations; no one would coolly allow an Invisible to jab out his eyes; no one would tolerate an Invisible's invasion of his home. There were ways of coping with such infringements without appearing to recognize the existence of the Invisible, as I have mentioned.

Still, it was possible to get away with a great deal. I declined to try. Somewhere Dostoyevski has written, "Without God, all things are possible." I can amend that. "To the invisible man, all things are possible—and uninteresting." So it was.

The weary months passed.

I did not count the minutes till my release. To be precise, I wholly forgot that my term was due to end. On the day itself, I was reading in my room, morosely turning page after page, when the annunciator chimed.

It had not chimed for a full year. I had almost forgotten the meaning of the sound.

But I opened the door. There they stood, the men of the law. Wordlessly, they broke the seal that held the mark to my forehead. The emblem dropped away and shattered.

"Hello, citizen," they said to me.

I nodded gravely. "Yes. Hello."

"May 11, 2105. Your term is up. You are restored to society. You have paid your debt."

"Thank you. Yes."

"Come for a drink with us."

"I'd sooner not."

"It's the tradition. Come along."

I went with them. My forehead felt strangely naked now, and I glanced in the mirror to see that there was a pale spot where the emblem had been. They took me to a bar nearby, and treated me to synthetic whiskey, raw, powerful. The bartender grinned at me. Someone on the next stool clapped me on the shoulder and asked me who I liked in tomorrow's jet races. I had no idea, and I said so.

"You mean it? I'm backing Kelso. Four to one, but he's got terrific spurt power."

"I'm sorry," I said.

"He's been away for a while," one of the government men said softly.

The euphemism was unmistakable. My neighbor glanced at my forehead and nodded at the pale spot. He offered to buy me a drink too. I accepted, though I was already feeling the effects of the first one. I was a human being again. I was visible.

I did not dare spurn him, anyway. It might have been construed as a crime of coldness once again. My fifth offence would have meant five years of Invisibility. I had learned humility.

Returning to visibility involved an awkward transition, of course. Old friends to meet, lame conversations to hold, shattered relationships to renew. I had been an exile in my own city for a year, and coming back was not easy.

No one referred to my time of invisibility, naturally. It was treated as an affliction best left unmentioned. Hypocrisy, I thought, but I accepted it. Doubtless they were all trying to spare my feelings. Does one tell a man whose cancerous stomach has been replaced, "I hear you had a narrow escape just now?" Does one say to a man whose aged father has tottered off toward a euthanasia house, "Well, he was getting pretty feeble anyway, wasn't he?"

No. Of course not.

So there was this hole in our shared experience, this void, this blankness. Which left me little to talk about with my friends, in particular since I had lost the knack of conversation entirely. The period of readjustment was a trying one.

But I persevered, for I was no longer the same haughty, aloof person I had been before my conviction. I had learned humility in the hardest of schools.

Now and then I noticed an Invisible on the streets, of course. It was impossible to avoid them. But, trained as I had been trained, I quickly glanced away, as though my eyes had come momentarily to rest on some shambling, festering horror from another world.

It was in the fourth month of my return to visibility that the ultimate lesson of my sentence struck home, though. I was in the vicinity of the City Tower, having returned to my old job in the documents division of the municipal government. I had left work for the day and was walking toward the tubes when a hand emerged from the crowd, caught my arm.

"Please," the soft voice said. "Wait a minute. Don't be afraid."

I looked up, startled. In our city strangers do not accost strangers.

I saw the gleaming emblem of invisibility on the man's forehead. Then I recognized him—the slim man I had accosted more than half a year before on that deserted street. He had grown haggard; his eyes were wild, his brown hair flecked with gray. He must have been at the beginning of his term, then. Now he must have been near its end.

He held my arm. I trembled. This was no deserted street. This was the most crowded square of the city. I pulled my arm away from his grasp and started to turn away.

"No—don't go," he cried. "Can't you pity me? You've been there yourself."

I took a faltering step. Then I remembered how I had cried out to him, how I had begged him not to spurn me. I remembered my own miserable loneliness.

I took another step away from him.

"Coward!" he shrieked after me. "Talk to me! I dare you! Talk to me, coward!"

It was too much. I was touched. Sudden tears stung my eyes, and I turned to him, stretched out a hand to his. I caught his thin wrist. The contact seemed to electrify him. A moment later, I held him in my arms, trying to draw some of the misery from his frame to mine.

The security robots closed in, surrounding us. He was hurled to one side, I was taken into custody. They will try me again—not for the crime of coldness, this time, but for a crime of warmth. Perhaps they will find extenuating circumstances and release me; perhaps not.

I do not care. If they condemn me, this time I will wear my invisibility like a shield of glory.

FLIES (1965)

INTRODUCTION

So I was writing sf again, slowly at first, then with greater frequency as I began to savor the advantages of my deal with Fred Pohl. Now that I had had a taste of what tackling complex science-fictional themes or modes of narrative without fear of rejection was like, I grew more and more enthusiastic about writing stories for him. Next I did a story called "The Pain Peddlers," and then one called "Neighbor," and in February, 1964, a fourth, "The Sixth Palace." But those four did not represent a return to my old bang-'em-out prolificity of the 1950s. Each was carefully planned and closely revised. They showed the new pride I was taking in my work.

Fred was pleased with them too. He encouraged me to keep going. By the summer of 1964 he and I were discussing my doing a series of five novellas for him — the "Blue Fire" stories, which became the novel *To Open the Sky*. I had told him at the outset that my contributions to his magazine would probably be few and far between, because I was more interested in writing nonfiction — I had launched a new career as a successful writer of popular books on archaeolgical subjects — and at the beginning that was true: but, bit by bit, he had lured me back into science fiction. (Or I had lured myself.) I did the first of the "Blue Fire" stories in November, 1964, the second in December, the third in March, 1965. For someone who planned to dabble in sf on a purely part-time basis, I was suddenly getting very active again after six or seven years away from the center of the scene.

I was beginning to edit anthologies, too. A book called *Earthmen and Strangers* was the first, and for my sins I chose to reprint a story by Harlan Ellison in it. Ellison was willing to grant me permission to use his story, but not without a lot of heavy muttering and grumbling about the terms of the contract, to which I replied on October 2, 1965:

"Dear Harlan: You'll be glad to know that in the course of a long and wearying dream last night I watched you win *two* Hugos at last year's WorldCon. [He had never won an award at this point in his career.] You acted pretty smug about it, too. I'm not sure which categories you led, but one of them was probably Unfounded Bitching. Permit me a brief and fatherly lecture in response to your letter of permission on the anthology...."

Whereupon I dealt with his complaints at some length, and then, almost gratuitously, threw in a postscript:

"Why *don't* you do an anthology? *Harlan Ellison Picks Offbeat Classics of SF,* or something…."

From the placement of the italicized word in that sentence, I suppose I must already have suggested to Harlan that he edit an anthology of controversial sf—he was running a paperback line then called Regency Books, published out of Chicago—but for some reason he had brushed the idea aside. Now, though, it kindled something in him. He was back to me right away, by telephone this time, to tell me that he *would* do a science-fiction anthology, all right, but for a major publishing house instead of little Regency, and instead of putting together a mere compilation of existing material he would solicit previously unpublished stories, the kind of sf that no magazine of that era would *dare* to publish. Truly dangerous stories, Harlan said—a book of dangerous visions. "In fact, that's what I'll call it," he told me, in mounting excitement. "*Dangerous Visions.* I want you to write a story for it, too."

And so I unwittingly touched off a publishing revolution.

By the eighteenth of October Harlan had sold the book to Doubleday and was soliciting stories far and wide. Requests for material—material of the boldest, most uncompromising kind—went out to the likes of Theodore Sturgeon, Frederik Pohl, Poul Anderson, Philip K. Dick, Philip Jose Farmer, Fritz Leiber, J. G. Ballard, Norman Spinrad, Brian Aldiss, Lester del Rey, Larry Niven, R. A. Lafferty, John Brunner, Roger Zelazny, and Samuel R. Delany. Dick, Pohl, Sturgeon, Anderson, del Rey, Farmer, Brunner, Aldiss, and Leiber were well-established authors, but the work of Ballard, Zelazny, Delany, Niven, and Spinrad, believe it or not, was only just beginning to be known in the United States in 1965. Harlan's eye for innovative talent had always been formidably keen.

As the accidental instigator of the whole thing—and the quickest man with an sf story since Henry Kuttner in his prime—I sat down right away and wrote the very first dangerous vision, "Flies," in November of 1965, just as soon as Harlan told me the deal was set. It was about as dangerous as I could manage: a demonstration of the random viciousness of the universe and a little blasphemy on the side. (I would return to both these themes again and again in the years ahead: my novel *Thorns* of 1966 was essentially a recasting of the underlying material of "Flies" at greater length.) Back at once came Harlan's check for $88.

Which was the first of many, for *Dangerous Visions* would turn out to be the most significant sf anthology of the decade, and was destined to go through edition after edition. It is still in print, more than thirty-five years later. *All* of the extraordinary writers whose names I rattled off above came through with brilliant stories, along with fifteen or twenty others, some well known at the time but forgotten now, some obscure then and still obscure, but all of them fiercely determined to live up to Harlan's demand for the kind of stories that other sf editors would consider too hot to handle.

Dangerous Visions appeared in 1967. "An event," said the *New York Times*, "a jubilee of fresh ideas…what we mean when we say an important book." Its success led to the publication of an immense companion volume in 1972, *Again, Dangerous Visions* — 760 pages of stories by writers who hadn't contributed to the first book (Ursula K. Le Guin, Gene Wolfe, Kurt Vonnegut, Gregory Benford, James Tiptree, Jr….) And ultimately Harlan began to assemble the mammoth third book in the series, *The Last Dangerous Visions*, though the project became stalled and its publication now will be an event in some alternate universe.

I knew not what I was setting in motion with my casual postscript of October 2, 1965, suggesting that Harlan edit an anthology. Certainly I had no idea that I was nudging him toward one of the great enterprises of his career. Nor did I suspect that my own 4400-word contribution to the book would open a new and darker phase of my own career — in which, ultimately, almost everything I wrote would become a dangerous vision of sorts.

Here is Cassiday:

transfixed on a table.

There wasn't much left of him. A brain-box; a few ropes of nerves; limb. The sudden implosion had taken care of the rest. There was enough, though. The golden ones didn't need much to go by. They had found him in the wreckage of the drifting ship as it passed through their zone, back of Iapetus. He was alive. He could be repaired. The others on the ship were beyond hope.

Repair him? Of course. Did one need to be human in order to be humanitarian? Repair, yes. By all means. And change. The golden ones were creative.

What was left of Cassiday lay in drydock on a somewhere table in a golden sphere of force. There was no change of season here; only the sheen of the walls, the unvarying warmth. Neither day nor night, neither yesterday nor tomorrow. Shapes came and went about him. They were regenerating him, stage by stage, as he lay in complete unthinking tranquility. The brain was intact but not functioning. The rest of the man was growing back: tendon and ligament, bone and blood, heart and elbows. Elongated mounds of tissue sprouted tiny buds that enlarged into blobs of flesh. Paste cell to cell together, build a man from his own wreckage — that was no chore for the golden ones. They had their skills. But they had much to learn too, and this Cassiday could help them learn it.

Day by day Cassiday grew toward wholeness. They did not awaken him. He lay cradled in warmth, unmoving, unthinking, drifting on the tide. His new flesh was pink and smooth, like a baby's. The epithelial thickening came a little later. Cassiday served as his own blueprint. The golden ones replicated him from a shred of himself, built him back from his own polynucleotide chains, decoded the proteins and reassembled him from the template. An easy task, for them. Why not? Any blob of protoplasm could do it — for itself. The golden ones, who were not protoplasm, could do it for others.

They made some changes in the template. Of course. They were craftsmen. And there was a good deal they wanted to learn.

Look at Cassiday:
the dossier.

BORN 1 August 2316
PLACE Nyack, New York
PARENTS Various
ECONOMIC LEVEL Low
EDUCATIONAL LEVEL Middle
OCCUPATION Fuel technician
MARITAL STATUS Three legal liaisons, duration eight months, sixteen
    months, and two months
HEIGHT Two meters
WEIGHT 96 kg
HAIR COLOR Yellow
EYES Blue
BLOOD TYPE A+
INTELLIGENCE LEVEL High
SEXUAL INCLINATIONS Normal

Watch them now:
changing him.

The complete man lay before them, newly minted, ready for rebirth. Now came the final adjustments. They sought the gray brain within its pink wrapper, and entered it, and traveled through the bays and inlets of the mind, pausing now at this quiet cove, dropping anchor now at the base of that slab-sided cliff. They were operating, but doing it neatly. Here were no submucous resections, no glittering blades carving through gristle and bone, no sizzling lasers at work, no clumsy hammering at the tender meninges. Cold steel did not slash the synapses. The golden ones were subtler; they tuned the circuit that was Cassiday, boosted the gain, damped out the noise, and they did it very gently.

When they were finished with him, he was much more sensitive. He had several new hungers. They had granted him certain abilities.

Now they awakened him.

"You are alive, Cassiday," a feathery voice said. "Your ship was destroyed. Your companions were killed. You alone survived."

"Which hospital is this?"

"Not on Earth. You'll be going back soon. Stand up, Cassiday. Move your right hand. Your left. Flex your knees. Inflate your lungs. Open and close your eyes several times. What's your name, Cassiday?"

"Richard Henry Cassiday."

"How old?"

"Forty-one."

"Look at this reflection. Who do you see?"

"Myself."

"Do you have any further questions?"

"What did you do to me?"

"Repaired you, Cassiday. You were almost entirely destroyed."

"Did you change me any?"

"We made you more sensitive to the feelings of your fellow man."

"Oh," said Cassiday.

Follow Cassiday as he journeys:
> *back to Earth.*

He arrived on a day that had been programmed for snow. Light snow, quickly melting, an aesthetic treat rather than a true manifestation of weather. It was good to touch foot on the homeworld again. The golden ones had deftly arranged his return, putting him back aboard his wrecked ship and giving him enough of a push to get him within range of a distress sweep. The monitors had detected him and picked him up. How was it you survived the disaster unscathed, Spaceman Cassiday? Very simple, sir, I was outside the ship when it happened. It just went swoosh, and everybody was killed. And I only am escaped alone to tell thee.

They routed him to Mars and checked him out, and held him awhile in a decontamination lock on Luna, and finally sent him back to Earth. He stepped into the snowstorm, a big man with a rolling gait and careful calluses in all the right places. He had few friends, no relatives, enough cash units to see him through for a while, and a couple of ex-wives he could look up. Under the rules, he was entitled to a year off with full pay as his disaster allotment. He intended to accept the furlough.

He had not yet begun to make use of his new sensitivity. The golden ones had planned it so that his abilities would remain inoperative until he reached the homeworld. Now he had arrived, and it was time to begin using them, and the endlessly curious creatures who lived back of Iapetus waited patiently while Cassiday sought out those who had once loved him.

He began his quest in Chicago Urban District, because that was where the spaceport was, just outside of Rockford. The slidewalk took him quickly to the travertine tower, festooned with radiant inlays of ebony and violet-hued metal, and there, at the local Televector Central, Cassiday checked out the present whereabouts of his former wives. He was patient about it, a bland-faced, mild-eyed tower of flesh, pushing the right buttons and waiting placidly for the silken contacts to close somewhere in the depths

of the Earth. Cassiday had never been a violent man. He was calm. He
knew how to wait.

The machine told him that Beryl Fraser Cassiday Mellon lived in Boston
Urban District. The machine told him that Lureen Holstein Cassiday lived
in New York Urban District. The machine told him that Mirabel Gunryk
Cassiday Milman Reed lived in San Francisco Urban District.

The names awakened memories: warmth of flesh, scent of hair, touch
of hand, sound of voice. Whispers of passion. Snarls of contempt. Gasps of
love.

Cassiday, restored to life, went to see his ex-wives.

We find one now:
>   *safe and sound.*

Beryl's eyes were milky in the pupil, greenish where they should have
been white. She had lost weight in the last ten years, and now her face was
parchment stretched over bone, an eroded face, the cheekbones pressing
from within against the taut skin and likely to snap through at any moment.
Cassiday had been married to her for eight months when he was twenty-
four. They had separated after she insisted on taking the Sterility Pledge.
He had not particularly wanted children, but he was offended by her
maneuver all the same. Now she lay in a soothing cradle of webfoam, trying
to smile at him without cracking her lips.

"They said you'd been killed," she told him.

"I escaped. How have you been, Beryl?"

"You can see that. I'm taking the cure."

"Cure?"

"I was a triline addict. Can't you see? My eyes, my face? It melted me
away. But it was peaceful. Like disconnecting your soul. Only it would
have killed me, another year of it. Now I'm on the cure. They tapered me
off last month. They're building up my system with prosthetics. I'm full of
plastic now. But I'll live."

"You've remarried?" Cassiday asked.

"He split long ago. I've been alone five years. Just me and the triline.
But now I'm off that stuff." Beryl blinked laboriously. "You look so relaxed,
Dick. But you always were. So calm, so sure of yourself. *You'd* never get
yourself hooked on triline. Hold my hand, will you?"

He touched the withered claw. He felt the warmth come from her, the
need for love. Great throbbing waves came lalloping into him, low-
frequency pulses of yearning that filtered through him and went booming
onward to the watchers far away.

"You once loved me," Beryl said. "Then we were both silly. Love me
again. Help me get back on my feet. I need your strength."

"Of course I'll help you," Cassiday said.

He left her apartment and purchased three cubes of triline. Returning, he activated one of them and pressed it into Beryl's hand. The green-and-milky eyes roiled in terror.

"No," she whimpered.

The pain flooding from her shattered soul was exquisite in its intensity. Cassiday accepted the full flood of it. Then she clenched her fist, and the drug entered her metabolism, and she grew peaceful once more.

Observe the next one:
> *with a friend.*

The annunciator said, "Mr. Cassiday is here."

"Let him enter," replied Mirabel Gunryk Cassiday Milman Reed.

The door-sphincter irised open and Cassiday stepped through, into onyx and marble splendor. Beams of auburn palisander formed a polished wooden framework on which Mirabel lay, and it was obvious that she reveled in the sensation of hard wood against plump flesh. A cascade of crystal-colored hair tumbled to her shoulders. She had been Cassiday's for sixteen months in 2346, and she had been a slender, timid girl then, but now he could barely detect the outlines of that girl in this pampered mound.

"You've married well," he observed.

"Third time lucky," Mirabel said. "Sit down? Drink? Shall I adjust the environment?"

"It's fine." He remained standing. "You always wanted a mansion, Mirabel. My most intellectual wife, you were, but you had this love of comfort. You're comfortable now."

"Very."

"Happy?"

"I'm comfortable," Mirabel said. "I don't read much any more, but I'm comfortable."

Cassiday noticed what seemed to be a blanket crumpled in her lap—purple with golden threads, soft, idle, clinging close. It had several eyes. Mirabel kept her hands spread over it.

"From Ganymede?" he asked. "A pet?"

"Yes. My husband bought it for me last year. It's very precious to me."

"Very precious to anybody. I understand they're expensive."

"But lovable," said Mirabel. "Almost human. Quite devoted. I suppose you'll think I'm silly, but it's the most important thing in my life now. More than my husband, even. I love it, you see. I'm accustomed to having others love me, but there aren't many things that I've been able to love."

"May I see it?" Cassiday said mildly.

"Be careful."

"Certainly." He gathered up the Ganymedean creature. Its texture was extraordinary, the softest he had ever encountered. Something fluttered apprehensively within the flat body of the animal. Cassiday detected a parallel wariness coming from Mirabel as he handled her pet. He stroked the creature. It throbbed appreciatively. Bands of iridescence shimmered as it contracted in his hands.

She said, "What are you doing now, Dick? Still working for the spaceline?"

He ignored the "Tell me the line from Shakespeare, Mirabel. About flies. The flies and wanton boys."

Furrows sprouted in her pale brow. "It's from *Lear,*" she said. "Wait. Yes. *As flies to wanton boys are we to the gods. They kill us for their sport.*"

"That's the one," Cassiday said. His big hands knotted quickly about the blanketlike being from Ganymede. It turned a dull gray, and reedy fibers popped from its ruptured surface. Cassiday dropped it to the floor. The surge of horror and pain and loss that welled from Mirabel nearly stunned him, but he accepted it and transmitted it.

"Flies," he explained. "Wanton boys. My sport, Mirabel. I'm a god now, did you know that?" His voice was calm and cheerful. "Good-bye. Thank you."

One more awaits the visit:
Swelling with new life.

Lureen Holstein Cassiday, who was thirty-one years old, dark-haired, large-eyed, and seven months pregnant, was the only one of his wives who had not remarried. Her room in New York was small and austere. She had been a plump girl when she had been Cassiday's two-month wife five years ago, and she was even more plump now, but how much of the access of new meat was the result of the pregnancy Cassiday did not know.

"Will you marry now?" he asked.

Smiling, she shook her head. "I've got money, and I value my independence. I wouldn't let myself get into another deal like the one we had. Not with anyone."

"And the baby? You'll have it?"

She nodded savagely. "I worked hard to get it! You think it's easy? Two years of inseminations! A fortune in fees! Machines poking around in me—all the fertility boosters—oh no, you've got the picture wrong. This isn't an unwanted baby. This is a baby I sweated to have."

"That's interesting," said Cassiday. "I visited Mirabel and Beryl, too, and they each had their babies, too. Of sorts. Mirabel had a little beast from Ganymede. Beryl had a triline addiction that she was very proud of shaking.

And you've had a baby put in you, without any help from a man. All three of you seeking something. Interesting."

"Are you all right, Dick?"

"Fine."

"Your voice is so flat. You're just unrolling a lot of words. It's a little frightening."

"Mmm. Yes. Do you know the kind thing I did for Beryl? I bought her some triline cubes. And I took Mirabel's pet and wrung its — well, not its neck. I did it very calmly. I was never a passionate man."

"I think you've gone crazy, Dick."

"I feel your fear. You think I'm going to do something to your baby. Fear is of no interest, Lureen. But sorrow — yes, that's worth analyzing. Desolation. I want to study it. I want to help *them* study it. I think it's what they want to know about. Don't run from me, Lureen. I don't want to hurt you, not that way."

She was small-bodied and not very strong, and unwieldy in her pregnancy. Cassiday seized her gently by both wrists and drew her toward him. Already he could feel the new emotions coming from her, the self-pity behind the terror, and he had not even done anything to her.

How did you abort a fetus two months from term?

A swift kick in the belly might do it. Too crude, too crude. Yet Cassiday had not come armed with abortifacients, a handy ergot pill, a quick-acting spasmic inducer. So he brought his knee up sharply, deploring the crudity of it. Lureen sagged. He kicked her a second time. He remained completely tranquil as he did it, for it would be wrong to take joy in violence. A third kick seemed desirable. Then he released her.

She was still conscious, but she was writhing. Cassiday made himself receptive to the outflow. The child, he realized, was not yet dead within her. Perhaps it might not die at all. But it would certainly be crippled in some way. What he drained from Lureen was the awareness that she might bring forth a defective. The fetus would have to be destroyed. She would have to begin again. It was all quite sad.

"Why?" she muttered, "...why?"

Among the watchers:
> *the equivalent of dismay.*

Somehow it had not developed as the golden ones had anticipated. Even they could miscalculate, it appeared, and they found that a rewarding insight. Still, something had to be done about Cassiday.

They had given him powers. He could detect and transmit to them the raw emotions of others. That was useful to them, for from the data they could perhaps construct an understanding of human beings. But in rendering him a switching center for the emotions of others they had unavoidably been forced to blank out his own. And that was distorting the data.

He was too destructive now, in his joyless way. That had to be corrected. For now he partook too deeply of the nature of the golden ones themselves. *They* might have their sport with Cassiday, for he owed them a life. But he might not have his sport with others.

They reached down the line of communication to him and gave him his instructions.

"No," Cassiday said. "You're done with me now. There's no need to come back."

"Further adjustments are necessary."

"I disagree."

"You will not disagree for long."

Still disagreeing, Cassiday took ship for Mars, unable to stand aside from their command. On Mars he chartered a vessel that regularly made the Saturn run and persuaded it to come in by way of Iapetus. The golden ones took possession of him once he was within their immediate reach.

"What will you do to me?" Cassiday asked.

"Reverse the flow. You will no longer be sensitive to others. You will report to us on your own emotions. We will restore your conscience, Cassiday."

He protested. It was useless.

Within the glowing sphere of golden light they made their adjustments on him. They entered him and altered him and turned his perceptions inward, so that he might feed on his own misery like a vulture tearing at its entrails. That would be informative. Cassiday objected until he no longer had the power to object, and when his awareness returned it was too late to object.

"No," he murmured. In the yellow gleam he saw the faces of Beryl and Mirabel and Lureen. "You shouldn't have done this to me. You're torturing me...like you would a fly...."

There was no response. They sent him away, back to Earth. They returned him to the travertine towers and the rumbling slidewalks, to the house of pleasure on 485th Street, to the islands of light that blazed in the sky, to the eleven billion people. They turned him loose to go among them, and suffer, and report on his sufferings. And a time would come when they would release him, but not yet.

Here is Cassiday:
> *nailed to his cross.*

PASSENGERS (1967)

INTRODUCTION

1966—the year of "Hawksbill Station," *The Time Hoppers, Thorns,* and my big El Dorado book, *The Golden Dream*—was a watershed year for me. I had found my own voice as a writer and had attained a degree of skill surprising even to me; publishers were crowding around me, eager for my science fiction and for my nonfiction work as well; the days of grinding out hack assignments for magazines like *Trapped* or *True Men Adventures* were receding into history. And as the major works of 1966 began to find their way into print the following year, critics who had dismissed me as a cynical opportunist were taking a second look at what I was doing. I felt a heady sense of new beginnings, of having entered into a mature and fulfilling phase of my career. (I also managed to damage my health in the joyous overwork of it all, coming down with a bout of hyperthyroidism and spending most of the summer of 1966 as an invalid, frail and exhausted—a new experience for me. But by autumn I was back to normal and ready to tackle a full schedule, as the writing of a novel like *Thorns* in just ten working days in September of 1966 demonstrated. If that seems improbable to you, please accept my assurance that it seems pretty improbable to me, too. But the ledger entries are incontrovertibly there: ten working days.)

Suddenly, now, I found I had won the respect of my peers in the science-fiction world for something other than my ability to turn out salable work in high volume. Though barely into my thirties, I was elected president of the newly founded Science Fiction Writers of America early in 1967. I made my first appearance on the awards ballots since winning the Hugo as Most Promising New Author in 1956: *Thorns* was a Nebula nominee in 1967, and so was the novella version of "Hawksbill Station." (I finished second both times.) Both stories would be on the Hugo ballot as well, the following year, the Hugos following a somewhat different chronological schedule in those days. (More second-place finishes would be the result.)

And in January, 1967, I offered a story to the most difficult, cantankerous, demanding editor of the era—Damon Knight, famous for his well-aimed and ferocious attacks on all that was slovenly in science fiction. He had started an anthology of original fiction called *Orbit*. Selling a story to Damon struck me as a challenge that had to be surmounted; and so I sent him "Passengers," and on January 16 he sent it back, saying, "I can't fault this one technically, & it is surely dark & nasty enough to suit anybody, but I have a nagging feeling that there's something missing, and I'm not sure I can put my finger on it." But he offered some suggestions for revisions anyway, and I decided to try another draft, telling him on January 26, "You and your *Orbit* are a great tribulation to me. I suppose I could take "Passengers" and ship it off to Fred Pohl and collect my $120 and start all over trying to sell one to you, but I don't want to do that, because I believe this story represents just about the best I have in me, and if I can't get you to take it it's futile to go on submitting others."

The rewrite, Knight said, was close—not quite there. So I rewrote it again. And again. The hook was in me, and all I could do was wriggle. On March 22 he wrote to me again to say, "God help us both, I am going to ask you to revise this one more time. The love story now has every necessary element, but it seems to me it's an empty jug. Now I want you to put the love into it. I say this with a feeling of helplessness, because I don't know how to tell you to do it."

And then he proceeded to tell me, not how to do it, but why I should do it; and I did it and he bought the story, and published it in *Orbit* Four in 1968. And the following year it won me my first Nebula, for Best Short Story of the Year. (It was nominated for the Hugo, too, and should have won that as well—but it was beaten by a story from an earlier year that was technically ineligible for the ballot but got on it anyway.) Since then it has become a standard anthology piece, has been purchased by a Hollywood studio, has in general become one of my best known stories. The five drafts of it that I did between January and March of 1967 were an almighty nuisance but I have never regretted doing them.

There are only fragments of me left now. Chunks of memory have broken free and drifted away like calved glaciers. It is always like that when a Passenger leaves us. We can never be sure of all the things our borrowed bodies did. We have only the lingering traces, the imprints.

Like sand clinging to an ocean-tossed bottle. Like the throbbings of amputated legs.

I rise. I collect myself. My hair is rumpled; I comb it. My face is creased from too little sleep. There is sourness in my mouth. Has my Passenger been eating dung with my mouth? They do that. They do anything.

It is morning.

A gray, uncertain morning. I stare at it awhile, and then, shuddering, I opaque the window and confront instead the gray, uncertain surface of the inner panel. My room looks untidy. Did I have a woman here? There are ashes in the trays. Searching for butts, I find several with lipstick stains. Yes, a woman was here.

I touch the bedsheets. Still warm with shared warmth. Both pillows tousled. She has gone, though, and the Passenger is gone, and I am alone.

How long did it last, this time?

I pick up the phone and ring Central. "What is the date?"

The computer's bland feminine voice replies, "Friday, December fourth, nineteen eighty-seven."

"The time?"

"Nine fifty-one, Eastern Standard Time."

"The weather forecast?"

"Predicted temperature range for today thirty to thirty-eight. Current temperature, thirty-one. Wind from the north, sixteen miles an hour. Chances of precipitation slight."

"What do you recommend for a hangover?"

"Food or medication?"

"Anything you like," I say.

The computer mulls that one over for a while. Then it decides on both, and activates my kitchen. The spigot yields cold tomato juice. Eggs begin to fry. From the medicine slot comes a purplish liquid. The Central Computer is always so thoughtful. Do the Passengers ever ride it, I wonder?

What thrills could that hold for them? Surely it must be more exciting to borrow the million minds of Central than to live for a while in the faulty, short-circuited soul of a corroding human being!

December 4, Central said. Friday. So the Passenger had me for three nights.

I drink the purplish stuff and probe my memories in a gingerly way, as one might probe a festering sore.

I remember Tuesday morning. A bad time at work. None of the charts will come out right. The section manager irritable; he has been taken by Passengers three times in five weeks, and his section is in disarray as a result, and his Christmas bonus is jeopardized. Even though it is customary not to penalize a person for lapses due to Passengers, according to the system, the section manager seems to feel he will be treated unfairly. So he treats us unfairly. We have a hard time. Revise the charts, fiddle with the program, check the fundamentals ten times over. Out they come: the detailed forecasts for price variations of public utility securities, February-April 1988. That afternoon we are to meet and discuss the charts and what they tell us.

I do not remember Tuesday afternoon.

That must have been when the Passenger took me. Perhaps at work; perhaps in the mahogany-paneled boardroom itself, during the conference. Pink concerned faces all about me; I cough, I lurch, I stumble from my seat. They shake their heads sadly. No one reaches for me. No one stops me. It is too dangerous to interfere with one who has a Passenger. The chances are great that a second Passenger lurks nearby in the discorporate state, looking for a mount. So I am avoided. I leave the building.

After that, what?

Sitting in my room on bleak Friday morning, I eat my scrambled eggs and try to reconstruct the three lost nights.

Of course it is impossible. The conscious mind functions during the period of captivity, but upon withdrawal of the Passenger nearly every recollection goes too. There is only a slight residue, a gritty film of faint and ghostly memories. The mount is never precisely the same person afterwards; though he cannot recall the details of his experience, he is subtly changed by it.

I try to recall.

A girl? Yes: lipstick on the butts. Sex, then, here in my room. Young? Old? Blonde? Dark? Everything is hazy. How did my borrowed body behave? Was I a good lover? I try to be, when I am myself. I keep in shape. At 38, I can handle three sets of tennis on a summer afternoon without collapsing. I can make a woman glow as a woman is meant to glow. Not boasting: just categorizing. We have our skills. These are mine.

But Passengers, I am told, take wry amusement in controverting our skills. So would it have given my rider a kind of delight to find me a woman and force me to fail repeatedly with her?

I dislike that thought.

The fog is going from my mind now. The medicine prescribed by Central works rapidly. I eat, I shave, I stand under the vibrator until my skin is clean. I do my exercises. Did the Passenger exercise my body Wednesday and Thursday mornings? Probably not. I must make up for that. I am close to middle age, now; tonus lost is not easily regained.

I touch my toes twenty times, knees stiff.

I kick my legs in the air.

I lie flat and lift myself on pumping elbows.

The body responds, maltreated though it has been. It is the first bright moment of my awakening: to feel the inner tingling, to know that I still have vigor.

Fresh air is what I want next. Quickly I slip into my clothes and leave. There is no need for me to report to work today. They are aware that since Tuesday afternoon I have had a Passenger; they need not be aware that before dawn on Friday the Passenger departed. I will have a free day. I will walk the city's streets, stretching my limbs, repaying my body for the abuse it has suffered.

I enter the elevator. I drop fifty stories to the ground. I step out into the December dreariness.

The towers of New York rise about me.

In the street the cars stream forward. Drivers sit edgily at their wheels. One never knows when the driver of a nearby car will be borrowed, and there is always a moment of lapsed coordination as the Passenger takes over. Many lives are lost that way on our streets and highways; but never the life of a Passenger.

I begin to walk without purpose. I cross Fourteenth Street, heading north, listening to the soft violent purr of the electric engines. I see a boy jigging in the street and know he is being ridden. At Fifth and Twenty-second a prosperous-looking paunchy man approaches, his necktie askew, this morning's *Wall Street Journal* jutting from an overcoat pocket. He giggles. He thrusts out his tongue. Ridden. Ridden. I avoid him. Moving briskly, I come to the underpass that carries traffic below Thirty-fourth Street toward Queens, and pause for a moment to watch two adolescent girls quarreling at the rim of the pedestrian walk. One is a Negro. Her eyes are rolling in terror. The other pushes her closer to the railing. Ridden. But the Passenger does not have murder on its mind, merely pleasure. The Negro girl is released and falls in a huddled heap, trembling. Then she rises and runs. The other girl draws a long strand of gleaming hair into her mouth, chews on it, seems to awaken. She looks dazed.

I avert my eyes. One does not watch while a fellow sufferer is awakening. There is a morality of the ridden; we have so many new tribal mores in these dark days.

I hurry on.

Where am I going so hurriedly? Already I have walked more than a mile. I seem to be moving toward some goal, as though my Passenger still hunches in my skull, urging me about. But I know that is not so. For the moment, at least, I am free.

Can I be sure of that?

Cogito ergo sum no longer applies. We go on thinking even while we are ridden, and we live in quiet desperation, unable to halt our courses no matter how ghastly, no matter how self-destructive. I am certain that I can distinguish between the condition of bearing a Passenger and the condition of being free. But perhaps not. Perhaps I bear a particularly devilish Passenger which has not quitted me at all, but which merely has receded to the cerebellum, leaving me the illusion of freedom while all the time surreptitiously driving me onward to some purpose of its own.

Did we ever have more than that: the illusion of freedom?

But this is disturbing, the thought that I may be ridden without realizing it. I burst out in heavy perspiration, not merely from the exertion of walking. Stop. Stop here. Why must you walk? You are at Forty-second Street. There is the library. Nothing forces you onward. Stop a while, I tell myself. Rest on the library steps.

I sit on the cold stone and tell myself that I have made this decision for myself.

Have I? It is the old problem, free will versus determinism, translated into the foulest of forms. Determinism is no longer a philosopher's abstraction; it is cold alien tendrils sliding between the cranial sutures. The Passengers arrived three years ago. I have been ridden five times since then. Our world is quite different now. But we have adjusted even to this. We have adjusted. We have our mores. Life goes on. Our governments rule, our legislatures meet, our stock exchanges transact business as usual, and we have methods for compensating for the random havoc. It is the only way. What else can we do? Shrivel in defeat? We have an enemy we cannot fight; at best we can resist through endurance. So we endure.

The stone steps are cold against my body. In December few people sit here.

I tell myself that I made this long walk of my own free will, that I halted of my own free will, that no Passenger rides my brain now. Perhaps. Perhaps. I cannot let myself believe that I am not free.

Can it be, I wonder, that the Passenger left some lingering command in me? Walk to this place, halt at this place? That is possible too.

I look about me at the others on the library steps.

An old man, eyes vacant, sitting on newspaper. A boy of thirteen or so with flaring nostrils. A plump woman. Are all of them ridden? Passengers seem to cluster about me today. The more I study the ridden ones, the more convinced I become that I am, for the moment, free. The last time, I had three months of freedom between rides. Some people, they say, are scarcely ever free. Their bodies are in great demand, and they know only scattered bursts of freedom, a day here, a week there, an hour. We have never been able to determine how many Passengers infest our world. Millions, maybe. Or maybe five. Who can tell?

A wisp of snow curls down out of the gray sky. Central had said the chance of precipitation was slight. Are they riding Central this morning too?

I see the girl.

She sits diagonally across from me, five steps up and a hundred feet away, her black skirt pulled up on her knees to reveal handsome legs. She is young. Her hair is deep, rich auburn. Her eyes are pale; at this distance, I cannot make out the precise color. She is dressed simply. She is younger than thirty. She wears a dark green coat and her lipstick has a purplish tinge. Her lips are full, her nose slender, high-bridged, her eyebrows carefully plucked.

I know her.

I have spent the past three nights with her in my room. She is the one. Ridden, she came to me, and ridden, I slept with her. I am certain of this. The veil of memory opens; I see her slim body naked on my bed.

How can it be that I remember this?

It is too strong to be an illusion. Clearly this is something that I have been *permitted* to remember for reasons I cannot comprehend. And I remember more. I remember her soft gasping sounds of pleasure. I know that my own body did not betray me those three nights, nor did I fail her need.

And there is more. A memory of sinuous music; a scent of youth in her hair; the rustle of winter trees. Somehow she brings back to me a time of innocence, a time when I am young and girls are mysterious, a time of parties and dances and warmth and secrets.

I am drawn to her now.

There is an etiquette about such things, too. It is in poor taste to approach someone you have met while being ridden. Such an encounter gives you no privilege; a stranger remains a stranger, no matter what you and she may have done and said during your involuntary time together.

Yet I am drawn to her.

Why this violation of taboo? Why this raw breach of etiquette? I have never done this before. I have been scrupulous.

But I get to my feet and walk along the step on which I have been sitting, until I am below her, and I look up, and automatically she folds her ankles together and angles her knees as if in awareness that her position is not a modest one. I know from that gesture that she is not ridden now. My eyes meet hers. Her eyes are hazy green. She is beautiful, and I rack my memory for more details of our passion.

I climb step by step until I stand before her.

"Hello," I say.

She gives me a neutral look. She does not seem to recognize me. Her eyes are veiled, as one's eyes often are, just after the Passenger has gone. She purses her lips and appraises me in a distant way.

"Hello," she replies coolly. "I don't think I know you."

"No. You don't. But I have the feeling you don't want to be alone just now. And I know I don't." I try to persuade her with my eyes that my motives are decent. "There's snow in the air," I say. "We can find a warmer place. I'd like to talk to you."

"About what?"

"Let's go elsewhere, and I'll tell you. I'm Charles Roth."

"Helen Martin."

She gets to her feet. She still has not cast aside her cool neutrality; she is suspicious, ill at ease. But at least she is willing to go with me. A good sign.

"Is it too early in the day for a drink?" I ask.

"I'm not sure. I hardly know what time it is."

"Before noon."

"Let's have a drink anyway," she says, and we both smile.

We go to a cocktail lounge across the street. Sitting face to face in the darkness, we sip drinks, daiquiri for her, Bloody Mary for me. She relaxes a little. I ask myself what it is I want from her. The pleasure of her company, yes. Her company in bed? But I have already had that pleasure, three nights of it, though she does not know that. I want something more. Something more. What?

Her eyes are bloodshot. She has had little sleep these past three nights.

I say, "Was it very unpleasant for you?"

"What?"

"The Passenger."

A whiplash of reaction crosses her face. "How did you know I've had a Passenger?"

"I know."

"We aren't supposed to talk about it."

"I'm broadminded," I tell her. "My Passenger left me some time during the night. I was ridden since Tuesday afternoon."

"Mine left me about two hours ago, I think." Her cheeks color. She is doing something daring, talking like this. "I was ridden since Monday night. This was my fifth time."

"Mine also."

We toy with our drinks. Rapport is growing, almost without the need of words. Our recent experiences with Passengers give us something in common, although Helen does not realize how intimately we shared those experiences.

We talk. She is a designer of display windows. She has a small apartment several blocks from here. She lives alone. She asks me what I do. "Securities analyst," I tell her. She smiles. Her teeth are flawless. We have a second round of drinks. I am positive, now, that this is the girl who was in my room while I was ridden.

A seed of hope grows in me. It was a happy chance that brought us together again, so soon after we parted as dreamers. A happy chance, too, that some vestige of the dream lingered in my mind.

We have shared something, who knows what, and it must have been good to leave such a vivid imprint on me, and now I want to come to her conscious, aware, my own master, and renew that relationship, making it a real one this time. It is not proper, for I am trespassing on a privilege that is not mine except by virtue of our Passengers' brief presence in us. Yet I need her. I want her.

She seems to need me, too, without realizing who I am. But fear holds her back.

I am frightened of frightening her, and I do not try to press my advantage too quickly. Perhaps she would take me to her apartment with her now, perhaps not, but I do not ask. We finish our drinks. We arrange to meet by the library steps again tomorrow. My hand momentarily brushes hers. Then she is gone.

I fill three ashtrays that night. Over and over I debate the wisdom of what I am doing. But why not leave her alone? I have no right to follow her. In the place our world has become, we are wisest to remain apart.

And yet — there is that stab of half-memory when I think of her. The blurred lights of lost chances behind the stairs, of girlish laughter in second-floor corridors, of stolen kisses, of tea and cake. I remember the girl with the orchid in her hair, and the one in the spangled dress, and the one with the child's face and the woman's eyes, all so long ago, all lost, all gone, and I tell myself that this one I will not lose, I will not permit her to be taken from me.

Morning comes, a quiet Saturday. I return to the library, hardly expecting to find her there, but she is there, on the steps, and the sight of her is like a reprieve. She looks wary, troubled; obviously she has done much thinking, little sleeping. Together we walk along Fifth Avenue. She is quite close to me, but she does not take my arm. Her steps are brisk, short, nervous.

I want to suggest that we go to her apartment instead of to the cocktail lounge. In these days we must move swiftly while we are free. But I know it would be a mistake to think of this as a matter of tactics. Coarse haste would be fatal, bringing me perhaps an ordinary victory, a numbing defeat within it. In any event her mood hardly seems promising. I look at her, thinking of string music and new snowfalls, and she looks toward the gray sky.

She says, "I can feel them watching me all the time. Like vultures swooping overhead, waiting, waiting. Ready to pounce."

"But there's a way of beating them. We can grab little scraps of life when they're not looking."

"They're *always* looking."

"No," I tell her. "There can't be enough of them for that. Sometimes they're looking the other way. And while they are, two people can come together and try to share warmth."

"But what's the use?"

"You're too pessimistic, Helen. They ignore us for months at a time. We have a chance. We have a chance."

But I cannot break through her shell of fear. She is paralyzed by the nearness of the Passengers, unwilling to begin anything for fear it will be snatched away by our tormentors. We reach the building where she lives, and I hope she will relent and invite me in. For an instant she wavers, but only for an instant: she takes my hand in both of hers, and smiles, and the smile fades, and she is gone, leaving me only with the words, "Let's meet at the library again tomorrow. Noon."

I make the long chilling walk home alone.

Some of her pessimism seeps into me that night. It seems futile for us to try to salvage anything. More than that: wicked for me to seek her out, shameful to offer a hesitant love when I am not free. In this world, I tell myself, we should keep well clear of others, so that we do not harm anyone when we are seized and ridden.

I do not go to meet her in the morning.

It is best this way, I insist. I have no business trifling with her. I imagine her at the library, wondering why I am late, growing tense, impatient, then annoyed. She will be angry with me for breaking our date, but her anger will ebb, and she will forget me quickly enough.

Monday comes. I return to work.

Naturally, no one discusses my absence. It is as though I have never been away. The market is strong that morning. The work is challenging; it is midmorning before I think of Helen at all. But once I think of her, I can think of nothing else. My cowardice in standing her up. The childishness of Saturday night's dark thoughts. Why accept fate so passively? Why give in? I want to fight, now, to carve out a pocket of security despite the odds. I feel a deep conviction that it can be done. The Passengers may never bother the two of us again, after all. And that flickering smile of hers outside her building Saturday, that momentary glow — it should have told me that behind her wall of fear she felt the same hopes. She was waiting for me to lead the way. And I stayed home instead.

At lunchtime I go to the library, convinced it is futile.

But she is there. She paces along the steps; the wind slices at her slender figure. I go to her.

She is silent a moment. "Hello," she says finally.

"I'm sorry about yesterday."

"I waited a long time for you."

I shrug. "I made up my mind that it was no use to come. But then I changed my mind again."

She tries to look angry. But I know she is pleased to see me again — else why did she come here today? She cannot hide her inner pleasure. Nor can I. I point across the street to the cocktail lounge.

"A daiquiri?" I say. "As a peace offering?"

"All right."

Today the lounge is crowded, but we find a booth somehow. There is a brightness in her eyes that I have not seen before. I sense that a barrier is crumbling within her.

"You're less afraid of me, Helen," I say.

"I've never been afraid of you. I'm afraid of what could happen if we take the risks."

"Don't be. Don't be."

"I'm trying not to be afraid. But sometimes it seems so hopeless. Since *they* came here —"

"We can still try to live our own lives."

"Maybe."

"We have to. Let's make a pact, Helen. No more gloom. No more worrying about the terrible things that might just maybe happen. All right?"

A pause. Then a cool hand against mine.

"All right."

We finish our drinks, and I present my Credit Central to pay for them, and we go outside. I want her to tell me to forget about this afternoon's work and come home with her. It is inevitable, now, that she will ask me, and better sooner than later.

We walk a block. She does not offer the invitation. I sense the struggle inside her, and I wait, letting that struggle reach its own resolution without interference from me. We walk a second block. Her arm is through mine, but she talks only of her work, of the weather, and it is a remote, arm's-length conversation. At the next corner she swings around, away from her apartment, back toward the cocktail lounge. I try to be patient with her.

I have no need to rush things now, I tell myself. Her body is not a secret to me. We have begun our relationship topsy-turvy, with the physical part first; now it will take time to work backward to the more difficult part that some people call love.

But of course she is not aware that we have known each other that way. The wind blows swirling snowflakes in our faces, and somehow the cold sting awakens honesty in me. I know what I must say. I must relinquish my unfair advantage.

I tell her, "While I was ridden last week, Helen, I had a girl in my room."

"Why talk of such things now?"

"I have to, Helen. You were the girl."

She halts. She turns to me. People hurry past us in the street. Her face is very pale, with dark red spots growing in her cheeks.

"That's not funny, Charles."

"It wasn't meant to be. You were with me from Tuesday night to early Friday morning."

"How can you possibly know that?"

"I do. I do. The memory is clear. Somehow it remains, Helen. I see your whole body."

"Stop it, Charles."

"We were very good together," I say. "We must have pleased our Passengers because we were so good. To see you again — it was like waking from a dream, and finding that the dream was real, the girl right there — "

"No!"

"Let's go to your apartment and begin again."

She says, "You're being deliberately filthy, and I don't know why, but there wasn't any reason for you to spoil things. Maybe I was with you and maybe I wasn't, but you wouldn't know it, and if you did know it you should keep your mouth shut about it, and — "

"You have a birthmark the size of a dime," I say, "about three inches below your left breast."

She sobs and hurls herself at me, there in the street. Her long silvery nails rake my cheeks. She pummels me. I seize her. Her knees assail me. No one pays attention; those who pass by assume we are ridden, and turn their heads. She is all fury, but I have my arms around hers like metal bands, so that she can only stamp and snort, and her body is close against mine. She is rigid, anguished.

In a low, urgent voice I say, "We'll defeat them, Helen. We'll finish what they started. Don't fight me. There's no reason to fight me. I know, it's a fluke that I remember you, but let me go with you and I'll prove that we belong together."

"Let—go—"

"Please. Please. Why should we be enemies? I don't mèan you any harm. I love you, Helen. Do you remember, when we were kids, we could play at being in love? I did; you must have done it too. Sixteen, seventeen years old. The whispers, the conspiracies—all a big game, and we knew it. But the game's over. We can't afford to tease and run. We have so little time, when we're free—we have to trust, to open ourselves—"

"It's wrong."

"No. Just because it's the stupid custom for two people brought together by Passengers to avoid one another, that doesn't mean we have to follow it. Helen—Helen—"

Something in my tone registers with her. She ceases to struggle. Her rigid body softens. She looks up at me, her tearstreaked face thawing, her eyes blurred.

"Trust me," I say. "Trust me, Helen!"

She hesitates. Then she smiles.

***

In that moment I feel the chill at the back of my skull, the sensation as of a steel needle driven deep through bone. I stiffen. My arms drop away from her. For an instant, I lose touch, and when the mists clear all is different.

"Charles?" she says. *"Charles?"*

Her knuckles are against her teeth. I turn, ignoring her, and go back into the cocktail lounge. A young man sits in one of the front booths. His dark hair gleams with pomade; his cheeks are smooth. His eyes meet mine.

I sit down. He orders drinks. We do not talk.

My hand falls on his wrist, and remains there. The bartender, serving the drinks, scowls but says nothing. We sip our cocktails and put the drained glasses down.

"Let's go," the young man says.

I follow him out.

NIGHTWINGS (1968)

INTRODUCTION

The messy, chaotic, and ultimately well-nigh apocalyptic year of 1968 — the year of the Tet offensive and other dismal military events in Vietnam, the year Robert F. Kennedy and Martin Luther King, Jr. were assassinated, the year when student protesters turned universities all over the world into armed camps, when Soviet troops marched into Prague to snuff out Czech liberty, when the Democratic Party's national convention produced open warfare in the streets of Chicago — gave me a private foretaste of the turmoil it was destined to bring when, on a bitterly cold February night, I awakened at half past three in the morning to discover that my house was on fire.

By dawn I knew the worst. The roof was gone; the attic, where I kept a reference library, had been gutted; my third-floor office was partially destroyed; the lower floors of the house had suffered such extensive water damage that the entire structure would have to be rebuilt from within. And so, amidst the general lunacy and nightmarish frenzy of that strange year, I would for nine months find myself living in exile from that splendid house in one of New York City's loveliest neighborhoods — nine months of exhaustion, depression, improvised quarters, cartons and packing crates, limited access to the reference materials I needed in my work, to my own files and notes, to everything that was part of an inordinately active literary career. While the rest of the world was exuberantly taking leave of its sanity, that year of 1968, I was struggling to hang on to mine.

The cost of rebuilding the house was immense (and kept climbing from week to week as the roaring war-driven inflation of the Vietnam years took hold.) The insurance money would, as it always does, fall short of the actual expense; and the first payment was delayed by the usual bureaucratic snafus for three full months. Though the impact of the fire on every aspect of my life had left me drained of energy, I had no choice but to get back to work as soon as I could replace my typewriter and find a flat surface on which to place it.

The first thing I wrote after the fire — I began it about ten days later, and completed it, groggy as I was, in something like five days — was a 19,000-word novella called "Nightwings."

I had no idea that I was beginning a novel, then. I was too weary to think about anything so long term. A quick story for one of the top-level science-fiction magazines would bring me about $500—something like $5000 in modern purchasing power—and that would get me through the basic living expenses of the first few weeks. The story came to me, as so many of mine do, with the title first—"'Nightwings,'" I asked myself. "What could that possibly refer to?"—and then a group of images, a winged girl, a sky full of invading alien ships, a blinded prince. Within moments a story had come together in my mind, by a process I have never dared to try to understand. I knew that I would set it in the very far future and try for a certain romantic, incantatory tone. Even the first sentence arrived in that early wonderful rush: "Roum is a city built on seven hills."

I sat down and wrote it as fast as I could. And sent it to Frederik Pohl of *Galaxy* early in March, 1968, and Fred, who had had a house fire of his own and knew precisely what I was going through, sent me a check by return mail. What he didn't manage to tell me was just how much he liked the story. As he explained in some chagrin a couple of months later, "I just discovered that I dictated a letter to you on 'Nightwings' when I got it, and it was never typed up. This is a serious oversight, because what I said in the letter was that I thought it was a great story and admired you enormously for having written it."

That was a good thing to hear, because Fred and I had had some pretty heated correspondence in the interim about the two sequels to the original story that I had written for him by then, and I welcomed this pacifying gesture. But at the time I wrote the original one I had no time to worry about whether it was a great story, or even a good one, or whether Fred Pohl really and truly loved it. What mattered was the check for $513 that the story produced, which would pay several weeks' rent at my current temporary quarters.

I went on quickly to write a story called "Ishmael in Love" for *Fantasy & Science Fiction*, one of the other top sf magazines of the time, and then a short book on the wonders of ancient Chinese science for young readers. At the pace I worked back then, I got both of these projects out of the way before the end of March. By that time it had occurred to me that the "Nightwings" novella was, in fact, the opening section of a three-part novel that would carry my protagonist deeper and deeper into the strange world I had created until he, and the entire conquered Earth, attained rebirth and redemption. And so on March 18 I told Fred Pohl—who tended to like series stories anyway—that I was going to write two sequels of about the same length as the first story. "Go ahead," he told me. Which is how, eventually, the novel-length book called *Nightwings*, of which the novella of the same title is the opening sequence, came into being.

The world outside was a pretty wild place while I was writing those stories. Police stormed five student-occupied buildings at my alma mater,

Columbia University, to end a sit-in by war protesters; all of France was paralyzed by a general strike; the U. S. Supreme Court upheld a new law making it illegal to burn draft cards; and Robert F. Kennedy was assassinated while campaigning for the Presidency in Los Angeles. Against this background of personal stress and mounting global madness I wrote the second and third of my three stories about the far-future civilization of Earth's Third Cycle.

"Nightwings," the first of the three, was published in July, in the edition of *Galaxy* dated September, 1968. It won immediate reader acclaim, and when I showed up at that year's World Science Fiction Convention in Berkeley, California (where the People's Park riots were going on practically next door, and whiffs of tear gas drifted through the convention hotel), I heard much in its praise. Story number two, called "Perris Way," appeared in the issue after next, dated November, 1968. The final story, "To Jorslem," followed in the February, 1969 issue.

In the spring of 1969 "Nightwings" was one of five stories to make the final Nebula Award ballot in the Best Novella category, but finished second to Anne McCaffrey's "Dragonrider." Then, a few months later, running against the same group of stories, it won me that year's Best Novella Hugo award — my first Hugo award for a specific piece of fiction. (An earlier one, in 1956, was for being the best new writer of the year.) As for the novel that I made out of the three magazine stories by dint of slight revisions and the addition of a small amount of new connective tissue, it was published in September, 1969, has been translated into many languages and mentioned in various lists of great science fiction novels, and remains in print to this day.

ONE

Roum is a city built on seven hills. They say it was a capital of man in one of the earlier cycles. I did not know of that, for my guild was Watching, not Remembering; but yet as I had my first glimpse of Roum, coming upon it from the south at twilight, I could see that in former days it must have been of great significance. Even now it was a mighty city of many thousands of souls.

Its bony towers stood out sharply against the dusk. Lights glimmered appealingly. On my left hand the sky was ablaze with splendor as the sun relinquished possession; streaming bands of azure and violet and crimson folded and writhed about one another in the nightly dance that brings the darkness. To my right, blackness had already come. I attempted to find the seven hills, and failed, and still I knew that this was that Roum of majesty toward which all roads are bent, and I felt awe and deep respect for the works of our bygone fathers.

We rested by the long straight road, looking up at Roum. I said, "It is a goodly city. We will find employment there." Beside me, Avluela fluttered her lacy wings. "And food?" she asked in her high, fluty voice. "And shelter? And wine?"

"Those too," I said. "All of those."

"How long have we been walking, Watcher?" she asked.

"Two days. Three nights."

"If I had been flying, it would have been more swift."

"For you," I said. "You would have left us far behind and never seen us again. Is that your desire?"

She came close to me and rubbed the rough fabric of my sleeve, and then she pressed herself at me the way a flirting cat might do. Her wings unfolded into two broad sheets of gossamer through which I could still see the sunset and the evening lights, blurred, distorted, magical. I sensed the fragrance of her midnight hair. I put my arms to her and embraced her slender, boyish body.

She said, "You know it is my desire to remain with you always, Watcher. Always!"

"Yes, Avluela."

"Will we be happy in Roum?"

"We will be happy," I said, and released her.

"Shall we go into Roum now?"

"I think we should wait for Gormon," I said, shaking my head. "He'll be back soon from his explorations." I did not want to tell her of my weariness. She was only a child, seventeen summers old; what did she know of weariness or of age? And I was old. Not as old as Roum, but old enough.

"While we wait," she said, "may I fly?"

"Fly, yes."

I squatted beside our cart and warmed my hands at the throbbing generator while Avluela prepared to fly. First she removed her garments, for her wings have little strength and she cannot lift such extra baggage. Lithely, deftly, she peeled the glassy bubbles from her tiny feet and wriggled free of her crimson jacket and her soft, furry leggings. The vanishing light in the west sparkled over her slim form. Like all Fliers, she carried no surplus body tissue: her breasts were mere bumps, her buttocks flat, her thighs so spindly that there was a span of inches between them when she stood. Could she have weighed more than a quintal? I doubt it. Looking at her, I felt, as always, gross and earthbound, a thing of loathsome flesh, and yet I am not a heavy man.

By the roadside she genuflected, knuckles to the ground, head bowed to knees, as she said whatever ritual it is that the Fliers say. Her back was to me. Her delicate wings fluttered, filled with life, rose about her like a cloak whipped up by the breeze. I could not comprehend how such wings could possibly lift even so slight a form as Avluela's. They were not hawk wings but butterfly wings, veined and transparent, marked here and there with blotches of pigment, ebony and turquoise and scarlet. A sturdy ligament joined them to the two flat pads of muscle beneath her sharp shoulder blades; but what she did not have was the massive breastbone of a flying creature, the bands of corded muscle needed for flight. Oh, I know that the Fliers use more than muscle to get aloft, that there are mystical disciplines in their mystery. Even so, I, who was of the Watchers, remained skeptical of the more fantastic guilds.

Avluela finished her words. She rose; she caught the breeze with her wings; she ascended several feet. There she remained, suspended between earth and sky, while her wings beat frantically. It was not yet night, and Avluela's wings were merely nightwings. By day she could not fly, for the terrible pressure of the solar wind would hurl her to the ground. Now, midway between dusk and dark, it was still not the best time for her to go up. I saw her thrust toward the east by the remnant of light in the sky. Her arms as well as her wings thrashed; her small pointed face was grim with concentration; on her thin lips were the words of her guild. She doubled her body and shot it out, head going one way, rump the other; and abruptly she hovered horizontally, looking groundward, her wings thrashing against the air. *Up, Avluela! Up!*

Up it was, as by will alone she conquered the vestige of light that still glowed.

With pleasure I surveyed her naked form against the darkness. I could see her clearly, for a Watcher's eyes are keen. She was five times her own height in the air now, and her wings spread to their full expanse, so that the towers of Roum were in partial eclipse for me. She waved. I threw her a kiss and offered words of love. Watchers do not marry, nor do they engender children, but yet Avluela was as a daughter to me, and I took pride in her flight. We had traveled together a year now, since we had first met in Agupt, and it was as though I had known her all my long life. From her I drew a renewal of strength. I do not know what it was she drew from me; security, knowledge, a continuity with the days before her birth. I hoped only that she loved me as I loved her.

Now she was far aloft. She wheeled, soared, dived, pirouetted, danced. Her long black hair streamed from her scalp. Her body seemed only an incidental appendage to those two great wings which glistened and throbbed and gleamed in the night. Up she rose, glorying in her freedom from gravity, making me feel all the more leaden-footed; and like some slender rocket she shot abruptly away in the direction of Roum. I saw the soles of her feet, the tips of her wings; then I saw her no more.

I sighed. I thrust my hands into the pits of my arms to keep them warm. How is it that I felt a winter chill while the girl Avluela could soar joyously bare through the sky?

It was now the twelfth of the twenty hours, and time once again for me to do the Watching. I went to the cart, opened my cases, prepared the instruments. Some of the dial covers were yellowed and faded; the indicator needles had lost their luminous coating; sea stains defaced the instrument housings, a relic of the time that pirates had assailed me in Earth Ocean. The worn and cracked levers and nodes responded easily to my touch as I entered the preliminaries. First one prays for a pure and perceptive mind; then one creates the affinity with one's instruments; then one does the actual Watching, searching the starry heavens for the enemies of man. Such was my skill and my craft. I grasped handles and knobs, thrust things from my mind, prepared myself to become an extension of my cabinet of devices.

I was only just past my threshold and into the first phase of Watchfulness when a deep and resonant voice behind me said, "Well, Watcher, how goes it?"

I sagged against the cart. There is a physical pain in being wrenched so unexpectedly from one's work. For a moment I felt claws clutching at my heart. My face grew hot; my eyes would not focus; the saliva drained from my throat. As soon as I could, I took the proper protective measures to ease the metabolic drain, and severed myself from my instruments. Hiding my trembling as much as possible, I turned around.

Gormon, the other member of our little band, had appeared and stood jauntily beside me. He was grinning, amused at my distress, but I could not feel angry with him. One does not show anger at a guildless person no matter what the provocation.

Tightly, with effort, I said, "Did you spend your time rewardingly?"

"Very. Where's Avluela?"

I pointed heavenward. Gormon nodded.

"What have you found?" I asked.

"That this city is definitely Roum."

"There never was doubt of that."

"For me there was. But now I have proof."

"Yes?"

"In the overpocket. Look!"

From his tunic he drew his overpocket, set it on the pavement beside me, and expanded it so that he could insert his hands into its mouth. Grunting a little, he began to pull something heavy from the pouch— something of white stone—a long marble column, I now saw, fluted, pocked with age.

"From a temple of Imperial Roum!" Gormon exulted.

"You shouldn't have taken that."

"Wait!" he cried, and reached into the overpocket once more. He took from it a handful of circular metal plaques and scattered them jingling at my feet. "Coins! Money! Look at them, Watcher! The faces of the Caesars!"

"Of whom?"

"The ancient rulers. Don't you know your history of past cycles?"

I peered at him curiously. "You claim to have no guild, Gormon. Could it be you are a Rememberer and are concealing it from me?"

"Look at my face, Watcher. Could I belong to any guild? Would a Changeling be taken?"

"True enough," I said, eyeing the golden hue of him, the thick waxen skin, the red-pupiled eyes, the jagged mouth. Gormon had been weaned on teratogenetic drugs; he was a monster, handsome in his way, but a monster nevertheless, a Changeling, outside the laws and customs of man as they are practiced in the Third Cycle of civilization. And there is no guild of Changelings.

"There's more," Gormon said. The overpocket was infinitely capacious; the contents of a world, if need be, could be stuffed into its shriveled gray maw, and still it would be no longer than a man's hand. Gormon took from it bits of machinery, reading spools, an angular thing of brown metal that might have been an ancient tool, three squares of shining glass, five slips of paper — *paper!* — and a host of other relics of antiquity. "See?" he said. "A fruitful stroll, Watcher! And not just random booty. Everything recorded, everything labeled, stratum, estimated age, position when *in situ.* Here we have many thousands of years of Roum."

"Should you have taken these things?" I asked doubtfully.

"Why not? Who is to miss them? Who of this cycle cares for the past?"

"The Rememberers."

"They don't need solid objects to help them do their work."

"Why do you want these things, though?"

"The past interests me, Watcher. In my guildless way I have my scholarly pursuits. Is that wrong? May not even a monstrosity seek knowledge?"

"Certainly, certainly. Seek what you wish. Fulfill yourself in your own way. This is Roum. At dawn we enter. I hope to find employment here."

"You may have difficulties."

"How so?"

"There are many Watchers already in Roum, no doubt. There will be little need for your services."

"I'll seek the favor of the Prince of Roum," I said.

"The Prince of Roum is a hard and cold and cruel man."

"You know of him?"

Gormon shrugged. "Somewhat." He began to stuff his artifacts back in the overpocket. "Take your chances with him, Watcher. What other choice do you have?"

"None," I said, and Gormon laughed, and I did not.

He busied himself with his ransacked loot of the past. I found myself deeply depressed by his words. He seemed so sure of himself in an uncertain world, this guildless one, this mutated monster, this man of inhuman look; how could he be so cool, so casual? He lived without concern for calamity and mocked those who admitted to fear. Gormon had been traveling with us for nine days, now, since we had met him in the ancient city beneath the volcano to the south by the edge of the sea. I had not suggested that he join us; he had invited himself along, and at Avluela's bidding I had accepted. The roads are dark and cold at this time of year, and dangerous beasts of many species abound, and an old man journeying with a girl might well consider taking with him a brawny one like Gormon. Yet there were times I wished he had not come with us, and this was one.

Slowly I walked back to my equipment.

Gormon said, as though first realizing it, "Did I interrupt you at your Watching?"

I said mildly, "You did."

"Sorry. Go and start again. I'll leave you in peace." And he gave me his dazzling lopsided smile, so full of charm that it took the curse off the easy arrogance of his words.

I touched the knobs, made contact with the nodes, monitored the dials. But I did not enter Watchfulness, for I remained aware of Gormon's presence and fearful that he would break into my concentration once again at a painful moment, despite his promise. At length I looked away from the apparatus. Gormon stood at the far side of the road, craning his neck for some sight of Avluela. The moment I turned to him he became aware of me.

"Something wrong, Watcher?"

"No. The moment's not propitious for my work. I'll wait."

"Tell me," he said. "When Earth's enemies really do come from the stars, will your machines let you know it?"

"I trust they will."

"And then?"

"Then I notify the Defenders."

"After which your life's work is over?"

"Perhaps," I said.

"Why a whole guild of you, though? Why not one master center where the Watch is kept? Why a bunch of itinerant Watchers drifting from place to place?"

"The more vectors of detection," I said, "the greater the chance of early awareness of the invasion."

"Then an individual Watcher might well turn his machines on and not see anything, with an invader already here."

"It could happen. And so we practice redundancy."

"You could carry it to an extreme, I sometimes think." Gormon laughed. "Do you actually believe an invasion is coming?"

"I do," I said stiffly. "Else my life was a waste."

"And why should the star people want Earth? What do we have here besides the remnants of old empires? What would they do with miserable Roum? With Perris? With Jorslem? Rotting cities! Idiot princes! Come, Watcher, admit it: the invasion's a myth, and you go through meaningless motions four times a day. Eh?"

"It is my craft and my science to Watch. It is yours to jeer. Each of us to our specialty, Gormon."

"Forgive me," he said with mock humility. "Go, then, and Watch."

"I shall."

Angrily I turned back to my cabinet of instruments, determined now to ignore any interruption, no matter how brutal. The stars were out; I gazed at the glowing constellations, and automatically my mind registered the many worlds. Let us Watch, I thought. Let us keep our vigil despite the mockers.

I entered full Watchfulness.

I clung to the grips and permitted the surge of power to rush through me. I cast my mind to the heavens and searched for hostile entities. What ecstasy! What incredible splendor! I who had never left this small planet roved the black spaces of the void, glided from star to burning star, saw the planets spinning like tops. Faces stared back at me as I journeyed, some without eyes, some with many eyes, all the complexity of the many-peopled galaxy accessible to me. I spied out possible concentrations of inimitable force. I inspected drilling-grounds and military encampments. I sought, as I had sought four times daily for all my adult life, for the invaders who had been promised us, the conquerors who at the end of the days were destined to seize our tattered world.

I found nothing, and when I came up from my trance, sweaty and drained, I saw Avluek descending.

Feather-light she landed. Gormon called to her, and she ran, bare, her little breasts quivering, and he enfolded her smallness in his powerful arms, and they embraced, not passionately but joyously. When he released her she turned to me.

"Roum," she gasped. *"Roum!"*

"You saw it?"

"Everything! Thousands of people! Lights! Boulevards! A market! Broken buildings many cycles old! Oh, Watcher, how wonderful Roum is!"

"Your flight was a good one, then," I said.

"A miracle!"

"Tomorrow we go to dwell in Roum."

"No, Watcher, tonight, tonight!" She was girlishly eager, her face bright with excitement. "It's just a short journey more! Look, it's just over there!"

"We should rest first," I said. "We do not want to arrive weary in Roum."

"We can rest when we get there," Avluela answered. "Come! Pack everything! You've done your Watching, haven't you?"

"Yes. Yes."

"Then let's go. To Roum! To Roum!"

I looked in appeal at Gormon. Night had come; it was time to make camp, to have our few hours of sleep.

For once Gormon sided with me. He said to Avluela, "The Watcher's right. We can all use some rest. We'll go into Roum at dawn."

Avluela pouted. She looked more like a child than ever. Her wings drooped; her underdeveloped body slumped. Petulantly she closed her wings until they were mere fist-sized humps on her back, and picked up the garments she had scattered on the road. She dressed while we made camp. I distributed food tablets; we entered our receptacles; I fell into troubled sleep and dreamed of Avluela limned against the crumbling moon, and Gormon flying beside her. Two hours before dawn I arose and performed my first Watch of the new day while they still slept. Then I aroused them, and we went onward toward the fabled imperial city, onward toward Roum.

TWO

The morning's light was bright and harsh, as though this were some young world newly created. The road was all but empty; people do not travel much in these latter days unless, like me, they are wanderers by habit and profession. Occasionally we stepped aside to let a chariot of some member of the guild of Masters go by, drawn by a dozen expressionless neuters harnessed in series. Four such vehicles went by in the first two hours of the day, each shuttered and sealed to hide the Master's proud features from the gaze of such common folk as we. Several rollerwagons laden with produce passed us, and a number of floaters soared overhead. Generally we had the road to ourselves, however.

The environs of Roum showed vestiges of antiquity: isolated columns, the fragments of an aqueduct transporting nothing from nowhere to nowhere, the portals of a vanished temple. That was the oldest Roum we saw, but there were accretions of the later Roums of subsequent cycles: the huts of peasants, the domes of power drains, the hulls of dwelling-towers. Infrequently we met with the burned-out shell of some ancient airship. Gormon examined everything, taking samples from time to time. Avluela looked, wide-eyed, saying nothing. We walked on, until the walls of the city loomed before us.

They were of a blue glossy stone, neatly joined, rising to a height of perhaps eight men. Our road pierced the wall through a corbelled arch; the gate stood open. As we approached the gate, a figure came toward us; he was hooded, masked, a man of extraordinary height wearing the somber garb of the guild of Pilgrims. One does not approach such a person oneself, but one heeds him if he beckons. The Pilgrim beckoned.

Through his speaking grille he said, "Where from?"

"The south. I lived in Agupt awhile, then crossed Land Bridge to Talya," I replied.

"Where bound?"

"Roum, awhile."

"How goes the Watch?"

"As customary."

"You have a place to stay in Roum?" the Pilgrim asked.

I shook my head. "We trust to the kindness of the Will."

"The Will is not always kind," said the Pilgrim absently. "Nor is there much need of Watchers in Roum. Why do you travel with a Flier?"

"For company's sake. And because she is young and needs protection."

"Who is the other one?"

"He is guildless, a Changeling."

"So I can see. But why is he with you?"

"He is strong and I am old, and so we travel together. Where are you bound, Pilgrim?"

"Jorslem. Is there another destination for my guild?"

I conceded the point with a shrug.

The Pilgrim said, "Why do you not come to Jorslem with me?"

"My road lies north now. Jorslem is in the south, close by Agupt."

"You have been to Agupt and not to Jorslem?" he said, puzzled.

"Yes. The time was not ready for me to see Jorslem."

"Come now. We will walk together on the road, Watcher, and we will talk of the old times and of the times to come, and I will assist you in your Watching, and you will assist me in my communions with the Will. Is it agreed?"

It was a temptation. Before my eyes flashed the image of Jorslem the Golden, its holy buildings and shrines, its places of renewal where the old are made young, its spires, its tabernacles. Even though I am a man set in his ways, I was willing at the moment to abandon Roum and go with the Pilgrim to Jorslem.

I said, "And my companions—"

"Leave them. It is forbidden for me to travel with the guildless, and I do not wish to travel with a female. You and I, Watcher, will go to Jorslem together."

Avluela, who had been standing to one side frowning through all this colloquy, shot me a look of sudden terror.

"I will not abandon them," I said.

"Then I go to Jorslem alone," said the Pilgrim. Out of his robe stretched a bony hand, the fingers long and white and steady. I touched my fingers reverently to the tips of his, and the Pilgrim said, "Let the Will give you mercy, friend Watcher. And when you reach Jorslem, search for me."

He moved on down the road without further conversation.

Gormon said to me, "You would have gone with him, wouldn't you?"

"I considered it."

"What could you find in Jorslem that isn't here? That's a holy city and so is this. Here you can rest awhile. You're in no shape for more walking now."

"You may be right," I conceded, and with the last of my energy I strode toward the gate of Roum.

Watchful eyes scanned us from slots in the wall. When we were at midpoint in the gate, a fat, pockmarked Sentinel with sagging jowls halted us and asked our business in Roum. I stated my guild and purpose, and he gave a snort of disgust.

"Go elsewhere, Watcher! We need only useful men here."

"Watching has its uses," I said mildly.

"No doubt. No doubt." He squinted at Avluela. "Who's this? Watchers are celibates, no?"

"She is nothing more than a traveling companion."

The Sentinel guffawed coarsely. "It's a route you travel often, I wager! Not that there's much to her. What is she, thirteen, fourteen? Come here, child. Let me check you for contraband." He ran his hands quickly over her, scowling as he felt her breasts, then raising an eyebrow as he encountered the mounds of her wings below her shoulders. "What's this? What's this? More in back than in front! A Flier, are you? Very dirty business, Fliers consorting with foul old Watchers." He chuckled and put his hand on Avluela's body in a way that sent Gormon starting forward in fury, murder in his fire-circled eyes. I caught him in time and grasped his wrist with all my strength, holding him back lest he ruin the three of us by an attack on the Sentinel. He tugged at me, nearly pulling me over; then he grew calm and subsided, icily watching as the fat one finished checking Avluela for "contraband."

At length the Sentinel turned in distaste to Gormon and said, "What kind of thing are you?"

"Guildless, your mercy," Gormon said in sharp tones. "The humble and worthless product of teratogenesis, and yet nevertheless a free man who desires entry to Roum."

"Do we need more monsters here?"

"I eat little and work hard."

"You'd work harder still, if you were neutered," said the Sentinel.

Gormon glowered. I said, "May we have entry?"

"A moment." The Sentinel donned his thinking cap and narrowed his eyes as he transmitted a message to the memory tanks. His face tensed with the effort; then it went slack, and moments later came the reply. We could not hear the transaction at all; but from his disappointed look, it appeared evident that no reason had been found to refuse us admission to Roum.

"Go on in," he said. "The three of you. Quickly!"

We passed beyond the gate.

Gormon said, "I could have split him open with a blow."

"And be neutered by nightfall. A little patience, and we've come into Roum."

"The way he handled her—!"

"You take a very possessive attitude toward Avluela," I said. "Remember that she's a Flier, and not sexually available to the guildless."

Gormon ignored my thrust. "She arouses me no more than you do, Watcher. But it pains me to see her treated that way. I would have killed him if you hadn't held me back."

Avluela said, "Where shall we stay, now that we're in Roum?"

"First let me find the headquarters of my guild," I said. "I'll register at the Watchers' Inn. After that, perhaps we'll hunt up the Fliers' Lodge for a meal."

"And then," said Gormon dryly, "we'll go to the Guildless Gutter and beg for coppers."

"I pity you because you are a Changeling," I told him, "but I find it ungraceful of you to pity yourself. Come."

We walked up a cobbled, winding street away from the gate and into Roum itself. We were in the outer ring of the city, a residential section of low, squat houses topped by the unwieldy bulk of defense installations. Within lay the shining towers we had seen from the fields the night before; the remnant of ancient Roum carefully preserved across ten thousand years or more; the market, the factory zone, the communications hump, the temples of the Will, the memory tanks, the sleepers' refuges, the outworlders' brothels, the government buildings, the headquarters of the various guilds.

At the corner, beside a Second Cycle building with walls of rubbery texture, I found a public thinking cap and slipped it on my forehead. At once my thoughts raced down the conduit until they came to the interface that gave them access to one of the storage brains of a memory tank. I pierced the interface and saw the wrinkled brain itself, pale gray against the deep green of its housing. A Rememberer once told me that, in cycles past, men built machines to do their thinking for them, although these machines were hellishly expensive and required vast amounts of space and drank power gluttonously. That was not the worst of our forefathers' follies; but why build artificial brains when death each day liberates scores of splendid natural ones to hook into the memory tanks? Was it that they lacked the knowledge to use them? I find that hard to believe.

I gave the brain my guild identification and asked the coordinates of our inn. Instantly I received them, and we set out, Avluela on one side of me, Gormon on the other, myself wheeling, as always, the cart in which my instruments resided.

The city was crowded. I had not seen such throngs in sleepy, heat-fevered Agupt, nor at any other point on my northward journey. The streets were full of Pilgrims, secretive and masked. Jostling through them went busy Rememberers and glum Merchants and now and then the litter of a Master. Avluela saw a number of Fliers, but was barred by the tenets of her guild from greeting them until she had undergone her ritual purification. I regret to say that I spied many Watchers, all of whom looked upon me disdainfully and without welcome. I noted a good many Defenders and ample representation of such lesser guilds as Vendors, Servitors, Manufactories, Scribes, Communicants, and Transporters. Naturally, a host of neuters went silently about their humble business, and numerous outworlders of all descriptions flocked the streets, most of them probably tourists, some here to do what business could be done with the sullen, poverty-blighted people of Earth. I noticed many Changelings limping furtively through the crowd, not one of them as proud of bearing as Gormon beside me. He was unique among his kind; the others, dappled and piebald and asymmetrical, limbless or overlimbed, deformed in a thousand imaginative and artistic ways, were slinkers, squinters, shufflers, hissers, creepers; they were cutpurses, brain-drainers, organ-peddlers, repentance-mongers, gleam-buyers, but none held himself upright as though he thought he were a man.

The guidance of the brain was exact, and in less than an hour of walking we arrived at the Watchers' Inn. I left Gormon and Avluela outside and wheeled my cart within.

Perhaps a dozen members of my guild lounged in the main hall. I gave them the customary sign, and they returned it languidly. Were these the guardians on whom Earth's safety depended? Simpletons and weaklings!

"Where may I register?" I asked.

"New? Where from?"

"Agupt was my last place of registry."

"Should have stayed there. No need of Watchers here."

"Where may I register?" I asked again.

A foppish youngster indicated a screen in the rear of the great room. I went to it, pressed my fingertips against it, was interrogated, and gave my name, which a Watcher may utter only to another Watcher and only within the precincts of an inn. A panel shot open, and a puffy-eyed man who wore the Watcher emblem on his right cheek and not on the left, signifying his high rank in the guild, spoke my name and said, "You should have known better than to come to Roum. We're over our quota."

"I claim lodging and employment nonetheless."

"A man with your sense of humor should have been born into the guild of Clowns," he said.

"I see no joke."

"Under laws promulgated by our guild in the most recent session, an inn is under no obligation to take new lodgers once it has reached its assigned capacity. We are at our assigned capacity. Farewell, my friend."

I was aghast. "I know of no such regulation! This is incredible! For a guild to turn away a member from its own inn—when he arrives footsore and numb! A man of my age, having crossed Land Bridge out of Agupt, here as a stranger and hungry in Roum—

"Why did you not check with us first?"

"I had no idea it would be necessary."

"The new regulations—"

"May the Will shrivel the new regulations!" I shouted. "I demand lodging! To turn away one who has Watched since before you were born—"

"Easy, brother, easy."

"Surely you have some corner where I can sleep—some crumbs to let me eat—"

Even as my tone had changed from bluster to supplication, his expression softened from indifference to mere disdain. "We have no room. We have no food. These are hard times for our guild, you know. There is talk that we will be disbanded altogether, as a useless luxury, a drain upon the Will's resources. We are very limited in our abilities. Because Roum has a surplus of Watchers, we all are on short rations as it is, and if we admit you our rations will be all the shorter."

"But where will I go? What shall I do?"

"I advise you," he said blandly, "to throw yourself upon the mercy of the Prince of Roum."

THREE

Outside, I told that to Gormon, and he doubled with laughter, guffawing so furiously that the striations on his lean cheeks blazed like bloody stripes. "The mercy of the Prince of Roum!" he repeated. "The mercy—of the Prince of Roum—"

"It is customary for the unfortunate to seek the aid of the local ruler," I said coldly.

"The Prince of Roum knows no mercy," Gormon told me. "The Prince of Roum will feed you your own limbs to ease your hunger!"

"Perhaps," Avluela put in, "we should try to find the Fliers' Lodge. They'll feed us there."

"Not Gormon," I observed. "We have obligations to one another."

"We could bring food out to him," she said.

"I prefer to visit the court first," I insisted. "Let us make sure of our status. Afterward we can improvise living arrangements, if we must."

She yielded, and we made our way to the palace of the Prince of Roum, a massive building fronted by a colossal column-ringed plaza, on the far side of the river that splits the city. In the plaza we were accosted by mendicants of many sorts, some not even Earthborn; something with ropy tendrils and a corrugated, noseless face thrust itself at me and jabbered for alms until Gormon pushed it away, and moments later a second creature, equally strange, its skin pocked with luminescent craters and its limbs studded with eyes, embraced my knees and pleaded in the name of the Will for my mercy. "I am only a poor Watcher," I said, indicating my cart, "and am here to gain mercy myself." But the being persisted, sobbing out its misfortunes in a blurred, feathery voice, and in the end, to Gormon's immense disgust, I dropped a few food tablets into the shelflike pouch on its chest. Then we muscled on toward the doors of the palace. At the portico a more horrid sight presented itself: a maimed Flier, fragile limbs bent and twisted, one wing half unfolded and severely cropped, the other missing altogether. The Flier rushed upon Avluela, called her by a name not hers, moistened her leggings with tears so copious that the fur of them matted and stained. "Sponsor me to the lodge," he appealed. "They have turned me away because I am crippled, but if you sponsor me—" Avluela explained that she could do nothing, that she was a stranger to this lodge. The broken flier would not release her, and Gormon with great delicacy lifted him like the bundle of dry bones that he was and set him aside. We stepped up onto the portico and at once were confronted by a trio of soft-faced neuters, who asked our business and admitted us quickly to the next line of barrier, which was manned by a pair of wizened Indexers. Speaking in unison, they queried us.

"We seek audience," I said. "A matter of mercy."

"The day of audience is four days hence," said the Indexer on the right. "We will enter your request on the rolls."

"We have no place to sleep!" Avluela burst out. "We are hungry! We—"

I hushed her. Gormon, meanwhile, was groping in the mouth of his overpocket. Bright things glimmered in his hand: pieces of gold, the eternal metal, stamped with hawk-nosed, bearded faces. He had found them rubbing in the ruins. He tossed one coin to the Indexer who had refused us. The man snapped it from the air, rubbed his thumb roughly across its shining obverse, and dropped it instantly into a fold of his garment. The second Indexer waited expectantly. Smiling, Gormon gave him his coin.

"Perhaps," I said, "we can arrange for a special audience within."

"Perhaps you can," said one of the Indexers. "Go through."

And so we passed into the nave of the palace itself and stood in the great, echoing space, looking down the central aisle toward the shielded throne-chamber at the apse. There were more beggars in here — licensed ones holding hereditary concessions — and also throngs of Pilgrims, Communicants, Rememberers, Musicians, Scribes, and Indexers. I heard muttered prayers: I smelled the scent of spicy incense; I felt the vibration of subterranean gongs. In cycles past, this building had been a shrine of one of the old religions — the Christers, Gormon told me, making me suspect once more that he was a Rememberer masquerading as a Changeling — and it still maintained something of its holy character even though it served as Roum's seat of secular government. But how were we to get to see the Prince? To my left I saw a small ornate chapel which a line of prosperous-looking Merchants and Landholders was slowly entering. Peering past them, I noted three skulls mounted on an interrogation fixture — a memory-tank input — and beside them, a burly Scribe. Telling Gormon and Avluela to wait for me in the aisle, I joined the line.

It moved infrequently, and nearly an hour passed before I reached the interrogation fixture. The skulls glared sightlessly at me; within their sealed crania, nutrient fluids bubbled and gurgled, caring for the dead, yet still functional, brains whose billion billion synaptic units now served as incomparable mnemonic devices. The Scribe seemed aghast to find a Watcher in this line, but before he could challenge me I blurted, "I come as a stranger to claim the Prince's mercy. I and my companions are without lodging. My own guild has turned me away. What shall I do? How may I gain an audience?"

"Come back in four days."

"I've slept on the road for more days than that. Now I must rest more easily."

"A public inn — "

"But I am guilded!" I protested. "The public inns would not admit me while my guild maintains an inn here, and my guild refuses me because of some new regulation, and — you see my predicament?"

In a wearied voice the Scribe said, "You may have application for a special audience. It will be denied, but you may apply."

"Where?"

"Here. State your purpose."

I identified myself to the skulls by my public designation, listed the name and status of my two companions, and explained my case. All this was absorbed and transmitted to the ranks of brains mounted somewhere in the depths of the city, and when I was done the Scribe said, "If the application is approved, you will be notified."

"Meanwhile where shall I stay?"

"Close to the palace, I would suggest." I understood. I could join that legion of unfortunates packing the plaza. How many of them had requested some special favor of the Prince and were still there, months or years later, waiting to be summoned to the Presence? Sleeping on stone, begging for crusts, living in foolish hope!

But I had exhausted my avenues. I returned to Gormon and Avluela, told them of the situation, and suggested that we now attempt to hunt whatever accommodations we could. Gormon, guildless, was welcome at any of the squalid public inns maintained for his kind; Avluela could probably find residence at her own guild's lodge; only I would have to sleep in the streets — and not for the first time. But I hoped that we would not have to separate. I had come to think of us as a family, strange thought though that was for a Watcher.

As we moved toward the exit, my timepiece told me softly that the hour of Watching had come round again. It was my obligation and my privilege to tend to my Watching wherever I might be, regardless of the circumstances, whenever my hour came round; and so I halted, opened the cart, activated the equipment. Gorman and Avluela stood beside me. I saw smirks and open mockery on the faces of those who passed in and out of the palace; Watching was not held in very high repute, for we had Watched so long, and the promised enemy had never come. Yet one has one's duties, comic though they may seem to others. What is a hollow ritual to some is a life's work to others. Doggedly I forced myself into a state of Watchfulness. The world melted away from me, and I plunged into the heavens. The familiar joy engulfed me; and I searched the familiar places, and some that were not so familiar, my amplified mind leaping through the galaxies in wild swoops. Was an armada massing? Were troops drilling for the conquest of Earth? Four times a day I Watched, and the other members of my guild did the same, each at slightly different hours, so that no moment went by without some vigilant mind on guard. I do not believe that that was a foolish calling.

When I came up from my trance, a brazen voice was crying, " — for the Prince of Roum! Make way for the Prince of Roum!"

I blinked and caught my breath and fought to shake off the last strands of my concentration. A gilded palanquin borne by a phalanx of neuters had emerged from the rear of the palace and was proceeding down the nave toward me. Four men in the elegant costumes and brilliant masks of the guild of Masters flanked the litter, and it was preceded by a trio of Changelings, squat and broad, whose throats were so modified to imitate the sounding-boxes of bullfrogs; they emitted a trumpetlike boom of majestic sound as they advanced. It struck me as most strange that a prince would admit Changelings to his service, even ones as gifted as these.

My cart was blocking the progress of this magnificent procession, and hastily I struggled to close it and move it aside before the parade swept down upon me. Age and fear made my fingers tremble, and I could not make the sealings properly; while I fumbled in increasing clumsiness, the strutting Changelings drew so close that the blare of their throats was deafening, and Gormon attempted to aid me, forcing me to hiss at him that it is forbidden for anyone not of my guild to touch the equipment. I pushed him away; and an instant later a vanguard of neuters descended on me and prepared to scourge me from the spot with sparkling whips. "In the Will's name," I cried, "I am a Watcher!"

And in antiphonal response came the deep, calm, enormous reply, "Let him be. He is a Watcher."

All motion ceased. The Prince of Roum had spoken.

The neuters drew back. The Changelings halted their music. The bearers of the palanquin eased it to the floor. All those in the nave of the palace had pulled back, save only Gormon and Avluela and myself. The shimmering chain-curtains of the palanquin parted. Two of the Masters hurried forward and thrust their hands through the sonic barrier within, offering aid to their monarch. The barrier died away with a whimpering buzz.

The Prince of Roum appeared.

He was so young! He was nothing more than a boy, his hair full and dark, his face unlined. But he had been born to rule, and for all his youth he was as commanding as anyone I had ever seen. His lips were thin and tightly compressed; his aquiline nose was sharp and aggressive; his eyes, deep and cold, were infinite pools. He wore the jeweled garments of the guild of Dominators, but incised on his cheek was the double-barred cross of the Defenders, and around his neck he carried the dark shawl of the Rememberers. A Dominator may enroll in as many guilds as he pleases, and it would be a strange thing for a Dominator not also to be a Defender; but it startled me to find this prince a Rememberer as well. That is not normally a guild for the fierce.

He looked at me with little interest and said, "You choose an odd place to do your Watching, old man."

"The hour chose the place, sire," I replied. "I was here, and my duty compelled me. I had no way of knowing that you were about to come forth."

"Your Watching found no enemies?"

"None, sire."

I was about to press my luck, to take advantage of the unexpected appearance of the Prince to beg for his aid; but his interest in me died like a guttering candle as I stood there, and I did not dare call to him when his head had turned. He eyed Gormon a long moment, frowning and tugging at his chin. Then his gaze fell on Avluela. His eyes brightened. His jaw muscles flickered. His delicate nostrils widened. "Come up here, little Flier," he said, beckoning. "Are you this Watcher's friend?"

She nodded, terrified.

The Prince held out a hand to her and grasped; she floated up onto
the palanquin, and with a grin so evil it seemed a parody of wickedness,
the young Dominator drew her through the curtain. Instantly a pair of
Masters restored the sonic barrier, but the procession did not move on. I
stood mute. Gormon beside me was frozen, his powerful body rigid as a
rod. I wheeled my cart to a less conspicuous place. Long moments passed.
The courtier remained silent, discreetly looking away from the palanquin.

At length the curtain parted once more. Avluela came stumbling out,
her face pale, her eyes blinking rapidly. She seemed dazed. Streaks of sweat
gleamed on her cheeks. She nearly fell, and a neuter caught her and swung
her down to floor level. Beneath her jacket her wings were partly erect,
giving her a hunchbacked look and telling me that she was in great
emotional distress. In ragged, sliding steps she came to us, quivering,
wordless; she darted a glance at me and flung herself against Gormon's
broad chest.

The bearers lifted the palanquin. The Prince of Roum went out from
his palace.

When he was gone, Avluela stammered hoarsely, "The Prince has
granted us lodging in the royal hostelry!"

FOUR

The hostelkeepers, of course, would not believe us.

Guests of the Prince were housed in the royal hostelry, which was to
the rear of the palace in a small garden of frostflowers and blossoming
ferns. The usual inhabitants of such a hostelry were Masters and an
occasional Dominator; sometimes a particularly important Rememberer
on an errand of research would win a niche there, or some highly placed
Defender visiting for purposes of strategic planning. To house a Flier in a
royal hostelry was distinctly odd; to admit a Watcher was unlikely; to
take in a Changeling or some other guildless person was improbable
beyond comprehension. When we presented ourselves, therefore, we were
met by Servitors whose attitude was at first one of high good humor at
our joke, then of irritation, finally of scorn. "Get away," they told us
ultimately. "Scum! Rabble!"

Avluela said in a grave voice, "The Prince has granted us lodging here,
and you may not refuse us."

"Away! Away!"

One snaggle-toothed Servitor produced a neural truncheon and
brandished it in Gormon's face, passing a foul remark about his
guildlessness. Gormon slapped the truncheon from the man's grasp,
oblivious to the painful sting, and kicked him in the gut, so that he coiled

and fell over, puking. Instantly a throng of neuters came rushing from within the hostelry. Gormon seized another of the Servitors and hurled him into the midst of them, turning them into a muddled mob. Wild shouts and angry cursing cries attracted the attention of a venerable Scribe who waddled to the door, bellowed for silence, and interrogated us. "That's easily checked," he said, when Avluela had told the story. To a Servitor he said contemptuously, "Send a think to the Indexers, fast!"

In time the confusion was untangled and we were admitted. We were given separate, but adjoining rooms. I had never known such luxury before, and perhaps never shall again. The rooms were long, high, and deep. One entered them through telescopic pits keyed to one's own thermal output, to assure privacy. Lights glowed at the resident's merest nod, for hanging from ceiling globes and nestling in cupolas on the walls were spicules of slave-light from one of the Brightstar worlds, trained through suffering to obey such commands. The windows came and went at the dweller's whim; when not in use, they were concealed by streamers of quasi-sentient out-world gauzes, which not only were decorative in their own right, but which functioned as monitors to produce lightful scents according to requisitioned patterns. The rooms were equipped with individual thinking caps connected to the main memory banks. They likewise had conduits that summoned Servitors, Scribes, Indexers, and Musicians as required. Of course, a man of my own humble guild would not deign to make use of other human beings that way, out of fear of their glowering resentment: but in any case I had little need of them.

I did not ask of Avluela what had occurred in the Prince's palanquin to bring us such bounty. I could well imagine, as could Gormon, whose barely suppressed inner rage was eloquent of his never-admitted love for the pale, slender little Flier.

We settled in. I placed my cart beside the window, draped it with gauzes, and left it in readiness for the next period of Watching. I cleaned my body of grime while entities mounted in the wall sang me to peace. Later I ate. Afterwards Avluela came to me, refreshed and relaxed, and sat beside me in my room as we talked of our experiences. Gormon did not appear for hours. I thought that perhaps he had left this hostelry altogether, finding the atmosphere too rarefied for him, and had sought company among his own guildless kind. But at twilight, Avluela and I walked in the cloistered courtyard of the hostelry and mounted a ramp to watch the stars emerge in Roum's sky, and Gormon was there. With him was a lanky and emaciated man in a Rememberer's shawl; they were talking in low tones.

Gormon nodded to me and said, "Watcher, meet my new friend."

The emaciated one fingered his shawl. "I am the Rememberer Basil," he intoned, in a voice as thin as a fresco that has been peeled from its wall.

"I have come from Perris to delve into the mysteries of Roum. I shall be here many years."

"The Rememberer has fine stories to tell," said Gormon. "He is among the foremost of his guild. As you approached, he was describing to me the techniques by which the past is revealed. They drive a trench through the strata of Third Cycle deposits, you see, and with vacuum cores they lift the molecules of earth to lay bare the ancient layers."

"We have found," Basil said, "the catacombs of Imperial Roum, and the rubble of the Time of Sweeping, the books inscribed on slivers of white metal, written toward the close of the Second Cycle. All these go to Perris for examination and classification and decipherment; then they return. Does the past interest you, Watcher?"

"To some extent." I smiled. "This Changeling here shows much more fascination for it. I sometimes suspect his authenticity. Would you recognize a Rememberer in disguise?"

Basil scrutinized Gormon; he lingered over the bizarre features, the excessively muscular frame. "He is no Rememberer," he said at length. "But I agree that he has antiquarian interests. He has asked me many profound questions."

"Such as?"

"He wishes to know the origin of guilds. He asks the name of the genetic surgeon who crafted the first true-breeding Fliers. He wonders why there are Changelings, and if they are truly under the curse of the Will."

"And do you have answers for these?" I asked.

"For some," said Basil. "For some."

"The origin of guilds?"

"To give structure and meaning to a society that has suffered defeat and destruction," said the Rememberer. "At the end of the Second Cycle all was in flux. No man knew his rank nor his purpose. Through our world strode haughty outworlders who looked upon us all as worthless. It was necessary to establish fixed frames of reference by which one man might know his value beside another. So the first guilds appeared: Dominators, Masters, Merchants, Landholders, Vendors and Servitors. Then came Scribes, Musicians, Clowns and Transporters. Afterward Indexers became necessary, and then Watchers and Defenders. When the Years of Magic gave us Fliers and Changelings, those guilds were added, and then the guildless ones, the neuters, were produced, so that—"

"But surely the Changelings are guildless too!" said Avluela.

The Rememberer looked at her for the first time. "Who are you, child?"

"Avluela of the Fliers. I travel with this Watcher and this Changeling."

Basil said, "As I have been telling the Changeling here, in the early days his kind was guilded. The guild was dissolved a thousand years ago by the order of the Council of Dominators after an attempt by a disreputable Changeling faction to seize control of the holy places of Jorslem, and since that time Changelings have been guildless, ranking only above neuters."

"I never knew that," I said.

"You are no Rememberer," said Basil smugly. "It is our craft to uncover the past."

"True. True."

Gormon said, "And today, how many guilds are there?"

Discomfited, Basil replied vaguely, "At least a hundred, my friend. Some are quite small; some are local. I am concerned only with the original guilds and their immediate successors; what has happened in the past few hundred years is in the province of others. Shall I requisition an information for you?"

"Never mind," Gormon said. "It was only an idle question."

"Your curiosity is well developed," said the Rememberer.

"I find the world and all it contains extremely fascinating. Is this sinful?"

"It is strange," said Basil. "The guildless rarely look beyond their own horizons."

A Servitor appeared. With a mixture of awe and contempt he genuflected before Avluela and said, "The Prince has returned. He desires your company in the palace at this time."

Terror glimmered in Avluela's eyes. But to refuse was inconceivable. "Shall I come with you?" she asked.

"Please. You must be robed and perfumed. He wishes you to come to him with your wings open, as well."

Avluela nodded. The Servitor led her away.

We remained on the ramp a while longer; the Rememberer Basil talked of the old days of Roum, and I listened, and Gormon peered into the gathering darkness. Eventually, his throat dry, the Rememberer excused himself and moved solemnly away. A few moments later, in the courtyard below us, a door opened and Avluela emerged, walking as though she were of the guild of Somnambulists, not of Fliers. She was nude under transparent draperies, and her fragile body gleamed ghostly white in the starbeams. Her wings were spread and fluttered slowly in a somber systole and diastole. One Servitor grasped each of her elbows: they seemed to be propelling her toward the palace as though she were but a dreamed facsimile of herself and not a real woman.

"Fly, Avluela, fly," Gormon growled. "Escape while you can!"

She disappeared into a side entrance of the palace.

The Changeling looked at me. "She has sold herself to the Prince to provide lodging for us."

"So it seems."

"I could smash down that palace!"

"You love her?"

"It should be obvious."

"Cure yourself," I advised. "You are an unusual man, but still a Flier is not for you. Particularly a Flier who has shared the bed of the Prince of Roum."

"She goes from my arms to his."

I was staggered. "You've known her?"

"More than once," he said, smiling sadly. "At the moment of ecstasy her wings thrash like leaves in a storm."

I gripped the railing of the ramp so that I would not tumble into the courtyard. The stars whirled overhead; the old moon and its two blank-faced consorts leaped and bobbed. I was shaken without fully understanding the cause of my emotion. Was it wrath that Gormon had dared to violate a canon of the law? Was it a manifestation of those pseudo-parental feelings I had toward Avluela? Or was it mere envy of Gormon for daring to commit a sin beyond my capacity, though not beyond my desires?

I said, "They could burn your brain for that. They could mince your soul. And now you make me an accessory."

"What of it? The Prince commands, and he gets—but others have been there before him. I had to tell someone."

"Enough. Enough."

"Will we see her again?"

"Princes tire quickly of their women. A few days, perhaps a single night—then he will throw her back to us. And perhaps then we shall have to leave this hostelry." I sighed. "At least we'll know it a few nights more than we deserved."

"Where will you go then?" Gormon asked.

"I will stay in Roum awhile."

"Even if you sleep in the streets? There does not seem to be much demand for Watchers here."

"I'll manage," I said. "Then I may go toward Perris."

"To learn from the Rememberers?"

"To see Perris. What of you? What do you want in Roum?"

"Avluela."

"Stop that talk!"

"Very well," he said, and his smile was bitter. "But I will stay here until the Prince is through with her. Then she will be mine, and we'll find ways to survive. The guildless are resourceful. They have to be. Maybe we'll scrounge lodgings in Roum awhile, and then follow you to Perris. If you're willing to travel with monsters and faithless Fliers."

I shrugged. "We'll see about that when the time comes."

"Have you ever been in the company of a Changeling before?"

"Not often. Not for long."

"I'm honored." He drummed on the parapet. "Don't cast me off, Watcher. I have a reason for wanting to stay with you."

"Which is?"

"To see your face on the day your machines tell you that the invasion of Earth has begun."

I let myself sag forward, shoulders drooping. "You'll stay with me a long time, then."

"Don't you believe the invasion is coming?"

"Someday. Not soon."

Gormon chuckled. "You're wrong. It's almost here."

"You don't amuse me."

"What is it, Watcher? Have you lost your faith? It's been known for a thousand years: another race covets Earth and owns it by treaty, and will someday come to collect. That much was decided at the end of the Second Cycle."

"I know all that, and I am no Rememberer." Then I turned to him and spoke words I never thought I would say aloud. "For twice your lifetime, Changeling, I've listened to the stars and done my Watching. Something done that often loses meaning. Say your own name ten thousand times and it will be an empty sound. I have Watched, and Watched well, and in the dark hours of the night I sometimes think I Watch for nothing, that I have wasted my life. There is a pleasure in Watching, but perhaps there is no real purpose."

His hand encircled my wrist. "Your confession is as shocking as mine. Keep your faith, Watcher. The invasion comes!"

"How could you possibly know?"

"The guildless also have their skills."

The conversation troubled me. I said, "Is it painful to be guildless?"

"One grows reconciled. And there are certain freedoms to compensate for the lack of status. I may speak freely to all."

"I notice."

"I move freely. I am always sure of food and lodging, though the food may be rotten and the lodging poor. Women are attracted to me despite all prohibitions. Because of them, perhaps. I am untroubled by ambitions."

"Never desire to rise above your rank?"

"Never."

"You might have been happier as a Rememberer."

"I am happy now. I can have a Rememberer's pleasures without his responsibility."

"How smug you are!" I cried. "To make a virtue of guildlessness!"

"How else does one endure the weight of the Will?" He looked toward the palace. "The humble rise. The mighty fall. Take this as prophecy, Watcher: that lusty Prince in there will know more of life before summer comes. I'll rip out his eyes for taking Avluela!"

"Strong words. You bubble with treason tonight."

"Take it as prophecy."

"You can't get close to him," I said. Then, irritated for taking his foolishness seriously, I added, "And why blame him? He only does as princes do. Blame the girl for going to him. She might have refused."

"And lost her wings. Or died. No, she had no choice. I do!" In a sudden, terrible gesture the Changeling held out thumb and forefinger, double-jointed, long-nailed, and plunged them forward into imagined eyes. "Wait," he said. "You'll see!"

In the courtyard two Chronomancers appeared, set up the apparatus of their guild, and lit tapers by which to read the shape of tomorrow. A sickly odor of pallid smoke rose to my nostrils. I had now lost further desire to speak with the Changeling.

"It grows late," I said. "I need rest, and soon I must do my Watching."

"Watch carefully," Gormon told me.

FIVE

At night in my chamber I performed my fourth and last Watch of that long day, and for the first time in my life I detected an anomaly. I could not interpret it. It was an obscure sensation, a mingling of tastes and sounds, a feeling of being in contact with some colossal mass. Worried, I clung to my instruments far longer than usual, but perceived no more clearly at the end of my séance than at its commencement.

Afterward I wondered about my obligations.

Watchers are trained from childhood to be swift to sound the alarm, and the alarm must be sounded when the Watcher judges the world in peril. Was I now obliged to notify the Defenders? Four times in my life the alarm had been given, on each occasion in error; and each Watcher who had thus touched off a false mobilization had suffered a fearful loss of status. One had contributed his brain to the memory tanks; one had become a neuter out of shame; one had smashed his instruments and gone to live among the guildless; and one, vainly attempting to continue in his profession, had discovered himself mocked by all his comrades. I saw no virtue in scorning one who had delivered a false alarm, for was it not preferable for a Watcher to cry out too soon than not at all? But those were the customs of our guild, and I was constrained by them.

I evaluated my position and decided that I did not have valid grounds for an alarm.

I reflected that Gormon had placed suggestive ideas in my mind that evening. I might possibly be reacting only to his jeering talk of imminent invasion.

I could not act. I dared not jeopardize my standing by hasty outcry. I mistrusted my own emotional state.

I gave no alarm.

Seething, confused, my soul roiling, I closed my cart and let myself sink into a drugged sleep.

At dawn I woke and rushed to the window, expecting to find invaders in the streets. But all was still: a winter grayness hung over the courtyard, and sleepy Servitors pushed passive neuters about. Uneasily I did my first Watching of the day, and to my relief the strangenesses of the night before did not return, although I had it in mind that my sensitivity is always greater at night than upon arising.

I ate and went to the courtyard. Gormon and Avluela were already there. She looked fatigued and downcast, depleted by her night with the Prince of Roum, but I said nothing to her about it. Gormon, slouching disdainfully against a wall embellished with the shells of radiant mollusks, said to me, "Did your Watching go well?"

"Well enough."

"What of the day?"

"Out to roam Roum," I said. "Will you come? Avluela? Gormon?"

"Surely," he said, and she gave a faint nod; and, like the tourists we were, we set off to inspect the splendid city of Roum.

Gormon acted as our guide to the jumbled pasts of Roum, belying his claim never to have been here before. As well as any Rememberer he described the things we saw as we walked the winding streets. All the scattered levels of thousands of years were exposed. We saw the power domes of the Second Cycle, and the Colosseum where at an unimaginably early date man and beast contended like jungle creatures. In the broken hull of that building of horrors Gormon told us of the savagery of that unimaginably ancient time. "They fought," he said, "naked before huge throngs. With bare hands men challenged beasts called lions, great hairy cats with swollen heads; and when the lion lay in its gore, the victor turned to the Prince of Roum and asked to be pardoned for whatever crime it was that had cast him into the arena. And if he had fought well, the Prince made a gesture with his hand, and the man was freed." Gormon made the gesture for us: a thumb upraised and jerked backward over the right shoulder several times. "But if the man had shown cowardice, or if the lion had distinguished itself in the manner of its dying, the Prince made another gesture, and the man was condemned to be slain by a second beast." Gormon showed us that gesture too: the middle finger jutting upward from a clenched fist and lifted in a short sharp thrust.

"How are these things known?" Avluela asked, but Gormon pretended not to hear her.

We saw the line of fusion-pylons built early in the Third Cycle to draw energy from the world's core; they were still functioning, although stained and corroded. We saw the shattered stump of a Second Cycle weather machine, still a mighty column at least twenty men high. We saw a hill on which white marble relics of First Cycle Roum sprouted like pale clumps of winter deathflowers. Penetrating toward the inner part of the city, we came upon the embankment of defensive amplifiers waiting in readiness to hurl the full impact of the Will against invaders. We viewed a market where visitors from the stars haggled with peasants for excavated fragments of antiquity. Gormon strode into the crowd and made several purchases. We came to a fleshhouse for travelers from afar, where one could buy anything from quasi-life to mounds of passion-ice. We ate at a small restaurant by the edge of the River Tver, where guildless ones were served without ceremony, and at Gormon's insistence we dined on mounds of a soft doughy substance and drank a tart yellow wine, local specialties.

Afterward we passed through a covered arcade in whose many aisles plump Vendors peddled star-goods, costly trinkets from Afreek, and the flimsy constructs of the local Manufactories. Just beyond we emerged in a plaza that contained a fountain in the shape of a boat, and to the rear of this rose a flight of cracked and battered stone stairs ascending to a zone of rubble and weeds. Gormon beckoned, and we scrambled into this dismal area, then passed rapidly through it to a place where a sumptuous palace, by its looks early Second Cycle or even First, brooded over a sloping vegetated hill.

"They say this is the center of the world," Gormon declared. "In Jorslem one finds another place that also claims the honor. They mark the spot here by a map."

"How can the world have one center," Avluela asked, "when it is round?"

Gormon laughed. We went in. Within, in wintry darkness, there stood a colossal jeweled globe lit by some inner glow.

"Here is your world," said Gormon, gesturing grandly.

"Oh!" Avluela gasped. "Everything! Everything is here!"

The map was a masterpiece of craftmanship. It showed natural contours and elevations, its seas seemed deep liquid pools, its deserts were so parched as to make thirst spring in one's mouth, its cities swirled with vigor and life. I beheld the continents, Eyrop, Afreek, Ais, Stralya. I saw the vastness of Earth Ocean. I traversed the golden span of Land Bridge, which I had crossed so toilfully on foot not long before. Avluela rushed forward and pointed to Roum, to Agupt, to Jorslem, to Perris. She tapped the globe at the high mountains north of Hind and said softly, "This is where I was born, where the ice lives, where the mountains touch the moons. Here is where the Fliers have their kingdom." She ran a finger westward toward Fars and beyond it into the terrible Arban Desert, and on to Agupt. "This is where I flew. By night, when I left my girlhood. We all must fly, and I flew here. A hundred times I thought I would die. Here, here in the desert, sand in my throat as I flew, and beating against my wings—I was forced down, I lay naked on the hot sand for days, and another Flier saw me, he came down to me and pitied me, and lifted me up, and when I was aloft my strength returned, and we flew on toward Agupt. And he died over the sea, his life stopped though he was young and strong, and he fell down into the sea, and I flew down to be with him, and the water was hot even at night. I drifted, and morning came, and I saw the living stones growing like trees in the water, and the fish of many colors, and they came to him and pecked at his flesh as he floated with his wings outspread on the water, and I left him, I thrust him down to rest there, and I rose, and I flew on to Agupt, alone, frightened, and there I met you, Watcher." Timidly she smiled to me. "Show us the place where you were young, Watcher."

Painfully, for I was suddenly stiff at the knees, I hobbled to the far side of the globe. Avluela followed me; Gormon hung back, as though not interested at all. I pointed to the scattered islands rising in two long strips from Earth Ocean—the remnants of the Lost Continents.

"Here," I said, indicating my native island in the west. "I was born here."

"So far away!" Avluela cried.

"And so long ago," I said. "In the middle of the Second Cycle, it sometimes seems to me."

"No! That is not possible!" But she looked at me as though it might just be true that I was thousands of years old.

I smiled and touched her satiny cheek. "It only seems that way to me," I said.

"When did you leave your home?"

"When I was twice your age," I said. "I came first to here—" I indicated the eastern group of islands. "I spent a dozen years as a Watcher on Palash. Then the Will moved me to cross Earth Ocean to Afreek. I came. I lived awhile in the hot countries. I went on to Agupt. I met a certain small Flier." Falling silent, I looked a long while at the islands that had been my home, and within my mind my image changed from the gaunt and eroded thing I now had become, and I saw myself young and well-fleshed, climbing the green mountains and swimming in the chill sea, doing my Watching at the rim of a white beach hammered by surf.

While I brooded Avluela turned away from me to Gormon and said, "Now you. Show us where you came from, Changeling!"

Gormon shrugged. "The place does not appear to be on this globe."

"But that's *impossible!*"

"Is it?" he asked.

She pressed him, but he evaded her, and we passed through a side exit and into the streets of Roum.

I was growing tired, but Avluela hungered for this city and wished to devour it all in an afternoon, and so we went on through a maze of interlocking streets, through a zone of sparkling mansions of Masters and Merchants, and through a foul den of Servitors and Vendors that extended into subterranean catacombs, and to a place where Clowns and Musicians resorted, and to another where the guild of Somnambulists offered its doubtful wares. A bloated female Somnambulist begged us to come inside and buy the truth that comes with trances, and Avluela urged us to go, but Gormon shook his head and I smiled, and we moved on. Now we were at the edge of a park close to the city's core. Here the citizens of Roum promenaded with an energy rarely seen in hot Agupt, and we joined the parade.

"Look there!" Avluela said. "How bright it is!"

She pointed toward the shining arc of a dimensional sphere enclosing some relic of the ancient city; shading my eyes, I could make out a weathered stone wall within, and a knot of people. Gormon said, "It is the Mouth of Truth."

"What is that?" Avluela asked.

"Come. See."

A line progressed into the sphere. We joined it and soon were at the lip of the interior, peering at the timeless region just across the threshold. Why this relic and so few others had been accorded such special protection I did not know, and I asked Gormon, whose knowledge was so unaccountably as profound as any Rememberer's, and he replied, "Because this is the realm of certainty, where what one says is absolutely congruent with what actually is the case."

"I don't understand," said Avluela.

"It is impossible to lie in this place," Gormon told her. "Can you imagine any relic more worthy of protection?" He stepped across the entry duct, blurring as he did so, and I followed him quickly within. Avluela hesitated. It was a long moment before she entered; pausing a moment on the very threshold, she seemed buffeted by the wind that blew along the line of demarcation between the outer world and the pocket universe in which we stood.

An inner compartment held the Mouth of Truth itself. The line extended toward it, and a solemn Indexer was controlling the flow of entry to the tabernacle. It was a while before we three were permitted to go in. We found ourselves before the ferocious head of a monster in high relief, affixed to an ancient wall pockmarked by time. The monster's jaws gaped; the open mouth was a dark and sinister hole. Gormon nodded, inspecting it, as though he seemed pleased to find it exactly as he had thought it would be.

"What do we do?" Avluela asked.

Gormon said, "Watcher, put your right hand into the Mouth of Truth." Frowning, I complied.

"Now," said Gormon, "one of us asks a question. You must answer it. If you speak anything but the truth, the mouth will close and sever your hand."

"No!" Avluela cried.

I stared uneasily at the stone jaws rimming my wrist. A Watcher without both his hands is a man without a craft; in Second Cycle days one might have obtained a prosthesis more artful than one's original hand, but the Second Cycle had long ago been concluded, and such niceties were not to be purchased on Earth nowadays.

"How is such a thing possible?" I asked.

"The Will is unusually strong in these precincts," Gormon replied. "It distinguishes sternly between truth and untruth. To the rear of this wall sleeps a trio of Somnambulists through whom the Will speaks, and they control the Mouth. Do you fear the Will, Watcher?"

"I fear my own tongue."

"Be brave. Never has a lie been told before this wall. Never has a hand been lost."

"Go ahead, then," I said. "Who will ask me a question?"

"I," said Gormon. "Tell me, Watcher: all pretense aside, would you say that a life spent in Watching has been a life spent wisely?"

I was silent a long moment, rotating my thought, eyeing the jaws.

At length I said, "To devote oneself to vigilance on behalf of one's fellow man is perhaps the noblest purpose one can serve."

"Careful!" Gormon cried in alarm.

"I am not finished," I said.

"Go on."

"But to devote oneself to vigilance when the enemy is an imaginary one is idle, and to congratulate oneself for looking long and well for a foe that is not coming is foolish and sinful. My life has been a waste."

The jaws of the Mouth of Truth did not quiver.

I removed my hand. I stared at it as though it had newly sprouted from my wrist. I felt suddenly several cycles old. Avluela, her eyes wide, her hands to her lips, seemed shocked by what I had said. My own words appeared to hang congealed in the air before the hideous idol.

"Spoken honestly," said Gormon, "although without much mercy for yourself. You judge yourself too harshly, Watcher."

"I spoke to save my hand," I said. "Would you have had me lie?"

He smiled. To Avluela the Changeling said, "Now it's your turn."

Visibly frightened, the little Flier approached the Mouth. Her dainty hand trembled as she inserted it between the slabs of cold stone. I fought back an urge to rush toward her and pull her free of that devilish grimacing head.

"Who will question her?" I asked.

"I," said Gormon.

Avluela's wings stirred faintly beneath her garments. Her face grew pale; her nostrils flickered; her upper lip slid over the lower one. She stood slouched against the wall and stared in horror at the termination of her arm. Outside the chamber vague faces peered at us; lips moved in what no doubt were expressions of impatience over our lengthy visit to the Mouth; but we heard nothing. The atmosphere around us was warm and clammy, with a musty tang like that which would come from a well that was driven through the structure of Time.

Gormon said slowly, "This night past you allowed your body to be possessed by the Prince of Roum. Before that, you granted yourself to the Changeling Gormon, although such liaisons are forbidden by custom and law. Much prior to that you were the mate of a Flier, now deceased. You may have had other men, but I know nothing of them, and for the purposes of my question they are not relevant. Tell me this, Avluela: which of the three gave you the most intense physical pleasure, which of the three aroused your deepest emotions, and which of the three would you choose as a mate, if you were choosing a mate?"

I wanted to protest that the Changeling had asked her three questions, not one, and so had taken unfair advantage. But I had no chance to speak, because Avluela replied unfalteringly, hand wedged deep into the Mouth of Truth, "The Prince of Roum gave me greater pleasure of the body than I had ever known before, but he is cold and cruel, and I despise him. My dead Flier I loved more deeply than any person before or since, but he was weak, and I would not have wanted a weakling as a mate. You, Gormon, seem almost a stranger to me even now, and I feel that I know neither your body nor your soul, and yet, though the gulf between us is so wide, it is you with whom I would spend my days to come."

She drew her hand from the Mouth of Truth.

"Well spoken!" said Gormon, though the accuracy of her words had clearly wounded as well as pleased him. "Suddenly you find eloquence, eh, when the circumstances demand it. And now the turn is mine to risk my hand."

He neared the Mouth. I said, "You have asked the first two questions. Do you wish to finish the job and ask the third as well?"

"Hardly," he said. He made a negligent gesture with his free hand. "Put your heads together and agree on a joint question."

Avluela and I conferred. With uncharacteristic forwardness she proposed a question; and since it was the one I would have asked, I accepted it and told her to ask it.

She said, "When we stood before the globe of the world, Gormon, I asked you to show me the place where you were born, and you said you were unable to find it on the map. That seemed most strange. Tell me now: are you what you say you are, a Changeling who wanders the world?"

He replied, "I am not."

In a sense he had satisfied the question as Avluela had phrased it, but it went without saying that his reply was inadequate, and he kept his hand in the Mouth of Truth as he continued, "I did not show my birthplace to you on the globe because I was born nowhere on this globe, but on a world of a star I must not name. I am no Changeling in your meaning of the word, though by some definitions I am, for my body is somewhat disguised, and on my own world I wear a different flesh. I have lived here ten years."

"What was your purpose in coming to Earth?" I asked.

"I am obliged only to answer one question," said Gormon. Then he smiled. "But I give you an answer anyway: I was sent to Earth in the capacity of a military observer, to prepare the way for the invasion for which you have Watched so long and in which you have ceased to believe, and which will be upon you in a matter now of some hours."

"Lies!" I bellowed. *"Lies!"*

Gormon laughed. And drew his hand from the Mouth of Truth, intact, unharmed.

SIX

Numb with confusion, I fled with my cart of instruments from that gleaming sphere and emerged into a street suddenly cold and dark. Night had come with winter's swiftness; it was almost the ninth hour, and almost the time for me to Watch once more.

Gormon's mockery thundered in my brain. He had arranged everything: he had maneuvered us into the Mouth of Truth; he had wrung a confession of lost faith from me and a confession of a different sort from Avluela; he had mercilessly volunteered information he need not have revealed, spoken words calculated to split me to the core.

Was the Mouth of Truth a fraud? Could Gormon lie and emerge unscathed?

Never since I first took up my tasks had I Watched at anything but my appointed hours. This was a time of crumbling realities; I could not wait for the ninth hour to come round; crouching in the windy street, I opened my cart, readied my equipment, and sank like a diver into Watchfulness.

My amplified consciousness roared toward the stars.

Godlike I roamed infinity. I felt the rush of the solar wind, but I was no Flier to be hurled to destruction by that pressure, and I soared past it, beyond the reach of those angry particles of light, into the blackness at the edge of the sun's dominion. Down upon me there beat a different pressure.

Starships coming near.

Not the tourist lines bringing sightseers to gape at our diminished world. Not the registered mercantile transport vessels, nor the scoop ships that collect the interstellar vapors, nor the resort craft on their hyperbolic orbits.

These were military craft, dark, alien, menacing. I could not tell their number; I knew only that they sped Earthward at many lights, nudging a cone of deflected energies before them; and it was that cone that I had sensed, that I had felt also the night before, booming into my mind through my instruments, engulfing me like a cube of crystal through which stress patterns play and shine.

All my life I had Watched for this.

I had been trained to sense it. I had prayed that I never would sense it, and then in my emptiness I had prayed that I *would* sense it, and then I had ceased to believe in it. And then by grace of the Changeling Gormon, I had sensed it after all, Watching ahead of my hour, crouching in a cold Roumish street just outside the Mouth of Truth.

In his training, a Watcher is instructed to break from his Watchfulness as soon as his observations are confirmed by a careful check, so that he can sound the alarm. Obediently I made my check by shifting from one channel to another to another, triangulating and still picking up that foreboding sensation of titanic force rushing upon Earth at unimaginable speed.

Either I was deceived, or the invasion was come. But I could not shake from my trance to give the alarm.

Lingeringly, lovingly, I drank in the sensory data for what seemed like hours. I fondled my equipment; I drained from it the total affirmation of faith that my readings gave me. Dimly I warned myself that I was wasting vital time, that it was my duty to leave this lewd caressing of destiny to summon the Defenders.

And at last I burst free of Watchfulness and returned to the world I was guarding.

Avluela was beside me; she was dazed, terrified, her knuckles to her teeth, her eyes blank.

"Watcher! Watcher, do you hear me? What's happening? What's going to happen?"

"The invasion," I said. "How long was I under?"

"About half a minute. I don't know. Your eyes were closed. I thought you were dead."

"Gormon was speaking the truth! The invasion is almost here. Where is he? Where did he go?"

"He vanished as we came away from that place with the Mouth," Avluela whispered. "Watcher, I'm frightened. I feel everything collapsing. I have to fly—I can't stay down here now!"

"Wait," I said, clutching at her and missing her arm. "Don't go now. First I have to give the alarm, and then—"

But she was already stripping off her clothing. Bare to the waist, her pale body gleamed in the evening light, while about us people were rushing to and fro in ignorance of all that was about to occur. I wanted to keep Avluela beside me, but I could delay no longer in giving the alarm, and I turned away from her, back to my cart.

As though caught up in a dream born of overripe longings I reached for the node that I had never used, the one that would send forth a planetwide alert to the Defenders.

Had the alarm already been given? Had some other Watcher sensed what I had sensed, and, less paralyzed by bewilderment and doubt, performed a Watcher's final task?

No. No. For then I would be hearing the sirens' shriek reverberating from the orbiting loudspeakers above the city.

I touched the node. From the corner of my eye I saw Avluela, free of her encumbrances now, kneeling to say her words, filling her tender wings with strength. In a moment she would be in the air, beyond my grasp.

With a single swift tug I activated the alarm.

In that instant I became aware of a burly figure striding toward us. Gormon, I thought; and as I rose from my equipment I reached out to him; I wanted to seize him and hold him fast. But he who approached was not Gormon but some officious dough-faced Servitor who said to Avluela, "Go easy, Flier, let your wings drop. The Prince of Roum sends me to bring you to his presence."

He grappled with her. Her little breasts heaved; her eyes flashed anger at him.

"Let go of me! I'm going to fly!"

"The Prince of Roum summons you," the Servitor said, enclosing her in his heavy arms.

"The Prince of Roum will have other distractions tonight," I said. "He'll have no need of her."

As I spoke, the sirens began to sing from the skies.

The Servitor released her. His mouth worked noiselessly for an instant; he made one of the protective gestures of the Will; he looked skyward and grunted, "The alarm! Who gave the alarm? You, old Watcher?"

Figures rushed about insanely in the streets.

Avluela, freed, sped past me—on foot, her wings but half-furled—and was swallowed up in the surging throng. Over the terrifying sound of the sirens came booming messages from the public annunciators, giving instructions for defense and safety. A lanky man with the mark of the guild of Defenders upon his cheek rushed up to me, shouted words too incoherent to be understood, and sped on down the street. The world seemed to have gone mad.

Only I remained calm. I looked to the skies, half-expecting to see the invaders' black ships already hovering above the towers of Roum. But I saw nothing except the hovering nightlights and the other objects one might expect overhead.

"Gormon?" I called. "Avluela?"

I was alone.

A strange emptiness swept over me. I had given the alarm; the invaders were on their way; I had lost my occupation. There was no need of Watchers now.

Almost lovingly I touched the worn cart that had been my companion for so many years. I ran my fingers over its stained and pitted instruments; and then I looked away, abandoning it, and went down the dark streets cartless, burdenless, a man whose life had found and lost meaning in the same instant. And about me raged chaos.

SEVEN

It was understood that when the moment of Earth's final battle arrived, all guilds would be mobilized, the Watchers alone exempted. We who had manned the perimeter of defense for so long had no part in the strategy of combat; we were discharged by the giving of a true alarm. Now it was the time of the guild of Defenders to show its capabilities. They had planned for half a cycle what they would do in time of war. What plans would they call forth now? What deeds would they direct?

My only concern was to return to the royal hostelry and wait out the crisis. It was hopeless to think of finding Avluela, and I pummeled myself savagely for having let her slip away, naked and without a protector, in that confused moment. Where would she go? Who would shield her?

A fellow Watcher, pulling his cart madly along, nearly collided with me. "Careful!" I snapped.

He looked up, breathless, stunned. "Is it true?" he asked. "The alarm?"

"Can't you hear?"

"But is it real?"

I pointed to his cart. "You know how to find that out."

"They say the man who gave the alarm was drunk, an old fool who was turned away from the inn yesterday."

"It could be so," I admitted.

"But if the alarm is real—!"

Smiling, I said, "If it is, now we all may rest. Good day to you, Watcher."

"Your cart! Where's your cart?" he shouted at me.

But I had moved past him, toward the mighty carven stone pillar of some relic of Imperial Roum.

Ancient images were carved on that pillar: battles and victories, foreign monarchs marching in the chains of disgrace through the streets of Roum, triumphant eagles celebrating imperial grandeur. In my strange new calmness I stood awhile before the column of stone and admired its elegant engravings. Toward me rushed a frenzied figure whom I recognized as the Rememberer Basil; I hailed him, saying, "How timely you come! Do me the kindness of explaining these images, Rememberer. They fascinate me, and my curiosity is aroused."

"Are you insane? Can't you hear the alarm?"

"I gave the alarm, Rememberer."

"Flee, then! Invaders come! We must fight!"

"Not I, Basil. Now my time is over. Tell me of these images. These beaten kings, these broken emperors. Surely a man of your years will not be doing battle."

"All are mobilized now!"

"All but Watchers," I said. "Take a moment. Yearning for the past is born in me. Gormon has vanished; be my guide to these lost cycles."

The Rememberer shook his head wildly, circled around me, and tried to get away. Hoping to seize his skinny arm and pin him to the spot, I made a lunge at him; but he eluded me and I caught only his dark shawl, which pulled free and came loose in my hands. Then he was gone, his spindly limbs pumping madly as he fled down the street and left my view. I shrugged and examined the shawl I had so unexpectedly acquired. It was shot through with glimmering threads of metal arranged in intricate patterns that teased the eye: it seemed to me that each strand disappeared into the weave of the fabric, only to reappear at some improbable point, like the lineage of dynasties unexpectedly revived in distant cities. The workmanship was superb. Idly I draped the shawl about my shoulders.

I walked on.

My legs, which had been on the verge of failing me earlier in the day, now served me well. With renewed youthfulness I made my way through the chaotic city, finding no difficulties in choosing my route. I headed for the river, then crossed it and, on the Tver's far side, sought the palace of the Prince. The night had deepened, for most lights were extinguished under the mobilization orders; and from time to time a dull boom signaled the explosion of a screening bomb overhead, liberating clouds of murk that shielded the city from most forms of long-range scrutiny. There were fewer pedestrians in the streets. The sirens still cried out. Atop the buildings the defensive installations were going into action; I heard the bleeping sounds of repellors warming up, and I saw long spidery arms of amplification booms swinging from tower to tower as they linked for maximum output. I had no doubt now that the invasion actually was coming. My own instruments might have been fouled by inner confusion, but they would not have proceeded thus far with the mobilization if the initial report had not been confirmed by the findings of hundreds of other members of my guild.

As I neared the palace a pair of breathless Rememberers sped toward me, their shawls flapping behind them. They called to me in words I did not comprehend—some code of their guild, I realized, recollecting that I wore Basil's shawl. I could not reply, and they rushed upon me, still gabbling; and switching to the language of ordinary men they said, "What is the matter with you? To your post! We must record! We must comment! We must observe!"

"You mistake me," I said mildly. "I keep this shawl only for your brother Basil, who left it in my care. I have no post to guard at this time."

"A Watcher," they cried in unison, and cursed me separately, and ran on. I laughed and went to the palace.

Its gates stood open. The neuters who had guarded the outer portal were gone, as were the two Indexers who had stood just within the door. The beggars that had thronged the vast plaza had jostled their way into the building itself to seek shelter; this had awakened the anger of the licensed hereditary mendicants whose customary stations were in that part of the building, and they had fallen upon the inflowing refugees with fury and unexpected strength. I saw cripples lashing out with their crutches held as clubs; I saw blind men landing blows with suspicious accuracy; meek penitents were wielding a variety of weapons ranging from stilettos to sonic pistols. Holding myself aloof from this shameless spectacle, I penetrated to the inner recesses of the palace and peered into chapels, where I saw Pilgrims beseeching the blessings of the Will and Communicants desperately seeking spiritual guidance as to the outcome of the conflict.

Abruptly I heard the blare of trumpets and cries of, "Make way! Make way!"

A file of sturdy Servitors marched into the palace, striding toward the Prince's chambers in the apse. Several of them held a struggling, kicking, frantic figure with half-unfolded wings: Avluela! I called out to her, but my voice died in the din, nor could I reach her. The Servitors shoved me aside. The procession vanished into the princely chambers. I caught a final glimpse of the little Flier, pale and small in the grip of her captors, and then she was gone once more.

I seized a bumbling neuter who had been moving uncertainly in the wake of the Servitors.

"That Flier! Why was she brought here?"

"Ha — he — they — "

"Tell me!"

"The Prince — his woman — in his chariot — he — he — they — the invaders — "

I pushed the flabby creature aside and rushed toward the apse. A brazen wall ten times my own height confronted me. I pounded on it. "Avluela!" I shouted hoarsely. "Av...lu...ela...!"

I was neither thrust away nor admitted. I was ignored. The bedlam at the western doors of the palace had extended itself now to the nave and aisles, and as the ragged beggars boiled toward me I executed a quick turn and found myself passing through one of the side doors of the palace.

Suspended and passive, I stood in the courtyard that led to the hostelry. A strange electricity crackled in the air. I assumed it to be an emanation from one of Roum's defense installations, some kind of beam designed to screen the city from attack. But an instant later I realized that it presaged the actual arrival of the invaders.

Starships blazed in the heavens.

When I had perceived them in my Watching they had appeared black against the infinite blackness, but now they burned with the radiance of suns. A stream of bright, hard, jewel-like globes bedecked the sky; they were ranged side by side, stretching from east to west in a continuous band, filling all the celestial arch, and as they erupted simultaneously into being it seemed to me that I heard the crash and throb of an invisible symphony heralding the arrival of the conquerors of earth.

I do not know how far above me the starships were, nor how many of them hovered there, nor any of the details of their design. I know only that in sudden massive majesty they were there, and that if I had been a Defender my soul would have withered instantly at the sight.

Across the heavens shot light of many hues. The battle had been joined. I could not comprehend the actions of our warriors, and I was equally baffled by the maneuvers of those who had come to take possession of

our history-crusted but time-diminished planet. To my shame I felt not
only out of the struggle but above the struggle, as though this were no
quarrel of mine. I wanted Avluela beside me, and she was somewhere
within the depths of the palace of the Prince of Roum. Even Gormon would
have been a comfort now, Gormon the Changeling, Gormon the spy,
Gormon the monstrous betrayer of our world.

Gigantic amplified voices bellowed, "Make way for the Prince of
Roum! The Prince of Roum leads the Defenders in the battle for the
fatherworld!"

From the palace emerged a shining vehicle the shape of a teardrop, in
whose bright-metaled roof a transparent sheet had been mounted so that
all the populace could see and take heart in the presence of the ruler. At
the controls of the vehicle sat the Prince of Roum, proudly erect, his cruel,
youthful features fixed in harsh determination; and beside him, robed like
an empress, I beheld the slight figure of the Flier Avluela. She seemed in a
trance.

The royal chariot soared upward and was lost in the darkness.

It seemed to me that a second vehicle appeared and followed its path,
and that the Prince's reappeared, and that the two flew in tight circles,
apparently locked in combat. Clouds of blue sparks wrapped both chariots
now; and then they swung high and far and were lost to me behind one of
the hills of Roum.

Was the battle now raging all over the planet? Was Perris in jeopardy,
and holy Jorslem, and even the sleepy isles of the Lost Continents? Did
starships hover everywhere? I did not know. I perceived events in only
one small segment of the sky over Roum, and even there my awareness of
what was taking place was dim, uncertain, and ill-informed. There were
momentary flashes of light in which I saw battalions of Fliers streaming
across the sky; and then darkness returned as though a velvet shroud had
been hurled over the city. I saw the great machines of our defense firing in
fitful bursts from the tops of our towers; and yet I saw the starships
untouched, unharmed, unmoved above. The courtyard in which I stood
was deserted, but in the distance I heard voices, full of fear and foreboding,
shouting in tinny tones that might have been the screeching of birds.
Occasionally there came a booming sound that rocked all the city. Once a
platoon of Somnambulists was driven past where I was; in the plaza
fronting the palace I observed what appeared to be an array of Clowns
unfolding some sort of sparkling netting of a military look; by one flash of
lightning I was able to see a trio of Rememberers making copious notes of
all that elapsed as they soared aloft on the gravity plate. It seemed—I was
not sure—that the vehicle of the Prince of Roum returned, speeding across
the sky with its pursuer clinging close. "Avluela," I whispered, as the twin
dots of light left my sight. Were the starships disgorging troops? Did

colossal pylons of force spiral down from those orbiting brightnesses to touch the surface of the Earth? Why had the Prince seized Avluela? Where was Gormon? What were our Defenders doing? Why were the enemy ships not blasted from the sky?

Rooted to the ancient cobbles of the courtyard, I observed the cosmic battle in total lack of understanding throughout the long night.

Dawn came. Strands of pale light looped from tower to tower. I touched fingers to my eyes, realizing that I must have slept while standing. Perhaps I should apply for membership in the guild of Somnambulists, I told myself lightly. I put my hands to the Rememberer's shawl about my shoulders and wondered how I managed to acquire it, and the answer came.

I looked toward the sky.

The alien starships were gone. I saw only the ordinary morning sky, gray with pinkness breaking through. I felt the jolt of compulsion and looked about for my cart, and reminded myself that I need do no more Watching, and I felt more empty than one would ordinarily feel at such an hour.

Was the battle over?

Had the enemy been vanquished?

Were the ships of the invaders blasted from the sky and lying in charred ruin outside Roum?

All was silent. I heard no more celestial symphonies. Then out of the eerie stillness there came a new sound, a rumbling noise as of wheeled vehicles, passing through the streets of the city. And the invisible Musicians played one final note, deep and resonant, which trailed away jaggedly as though every string had been broken at once.

Over the speakers used for public announcements came quiet words. "Roum is fallen. Roum is fallen."

EIGHT

The royal hostelry was untended. Neuters and members of the servant guilds all had fled. Defenders, Masters, and Dominators must have perished honorably in combat. Basil the Rememberer was nowhere about; likewise none of his brethren. I went to my room, cleansed and refreshed and fed myself, gathered my few possessions, and bade farewell to the luxuries I had known so briefly. I regretted that I had had such a short time to visit Roum; but at least Gormon had been a most excellent guide, and I had seen a great deal.

Now I proposed to move on.

It did not seem prudent to remain in a conquered city. My room's thinking cap did not respond to my queries, and so I did not know what the extent of the defeat was, here or in other regions, but it was evident to me that Roum at least had passed from human control, and I wished to depart quickly. I weighed the thought of going to Jorslem, as that tall Pilgrim had suggested upon my entry into Roum; but then I reflected and chose a westward route, toward Perris, which not only was closer but held the headquarters of the Rememberers. My own occupation had been destroyed; but on this first morning of Earth's conquest I felt a sudden powerful and strange yearning to offer myself humbly to the Rememberers and seek with them knowledge of our more glittering yesterdays.

At midday I left the hostelry. I walked first to the palace, which still stood open. The beggars lay strewn about, some drugged, some sleeping, most dead; from the crude manner of their death I saw that they must have slain one another in their panic and frenzy. A despondent-looking Indexer squatted beside the three skulls of the interrogation fixture in the chapel. As I entered he said, "No use. The brains do not reply."

"How goes it with the Prince of Roum?"

"Dead. The invaders shot him from the sky."

"A young Flier rode beside him. What do you know of her?"

"Nothing. Dead, I suppose."

"And the city?"

"Fallen. Invaders are everywhere."

"Killing?"

"Not even looting," the Indexer said. "They are most gentle. They have *collected* us."

"In Roum alone, or everywhere?"

The man shrugged. He began to rock rhythmically back and forth. I let him be, and walked deeper into the palace. To my surprise, the imperial chambers of the Prince were unsealed. I went within; I was awed by the sumptuous luxury of the hangings, the draperies, the lights, the furnishings. I passed from room to room, coming at last to the royal bed, whose coverlet was the flesh of a colossal bivalve of the planet of another star, and as the shell yawned for me I touched the infinitely soft fabric under which the Prince of Roum had lain, and I recalled that Avluela too had lain here, and if I had been a younger man I would have wept.

I left the palace and slowly crossed the plaza to begin my journey toward Perris.

As I departed I had my first glimpse of our conquerors. A vehicle of alien design drew up at the plaza's rim and perhaps a dozen figures emerged. They might almost have been human. They were tall and broad, deep-chested, as Gormon had been, and only the extreme length of their arms marked them instantly as alien. Their skins were of strange texture, and if I had been closer I suspect I would have seen eyes and lips and nostrils that were not of a human design. Taking no notice of me, they crossed the plaza, walking in a curiously loose-jointed loping way that reminded me irresistibly of Gormon's stride, and entered the palace. They seemed neither swaggering nor belligerent.

Sightseers. Majestic Roum once more exerted its magnetism upon strangers.

Leaving our new masters to their amusement, I walked off, toward the outskirts of the city. The bleakness of eternal winter crept into my soul. I wondered: did I feel sorrow that Roum had fallen? Or did I mourn the loss of Avluela? Or was it only that I now had missed three successive Watchings, and like an addict I was experiencing the pangs of withdrawal?

It was all of these that pained me, I decided. But mostly the last.

No one was abroad in the city as I made for the gates. Fear of the new masters kept the Roumish in hiding, I supposed. From time to time one of the alien vehicles hummed past, but I was unmolested. I came to the city's western gate late in the afternoon. It was open, revealing to me a gently rising hill on whose breast rose trees with dark green crowns. I passed through and saw, a short distance beyond the gate, the figure of a Pilgrim who was shuffling slowly away from the city.

I overtook him easily.

His faltering, uncertain walk seemed strange to me, for not even his thick brown robes could hide the strength and youth of his body: he stood erect, his shoulders square and his back straight, and yet he walked with the hesitating, trembling step of an old man. When I drew abreast of him and peered under his hood I understood, for affixed to the bronze mask all Pilgrims wear was a reverberator, such as is used by blind men to warn them of obstacles and hazards. He became aware of me and said, "I am a sightless Pilgrim. I pray you do not molest me."

It was not a Pilgrim's voice. It was a strong and harsh and imperious voice.

I replied, "I molest no one. I am a Watcher who has lost his occupation this night past."

"Many occupations were lost this night past, Watcher."

"Surely not a Pilgrim's."

"No," he said. "Not a Pilgrim's."

"Where are you bound?"

"Away from Roum."

"No particular destination?"

"No," the Pilgrim said. "None. I will wander."

"Perhaps we should wander together," I said, for it is accounted good luck to travel with a Pilgrim and shorn of my Flier and my Changeling, I would otherwise have traveled alone. "My destination is Perris. Will you come?"

"There as well as anywhere else," he said bitterly "Yes. We will go to Perris together. But what business does a Watcher have there?"

"A Watcher has no business anywhere. I go to Perris to offer myself in service to the Rememberers.

"Ah," he said. "I was of that guild too, but it was only honorary."

"With Earth fallen, I wish to learn more of Earth in its pride."

"Is all Earth fallen, then, and not only Roum?"

"I think it is so," I said.

"Ah," replied the Pilgrim. "Ah!"

He fell silent and we went onward. I gave him my arm, and now he shuffled no longer, but moved with a young man's brisk stride. From time to time he uttered what might have been a sigh or a smothered sob. When I asked him details of his Pilgrimage, he answered obliquely or not at all. When we were a hour's journey outside Roum, and already amid forests, he said suddenly, "This mask gives me pain. Will you help me adjust it?"

To my amazement he began to remove it. I gasped, for it is forbidden for a Pilgrim to reveal his face. Had he forgotten that I was not sightless too?

As the mask came away he said, "You will welcome this sight."

The bronze grillwork slipped down from his forehead, and I saw first eyes that had been newly blinded, gaping holes where no surgeon's knife, but possibly thrusting fingers, had penetrated, and then the sharp regal nose, and finally the quirked, taut lips of the Prince of Roum.

"Your Majesty!" I cried.

Trails of dried blood ran down his cheeks. About the raw sockets themselves were smears of ointment. He felt little pain, I suppose, for he had killed it with those green smears, but the pain that burst through me was real and potent.

"Majesty no longer," he said. "Help me with the mask!" His hands trembled as he held it forth. "These flanges must be widened. They press cruelly at my cheeks. Here—here—"

Quickly I made the adjustments, so that I would not have to see his ruined face for long.

He replaced the mask. "I am a Pilgrim now," he said quietly. "Roum is without its Prince. Betray me if you wish, Watcher; otherwise help me to Perris; and if ever I regain my power you will be well rewarded."

"I am no betrayer," I told him.

In silence we continued. I had no way of making small talk with such a man. It would be a somber journey for us to Perris: but I was committed now to be his guide. I thought of Gormon and how well he had kept his vows. I thought too of Avluela, and a hundred times the words leaped to my tongue to ask the fallen Prince how his consort the Flier had fared in the night of defeat, but I did not ask.

Twilight gathered, but the sun still gleamed golden-red before us in the west. And suddenly I halted and made a hoarse sound of surprise deep in my throat as a shadow passed overhead.

High above me Avluela soared. Her skin was stained by the colors of the sunset, and her wings were spread to their fullest, radiant with every hue of the spectrum. She was already at least the height of a hundred men above the ground, and still climbing, and to her I must have been only a speck among the trees.

"What is it?" the Prince asked. "What do you see?"

"Nothing."

"Tell me what you see!"

I could not deceive him. "I see a Flier, your Majesty. A slim girl far aloft."

"Then the night must have come."

"No," I said. "The sun is still above the horizon."

"How can that be? She can have only nightwings. The sun would hurl her to the ground."

I hesitated. I could not bring myself to explain how it was that Avluela flew by day, though she had only nightwings. I could not tell the Prince of Roum that beside her, wingless, flew the invader Gormon, effortlessly moving through the air, his arm about her thin shoulders, steadying her, supporting her, helping her resist the pressure of the solar wind. I could not tell him that his nemesis flew with the last of his consorts above his head.

"Well?" he demanded. "How does she fly by day?"

"I do not know," I said. "It is a mystery to me. There are many things nowadays I can no longer understand."

The Prince appeared to accept that. "Yes, Watcher. Many things none of us can understand."

He fell once more into silence. I yearned to call out to Avluela, but I knew she could not and would not hear me, and so I walked on toward the sunset, toward Perris, leading the blind Prince. And over us Avluela and Gormon sped onward, limned sharply against the day's last glow, until they climbed so high they were lost to my sight.

SUNDANCE (1968)

INTRODUCTION

This was another product of the dark year of 1968 — written for Edward L. Ferman, the publisher and now also the editor of *Fantasy & Science Fiction*, in late September, a couple of months after I finished the *Nightwings* sequence. I was still living in rented quarters — in exile, that was exactly how I thought of it — but I had begun to adapt by that time to the changed circumstances that the fire had brought, and I was working at something like the old pace. Since I was writing too many stories for Fred Pohl to handle all at once, I began offering every other one to Ferman. I was working at a new level of complexity, too — sure of myself and my technique, willing now to push the boundaries of the short-story form in any direction that seemed worth exploring. I had always been interested, from the beginning of my career, in technical experimentation, when and as the restrictions imposed on me by my pulp-magazine editors allowed any. But now I was in my thirties and approaching the height of my powers as a writer. So I did "Sundance" by way of producing a masterpiece in the old sense of the word — that is, a piece of work which is intended to demonstrate to a craftsman's peers that he has ended his apprenticeship and has fully mastered the intricacies of his trade.

Apparently I told Ed Ferman something about the story's nature while I was working on it, and he must have reacted with some degree of apprehensiveness, because the letter I sent him on October 22, 1968, accompanying the submitted manuscript, says, "I quite understand your hesitation to commit yourself in advance to a story when you've been warned it's experimental; but it's not all *that* experimental....I felt that the only way I could properly convey the turmoil in the protagonist's mind, the gradual dissolution of his hold on reality, was through the constant changing of persons and tenses; but as I read it through I think everything remains clear despite the frequent derailments of the reader." And I added, "I don't mean to say that I intend to disappear over the deep end of experimentalism. I don't regard myself as a member of any 'school' of sf, and don't value obscurity for its own sake. Each story is a technical challenge unique unto itself, and I have to go where the spirit moves me. Sometimes it moves me to a relatively conventional strong-narrative item...and sometimes to a relatively avant-garde item like this present 'Sundance;' I'm just after the best way of telling my story, in each case."

Ferman responded on Nov 19 with: "You should do more of this sort of thing. 'Sundance' is by far the best of the three I've seen recently. It not only works; it works beautifully. The ending — with the trapdoor image and that last line — is perfectly consistent, and just fine." He had only one suggestion: that I simplify the story's structure a little, perhaps by eliminating the occasional use of second-person narrative. But I wasn't about to do that. I replied with an explanation of *why* the story kept switching about between first person narrative, second person, third person present tense, and third person past tense. Each mode had its particular narrative significance in conveying the various reality-levels of the story, I told him: the first-person material was the protagonist's interior monolog, progressively more incoherent and untrustworthy; the second-person passages provided objective description of his actions, showing his breakdown from the outside, but not so far outside as third person would be — and so forth. Ferman was convinced, and ran the story as is.

And it became something of a classic almost immediately after Ed ran it in his June,1969 issue. Though it was certainly a kind of circus stunt, it was a stunt that worked, and it attracted widespread attention, including a place on the ballot for the Nebula award the following year. (But I had "Passengers" on the same ballot, and had no wish to compete with myself. Shrewdly if somewhat cynically, I calculated that the more accessible "Passengers" had a better chance of winning the award, and had "Sundance" removed from the ballot. And that was how I came to win a Nebula with my second-best story of 1969.) "Sundance" has since been reprinted dozens of times, both in science-fiction anthologies and in textbooks of literature. Here it is once more.

Today you liquidated about 50,000 Eaters in Sector A, and now you are spending an uneasy night. You and Herndon flew east at dawn, with the green-gold sunrise at your backs, and sprayed the neural pellets over a thousand hectares along the Forked River. You flew on into the prairie beyond the river, where the Eaters have already been wiped out, and had lunch sprawled on that thick, soft carpet of grass where the first settlement is expected to rise. Herndon picked some juiceflowers, and you enjoyed half an hour of mild hallucinations. Then, as you headed toward the copter to begin an afternoon of further pellet spraying, he said suddenly, "Tom, how would you feel about this if it turned out that the Eaters weren't just animal pests? That they were *people,* say, with a language and rites and a history and all?"

You thought of how it had been for your own people.

"They aren't," you said.

"Suppose they were. Suppose the Eaters—"

"They aren't. Drop it.

Herndon has this streak of cruelty in him that leads him to ask such questions. He goes for the vulnerabilities; it amuses him. All night now his casual remark has echoed in your mind. Suppose the Eaters...suppose the eaters...suppose...suppose....

You sleep for a while, and dream, and in your dreams you swim through rivers of blood.

Foolishness. A feverish fantasy. You know how important it is to exterminate the Eaters fast, before the settlers get here. They're just animals, and not even harmless animals at that; ecology-wreckers is what they are, devourers of oxygen-liberating plants, and they have to go. A few have been saved for zoological study. The rest must be destroyed. Ritual extirpation of undesirable beings, the old, old story. But let's not complicate our job with moral qualms, you tell yourself. Let's not dream of rivers of blood.

The Eaters don't even *have* blood, none that could flow in rivers, anyway. What they have is, well, a kind of lymph that permeates every tissue and transmits nourishment along the interfaces. Waste products go out the same way, osmotically. In terms of process, it's structurally analogous to your own kind of circulatory system, except there's no network of blood vessels hooked to a master pump. The life-stuff just oozes through their bodies as though they were amoebas or sponges or some other low-phylum form. Yet they're definitely high-phylum in nervous system, digestive setup, limb-and-organ template, etc. Odd, you think. The thing about aliens is that they're alien, you tell yourself, not for the first time.

The beauty of their biology for you and your companions is that it lets you exterminate them so neatly.

You fly over the grazing grounds and drop the neural pellets. The Eaters find and ingest them. Within an hour the poison has reached all sectors of the body. Life ceases; a rapid breakdown of cellular matter follows, the Eater literally falling apart molecule by molecule the instant that nutrition is cut off; the lymph-like stuff works like acid; a universal lysis occurs; flesh and even the bones, which are cartilaginous, dissolve. In two hours, a puddle on the ground. In four, nothing at all left. Considering how many millions of Eaters you've scheduled for extermination here, it's sweet of the bodies to be self-disposing. Otherwise what a charnel house this world would become!

Suppose the Eaters....

Damn Herndon. You almost feel like getting a memory-editing in the morning. Scrape his stupid speculations out of your head. If you dared. If you dared.

***

In the morning he does not dare. Memory-editing frightens him; he will try to shake free of his new-found guilt without it. The Eaters, he explains to himself, are mindless herbivores, the unfortunate victims of human expansionism, but not really deserving of passionate defense. Their extermination is not tragic; it's just too bad. If Earthmen are to have this world, the Eaters must relinquish it. There's a difference, he tells himself, between the elimination of the Plains Indians from the American prairie in the nineteenth century and the destruction of the bison on that same prairie. One feels a little wistful about the slaughter of the thundering herds; one regrets the butchering of millions of the noble brown woolly beasts, yes. But one feels outrage, not mere wistful regret, at what was done to the Sioux. There's a difference. Reserve your passions for the proper cause.

He walks from his bubble at the edge of the camp toward the center of things. The flagstone path is moist and glistening. The morning fog has not yet lifted, and every tree is bowed, the long, notched leaves heavy with droplets of water. He pauses, crouching, to observe a spider-analog spinning its asymmetrical web. As he watches, a small amphibian, delicately shaded turquoise, glides as inconspicuously as possible over the mossy ground.

Not inconspicuously enough; he gently lifts the little creature and puts it on the back of his hand. The gills flutter in anguish, and the amphibian's sides quiver. Slowly, cunningly, its color changes until it matches the coppery tone of the hand. The camouflage is excellent. He lowers his hand and the amphibian scurries into a puddle. He walks on.

He is forty years old, shorter than most of the other members of the expedition, with wide shoulders, a heavy chest, dark glossy hair, a blunt, spreading nose. He is a biologist. This is his third career, for he has failed as an anthropologist and as a developer of real estate.

His name is Tom Two Ribbons. He has been married twice but has had no children. His great-grandfather died of alcoholism; his grandfather was addicted to hallucinogens; his father had compulsively visited cheap memory-editing parlors. Tom Two Ribbons is conscious that he is failing a family tradition, but he has not yet found his own mode of self-destruction.

In the main building he discovers Herndon, Julia, Ellen, Schwartz, Chang, Michaelson, and Nichols. They are eating breakfast; the others are already at work. Ellen rises and comes to him and kisses him. Her short soft yellow hair tickles his cheeks. "I love you," she whispers. She has spent the night in Michaelson's bubble. "I love you," he tells her, and draws a quick vertical line of affection between her small pale breasts. He winks at Michaelson, who nods, touches the tops of two fingers to his lips, and blows them a kiss. We are all good friends here, Tom Two Ribbons thinks.

"Who drops pellets today?" he asks.

"Mike and Chang," says Julia. "Sector C."

Schwartz says, "Eleven more days and we ought to have the whole peninsula clear. Then we can move inland."

"If our pellet supply holds up," Chang points out.

Herndon says, "Did you sleep well, Tom?"

"No," says Tom. He sits down and taps out his breakfast requisition. In the west, the fog is beginning to burn off the mountains. Something throbs in the back of his neck. He has been on this world nine weeks now, and in that time it has undergone its only change of season, shading from dry weather to foggy. The mists will remain for many months. Before the plains parch again, the Eaters will be gone and the settlers will begin to arrive. His food slides down the chute and he seizes it. Ellen sits beside him. She is a little more than half his age; this is her first voyage; she is their keeper of records, but she is also skilled at editing. "You look troubled," Ellen tells him. "Can I help you?"

"No. Thank you."

"I hate it when you get gloomy."

"It's a racial trait," says Tom Two Ribbons.

"I doubt that very much."

"The truth is that maybe my personality reconstruct is wearing thin. The trauma level was so close to the surface. I'm just a walking veneer, you know."

Ellen laughs prettily. She wears only a spray-on half-wrap. Her skin looks damp; she and Michaelson have had a swim at dawn. Tom Two Ribbons is thinking of asking her to marry him, when this job is over. He has not been married since the collapse of the real estate business. The therapist suggested divorce as part of the reconstruct. He sometimes wonders where Terry has gone and whom she lives with now. Ellen says, "You seem pretty stable to me, Tom."

"Thank you," he says. She is young. She does not know.

"If it's just a passing gloom I can edit it out in one quick snip."

"Thank you," he says. "No."

"I forgot. You don't like editing."

"My father—"

"Yes?"

"In fifty years he pared himself down to a thread," Tom Two Ribbons says. "He had his ancestors edited away, his whole heritage, his religion, his wife, his sons, finally his name. Then he sat and smiled all day. Thank you, no editing."

"Where are you working today?" Ellen asks.

"In the compound, running tests."

"Want company? I'm off all morning."

"Thank you, no," he says, too quickly. She looks hurt. He tries to remedy his unintended cruelty by touching her arm lightly and saying, "Maybe this afternoon, all right? I need to commune a while. Yes?"

"Yes," she says, and smiles, and shapes a kiss with her lips.

After breakfast he goes to the compound. It covers a thousand hectares east of the base; they have bordered it with neural-field projectors at intervals of eighty meters, and this is a sufficient fence to keep the captive population of two hundred Eaters from straying. When all the others have been exterminated, this study group will remain. At the southwest corner of the compound stands a lab bubble from which the experiments are run: metabolic, psychological, physiological, ecological. A stream crosses the compound diagonally. There is a low ridge of grassy hills at its eastern edge. Five distinct copses of tightly clustered knifeblade trees are separated by patches of dense savanna. Sheltered beneath the grass are the oxygen-plants, almost completely hidden except for the photosynthetic spikes that adjust to heights of three or four meters at regular intervals, and for the lemon-colored respiratory bodies, chest high, that make the grassland sweet and dizzying with exhaled gases. Through the fields move the Eaters in a straggling herd, nibbling delicately at the respiratory bodies.

Tom Two Ribbons spies the herd beside the stream and goes toward it. He stumbles over an oxygen-plant hidden in the grass but deftly recovers his balance and, seizing the puckered orifice of the respiratory body, inhales deeply. His despair lifts. He approaches the Eaters. They are spherical, bulky, slow-moving creatures, covered by masses of coarse orange fur. Saucerlike eyes protrude above narrow rubbery lips. Their legs are thin and scaly, like a chicken's, and their arms are short and held close to their bodies. They regard him with bland lack of curiosity. "Good morning, brothers!" is the way he greets them this time, and he wonders why.

***

I noticed something strange today. Perhaps I simply sniffed too much oxygen in the fields; maybe I was succumbing to a suggestion Herndon planted; or possibly it's the family masochism cropping out. But while I was observing the Eaters in the compound, it seemed to me, for the first time, that they were behaving intelligently, that they were functioning in a ritualized way.

I followed them around for three hours. During that time they uncovered half a dozen outcroppings of oxygen-plants. In each case they went through a stylized pattern of action before starting to munch. They:

Formed a straggly circle around the plants.

Looked toward the sun.

Looked toward their neighbors on left and right around the circle.

Made fuzzy neighing sounds *only* after having done the foregoing.

Looked toward the sun again.

Moved in and ate.

If this wasn't a prayer of thanksgiving, a saying of grace, then what was it? And if they're advanced enough spiritually to say grace, are we not therefore committing genocide here? Do chimpanzees say grace? Christ, we wouldn't even wipe out chimps the way we're cleaning out the Eaters! Of course, chimps don't interfere with human crops, and some kind of coexistence would be possible, whereas Eaters and human agriculturalists simply can't function on the same planet. Nevertheless, there's a moral issue here. The liquidation effort is predicated on the assumption that the intelligence level of the Eaters is about on a par with that of oysters, or, at best, sheep. Our consciences stay clear because our poison is quick and painless and because the Eaters thoughtfully dissolve upon dying, sparing us the mess of incinerating millions of corpses. But if they pray—

I won't say anything to the others just yet. I want more evidence, hard, objective. Films, tapes, record cubes. Then we'll see. What if I can show that we're exterminating intelligent beings? My family knows a little about genocide, after all, having been on the receiving end just a few centuries back. I doubt that I could halt what's going on here. But at the very least I could withdraw from the operation. Head back to Earth and stir up public outcries. I hope I'm imagining this.

***

I'm not imagining a thing. They gather in circles; they look to the sun; they neigh and pray. They're only balls of jelly on chicken legs, but they give thanks for their food. Those big round eyes now seem to stare accusingly at me. Our tame herd here knows what's going on: that we have descended from the stars to eradicate their kind, and that they alone will be spared. They have no way of fighting back or even of communicating their displeasure, but they *know*. And hate us. Jesus, we have killed two million of them since we got here, and in a metaphorical sense I'm stained with blood, and what will I do, what can I do?

I must move very carefully, or I'll end up drugged and edited.

I can't let myself seem like a crank, a quack, an agitator. I can't stand up and *denounce!* I have to find allies. Herndon, first. He surely is onto the truth; he's the one who nudged *me* to it, that day we dropped pellets. And I thought he was merely being vicious in his usual way!

I'll talk to him tonight.

He says, "I've been thinking about that suggestion you made. About the Eaters. Perhaps we haven't made sufficiently close psychological studies. I mean, if they really *are* intelligent—"

Herndon blinks. He is a tall man with glossy dark hair, a heavy beard, sharp cheekbones. "Who says they are, Tom?"

"You did. On the far side of the Forked River, you said—"

"It was just a speculative hypothesis. To make conversation."

"No, I think it was more than that. You really believed it."

Herndon looks troubled. "Tom, I don't know what you're trying to start, but don't start it. If I for a moment believed we were killing intelligent creatures, I'd run for an editor so fast I'd start an implosion wave."

"Why did you ask me that thing, then?" Tom Two Ribbons says.

"Idle chatter."

"Amusing yourself by kindling guilts in somebody else? You're a bastard, Herndon. I mean it."

"Well, look, Tom, if I had any idea that you'd get so worked up about a hypothetical suggestion—" Herndon shakes his head. "The Eaters aren't intelligent beings. Obviously. Otherwise we wouldn't be under orders to liquidate them."

"Obviously," says Tom Two Ribbons.

***

Ellen said, "No, I don't know what Tom's up to. But I'm pretty sure he needs a rest. It's only a year and a half since his personality reconstruct, and he had a pretty bad breakdown back then."

Michaelson consulted a chart. "He's refused three times in a row to make his pellet-dropping run. Claiming he can't take time away from his research. Hell, we can fill in for him, but it's the idea that he's ducking chores that bothers me."

"What kind of research is he doing?" Nichols wanted to know.

"Not biological," said Julia. "He's with the Eaters in the compound all the time, but I don't see him making any tests on them. He just watches them."

"And talks to them," Chang observed.

"And talks, yes," Julia said.

"About what?" Nicholas asked.

"Who knows?"

Everyone looked at Ellen. "You're closest to him," Michaelson said. "Can't you bring him out of it?"

"I've got to know what he's in, first," Ellen said. "He isn't saying a thing."

***

You have done probing of your own—subtly, you hope. And you are aware that you can do nothing to save the Eaters. An irrevocable commitment has been made. It is 1876 all over again; these are the bison, these are the Sioux, and they must be destroyed, for the railroad is on its way. If you speak out here, your friends will calm you and pacify you and edit you, for they do not see what you see. If you return to Earth to agitate, you will be mocked and recommended for another reconstruct. You can do nothing. You can do nothing.

You cannot save, but perhaps you can record.

Go out into the prairie. Live with the Eaters; make yourself their friend; learn their ways. Set it down, a full account of their culture, so that at least that much will not be lost. You know the techniques of field anthropology. As was done for your people in the old days, do now for the Eaters.

***

He finds Michaelson. "Can you spare me for a few weeks?" he asks.

"Spare you, Tom? What do you mean?"

"I've got some field studies to do. I'd like to leave the base and work with Eaters in the wild."

"What's wrong with the ones in the compound?"

"It's the last chance with wild ones, Mike. I've got to go."

"Alone, or with Ellen?"

"Alone."

Michaelson nods slowly. "All right, Tom. Whatever you want. Go. I won't hold you here."

***

I dance in the prairie under the green-gold sun. About me the Eaters gather. I am stripped; sweat makes my skin glisten; my heart pounds. I talk to them with my feet, and they understand.

They understand.

They have a language of soft sounds. They have a god. They know love and awe and rapture. They have rites. They have names. They have a history. Of all this I am convinced.

I dance on thick grass.

How can I reach them? With my feet, with my hands, with my grunts, with my sweat. They gather by the hundreds, by the thousands, and I dance. I must not stop. They cluster about me and make their sounds. I am a conduit for strange forces. My great-grandfather should see me now! Sitting on his porch in Wyoming, the firewater in his hand, his brain rotting—see me now, old one! See the dance of Tom Two Ribbons! I talk to these strange ones with my feet under a sun that is the wrong color. I dance. I dance.

"Listen to me," I say. "I am your friend, I alone, the only one you can trust. Trust me, talk to me, teach me. Let me preserve your ways, for soon the destruction will come."

I dance, and the sun climbs, and the Eaters murmur.

There is the chief. I dance toward him, back, toward, I bow, I point to the sun, I imagine the being that lives in that ball of flame, I imitate the sounds of these people, I kneel, I rise, I dance. Tom Two Ribbons dances for you.

I summon skills my ancestors forgot. I feel the power flowing in me. As they danced in the days of the bison, I dance now, beyond the Forked River.

I dance, and now the Eaters dance too. Slowly, uncertainly, they move toward me, they shift their weight, lift leg and leg, sway about. "Yes, like that!" I cry. "Dance!"

We dance together as the sun reaches noon height.

Now their eyes are no longer accusing. I see warmth and kinship. I am their brother, their redskinned tribesman, he who dances with them. No longer do they seem clumsy to me. There is a strange ponderous grace in their movements. They dance. They dance. They caper about me. Closer, closer, closer!

We move in holy frenzy.

They sing, now, a blurred hymn of joy. They throw forth their arms, unclench their little claws. In unison they shift weight, left foot forward, right, left, right. Dance, brothers, dance, dance, dance! They press against me. Their flesh quivers; their smell is a sweet one. They gently thrust me across the field, to a part of the meadow where the grass is deep and untrampled. Still dancing, we seek for the oxygen-plants, and find clumps of them beneath the grass, and they make their prayer and seize them with their awkward arms, separating the respiratory bodies from the photosynthetic spikes. The plants, in anguish, release floods of oxygen. My mind reels. I laugh and sing. The Eaters are nibbling the lemon-colored perforated globes, nibbling the stalks as well. They thrust their plants at me. It is a religious ceremony, I see. Take from us, eat with us, join with us, this is the body, this is the blood, take, eat, join. I bend forward and put a lemon-colored globe to my lips. I do not bite; I nibble, as they do, my teeth slicing away the skin of the globe. Juice spurts into my mouth while oxygen drenches my nostrils. The Eaters sing hosannas. I should be in full paint for this, paint of my forefathers, feathers too, meeting their religion in the regalia of what should have been mine. Take, eat, join. The juice of the oxygen-plant flows in my veins. I embrace my brothers. I sing, and as my voice leaves my lips it becomes an arch that glistens like new steel, and I pitch my song lower, and the arch turns to tarnished silver. The Eaters crowd close. The scent of their bodies is fiery red to me. Their soft cries are puffs of steam. The sun is very warm; its rays are tiny jagged pings of puckered sound, close to the top of my range of hearing, plink! plink! plink! The thick grass hums to me, deep and rich, and the wind hurls points of flame along the prairie. I devour another oxygen-plant, and then a third. My brothers laugh and shout. They tell me of their gods, the god of warmth, the god of food, the god of pleasure, the god of death, the god of holiness, the god of wrongness, and the others. They recite for me the names of their kings, and I hear their voices as splashes of green mold on the clean sheet of the sky. They instruct me in their holy rites. I must remember this, I tell myself, for when it is gone it will never come again. I continue to dance. They continue to dance. The color of the hills becomes rough and coarse, like abrasive gas. Take, eat, join. Dance. They are so gentle!

I hear the drone of the copter, suddenly.

It hovers far overhead. I am unable to see who flies in it. "No!" I scream. "Not here! Not these people! Listen to me! This is Tom Two Ribbons! Can't you hear me? I'm doing a field study here! You have no right—!"

My voice makes spirals of blue moss edged with red sparks. They drift upward and are scattered by the breeze.

I yell, I shout, I bellow. I dance and shake my fists. From the wings of the copter the jointed arms of the pellet-distributors unfold. The gleaming spigots extend and whirl. The neural pellets rain down into the meadow, each tracing a blazing track that lingers in the sky. The sound of the copter becomes a furry carpet stretching to the horizon, and my shrill voice is lost in it.

The Eaters drift away from me, seeking the pellets, scratching at the roots of the grass to find them. Still dancing, I spring into their midst, striking the pellets from their hands, hurling them into the stream, crushing them to powder. The Eaters growl black needles at me. They turn away and search for more pellets. The copter turns and flies off, leaving a trail of dense oily sound. My brothers are gobbling the pellets eagerly.

There is no way to prevent it.

Joy consumes them and they topple and lie still. Occasionally a limb twitches; then even this stops. They begin to dissolve. Thousands of them melt on the prairie, sinking into shapelessness, losing their spherical forms, flattening, ebbing into the ground. The bonds of the molecules will no longer hold. It is the twilight of protoplasm. They perish. They vanish. For hours I walk the prairie. Now I inhale oxygen; now I eat a lemon-colored globe. Sunset begins with the ringing of leaden chimes. Black clouds make brazen trumpet calls in the east and the deepening wind is a swirl of coaly bristles. Silence comes. Night falls. I dance. I am alone.

The copter comes again, and they find you, and you do not resist as they gather you in. You are beyond bitterness. Quietly you explain what you have done and what you have learned, and why it is wrong to exterminate these people. You describe the plant you have eaten and the way it affects your senses, and as you talk of the blessed synesthesia, the texture of the wind and the sound of the clouds and the timbre of the sunlight, they nod and smile and tell you not to worry, that everything will be all right soon, and they touch something cold to your forearm, so cold that it is a whir and a buzz and the deintoxicant sinks into your vein and soon the ecstasy drains away, leaving only the exhaustion and the grief.

***

He says, "We never learn a thing, do we? We export all our horrors to the stars. Wipe out the Armenians, wipe out the Jews, wipe out the Tasmanians, wipe out the Indians, wipe out everyone who's in the way, and then come out here and do the same damned murderous thing. You weren't with me out there. You didn't dance with them. You didn't see what a rich, complex culture the Eaters have. Let me tell you about their tribal structure. It's dense: seven levels of matrimonial relationships, to begin with, and an exogamy factor that requires—"

Softly Ellen says, "Tom, darling, nobody's going to harm the Eaters."

"And the religion," he goes on. "Nine gods, each one an aspect of *the* god. Holiness and wrongness both worshiped. They have hymns, prayers, a theology. And we, the emissaries of the god of wrongness—"

"We're not exterminating them," Michaelson says. "Won't you understand that, Tom? This is all a fantasy of yours. You've been under the influence of drugs, but now we're clearing you out. You'll be clean in a little while. You'll have perspective again."

"A fantasy?" he says bitterly. "A drug dream? I stood out in the prairie and saw you drop pellets. And I watched them die and melt away. I didn't dream that."

"How can we convince you?" Chang asks earnestly. "What will make you believe? Shall we fly over the Eater country with you and show you how many millions there are?"

"But how many millions have been destroyed?" he demands.

They insist that he is wrong. Ellen tells him again that no one has ever desired to harm the Eaters. "This is a scientific expedition, Tom. We're here to *study* them. It's a violation of all we stand for to injure intelligent lifeforms."

"You admit that they're intelligent?"

"Of course. That's never been in doubt."

"Then why drop the pellets?" he asks. "Why slaughter them?"

"None of that has happened, Tom," Ellen says. She takes his hand between her cool palms. "Believe us. Believe us."

He says bitterly, "If you want me to believe you, why don't you do the job properly? Get out the editing machine and go to work on me. You can't simply *talk* me into rejecting the evidence of my own eyes."

"You were under drugs all the time," Michaelson says.

"I've never taken drugs! Except for what I ate in the meadow, when I danced—and that came after I had watched the massacre going on for weeks and weeks. Are you saying that it's a retroactive delusion?"

"No, Tom," Schwartz says. "You've had this delusion all along. It's part of your therapy, your reconstruct. You came here programmed with it."

"Impossible," he says.

Ellen kisses his fevered forehead. "It was done to reconcile you to mankind, you see. You had this terrible resentment of the displacement of your people in the nineteenth century. You were unable to forgive the industrial society for scattering the Sioux, and you were terribly full of hate. Your therapist thought that if you could be made to participate in an imaginary modern extermination, if you could come to see it as a necessary operation, you'd be purged of your resentment and able to take your place in society as—"

He thrusts her away. "Don't talk idiocy! If you knew the first thing about reconstruct therapy, you'd realize that no reputable therapist could be so shallow. There are no one-to-one correlations in reconstructs. No, don't touch me. Keep away. Keep away."

He will not let them persuade him that this is merely a drug-born dream. It is no fantasy, he tells himself, and it is no therapy. He rises. He goes out. They do not follow him. He takes a copter and seeks his brothers.

***

Again I dance. The sun is much hotter today. The Eaters are more numerous. Today I wear paint, today I wear feathers. My body shines with my sweat. They dance with me, and they have a frenzy in them that I have never seen before. We pound the trampled meadows with our feet. We clutch for the sun with our hands. We sing, we shout, we cry. We will dance until we fall.

This is no fantasy. These people are real, and they are intelligent, and they are doomed. This I know.

We dance. Despite the doom, we dance.

My great-grandfather comes and dances with us. He too is real. His nose is like a hawk's, not blunt like mine, and he wears the big headdress, and his muscles are like cords under his brown skin. He sings, he shouts, he cries.

Others of my family join us.

We eat the oxygen-plants together. We embrace the Eaters. We know, all of us, what it is to be hunted.

The clouds make music and the wind takes on texture and the sun's warmth has color.

We dance. We dance. Our limbs know no weariness. Eaters now, only my own people, my father's fathers across the centuries, thousands of gleaming skins, thousands of hawk's noses, and we eat the plants, and we find sharp sticks and thrust them into our flesh, and the sweet blood flows and dries in the blaze of the sun, and we dance, and we dance, and some of us fall from weariness, and we dance, and the prairie is a sea of bobbing headdresses, an ocean of feathers, and we dance, and my heart makes thunder, and my knees become water, and the sun's fire engulfs me, and I dance, and I fall, and I dance, and I fall, and I fall, and I fall.

***

Again they find you and bring you back. They give you the cool snout on your arm to take the oxygen-plant drug from your veins, and then they give you something else so you will rest. You rest and you are very calm.

Ellen kisses you and you stroke her soft skin, and then the others come in and they talk to you, saying soothing things, but you do not listen, for you are searching for realities. It is not an easy search. It is like falling through many trapdoors, looking for the one room whose floor is not hinged. Everything that has happened on this planet is your therapy, you tell yourself, designed to reconcile an embittered aborigine to the white man's conquest; nothing is really being exterminated here. You reject that and fall through and realize that this must be the therapy of your friends; they carry the weight of accumulated centuries of guilts and have come here to shed that load, and you are here to ease them of their burden, to draw their sins into yourself and give them forgiveness. Again you fall through, and see that the Eaters are mere animals who threaten the ecology and must be removed; the culture you imagined for them is your hallucination, kindled out of old churnings. You try to withdraw your objections to this necessary extermination, but you fall through again and discover that there is no extermination except in your mind, which is troubled and disordered by your obsession with the crime against your ancestors, and you sit up, for you wish to apologize to these friends of yours, these innocent scientists whom you have called murderers. And you fall through.

THREE

The 1970s

THE 1970s

Then the war in Vietnam was over, the cultural revolutions of the so-called Sixties had burned themselves out, and I felt pretty burned out myself as the new decade began, both metaphorically and literally. The rebuilding of my house had created terrible strains on my finances and my nervous system; my marriage, now in its second decade, was obviously crumbling; and the vast productivity of my writing career over fifteen years had left me exhausted. Something had to give. *Everything* had to give. A period of upheaval and transition was descending on me. The title of a novel I wrote in April, 1970 — *A Time of Changes* — told the whole story.

GOOD NEWS FROM THE VATICAN (1971)

INTRODUCTION

Ever since I read Baron Corvo's remarkable novel *Hadrian the Seventh* in 1955 I have amused myself with the fantasy of being elected Pope—an ambition complicated to some degree by the fact that I am not in holy orders, nor a Roman Catholic, nor, indeed, any kind of Christian at all. As my friends know, I duly submit an application whenever a vacancy occurs at the Vatican, but as of this date the Church has not yet seen fit to make use of my services.

All the same, I keep close watch over events in the Holy City as I bide my time, and in the pursuit of this not entirely serious career plan I've learned a good deal about the rituals and tensions surrounding the elections of a pontiff. This led me, one chilly but lighthearted day in February, 1971, to produce this sly, playful story of the accession of the first robot to the Holy See. (The robot is, in fact, meant to be my own successor, though the point is made only through an oblique private reference in the final paragraph.)

At that time a year and a half had passed since the completion of rebuilding work on my New York house, and it was even more handsome than it had been before the fire. I assumed I would live there for the rest of my life. But some sort of uneasiness was stirring in my soul even then, for the winter of 1970-71 was unusually snowy in New York, and as the white drifts piled up outside the door I began to tell people that I yearned for some warmer climate. On the February day when Terry Carr called to ask me to write a story for *Universe,* his new anthology of previously unpublished short stories, I was, as a matter of fact, writing *The Book of Skulls,* a novel set in the torrid Arizona desert.

Carr, then at the peak of his distinguished career as a science-fiction editor for Ace Books, told me that he was approaching the deadline for delivery of the first volume of *Universe* and was badly in need of work by authors with recognizable names. He had been asking me for a story for weeks, but I was busy with my novel, and I put him off; but now he appealed bluntly to me to help him out. Since Terry was a persuasive man and a close friend besides, I agreed to do a quick short story for him.

What to write about? Well, I thought, casting about quickly, suppose they elect a robot as Pope? That ought to be worth 3000 words or so of amiable foolery, right? My own pretense of interest in attaining the Papacy and my knowledge of the mechanics of Papal elections would help me make the story reasonably convincing. A couple of hours' work and Terry and his new anthology would be off my conscience.

So I sat down and wrote "Good News from the Vatican" just about as fast as I could type it out. Terry was amused by its cool, detached, tongue-in-cheek mode of irony (which I was beginning to employ more and more, as I entered my third decade as a writer) and published it in the first issue of *Universe* with a brief introduction noting that although my stories were usually quite serious in tone, this one was a bit on the silly side, although nevertheless quite thoughtful and ingenious, et cetera, et cetera.

A couple of unexpected ironies proceeded from this enterprise. The little story I had written so quickly that snowy February day caught everybody's attention, was nominated for a Nebula award, and won the trophy for me — the second of, ultimately, five Nebulas — the following spring. (I won my third the same night, for the novel *A Time of Changes*.) I collected my awards not in New York but at a ceremony held in California, for, much to my astonishment, the inner uneasiness of February had culminated by late summer in a series of explosive personal upheavals that had caused me to sell my New York house and move westward, a few months after Terry Carr himself had done the very same thing.

And also — rather sadly, actually — a decade and a half after I had helped Terry get *Universe* started by hastily writing an award-winning story for his first issue, I found myself taking his place as its editor, when his publisher decided to continue the anthology as a memorial to him following his untimely death in 1987.

Good News from the Vatican

This is the morning everyone has waited for, when at last the robot cardinal is to be elected pope. There can no longer be any doubt of the outcome. The conclave has been deadlocked for many days between the obstinate advocates of Cardinal Asciuga of Milan and Cardinal Carciofo of Genoa, and word has gone out that a compromise is in the making. All factions now are agreed on the selection of the robot. This morning I read in *Osservatore Romano* that the Vatican computer itself has taken a hand in the deliberations. The computer has been strongly urging the candidacy of the robot. I suppose we should not be surprised by this loyalty among machines. Nor should we let it distress us. We *absolutely must not* let it distress us.

"Every era gets the pope it deserves," Bishop FitzPatrick observed somewhat gloomily today at breakfast. "The proper pope for our times is a robot, certainly. At some future date it may be desirable for the pope to be a whale, an automobile, a cat, a mountain." Bishop FitzPatrick stands well over two meters in height and his normal facial expression is a morbid, mournful one. Thus it is impossible for us to determine whether any particular pronouncement of his reflects existential despair or placid acceptance. Many years ago he was a star player for the Holy Cross championship basketball team. He has come to Rome to do research for a biography of St. Marcellus the Righteous.

We have been watching the unfolding drama of the papal election from an outdoor cafe several blocks from the Square of St. Peter's. For all of us, this has been an unexpected dividend of our holiday in Rome; the previous pope was reputed to be in good health and there was no reason to suspect that a successor would have to be chosen for him this summer.

Each morning we drive across by taxi from our hotel near the Via Veneto and take up our regular positions around "our" table. From where we sit, we all have a clear view of the Vatican chimney through which the smoke of the burning ballots rises: black smoke if no pope has been elected, white if the conclave has been successful. Luigi, the owner and headwaiter, automatically brings us our preferred beverages: fernet branca for Bishop FitzPatrick, campari and soda for Rabbi Mueller, Turkish coffee for Miss Harshaw, lemon squash for Kenneth and Beverly, and pernod on the rocks

197

for me. We take turns paying the check, although Kenneth has not paid it even once since our vigil began. Yesterday, when Miss Harshaw paid, she emptied her purse and found herself 350 lire short; she had nothing else except hundred-dollar travelers' checks. The rest of us looked pointedly at Kenneth but he went on calmly sipping his lemon squash. After a brief period of tension Rabbi Mueller produced a 500-lire coin and rather irascibly slapped the heavy silver piece against the table. The rabbi is known for his short temper and vehement style. He is twenty-eight years old, customarily dresses in a fashionable plaid cassock and silvered sunglasses, and frequently boasts that he has never performed a bar mitzvah ceremony for his congregation, which is in Wicomico County, Maryland. He believes that the rite is vulgar and obsolete, and invariably farms out all his bar mitzvahs to a franchised organization of itinerant clergymen who handle such affairs on a commission basis. Rabbi Mueller is an authority on angels.

Our group is divided over the merits of electing a robot as the new pope. Bishop FitzPatrick, Rabbi Mueller, and I are in favor of the idea. Miss Harshaw, Kenneth, and Beverly are opposed. It is interesting to note that both of our gentlemen of the cloth, one quite elderly and one fairly young, support this remarkable departure from tradition. Yet the three "swingers" among us do not.

I am not sure why I align myself with the progressives. I am a man of mature years and fairly sedate ways. Nor have I ever concerned myself with the doings of the Church of Rome. I am unfamiliar with Catholic dogma and unaware of recent currents of thought within the Church. Still, I have been hoping for the election of the robot since the start of the conclave.

Why, I wonder? Is it because the image of a metal creature upon the Throne of St. Peter's stimulates my imagination and tickles my sense of the incongruous? That is, is my support of the robot purely an aesthetic matter? Or is it, rather, a function of my moral cowardice? Do I secretly think that this gesture will buy the robots off? Am I privately saying, Give them the papacy and maybe they won't want other things for a while? No. I can't believe anything so unworthy of myself. Possibly I am for the robot because I am a person of unusual sensitivity to the needs of others.

"If he's elected," says Rabbi Mueller, "he plans an immediate time-sharing agreement with the Dalai Lama and a reciprocal plug-in with the head programmer of the Greek Orthodox Church, just for starters. I'm told he'll make ecumenical overtures to the Rabbinate as well, which is certainly something for all of us to look forward to."

"I don't doubt that there'll be many corrections in the customs and practices of the hierarchy," Bishop FitzPatrick declares. "For example we can look forward to superior information-gathering techniques as the

Vatican computer is given a greater role in the operations of the Curia. Let me illustrate by — "

"What an utterly ghastly notion," Kenneth says. He is a gaudy young man with white hair and pink eyes. Beverly is either his wife or his sister. She rarely speaks. Kenneth makes the sign of the Cross with offensive brusqueness and murmurs, "In the name of the Father, the Son, and the Holy Automaton." Miss Harshaw giggles but chokes the giggle off when she sees my disapproving face.

Dejectedly, but not responding at all to the interruption, Bishop FitzPatrick continues, "Let me illustrate by giving you some figures I obtained yesterday afternoon. I read in the newspaper *Oggi* that during the last five years, according to a spokesman for the *Missiones Catholicae,* the Church has increased its membership in Yugoslavia from 19,381,403 to 23,501,062. But the government census taken last year gives the total population of Yugoslavia at 23,575,194. That leaves only 74,132 for the other religious and 'irreligious bodies.' Aware of the large Muslim population of Yugoslavia, I suspected an inaccuracy in the published statistics and consulted the computer in St. Peter's, which informed me" — the bishop, pausing, produces a lengthy printout and unfolds it across much of the table — "that the last count of the Faithful in Yugoslavia, made a year and a half ago, places our numbers at 14,206,198. Therefore an overstatement of 9,294,864 has been made. Which is absurd. And perpetuated. Which is damnable."

"What does he look like?" Miss Harshaw asks. "Does anyone have any idea?"

"He's like all the rest," says Kenneth. "A shiny metal box with wheels below and eyes on top."

"You haven't seen him," Bishop FitzPatrick interjects. "I don't think it's proper for you to assume that — "

"They're all alike," Kenneth says. "Once you've seen one, you've seen all of them. Shiny boxes. Wheels. Eyes. And voices coming out of their bellies like mechanized belches. Inside, they're all cogs and gears." Kenneth shudders delicately. "It's too much for me to accept. Let's have another round of drinks, shall we?"

Rabbi Mueller says, "It so happens that I've seen him with my own eyes."

"You *have?*" Beverly exclaims.

Kenneth scowls at her. Luigi, approaching, brings a tray of new drinks for everyone. I hand him a 5,000-lire note. Rabbi Mueller removes his sunglasses and breathes on their brilliantly reflective surfaces. He has small, watery gray eyes and a bad squint. He says, "The cardinal was the keynote speaker at the Congress of World Jewry that was held last fall in Beirut. His theme was 'Cybernetic Ecumenicism for Contemporary Man.'

I was there. I can tell you that His Eminency is tall and distinguished, with a fine voice and a gentle smile. There's something inherently melancholy about his manner that reminds me greatly of our friend the bishop, here. His movements are graceful and his wit is keen."

"But he's mounted on wheels, isn't he?" Kenneth persists.

"On treads," replies the rabbi, giving Kenneth a fiery, devastating look and resuming his sunglasses. "Treads, like a tractor has. But I don't think that treads are spiritually inferior to feet, or, for that matter, to wheels. If I were a Catholic I'd be proud to have a man like that as my pope."

"Not a man," Miss Harshaw puts in. A giddy edge enters her voice whenever she addresses Rabbi Mueller. "A robot," she says. "He's not a man, remember?"

"A *robot* like that as my pope, then," Rabbi Mueller says, shrugging at the correction. He raises his glass. "To the new pope!"

"To the new pope!" cries Bishop FitzPatrick.

Luigi comes rushing from his cafe. Kenneth waves him away, "Wait a second," Kenneth says. "The election isn't over yet. How can you be so sure?"

"The *Osservatore Romano*," I say, "indicates in this morning's edition that everything will be decided today. Cardinal Carciofo has agreed to withdraw in his favor, in return for a larger real-time allotment when the new computer hours are decreed at next year's consistory."

"In other words, the fix is in," Kenneth says.

Bishop FitzPatrick sadly shakes his head. "You state things much too harshly, my son. For three weeks now we have been without a Holy Father. It is God's Will that we shall have a pope. The conclave, unable to choose between the candidacies of Cardinal Carciofo and Cardinal Asciuga, thwarts that Will. If necessary, therefore, we must make certain accommodations with the realities of the times so that His Will shall not be further frustrated. Prolonged politicking within the conclave now becomes sinful. Cardinal Carciofo's sacrifice of his personal ambitions is not as self-seeking an act as you would claim."

Kenneth continues to attack poor Carciofo's motives for withdrawing. Beverly occasionally applauds his cruel sallies. Miss Harshaw several times declares her unwillingness to remain a communicant of a Church whose leader is a machine. I find this dispute distasteful and swing my chair away from the table to have a better view of the Vatican. At this moment the cardinals are meeting in the Sistine Chapel. How I wish I were there! What splendid mysteries are being enacted in that gloomy, magnificent room! Each prince of the Church now sits on a small throne surmounted by a violet-hued canopy. Fat wax tapers glimmer on the desk before each throne. Masters of ceremonies move solemnly through the vast chamber, carrying the silver basins in which the blank ballots repose. These basins are placed on the table before the altar. One by one the cardinals advance to the table, take ballots, return to their desks. Now, lifting their quill pens, they begin to write. "I, Cardinal _____, elect to the Supreme Pontificate the Most Reverend Lord my Lord Cardinal _____." What name do they fill in? Is it Carciofo? Is it Asciuga? Is it the name of some obscure and shriveled prelate from Madrid or Heidelberg, some last-minute choice of the anti-robot faction in its desperation? Or are they writing *his* name? The sound of scratching pens is loud in the chapel. The cardinals are completing their ballots, sealing them at the ends, folding them, folding them again and again, carrying them to the altar, dropping them into the great gold chalice. So have they done every morning and every afternoon for days, as the deadlock has prevailed.

"I read in the *Herald-Tribune* a couple of days ago," says Miss Harshaw, "that a delegation of two hundred and fifty young Catholic robots from Iowa is waiting at the Des Moines airport for news of the election. If their man gets in, they've got a chartered flight ready to leave, and they intend to request that they be granted the Holy Father's first public audience."

"There can be no doubt," Bishop FitzPatrick agrees, "that his election will bring a great many people of synthetic origin into the fold of the Church."

"While driving out plenty of flesh and blood people!" Miss Harshaw says shrilly.

"I doubt that," says the bishop. "Certainly there will be some feelings of shock, of dismay, of injury, of loss, for some of us at first. But these will pass. The inherent goodness of the new pope, to which Rabbi Mueller alluded, will prevail. Also I believe that technologically minded young folk everywhere will be encouraged to join the Church. Irresistible religious impulses will be awakened throughout the world."

"Can you imagine two hundred and fifty robots clanking into St. Peter's?" Miss Harshaw demands.

I contemplate the distant Vatican. The morning sunlight is brilliant and dazzling, but the assembled cardinals, walled away from the world, cannot enjoy its gay sparkle. They all have voted, now. The three cardinals who were chosen by lot as this morning's scrutators of the vote have risen. One of them lifts the chalice and shakes it, mixing the ballots. Then he places it on the table before the altar; a second scrutator removes the ballots and counts them. He ascertains that the number of ballots is identical to the number of cardinals present. The ballots now have been transferred to a ciborium, which is a goblet ordinarily used to hold the consecrated bread of the Mass. The first scrutator withdraws a ballot, unfolds it, reads its inscription; passes it to the second scrutator, who reads it also; then it is given to the third scrutator, who reads the name aloud. Asciuga? Carciofo? Some other? *His?*

Rabbi Mueller is discussing angels. "Then we have the Angels of the Throne, known in Hebrew as *arelim* or *ophanim*. There are seventy of them noted primarily for their steadfastness. Among them are the angels Orifiel, Ophaniel, Zabkiel, Jophiel, Ambriel, Tychagar, Barael, Quelamia, Paschar, Boel, and Raum. Some of these are no longer found in Heaven and are numbered among the fallen angels in Hell."

"So much for their steadfastness," says Kenneth.

"Then, too," the rabbi goes on, "there are the Angels of the Presence, who apparently were circumcized at the moment of their creation. These are Michael, Metatron, Suriel, Sandalphon, Uriel, Saraqael, Astanphaeus, Phanuel, Jehoel, Zagzagael, Yefefiah, and Akatriel. But I think my favorite of the whole group is the Angel of Lust, who is mentioned in Talmud *Bereshith Rabba* 85 as follows, that when Judah was about to pass by — "

They have finished counting the votes by this time, surely. An immense throng has assembled in the Square of St. Peter's. The sunlight gleams off hundreds if not thousands of steel-jacketed craniums. This must be a wonderful day for the robot population of Rome. But most of those in the piazza are creatures of flesh and blood: old women in black, gaunt young pickpockets, boys with puppies, plump vendors of sausages, and an assortment of poets, philosophers, generals, legislators, tourists, and fishermen. How has the tally gone? We will have our answer shortly. If no candidate has had a majority, they will mix the ballots with wet straw before casting them into the chapel stove, and black smoke will billow from the chimney. But if a pope has been elected, the straw will be dry, the smoke will be white.

The system has agreeable resonances. I like it. It gives me the satisfactions one normally derives from a flawless work of art: the *Tristan* chord, let us say, or the teeth of the frog in Bosch's *Temptation of St. Anthony*. I await the outcome with fierce concentration. I am certain of the result; I can already feel the irresistible religious impulses awakening in me. Although I feel, also, an odd nostalgia for the days of flesh and blood popes. Tomorrow's newspapers will have no interviews with the Holy Father's aged mother in Sicily, nor with his proud younger brother in San Francisco. And will this grand ceremony of election ever be held again? Will we need another pope, when this one whom we will soon have can be repaired so easily?

Ah. The white smoke! The moment of revelation comes!

A figure emerges on the central balcony of the facade of St. Peter's, spreads a web of cloth-of-gold, and disappears. The blaze of light against that fabric stuns the eye. It reminds me perhaps of moonlight coldly kissing the sea at Castellamare, or, perhaps even more, of the noonday glare rebounding from the breast of the Caribbean off the coast of St. John. A second figure, clad in ermine and vermilion, has appeared on the balcony.

"The cardinal-archdeacon," Bishop FitzPatrick whispers. People have started to faint. Luigi stands beside me, listening to the proceedings on a tiny radio. Kenneth says "It's all been fixed." Rabbi Mueller hisses at him to be still. Miss Harshaw begins to sob. Beverly softly recites the Pledge of Allegiance, crossing herself throughout. This is a wonderful moment for me. I think it is the most truly contemporary moment I have ever experienced.

The amplified voice of the cardinal-archdeacon cries, "I announce to you great joy. We have a pope."

Cheering commences, and grows in intensity as the cardinal-archdeacon tells the world that the newly chosen pontiff is indeed *that* cardinal, that noble and distinguished person, that melancholy and austere individual, whose elevation to the Holy See we have all awaited so intensely for so long. "He has imposed upon himself," says the cardinal-archdeacon, "the name of—"

Lost in the cheering. I turn to Luigi. "Who? What name?"

"Sisto Settimo," Luigi tells me.

Yes, and there he is, Pope Sixtus the Seventh, as we now must call him. A tiny figure clad in the silver and gold papal robes, arms outstretched to the multitude, and, yes! the sunlight glints on his cheeks, his lofty forehead, there is the brightness of polished steel. Luigi is already on his knees. I kneel beside him. Miss Harshaw, Beverly, Kenneth, even the rabbi, all kneel, for beyond doubt this is a miraculous event. The pope comes forward on his balcony. Now he will deliver the traditional apostolic benediction to the city and to the world. "Our help is in the Name of the Lord," he declares gravely. He activates the levitator jets beneath his arms; even at this distance I can see the two small puffs of smoke. White smoke, again. He begins to rise into the air. "Who hath made heaven and earth," he says. "May Almighty God, Father, Son, and Holy Ghost, bless you." His voice rolls majestically toward us. His shadow extends across the whole piazza. Higher and higher he goes, until he is lost to sight. Kenneth taps Luigi. "Another round of drinks," he says, and presses a bill of high denomination into the innkeeper's fleshy palm. Bishop FitzPatrick weeps. Rabbi Mueller embraces Miss Harshaw. The new pontiff, I think, has begun his reign in an auspicious way.

CAPRICORN GAMES (1972)

INTRODUCTION

Jesus was a Capricorn; so was Richard M. Nixon; and so am I. I am not much of a believer in the astrological sciences — the whole theory that the stars govern our lives makes no sense whatever to me — but I do accept, however inconsistent with the previous statement it may be, the conventional notion of the sort of people those born under the sign of Capricorn tend to be. (Stubborn, dedicated, talented, self-centered, always planning things out ahead of time. I think of Capricorns as being excellent chess players, though I'm a terrible one myself.) I look upon Capricorns as somewhat manipulative, which is not necessarily a negative attribute: "manipulative" is a term that can be applied to jugglers, novelists, surgeons, musicians, and others who are quick with their hands in a literal rather than metaphorical sense. But some of the Capricorn energy does flow into the work of organizing other human beings into patterns that serve the needs of the Capricorn, I feel. Certainly that's the sort of Capricorn that Nikki is in this story, which dates from October, 1972. I was a Californian by the time I wrote it, and you know how Californians are about things like astrology.

I was also at the beginning of a serious slowdown in my productivity, after a decade and a half's output of short stories and novels at a fantastic and almost unreal pace. After the heavy exertions of 1971, a year in which I wrote the novels *The Book of Skulls* and *Dying Inside* and nine or ten lesser items while in the midst of moving myself from New York to California, I wrote no novels at all in 1972, only short stories and novelets. (I did manage to produce fifteen of them during the year, a pretty hefty rate of production by the standards of normal writers, and far more than I've done in any year since, but nothing at all compared with what I was routinely doing in 1956 or 1957.) The early 1970s were the heyday of hardcover anthologies of original science fiction, a peculiar publishing phenomenon that had, so far as I could tell, no economic justification whatever for its existence. A go-getter named Roger Elwood was editing eight or ten such books a year, and much of my 1972 output was written for him — "Capricorn Games" for a collection called *The Far Side of Time*, published by the now-forgotten house of Dodd, Mead.

This story has always been a particular favorite of mine, and not just because its January-born author often sees himself as sitting at the keyboard playing games with his characters, playing games with his readers' minds. Nikki's birthdate happens to be — by sheer one-out-of-365 coincidence — to be the same as that of a young woman who was living in Houston, Texas, in 1981, when I — also by sheer coincidence — was in town to speak at the local university. She came upon the story somehow, was startled and amused to find that she shared a birthdate with its protagonist and that the author of the story was making a public appearance locally, and went to meet him. It turned out that we had a lot to say to each other. Her name was Karen Haber and — to make a long story short — we play our Capricorn games under the same roof these days.

Capricorn Games

Nikki stepped into the conical field of the ultrasonic cleanser, wriggling so that the unheard droning out of the machine's stubby snout could more effectively shear her skin of dead epidermal tissue, globules of dried sweat, dabs of yesterday's scents, and other debris; after three minutes she emerged clean, bouncy, ready for the party. She programmed her party outfit: green buskins, lemon-yellow tunic of gauzy film, pale orange cape soft as a clam's mantle, and nothing underneath but Nikki—smooth, glistening, satiny Nikki. Her body was tuned and fit. The party was in her honor, though she was the only one who knew that. Today was her birthday, the seventh of January, 1999: twenty-four years old, no sign yet of bodily decay. Old Steiner had gathered an extraordinary assortment of guests: he promised to display a reader of minds, a billionaire, an authentic Byzantine duke, an Arab rabbi, a man who had married his own daughter, and other marvels. All of these, of course, subordinate to the true guest of honor, the evening's prize, the real birthday boy, the lion of the season—the celebrated Nicholson, who had lived a thousand years and who said he could help others to do the same. Nikki…Nicholson. Happy assonance, portending close harmony. You will show me, dear Nicholson, how I can live forever and never grow old. A cozy, soothing idea.

The sky beyond the sleek curve of her window was black, snow-dappled; she imagined she could hear the rusty howl of the wind and feel the sway of the frost-gripped building, ninety stories high. This was the worst winter she had ever known. Snow fell almost every day, a planetary snow, a global shiver, not even sparing the tropics. Ice hard as iron bands bound the streets of New York. Walls were slippery, the air had a cutting edge. Tonight Jupiter gleamed fiercely in the blackness like a diamond in a raven's forehead. Thank God she didn't have to go outside. She could wait out the winter within this tower. The mail came by pneumatic tube. The penthouse restaurant fed her. She had friends on a dozen floors. The building was a world, warm, snug. Let it snow. Let the sour gales come. Nikki checked herself in the all-around mirror: very nice, very very nice. Sweet filmy yellow folds. Hint of thigh, hint of breasts. More than a hint when there's a light-source behind her. She glowed. Fluffed her short glossy black hair. Dab of scent. Everyone loved her. Beauty is a magnet: repels some, attracts many, leaves no one unmoved. It was nine o'clock.

"Upstairs," she said to the elevator. "Steiner's place."

"Eighty-eighth floor," the elevator said.

"I know that. You're so sweet."

Music in the hallway: Mozart, crystalline and sinuous. The door to Steiner's apartment was a half-barrel of chromed steel, like the entrance to a bank vault. Nikki smiled into the scanner. The barrel revolved. Steiner held his hands like cups, centimeters from her chest, by way of greeting. "Beautiful," he murmured.

"So glad you asked me to come."

"Practically everybody's here already. It's a wonderful party, love."

She kissed his shaggy cheek. In October they had met in the elevator. He was past sixty and looked less than forty. When she touched his body she perceived it as an object encased in milky ice, like a mammoth fresh out of the Siberian permafrost. They had been lovers for two weeks. Autumn had given way to winter and Nikki had passed out of his life, but he had kept his word about the parties: here she was, invited.

"Alexius Ducas," said a short, wide man with a dense black beard, parted in the middle. He bowed. A good flourish. Steiner evaporated and she was in the keeping of the Byzantine duke. He maneuvered her at once across the thick white carpet to a place where clusters of spotlights, sprouting like angry fungi from the wall, revealed the contours of her body. Others turned to look. Duke Alexius favored her with a heavy stare. But she felt no excitement. Byzantium had been over for a long time. He brought her a goblet of chilled green wine and said, "Are you ever in the Aegean Sea? My family has its ancestral castle on an island eighteen kilometers east of —"

"Excuse me, but which is the man named Nicholson?"

"Nicholson is merely the name he currently uses. He claims to have had a shop in Constantinople during the reign of my ancestor the Basileus Manuel Comnenus." A patronizing click, tongue on teeth. "Only a shopkeeper." The Byzantine eyes sparkled ferociously. "How beautiful you are!"

"Which one is he?"

"There. By the couch."

Nikki saw only a wall of backs. She tilted to the left and peered. No use. She would get to him later. Alexius Ducas continued to offer her his body with his eyes. She whispered languidly, "Tell me all about Byzantium."

He got as far as Constantine the Great before he bored her. She finished her wine, and, coyly extending the glass, persuaded a smooth young man passing by to refill it for her. The Byzantine looked sad. "The empire then was divided," he said, "among—"

"This is my birthday," she announced.

"Yours also? My congratulations. Are you as old as—"

"Not nearly. Not by half. I won't even be five hundred for some time," she said, and turned to take her glass. The smooth young man did not wait to be captured. The party engulfed him like an avalanche. Sixty, eighty guests, all in motion. The draperies were pulled back, revealing the full fury of the snowstorm. No one was watching it. Steiner's apartment was like a movie set: great porcelain garden stools, Ming or even Sung; walls painted with flat sheets of bronze and scarlet; pre-Columbian artifacts in spotlit niches; sculptures like aluminum spiderwebs; Dürer etchings—the loot of the ages. Squat shaven-headed servants, Mayans or Khmers or perhaps Olmecs, circulated impassively offering trays of delicacies: caviar, sea urchins, bits of roasted meat, tiny sausages, burritos in startling chili sauce. Hands darted unceasingly from trays to lips. This was a gathering of life-eaters, world-swallowers. Duke Alexius was stroking her arm. "I will leave at midnight," he said gently. "It would be a delight if you left with me."

"I have other plans," she told him.

"Even so." He bowed courteously, outwardly undisappointed. "Possibly another time. My card?" It appeared as if by magic in his hand: a sliver of tawny cardboard, elaborately engraved. She put it in her purse and the room swallowed him. Instantly a big, wild-eyed man took his place before her. "You've never heard of me," he began.

"Is that a boast or an apology?"

"I'm quite ordinary. I work for Steiner. He thought it would be amusing to invite me to one of his parties."

"What do you do?"

"Invoices and debarkations. Isn't this an amazing place?"

"What's your sign?" Nikki asked him.

"Libra."

"I'm Capricorn. Tonight's my birthday as well as *his*. If you're really Libra, you're wasting your time with me. Do you have a name?"

"Martin Bliss."

"Nikki."

"There isn't any Mrs. Bliss, hah-hah."

Nikki licked her lips. "I'm hungry. Would you get me some canapés?"

She was gone as soon as he moved toward the food. Circumnavigating the long room—past the string quintet, past the bartender's throne, past the window—until she had a good view of the man called Nicholson. He didn't disappoint her. He was slender, supple, not tall, strong in the shoulders. A man of presence and authority. She wanted to put her lips to

him and suck immortality out. His head was a flat triangle, brutal
cheekbones, thin lips, dark mat of curly hair, no beard, no mustache. His
eyes were keen, electric, intolerably wise. He must have seen everything
twice, at the very least. Nikki had read his book. Everyone had. He had
been a king, a lama, a slave trader, a slave. Always taking pains to conceal
his implausible longevity, now offering his terrible secret freely to the
members of the Book-of-the-Month Club. Why had he chosen to surface
and reveal himself? Because this is the necessary moment of revelation,
he had said. When he must stand forth as what he is, so that he might
impart his gift to others, lest he lose it. Lest he lose it. At the stroke of the
new century he must share his prize of life. A dozen people surrounded
him, catching his glow. He glanced through a palisade of shoulders and
locked his eyes on hers; Nikki felt impaled, exalted, chosen. Warmth spread
through her loins like a river of molten tungsten, like a stream of hot honey.
She started to go to him. A corpse got in her way. Death's-head, parchment
skin, nightmare eyes. A scaly hand brushed her bare biceps. A frightful
eroded voice croaked, "How old do you think I am?"

"Oh, God!"

"How old?"

"Two thousand?"

"I'm fifty-eight. I won't live to see fifty-nine. Here, smoke one of these."

With trembling hands he offered her a tiny ivory tube. There was a
Gothic monogram near one end — FXB — and a translucent green capsule
at the other. She pressed the capsule, and a flickering blue flame sprouted.
She inhaled. "What is it?" she asked.

"My own mixture. Soma Number Five. You like it?"

"I'm smeared," she said. "Absolutely smeared. Oh, God!" The walls
were flowing. The snow had turned to tinfoil. An instant hit. The corpse
had a golden halo. Dollar signs rose into view like stigmata on his furrowed
forehead. She heard the crash of the surf, the roar of the waves. The deck
was heaving. The masts were cracking. *Woman overboard!* she cried, and
heard her inaudible voice disappearing down a tunnel of echoes, boingg
boingg boingg. She clutched at his frail wrists. "You bastard, what did
you *do* to me?"

"I'm Francis Xavier Byrne."

Oh. The billionaire. Byrne Industries, the great conglomerate. Steiner
had promised her a billionaire tonight.

"Are you going to die soon?" she asked.

"No later than Easter. Money can't help me now. I'm a walking
metastasis." He opened his ruffled shirt. Something bright and metallic,
like chain mail, covered his chest. "Life-support system," he confided. "It
operates me. Take it off for half an hour and I'd be finished. Are you a
Capricorn?"

"How did you know?"

"I may be dying, but I'm not stupid. You have the Capricorn gleam in your eyes. What am I?"

She hesitated. His eyes were gleaming too. Self-made man, fantastic business sense, energy, arrogance. Capricorn, of course. No, too easy. "Leo," she said.

"No. Try again." He pressed another monogrammed tube into her hand and strode away. She hadn't yet come down from the last one, although the most flamboyant effects had ebbed. Party guests swirled and flowed around her. She no longer could see Nicholson. The snow seemed to be turning to hail, little hard particles spattering the vast windows and leaving white abraded tracks: or were her perceptions merely sharper? The roar of conversation seemed to rise and fall as if someone were adjusting a volume control. The lights fluctuated in a counterpointed rhythm. She felt dizzy. A tray of golden cocktails went past her and she hissed, "Where's the bathroom?"

Down the hall. Five strangers clustered outside it, talking in scaly whispers. She floated through them, grabbed the sink's cold edge, thrust her face to the oval concave mirror. A death's-head. Parchment skin, nightmare eyes. No! No! She blinked and her own features reappeared. Shivering, she made an effort to pull herself together. The medicine cabinet held a tempting collection of drugs, Steiner's all-purpose remedies. Without looking at labels Nikki seized a handful of vials and gobbled pills at random. A flat red one, a tapering green one, a succulent yellow gelatin capsule. Maybe headache remedies, maybe hallucinogens. Who knows, who cares? We Capricorns are not always as cautious as you think.

Someone knocked at the bathroom door. She answered and found the bland, hopeful face of Martin Bliss hovering near the ceiling. Eyes protruding faintly, cheeks florid. "They said you were sick. Can I do anything for you?" So kind, so sweet. She touched his arm, grazed his cheek with her lips. Beyond him in the hall stood a broad-bodied man with close-cropped blonde hair, glacial blue eyes, a plump perfect face. His smile was intense and brilliant. "That's easy," he said. "Capricorn."

"You can guess my —" She stopped, stunned. "Sign?" she finished, voice very small. "How did you do that? Oh."

"Yes. I'm that one."

She felt more than naked, stripped down to the ganglia, to the synapses. "What's the trick?"

"No trick. I listen. I hear."

"You hear people thinking?"

"More or less. Do you think it's a party game?" He was beautiful but terrifying, like a Samurai sword in motion. She wanted him but she didn't dare. He's got my number, she thought. I would never have any secrets

from him. He said sadly, "I don't mind that. I know I frighten a lot of
people. Some don't care."

"What's your name?"

"Tom," he said. "Hello, Nikki."

"I feel very sorry for you."

"Not really. You can kid yourself if you need to. But you can't kid me.
Anyway, you don't sleep with men you feel sorry for."

"I don't sleep with you."

"You will," he said.

"I thought you were just a mind reader. They didn't tell me you did
prophecies too."

He leaned close and smiled. The smile demolished her. She had to
fight to keep from falling. "I've got your number, all right," he said in a
low, harsh voice. "I'll call you next Tuesday." As he walked away he said,
"You're wrong. I'm a Virgo. Believe it or not."

Nikki returned, numb, to the living room. "…the figure of the
mandala," Nicholson was saying. His voice was dark, focused, a pure
basso cantante. "The essential thing that every mandala has is a center —
the place where everything is born, the eye of God's mind, the heart of
darkness and of light, the core of the storm. All right. You must move
toward the center, find the vortex at the boundary of Yang and Yin, place
yourself right at the mandala's midpoint. *Center yourself.* Do you follow
the metaphor? Center yourself at *now,* the eternal *now.* To move off-center
is to move forward toward death, backward toward birth, always the fatal
polar swings. But if you're capable of positioning yourself constantly at
the focus of the mandala, right on center, you have access to the fountain
of renewal, you become an organism capable of constant self-healing,
constant self-replenishment, constant expansion into regions beyond self.
Do you follow? The power of…"

Steiner, at her elbow, said tenderly, "How beautiful you are in the first
moments of erotic fixation."

"It's a marvelous party."

"Are you meeting interesting people?"

"Is there any other kind?" she asked.

Nicholson abruptly detached himself from the circle of his audience
and strode across the room, alone, in a quick decisive knight's move toward
the bar. Nikki, hurrying to intercept him, collided with a shaven-headed
tray-bearing servant. The tray slid smoothly from the man's thick fingertips
and launched itself into the air like a spinning shield; a rainfall of skewered
meat in an oily green curry sauce spattered the white carpet. The servant
was utterly motionless. He stood frozen like some sort of Mexican stone
idol, thick-necked, flat-nosed, for a long painful moment; then he turned
his head slowly to the left and regretfully contemplated his rigid outspread

hand, shorn of its tray; finally he swung his head toward Nikki, and his normally expressionless granite face took on for a quick flickering instant a look of total hatred, a coruscating emanation of contempt and disgust that faded immediately. He laughed: hu-hu-hu, a neighing snicker. His superiority was overwhelming. Nikki floundered in quicksands of humiliation. Hastily she escaped, a zig and a zag, around the tumbled goodies and across to the bar. Nicholson, still by himself. Her face went crimson. She felt short of breath. Hunting for words, tongue all thumbs. Finally, in a catapulting blurt: "Happy birthday!"

"Thank you," he said solemnly.

"Are you enjoying your birthday?"

"Very much."

"I'm amazed that they don't bore you. I mean, having had so many of them."

"I don't bore easily." He was awesomely calm, drawing on some bottomless reservoir of patience. He gave her a look that was at the same time warm and impersonal. "I find everything interesting," he said.

"That's curious. I said more or less the same thing to Steiner just a few minutes ago. You know, it's my birthday too."

"Really?"

"The seventh of January, 1975, for me."

"Hello, 1975. I'm —" He laughed. "It sounds absolutely absurd, doesn't it?"

"The seventh of January, 982."

"You've been doing your homework."

"I've read your book," she said. "Can I make a silly remark? My God, you don't *look* like you're a thousand and seventeen years old."

"How should I look?"

"More like him," she said, indicating Francis Xavier Byrne.

Nicholson chuckled. She wondered if he liked her. Maybe. Maybe. Nikki risked some eye contact. He was hardly a centimeter taller than she was, which made it a terrifyingly intimate experience. He regarded her steadily, centeredly; she imagined a throbbing mandala surrounding him, luminous turquoise spokes emanating from his heart, radiant red and green spiderweb rings connecting them. Reaching from her loins, she threw a loop of desire around him. Her eyes were explicit. His were veiled. She felt him calmly retreating. Take me inside, she pleaded, take me to one of the back rooms. Pour life into me. She said, "How will you choose the people you're going to instruct in the secret?"

"Intuitively."

"Refusing anybody who asks directly, of course."

"Refusing anybody who asks."

"Did *you* ask?"

"You said you read my book."

"Oh. Yes. I remember—you didn't know what was happening, you didn't understand anything until it was over."

"I was a simple lad," he said. "That was a long time ago." His eyes were alive again. He's drawn to me. He sees that I'm his kind, that I deserve him. Capricorn, Capricorn, Capricorn, you and me, he-goat and she-goat. Play my game, Cap. "How are you named?" he asked.

"Nikki."

"A beautiful name. A beautiful woman."

The emptiness of the compliments devastated her. She realized she had arrived with mysterious suddenness at a necessary point of tactical withdrawal; retreat was obligatory, lest she push too hard and destroy the tenuous contact so tensely established. She thanked him with a glance and gracefully slipped away, pivoting toward Martin Bliss, slipping her arm through his. Bliss quivered at the gesture, glowed, leaped into a higher energy state. She resonated to his vibrations, going up and up. She was at the heart of the party, the center of the mandala: standing flat-footed, legs slightly apart, making her body a polar axis, with lines of force zooming up out of the earth, up through the basement levels of this building, up the eighty-eight stories of it, up through her sex, her heart, her head. This is how it must feel, she thought, when undyingness is conferred on you. A moment of spontaneous grace, the kindling of an inner light. She looked love at poor sappy Bliss. You dear heart, you dumb walking pun. The string quintet made molten sounds. "What is that?" she asked. "Brahms?" Bliss offered to find out. Alone, she was vulnerable to Francis Xavier Byrne, who brought her down with a single cadaverous glance.

"Have you guessed it yet?" he asked. "The sign."

She stared through his ragged cancerous body, blazing with decomposition. "Scorpio," she told him hoarsely.

"Right! Right!" He pulled a pendant from his breast and draped its golden chain over her head. "For you," he rasped, and fled. She fondled it. A smooth green stone. Jade? Emerald? Lightly engraved on its domed face was the looped cross, the crux ansata. Beautiful. The gift of life, from the dying man. She waved fondly to him across a forest of heads and winked. Bliss returned.

"They're playing something by Schonberg," he reported. *"Verklärte Nacht."*

"How lovely." She flipped the pendant and let it fall back against her breasts. "Do you like it?"

"I'm sure you didn't have it a moment ago."

"It sprouted," she told him. She felt high, but not as high as she had been just after leaving Nicholson. That sense of herself as focal point had departed. The party seemed chaotic. Couples were forming, dissolving,

reforming; shadowy figures were stealing away in twos and threes toward
the bedrooms; the servants were more obsessively thrusting their trays of
drinks and snacks at the remaining guests; the hail had reverted to snow,
and feathery masses silently struck the windows, sticking there, revealing
their glistening mandalic structures for painfully brief moments before
they deliquesced. Nikki struggled to regain her centered position. She
indulged in a cheering fantasy: Nicholson coming to her, formally touching
her cheek, telling her, "You will be one of the elect." In less than twelve
months the time would come for him to gather with his seven still unnamed
disciples to see in the new century, and he would take their hands into his
hands, he would pump the vitality of the undying into their bodies, sharing
with them the secret that had been shared with him a thousand years ago.
Who? Who? Who? Me. Me. Me. But where had Nicholson gone? His aura,
his glow, that cone of imaginary light that had appeared to surround him—
nowhere.

A man in a lacquered orange wig began furiously to quarrel, almost
under Nikki's nose, with a much younger woman wearing festoons of
bioluminescent pearls. Man and wife, evidently. They were both sharp
featured, with glossy, protuberant eyes, rigid faces, cheek muscles working
intensely. Live together long enough, come to look alike. Their dispute
had a stale, ritualistic flavor, as though they had staged it all too many
times before. They were explaining to each other the events that had caused
the quarrel, interpreting them, recapitulating them, shading them,
justifying, attacking, defending—you said this because and that led me to
respond that way because...no, on the contrary, I said this because you
said that—all of it in a quiet screechy tone, sickening, agonizing, pure
death.

"He's her biological father," a man next to Nikki said. "She was one of
the first of the in vitro babies, and he was the donor, and five years ago he
tracked her down and married her. A loophole in the law." Five years?
They sounded as if they had been married for fifty. Walls of pain and
boredom encased them. Only their eyes were alive. Nikki found it
impossible to imagine those two in bed, bodies entwined in the act of
love. Act of love, she thought, and laughed. Where was Nicholson? Duke
Alexius, flushed and sweat-beaded, bowed to her. "I will leave soon," he
announced, and she received the announcement gravely but without
reacting, as though he had merely commented on the fluctuations of the
storm, or had spoken in Greek. He bowed again and went away. Nicholson?
Nicholson? She grew calm again, finding her center. He will come to me
when he is ready. There was contact between us, and it was real and good.

Bliss, beside her, gestured and said, "A rabbi of Syrian birth, formerly
Muslim, highly regarded among Jewish theologians."

She nodded but didn't look.

"An astronaut just back from Mars. I've never seen anyone's skin tanned quite that color."

The astronaut held no interest for her. She worked at kicking herself back into high. The party was approaching a climactic moment, she felt, a time when commitments were being made and decisions taken. The clink of ice in glasses, the foggy vapors of psychedelic inhalants, the press of warm flesh all about her—she was wired into everything, she was alive and receptive, she was entering into the twitching hour, the hour of galvanic jerks. She grew wild and reckless. Impulsively she kissed Bliss, straining on tiptoes, jabbing her tongue deep into his startled mouth. Then she broke free. Someone was playing with the lights: they grew redder, then gained force and zoomed to blue-white ferocity. Far across the room a crowd was surging and billowing around the fallen figure of Francis Xavier Byrne, slumped loose-jointedly against the base of the bar. His eyes were open but glassy. Nicholson crouched over him, reaching into his shirt, making delicate adjustments of the controls of the chain mail beneath. "It's all right," Steiner was saying. "Give him some air. It's all right!" Confusion. Hubbub. A torrent of tangled input.

" —they say there's been a permanent change in the weather patterns. Colder winters from now on, because of accumulations of dust in the atmosphere that screen the sun's rays. Until we freeze altogether by around the year 2200—"

" —but the carbon dioxide is supposed to start a greenhouse effect that's causing *warmer* weather, I thought, and—"

" —the proposal to generate electric power from—"

" —the San Andreas fault—"

" —financed by debentures convertible into—"

" —capsules of botulism toxin—"

" —to be distributed at a ratio of one per thousand families, throughout Greenland and the Kamchatka Metropolitan Area—"

" —in the sixteenth century, when you could actually hope to found your own empire in some unknown part of the—"

" —unresolved conflicts of Capricorn personality—"

" —intense concentration and meditation upon the completed mandala so that the contents of the work are transferred to and identified with the mind and body of the beholder. I mean, technically what occurs is the reabsorption of cosmic forces. In the process of construction these forces—"

" —butterflies, which are no longer to be found anywhere in—"

" —were projected out from the chaos of the unconscious; in the process of absorption, the powers are drawn back in again—"

" —reflecting transformations of the DNA in the light-collecting organ, which—"

" — the snow — "

" — a thousand years, can you imagine that? And — "

" — her body — "

" — formerly a toad — "

" — just back from Mars, and there's that *look* in his eye — "

"Hold me," Nikki said. "Just hold me. I'm very dizzy."

"Would you like a drink?"

"Just hold me." She pressed against cool sweet-smelling fabric. His chest unyielding beneath it. Steiner. Very male. He steadied her, but only for a moment. Other responsibilities summoned him. When he released her, she swayed. He beckoned to someone else, blonde, soft-faced. The mind reader, Tom. Passing her along the chain from man to man.

"You feel better now," the telepath told her.

"Are you positive of that?"

"Very."

"Can you read any mind in the room?" she asked.

He nodded.

"Even *his?*"

Again a nod. "He's the clearest of all. He's been using it so long, all the channels are worn deep."

"Then he really is a thousand years old?"

"You didn't believe it?"

Nikki shrugged. "Sometimes I don't know what I believe."

"He's *old*."

"You'd be the one to know."

"He's a phenomenon. He's absolutely extraordinary." A pause — quick, stabbing. "Would you like to see into his mind?"

"How can I?"

"I'll patch you right in, if you'd like me to." The glacial eyes flashed sudden mischievous warmth. "Yes?"

"I'm not sure I want to."

"You're very sure. You're curious as hell. Don't kid me. Don't play games, Nikki. You want to see into him."

"Maybe." Grudgingly.

"You do. Believe me, you do. Here. Relax, let your shoulders slump a little, loosen up, make yourself receptive, and I'll establish the link."

"Wait," she said.

But it was too late. The mind reader serenely parted her consciousness like Moses doing the Red Sea and rammed something into her forehead, something thick but insubstantial, a truncheon of fog. She quivered and recoiled. She felt violated. It was like her first time in bed, in that moment when all the fooling around at last was over, the kissing and the nibbling and the stroking, and suddenly there was this object deep inside her body.

She had never forgotten that sense of being impaled. But of course it had
been not only an intrusion but also a source of ecstasy. As was this. The
object within her was the consciousness of Nicholson. In wonder she
explored its surface, rigid and weathered, pitted with the myriad ablations
of reentry. Ran her trembling hands over its bronzy roughness. Remained
outside it. Tom, the mind reader gave her a nudge. Go on, go on. Deeper.
Don't hold back. She folded herself around Nicholson and drifted into
him like ectoplasm seeping into sand. Suddenly she lost her bearings. The
discrete and impermeable boundary marking the end of her self and the
beginning of his became indistinct. It was impossible to distinguish
between her experiences and his, nor could she separate the pulsations of
her nervous system from the impulses traveling along his. Phantom
memories assailed and engulfed her. She was transformed into a node of
pure perception: a steady, cool, isolated eye, surveying and recording.
Images flashed. She was toiling upward along a dazzling snowy crest,
with jagged Himalayan fangs hanging above her in the white sky and a
warm-muzzled yak snuffling wearily at her side.

A platoon of swarthy little men accompanied her, slanty eyes, heavy
coats, thick boots. The stink of rancid butter, the cutting edge of an
impossible wind: and there, gleaming in the sudden sunlight, a pile of
fire-bright yellow plaster with a thousand winking windows, a building,
a lamasery strung along a mountain ridge. The nasal sound of distant
horns and trumpets. The hoarse chanting of lotus-legged monks. What
were they chanting? Om? Om? Om! *Om*, and flies buzzed around her nose,
and she lay hunkered in a flimsy canoe, coursing silently down a midnight
river in the heart of Africa, drowning in humidity. Brawny naked men
with purple-black skins crouching close. Sweaty fronds dangling from
flamboyantly excessive shrubbery; the snouts of crocodiles rising out of
the dark water like toothy flowers; great nauseating orchids blossoming
high in the smooth-shanked trees. And on shore, five white men in
Elizabethan costume, wide-brimmed hats, drooping sweaty collars, lace,
fancy buckles, curling red beards. Errol Flynn as Sir Francis Drake,
blunderbuss dangling in crook of arm. The white men laughing, beckoning,
shouting to the men in the canoe. Am I slave or slavemaster? No answer.
Only a blurring and a new vision: autumn leaves blowing across the open
doorways of straw-thatched huts, shivering oxen crouched in bare stubble-
strewn fields, grim long-mustachioed men with close-cropped hair riding
diagonal courses toward the horizon. Crusaders, are they? Or warriors of
Hungary on their way to meet the dread Mongols? Defenders of the
imperiled Anglo-Saxon realm against the Norman invaders? They could
be any of these. But always that steady cool eye, always that unmoving
consciousness at the center of every scene. *Him*, eternal, all-enduring. And
then: the train rolling westward, belching white smoke, the plains unrolling

infinityward, the big brown fierce-eyed bison standing in shaggy clumps along the right of way, the man with turbulent shoulder-length hair laughing, slapping a twenty-dollar gold piece on the table. Picking up his rifle—a .50-caliber breech-loading Springfield—he aims casually through the door of the moving train, he squeezes off a shot, another, another. Three shaggy brown corpses beside the tracks, and the train rolls onward, honking raucously.

Her arm and shoulder tingled with the impact of those shots. Then: a fetid waterfront, bales of cloves and peppers and cinnamon, small brown-skinned men in turbans and loincloths arguing under a terrible sun. Tiny irregular silver coins glittering in the palm of her hand. The jabber of some Malabar dialect counterpointed with fluid mocking Portuguese. Do we sail now with Vasco da Gama? Perhaps. And then a gray Teutonic street, windswept, medieval, bleak Lutheran faces scowling from leaded windows. And then the Gobi steppe, with horsemen and campfires and dark tents. And then New York City, unmistakably New York City, with square black automobiles scurrying between the stubby skyscrapers like glossy beetles, a scene out of some silent movie. And then. And then. Everywhere, everything, all times, all places, a discontinuous flow of events but always that clarity of vision, that rock-steady perception, that solid mind at the center, that unshakeable identity, that unchanging self—with whom I am inextricably enmeshed—

There was no "I," there was no "he," there was only the one ever-perceiving point of view. But abruptly she felt a change of focus, a distancing effect, a separation of self and self, so that she was looking at him as he lived his many lives, seeing him from the outside, seeing him plainly changing identities as others might change clothing, growing beards and mustaches, shaving them, cropping his hair, letting his hair grow, adopting new fashions, learning languages, forging documents. She saw him in all his thousand years of guises and subterfuges, saw him real and unified and centered beneath his obligatory camouflages—and saw him seeing her.

Instantly contact broke. She staggered. Arms caught her. She pulled away from the smiling plump-faced blonde man, muttering, "What have you done? You didn't tell me you'd show *me* to *him*."

"How else can there be a linkage?" the telepath asked.

"You didn't tell me. You should have told me." Everything was lost. She couldn't bear to be in the same room as Nicholson now. Tom reached for her, but she stumbled past him, stepping on people. They winked up at her. Someone stroked her leg. She forced her way through improbable laocoons, three women and two servants, five men and a tablecloth. A glass door, a gleaming silvery handle: she pushed. Out onto the terrace. The purity of the gale might cleanse her. Behind her, faint gasps, a few

shrill screams, annoyed expostulations: "Close that thing!" She slammed
it. Alone in the night, eighty-eight stories above street level, she offered
herself to the storm. Her filmy tunic shielded her not at all. Snowflakes
burned against her breasts. Her nipples hardened and rose like fiery
beacons, jutting against the soft fabric. The snow stung her throat, her
shoulders, her arms. Far below, the wind churned newly fallen crystals
into spiral galaxies. The street was invisible. Thermal confusions brought
updrafts that seized the edge of her tunic and whipped it outward from
her body. Fierce, cold particles of hail were driven into her bare pale thighs.
She stood with her back to the party. Did anyone in there notice her? Would
someone think she was contemplating suicide and come rushing gallantly
out to save her? Capricorns didn't commit suicide. They might threaten it,
yes, they might even tell themselves quite earnestly that they were really
going to do it, but it was only a game, only a game. No one came to her.
She didn't turn. Gripping the railing, she fought to calm herself.

No use. Not even the bitter air could help. Frost in her eyelashes, snow
on her lips. The pendant Byrne had given her blazed between her breasts.
The air was white with a throbbing green underglow. It seared her eyes.
She was off-center and floundering. She felt herself still reverberating
through the centuries, going back and forth across the orbit of Nicholson's
interminable life. What year is this? Is it 1386, 1912, 1532, 1779, 1043, 1977,
1235, 1129, 1836? So many centuries. So many lives. And yet always the
one true self, changeless, unchangeable.

Gradually the resonances died away. Nicholson's unending epochs
no longer filled her mind with terrible noise. She began to shiver, not from
fear but merely from cold, and tugged at her moist tunic, trying to shield
her nakedness. Melting snow left hot clammy tracks across her breasts
and belly. A halo of steam surrounded her. Her heart pounded.

She wondered if what she had experienced had been genuine contact
with Nicholson's soul, or rather only some trick of Tom's, a simulation of
contact. Was it possible, after all, even for Tom to create a linkage between
two nontelepathic minds such as hers and Nicholson's? Maybe Tom had
fabricated it all himself, using images borrowed from Nicholson's book.

In that case there might still be hope for her.

A delusion, she knew. A fantasy born of the desperate optimism of the
hopeless. But nevertheless—

She found the handle, let herself back into the party. A gust
accompanied her, sweeping snow inward. People stared. She was like death
arriving at the feast. Doglike, she shook off the searing snowflakes. Her
clothes were wet and stuck to her skin; she might as well have been naked.
"You poor shivering thing," a woman said. She pulled Nikki into a tight
embrace. It was the sharp-faced woman, the bulgy-eyed bottle-born one,
bride of her own father. Her hands traveled swiftly over Nikki's body,

caressing her breasts, touching her cheek, her forearm, her haunch. "Come inside with me," she crooned. "I'll make you warm." Her lips grazed Nikki's. A playful tongue sought hers.

For a moment, needing the warmth, Nikki gave herself to the embrace. Then she pulled away. "No," she said. "Some other time. Please." Wriggling free, she started across the room. An endless journey. Like crossing the Sahara by pogo stick. Voices, faces, laughter. A dryness in her throat. Then she was in front of Nicholson.

Well. Now or never.

"I have to talk to you," she said.

"Of course." His eyes were merciless. No wrath in them, not even disdain, only an incredible patience more terrifying than anger or scorn. She would not let herself bend before that cool level gaze.

She said, "A few minutes ago, did you have an odd experience, a sense that someone was — well, looking into your mind? I know it sounds foolish, but —"

"Yes. It happened." So calm. How did he stay that close to his center? That unwavering eye, that uniquely self-contained self, perceiving all: the lamasery, the slave depot, the railroad train, everything, all time gone by, all time to come — how did he manage to be so tranquil? She knew she never could learn such calmness. She knew he knew it. *He has my number, all right.* She found that she was looking at his cheekbones, at his forehead, at his lips. Not into his eyes.

"You have the wrong image of me," she told him.

"It isn't an image," he said. "What I have is you."

"No."

"Face yourself, Nikki. If you can figure out where to look." He laughed. Gently, but she was demolished.

An odd thing, then. She forced herself to stare into his eyes and felt a snapping of awareness from one mode into some other, and he turned into an old man. That mask of changeless early maturity dissolved and she saw the frightening yellowed eyes, the maze of furrows and gullies, the toothless gums, the drooling lips, the hollow throat, the self beneath the face. A thousand years, a thousand years! And every moment of those thousand years was visible. "You're old," she whispered. "You disgust me. I wouldn't want to be like you, not for anything!" She backed away, shaking. "An old, old, old man. All a masquerade!"

He smiled. "Isn't that pathetic?"

"Me or you? *Me or you?*"

He didn't answer. She was bewildered. When she was five paces away from him there came another snapping of awareness, a second changing of phase, and suddenly he was himself again, taut-skinned, erect, appearing to be perhaps thirty-five years old. A globe of silence hung between them. The force of his rejection was withering. She summoned her last strength for a parting glare. *I didn't want you either, friend, not any single part of you.* He saluted cordially. Dismissal.

Martin Bliss, grinning vacantly, stood near the bar. "Let's go," she said savagely. "Take me home!"

"But—"

"It's just a few floors below." She thrust her arm through his. He blinked, shrugged, fell into step.

"I'll call you Tuesday, Nikki," Tom said as they swept past him.

Downstairs, on her home turf, she felt better. In the bedroom they quickly dropped their clothes. His body was pink, hairy, serviceable. She turned the bed on, and it began to murmur and throb. "How old do you think I am?" she asked.

"Twenty-six?" Bliss said vaguely.

"Bastard!" She pulled him down on top of her. Her hands raked his skin. Her thighs parted. Go on. Like an animal, she thought. Like an animal! She was getting older moment by moment, she was dying in his arms.

"You're much better than I expected," she said eventually.

He looked down, baffled, amazed. "You could have chosen anyone at that party. Anyone."

"Almost anyone," she said.

When he was asleep she slipped out of bed. Snow was still falling. She heard the thunk of bullets and the whine of wounded bison. She heard the clangor of swords on shields. She heard lamas chanting: Om, Om, Om. No sleep for her this night, none. The clock was ticking like a bomb. The century was flowing remorselessly toward its finish. She checked her face for wrinkles in the bathroom mirror. Smooth, smooth, all smooth under the blue fluorescent glow. Her eyes looked bloody. Her nipples were still hard. She took a little alabaster jar from one of the bathroom cabinets and three slender red capsules fell out of it, into her palm. Happy birthday, dear Nikki, happy birthday to you. She swallowed all three. Went back to bed. Waited, listening to the slap of snow on glass, for the visions to come and carry her away.

BORN WITH THE DEAD (1973)

INTRODUCTION

The slowdown in my productivity continued in 1973. Life was pretty crazy for most of us that year — the United States was suffering the gigantic hangover of the post-Vietnam years, and even for the most prosaic suburban people it was a time of weird clothing, weird hairstyles, massive drug consumption, and outlandish sexual revelry. Here in California we were churning through some sort of societal revolution every six weeks or so. My first marriage was falling apart, besides. And I was simply worn out after years and years of super-prolific writing. All that work had left me fairly independent financially, however, and although I was not yet 40 I was beginning to think of abandoning my career and spending the rest of my life traveling, reading, and caring for my new Californian garden of exotic semitropical plants.

As a result I wrote practically nothing in 1973 — my output for the entire year was a piddling 81,000 words, which would have been two weeks' work ten years before. Though whatever work I did manage to produce was of a high level of quality, every word was an effort and it was only the pressure of other people's deadlines that got me to do anything at all.

Nevertheless, in the middle of that deadly year I embarked on a long story that surely ranks near the top of my entire vast array of work. Weary as I was, reluctant to work as I was, I found myself unable to keep this one from coming into being — thanks to a little timely encouragement from Ed Ferman of *Fantasy & Science Fiction*.

For most of its half-century-plus of existence the magazine that is formally known as *The Magazine of Fantasy & Science Fiction*, but more usually *F&SF*, has been a bastion of civilized and cultivated material. That was true under its founding editors, Anthony Boucher and J. Francis McComas, and under such succeeding editors as Robert P. Mills and Avram Davidson. By the 1970s, editorial control had passed into the hands of Ed Ferman, who also happened to be the publisher of the magazine, and who functioned in admirable fashion in both capacities for many years thereafter.

My fiction had been appearing on and off in *F&SF* since the days of the Boucher-McComas administration; but it was Ed Ferman who turned me into a steady contributor. He published a flock of my short stories in the magazines in the 1960s, of which the best known was the much-anthologized

"Sundance," and then, as I began to turn away from shorter fiction in favor of novellas and novels, Ferman let me know that he would be interested in publishing some of my longer work also.

In December, 1972, just after the publication of my novel *Dying Inside*, I got a note from Ed saying that he had just received a review copy of that book. "I simply wanted to tell you what a fine and moving and painful experience it was to read it," he wrote, going on to compare the novel favorably to recent works by Bernard Malamud and Chaim Potok. And he added in a postscript, "The editor in me has just popped up, and I can't help asking what I have to do to see your next novel. If it's anything near the quality of *Dying Inside*, I'll go higher than our top rate."

I already knew that I wasn't going to write another novel just then, not with all the turbulence going on in my life, and perhaps would never write one ever again. Therefore I felt uneasy about committing myself to any very lengthy work. And I was already working on a longish short story called "Trips" for an anthology Ferman was editing in collaboration with Barry Malzberg. But despite everything, I did have another long story in mind to write after that, one that would probably run to novella length, and I could not keep myself from telling Ferman it was his if he wanted it. He replied at once that he did.

The story was "Born With the Dead".

It had the feel of a major story from the moment I conceived it. I had played with the idea of the resuscitation of the dead in fiction since my 1957 novel *Recalled To Life,* and now, I felt, I was ready to return to it with a kind of culminating statement on the subject. A few days after I began work on it I let Ferman know that it was going to be a big one. To which he replied on April 16, 1973 that I should make it as big as it needed to be, because he proposed to make the story the centerpiece of a special Robert Silverberg issue of the magazine.

That had real impact on me. Over the years *F&SF* had done a handful of special issues honoring its favorite contributors — Theodore Sturgeon, Ray Bradbury, Fritz Leiber, Poul Anderson, James Blish, and one or two others. Each special issue featured a portrait of the writer on the cover, a major new story by him, several critical essays, and a bibliography. All of the writers chosen had been favorites of mine since my days as an avid adolescent reader; and now, suddenly, in my mid-thirties and at what plainly was the peak of my career, I found myself chosen to join their company. It gave me a nice shiver down the spine.

But of course I had to write a story *worthy* of that company — and this at a time when my private life was in chaos and the world about me, there in the apocalyptic days of the late Nixon era, was pretty chaotic too. So every day's work was an ordeal. Sometimes I managed no more than a couple of paragraphs. At best I averaged about a page a day. Writing it required me to do battle with all kinds of internal demons, for the story springs from areas within me that I found it taxing to explore: I had to confront my own attitudes toward death, love, marriage, responsibility, and the like in every paragraph. I was, in addition, growing ever more uneasy about my relationship to the science-fiction readership, and found myself wondering constantly whether one more Silverbergian exploration of the dark side of existence might not be asking too much. And I was mentally exhausted besides.

The weeks dragged by; I entered the second month of the project with more than half the story still to tell. (By way of comparison: *Dying Inside,* also a difficult thing to write and three times as long, took me just nine weeks.) And now it was the middle of May; I had begun the story in late March. But somehow, finally, I regained my stride in early June, and the closing scenes, grim as their content was, were much easier to write than those that had gone before. One night in early June I was at the movies — Marlon Brando's *Last Tango in Paris,* it was — when the closing paragraphs of the story began to form in my mind. I turned to my wife and asked her for the notebook she always carried, and began to scribble sentences in the dark during the final minutes of the film. The movie ended; the lights came on; the theater emptied; and there I sat, still writing. "Are you a movie critic?" an usher asked me. I shook my head and went on writing.

So the thing was done, and I knew that I had hooked me a big fish. The next day I typed out what I had written in the theater, and set about preparing a final draft for Ed Ferman, and on June 16, 1973 I sent it to him with a note that said, "Here It Is. I feel exhausted, drained, relieved, pleased, proud, etc. I hope the thing is worthy of all the sweat that went into it. What I'm going to do tomorrow is don my backpack and head for the Sierra for a week in the back country at 10,000 feet, a kind of rite of purification after all these months of crazy intense typing."

"I could not be more pleased with "Born With the Dead,"" Ferman replied four days later. (E-mail was mere science fiction in those days.) "It seems to me that it brings to a peak the kind of thing you've been doing with *Book of Skulls* and *Dying Inside.*" (I had not noticed until that moment the string of death-images running through the titles of those three practically consecutive works of mine.) "I don't think there is a wrong move in this story, and it comes together beautifully in the ending, which I found perfect and quite moving."

The story appeared in the April, 1974 *F&SF,* which was indeed the special Robert Silverberg issue, with an Ed Emshwiller portrait of me on the cover in my best long-haired 1970s psychedelic mode, and essays about me within by Barry Malzberg and Tom Clareson, along with a Silverberg bibliography in very small type (so it didn't fill half the issue.) "Born With the Dead" went on to win the Nebula award in 1975 and the Locus award as well. In the Hugo voting, though, it finished second, an event which seemed to confirm what I had already come to believe, that my current output was far removed from the needs and interests of the science-fiction mass audience. But, Hugo or no, the story has, since then, been generally acclaimed as a classic. It has been reprinted in innumerable anthologies, translated into ten foreign languages, and optioned for motion picture production. I have rarely had so much difficulty writing a story as I had with this one; but the anguish and trauma that it cost me now lie three full decades behind me, and the story is still here, to my great delight as its creator and, I hope, to yours as reader.

ONE

And what the dead had no speech for, when living,
They can tell you, being dead: the communication
Of the dead is tongued with fire beyond the language
of the living.

Eliot: *Little Gidding*

Supposedly his late wife Sybille was on her way to Zanzibar. That
was what they told him, and he believed it. Jorge Klein was at that stage
in his search when he would believe anything, if belief would only lead
him to Sybille. Anyway, it wasn't so absurd that she would go to Zanzibar.
Sybille had always wanted to go there. In some unfathomable obsessive
way the place had seized the center of her consciousness long ago. When
she was alive it hadn't been possible for her to go there, but now, loosed
from all bonds, she would be drawn toward Zanzibar like a bird to its
nest, like Ulysses to Ithaca, like a moth to a flame.

***

The plane, a small Air Zanzibar Havilland FP-803, took off more than
half empty from Dar es Salaam at 0915 on a mild bright morning, gaily
circled above the dense masses of mango trees, red-flowering flamboyants,
and tall coconut palms along the aquamarine shores of the Indian Ocean,
and headed northward on the short hop across the strait to Zanzibar. This
day—Tuesday, the ninth of March, 1993—would be an unusual one for
Zanzibar: five deads were aboard the plane, the first of their kind ever to
visit that fragrant isle. Daud Mahmoud Barwani, the health officer on duty
that morning at Zanzibar's Karume Airport, had been warned of this by
the emigration officials on the mainland. He had no idea how he was going
to handle the situation, and he was apprehensive: these were tense times
in Zanzibar. Times are always tense in Zanzibar. Should he refuse them

entry? Did deads pose any threat to Zanzibar's ever-precarious political stability? What about subtler menaces? Deads might be carriers of dangerous spiritual maladies. Was there anything in the Revised Administrative Code about refusing visas on grounds of suspected contagions of the spirit? Daud Mahmoud Barwani nibbled moodily at his breakfast—a cold chapatti, a mound of cold curried potato—and waited without eagerness for the arrival of the deads.

***

Almost two and a half years had passed since Jorge Klein had last seen Sybille: the afternoon of Saturday, October 13, 1990, the day of her funeral. That day she lay in her casket as though merely asleep, her beauty altogether unmarred by her final ordeal: pale skin, dark lustrous hair, delicate nostrils, full lips. Iridescent gold and violet fabric enfolded her serene body; a shimmering electrostatic haze, faintly perfumed with a jasmine fragrance, protected her from decay. For five hours she floated on the dais while the rites of parting were read and the condolences were offered—offered almost furtively, as if her death were a thing too monstrous to acknowledge with a show of strong feeling; then, when only a few people remained, the inner core of their circle of friends, Klein kissed her lightly on the lips and surrendered her to the silent dark-clad men whom the Cold Town had sent. She had asked in her will to be rekindled; they took her away in a black van to work their magic on her corpse. The casket, retreating on their broad shoulders, seemed to Klein to be disappearing into a throbbing gray vortex that he was helpless to penetrate. Presumably he would never hear from her again. In those days the deads kept strictly to themselves, sequestered behind the walls of their self-imposed ghettos; it was rare ever to see one outside the Cold Towns, rare even for one of them to make oblique contact with the world of the living.

So a redefinition of their relationship was forced on him. For nine years it had been Jorge and Sybille, Sybille and Jorge, I and thou forming *we*, above all *we*, a transcendental *we*. He had loved her with almost painful intensity. In life they had gone everywhere together, had done everything together, shared research tasks and classroom assignments, thought interchangeable thoughts, expressed tastes that were nearly always identical, so completely had each permeated the other. She was a part of him, he of her, and until the moment of her unexpected death he had assumed it would be like that forever. They were still young, he thirty-eight, she thirty-four, decades to look forward to. Then she was gone. And now they were mere anonymities to one another, she not Sybille but only a dead, he not Jorge but only a warm. She was somewhere on the North American continent, walking about, talking, eating, reading, and yet she was gone, lost to him, and it behooved him to accept that alteration in his life, and outwardly he did accept it, but yet, though he knew he could never again have things as they once had been, he allowed himself the indulgence of a lingering wistful hope of regaining her.

***

Shortly the plane was in view, dark against the brightness of the sky, a suspended mote, an irritating fleck in Barwani's eye, growing larger, causing him to blink and sneeze. Barwani was not ready for it. When Ameri Kombo, the flight controller in the cubicle next door, phoned him with the routine announcement of the landing, Barwani replied, "Notify the pilot that no one is to debark until I have given clearance. I must consult the regulations. There is possibly a peril to public health." For twenty minutes he let the plane sit, all hatches sealed, on the quiet runway. Wandering goats emerged from the shrubbery and inspected it. Barwani consulted no regulations. He finished his modest meal; then he folded his arms and sought to attain the proper state of tranquility. These deads, he told himself, could do no harm. They were people like all other people, except that they had undergone extraordinary medical treatment. He must overcome his superstitious fear of them: he was no peasant, no silly clove-picker, nor was Zanzibar an abode of primitives. He would admit them, he would give them their anti-malaria tablets as though they were ordinary tourists, he would send them on their way. Very well. Now he was ready. He phoned Ameri Kombo. "There is no danger," he said. "The passengers may exit."

There were nine altogether, a sparse load. The four warms emerged first, looking somber and a little congealed, like people who had had to travel with a party of uncaged cobras. Barwani knew them all: the German consul's wife, the merchant Chowdhary's son, and two Chinese engineers, all returning from brief holidays in Dar. He waved them through the gate without formalities. Then came the deads, after an interval of half a minute: probably they had been sitting together at one end of the nearly empty plane and the others had been at the other. There were two women, three men, all of them tall and surprisingly robust-looking. He had expected them to shamble, to shuffle, to limp, to falter, but they moved with aggressive strides, as if they were in better health now than when they had been alive. When they reached the gate, Barwani stepped forward to greet them, saying softly, "Health regulations, come this way, kindly." They were breathing, undoubtedly breathing: he tasted an emanation of liquor from the big red-haired man, a mysterious and pleasant sweet flavor, perhaps anise, from the dark-haired woman. It seemed to Barwani that their skins had an odd waxy texture, an unreal glossiness, but possibly that was his imagination; white skins had always looked artificial to him.

The only certain difference he could detect about the deads was in their eyes, a way they had of remaining unnervingly fixed in a single intense gaze for many seconds before shifting. Those were the eyes, Barwani thought, of people who had looked upon the Emptiness without having been swallowed into it. A turbulence of questions erupted within him: What is it like, how do you feel, what do you remember, where did you go? He left them unspoken. Politely he said, "Welcome to the isle of cloves. We ask you to observe that malaria has been wholly eradicated here through extensive precautionary measures, and to prevent recurrence of unwanted disease we require of you that you take these tablets before proceeding further." Tourists often objected to that; these people swallowed their pills without a word of protest. Again Barwani yearned to reach toward them, to achieve some sort of contact that might perhaps help him to transcend the leaden weight of being. But an aura, a shield of strangeness, surrounded these five, and though he was an amiable man who tended to fall into conversations easily with strangers, he passed them on in silence to Mponda the immigration man.

Mponda's high forehead was shiny with sweat, and he chewed at his lower lip; evidently he was as disturbed by the deads as Barwani. He fumbled forms, he stamped a visa in the wrong place, he stammered while telling the deads that he must keep their passports overnight. "I shall post them by messenger to your hotel in the morning," Mponda promised them, and sent the visitors onward to the baggage pickup area with undue haste.

***

Klein had only one friend with whom he dared talk about it, a colleague of his at UCLA, a sleek supple Parsee sociologist from Bombay named Framji Jijibhoi, who was as deep into the elaborate new subculture of the deads as a warm could get. "How can I accept this?" Klein demanded. "I can't accept it at all. She's out there somewhere, she's alive, she's—"

Jijibhoi cut him off with a quick flick of his fingertips. "No, dear friend," he said sadly, "not alive, not alive at all, merely rekindled. You must learn to grasp the distinction."

Klein could not learn to grasp the distinction. Klein could not learn to grasp anything having to do with Sybille's death. He could not bear to think that she had passed into another existence from which he was totally excluded. To find her, to speak with her, to participate in her experience of death and whatever lay beyond death, became his only purpose. He was inextricably bound to her, as though she were still his wife, as though Jorge-and-Sybille still existed in any way.

He waited for letters from her, but none came. After a few months he began trying to trace her, embarrassed by his own compulsiveness and by his increasingly open breaches of the etiquette of this sort of widowerhood. He traveled from one Cold Town to another—Sacramento, Boise, Ann Arbor, Louisville—but none would admit him, none would even answer his questions. Friends passed on rumors to him, that she was living among the deads of Tucson, of Roanoke, of Rochester, of San Diego, but nothing came of these tales; then Jijibhoi, who had tentacles into the world of the rekindled in many places, and who was aiding Klein in his quest even though he disapproved of its goal, brought him an authoritative-sounding report that she was at Zion Cold Town in southeastern Utah. They turned him away there too, but not entirely cruelly, for he did manage to secure plausible evidence that that was where Sybille really was.

In the summer of '92 Jijibhoi told him that Sybille had emerged from Cold Town seclusion. She had been seen, he said, in Newark, Ohio, touring the municipal golf course at Octagon State Memorial in the company of a swaggering red-haired archaeologist named Kent Zacharias, also a dead, formerly a specialist in the mound-building Hopewellian cultures of the Ohio Valley. "It is a new phase," said Jijibhoi, "not unanticipated. The deads are beginning to abandon their early philosophy of total separatism. We have started to observe them as tourists visiting our world—exploring the life-death interface, as they like to term it. It will be very interesting, dear friend." Klein flew at once to Ohio and without ever actually seeing her, tracked her from Newark to Chillicothe, from Chillicothe to Marietta, from Marietta into West Virginia, where he lost her trail somewhere between Moundsville and Wheeling. Two months later she was said to be in London, then in Cairo, then Addis Ababa. Early in '93 Klein learned, via the scholarly grapevine—an ex-Californian now at Nyerere University in Arusha—that Sybille was on safari in Tanzania and was planning to go, in a few weeks, across to Zanzibar.

Of course. For ten years she had been working on a doctoral thesis on the establishment of the Arab Sultanate in Zanzibar in the early nineteenth century—studies unavoidably interrupted by other academic chores, by love affairs, by marriage, by financial reverses, by illnesses, death, and other responsibilities—and she had never actually been able to visit the island that was so central to her. Now she was free of all entanglements. Why shouldn't she go to Zanzibar at last? Why not? Of course: she was heading for Zanzibar. And so Klein would go to Zanzibar too, to wait for her.

As the five disappeared into taxis, something occurred to Barwani. He asked Mponda for the passports and scrutinized the names. Such strange ones: Kent Zacharias, Nerita Tracy, Sybille Klein, Anthony Gracchus, Laurence Mortimer. He had never grown accustomed to the names of Europeans. Without the photographs he would be unable to tell which were the women, which the men. Zacharias, Tracy, Klein...ah. *Klein.*

He checked a memo, two weeks old, tacked to his desk. Klein, yes. Barwani telephoned the Shirazi Hotel — a project that consumed several minutes — and asked to speak with the American who had arrived ten days before, that slender man whose lips had been pressed tight in tension, whose eyes had glittered with fatigue, the one who had asked a little service of Barwani, a special favor, and had dashed him a much-needed hundred shillings as payment in advance. There was a lengthy delay, no doubt while porters searched the hotel, looking in the men's room, the bar, the lounge, the garden, and then the American was on the line. "The person about whom you inquired has just arrived, sir," Barwani told him.

TWO

The dance begins. Worms underneath fingertips, lips beginning
to pulse, heartache and throat-catch. All slightly out of step and
out of key, each its own tempo and rhythm. Slowly, connections.
Lip to lip, heart to heart, finding self in other, dreadfully, tentatively,
burning…notes finding themselves in chords, chords in sequence,
cacophony turning to polyphonous contrapuntal chorus, a diapason
of celebration.

R. D. Laing: *The Bird of Paradise*

Sybille stands timidly at the edge of the municipal golf course at Octagon State Memorial in Newark, Ohio, holding her sandals in her hand and surreptitiously working her toes into the lush, immaculate carpet of dense, close-cropped lime-green grass. It is a summer afternoon in 1992, very hot; the air, beautifully translucent, has that timeless midwestern shimmer, and the droplets of water from the morning sprinkling have not burned off the lawn. Such extraordinary grass! She hadn't often seen grass like that in California, and certainly not at Zion Cold Town in thirsty Utah. Kent Zacharias, towering beside her, shakes his head sadly. "A golf course!" he mutters. "One of the most important prehistoric sites in North America and they make a golf course out of it! Well, I suppose it could have been worse. They might have bulldozed the whole thing and turned it into a municipal parking lot. Look, there, do you see the earthworks?"

She is trembling. This is her first extended journey outside the Cold Town, her first venture into the world of the warms since her rekindling, and she is picking up threatening vibrations from all the life that burgeons about her. The park is surrounded by pleasant little houses, well kept. Children on bicycles rocket through the streets. In front of her, golfers are

merrily slamming away. Little yellow golf carts clamber with lunatic energy
over the rises and dips of the course. There are platoons of tourists who,
like herself and Zacharias, have come to see the Indian mounds. There are
dogs running free. All this seems menacing to her. Even the vegetation —
the thick grass, the manicured shrubs, the heavy-leafed trees with low-
hanging boughs — disturbs her. Nor is the nearness of Zacharias reassuring,
for he too seems inflamed with undeadlike vitality; his face is florid, his
gestures are broad and overanimated, as he points out the low flat-topped
mounds, the grassy bumps and ridges making up the giant joined circle
and octagon of the ancient monument. Of course, these mounds are the
mainspring of his being, even now, five years post mortem. Ohio is his
Zanzibar.

"—once covered four square miles. A grand ceremonial center, the
Hopewellian equivalent of Chichén Itzá, of Luxor, of—" He pauses.
Awareness of her distress has finally filtered through the intensity of his
archaeological zeal. "How are you doing?" he asks gently.

She smiles a brave smile. Moistens her lips. Inclines her head toward
the golfers, toward the tourists, toward the row of darling little houses
outside the rim of the park. Shudders.

"Too cheery for you, is it?"

"Much," she says.

Cheery. Yes. A cheery little town, a magazine-cover town, a chamber-
of-commerce town. Newark lies becalmed on the breast of the sea of time:
but for the look of the automobiles, this could be 1980 or 1960 or perhaps
1940. Yes. Motherhood, baseball, apple pie, church every Sunday. Yes.
Zacharias nods and makes one of the signs of comfort at her. "Come," he
whispers. "Let's go toward the heart of the complex. We'll lose the twentieth
century along the way."

With brutal imperial strides he plunges into the golf course. Long-
legged Sybille must work hard to keep up with him. In a moment they are
within the embankment, they have entered the sacred octagon, they have
penetrated the vault of the past, and at once Sybille feels they have achieved
a successful crossing of the interface between life and death. How still it is
here! She senses the powerful presence of the forces of death, and those
dark spirits heal her unease. The encroachments of the world of the living
on these precincts of the dead become insignificant: the houses outside
the park are no longer in view, the golfers are mere foolish incorporeal
shadows, the bustling yellow golf carts become beetles, the wandering
tourists are invisible.

She is overwhelmed by the size and symmetry of the ancient site. What
spirits sleep here? Zacharias conjures them, waving his hands like a
magician. She has heard so much from him already about these people,
these Hopewellians — What did they call themselves? How can we ever

know? — who heaped up these ramparts of earth twenty centuries ago. Now
he brings them to life for her with gestures and low urgent words. He
whispers fiercely:

— Do you see them?

And she does see them. Mists descend. The mounds reawaken; the
mound-builders appear. Tall, slender, swarthy, nearly naked, clad in
shining copper breastplates, in necklaces of flint disks, in bangles of bone
and mica and tortoise shell, in heavy chains of bright lumpy pearls, in
rings of stone and terra cotta, in armlets of bears' teeth and panthers' teeth,
in spool-shaped metal ear ornaments, in furry loincloths. Here are priests
in intricately woven robes and awesome masks. Here are chieftains with
crowns of copper rods, moving in frosty dignity along the long earthen-
walled avenue. The eyes of these people glow with energy. What an
enormously vital, enormously profligate culture they sustain here! Yet
Sybille is not alienated by their throbbing vigor, for it is the vigor of the
dead, the vitality of the vanished.

Look, now. Their painted faces, their unblinking gazes. This is a funeral
procession. The Indians have come to these intricate geometrical enclosures
to perform their acts of worship, and now, solemnly parading along the
perimeters of the circle and the octagon, they pass onward, toward the
mortuary zone beyond. Zacharias and Sybille are left alone in the middle
of the field. He murmurs to her:

— Come. We'll follow them.

He makes it real for her. Through his cunning craft she has access to
this community of the dead. How easily she has drifted backward across
time! She learns here that she can affix herself to the sealed past at any
point; it's only the present, open-ended and unpredictable, that is
troublesome. She and Zacharias float through the misty meadow, no
sensation of feet touching ground; leaving the octagon, they travel now
down a long grassy causeway to the place of the burial mounds, at the
edge of a dark forest of wide-crowned oaks. They enter a vast clearing. In
the center the ground has been plastered with clay, then covered lightly
with sand and fine gravel; on this base the mortuary house, a roofless
four-sided structure with walls consisting of rows of wooden palisades,
has been erected. Within this is a low clay platform topped by a rectangular
tomb of log cribbing, in which two bodies can be seen: a young man, a
young woman, side by side, bodies fully extended, beautiful even in death.
They wear copper breastplates, copper ear ornaments, copper bracelets,
necklaces of gleaming yellowish bears' teeth.

Four priests station themselves at the corners of the mortuary house.
Their faces are covered by grotesque wooden masks topped by great
antlers, and they carry wands two feet long, effigies of the death-cup
mushroom in wood sheathed with copper. One priest commences a harsh,

percussive chant. All four lift their wands and abruptly bring them down. It is a signal; the depositing of grave-goods begins. Lines of mourners bowed under heavy sacks approach the mortuary house. They are unweeping, even joyful, faces ecstatic, eyes shining, for these people know what later cultures will forget, that death is no termination but rather a natural continuation of life. Their departed friends are to be envied. They are honored with lavish gifts, so that they may live like royalty in the next world: out of the sacks come nuggets of copper, meteoric iron, and silver, thousands of pearls, shell beads, beads of copper and iron, buttons of wood and stone, heaps of metal ear-spools, chunks and chips of obsidian, animal effigies carved from slate and bone and tortoise shell, ceremonial copper axes and knives, scrolls cut from mica, human jawbones inlaid with turquoise, dark coarse pottery, needles of bone, sheets of woven cloth, coiled serpents fashioned from dark stone, a torrent of offerings, heaped up around and even upon the two bodies.

At length the tomb is choked with gifts. Again there is a signal from the priests. They elevate their wands and the mourners, drawing back to the borders of the clearing, form a circle and begin to sing a somber, throbbing funereal hymn. Zacharias, after a moment, sings with them, wordlessly embellishing the melody with heavy melismas. His voice is a rich *basso cantante*, so unexpectedly beautiful that Sybille is moved almost to confusion by it, and looks at him in awe. Abruptly he breaks off, turns to her, touches her arm, leans down to say:

— You sing too.

Sybille nods hesitantly. She joins the song, falteringly at first, her throat constricted by self-consciousness; then she finds herself becoming part of the rite, somehow, and her tone becomes more confident. Her high clear soprano soars brilliantly above the other voices.

Now another kind of offering is made: boys cover the mortuary house with heaps of kindling — twigs, dead branches, thick boughs, all sorts of combustible debris — until it is quite hidden from sight, and the priests cry a halt. Then, from the forest, comes a woman bearing a blazing firebrand, a girl, actually, entirely naked, her sleek fair-skinned body painted with bizarre horizontal stripes of red and green on breasts and buttocks and thighs, her long glossy black hair flowing like a cape behind her as she runs. Up to the mortuary house she sprints; breathlessly she touches the firebrand to the kindling, here, here, here, performing a wild dance as she goes, and hurls the torch into the center of the pyre. Skyward leap the flames in a ferocious rush. Sybille feels seared by the blast of heat. Swiftly the house and tomb are consumed.

While the embers still glow, the bringing of earth gets under way. Except for the priests, who remain rigid at the cardinal points of the site, and the girl who wielded the torch, who lies like discarded clothing at the edge of the clearing, the whole community takes part. There is an open pit behind a screen of nearby trees; the worshipers, forming lines, go to it and scoop up soil, carrying it to the burned mortuary house in baskets, in buckskin aprons, in big moist clods held in their bare hands. Silently they dump their burdens on the ashes and go back for more.

Sybille glances at Zacharias; he nods; they join the line. She goes down into the pit, gouges a lump of moist black clayey soil from its side, takes it to the growing mound. Back for another, back for another. The mound rises rapidly, two feet above ground level now, three, four, a swelling circular blister, its outlines governed by the unchanging positions of the four priests, its tapering contours formed by the tamping of scores of bare feet. Yes, Sybille thinks, this is a valid way of celebrating death, this is a fitting rite. Sweat runs down her body, her clothes become stained and muddy, and still she runs to the earth-quarry, runs from there to the mound, runs to the quarry, runs to the mound, runs, runs, transfigured, ecstatic.

Then the spell breaks. Something goes wrong, she does not know what, and the mists clear, the sun dazzles her eyes, the priests and the mound-builders and the unfinished mound disappear. She and Zacharias are once again in the octagon, golf carts roaring past them on every side. Three children and their parents stand just a few feet from her, staring, staring, and a boy about ten years old points to Sybille and says in a voice that reverberates through half of Ohio, "Dad, what's wrong with those people? Why do they look so weird?"

Mother gasps and cries, "*Quiet,* Tommy, don't you have any manners?" Dad, looking furious, gives the boy a stinging blow across the face with the tips of his fingers, seizes him by the wrist, tugs him toward the other side of the park, the whole family following in their wake.

Sybille shivers convulsively. She turns away, clasping her hands to her betraying eyes. Zacharias embraces her. "It's all right," he says tenderly. "The boy didn't know any better. It's all right."

"Take me away from here!"

"I want to show you—"

"Some other time. Take me away. To the motel. I don't want to see anything. I don't want anybody to see me."

He takes her to the motel. For an hour she lies face down on the bed, racked by dry sobs. Several times she tells Zacharias she is unready for this tour, she wants to go back to the Cold Town, but he says nothing, simply strokes the tense muscles of her back, and after a while the mood passes. She turns to him and their eyes meet and he touches her and they make love in the fashion of the deads.

THREE

Newness is renewal: *ad hoc enim venit, ut renovemur in illo;*
making it new again, as on the first day; *herrlich wie am ersten
Tag.* Reformation, or renaissance; rebirth. Life is Phoenix-like,
always being born again out of its own death. The true nature of
life is resurrection; all life is life after death, a second life,
reincarnation. *Totus hie ordo revolubilis testatio est resurrectionis
mortuorum.* The universal pattern of recurrence bears witness to
the resurrection of the dead.

Norman O. Brown: *Love's Body*

"The rains shall be commencing shortly, gentleman and lady," the taxi
driver said, speeding along the narrow highway to Zanzibar Town. He
had been chattering steadily, wholly unafraid of his passengers. He must
not know what we are, Sybille decided. "Perhaps in a week or two they
begin. These shall be the long rains. The short rains come in the last of
November and December."

"Yes, I know," Sybille said.

"Ah, you have been to Zanzibar before?"

"In a sense," she replied. In a sense she had been to Zanzibar many
times, and how calmly she was taking it, now that the true Zanzibar was
beginning to superimpose itself on the template in her mind, on that dream-
Zanzibar she had carried about so long! She took everything calmly now:
nothing excited her, nothing aroused her. In her former life the delay at
the airport would have driven her into a fury: a ten-minute flight, and
then to be trapped on the runway twice as long! But she had remained
tranquil throughout it all, sitting almost immobile, listening vaguely to
what Zacharias was saying and occasionally replying as if sending
messages from some other planet. And now Zanzibar, so placidly accepted.
In the old days she had felt a sort of paradoxical amazement whenever
some landmark familiar from childhood geography lessons or the movies
or travel posters — the Grand Canyon, the Manhattan skyline, Taos
Pueblo — turned out in reality to look exactly as she imagined it would;
but now here was Zanzibar, unfolding predictably and unsurprisingly
before her, and she observed it with a camera's cool eye, unmoved,
unresponsive.

The soft, steamy air was heavy with a burden of perfumes, not only
the expected pungent scent of cloves but also creamier fragrances which

perhaps were those of hibiscus, frangipani, jacaranda, bougainvillea, penetrating the cab's open window like probing tendrils. The imminence of the long rains was a tangible pressure, a presence, a heaviness in the atmosphere: at any moment a curtain might be drawn aside and the torrents would start. The highway was lined by two shaggy green walls of palms broken by tin-roofed shacks; behind the palms were mysterious dark groves, dense and alien. Along the edge of the road was the usual tropical array of obstacles: chickens, goats, naked children, old women with shrunken, toothless faces, all wandering around untroubled by the taxi's encroachment on their right-of-way. On through the rolling flatlands the cab sped, out onto the peninsula on which Zanzibar Town sits. The temperature seemed to be rising perceptibly minute by minute; a fist of humid heat was clamping tight over the island. "Here is the waterfront, gentleman and lady," the driver said. His voice was an intrusive hoarse purr, patronizing, disturbing. The sand was glaringly white, the water a dazzling glassy blue; a couple of dhows moved sleepily across the mouth of the harbor, their lateen sails bellying slightly as the gentle sea breeze caught them. "On this side, please—" An enormous white wooden building, four stories high, a wedding cake of long verandahs and cast-iron railings, topped by a vast cupola. Sybille, recognizing it, anticipated the driver's spiel, hearing it like a subliminal pre-echo: "Beit al-Ajaib, the House of Wonders, former government house. Here the Sultan was often make great banquets, here the famous of all Africa came homaging. No longer in use. Next door the old Sultan's Palace, now Palace of People. You wish to go in House of Wonders? Is open: we stop, I take you now."

"Another time," Sybille said faintly. "We'll be here awhile."

"You not here just a day like most?"

"No, a week or more. I've come to study the history of your island. I'll surely visit the Beit al-Ajaib. But not today."

"Not today, no. Very well: you call me, I take you anywhere. I am Ibuni." He gave her a gallant toothy grin over his shoulder and swung the cab inland with a ferocious lurch, into the labyrinth of winding streets and narrow alleys that was Stonetown, the ancient Arab quarter.

All was silent here. The massive white stone buildings presented blank faces to the streets. The windows, mere slits, were shuttered. Most doors — the famous paneled doors of Stonetown, richly carved, studded with brass, cunningly inlaid, each door an ornate Islamic masterpiece—were closed and seemed to be locked. The shops looked shabby, and the small display windows were speckled with dust. Most of the signs were so faded Sybille could barely make them out:

PREMCHAND'S EMPORIUM
MONJI'S CURIOS

ABDULLAH'S BROTHERHOOD STORE

MOTILAL'S BAZAAR

The Arabs were long since gone from Zanzibar. So were most of the Indians, though they were said to be creeping back. Occasionally, as it pursued its intricate course through the maze of Stonetown, the taxi passed elongated black limousines, probably of Russian or Chinese make, chauffeur-driven, occupied by dignified self-contained dark-skinned men in white robes. Legislators, so she supposed them to be, en route to meetings of state. There were no other vehicles in sight, and no pedestrians except for a few women, robed entirely in black, hurrying on solitary errands. Stonetown had none of the vitality of the countryside; it was a place of ghosts, she thought, a fitting place for vacationing deads. She glanced at Zacharias, who nodded and smiled, a quick quirky smile that acknowledged her perception and told her that he too had had it. Communication was swift among the deads and the obvious rarely needed voicing.

The route to the hotel seemed extraordinarily involuted, and the driver halted frequently in front of shops, saying hopefully, "You want brass chests, copper pots, silver curios, gold chains from China?" Though Sybille gently declined his suggestions, he continued to point out bazaars and emporiums, offering earnest recommendations of quality and moderate price, and gradually she realized, getting her bearings in the town, that they had passed certain corners more than once. Of course: the driver must be in the pay of shopkeepers who hired him to lure tourists.

"Please take us to our hotel," Sybille said, and when he persisted in his huckstering— "Best ivory here, best lace" —she said it more firmly, but she kept her temper. Jorge would have been pleased by her transformation, she thought; he had all too often been the immediate victim of her fiery impatience. She did not know the specific cause of the change. Some metabolic side effect of the rekindling process, maybe, or maybe her two years of communion with Guidefather at the Cold Town, or was it, perhaps, nothing more than the new knowledge that all of time was hers, that to let oneself feel hurried now was absurd?

"Your hotel is this," Ibuni said at last.

It was an old Arab mansion—high arches, innumerable balconies, musty air, electric fans turning sluggishly in the dark hallways. Sybille and Zacharias were given a sprawling suite on the third floor, overlooking a courtyard lush with palms, vermilion nandi, kapok trees, poinsettia, and agapanthus. Mortimer, Gracchus, and Nerita had long since arrived in the other cab and were in an identical suite one floor below. "I'll have a bath," Sybille told Zacharias. "Will you be in the bar?"

"Very likely. Or strolling in the garden."

He went out. Sybille quickly shed her travel-sweaty clothes. The bathroom was a Byzantine marvel, elaborate swirls of colored tile, an immense yellow tub standing high on bronze eagle-claw-and-globe legs. Lukewarm water dribbled in slowly when she turned the tap. She smiled at her reflection in the tall oval mirror. There had been a mirror somewhat like it at the rekindling house. On the morning after her awakening, five or six deads had come into her room to celebrate with her her successful transition across the interface, and they had had that big mirror with them; delicately, with great ceremoniousness, they had drawn the coverlet down to show herself to her in it, naked, slender, narrow-waisted, high-breasted, the beauty of her body unchanged, marred neither by dying nor by rekindling, indeed enhanced by it, so that she had become more youthful-looking and even radiant in her passage across that terrible gulf.

— You're a very beautiful woman. That was Pablo. She would learn his name and all the other names later.

— I feel such a flood of relief. I was afraid I'd wake up and find myself a shriveled ruin.

— That could not have happened, Pablo said.

— And never will happen, said a young woman. Nerita, she was.

— But deads do age, don't they?

— Oh, yes, we age, just as the warms do. But not *just* as.

— More slowly?

— Very much more slowly. And differently. All our biological processes operate more slowly, except the functions of the brain, which tend to be quicker than they were in life.

— Quicker?

— You'll see.

— It all sounds ideal.

— We are extremely fortunate. Life has been kind to us. Our situation is, yes, ideal. We are the new aristocracy.

— The new aristocracy —

                                    ***

Sybille slipped slowly into the tub, leaning back against the cool porcelain, wriggling a little, letting the tepid water slide up as far as her throat. She closed her eyes and drifted peacefully. All of Zanzibar was waiting for her. *Streets I never thought I should visit.* Let Zanzibar wait. Let Zanzibar wait. *Words I never thought to speak. When I left my body on a distant shore.* Time for everything, everything in its due time.

— *You're a very beautiful woman,* Pablo had told her, not meaning to flatter.

Yes. She had wanted to explain to them, that first morning, that she didn't really care all that much about the appearance of her body, that her real priorities lay elsewhere, were "higher," but there hadn't been any need to tell them that. They understood. They understood everything. Besides, she *did* care about her body. Being beautiful was less important to her than it was to those women for whom physical beauty was their only natural advantage, but her appearance mattered to her; her body pleased her and she knew it was pleasing to others, it gave her access to people, it was a means of making connections, and she had always been grateful for that. In her other existence her delight in her body had been flawed by the awareness of the inevitability of its slow steady decay, the certainty of the loss of that accidental power that beauty gave her, but now she had been granted exemption from that: she would change with time but she would not have to feel, as warms must feel, that she was gradually falling apart. Her rekindled body would not betray her by turning ugly. No.

—We are the new aristocracy—

After her bath she stood a few minutes by the open window, naked to the humid breeze. Sounds came to her: distant bells, the bright chatter of tropical birds, the voices of children singing in a language she could not identify. Zanzibar! Sultans and spices, Livingstone and Stanley, Tippu Tib the slaver, Sir Richard Burton spending a night in this very hotel room, perhaps. There was a dryness in her throat, a throbbing in her chest: a little excitement coming alive in her after all. She felt anticipation, even eagerness. All Zanzibar lay before her. Very well. Get moving, Sybille, put some clothes on, let's have lunch, a look at the town.

She took a light blouse and shorts from her suitcase. Just then Zacharias returned to the room, and she said, not looking up, "Kent, do you think it's all right for me to wear these shorts here? They're—" A glance at his face and her voice trailed off. "What's wrong?"

"I've just been talking to your husband."

"He's *here?*"

"He came up to me in the lobby. Knew my name. 'You're Zacharias,' he said, with a Bogarty little edge to his voice, like a deceived movie husband confronting the Other Man. 'Where is she? I have to see her.'"

"Oh, no, Kent."

"I asked him what he wanted with you. 'I'm her husband,' he said, and I told him, 'Maybe you were her husband once, but things have changed,' and then—"

"I can't imagine Jorge talking tough. He's such a *gentle* man, Kent! How did he look?"

"Schizoid," Zacharias said. "Glassy eyes, muscles bunching in his jaws, signs of terrific pressure all over him. He knows he's not supposed to do things like this, doesn't he?"

"Jorge knows exactly how he's supposed to behave. Oh, Kent, what a stupid mess! Where is he now?"

"Still downstairs. Nerita and Laurence are talking to him. You don't want to see him, do you?"

"Of course not."

"Write him a note to that effect and I'll take it down to him. Tell him to clear off."

Sybille shook her head. "I don't want to hurt him."

"Hurt him? He's followed you halfway around the world like a lovesick boy, he's tried to violate your privacy, he's disrupted an important trip, he's refused to abide by the conventions that govern the relationships of warms and deads, and you —"

"He loves me, Kent."

"He loved you. All right, I concede that. But the person he loved doesn't exist any more. He has to be made to realize that."

Sybille closed her eyes. "I don't want to hurt him. I don't want you to hurt him either."

"I won't hurt him. Are you going to see him?"

"No," she said. She grunted in annoyance and threw her shorts and blouse into a chair. There was a fierce pounding at her temples, a sensation of being challenged, of being threatened, that she had not felt since that awful day at the Newark mounds. She strode to the window and looked out, half expecting to see Jorge arguing with Nerita and Laurence in the courtyard. But there was no one down there except a houseboy who looked up as if her bare breasts were beacons and gave her a broad dazzling smile. Sybille turned her back to him and said dully, "Go back down. Tell him that it's impossible for me to see him. Use that word. Not that I *won't* see him, not that I *don't want to* see him, not that it isn't *right* for me to see him, just that it's impossible. And then phone the airport. I want to go back to Dar on the evening plane."

"But we've only just arrived!"

"No matter. We'll come back some other time. Jorge is very persistent; he won't accept anything but a brutal rebuff, and I can't do that to him. So we'll leave."

***

Klein had never seen deads at close range before. Cautiously, uneasily, he stole quick intense looks at Kent Zacharias as they sat side by side on rattan chairs among the potted palms in the lobby of the hotel. Jijibhoi had told him that it hardly showed, that you perceived it more subliminally than by any outward manifestation, and that was true; there was a certain look about the eyes, of course, the famous fixity of the deads, and there was something oddly pallid about Zacharias' skin *beneath* the florid complexion, but if Klein had not known what Zacharias was, he might not have guessed it. He tried to imagine this man, this red-haired red-faced dead archaeologist, this digger of dirt mounds, in bed with Sybille. Doing with her whatever it was that the deads did in their couplings. Even Jijibhoi wasn't sure. Something with hands, with eyes, with whispers and smiles, not at all genital — so Jijibhoi believed. *This is Sybille's lover I'm talking to. This is Sybille's lover.* How strange that it bothered him so. She had had affairs when she was living; so had he; so had everyone; it was the way of life. But he felt threatened, overwhelmed, defeated, by this walking corpse of a lover.

Klein said, "Impossible?"

"That was the word she used."

"Can't I have ten minutes with her?"

"Impossible."

"Would she let me see her for a few moments, at least? I'd just like to find out how she looks."

"Don't you find it humiliating, doing all this scratching around just for a glimpse of her?"

"Yes."

"And you still want it?"

"Yes."

Zacharias sighed. "There's nothing I can do for you. I'm sorry."

"Perhaps Sybille is tired from having done so much traveling. Do you think she might be in a more receptive mood tomorrow?"

"Maybe," Zacharias said. "Why don't you come back then?"

"You've been very kind."

"De nada."

"Can I buy you a drink?"

"Thanks, no," Zacharias said. "I don't indulge any more. Not since —" He smiled.

Klein could smell whiskey on Zacharias' breath. All right, though. All right. He would go away. A driver waiting outside the hotel grounds poked his head out of his cab window and said hopefully, "Tour of the island, gentleman? See the clove plantations, see the athlete stadium?"

"I've seen them already," Klein said. He shrugged. "Take me to the beach."

He spent the afternoon watching turquoise wavelets lapping pink sand. The next morning he returned to Sybille's hotel, but they were gone, all five of them, gone. On last night's flight to Dar, said the apologetic desk clerk. Klein asked if he could make a telephone call, and the clerk showed him an ancient instrument in an alcove near the bar. He phoned

Barwani. "What's going on?" he demanded. "You told me they'd be staying at least a week!"

"Oh, sir, things change," Barwani said softly.

FOUR

> What portends? What will the future bring? I do not
> know, I have no presentiment. When a spider hurls
> itself down from some fixed point, consistently with
> its nature, it always sees before it only an empty space
> wherein it can find no foothold however much it sprawls.
> And so it is with me: always before me an empty space;
> what drives me forward is a consistency which lies behind
> me. This life is topsy-turvy and terrible, not to be endured.

> Soren Kierkegaard: *Either/Or*

Jijibhoi said, "In the entire question of death who is to say what is right, dear friend? When I was a boy in Bombay it was not unusual for our Hindu neighbors to practice the rite of suttee, that is, the burning of the widow on her husband's funeral pyre, and by what presumption may we call them barbarians? Of course" — his dark eyes flashed mischievously — "we *did* call them barbarians, though never when they might hear us. Will you have more curry?"

Klein repressed a sigh. He was getting full, and the curry was fiery stuff, of an incandescence far beyond his usual level of tolerance; but Jijibhoi's hospitality, unobtrusively insistent, had a certain hieratic quality about it that made Klein feel like a blasphemer whenever he refused anything in his home. He smiled and nodded, and Jijibhoi, rising, spooned a mound of rice into Klein's plate, buried it under curried lamb, bedecked it with chutneys and sambals. Silently, unbidden, Jijibhoi's wife went to the kitchen and returned with a cold bottle of Heinekens. She gave Klein a shy grin as she set it down before him. They worked well together, these two Parsees, his hosts.

They were an elegant couple — striking, even. Jijibhoi was a tall, erect man with a forceful aquiline nose, dark Levantine skin, jet-black hair, a formidable mustache. His hands and feet were extraordinarily small; his manner was polite and reserved; he moved with a quickness of action bordering on nervousness. Klein guessed that he was in his early forties, though he suspected his estimate could easily be off by ten years in either direction. His wife — strangely, Klein had never been told her name — was younger than her husband, nearly as tall, fair of complexion—a light-olive tone—and voluptuous of figure. She dressed invariably in flowing silken saris; Jijibhoi affected western business dress, suits and ties in styles twenty years out of date. Klein had never seen either of them bareheaded: she wore a kerchief of white linen, he a brocaded skullcap that might lead people to mistake him for an Oriental Jew. They were childless and self-sufficient, forming a closed dyad, a perfect unit, two segments of the same entity, conjoined and indivisible, as Klein and Sybille once had been. Their harmonious interplay of thought and gesture made them a trifle disconcerting, even intimidating, to others. As Klein and Sybille once had been.

Klein said, "Among your people—"

"Oh, very different, very different, quite unique. You know of our funeral custom?"

"Exposure of the dead, isn't it?"

Jijibhoi's wife giggled. "A very ancient recycling scheme!"

"The Towers of Silence," Jijibhoi said. He went to the dining room's vast window and stood with his back to Klein, staring out at the dazzling lights of Los Angeles. The Jijibhois' house, all redwood and glass, perched precariously on stilts near the crest of Benedict Canyon, just below Mulholland: the view took in everything from Hollywood to Santa Monica. "There are five of them in Bombay," said Jijibhoi, "on Malabar Hill, a rocky ridge overlooking the Arabian Sea. They are centuries old, each one circular, several hundred feet in circumference, surrounded by a stone wall twenty or thirty feet high. When a Parsee dies—do you know of this?"

"Not as much as I'd like to know."

"When a Parsee dies, he is carried to the Towers on an iron bier by professional corpse-bearers; the mourners follow in procession, two by two, joined hand to hand by holding a white handkerchief between them. A beautiful scene, dear Jorge. There is a doorway in the stone wall through which the corpse-bearers pass, carrying their burden. No one else may enter the Tower. Within is a circular platform paved with large stone slabs and divided into three rows of shallow, open receptacles. The outer row is used for the bodies of males, the next for those of females, the innermost one for children. The dead one is given a resting-place; vultures rise from the lofty palms in the gardens adjoining the Towers; within an hour or two, only bones remain. Later, the bare, sun-dried skeleton is cast into a pit at the center of the Tower. Rich and poor crumble together there into dust."

"And all Parsees are—ah—buried in this way?"

"Oh, no, no, by no means," Jijibhoi said heartily. "All ancient traditions are in disrepair nowadays, do you not know? Our younger people advocate cremation or even conventional interment. Still, many of us continue to see the beauty of our way."

" —beauty?—"

Jijibhoi's wife said in a quiet voice, "To bury the dead in the ground, in a moist tropical land where diseases are highly contagious, seems not sanitary to us. And to burn a body is to waste its substance. But to give the bodies of the dead to the efficient hungry birds—quickly, cleanly, without fuss—is to us a way of celebrating the economy of nature. To have one's bones mingle in the pit with the bones of the entire community is, to us, the ultimate democracy."

"And the vultures spread no contagions themselves, feeding as they do on the bodies of—"

"Never," said Jijibhoi firmly. "Nor do they contract our ills."

"And I gather that you both intend to have your bodies returned to Bombay when you—" Aghast, Klein paused, shook his head, coughed in embarrassment, forced a weak smile. "You see what this radioactive curry of yours has done to my manners? Forgive me. Here I sit, a guest at your dinner table, quizzing you about your funeral plans!"

Jijibhoi chuckled. "Death is not frightening to us, dear friend. It is— one hardly needs say it, does one?—it is a natural event. For a time we are here, and then we go. When our time ends, yes, she and I will give ourselves to the Towers of Silence."

His wife added sharply, "Better there than the Cold Towns! Much better!"

Klein had never observed such vehemence in her before.

Jijibhoi swung back from the window and glared at her. Klein had never seen that before either. It seemed as if the fragile web of elaborate courtesy that he and these two had been spinning all evening was suddenly unraveling, and that even the bonds between Jijibhoi and his wife were undergoing strain. Agitated now, fluttery, Jijibhoi began to collect the empty dishes, and after a long awkward moment said, "She did not mean to give offense."

"Why should I be offended?"

"A person you love chose to go to the Cold Towns. You might think there was implied criticism of her in my wife's expression of distaste for—"

Klein shrugged. "She's entitled to her feelings about rekindling. I wonder, though—"

He halted, uneasy, fearing to probe too deeply.

"Yes?"

"It was irrelevant."

"Please," Jijibhoi said. "We are old friends."

"I was wondering," said Klein slowly, "if it doesn't make things hard for you, spending all your time among deads, studying them, mastering their ways, devoting your whole career to them, when your wife evidently despises the Cold Towns and everything that goes on in them. If the theme of your work repels her, you must not be able to share it with her."

"Oh," Jijibhoi said, tension visibly going from him, "if it comes to that, I have even less liking for the entire rekindling phenomenon than she."

"You do?" This was a side of Jijibhoi that Klein had never suspected. "It repels you? Then why did you choose to make such an intensive survey of it?"

Jijibhoi looked genuinely amazed. "What? Are you saying one must have personal allegiance to the subject of one's field of scholarship?" He laughed. "You are of Jewish birth, I think, and yet your doctoral thesis was concerned, was it not, with the early phases of the Third Reich?"

Klein winced. "Touché!"

"I find the subculture of the deads irresistible, as a sociologist," Jijibhoi went on. "To have such a radical new aspect of human existence erupt during one's career is an incredible gift. There is no more fertile field for me to investigate. Yet I have no wish, none at all, ever to deliver myself up for rekindling. For me, for my wife, it will be the Towers of Silence, the hot sun, the obliging vultures — and finis, the end, no more, terminus."

"I had no idea you felt this way. I suppose if I'd known more about Parsee theology, I might have realized —"

"You misunderstand. Our objections are not theological. It is that we share a wish, an idiosyncratic whim, not to continue beyond the allotted time. But also I have serious reservations about the impact of rekindling on our society. I feel a profound distress at the presence among us of these deads, I feel a purely private fear of these people and the culture they are creating, I feel even an abhorrence for —" Jijibhoi cut himself short. "Your pardon. That was perhaps too strong a word. You see how complex my attitudes are toward this subject, my mixture of fascination and repulsion? I exist in constant tension between those poles. But why do I tell you all this, which if it does not disturb you, must surely bore you? Let us hear about your journey to Zanzibar."

"What can I say? I went, I waited a couple of weeks for her to show up, I wasn't able to get near her at all, and I came home. All the way to Africa and I never even had a glimpse of her."

"What a frustration, dear Jorge!"

"She stayed in her hotel room. They wouldn't let me go upstairs to her."

"They?"

"Her entourage," Klein said. "She was traveling with four other deads, a woman and three men. Sharing her room with the archaeologist,

Zacharias. He was the one who shielded her from me, and did it very cleverly, too. He acts as though he owns her. Perhaps he does. What can you tell me, Framji? Do the deads marry? Is Zacharias her new husband?"

"It is very doubtful. The terms 'wife' and 'husband' are not in use among the deads. They form relationships, yes, but pair-bonding seems to be uncommon among them, possibly altogether unknown. Instead they tend to create supportive pseudo-familial groupings of three or four or even more individuals, who—"

"Do you mean that all four of her companions in Zanzibar are her lovers?"

Jijibhoi gestured eloquently. "Who can say? If you mean in a physical sense, I doubt it, but one can never be sure. Zacharias seems to be her special companion, at any rate. Several of the others may be part of her pseudo-family also, or all, or none. I have reason to think that at certain times every dead may claim a familial relationship to all others of his kind. Who can say? We perceive the doings of these people, as they say, through a glass, darkly."

"I don't see Sybille even that well. I don't even know what she looks like now."

"She has lost none of her beauty."

"So you've told me before. But I want to see her myself. You can't really comprehend, Framji, how much I want to see her. The pain I feel, not able—"

"Would you like to see her right now?"

Klein shook in a convulsion of amazement. "What? What do you mean? Is she—"

"Hiding in the next room? No, no, nothing like that. But I do have a small surprise for you. Come into the library." Smiling expansively, Jijibhoi led the way from the dining room to the small study adjoining it, a room densely packed from floor to ceiling with books in an astonishing range of languages—not merely English, French, and German, but also Sanskrit, Hindi, Gujerati, Farsi, the tongues of Jijibhoi's polyglot upbringing among the tiny Parsee colony of Bombay, a community in which no language once cherished was ever discarded. Pushing aside a stack of dog-eared professional journals, he drew forth a glistening picture-cube, activated its inner light with a touch of his thumb, and handed it to Klein.

The sharp, dazzling holographic image showed three figures in a broad grassy plain that seemed to have no limits and was without trees, boulders, or other visual interruptions, an endlessly unrolling green carpet under a blank death-blue sky. Zacharias stood at the left, his face averted from the camera; he was looking down, tinkering with the action of an enormous rifle. At the far right stood a stocky, powerful-looking dark-haired man whose pale, harsh-featured face seemed all beard and nostrils. Klein

recognized him: Anthony Gracchus, one of the deads who had accompanied
Sybille to Zanzibar. Sybille stood beside him, clad in khaki slacks and a
crisp white blouse. Gracchus' arm was extended; evidently he had just
pointed out a target to her, and she was intently aiming a gun nearly as big
as Zacharias'.

Klein shifted the cube about, studying her face from various angles,
and the sight of her made his fingers grow thick and clumsy, his eyelids to
quiver. Jijibhoi had spoken truly: she had lost none of her beauty. Yet she
was not at all the Sybille he had known. When he had last seen her, lying
in her casket, she had seemed to be a flawless marble image of herself,
and she had that same surreal statuary appearance now. Her face was an
expressionless mask, calm, remote, aloof; her eyes were glossy mysteries;
her lips registered a faint, enigmatic, barely perceptible smile. It frightened
him to behold her this way, so alien, so unfamiliar. Perhaps it was the
intensity of her concentration that gave her that forbidding marmoreal
look, for she seemed to be pouring her entire being into the task of taking
aim. By tilting the cube more extremely, Klein was able to see what she
was aiming at: a strange awkward bird moving through the grass at the
lower left, a bird larger than a turkey, round as a sack, with ash-gray
plumage, a whitish breast and tail, yellow-white wings, and short, comical
yellow legs. Its head was immense and its black bill ended in a great
snubbed hook. The creature seemed solemn, rather dignified, and faintly
absurd; it showed no awareness that its doom was upon it. How odd that
Sybille should be about to kill it, she who had always detested the taking
of life: Sybille the huntress now, Sybille the lunar goddess, Sybille-Diana!
Shaken, Klein looked up at Jijibhoi and said, "Where was this taken? On
that safari in Tanzania, I suppose."

"Yes. In February. This man is the guide, the white hunter."

"I saw him in Zanzibar. Gracchus, his name is. He was one of the
deads traveling with Sybille."

"He operates a hunting preserve not far from Kilimanjaro," Jijibhoi
said, "that is set aside exclusively for the use of the deads. One of the
more bizarre manifestations of their subculture, actually. They hunt only
those animals which—"

Klein said impatiently, "How did you get this picture?"

"It was taken by Nerita Tracy, who is one of your wife's companions."

"I met her in Zanzibar too. But how—"

"A friend of hers is an acquaintance of mine, one of my informants, in
fact, a valuable connection in my researches. Some months ago I asked
him if he could obtain something like this for me. I did not tell him, of
course, that I meant it for you." Jijibhoi looked close. "You seem troubled,
dear friend."

Klein nodded. He shut his eyes as though to protect them from the glaring surfaces of Sybille's photograph. Eventually he said in a flat, toneless voice, "I have to get to see her."

"Perhaps it would be better for you if you would abandon—"

"No."

"Is there no way I can convince you that it is dangerous for you to pursue your fantasy of—"

"No," Klein said. "Don't even try. It's necessary for me to reach her. Necessary."

"How will you accomplish this, then?"

Klein said mechanically, "By going to Zion Cold Town."

"You have already done that. They would not admit you."

"This time they will. They don't turn away deads."

The Parsee's eyes widened. "You will surrender your own life? Is this your plan? What are you saying, Jorge?"

Klein, laughing, said, "That isn't what I meant at all."

"I am bewildered."

"I intend to infiltrate. I'll disguise myself as one of them. I'll slip into the Cold Town the way an infidel slips into Mecca." He seized Jijibhoi's wrist. "Can you help me? Coach me in their ways, teach me their jargon?"

"They'll find you out instantly."

"Maybe not. Maybe I'll get to Sybille before they do."

"This is insanity," Jijibhoi said quietly.

"Nevertheless. You have the knowledge. Will you help me?"

Gently Jijibhoi withdrew his arm from Klein's grasp. He crossed the room and busied himself with an untidy bookshelf for some moments, fussily arranging and rearranging. At length he said, "There is little I can do for you myself. My knowledge is broad but not deep, not deep enough. But if you insist on going through with this, Jorge, I can introduce you to someone who may be able to assist you. He is one of my informants, a dead, a man who has rejected the authority of the Guidefathers, a person who is *of* the deads but not *with* them, possibly he can instruct you in what you would need to know."

"Call him," Klein said.

"I must warn you he is unpredictable, turbulent, perhaps even treacherous. Ordinary human values are without meaning to him in his present state."

"Call him."

"If only I could discourage you from—"

"Call him."

FIVE

Quarreling brings trouble. These days lions roar a great
deal. Joy follows grief. It is not good to beat children
much. You had better go away now and go home. It is
impossible to work today. You should go to school every
day. It is not advisable to follow this path, there is water
in the way. Never mind, I shall be able to pass. We had
better go back quickly. These lamps use a lot of oil.
There are no mosquitoes in Nairobi. There are no lions
here. There are people here, looking for eggs. Is there
water in the well? No, there is none. If there are only
three people, work will be impossible today.

D.V. Perrott: *Teach Yourself Swahili*

Gracchus signals furiously to the porters and bellows, *"Shika njia hii
hii!"* Three turn, two keep trudging along. *"Nmyi nyote!"* he calls. *"Fanga
kama hivi!"* He shakes his head, spits, flicks sweat from his forehead. He
adds, speaking in a lower voice and in English, taking care that they will
not hear him, "Do as I say, you malevolent black bastards, or you'll be
deader than I am before sunset!"

Sybille laughs nervously. "Do you always talk to them like that?"

"I try to be easy on them. But what good does it do, what good does
any of it do? Come on, let's keep up with them."

It is less than an hour after dawn, but already the sun is very hot, here
in the flat dry country between Kilimanjaro and Serengeti. Gracchus is
leading the party northward across the high grass, following the spoor of
what he thinks is a quagga, but breaking a trail in the high grass is hard
work and the porters keep veering away toward a ravine that offers the
tempting shade of a thicket of thorn trees, and he constantly has to harass
them in order to hold them to the route he wants. Sybille has noticed that
Gracchus shouts fiercely to his blacks, as if they were no more than
recalcitrant beasts, and speaks of them behind their backs with a rough
contempt, but it all seems done for show, all part of his white-hunter role:
she has also noticed, at times when she was not supposed to notice, that
privately Gracchus is in fact gentle, tender, even loving among the porters,
teasing them—she supposes—with affectionate Swahili banter and playful
mock-punches. The porters are role-players too: they behave in the
traditional manner of their profession, alternately deferential and
patronizing to the clients, alternately posing as all-knowing repositories

of the lore of the bush and as simple, guileless savages fit only for carrying burdens. But the clients they serve are not quite like the sportsmen of Hemingway's time, since they are deads, and secretly the porters are terrified of the strange beings whom they serve. Sybille has seen them muttering prayers and fondling amulets whenever they accidentally touch one of the deads, and has occasionally detected an unguarded glance conveying unalloyed fear, possibly revulsion. Gracchus is no friend of theirs, however jolly he may get with them: they appear to regard him as some sort of monstrous sorcerer and the clients as fiends made manifest.

Sweating, saying little, the hunters move in single file, first the porters with the guns and supplies, then Gracchus, Zacharias, Sybille, Nerita constantly clicking her camera, and Mortimer. Patches of white cloud drift slowly across the immense arch of the sky. The grass is lush and thick, for the short rains were unusually heavy in December. Small animals scurry through it, visible only in quick flashes, squirrels and jackals and guinea-fowl. Now and then larger creatures can be seen: three haughty ostriches, a pair of snuffling hyenas, a band of Thomson gazelles flowing like a tawny river across the plain. Yesterday Sybille spied two warthogs, some giraffes, and a serval, an elegant big-eared wildcat that slithered along like a miniature cheetah. None of these beasts may be hunted, but only those special ones that the operators of the preserve have introduced for the special needs of their clients; anything considered native African wildlife, which is to say anything that was living here before the deads leased this tract from the Masai, is protected by government decree. The Masai themselves are allowed to do some lion-hunting, since this is their reservation, but there are so few Masai left that they can do little harm. Yesterday, after the warthogs and before the giraffes, Sybille saw her first Masai, five lean, handsome, long-bodied men, naked under skimpy red robes, drifting silently through the bush, pausing frequently to stand thoughtfully on one leg, propped against their spears. At close range they were less handsome—toothless, fly-specked, herniated. They offered to sell their spears and their beaded collars for a few shillings, but the safarigoers had already stocked up on Masai artifacts in Nairobi's curio shops, at astonishingly higher prices.

All through the morning they stalk the quagga, Gracchus pointing out hoofprints here, fresh dung there. It is Zacharias who has asked to shoot a quagga. "How can you tell we're not following a zebra?" he asks peevishly.

Gracchus winks. "Trust me. We'll find zebras up ahead too. But you'll get your quagga. I guarantee it."

Ngiri, the head porter, turns and grins. *"Piga quagga m'uzuri, bwana,"* he says to Zacharias, and winks also, and then—Sybille sees it plainly—

his jovial confident smile fades as though he has had the courage to sustain it only for an instant, and a veil of dread covers his dark glossy face.

"What did he say?" Zacharias asks.

"That you'll shoot a fine quagga," Gracchus replies.

Quaggas. The last wild one was killed about 1870, leaving only three in the world, all females, in European zoos. The Boers had hunted them to the edge of extinction in order to feed their tender meat to Hottentot slaves and to make from their striped hides sacks for Boer grain, leather *veldschoen* for Boer feet. The quagga of the London zoo died in 1872, that in Berlin in 1875, the Amsterdam quagga in 1883, and none was seen alive again until the artificial revival of the species through breedback selection and genetic manipulation in 1990, when this hunting preserve was opened to a limited and special clientele.

It is nearly noon, now, and not a shot has been fired all morning. The animals have begun heading for cover; they will not emerge until the shadows lengthen. Time to halt, pitch camp, break out the beer and sandwiches, tell tall tales of harrowing adventures with maddened buffaloes and edgy elephants. But not quite yet. The marchers come over a low hill and see, in the long sloping hollow beyond, a flock of ostriches and several hundred grazing zebras. As the humans appear, the ostriches begin slowly and warily to move off, but the zebras, altogether unafraid, continue to graze. Ngiri points and says, *"Piga quagga, bwana."*

"Just a bunch of zebras," Zacharias says.

Gracchus shakes his head. "No. Listen. You hear the sound?"

At first no one perceives anything unusual. But then, yes, Sybille hears it: a shrill barking neigh, very strange, a sound out of lost time, the cry of some beast she has never known. It is a song of the dead. Nerita hears it too, and Mortimer, and finally Zacharias. Gracchus nods toward the far side of the hollow. There, among the zebras, are half a dozen animals that might almost be zebras, but are not—unfinished zebras, striped only on their heads and foreparts; the rest of their bodies are yellowish brown, their legs are white, their manes are dark-brown with pale stripes. Their coats sparkle like mica in the sunshine. Now and again they lift their heads, emit that weird percussive whistling snort, and bend to the grass again. Quaggas. Strays out of the past, relicts, rekindled specters. Gracchus signals and the party fans out along the peak of the hill. Ngiri hands Zacharias his colossal gun. Zacharias kneels, sights.

"No hurry," Gracchus murmurs. "We have all afternoon."

"Do I seem to be hurrying?" Zacharias asks. The zebras now block the little group of quaggas from his view, almost as if by design. He must not shoot a zebra, of course, or there will be trouble with the rangers. Minutes go by. Then the screen of zebras abruptly parts and Zacharias squeezes his trigger. There is a vast explosion; zebras bolt in ten directions, so that the eye is bombarded with dizzying stroboscopic waves of black and white; when the convulsive confusion passes, one of the quaggas is lying on its side, alone in the field, having made the transition across the interface. Sybille regards it calmly. Death once dismayed her, death of any kind, but no longer.

"*Piga m'uzuri!*" the porters cry exultantly.

"*Kufa,*" Gracchus says. "Dead. A neat shot. You have your trophy."

Ngiri is quick with the skinning-knife. That night, camping below Kilimanjaro's broad flank, they dine on roast quagga, deads and porters alike. The meat is juicy, robust, faintly tangy.

***

Late the following afternoon, as they pass through cooler stream-broken country thick with tall, scrubby gray-green vase-shaped trees, they come upon a monstrosity, a shaggy shambling thing twelve or fifteen feet high, standing upright on ponderous hind legs and balancing itself on an incredibly thick, heavy tail. It leans against a tree, pulling at its top branches with long forelimbs that are tipped with ferocious claws like a row of sickles; it munches voraciously on leaves and twigs. Briefly it notices them, and looks around, studying them with small stupid yellow eyes; then it returns to its meal.

"A rarity," Gracchus says. "I know hunters who have been all over this park without ever running into one. Have you ever seen anything so ugly?"

"What is it?" Sybille asks.

"Megatherium. Giant ground sloth. South American, really, but we weren't fussy about geography when we were stocking this place. We have only four of them, and it costs God knows how many thousands of dollars to shoot one. Nobody's signed up for a ground sloth yet. I doubt anyone will."

Sybille wonders where the beast might be vulnerable to a bullet: surely not in its dim peanut-sized brain. She wonders, too, what sort of sportsman would find pleasure in killing such a thing. For a while they watch as the sluggish monster tears the tree apart. Then they move on.

Gracchus shows them another prodigy at sundown: a pale dome, like some huge melon, nestling in a mound of dense grass beside a stream. "Ostrich egg?" Mortimer guesses.

"Close. Very close. It's a moa egg. World's biggest bird. From New Zealand, extinct since about the eighteenth century."

Nerita crouches and lightly taps the egg. "What an omelet we could make!"

"There's enough there to feed seventy-five of us," Gracchus says. "Two gallons of fluid, easy. But of course we mustn't meddle with it. Natural increase is very important in keeping this park stocked."

"And where's mama moa?" Sybille asks. "Should she have abandoned the egg?"

"Moas aren't very bright," Gracchus answers. "That's one good reason why they became extinct. She must have wandered off to find some dinner. And—"

"Good God," Zacharias blurts.

The moa has returned, emerging suddenly from a thicket. She stands like a feathered mountain above them, limned by the deep-blue of twilight: an ostrich, more or less, but a magnified ostrich, an ultimate ostrich, a bird a dozen feet high, with a heavy rounded body and a great thick hose of a neck and taloned legs sturdy as saplings. Surely this is Sinbad's rukh, that can fly off with elephants in its grasp! The bird peers at them, sadly contemplating the band of small beings clustered about her egg; she arches her neck as though readying for an attack, and Zacharias reaches for one of the rifles, but Gracchus checks his hand, for the moa is merely rearing back to protest. It utters a deep mournful mooing sound and does not move. "Just back slowly away," Gracchus tells them. "It won't attack. But keep away from the feet; one kick can kill you."

"I was going to apply for a license on a moa," Mortimer says.

"Killing them's a bore," Gracchus tells him. "They just stand there and let you shoot. You're better off with what you signed up for."

***

What Mortimer has signed up for is an aurochs, the vanished wild ox of the European forests, known to Caesar, known to Pliny, hunted by the hero Siegfried, altogether exterminated by the year 1627. The plains of East Africa are not a comfortable environment for the aurochs and the herd that has been conjured by the genetic necromancers keeps to itself in the wooded highlands, several days' journey from the haunts of quaggas and ground sloths. In this dark grove the hunters come upon troops of chattering baboons and solitary big-eared elephants and, in a place of broken sunlight and shadow, a splendid antelope, a bull bongo with a fine curving pair of horns. Gracchus leads them onward, deeper in. He seems tense: there is peril here. The porters slip through the forest like black wraiths, spreading out in arching crab-claw patterns, communicating with one another and with Gracchus by whistling. Everyone keeps weapons ready in here. Sybille half expects to see leopards draped on overhanging branches, cobras slithering through the undergrowth. But she feels no fear.

They approach a clearing.

"Aurochs," Gracchus says.

A dozen of them are cropping the shrubbery: big short-haired long-horned cattle, muscular and alert. Picking up the scent of the intruders, they lift their heavy heads, sniff, glare. Gracchus and Ngiri confer with eyebrows. Nodding, Gracchus mutters to Mortimer, "Too many of them. Wait for them to thin off." Mortimer smiles. He looks a little nervous. The aurochs has a reputation for attacking without warning. Four, five, six of the beasts slip away, and the others withdraw to the edge of the clearing, as if to plan strategy; but one big bull, sour-eyed and grim, stands his ground, glowering. Gracchus rolls on the balls of his feet. His burly body seems, to Sybille, a study in mobility, in preparedness.

"Now," he says.

In the same moment the bull aurochs charges, moving with extraordinary swiftness, head lowered, horns extended like spears. Mortimer fires. The bullet strikes with a loud whonking sound, crashing into the shoulder of the aurochs, a perfect shot, but the animal does not fall, and Mortimer shoots again, less gracefully ripping into the belly, and then Gracchus and Ngiri are firing also, not at Mortimer's aurochs but over the heads of the others, to drive them away, and the risky tactic works, for the other animals go stampeding off into the woods. The one Mortimer has shot continues toward him, staggering now, losing momentum, and falls practically at his feet, rolling over, knifing the forest floor with its hooves.

"*Kufa,*" Ngiri says. "*Piga nyati m'uzuri, bwana.*"

Mortimer grins. "*Piga,*" he says.

Gracchus salutes him. "More exciting than moa," he says.

***

"And these are mine," says Nerita three hours later, indicating a tree at the outer rim of the forest. Several hundred large pigeons nest in its boughs, so many of them that the tree seems to be sprouting birds rather than leaves. The females are plain—light-brown above, gray below—but the males are flamboyant, with rich, glossy blue plumage on their wings and backs, breasts of a wine-red chestnut color, iridescent spots of bronze and green on their necks, and weird, vivid eyes of a bright, fiery orange. Gracchus says, "Right. You've found your passenger pigeons."

"Where's the thrill in shooting pigeons out of a tree?" Mortimer asks.

Nerita gives him a withering look. "Where's the thrill in gunning down a charging bull?" She signals to Ngiri, who fires a shot into the air. The startled pigeons burst from their perches and fly in low circles. In the old days, a century and a half ago in the forests of North America, no one troubled to shoot passenger pigeons on the wing: the pigeons were food, not sport, and it was simpler to blast them as they sat, for that way a single hunter might kill thousands of birds in one day. Thus it took only fifty years to reduce the passenger pigeon population from uncountable sky-blackening billions to zero. Nerita is more sporting. This is a test of her skill, after all. She aims her shotgun, shoots, pumps, shoots, pumps. Stunned birds drop to the ground. She and her gun are a single entity, sharing one purpose. In moments it is all over. The porters retrieve the fallen birds and snap their necks. Nerita has the dozen pigeons her license allows: a pair to mount, the rest for tonight's dinner. The survivors have returned to their tree and stare placidly, unreproachfully, at the hunters.

"They breed so damned fast," Gracchus mutters. "If we aren't careful, they'll be getting out of the preserve and taking over all of Africa."

Sybille laughs. "Don't worry. We'll cope. We wiped them out once and we can do it again, if we have to."

***

Sybille's prey is a dodo. In Dar, when they were applying for their licenses, the others mocked her choice: a fat flightless bird, unable to run or fight, so feeble of wit that it fears nothing. She ignored them. She wants a dodo because to her it is the essence of extinction, the prototype of all that is dead and vanished. That there is no sport in shooting foolish dodos means little to Sybille. Hunting itself is meaningless for her.

Through this vast park she wanders as in a dream. She sees ground sloths, great auks, quaggas, moas, heath hens, Javan rhinos, giant armadillos, and many other rarities. The place is an abode of ghosts. The ingenuities or the genetic craftsmen are limitless; someday, perhaps, the preserve will offer trilobites, tyrannosaurs, mastodons, saber-toothed cats, baluchitheria, even — why not? — packs of Australopithecines, tribes of Neanderthals, for the amusement of the deads, whose games tend to be somber. Sybille wonders whether it can really be considered killing, this slaughter of laboratory-spawned novelties. Are these animals real or artificial? Living things, or cleverly animated constructs? Real, she decides. Living. They eat, they metabolize, they reproduce. They must seem real to themselves, and so they are real, realer, maybe, than dead human beings who walk again in their own cast-off bodies.

"Shotgun," Sybille says to the closest porter.

There is the bird, ugly, ridiculous, waddling laboriously through the tall grass. Sybille accepts a weapon and sights along its barrel. "Wait," Nerita says. "I'd like to get a picture of this." She moves slantwise around the group, taking exaggerated care not to frighten the dodo, but the dodo does not seem to be aware of any of them. Like an emissary from the realm

of darkness, carrying good news of death to those creatures not yet extinct,
it plods diligently across their path. "Fine," Nerita says. "Anthony, point
at the dodo, will you, as if you've just noticed it? Kent, I'd like you to look
down at your gun, study its bolt or something. Fine. And Sybille, just hold
that pose — aiming — yes —"

Nerita takes the picture.

Calmly Sybille pulls the trigger.

"*Kazi imekwisha,*" Gracchus says. "The work is finished."

SIX

Although to be driven back upon oneself is an uneasy
affair at best, rather like trying to cross a border with
borrowed credentials, it seems to be now the one condition
necessary to the beginnings of real self-respect. Most of
our platitudes notwithstanding, self-deception remains the
most difficult deception. The tricks that work on others
count for nothing in that very well-lit back alley where
one keeps assignations with oneself: no winning smiles
will do here, no prettily drawn lists of good intentions.

Joan Didion: *On Self-Respect*

You better believe what Jeej is trying to tell you," Dolorosa said. "Ten
minutes inside the Cold Town, they'll have your number. Five minutes."

Jijibhoi's man was small, rumpled-looking, forty or fifty years old,
with untidy long dark hair and wide-set smoldering eyes. His skin was
sallow and his face was gaunt. Such other deads as Klein had seen at close
range about them an air of unearthly serenity, but not this one: Dolorosa
was tense, fidgety, a knuckle-cracker, a lip-gnawer. Yet somehow there
could be no doubt he was a dead, as much a dead as Zacharias, as Gracchus,
as Mortimer.

"They'll have my what?" Klein asked.

"Your number. Your number. They'll know you aren't a dead, because
it can't be faked. Jesus, don't you even speak English? Jorge, that's a foreign
name. I should have known. Where are you from?"

"Argentina, as a matter of fact, but I was brought to California when I
was a small boy. In 1955. Look, if they catch me, they catch me. I just want
to get in there and spend half an hour talking with my wife."

"Mister, you don't have any wife any more."

"With Sybille," Klein said, exasperated. "To talk with Sybille, my — my former wife."

"All right. I'll get you inside."

"What will it cost?"

"Never mind that," Dolorosa said. "I owe Jeej here a few favors. More than a few. So I'll get you the drug—"

"Drug?"

"The drug the Treasury agents use when they infiltrate the Cold Towns. It narrows the pupils, contracts the capillaries, gives you that good old zombie look. The agents always get caught and thrown out, and so will you, but at least you'll go in there feeling that you've got a convincing disguise. Little oily capsule, one every morning before breakfast."

Klein looked at Jijibhoi. "Why do Treasury agents infiltrate the Cold Towns?"

"For the same reasons they infiltrate anywhere else," Jijibhoi said. "To spy. They are trying to compile dossiers on the financial dealings of the deads, you see, and until proper life-defining legislation is approved by Congress there is no precise way of compelling a person who is deemed legally dead to divulge—"

Dolorosa said, "Next, the background. I can get you a card of residence from Albany Cold Town in New York. You died last December, okay, and they rekindled you back east because — let's see —"

"I could have been attending the annual meeting of the American Historical Association in New York," Klein suggested. "That's what I do, you understand, professor of contemporary history at UCLA. Because of the Christmas holiday my body couldn't be shipped back to California, no room on any flight, and so they took me to Albany. How does that sound?"

Dolorosa smiled. "You really enjoy making up lies, Professor, don't you? I can dig that quality in you. Okay, Albany Cold Town, and this is your first trip out of there, your drying-off trip—that's what it's called, drying-off—you come out of the Cold Town like a new butterfly just out of its cocoon, all soft and damp, and you're on your own in a strange place. Now, there's a lot of stuff you'll need to know about how to behave, little mannerisms, social graces, that kind of crap, and I'll work on that with you tomorrow and Wednesday and Friday, three sessions; that ought to be enough. Meanwhile let me give you the basics. There are only three things you really have to remember while you're inside:

"(1) Never ask a direct question.

"(2) Never lean on anybody's arm. You know what I mean?

"(3) Keep in mind that to a dead the whole universe is plastic, nothing's real, nothing matters a hell of a lot, it's all only a joke. Only a joke, friend, only a joke."

***

Early in April he flew to Salt Lake City, rented a car, and drove out past Moab into the high plateau rimmed by red-rock mountains where the deads had built Zion Cold Town. This was Klein's second visit to the necropolis. The other had been in the late summer of '91, a hot, parched season when the sun filled half the sky and even the gnarled junipers looked dazed from thirst; but now it was a frosty afternoon, with faint pale light streaming out of the wintry western hills and occasional gusts of light snow whirling through the iron-blue air. Jijibhoi's route instructions pulsed from the memo screen on his dashboard. Fourteen miles from town, yes, narrow paved lane turns off highway, yes, discreet little sign announcing PRIVATE ROAD, NO ADMITTANCE, yes, a second sign a thousand yards in, ZION COLD TOWN, MEMBERS ONLY, yes, and then just beyond that the barrier of green light across the road, the scanner system, the roadblocks sliding like scythes out of the underground installations, a voice on an invisible loudspeaker saying, "If you have a permit to enter Zion Cold Town, please place it under your left-hand windshield wiper."

That other time he had had no permit, and he had gone no farther than this, though at least he had managed a little colloquy with the unseen gatekeeper out of which he had squeezed the information that Sybille was indeed living in that particular Cold Town. This time he affixed Dolorosa's forged card of residence to his windshield, and waited tensely, and in thirty seconds the roadblocks slid from sight. He drove on, along a winding road that followed the natural contours of a dense forest of scrubby conifers, and came at last to a brick wall that curved away into the trees as though it encircled the entire town. Probably it did. Klein had an overpowering sense of the Cold Town as a hermetic city, ponderous and sealed as old Egypt. There was a metal gate in the brick wall; green electronic eyes surveyed him, signaled their approval, and the wall rolled open.

He drove slowly toward the center of town, passing through a zone of what he supposed were utility buildings—storage depots, a power substation, the municipal waterworks, whatever, a bunch of grim windowless one-story cinderblock affairs—and then into the residential district, which was not much lovelier. The streets were laid out on a rectangular grid; the buildings were squat, dreary, impersonal, homogeneous. There was practically no automobile traffic, and in a dozen blocks he saw no more than ten pedestrians, who did not even glance at him. So this was the environment in which the deads chose to spend their second lives. But why such deliberate bleakness? "You will never understand us," Dolorosa had warned. Dolorosa was right. Jijibhoi had told him that Cold Towns were something less than charming, but Klein had not been prepared for this. There was a glacial quality about the place, as though it were wholly entombed in a block of clear ice: silence, sterility, a mortuary calm. Cold Town, yes, aptly named. Architecturally, the town looked like the worst of all possible cheap-and-sleazy tract developments, but the psychic texture it projected was even more depressing, more like that of one of those ghastly retirement communities, one of the innumerable Leisure Worlds or Sun Manors, those childless joyless retreats where colonies of that other kind of living dead collected to await the last trumpet. Klein shivered.

***

At last, another few minutes deeper into the town, a sign of activity, if not exactly of life: a shopping center, flat-topped brown stucco buildings around a U-shaped courtyard, a steady flow of shoppers moving about. All right. His first test was about to commence. He parked his car near the mouth of the U and strolled uneasily inward. He felt as if his forehead were a beacon, flashing glowing betrayals at rhythmic intervals:

FRAUD   INTRUDER   INTERLOPER   SPY

Go ahead, he thought, seize me, seize the impostor, get it over with, throw me out, string me up, crucify me. But no one seemed to pick up the signals. He was altogether ignored. Out of courtesy? Or just contempt? He stole what he hoped were covert glances at the shoppers, half expecting to run across Sybille right away. They all looked like sleepwalkers, moving in glazed silence about their errands. No smiles, no chatter: the icy aloofness of these self-contained people heightened the familiar suburban atmosphere of the shopping center into surrealist intensity, Norman Rockwell with an overlay of Dali or De Chirico. The shopping center looked like all other shopping centers: clothing stores, a bank, a record shop, snack bars, a florist, a TV-stereo outlet, a theater, a five-and-dime. One difference, though, became apparent as Klein wandered from shop to shop: the whole place was automated. There were no clerks anywhere, only the ubiquitous data screens, and no doubt a battery of hidden scanners to discourage shoplifters. (Or did the impulse toward petty theft perish with the body's first death?) The customers selected all the merchandise themselves, checked it out via data screens, touched their thumbs to charge-plates to debit their accounts. Of course. No one was going to waste his precious rekindled existence standing behind a counter to sell tennis shoes or cotton candy. Nor were the dwellers in the Cold Towns likely to dilute their isolation by hiring a labor force of imported warms. Somebody here had to do a little work, obviously — how did the merchandise get into the stores? — but, in general, Klein realized, what could not be done here by machines would not be done at all.

For ten minutes he prowled the center. Just when he was beginning to think he must be entirely invisible to these people, a short, broad-shouldered man, bald but with oddly youthful features, paused in front of him and said, "I am Pablo. I welcome you to Zion Cold Town." This unexpected puncturing of the silence so startled Klein that he had to fight to retain appropriate deadlike imperturbability. Pablo smiled warmly and touched both his hands to Klein's in friendly greeting, but his eyes were frigid, hostile, remote, a terrifying contradiction. "I've been sent to bring you to the lodging-place. Come: your car."

Other than to give directions, Pablo spoke only three times during the five-minute drive. "Here is the rekindling house," he said. A five-story building, as inviting as a hospital, with walls of dark bronze and windows black as onyx. "This is Guidefather's house," Pablo said a moment later. A modest brick building, like a rectory, at the edge of a small park. And, finally: "This is where you will stay. Enjoy your visit." Abruptly he got out of the car and walked rapidly away.

***

This was the house of strangers, the hotel for visiting deads, a long low cinderblock structure, functional and unglamorous, one of the least seductive buildings in this city of stark disagreeable buildings. However else it might be with the deads, they clearly had no craving for fancy architecture. A voice out of a data screen in the spartan lobby assigned him to a room: a white-walled box, square, high of ceiling. He had his own toilet, his own data screen, a narrow bed, a chest of drawers, a modest closet, a small window that gave him a view of a neighboring building just as drab as this. Nothing had been said about rental; perhaps he was a guest of the city. Nothing had been said about anything. It seemed that he had been accepted. So much for Jijibhoi's gloomy assurance that he would instantly be found out, so much for Dolorosa's insistence that they would have his number in ten minutes or less. He had been in Zion Cold Town for half an hour. Did they have his number?

***

"Eating isn't important among us," Dolorosa had said.
"But you do eat?"
"Of course we eat. It just isn't *important*."

It was important to Klein, though. Not *haute cuisine,* necessarily, but some sort of food, preferably three times a day. He was getting hungry now. Ring for room service? There were no servants in this city. He turned to the data screen. Dolorosa's first rule: *Never ask a direct question.* Surely that didn't apply to the data screen, only to his fellow deads. He didn't have to observe the niceties of etiquette when talking to a computer. Still, the voice behind the screen might not be that of a computer after all, so he tried to employ the oblique, elliptical conversational style that Dolorosa said the deads favored among themselves:

"Dinner?"

"Commissary."

"Where?"

"Central Four," said the screen.

Central Four? All right. He would find the way. He changed into fresh clothing and went down the long vinyl-floored hallway to the lobby. Night had come; street lamps were glowing; under cloak of darkness the city's ugliness was no longer so obtrusive, and there was even a kind of controlled beauty about the brutal regularity of its streets.

The streets were unmarked, though, and deserted. Klein walked at random for ten minutes, hoping to meet someone heading for the Central Four commissary. But when he did come upon someone, a tall and regal woman well advanced in years, he found himself incapable of approaching her. *(Never ask a direct question. Never lean on anybody's arm.)* He walked alongside her, in silence and at a distance, until she turned suddenly to enter a house. For ten minutes more he wandered alone again. This is ridiculous, he thought: dead or warm, I'm a stranger in town, I should be entitled to a little assistance. Maybe Dolorosa was just trying to complicate things. On the next corner, when Klein caught sight of a man hunched away from the wind, lighting a cigarette, he went boldly over to him. "Excuse me, but—"

The other looked up. "Klein?" he said. "Yes. Of course. Well, so you've made the crossing too!"

He was one of Sybille's Zanzibar companions, Klein realized. The quick-eyed, sharp-edged one—Mortimer. A member of her pseudo-familial grouping, whatever that might be. Klein stared sullenly at him. This had to be the moment when his imposture would be exposed, for only some six weeks had passed since he had argued with Mortimer in the gardens of Sybille's Zanzibar hotel, not nearly enough time for someone to have died and been rekindled and gone through his drying-off. But a moment passed and Mortimer said nothing. At length Klein said, "I just got here. Pablo showed me to the house of strangers and now I'm looking for the commissary."

Central Four? I'm going there myself. How lucky for you." No sign of suspicion in Mortimer's face. Perhaps an elusive smile revealed his awareness that Klein could not be what he claimed to be. *Keep in mind that to a dead the whole universe is plastic, it's all only a joke.* "I'm waiting for Nerita," Mortimer said. "We can all eat together."

Klein said heavily, "I was rekindled in Albany Cold Town. I've just emerged."

"How nice," Mortimer said.

Nerita Tracy stepped out of a building just beyond the corner — a slim, athletic-looking woman, about forty, with short reddish-brown hair. As she swept toward them, Mortimer said, "Here's Klein, who we met in Zanzibar. Just rekindled, out of Albany."

"Sybille will be amused."

"Is she in town?" Klein blurted.

Mortimer and Nerita exchanged sly glances. Klein felt abashed. *Never ask a direct question.* Damn Dolorosa!

Nerita said, "You'll see her before long. Shall we go to dinner?"

***

The commissary was less austere than Klein had expected: actually quite an inviting restaurant, elaborately constructed on five or six levels divided by lustrous dark hangings into small, secluded dining areas. It had the warm, rich look of a tropical resort. But the food, which came automat-style out of revolving dispensers, was prefabricated and cheerless — another jarring contradiction. *Only a joke, friend, only a joke.* In any case he was less hungry than he had imagined at the hotel. He sat with Mortimer and Nerita, picking at his meal, while their conversation flowed past him at several times the speed of thought. They spoke in fragments and ellipses, in periphrastics and aposiopeses, in a style abundant in chiasmus, metonymy, meiosis, oxymoron, and zeugma; their dazzling rhetorical techniques left him baffled and uncomfortable, which beyond much doubt was their intention. Now and again they would dart from a thicket of indirection to skewer him with a quick corroborative stab: Isn't that so, they would say, and he would smile and nod, nod and smile, saying, Yes, yes, absolutely. Did they know he was a fake, and were they merely playing with him, or had they, somehow, impossibly, accepted him as one of them? So subtle was their style that he could not tell. A very new member of the society of the rekindled, he told himself, would be nearly as much at sea here as a warm in deadface.

Then Nerita said — no verbal games, this time — "You still miss her terribly, don't you?"

"I do. Some things evidently never perish."

"Everything perishes," Mortimer said. "The dodo, the aurochs, the Holy Roman Empire, the T'ang Dynasty, the walls of Byzantium, the language of Mohenjo-daro."

"But not the Great Pyramid, the Yangtze, the coelacanth, or the skullcap of Pithecanthropus," Klein countered. "Some things persist and endure. And some can be regenerated. Lost languages have been deciphered. I believe the dodo and the aurochs are hunted in a certain African park in this very era."

"Replicas," Mortimer said.

"Convincing replicas. Simulations as good as the original."

"Is that what you want?" Nerita asked.

"I want what's possible to have."

"A convincing replica of lost love?"

"I might be willing to settle for five minutes of conversation with her."

"You'll have it. Not tonight. See? There she is. But don't bother her now." Nerita nodded across the gulf in the center of the restaurant; on the far side, three levels up from where they sat, Sybille and Kent Zacharias had appeared. They stood for a brief while at the edge of their dining alcove, staring blandly and emotionlessly into the restaurant's central well. Klein felt a muscle jerking uncontrollably in his cheek, a damning revelation of undeadlike uncoolness, and pressed his hand over it, so that it twanged and throbbed against his palm. She was like a goddess up there, manifesting herself in her sanctum to her worshipers, a pale shimmering figure, more beautiful even than she had become to him through the anguished enhancements of memory, and it seemed impossible to him that that being had ever been his wife, that he had known her when her eyes were puffy and reddened from a night of study, that he had looked down at her face as they made love and had seen her lips pull back in that spasm of ecstasy that is so close to a grimace of pain, that he had known her crotchety and unkind in her illness, short-tempered and impatient in health, a person of flaws and weaknesses, of odors and blemishes, in short a human being, this goddess, this unreal rekindled creature, this object of his quest, this Sybille. Serenely she turned, serenely she vanished into her cloaked alcove. "She knows you're here," Nerita told him. "You'll see her. Perhaps tomorrow." Then Mortimer said something maddeningly oblique, and Nerita replied with the same off-center mystification, and Klein once more was plunged into the river of their easy dancing wordplay, down into it, down and down and down, and as he struggled to keep from drowning, as he fought to comprehend their interchanges, he never once looked toward the place where Sybille sat, not even once, and congratulated himself on having accomplished that much at least in his masquerade.

***

That night, lying alone in his room at the house of strangers, he wonders what he will say to Sybille when they finally meet, and what she will say to him. Will he dare bluntly to ask her to describe to him the quality of her new existence? That is all that he wants from her, really, that knowledge, that opening of an aperture into her transfigured self; that is as much as he hopes to get from her, knowing as he does that there is scarcely a chance of regaining her, but will he dare to ask, will he dare even that? Of course his asking such things will reveal to her that he is still a warm, too dense and gross of perception to comprehend the life of a dead; but he is certain she will sense that anyway, instantly. What will he say, what will he say? He plays out an imagined script of their conversation in the theater of his mind:

— Tell me what it's like, Sybille, to be the way you are now.

— Like swimming under a sheet of glass.

— I don't follow.

— Everything is quiet where I am, Jorge. There's a peace that passeth all understanding. I used to feel sometimes that I was caught up in a great storm, that I was being buffeted by every breeze, that my life was being consumed by agitations and frenzies, but now, now, I'm at the eye of the storm, at the place where everything is always calm. I observe rather than let myself be acted upon.

— But isn't there a loss of feeling that way? Don't you feel that you're wrapped in an insulating layer? Like swimming under glass, you say — that conveys being insulated, being cut off, being almost numb.

— I suppose you might think so. The way it is, is that one no longer is affected by the unnecessary.

— It sounds to me like a limited existence.

— Less limited than the grave, Jorge.

— I never understood why you wanted rekindling. You were such a world-devourer, Sybille, you lived with such intensity, such passion. To settle for the kind of existence you have now, to be only half-alive —

— Don't be a fool, Jorge. To be half-alive is better than to be rotting in the ground. I was so young. There was so much else still to see and do.

— But to see it and do it half-alive?

— Those were your words, not mine. I'm not alive at all. I'm neither less nor more than the person you knew. I'm another kind of being altogether. Neither less nor more, only different.

— Are all your perceptions different?

— Very much so. My perspective is broader. Little things stand revealed as little things.

— Give me an example, Sybille.

—I'd rather not. How could I make anything clear to you? Die and be with us, and you'll understand.

—You know I'm not dead?

—Oh, Jorge, how funny you are!

—How nice that I can still amuse you.

—You look so hurt, so tragic. I could almost feel sorry for you. Come: ask me anything.

—Could you leave your companions and live in the world again?

—I've never considered that.

—Could you?

—I suppose I could. But why should I? This is my world now.

—This ghetto.

—Is that how it seems to you?

—You lock yourselves into a closed society of your peers, a tight subculture. Your own jargon, your own wall of etiquette and idiosyncrasy. Designed, I think, mainly to keep the outsiders off balance, to keep them feeling like outsiders. It's a defensive thing. The hippies, the blacks, the gays, the deads—same mechanism, same process.

—The Jews, too. Don't forget the Jews.

—All right, Sybille, the Jews. With their little tribal jokes, their special holidays, their own mysterious language, yes, a good case in point.

—So I've joined a new tribe. What's wrong with that?

—Did you need to be part of a tribe?

—What did I have before? The tribe of Californians? The tribe of academics?

—The tribe of Jorge and Sybille Klein.

—Too narrow. Anyway, I've been expelled from that tribe. I needed to join another one.

—Expelled?

—By death. After that there's no going back.

—You could go back. Any time.

—Oh, no, no, no, Jorge, I can't, I can't, I'm not Sybille Klein any more, I never will be again. How can I explain it to you? There's no way. Death brings on changes. Die and see, Jorge. Die and see.

***

Nerita said, "She's waiting for you in the lounge."

It was a big, coldly furnished room at the far end of the other wing of the house of strangers. Sybille stood by a window through which pale, chilly morning light was streaming. Mortimer was with her, and also Kent Zacharias. The two men favored Klein with mysterious oblique smiles—courteous or derisive, he could not tell which. "Do you like our town?"

Zacharias asked. "Have you been seeing the sights?" Klein chose not to reply. He acknowledged the question with a faint nod and turned to Sybille. Strangely, he felt altogether calm at this moment of attaining a years-old desire: he felt nothing at all in her presence, no panic, no yearning, no dismay, no nostalgia, nothing, nothing. As though he were truly a dead. He knew it was the tranquility of utter terror.

"We'll leave you two alone," Zacharias said. "You must have so much to tell each other." He went out, with Nerita and Mortimer. Klein's eyes met Sybille's and lingered there. She was looking at him coolly, in a kind of impersonal appraisal. That damnable smile of hers, Klein thought: dying turns them all into Mona Lisas.

She said, "Do you plan to stay here long?"

"Probably not. A few days, maybe a week." He moistened his lips. "How have you been, Sybille? How has it been going?"

"It's all been about as I expected."

What do you mean by that? Can you give me some details? Are you at all disappointed? Have there been any surprises? What has it been like for you, Sybille? Oh, Jesus —

— Never ask a direct question —

He said, "I wish you had let me visit with you in Zanzibar."

"That wasn't possible. Let's not talk about it now." She dismissed the episode with a casual wave. After a moment she said, "Would you like to hear a fascinating story I've uncovered about the early days of Omani influence in Zanzibar?"

The impersonality of the question startled him. How could she display such absolute lack of curiosity about his presence in Zion Cold Town, his claim to be a dead, his reasons for wanting to see her? How could she plunge so quickly, so coldly, into a discussion of archaic political events in Zanzibar?

"I suppose so," he said weakly.

"It's a sort of Arabian Nights story, really. It's the story of how Ahmad the Sly overthrew Abdullah ibn Muhammad Alawi."

The names were strange to him. He had indeed taken some small part in her historical researches, but it was years since he had worked with her, and everything had drifted about in his mind, leaving a jumbled residue of Ahmads and Hasans and Abdullahs. "I'm sorry," he said. "I don't recall who they were."

Unperturbed, Sybille said, "Certainly you remember that in the eighteenth and early nineteenth centuries the chief power in the Indian Ocean was the Arab state of Oman, ruled from Muscat on the Persian Gulf. Under the Busaidi dynasty, founded in 1744 by Ahmad ibn Said al-Busaidi, the Omani extended their power to East Africa. The logical capital for their African empire was the port of Mombasa, but they were unable to evict a rival dynasty reigning there, so the Busaidi looked toward nearby Zanzibar—a cosmopolitan island of mixed Arab, Indian, and African population. Zanzibar's strategic placement on the coast and its spacious and well-protected harbor made it an ideal base for the East African slave trade that the Busaidi of Oman intended to dominate."

"It comes back to me now, I think."

"Very well. The founder of the Omani Sultanate of Zanzibar was Ahmad ibn Majid the Sly, who came to the throne of Oman in 1811—do you remember?—upon the death of his uncle Abder-Rahman al-Busaidi."

"The names sound familiar," Klein said doubtfully.

"Seven years later," Sybille continued, "seeking to conquer Zanzibar without the use of force, Ahmad the Sly shaved his beard and mustache and visited the island disguised as a soothsayer, wearing yellow robes and a costly emerald in his turban. At that time most of Zanzibar was governed by a native ruler of mixed Arab and African blood, Abdullah ibn Muhammad Alawi, whose hereditary title was Mwenyi Mkuu. The Mwenyi Mkuu's subjects were mainly Africans, members of a tribe called the Hadimu. Sultan Ahmad, arriving in Zanzibar Town, gave a demonstration of his soothsaying skills on the waterfront and attracted so much attention that he speedily gained an audience at the court of the Mwenyi Mkuu. Ahmad predicted a glowing future for Abdullah, declaring that a powerful prince famed throughout the world would come to Zanzibar, make the Mwenyi Mkuu his high lieutenant, and confirm him and his descendants as lords of Zanzibar forever.

"'How do you know these things?' asked the Mwenyi Mkuu.

"'There is a potion I drink,' Sultan Ahmad replied, 'that enables me to see what is to come. Do you wish to taste of it?'

"'Most surely I do,' Abdullah said, and Ahmad thereupon gave him a drug that sent him into rapturous transports and showed him visions of paradise. Looking down from his place near the footstool of Allah, the Mwenyi Mkuu saw a rich and happy Zanzibar governed by his children's children's children. For hours he wandered in fantasies of almighty power.

"Ahmad then departed, and let his beard and mustache grow again, and returned to Zanzibar ten weeks later in his full regalia as Sultan of Oman, at the head of an imposing and powerful armada. He went at once to the court of the Mwenyi Mkuu and proposed, just as the soothsayer had prophesied, that Oman and Zanzibar enter into a treaty of alliance under which Oman would assume responsibility for much of Zanzibar's external relations—including the slave trade—while guaranteeing the authority of the Mwenyi Mkuu over domestic affairs. In return for his partial abdication of authority, the Mwenyi Mkuu would receive financial compensation from Oman. Remembering the vision the soothsayer had revealed to him, Abdullah at once signed the treaty, thereby legitimizing what was, in effect, the Omani conquest of Zanzibar. A great feast was held to celebrate the treaty, and, as a mark of honor, the Mwenyi Mkuu offered Sultan Ahmad a rare drug used locally, known as *borqash,* or 'the flower of truth.' Ahmad only pretended to put the pipe to his lips, for he loathed all mind-altering drugs, but Abdullah, as the flower of truth possessed him, looked at Ahmad and recognized the outlines of the soothsayer's face behind the Sultan's new beard. Realizing that he had been deceived, the Mwenyi Mkuu thrust his dagger, the tip of which was poisoned, deep into the Sultan's side and fled the banquet hall, taking up residence on the neighboring island of Pemba. Ahmad ibn Majid survived, but the poison consumed his vital organs and the remaining ten years of his life were spent in constant agony. As for the Mwenyi Mkuu, the Sultan's men hunted him down and put him to death along with ninety members of his family, and native rule in Zanzibar was therewith extinguished."

Sybille paused. "Is that not a gaudy and wonderful story?" she asked at last.

"Fascinating," Klein said. "Where did you find it?"

"Unpublished memoirs of Claude Richburn of the East India Company. Buried deep in the London archives. Strange that no historian ever came upon it before, isn't it? The standard texts simply say that Ahmad used his navy to bully Abdullah into signing the treaty, and then had the Mwenki Mkuu assassinated at the first convenient moment."

"Very strange," Klein agreed. But he had not come here to listen to romantic tales of visionary potions and royal treacheries. He groped for some way to bring the conversation to a more personal level. Fragments of his imaginary dialogue with Sybille floated through his mind. *Everything is quiet where I am, Jorge. There's a peace that passeth all understanding. Like swimming under a sheet of glass. The way it is, is that one no longer is affected by the unnecessary. Little things stand revealed as little things. Die and be with us, and you'll understand.* Yes. Perhaps. But did she really believe any of that? He had put all the words in her mouth; everything he had imagined her to say was his own construct, worthless as a key to the true Sybille. Where would he find the key, though?

She gave him no chance. "I will be going back to Zanzibar soon," she said. "There's much I want to learn about this incident from the people in the back country—old legends about the last days of the Mwenyi Mkuu, perhaps variants on the basic story—"

"May I accompany you?"

"Don't you have your own research to resume, Jorge?" she asked, and did not wait for an answer. She walked briskly toward the door of the lounge and went out, and he was alone.

SEVEN

I mean what they and their hired psychiatrists call "delusional
systems." Needless to say, "delusions" are always officially
defined. We don't have to worry about questions of real or unreal.
They only talk out of expediency. It's the *system* that matters. How
the data arrange themselves inside it. Some are consistent, others
fall apart.

Thomas Pynchon: *Gravity's Rainbow*

Once more the deads, this time only three of them, coming over on the
morning flight from Dar. Three was better than five, Daud Mahmoud
Barwani supposed, but three was still more than a sufficiency. Not that
those others, two months back, had caused any trouble, staying just the
one day and flitting off to the mainland again, but it made him
uncomfortable to think of such creatures on the same small island as
himself. With all the world to choose, why did they keep coming to
Zanzibar?

"The plane is here," said the flight controller.

Thirteen passengers. The health officer let the local people through
the gate first — two newspapermen and four legislators coming back from
the Pan-African Conference in Capetown — and then processed a party of
four Japanese tourists, unsmiling owlish men festooned with cameras. And
then the deads: and Barwani was surprised to discover that they were the
same ones as before, the red-haired man, the brown-haired man without
the beard, the black-haired woman. Did deads have so much money that
they could fly from America to Zanzibar every few months? Barwani had
heard a tale to the effect that each new dead, when he rose from his coffin,
was presented with bars of gold equal to his own weight, and now he
thought he believed it. No good will come of having such beings loose in
the world, he told himself, and certainly none from letting them into
Zanzibar. Yet he had no choice. "Welcome once again to the isle of cloves,"
he said unctuously, and smiled a bureaucratic smile, and wondered, not
for the first time, what would become of Daud Mahmoud Barwani once
his days on earth had reached their end.

***

" — Ahmad the Sly versus Abdullah Something," Klein said. "That's all she would talk about. The history of Zanzibar." He was in Jijibhoi's study. The night was warm and a late-season rain was falling, blurring the million sparkling lights of the Los Angeles basin. "It would have been, you know, gauche to ask her any direct questions. Gauche. I haven't felt so gauche since I was fourteen. I was helpless among them, a foreigner, a child."

"Do you think they saw through your disguise?" Jijibhoi asked.

"I can't tell. They seemed to be toying with me, to be having sport with me, but that may just have been their general style with any newcomer. Nobody challenged me. Nobody hinted I might be an impostor. Nobody seemed to care very much about me or what I was doing there or how I had happened to become a dead. Sybille and I stood face to face, and I wanted to reach out to her, I wanted her to reach out to me, and there was no contact, none, none at all, it was as though we had just met at some academic cocktail party and the only thing on her mind was the new nugget of obscure history she had just unearthed, and so she told me all about how Sultan Ahmad outfoxed Abdullah and Abdullah stabbed the Sultan." Klein caught sight of a set of familiar books on Jijibhoi's crowded shelves — Oliver and Mathew, *History of East Africa,* books that had traveled everywhere with Sybille in the years of their marriage. He pulled forth Volume I, saying, "She claimed that the standard histories give a sketchy and inaccurate description of the incident and that she's only now discovered the true story. For all I know, she was just playing a game with me, telling me a piece of established history as though it were something nobody knew till last week. Let me see — Ahmad, Ahmad, Ahmad — "

He examined the index. Five Ahmads were listed, but there was no entry for a Sultan Ahmad ibn Majid the Sly. Indeed, an Ahmad ibn Majid was cited, but he was mentioned only in a footnote and appeared to be an Arab chronicler. Klein found three Abdullahs, none of them a man of Zanzibar. "Something's wrong," he murmured.

"It does not matter, dear Jorge," Jijibhoi said mildly.

"It does. Wait a minute." He prowled the listings. Under *Zanzibar, Rulers,* he found no Ahmads, no Abdullahs; he did discover a Majid ibn Said, but when he checked the reference he found that he had reigned somewhere in the second half of the nineteenth century. Desperately Klein flipped pages, skimming, turning back, searching. Eventually he looked up and said, "It's all wrong!"

"The Oxford *History of East Africa?*"

"The details of Sybille's story. Look, she said this Ahmad the Sly gained the throne of Oman in 1811, and seized Zanzibar seven years later. But the book says that a certain Seyyid Said al-Busaidi became Sultan of Oman in 1806, and ruled for *fifty years.* He was the one, not this nonexistent Ahmad the Sly, who grabbed Zanzibar, but he did it in 1828, and the ruler he compelled to sign a treaty with him, the Mwenyi Mkuu, was named Hasan ibn Ahmad Alawi, and—" Klein shook his head. "It's an altogether different cast of characters. No stabbings, no assassinations, the dates are entirely different, the whole thing—"

Jijibhoi smiled sadly. "The deads are often mischievous."

"But why would she invent a complete fantasy and palm it off as a sensational new discovery? Sybille was the most scrupulous scholar I ever knew! She would never—"

"That was the Sybille you knew, dear friend. I keep urging you to realize that this is another person, a new person, within her body."

"A person who would lie about history?"

"A person who would tease," Jijibhoi said.

"Yes," Klein muttered. "Who would tease." *Keep in mind that to a dead the whole universe is plastic, nothing's real, nothing matters a hell of a lot.* "Who would tease a stupid, boring, annoyingly persistent ex-husband who has shown up in her Cold Town, wearing a transparent disguise and pretending to be a dead. Who would invent not only an anecdote but even its principals, as a joke, a game, a *jeu d'esprit*. Oh, God. Oh, God, how cruel she is, how foolish I was! It was her way of telling me she knew I was a phony dead. Quid pro quo, fraud for fraud!"

"What will you do?"

"I don't know," Klein said.

***

What he did, against Jijibhoi's strong advice and his own better judgment, was to get more pills from Dolorosa and return to Zion Cold Town. There would be a fitful joy, like that of probing the socket of a missing tooth, in confronting Sybille with the evidence of her fictional Ahmad, her imaginary Abdullah. Let there be no more games between us, he would say. Tell me what I need to know, Sybille, and then let me go away; but tell me only truth. All the way to Utah he rehearsed his speech, polishing and embellishing. There was no need for it, though, since this time the gate of Zion Cold Town would not open for him. The scanners scanned his forged Albany card and the loudspeaker said, "Your credentials are invalid."

Which could have ended it. He might have returned to Los Angeles and picked up the pieces of his life. All this semester he had been on sabbatical leave, but the summer term was coming and there was work to do. He did return to Los Angeles, but only long enough to pack a somewhat larger suitcase, find his passport, and drive to the airport. On a sweet May evening a BOAC jet took him over the Pole to London, where, barely pausing for coffee and buns at an airport shop, he boarded another plane that carried him southeast toward Africa. More asleep than awake, he

watched the dreamy landmarks drifting past: the Mediterranean, coming
and going with surprising rapidity, and the tawny carpet of the Libyan
Desert, and the mighty Nile, reduced to a brown thread's thickness when
viewed from a height of ten miles. Suddenly Kilimanjaro, mist-wrapped,
snowbound, loomed like a giant double-headed blister to his right, far
below, and he thought he could make out to his left the distant glare of the
sun on the Indian Ocean. Then the big needle-nosed plane began its abrupt
swooping descent, and he found himself, soon after, stepping out into the
warm humid air and dazzling sunlight of Dar es Salaam.

***

Too soon, too soon. He felt unready to go on to Zanzibar. A day or two
of rest, perhaps: he picked a Dar hotel at random, the Agip, liking the
strange sound of its name, and hired a taxi. The hotel was sleek and clean,
a streamlined affair in the glossy 1960s style, much cheaper than the
Kilimanjaro, where he had stayed briefly on the other trip, and located in
a pleasant leafy quarter of the city, near the ocean. He strolled about for a
short while, discovered that he was altogether exhausted, returned to his
room for a nap that stretched on for nearly five hours, and awakening
groggy, showered and dressed for dinner. The hotel's dining room was
full of beefy red-faced fair-haired men, jacketless and wearing open-
throated white shirts, all of whom reminded him disturbingly of Kent
Zacharias; but these were warms, Britishers from their accents, engineers,
he suspected, from their conversation. They were building a dam and a
power plant somewhere up the coast, it seemed, or perhaps a power plant
without a dam; it was hard to follow what they said. They drank a good
deal of gin and spoke in hearty booming shouts. There were also a good
many Japanese businessmen, of course, looking trim and restrained in
dark-blue suits and narrow ties, and at the table next to Klein's were five
tanned curly-haired men talking in rapid Hebrew — Israelis, surely. The
only Africans in sight were waiters and bartenders. Klein ordered Mombasa
oysters, steak, and a carafe of red wine, and found the food unexpectedly
good, but left most of it on his plate. It was late evening in Tanzania, but
for him it was ten o'clock in the morning, and his body was confused. He
tumbled into bed, meditated vaguely on the probable presence of Sybille
just a few air-minutes away in Zanzibar, and dropped into a sound sleep
from which he awakened, what seemed like many hours later, to discover
that it was still well before dawn.

He dawdled away the morning sightseeing in the old native quarter,
hot and dusty, with unpaved streets and rows of tin shacks, and at midday
returned to his hotel for a shower and lunch. Much the same national
distribution in the restaurant — British, Japanese, Israeli — though the faces

seemed different. He was on his second beer when Anthony Gracchus came in. The white hunter, broad-shouldered, pale, densely bearded, clad in khaki shorts, khaki shirt, seemed almost to have stepped out of the picture-cube Jijibhoi had once shown him. Instinctively Klein shrank back, turning toward the window, but too late: Gracchus had seen him. All chatter came to a halt in the restaurant as the dead man strode to Klein's table, pulled out a chair unasked, and seated himself; then, as though a motion-picture projector had been halted and started again, the British engineers resumed their shouting, sounding somewhat strained now.

"Small world," Gracchus said. "Crowded one, anyway. On your way to Zanzibar, are you, Klein?"

"In a day or so. Did you know I was here?"

"Of course not." Gracchus' harsh eyes twinkled slyly. "Sheer coincidence is what this is. She's there already."

"She is?"

"She and Zacharias and Mortimer. I hear you wiggled your way into Zion."

"Briefly," Klein said. "I saw Sybille. Briefly."

"Unsatisfactorily. So once again you've followed her here. Give it up, man. Give it up."

"I can't."

"*Can't!*" Gracchus scowled. "A neurotic's word, *can't.* What you mean is *won't.* A mature man can do anything he wants to that isn't a physical impossibility. Forget her. You're only annoying her, this way, interfering with her work, interfering with her—" Gracchus smiled. "With her life. She's been dead almost three years, hasn't she? Forget her. The world's full of other women. You're still young, you have money, you aren't ugly, you have professional standing—"

"Is this what you were sent here to tell me?"

"I wasn't sent here to tell you anything, friend. I'm only trying to save you from yourself. Don't go to Zanzibar. Go home and start your life again."

"When I saw her at Zion," Klein said, "she treated me with contempt. She amused herself at my expense. I want to ask her why she did that."

"Because you're a warm and she's a dead. To her you're a clown. To all of us you're a clown. It's nothing personal, Klein. There's simply a gulf in attitudes, a gulf too wide for you to cross. You went to Zion drugged up like a Treasury man, didn't you? Pale face, bulgy eyes? You didn't fool anyone. You certainly didn't fool *her.* The game she played with you was her way of telling you that. Don't you know that?"

"I know it, yes."

"What more do you want, then? More humiliation?"

Klein shook his head wearily and stared at the tablecloth. After a moment he looked up, and his eyes met those of Gracchus, and he was astounded to realize that he trusted the hunter, that for the first time in his dealings with the deads he felt he was being met with sincerity. He said in a low voice, "We were very close, Sybille and I, and then she died, and now I'm nothing to her. I haven't been able to come to terms with that. I need her, still. I want to share my life with her, even now."

"But you can't."

"I know that. And still I can't help doing what I've been doing."

"There's only one thing you *can* share with her," Gracchus said. "That's your death. She won't descend to your level: you have to climb to hers."

"Don't be absurd."

"Who's absurd, me or you? Listen to me, Klein. I think you're a fool, I think you're a weakling, but I don't dislike you, I don't hold you to blame for your own foolishness. And so I'll help you, if you'll allow me." He reached into his breast pocket and withdrew a tiny metal tube with a safety catch at one end. "Do you know what this is?" Gracchus asked. "It's a self-defense dart, the kind all the women in New York carry. A good many deads carry them, too, because we never know when the reaction will start, when the mobs will turn against us. Only we don't use anesthetic drugs in ours. Listen, we can walk into any tavern in the native quarter and have a decent brawl going in five minutes, and in the confusion I'll put one of these darts into you, and we'll have you in Dar General Hospital fifteen minutes after that, crammed into a deep-freeze unit, and for a few thousand dollars we can ship you unthawed to California, and this time Friday night you'll be undergoing rekindling in, say, San Diego Cold Town. And when you come out of it you and Sybille will be on the same side of the gulf, do you see? If you're destined to get back together with her, ever, that's the only way. That way you have a chance. This way you have none."

"It's unthinkable," Klein said.

"Unacceptable, maybe. But not unthinkable. Nothing's unthinkable once somebody's thought it. You think it some more. Will you promise me that? Think about it before you get aboard that plane for Zanzibar. I'll be staying here tonight and tomorrow, and then I'm going out to Arusha to meet some deads coming in for the hunting, and any time before then I'll do it for you if you say the word. Think about it. Will you think about it? Promise me that you'll think about it."

"I'll think about it," Klein said.

"Good. Good. Thank you. Now let's have lunch and change the subject. Do you like eating here?"

"One thing puzzles me. Why does this place have a clientele that's exclusively non-African? Does it dare to discriminate against blacks in a black republic?"

Gracchus laughed. "It's the blacks who discriminate, friend. This is considered a second-class hotel. All the blacks are at the Kilimanjaro or the Nyerere. Still, it's not such a bad place. I recommend the fish dishes, if you haven't tried them, and there's a decent white wine from Israel that—"

EIGHT

O Lord, methought what pain it was to drown!
What dreadful noise of water in mine ears!
What sights of ugly death within mine eyes!
Methoughts I saw a thousand fearful wracks;
A thousand men that fishes gnawed upon;
Wedges of gold, great anchors, heaps of pearl,
Inestimable stones, unvalued jewels,
All scatt'red in the bottom of the sea.
Some lay in dead men's skulls, and in the holes
Where eyes did once inhabit there were crept,
As 'twere in scorn of eyes, reflecting gems
That wooed the slimy bottom of the deep
And mocked the dead bones that lay scatt'red by.

Shakespeare: *Richard III*

" — Israeli wine," Mick Dongan was saying. "Well, I'll try anything once, especially if there's some neat little irony attached to it. I mean, there we were in Egypt, in *Egypt,* at this fabulous dinner party in the hills at Luxor, and our host is a Saudi prince, no less, in full tribal costume right down to the sunglasses, and when they bring out the roast lamb he grins devilishly and says, 'Of course we could always drink Mouton-Rothschild, but I do happen to have a small stock of select Israeli wines in my cellar, and because I think you are, like myself, a connoisseur of small incongruities, I've asked my steward to open a bottle or two of—' Klein, do you see that girl who just came in?" It is January, 1981, early afternoon, a fine drizzle in the air. Klein is lunching with six colleagues from the history department at the Hanging Gardens atop the Westwood Plaza. The hotel is a huge ziggurat on stilts; the Hanging Gardens is a rooftop restaurant, ninety stories up, in freaky neo-Babylonian decor, all winged bulls and snorting dragons of blue and yellow tile, waiters with long curly beards and scimitars at their hips — gaudy nightclub by dark, campy faculty hangout by day. Klein looks to his left. Yes, a handsome woman, mid-twenties, coolly beautiful, serious-looking, taking a seat by herself, putting a stack of books and cassettes down on the table before her. Klein does not pick up strange girls: a matter of moral policy, and also a matter of innate shyness. Dongan teases him. "Go on over, will you? She's your type, I swear. Her eyes are the right color for you, aren't they?"

Klein has been complaining, lately, that there are too many blue-eyed girls in southern California. Blue eyes are disturbing to him, somehow, even menacing. His own eyes are brown. So are hers: dark, warm, sparkling. He thinks he has seen her occasionally in the library. Perhaps they have even exchanged brief glances. "Go on," Dongan says. "Go *on*, Jorge. Go." Klein glares at him. He will not go. How can he intrude on this woman's privacy? To force himself on her—it would almost be like rape. Dongan smiles complacently; his bland grin is a merciless prod. Klein refuses to be stampeded. But then, as he hesitates, the girl smiles too, a quick shy smile, gone so soon he is not altogether sure it happened at all, but he is sure enough, and he finds himself rising, crossing the alabaster floor, hovering awkwardly over her, searching for some inspired words with which to make contact, and no words come, but still they make contact the old-fashioned way, eye to eye, and he is stunned by the intensity of what passes between them in that first implausible moment.

"Are you waiting for someone?" he mutters, shaken.

"No." The smile again, far less tentative. "Would you like to join me?"

She is a graduate student, he discovers quickly. Just got her master's, beginning now on her doctorate—the nineteenth-century East African slave trade, particular emphasis on Zanzibar. "How romantic," he says. "Zanzibar! Have you been there?"

"Never. I hope to go some day. Have you?"

"Not ever. But it always interested me, ever since I was a small boy collecting stamps. It was the last country in my album."

"Not in mine," she says. "Zululand was."

She knows him by name, it turns out. She had even been thinking of enrolling in his course on Nazism and Its Offspring. "Are you South American?" she asks.

"Born there. Raised here. My grandparents escaped to Buenos Aires in '37."

"Why Argentina? I thought that was a hotbed of Nazis."

"Was. Also full of German-speaking refugees, though. All their friends went there. But it was too unstable. My parents got out in '55, just before one of the big revolutions, and came to California. What about you?"

"British family. I was born in Seattle. My father's in the consular service. He—"

A waiter looms. They order sandwiches offhandedly. Lunch seems very unimportant now. The contact still holds. He sees Conrad's *Nostromo* in her stack of books; she is halfway through it, and he has just finished it, and the coincidence amuses them. Conrad is one of her favorites, she says. One of his, too. What about Faulkner? Yes, and Mann, and Virginia Woolf, and they share even a fondness for Hermann Broch, and a dislike for Hesse. How odd. Operas? *Freischiitz, Hollander, Fidelia,* yes. "We have very Teutonic tastes," she observes.

"We have very similar tastes," he adds. He finds himself holding her hand.

"Amazingly similar," she says.

Mick Dongan leers at him from the far side of the room; Klein gives him a terrible scowl. Dongan winks. "Let's get out of here," Klein says, just as she starts to say the same thing.

They talk half the night and make love until dawn. "You ought to know," he tells her solemnly over breakfast, "that I decided long ago never to get married and certainly never to have a child."

"So did I," she says. "When I was fifteen."

They were married four months later. Mick Dongan was his best man.

***

Gracchus said, as they left the restaurant, "You will think things over, won't you?"

"I will," Klein said. "I promised you that."

He went to his room, packed his suitcase, checked out, and took a cab to the airport, arriving in plenty of time for the afternoon flight to Zanzibar. The same melancholy little man was on duty as health officer when he landed, Barwani. "Sir, you have come back," Barwani said. "I thought you might. The other people have been here several days already."

"The other people?"

"When you were here last, sir, you kindly offered me a retainer in order that you might be informed when a certain person reached this island." Barwani's eyes gleamed. "That person, with two of her former companions, is here now."

Klein carefully placed a twenty-shilling note on the health officer's desk.

"At which hotel?"

Barwani's lips quirked. Evidently twenty shillings fell short of expectations. But Klein did not take out another banknote, and after a moment Barwani said, "As before. The Zanzibar House. And you, sir?"

"As before," Klein said. "I'll be staying at the Shirazi."

***

Sybille was in the garden of the hotel, going over that day's research notes, when the telephone call came from Barwani. "Don't let my papers blow away," she said to Zacharias, and went inside.

When she returned, looking bothered, Zacharias said, "Is there trouble?"

She sighed. "Jorge. He's on his way to his hotel now."

"What a bore," Mortimer murmured. "I thought Gracchus might have brought him to his senses."

"Evidently not," Sybille said. "What are we going to do?"

"What would you like to do?" Zacharias asked. She shook her head. "We can't allow this to go on, can we?"

***

The evening air was humid and fragrant. The long rains had come and gone, and the island was in the grip of the new season's lunatic fertility: outside the window of Klein's hotel room some vast twining vine was putting forth monstrous trumpet-shaped yellow flowers, and all about the hotel grounds everything was in blossom, everything was in a frenzy of moist young leaves. Klein's sensibility reverberated to that feeling of universal vigorous thrusting newness; he paced the room, full of energy, trying to devise some feasible stratagem. Go immediately to see Sybille? Force his way in, if necessary, with shouts and alarums, and demand to know why she had told him that fantastic tale of imaginary sultans? No. No. He would do no more confronting, no more lamenting; now that he was here, now that he was close by her, he would seek her out calmly, he would talk quietly, he would invoke memories of their old love, he would speak of Rilke and Woolf and Broch, of afternoons in Puerto Vallarta and nights in Santa Fe, of music heard and caresses shared, he would rekindle not their marriage, for that was impossible, but merely the remembrance of the bond that once had existed, he would win from her some acknowledgment of what had been, and then he would soberly and quietly exorcise that bond, he and she together, they would work to free him by speaking softly of the change that had come over their lives, until, after three hours or four or five, he had brought himself with her help to an acceptance of the unacceptable. That was all. He would demand nothing, he would beg for nothing, except only that she assist him for one evening in ridding his soul of this useless, destructive obsession. Even a dead, even a capricious, wayward, volatile, whimsical, wanton dead, would surely see the desirability of that, and would freely give him her cooperation. Surely. And then home, and then new beginnings, too long postponed.

He made ready to go out.

There was a soft knock at the door. "Sir? Sir? You have visitors downstairs."

"Who?" Klein asked, though he knew the answer.

"A lady and two gentlemen," the bellhop replied. "The taxi has brought them from the Zanzibar House. They wait for you in the bar."

"Tell them I'll be down in a moment."

He went to the iced pitcher on the dresser, drank a glass of cold water mechanically, unthinkingly, poured himself a second, drained that too. This visit was unexpected; and why had she brought her entourage along? He had to struggle to regain that centeredness, that sense of purpose understood, which he thought he had attained before the knock. Eventually he left the room.

They were dressed crisply and impeccably this damp night, Zacharias in a tawny frock coat and pale-green trousers, Mortimer in a belted white caftan trimmed with intricate brocade, Sybille in a simple lavender tunic. Their pale faces were unmarred by perspiration; they seemed perfectly composed, models of poise. No one sat near them in the bar. As Klein entered, they stood to greet him, but their smiles appeared sinister, having nothing of friendliness in them. Klein clung tight to his intended calmness. He said quietly, "It was kind of you to come. May I buy drinks for you?"

"We have ours already," Zacharias pointed out. "Let us be your hosts. What will you have?"

"Pimm's Number Six," Klein said. He tried to match their frosty smiles. "I admire your tunic, Sybille. You all look so debonair tonight that I feel shamed."

"You never were famous for your clothes," she said.

Zacharias returned from the counter with Klein's drink. He took it and toasted them gravely.

After a short while Klein said, "Do you think I could talk privately with you, Sybille?"

"There's nothing we have to say to one another that can't be said in front of Kent and Laurence."

"Nevertheless."

"I prefer not to, Jorge."

"As you wish." Klein peered straight into her eyes and saw nothing there, nothing, and flinched. All that he had meant to say fled his mind. Only churning fragments danced there: Rilke, Broch, Puerto Vallarta. He gulped at his drink.

Zacharias said, "We have a problem to discuss, Klein."

"Go on."

"The problem is you. You're causing great distress to Sybille. This is the second time, now, that you've followed her to Zanzibar, to the literal end of the earth, Klein, and you've made several attempts besides to enter a closed sanctuary in Utah under false pretenses, and this is interfering with Sybille's freedom, Klein, it's an impossible, intolerable interference."

"The deads are dead," Mortimer said. "We understand the depths of your feelings for your late wife, but this compulsive pursuit of her must be brought to an end."

"It will be," Klein said, staring at a point on the stucco wall midway between Zacharias and Sybille. "I want only an hour or two of private conversation with my—with Sybille, and then I promise you that there will be no further—"

"Just as you promised Anthony Gracchus," Mortimer said, "not to go to Zanzibar."

"I wanted—"

"We have our rights," said Zacharias. "We've gone through hell, literally through hell, to get where we are. You've infringed on our right to be left alone. You bother us. You bore us. You annoy us. We hate to be annoyed." He looked toward Sybille. She nodded. Zacharias' hand vanished into the breast pocket of his coat. Mortimer seized Klein's wrist with astonishing suddenness and jerked his arm forward. A minute metal tube glistened in Zacharias' huge fist. Klein had seen such a tube in the hand of Anthony Gracchus only the day before.

"No," Klein gasped. "I don't believe—*no!*"

Zacharias plunged the cold tip of the tube quickly into Klein's forearm.

***

"The freezer unit is coming," Mortimer said. "It'll be here in five minutes or less."

"What if it's late?" Sybille asked anxiously. "What if something irreversible happens to his brain before it gets here?"

"He's not even entirely dead yet," Zacharias reminded her. "There's time. There's ample time. I spoke to the doctor myself, a very intelligent Chinese, flawless command of English. He was most sympathetic. They'll have him frozen within a couple of minutes of death. We'll book cargo passage aboard the morning plane for Dar. He'll be in the United States within twenty-four hours, I guarantee that. San Diego will be notified. Everything will be all right, Sybille!"

Jorge Klein lay slumped across the table. The bar had emptied the moment he had cried out and lurched forward: the half-dozen customers had fled, not caring to mar their holidays by sharing an evening with the presence of death, and the waiters and bartenders, big-eyed, terrified, lurked in the hallway. A heart attack, Zacharias had announced, some kind of sudden attack, maybe a stroke, where's the telephone? No one had seen the tiny tube do its work.

Sybille trembled. "If anything goes wrong —"
"I hear the sirens now," Zacharias said.

                                        ***

From his desk at the airport Daud Mahmoud Barwani watched the bulky refrigerated coffin being loaded by grunting porters aboard the morning plane for Dar. And then, and then, and then? They would ship the dead man to the far side of the world, to America, and breathe new life into him, and he would go once more among men. Barwani shook his head. These people! The man who was alive is now dead, and these dead ones, who knows what they are? Who knows? Best that the dead remain dead, as was intended in the time of first things. Who could have foreseen a day when the dead returned from the grave? Not I. And who can foresee what we will all become, a hundred years from now? Not I. Not I. A hundred years from now I will sleep, Barwani thought. I will sleep, and it will not matter to me at all what sort of creatures walk the earth.

                                      NINE

We die with the dying:
See, they depart, and we go with them.
We are born with the dead:
See, they return, and bring us with them.

                            T.S. Eliot: *Little Gidding*

On the day of his awakening he saw no one except the attendants at the rekindling house, who bathed him and fed him and helped him to walk slowly around his room. They said nothing to him, nor he to them; words seemed irrelevant. He felt strange in his skin, too snugly contained, as though all his life he had worn ill-fitting clothes and now had for the first time encountered a competent tailor. The images that his eyes brought him were sharp, unnaturally clear, and faintly haloed by prismatic colors, an effect that imperceptibly vanished as the day passed. On the second day he was visited by the San Diego Guidefather, not at all the formidable patriarch he had imagined, but rather a cool, efficient executive, about fifty years old, who greeted him cordially and told him briefly of the disciplines and routines he must master before he could leave the Cold Town. "What month is this?" Klein asked, and Guidefather told him it was June, the seventeenth of June, 1993. He had slept four weeks.

Now it is the morning of the third day after his awakening, and he has guests: Sybille, Nerita, Zacharias, Mortimer, Gracchus. They file into his room and stand in an arc at the foot of his bed, radiant in the glow of light that pierces the narrow windows. Like demigods, like angels, glittering with a dazzling inward brilliance, and now he is of their company. Formally they embrace him, first Gracchus, then Nerita, then Mortimer. Zacharias advances next to his bedside, Zacharias who sent him into death, and he smiles at Klein and Klein returns the smile, and they embrace. Then it is Sybille's turn: she slips her hand between his, he draws her close, her lips brush his cheek, his touch hers, his arm encircles her shoulders.

"Hello," she whispers.

"Hello," he says.

They ask him how he feels, how quickly his strength is returning, whether he has been out of bed yet, how soon he will commence his drying-off. The style of their conversation is the oblique, elliptical style favored by the deads, but not nearly so clipped and cryptic as the way of speech they normally would use among themselves; they are favoring him, leading him inch by inch into their customs. Within five minutes he thinks he is getting the knack.

He says, using their verbal shorthand, "I must have been a great burden to you."

"You were, you were," Zacharias agrees. "But all that is done with now."

"We forgive you," Mortimer says.

"We welcome you among us," declares Sybille.

They talk about their plans for the months ahead. Sybille is nearly finished with her work on Zanzibar; she will retreat to Zion Cold Town for the summer months to write her thesis. Mortimer and Nerita are off to Mexico to tour the ancient temples and pyramids; Zacharias is going to Ohio, to his beloved mounds. In the autumn they will reassemble at Zion and plan the winter's amusement: a tour of Egypt, perhaps, or Peru, the heights of Machu Picchu. Ruins, archaeological sites, delight them; in the places where death has been busiest, their joy is most intense. They are flushed, excited, verbose — virtually chattering, now. Away we will go, to Zimbabwe, to Palenque, to Angkor, to Knossos, to Uxmal, to Nineveh, to Mohenjo-daro. And as they go on and on, talking with hands and eyes and smiles and even words, even words, torrents of words, they blur and become unreal to him, they are mere dancing puppets jerking about a badly painted stage, they are droning insects, wasps or bees or mosquitoes, with all their talk of travels and festivals, of Boghazkoy and Babylon, of Megiddo and Masada, and he ceases to hear them, he tunes them out, he lies there smiling, eyes glazed, mind adrift. It perplexes him that he has so little interest in them. But then he realizes that this a mark of his liberation.

He is freed of old chains now. Will he join their set? Why should he? Perhaps he will travel with them, perhaps not, as the whim takes him. More likely not. Almost certainly not. He does not need their company. He has his own interests. He will follow Sybille about no longer. He does not need, he does not want, he will not seek. Why should he become one of them, rootless, an amoral wanderer, a ghost made flesh? Why should he embrace the values and customs of these people who had given him to death as dispassionately as they might swat an insect, only because he had bored them, because he had annoyed them? He does not hate them for what they did to him, he feels no resentment that he can identify, he merely chooses to detach himself from them. Let them float on from ruin to ruin, let them pursue death from continent to continent; he will go his own way. Now that he has crossed the interface, he finds that Sybille no longer matters to him.

— *Oh, sir, things change* —

"We'll go now," Sybille says softly.

He nods. He makes no other reply.

"We'll see you after your drying-off," Zacharias tells him, and touches him lightly with his knuckles, a farewell gesture used only by the deads.

"See you," Mortimer says.

"See you," says Gracchus.

"Soon," Nerita says.

Never, Klein says, saying it without words, but so they will understand. Never. Never. Never. I will never see any of you. I will never see you, Sybille. The syllables echo through his brain, and the word, *never, never, never,* rolls over him like the breaking surf, cleansing him, purifying him, healing him. He is free. He is alone.

"Good-bye," Sybille calls from the hallway.

"Good-bye," he says.

***

It was years before he saw her again. But they spent the last days of '99 together, shooting dodos under the shadow of mighty Kilimanjaro.

SCHWARTZ BETWEEN THE GALAXIES (1973)

INTRODUCTION

In the two years since finishing *Dying Inside* in the fall of 1971, I wrote nothing but short stories and the novella "Born with the Dead." Despite the struggle that those stories, and "Born with the Dead" in particular had been, I allowed myself to take on commitments to write two more novels, which would eventually become *The Stochastic Man* and *Shadrach in the Furnace*. I also let two friends talk me into writing short stories for publications they were editing. But, even as I locked myself into these four projects, I felt an increasing certainty that I was going to give up writing science fiction once those jobs were done.

My own personal fatigue was only one factor in that decision. Another was my sense of having been on the losing side in a literary revolution.

Among the many revolutions that went on in the era known as the Sixties (which actually ran from about 1967 to 1972) there was one in science fiction. A host of gifted new writers, both in England and the United States, brought all manner of advanced literary techniques to bear on the traditional matter of sf, producing stories that were more deeply indebted to Joyce, Kafka, Faulkner, Mann, and even e.e. cummings than they were to Heinlein, Asimov, and Clarke. This period of stylistic and structural innovation, which reached its highest pitch of activity between 1966 and 1969, was a heady, exciting time for science-fiction writers, especially newer ones such as Thomas Disch, Samuel R. Delany, R. A. Lafferty, and Barry Malzberg, although some relatively well-established people like John Brunner, Harlan Ellison, and, yes, Robert Silverberg, joined in the fun. My stories grew more and more experimental in mode — you can see it beginning to happen in "Sundance" and "Good News from the Vatican" — and most of them were published, now, in anthologies of original stories rather than in the conventional sf magazines.

What was fun for the writers, though, turned out to be not so much fun for the majority of the readers, who quite reasonably complained that if they wanted to read Joyce and Kafka, they'd go and read Joyce and Kafka. They didn't want their sf to be Joycified and Kafkaized. So they stayed away from the new fiction in droves, and by 1972 the revolution was pretty much over. We were heading into the era of *Star Wars*, the trilogy craze, and the return of literarily conservative action-based science fiction to the center of the stage.

One of the most powerful figures in the commercialization of science fiction at that time was the diminutive Judy-Lynn del Rey, a charming and ferociously determined woman whose private reading tastes inclined toward *Ulysses* but who knew, perhaps better than anyone else ever had, what the majority of sf readers wanted to buy. As a kind of side enterprise during her dynamic remaking of the field, she started a paperback anthology series called *Stellar,* and — despite my recent identification with the experimental side of science fiction — asked me, in May, 1973, to do a story for it.

Her stated policy was to bring back the good old kind of sf storytelling, as exemplified in the magazines of the 1950s, a golden age for readers like me. "I don't want mood pieces without plots," she warned. "I don't want vignettes; I don't want character sketches; and I don't want obvious extrapolations of current fads and newspaper stories. These yarns should have beginnings, middles, and ends. I want the writers to solve the problems they postulate...."

Since most of what I had been writing recently embodied most of the characteristics she thus decried, there was a certain incompatibility between Judy-Lynn's strongly voiced requirements and her equally strong insistence on having a Silverberg story for her first issue. And yet I had no real problem with her stated policy. My own tastes in sf had been formed largely in the early 1950s, when such writers as C. M. Kornbluth, Alfred Bester, James Blish, Theodore Sturgeon, and Fritz Leiber had been at the top of their form. I had always felt more comfortable with their kind of fiction than with the wilder stuff of fifteen years later; I thought myself rather a reactionary writer alongside people like Disch, Lafferty, Malzberg, or J. G. Ballard. And I thought "Schwartz Between the Galaxies," which I wrote in October, 1973, was a reasonably conservative story, too — definitely a story of the 1970s but not particularly experimental in form or tone.

Judy-Lynn bought it — it would have been discourteous not to, after urging me so strenuously to write something for her — but she obviously felt let down, even betrayed. Here she was putting together her theme-setting first issue, and here I was still trying to write *literature.* To her surprise and chagrin, though, the story was extremely popular — one of the five contenders for the Hugo award the following year — and was fairly widely anthologized afterward.

So I won the skirmish; but Judy-Lynn, bless her, won the war. Our little literary revolution ended in total rout, with the space sagas and fantasy trilogies that she published sweeping the more highbrow kind of science fiction into oblivion, and many of the literary-minded writers left science fiction, never to return.

I was among those who left, although, as you will note, I did come back after a while. But it seemed certain to me as 1974 began that my days as a science-fiction writer were over forever. For one thing, the work had become terribly hard: my work-sheets indicate that "Schwartz Between the Galaxies" took me close to three weeks to write. In happier days I could have written a whole *novel*, and a good one, in that time. Then, too, despite that Hugo nomination, I felt that the readers were turning away from my work. I was still getting on the awards ballots as frequently as ever, but I wasn't winning anything. That seemed symptomatic. The readers no longer understood me, and I felt I understood them all too well.

So in late 1973 I wrote one more short story — "In the House of Double Minds" — because I had promised it to an editor, and then I swore a mighty oath that I would never write short sf again. In the spring of 1974 I wrote the first of my two promised novels, *The Stochastic Man*. About six months later I launched into the second one, *Shadrach in the Furnace*, and finished it in the spring of 1975 after a horrendous battle to get the words down on paper.

That was it. I had spent two decades as a science-fiction writer, and had emerged out of my early hackwork to win a considerable reputation among connoisseurs, and now it was all over. I would never write again, I told myself. (And told anyone else who would listen, too.)

And I didn't. For a while, anyway.

This much is reality: Schwartz sits comfortably cocooned — passive, suspended — in a first-class passenger rack aboard a Japan Air Lines rocket, nine kilometers above the Coral Sea. And this much is fantasy: the same Schwartz has passage on a shining starship gliding silkily through the interstellar depths, en route at nine times the velocity of light from Betelgeuse IX to Rigel XXI, or maybe from Andromeda to the Lesser Magellanic.

There are no starships. Probably there never will be any. Here we are, a dozen decades after the flight of Apollo 11, and no human being goes anywhere except back and forth across the face of the little O, the Earth, for the planets are barren and the stars are beyond reach. That little O is too small for Schwartz. Too often it glazes for him; it turns to a nugget of dead porcelain; and lately he has formed the habit, when the world glazes, of taking refuge aboard that interstellar ship. So what JAL Flight 411 holds is merely his physical self, his shell, occupying a costly private cubicle on a slender 200-passenger vessel which, leaving Buenos Aires shortly after breakfast, has sliced westward along the Tropic of Capricorn for a couple of hours and will soon be landing at Papua's Torres Skyport. But his consciousness, his *anima,* the essential Schwartzness of him, soars between the galaxies.

What a starship it is! How marvelous its myriad passengers! Down its crowded corridors swarms a vast gaudy heterogeny of galactic creatures, natives of the worlds of Capella, Arcturus, Altair, Canopus, Polaris, Antares, beings both intelligent and articulate, methane-breathing or nitrogen-breathing or argon-breathing, spiny-skinned or skinless, many-armed or many-headed or altogether incorporeal, each a product of a distinct and distinctly unique and alien cultural heritage. Among these varied folk moves Schwartz, that superstar of anthropologists, that true heir to Kroeber and Morgan and Malinowski and Mead, delightedly devouring their delicious diversity. Whereas aboard this prosaic rocket, this planet-locked stratosphere needle, one cannot tell the Canadians from the Portuguese, the Portuguese from the Romanians, the Romanians from the Irish, unless they open their mouths, and sometimes not always then.

In his reveries he confers with creatures from the Fomalhaut system about digital circumcision; he tapes the melodies of the Achernarnian eye-flute; he learns of the sneeze-magic of Acrux, the sleep-ecstasies of Aldebaran, the asteroid-sculptors of Thuban. Then a smiling JAL stewardess parts the curtain of his cubicle and peers in at him, jolting him from one reality to another. She is blue-eyed, frizzy-haired, straight-nosed, thin-lipped, bronze-skinned, a genetic mishmash, your standard twenty-first-century-model mongrel human, perhaps Melanesian-Swedish-Turkish-Bolivian, perhaps Polish-Berber-Tatar-Welsh. Cheap intercontinental transit has done its deadly work: all Earth is a crucible, all the gene pools have melted into one indistinguishable fluid. Schwartz wonders about the recessivity of those blue eyes and arrives at no satisfactory solution. She is beautiful, at any rate. Her name is Dawn—o sweet neutral nonculture-bound cognomen!—and they have played at a flirtation, he and she, Dawn and Schwartz, at occasional moments of this short flight. Twinkling, she says softly, "We're getting ready for our landing, Dr. Schwartz. Are your restrictors in polarity?"

"I never unfastened them."

"Good." The blue eyes, warm, interested, meet his. "I have a layover in Papua tonight," she says.

"That's nice."

"Let's have a drink while we're waiting for them to unload the baggage," she suggests with cheerful bluntness. "All right?"

"I suppose," he says casually. "Why not?" Her availability bores him: somehow he enjoys the obsolete pleasures of the chase. Once such easiness in a woman like this would have excited him, but no longer. Schwartz is forty years old, tall, square-shouldered, sturdy, a showcase for the peasant genes of his rugged Irish mother. His close-cropped black hair is flecked with gray; many women find that interesting. One rarely sees gray hair now. He dresses simply but well, in sandals and Socratic tunic. Predictably, his physical attractiveness, both within his domestic sixness and without, has increased with his professional success. He is confident, sure of his powers, and he radiates an infectious assurance. This month alone eighty million people have heard his lectures.

She picks up the faint weariness in his voice. "You don't sound eager. Not interested?"

"Hardly that."

"What's wrong, then? Feeling sub, Professor?"

Schwartz shrugs. "Dreadfully sub. Body like dry bone. Mind like dead ashes." He smiles, full force, depriving his words of all their weight.

She registers mock anguish. "That sounds bad," she says. "That sounds awful!"

"I'm only quoting Chuang Tzu. Pay no attention to me. Actually, I feel fine, just a little stale."

"Too many skyports?"

He nods. "Too much of a sameness wherever I go." He thinks of a star-bright, top-deck bubble dome where three boneless Spicans do a twining dance of propitiation to while away the slow hours of nine-light travel. "I'll be all right," he tells her. "It's a date."

Her hybrid face flows with relief and anticipation. "See you in Papua," she tells him, and winks, and moves jauntily down the aisle.

Papua. By cocktail time Schwartz will be in Port Moresby. Tonight he lectures at the University of Papua; yesterday it was Montevideo; the day after tomorrow it will be Bangkok. He is making the grand academic circuit. This is his year: he is very big, suddenly, in anthropological circles, since the publication of *The Mask Beneath the Skin*. From continent to continent he flashes, sharing his wisdom, Monday in Montreal, Tuesday Veracruz, Wednesday Montevideo, Thursday — Thursday? He crossed the international date line this morning, and he does not remember whether he has entered Thursday or Tuesday, though yesterday was surely Wednesday. Schwartz is certain only that this is July and the year is 2083, and there are moments when he is not even sure of that.

The JAL rocket enters the final phase of its landward plunge. Papua waits, sleek, vitrescent. The world has a glassy sheen again. He lets his spirit drift happily back to the gleaming starship making its swift way across the whirling constellations.

***

He found himself in the starship's busy lower-deck lounge, having a drink with his traveling companion, Pitkin, the Yale economist. Why Pitkin, that coarse, florid little man? With all of real and imaginary humanity to choose from, why had his unconscious elected to make him share this fantasy with such a boor?

"Look," Pitkin said, winking and leering. "There's your girlfriend."

The entry-iris had opened and the Antarean not-male had come in.

"Quit it," Schwartz snapped. "You know there's no such thing going on."

"Haven't you been chasing her for days?"

"She's not a 'her,'" Schwartz said.

Pitkin guffawed. "Such precision! Such scholarship! *She's* not a *her*, he says!" He gave Schwartz a broad nudge. "To you she's a she, friend, and don't try to kid me."

Schwartz had to admit there was some justice to Pitkin's vulgar innuendos. He did find the Antarean — a slim yellow-eyed ebony-skinned upright humanoid, sinuous and glossy, with tapering elongated limbs and a seal's fluid grace — powerfully attractive. Nor could he help thinking of the Antarean as feminine. That attitude was hopelessly culture-bound and species-bound, he knew; in fact the alien had cautioned him that terrestrial sexual distinctions were irrelevant in the Antares system, that if Schwartz insisted on thinking of "her" in genders, "she" could be considered only the negative of male, with no implication of biological femaleness.

He said patiently, "I've told you. The Antarean's neither male nor female as we understand those concepts. If we happen to perceive the Antarean as feminine, that's the result of our own cultural conditioning. If you want to believe that my interest in this being is sexual, go ahead, but I assure you that it's purely professional."

"Sure. You're only studying her."

"In a sense I am. And she's studying me. On her native world she has the status-frame of 'watcher-of-life,' which seems to translate into the Antarean equivalent of an anthropologist."

"How lovely for you both. She's your first alien and you're her first Jew."

"Stop calling her *her*," Schwartz hissed.

"But you've been doing it!"

Schwartz closed his eyes. "My grandmother told me never to get mixed up with economists. Their thinking is muddy and their breath is bad, she said. She also warned me against Yale men. Perverts of the intellect, she called them. So here I am cooped up on an interstellar ship with five hundred alien creatures and one fellow human, and he has to be an economist from Yale."

"Next trip travel with your grandmother instead."

"Go away," Schwartz said. "Stop lousing up my fantasies. Go peddle your dismal science somewhere else. You see those Delta Aurigans over there? Climb into their bottle and tell them all about the Gross Global Product." Schwartz smiled at the Antarean, who had purchased a drink, something that glittered an iridescent blue, and was approaching them. "Go on," Schwartz murmured.

"Don't worry," Pitkin said. "I wouldn't want to crowd you." He vanished into the motley crowd.

The Antarean said, "The Capellans are dancing, Schwartz."

"I'd like to see that. Too damned noisy in here anyway." Schwartz stared into the alien's vertical-slitted citreous eyes. Cat's eyes, he thought. Panther's eyes. The Antarean's gaze was focused, as usual, on Schwartz's mouth: other worlds, other customs. He felt a strange, unsettling tremor of desire. Desire of what, though? It was a sensation of pure need, nonspecific, certainly nonsexual. "I think I'll take a look. Will you come with me?"

***

The Papua rocket has landed. Schwartz, leaning across the narrow table in the skyport's lounge, says to the stewardess in a low, intense tone, "My life was in crisis. All my values were becoming meaningless. I was discovering that my chosen profession was empty, foolish, as useless as — as playing chess."

"How awful," Dawn whispers gently.

"You can see why. You go all over the world, you see a thousand skyports a year. Everything the same everywhere. The same clothes, the same slang, the same magazines, the same styles of architecture and decor."

"Yes."

"International homogeneity. Worldwide uniformity. Can you understand what it's like to be an anthropologist in a world where there are no primitives left, Dawn? Here we sit on the island of Papua — you know, headhunters, animism, body-paint, the drums at sunset, the bone through the nose — and look at the Papuans in their business robes all around us. Listen to them exchanging stock-market tips, talking baseball, recommending restaurants in Paris and barbers in Johannesburg. It's no different anywhere else. In a single century we've transformed the planet into one huge sophisticated plastic western industrial state. The TV relay satellites, the two-hour intercontinental rockets, the breakdown of religious exclusivism and genetic taboo have mongrelized every culture, don't you see? You visit the Zuni and they have plastic African masks on the wall. You visit the Bushmen and they have Japanese-made Hopi-motif ashtrays. It's all just so much interior decoration, and underneath the carefully selected primitive motifs there's the same universal pseudo-American sensibility, whether you're in the Kalahari or the Amazon rain forest. Do you comprehend what's happened, Dawn?"

"It's such a terrible loss," she says sadly. She is trying very hard to be sympathetic, but he senses she is waiting for him to finish his sermon and invite her to share his hotel room. He *will* invite her, but there is no stopping him once he has launched into his one great theme.

"Cultural diversity is gone from the world," he says. "Religion is dead; true poetry is dead; inventiveness is dead; individuality is dead. Poetry. Listen to this." In a high monotone he chants:

In beauty I walk
With beauty before me I walk
With beauty behind me I walk
With beauty above me I walk
With beauty above and about me I walk

It is finished in beauty
It is finished in beauty

He has begun to perspire heavily. His chanting has created an odd sphere of silence in his immediate vicinity; heads are turning, eyes are squinting. "Navaho," he says. "The Night Way, a nine-day chant, a vision, a spell. Where are the Navaho now? Go to Arizona and they'll chant for you, yes, for a price, but they don't know what the words mean, and chances are the singers are only one-fourth Navaho, or one-eighth, or maybe just Hopi hired to dress in Navaho costumes, because the real Navaho, if any are left, are off in Mexico City hired to be Aztecs. So much is gone. Listen." He chants again, more piercingly even than before:

The animal runs, it passes, it dies. And it is the great cold.
It is the great cold of the night, it is the dark.
The bird flies, it passes, it dies. And it is—

"JAL FLIGHT 411 BAGGAGE IS NOW UNLOADING ON CONCOURSE FOUR," a mighty mechanical voice cries.

—the great cold.
It is the great cold of the night, it is the dark.

"JAL FLIGHT 411 BAGGAGE..."

The fish flees, it passes, it dies. And—

"People are staring," Dawn says uncomfortably.
" —ON CONCOURSE FOUR."
"Let them stare. Do them some good. That's a Pygmy chant, from Gabon, in equatorial Africa. Pygmies? There are no more Pygmies. Everybody's two meters tall. And what do we sing? Listen. Listen." He gestures fiercely at the cloud of tiny golden loudspeakers floating near the ceiling. A mush of music comes from them: the current popular favorite. Savagely he mouths words: *"Star...far...here...near.* Playing in every skyport right now, all over the world." She smiles thinly. Her hand reaches toward his, covers it, presses against the knuckles. He is dizzy. The crowd, the eyes, the music, the drink. The plastic. Everything shines. Porcelain. Porcelain. The planet vitrifies. "Tom?" she asks uneasily. "Is anything the matter?" He laughs, blinks, coughs, shivers. He hears her calling for help, and then he feels his soul swooping outward, toward the galactic blackness.

***

With the Antarean not-male beside him, Schwartz peered through the viewport, staring in awe and fascination at the seductive vision of the Capellans coiling and recoiling outside the ship. Not all the passengers on this voyage had cozy staterooms like his. The Capellans were too big to come on board, and in any case they preferred never to let themselves be enclosed inside metal walls. They traveled just alongside the starship, basking like slippery whales in the piquant radiations of space. So long as they kept within twenty meters of the hull they would be inside the effective field of the Rabinowitz rive, which swept ship and contents and associated fellow travelers toward Rigel, or the Lesser Magellanic, or was it one of the Pleiades toward which they were bound at a cool nine lights?

He watched the Capellans moving beyond the shadow of the ship in tracks of shining white. Blue, glossy green, and velvet black, they coiled and swam, and every track was a flash of golden fire. "They have a dangerous beauty," Schwartz whispered. "Do you hear them calling? I do."

"What do they say?"

"They say, '*Come to me, come to me, come to me!*'"

"Go to them, then," said the Antarean simply. "Step through the hatch."

"And perish?"

"And enter into your next transition. Poor Schwartz! Do you love your present body so?"

"My present body isn't so bad. Do you think I'm likely to get another one some day?"

"No?"

"No," Schwartz said. "This one is all I get. Isn't it that way with you?"

"At the Time of Openings I receive my next housing. That will be fifty years from now. What you see is the fifth form I have been given to wear."

"Will the next be as beautiful as this?"

"All forms are beautiful," the Antarean said. "You find me attractive?"

"Of course."

A slitted wink. A bobbing nod toward the viewport. "As attractive as *those?*"

Schwartz laughed. "Yes. In a different way."

Coquettishly the Antarean said, "If I were out there, you would walk through the hatch into space?"

"I might. If they gave me a spacesuit and taught me how to use it."

"But not otherwise? Suppose I were out there right now. I could live in space five, ten, maybe fifteen minutes. I am there and I say, '*Come to me, Schwartz, come to me!*' What do you do?"

"I don't think I'm all that much self-destructive."

"To die for love, though! To make a transition for the sake of beauty."

"No. Sorry."

The Antarean pointed toward the undulating Capellans. "If *they* asked you, you would go."

"They are asking me," he said.

"And you refuse the invitation?"

"So far. So far."

The Antarean laughed an Antarean laugh, a thick silvery snort. "Our voyage will last many weeks more. One of these days, I think, you will go to them."

***

"You were unconscious at least five minutes," Dawn says. "You gave everyone a scare. Are you sure you ought to go through with tonight's lecture?

Nodding, Schwartz says, "I'll be all right. I'm a little tired, is all. Too many time zones this week." They stand on the terrace of his hotel room. Night is coming on, already, here in late afternoon: it is midwinter in the Southern Hemisphere, though the fragrance of tropic blossoms perfumes the air. The first few stars have appeared. He has never really known which star is which. That bright one, he thinks, could be Rigel, and that one Sirius, and perhaps this is Deneb over there. And this? Can this be red Antares, in the heart of the Scorpion, or is it only Mars? Because of his collapse at the skyport he has been able to beg off the customary faculty reception and the formal dinner; pleading the need for rest, he has arranged to have a simple snack at his hotel room, *a deux*. In two hours they will come for him and take him to the University to speak. Dawn watches him closely. Perhaps she is worried about his health, perhaps she is only waiting for him to make his move toward her. There's time for all that later, he figures. He would rather talk now. Warming up for the audience, he seizes his earlier thread:

"For a long time I didn't understand what had taken place. I grew up insular, cut off from reality, a New York boy, bright mind and a library card. I read all the anthropological classics, *Patterns of Culture* and *Coming of Age in Samoa* and *Life of a South African Tribe* and the rest, and I dreamed of field trips, collecting myths and grammars and folkways and artifacts and all that, until when I was twenty-five I finally got out into the field and started to discover I had gone into a dead science. We have only one worldwide culture now, with local variants but no basic divergences — there's nothing primitive left on Earth, *and there are no other planets*. Not inhabited ones. I can't go to Mars or Venus or Saturn and study the natives. What natives? And we can't reach the stars. All I have to work with is

Earth. I was thirty years old when the whole thing clicked together for me and I knew I had wasted my life."

She says, "But surely there was something for you to study on Earth."

"One culture, rootless and homogeneous. That's work for a sociologist, not for me. I'm a romantic, I'm an exotic, I want strangeness, difference. Look, we can never have any real perspective on our own time and lives. The sociologists try to attain it, but all they get is a mound of raw indigestible data. Insight comes later — two, five, ten generations later. But one way we've always been able to learn about ourselves is by studying alien cultures, studying them *completely,* and defining ourselves by measuring what they are that we aren't. The cultures have to be isolated, though. The anthropologist himself corrupts that isolation in the Heisenberg sense when he comes around with his camera and scanners and starts asking questions, but we can compensate, more or less, for the inevitable damage a lone observer causes. We can't compensate when our whole culture collides with another and absorbs and obliterates it. Which we technological-mechanical people now have done everywhere. One day I woke up and saw there were no alien cultures left. Hah! Crushing revelation! Schwartz's occupation is gone!"

"What did you do?"

"For years I was in an absolute funk. I taught, I studied, I went through the motions, knowing it was all meaningless. All I was doing was looking at records of vanished cultures left by earlier observers and trying to cudgel new meanings. Secondary sources, stale findings: I was an evaluator of dry bones, not a gatherer of evidence. Paleontology. Dinosaurs are interesting, but what do they tell you about the contemporary world and the meaning of its patterns? Dry bones, Dawn, dry bones. Despair. And then a clue. I had this Nigerian student, this Ibo — well, basically an Ibo, but she's got some Israeli in her and I think Chinese — and we grew very close, she was as close to me as anybody in my own sixness, and I told her my troubles. I'm going to give it all up, I said, because it isn't what I expected it to be. She laughed at me and said, What right do you have to be upset because the world doesn't live up to your expectations? Reshape your life, Tom; you can't reshape the world. I said, But how? And she said, Look inward, find the primitive in yourself, see what made you what you are, what made today's culture what it is, see how these alien streams have flowed together. Nothing's been lost here, only merged. Which made me think. Which gave me a new way of looking at things. Which sent me on an inward quest. It took me three years to grasp the patterns, to come to an understanding of what our planet has become, and only after I accepted the planet —"

It seems to him that he has been talking forever. Talking. Talking. But he can no longer hear his own voice. There is only a distant buzz.

"After I accepted —"
A distant buzz.
"What was I saying?" he asks.
"After you accepted the planet —"
"After I accepted the planet," he says, "that I could begin —" *Buzz.*
Buzz. "That I could begin to accept myself."

***

He was drawn toward the Spicans too, not so much for themselves —
they were oblique, elliptical characters, self-contained and self-satisfied,
hard to approach — as for the apparently psychedelic drug they took in
some sacramental way before the beginning of each of their interminable
ritual dances. Each time he had watched them take the drug, they had
seemingly made a point of extending it toward him, as if inviting him, as
if tempting him, before popping it into their mouths. He felt baited; he felt
pulled.

There were three Spicans on board, slender creatures two and a half
meters long, with flexible cylindrical bodies and small stubby limbs. Their
skins were reptilian, dry and smooth, deep green with yellow bands, but
their eyes were weirdly human, large liquid-brown eyes, sad Levantine
eyes, the eyes of unfortunate medieval travelers transformed by
enchantment into serpents. Schwartz had spoken with them several times.
They understood English well enough — all galactic races did; Schwartz
imagined it would become the interstellar *lingua franca* as it had on Earth —
but the construction of their vocal organs was such that they had no way
of speaking it, and they relied instead on small translating machines hung
around their necks that converted their soft whispered hisses into amber
words pulsing across a screen.

Cautiously, the third or fourth time he spoke with them, he expressed
polite interest in their drug. They told him it enabled them to make contact
with the central forces of the universe. He replied that there were such
drugs on Earth, too, and that he used them frequently, that they gave him
great insight into the workings of the cosmos. They showed some curiosity,
perhaps even intense curiosity: reading their eyes was difficult and the
tone of their voices gave no clues. He took his elegant leather-bound drug
case from his pouch and showed them what he had: learitonin,
psilocerebrin, siddharthin, and acid-57. He described the effects of each
and suggested an exchange, any of his for an equivalent dose of the
shriveled orange fungoid they nibbled. They conferred. Yes, they said, we
will do this. But not now. Not until the proper moment. Schwartz knew
better than to ask them when that would be. He thanked them and put his
drugs away.

Pitkin, who had watched the interchange from the far side of the lounge, came striding fiercely toward him as the Spicans glided off. "What are you up to now?" he demanded.

"How about minding your own business?" Schwartz said amiably.

"You're trading pills with those snakes, aren't you?"

"Let's call it field research."

"Research? Research? What are you going to do, trip on that orange stuff of theirs?"

"I might," Schwartz said.

"How do you know what its effects on the human metabolism might be? You could end up blind or paralyzed or crazy or—"

"—or illuminated," Schwartz said. "Those are the risks one takes in the field. The early anthropologists who unhesitatingly sampled peyote and yage and ololiuqui accepted those risks, and—"

"But those were drugs that *humans* were using. You have no way of telling how—oh, what's the use, Schwartz? Research, he calls it. Research." Pitkin sneered. *"Junkie!"*

Schwartz matched him sneer for sneer. *"Economist!"*

***

The house is a decent one tonight, close to three thousand, every seat in the University's great horseshoe-shaped auditorium taken, and a video relay besides, beaming his lecture to all Papua and half of Indonesia. Schwartz stands on the dais like a demigod under a brilliant no-glare spotlight. Despite his earlier weariness he is in good form now, gestures broad and forceful, eyes commanding, voice deep and resonant, words flowing freely. "Only one planet," he says, "one small and crowded planet, on which all cultures converge to a drab and depressing sameness. How sad that is! How tiny we make ourselves, when we make ourselves to resemble one another!" He flings his arms upward. "Look to the stars, the unattainable stars! Imagine, if you can, the millions of worlds that orbit those blazing suns beyond the night's darkness! Speculate with me on other peoples, other ways, other gods. Beings of every imaginable form, alien in appearance but not grotesque, not hideous, for all life is beautiful— beings that breathe gases strange to us, beings of immense size, beings of many limbs or of none, beings to whom death is a divine culmination of existence, beings who never die, beings who bring forth their young a thousand at a time, beings who do not reproduce—all the infinite possibilities of the infinite universe!

"Perhaps on each of those worlds it is as it has become here. One intelligent species, one culture, the eternal convergence. But the many worlds together offer a vast spectrum of variety. And now, share this vision with me! I see a ship voyaging from star to star, a spaceliner of the future, and aboard that ship is a sampling of many species, many cultures, a random scoop out of the galaxy's fantastic diversity. That ship is like a little cosmos, a small world, enclosed, sealed. How exciting to be aboard it, to encounter in that little compass such richness of cultural variation! Now our own world was once like that starship, a little cosmos, bearing with it all the thousands of Earthborn cultures. Hopi and Eskimo and Aztec and Kwakiutl and Arapesh and Orokolo and all the rest. In the course of our voyage we have come to resemble one another too much, and it has impoverished the lives of all of us, because—" He falters suddenly. He feels faint, and grasps the sides of the lectern. "Because—" The spotlight, he thinks. In my eyes. Not supposed to glare like that, but it's blinding. Got to have them move it. "In the course—the course of our voyage—" What's happening? Breaking into a sweat, now. Pain in my chest. My heart? Wait, slow up, catch your breath. That light in my eyes—

***

"Tell me," Schwartz said earnestly, "What it's like to know you'll have ten successive bodies and live more than a thousand years."

"First tell me," said the Antarean, "what it's like to know you'll live ninety years or less and perish forever."

***

Somehow he continues. The pain in his chest grows more intense, he cannot focus his eyes; he believes he will lose consciousness at any moment and may even have lost it already at least once, and yet he continues. Clinging to the lectern, he outlines the program he developed in *The Mask Beneath the Skin*. A rebirth of tribalism without a revival of ugly nationalism. The quest for a renewed sense of kinship with the past. A sharp reduction in nonessential travel, especially tourism. Heavy taxation of exported artifacts, including films and video shows. An attempt to create independent cultural units on Earth once again while maintaining present levels of economic and political interdependence. Relinquishment of materialistic technological-industrial values. New searches for fundamental meanings. An ethnic revival, before it is too late, among those cultures of mankind that have only recently shed their traditional folkways. (He repeats and embellishes this point particularly, for the benefit of the Papuans before him, the great-grandchildren of cannibals.)

The discomfort and confusion come and go as he unreels his themes. He builds and builds, crying out passionately for an end to the homogenization of Earth, and gradually the physical symptoms leave him, all but a faint vertigo. But a different malaise seizes him as he nears his peroration. His voice becomes, to him, a far-off quacking, meaningless and foolish. He has said all this a thousand times, always to great ovations, but who listens? Who listens? Everything seems hollow tonight, mechanical, absurd. An ethnic revival? Shall these people before him revert to their loincloths and their pig roasts? His starship is a fantasy; his dream of a diverse Earth is mere silliness. What is, will be. And yet he pushes on toward his conclusion. He takes his audience back to that starship, he creates a horde of fanciful beings for them. He completes the metaphor by sketching the structures of half a dozen vanished "primitive" cultures of Earth, he chants the chants of the Navaho, the Gabon Pygmies, the Ashanti, the Mundugumor. It is over. Cascades of applause engulf him. He holds his place until members of the sponsoring committee come to him and help him down: they have perceived his distress. "It's nothing," he gasps. "The lights—too bright—" Dawn is at his side. She hands him a drink, something cool. Two of the sponsors begin to speak of a reception for him in the Green Room. "Fine," Schwartz says. "Glad to." Dawn murmurs a protest. He shakes her off. "My obligation," he tells her. "Meet community leaders. Faculty people. I'm feeling better now. Honestly." Swaying, trembling, he lets them lead him away.

***

"A Jew," the Antarean said. "You call yourself a Jew, but what is this exactly? A clan, a sept, a moiety, a tribe, a nation, what? Can you explain?"

"You understand what a religion is?"

"Of course."

"Judaism—Jewishness—it's one of Earth's major religions."

"You are therefore a priest?"

"Not at all. I don't even practice Judaism. But my ancestors did, and therefore I consider myself Jewish, even though—"

"It is an hereditary religion, then," the Antarean said, "that does not require its members to observe its rites?"

"In a sense," said Schwartz desperately. "More an hereditary cultural group, actually, evolving out of a common religious outlook no longer relevant."

"Ah. And the cultural traits of Jewishness that define it and separate you from the majority of humankind are—?"

"Well—" Schwartz hesitated. "There's a complicated dietary code, a rite of circumcision for newborn males, a rite of passage for male adolescents, a language of scripture, a vernacular language that Jews all around the world more or less understand, and plenty more, including a certain intangible sense of clannishness and certain attitudes, such as a peculiar self-deprecating style of humor—"

"You observe the dietary code? You understand the language of scripture?"

"Not exactly," Schwartz admitted. "In fact I don't do anything that's specifically Jewish except think of myself as a Jew and adopt many of the characteristically Jewish personality modes, which however are not uniquely Jewish any longer—they can be traced among Italians, for example, and to some extent among Greeks. I'm speaking of Italians and Greeks of the late twentieth century, of course. Nowadays—" It was all becoming a terrible muddle. "Nowadays—"

"It would seem," said the Antarean, "that you are a Jew only because your maternal and paternal gene-givers were Jews, and they—"

"No, not quite. Not my mother, just my father, and he was Jewish only on his father's side, but even my grandfather never observed the customs, and—"

"I think this has grown too confusing," said the Antarean. "I withdraw the entire inquiry. Let us speak instead of my own traditions. The Time of Openings, for example, may be understood as—"

***

In the Green Room some eighty or a hundred distinguished Papuans press toward him, offering congratulations. "Absolutely right," they say. "A global catastrophe." "Our last chance to save our culture." Their skins are chocolate-tinted but their faces betray the genetic mishmash that is their ancestry: perhaps they call themselves Arapesh, Mundugumor, Tchambuli, Mafulu, in the way that he calls himself a Jew, but they have been liberally larded with chromosomes contributed by Chinese, Japanese, Europeans, Africans, everything. They dress in International Contemporary. They speak slangy, lively English. Schwartz feels seasick. "You look dazed," Dawn whispers. He smiles bravely. Body like dry bone. Mind like dead ashes. He is introduced to a tribal chieftain, tall, gray-haired, who looks and speaks like a professor, a lawyer, a banker. What, will these people return to the hills for the ceremony of the yam harvest? Will newborn girl-children be abandoned, cords uncut, skins unwashed, if their fathers do not need more girls? Will boys entering manhood submit to the expensive services of the initiator who scarifies them with the teeth of crocodiles? The crocodiles are gone. The shamans have become stockbrokers.

Suddenly he cannot breathe.

"Get me out of here," Schwartz mutters hoarsely, choking.

Dawn, with stewardess efficiency, chops a path for him through the mob. The sponsors, concerned, rush to his aid. He is floated swiftly back to the hotel in a glistening little bubble-car. Dawn helps him to bed. Reviving, he reaches for her.

"You don't have to," she says. "You've had a rough day."

He persists. He embraces her and takes her, quickly, fiercely, and they move together for a few minutes and it ends and he sinks back, exhausted, stupefied. She gets a cool cloth and pats his forehead and urges him to rest. "Bring me my drugs," he says. He wants siddharthin, but she misunderstands, probably deliberately, and offers him something blue and bulky, a sleeping pill, and, too weary to object, he takes it. Even so, it seems to be hours before sleep comes.

He dreams he is at the skyport, boarding the rocket for Bangkok, and instantly he is debarking at Bangkok—just like Port Moresby, only more humid—and he delivers his speech to a horde of enthusiastic Thais, while rockets flicker about him, carrying him to skyport after skyport, and the Thais blur and become Japanese, who are transformed into Mongols, who become Uighurs, who become Iranians, who become Sudanese, who become Zambians, who become Chileans, and all look alike, all look alike, all look alike.

***

The Spicans hovered above him, weaving, bobbing, swaying like cobras about to strike. But their eyes, warm and liquid, were sympathetic: loving, even. He felt the flow of their compassion. If they had had the sort of musculature that enabled them to smile, they would be smiling tenderly, he knew.

One of the aliens leaned close. The little translating device dangled toward Schwartz like a holy medallion. He narrowed his eyes, concentrating as intently as he could on the amber words flashing quickly across the screen.

"…has come. We shall…"

"Again, please," Schwartz said. "I missed some of what you were saying."

"The moment…has come. We shall…make the exchange of sacraments now."

"Sacraments?"

"Drugs."

"Drugs, yes. Yes. Of course." Schwartz groped in his pouch. He felt the cool, smooth leather skin of his drug case. Leather? Snakeskin, maybe. Anyway. He drew it forth. "Here," he said. "Siddharthin, learitonin, psilocerebrin, acid-57. Take your pick." The Spicans selected three small blue siddharthins. "Very good," Schwartz said. "The most transcendental of all. And now—"

The longest of the aliens proffered a ball of dried orange fungus the size of Schwartz's thumbnail.

"It is an equivalent dose. We give it to you."

"Equivalent to all three of my tablets, or to one?"

"Equivalent. It will give you peace."

Schwartz smiled. There was a time for asking questions and a time for unhesitating action. He took the fungus and reached for a glass of water.

"Wait!" Pitkin cried, appearing suddenly. "What are you—"

"Too late," Schwartz said serenely, and swallowed the Spican drug in one joyous gulp.

***

The nightmares go on and on. He circles the Earth like the Flying Dutchman, like the Wandering Jew, skyport to skyport to skyport, an unending voyage from nowhere to nowhere. Obliging committees meet him and convey him to his hotel. Sometimes the committee members are contemporary types, indistinguishable from one another, with standard faces, standard clothing, the all-purpose new-model hybrid unihuman, and sometimes they are consciously ethnic, elaborately decked out in feathers and paint and tribal emblems, but their faces, too, are standard behind the gaudy regalia, their slang is the slang of Uganda and Tierra del Fuego and Nepal, and it seems to Schwartz that these masqueraders are, if anything, less authentic, less honest, than the other sort, who at least are true representatives of their era. So it is hopeless either way. He lashes at his pillow, he groans, he wakens. Instantly Dawn's arms enfold him. He sobs incoherent phrases into her clavicle and she murmurs soothing sounds against his forehead. He is having some sort of breakdown, he realizes: a new crisis of values, a shattering of the philosophical synthesis that has allowed him to get through the last few years. He is bound to the wheel; he spins, he spins, he spins, traversing the continents, getting nowhere. There is no place to go. No. There is one, just one, a place where he will find peace, where the universe will be as he needs it to be. Go there, Schwartz. Go and stay as long as you can. "Is there anything I can *do?*" Dawn asks. He shivers and shakes his head. "Take this," she says, and gives him some sort of pill. Another tranquilizer. All right. All right. The world has turned to porcelain. His skin feels like a plastic coating. Away, away, to the ship. To the ship! "So long," Schwartz says.

***

Outside the ship the Capellans twist and spin in their ritual dance as, weightless and without mass, they are swept toward the rim of the galaxy at nine times the velocity of light. They move with a grace that is astonishing for creatures of such tremendous bulk. A dazzling light that emanates from the center of the universe strikes their glossy skin and, rebounding, resonates all up and down the spectrum, splintering into brilliant streamers of ultrared, infraviolet, exoyellow. All the cosmos glows and shimmers. A single perfect note of music comes out of the remote distance and, growing closer, swells in an infinite crescendo. Schwartz trembles at the beauty of all he perceives.

Beside him stands the seal-slick Antarean. She—definitely *she*, no doubt of it, *she*—plucks at his arm and whispers, "Will you go to them?"

"Yes. Yes, of course."

"So will I. Wherever you go."

"Now," Schwartz says. He reaches for the lever that opens the hatch. He pulls down. The side of the starship swings open.

The Antarean looks deep into his eyes and says blissfully, "I have never told you my name. My name is Dawn."

Together they float through the hatch into space.

The blackness receives them gently. There is no chill, no pressure at the lungs, no discomfort at all. He is surrounded by luminous surges, by throbbing mantles of pure color, as though he has entered the heart of an aurora. He and Dawn swim toward the Capellans, and the huge beings welcome them with deep, glad, booming cries. Dawn joins the dance at once, moving her sinuous limbs with extravagant ease; Schwartz will do the same in a moment, but first he turns to face the starship, hanging in space close by him like a vast coppery needle, and in a voice that could shake universes he calls, "Come, friends! Come, all of you! Come dance with us!" And they come, pouring through the hatch, the Spicans first, then all the rest, the infinite multitude of beings, the travelers from Fomalhaut and Achernar and Acrux and Aldebaran, from Thuban and Arcturus and Altair, from Polaris and Canopus and Sirius and Rigel, hundreds of star-creatures spilling happily out of the vessel, bursting forth, all of them, even Pitkin, poor little Pitkin, everyone joining hands and tentacles and tendrils and whatever, forming a great ring of light across space, everyone locked in a cosmic harmony, everyone dancing. Dancing. Dancing.

FOUR

The 1980s

THE 1980s

INTRODUCTION

The 1980s were a period of restabilization and reintegration, both for me and for the world in general, after the wilder times of the immediately previous years. Sure, plenty went wrong during the new decade. Plenty always does, decade in, decade out. But during the 1980s the economic troubles that had plagued the United States for fifteen years began to end: inflation, which had reached levels of historic horrendousness, leveled off and started to drop, and corporate productivity underwent a great increase, leading to a great surge in national prosperity. The ever-troublesome Soviet Union became less troublesome under its new leader, Mikhail Gorbachev, and, although we did not yet suspect that the USSR was entering its final days, international tensions eased noticeably. Some of the sociocultural dislocations of the previous decade were repaired: there was something of a boom in marriage and childbearing, both of which had been out of fashion for a long time. And so forth: not a perfect time, but a quieter time, at least, a time of healing for many.

My personal life became far less stormy as well. I extricated myself at last from my collapsed first marriage and established a relationship with the woman I had met years before in Houston, a writer named Karen Haber, who became my second wife in 1987. And, as I describe below, I emerged from a time of crisis in my writing career, came to terms (as well as I ever am likely to) with the complexities and contradictions of my goals as a science-fiction writer, and got back to work on a regular basis. As the publishing world changed, not necessarily for the better, I found it necessary to move from publisher to publisher, but always landed on my feet. New awards came to me — another Nebula, another Hugo. It was now more than thirty years since the publication of my first stories, and I was beginning to turn into something like an elder statesman of the field.

THE FAR SIDE OF THE BELL-SHAPED CURVE
(1980)

INTRODUCTION

After lying fallow for more than four years, my mind suddenly presented me with a novel that I could not refuse to write. And so I came out of my permanent and irrevocable retirement to produce *Lord Valentine's Castle*, which I completed in the spring of 1979.

Even after finishing that long and complicated novel, I had no desire to go back to short-story writing. Short-story writing is hard on the nerves: you have no room to make any real mistakes, by which I mean that every word has to count, every line of dialogue has to serve three or four simultaneous purposes, every scene has to sweep the story inexorably along toward the culminating moment of insight that is the classic short-story payoff. In a novel you can go off course for whole chapters at a time and no one will mind; you may even find yourself being praised for the wonderful breadth of your concept. But a short story with so much as half an irrelevant page is a sad, lame thing, and even the casual and uncritical reader is aware that something is wrong with it.

Having been through the tensions of short-story creation so many times over a twenty-year period, I resolved to excuse myself from further struggle with the form. In a collection of my stories published in 1978 I said, "I suppose I might someday write another short story, but it has been almost five years since the last and I see no sign that the impulse is coming over me."

I felt only relief, no regret, at giving up short stories. The short form was a challenge I felt no further need to meet. You needed a stunning idea, for one thing — the ideal science-fiction short story, I think, should amaze and delight — and you had to develop it with cunning and craft, working at the edge of your nervous system every moment, polishing and repolishing to hide all those extraneous knees and elbows. Doing a good short story meant a week or two of tough work, bringing an immediate cash reward of about $250, and then maybe $100 every year or two thereafter if you had written something that merited reprinting in anthologies. Though money isn't the most important factor in a writer's life (if it were, we'd all be writing the most debased junk possible), it is a consideration, especially when a good short story takes fifty or a hundred working hours, as mine were tending to take by 1973. At $2.50 an hour short stories hardly seemed worth the effort.

But then came a magazine called *Omni*.

It was printed on slick, shiny paper and its publishers understood a great deal about the techniques of promotion, and it started its life with a circulation about six times as great as any science-fiction magazine had ever managed to achieve. After some comings and goings in the editorial chair the job of fiction editor went to my old friend Ben Bova, who began to hint broadly that it would be a nice idea if I wrote a short story for him. He mentioned a sum of money. It was approximately as much as I had been paid for each of my novels prior to the year 1968. Though cash return, as I've just said, is not the most important factor in a writer's life, the amount of money Ben mentioned was at least capable of causing me to rethink my antipathy to short-story writing.

By the time I was through rethinking, however, Bova had moved upstairs to become *Omni*'s executive editor. The new fiction editor was another old friend of mine, the veteran science-fiction writer Robert Sheckley, who also thought I ought to be writing stories for *Omni*. All through 1979 he and Bova sang their siren song to me, and in the first month of the new year I gave in. I phoned Sheckley and somewhat timidly told him I was willing to risk my nervous system on one more short story after all. "He's going to do it," I heard Sheckley call across the office to Bova. It was as though they had just talked Laurence Olivier into doing one more Hamlet. So much fuss over one short story!

But for me it was a big thing indeed: at that moment short-story writing seemed to me more difficult than writing novels, more difficult than learning Sanskrit, more difficult than winning the Olympic broad-jump. I had promised to write a story, though; and I sat down to try. Though in an earlier phase of my career I had thought nothing of turning out three or four short stories a week, it took me about five working days to get the opening page of this one written satisfactorily, and I assure you that that week was no fun at all. But then, magically, the barriers dissolved, the words began to flow, and in a couple of days the rest of the story emerged. "Our Lady of the Sauropods," I called it, and when *Omni* published it in the September, 1980 issue, the cover announced, "Robert Silverberg Returns!" I imagined the puzzled readers of *Omni*, who surely were unaware that it was seven years since I had deigned to write short stories, turning to each other and saying, "Why, wherever has he been?"

Having done it once, I realized I could do it again. Bob Sheckley was asking for more; and in the summer of 1980 an idea for a fairly complex time-travel story wandered into my head. Since time travel is one of my favorite science-fiction themes, I set about immediately sketching it out.

It turned out to be the most ambitious story I had done in ten years or so, involving not only a very tricky plot but also a lot of historical and geographical research. (Sarajevo, where the story opens, would be all over the front pages of the newspapers a decade later, but this was 1980, remember, and the only thing anyone knew about the place then was that it was where the Austrian archduke Franz Ferdinand was assassinated in 1914, touching off the First World War.)

So I worked hard and long, with much revising along the way (a big deal, in those pre-computer days), and on August 16, 1980 I mailed it to Sheckley with a note that said, "Somehow I finished the story despite such distractions as the death of my cat and a visit from my mother and a lot of other headaches, some of which I'll tell you about as we sit sobbing into our drinks at the Boston convention and some of which I hope to have forgotten by then."

Though I was now writing regularly again—this was my fourth short story in eight months—I had not yet returned to full creative confidence, and, though I thought "Bell-Shaped Curve" was a fine story, I wasn't completely sure that Sheckley would agree. When we met two weeks later in Boston for that year's World Science Fiction Convention, though, he told me at once that he was going to publish it. But he hoped I'd take a second look at it and clean up some logical flaws.

"Sure," I said. "Just give me a list of them."

But Bob Sheckley, sweet man that he is, was not that sort of editor. He didn't have any list of the story's logical flaws—he simply felt sure there must be some. I was on my own. So after the Boston trip I went back to the story, giving it a very rigorous reading indeed, and, sure enough, there were places where the time-travel logic didn't make sense. That came as no surprise to me, because time-travel logic never does make sense, but I did see some ways of concealing, if not removing, the illogicalities. I revised the story and sent it back to him in late September, telling him this in my accompanying letter:

"I have reworked 'Bell-Shaped Curve' to handle most of the obvious problems, without pretending that I have made time travel into anything as plausible as the internal combustion engine. Aside from a bunch of tiny cosmetic changes, the main revision has been to eliminate the discussion between Reichenbach and Ilsabet about being wary of duplication; they now speak in much more general terms of paradox problems. But in fact they don't understand any more about time travel than I do about what's under the hood of my car....

"And remember that a story that may contain logical flaws is a story that will give the readers something to exercise their wits about. That will be pleasing to them. If they can come away from the issue feeling mentally superior to Robert Silverberg and the entire editorial staff of *Omni,* haven't they thereby had their two dollars' worth of gratification?"

Omni published the story in 1981. It's been reprinted in a lot of anthologies since then. And you all know what eventually happened to Sarajevo.

The Far Side of the Bell-Shaped Curve

Sarajevo was lovely on that early summer day. The air sparkled, the breeze off the mountains was strong and pungent, the whitewashed villas glittered in the morning sunlight. Reichenbach, enchanted by the beauty of the place and spurred by a sense of impending excitement, stepped buoyantly out of a dark cobbled alley and made his way in quick virile strides toward the river's right embankment. It was nearly 10:30.

A crowd of silent, sullen Bosnian burghers lined the embankment. The black-and-gold Hapsburg banners fluttered from every lamppost and balcony. In a little while the archduke Franz Ferdinand, the emperor's nephew and heir, would come this way with his duchess in their open-topped car. Venturing into dangerous territory, they were, into a province of disaffected and reluctant citizens.

The townsfolk stirred faintly. The townsfolk muttered. Like puddings, Reichenbach thought, they awaited in a dull, dutiful way their future monarch. But he knew they must be seething with revolutionary fervor inside.

Reichenbach looked about him for dark taut youths with the peculiar bright-eyed look of assassins. No one nearby seemed to fit the pattern. He let his gaze wander up the hills to the dense cypress groves, the ancient wooden houses, the old Turkish mosques topped by slender, splendid minarets and back down toward the river to the crowd again. And —

Who is she?

He noticed her for the first time, no more than a dozen meters to his left, in front of the Bank of Austria-Hungary building: a tall auburn-haired woman of striking presence and aura, who in this mob of coarse, rough folk radiated such supreme alertness and force that Reichenbach knew at once she must be of his sort. Yes! He had come here alone, certain he would find an appropriate companion, and that confidence now was affirmed.

He began to move toward her.

His eyes met hers and she nodded and smiled in recognition and acknowledgment.

"Have you just arrived?" Reichenbach asked in German.

She answered in Serbian. "Three days ago."

Smoothly he shifted languages. "How did I fail to see you?"

"You were looking everywhere else. I saw you at once. You came this morning?"

"Fifteen minutes ago."

"Does it please you so far?"

"Very much," he said. "Such a picturesque place. Like a medieval fantasy. Time stands still here."

Her eyes were mischievous. "Time stands still everywhere," she said, moving on into English.

Reichenbach smiled. Again he matched her change of language. "I take your meaning. And I think you take mine. This charming architecture, the little river, the ethnic costumes—it's hard to believe that a vast and hideous war is going to spring from so quaint a place."

"A nice irony, yes. And it's for ironies that we make these journeys, *n'est ce pas?*"

"*Vraiment.*"

They were standing quite close now. He felt a current flowing between them, a pulsating, almost tangible force.

"Join me later for a drink?" he said.

"Certainly. I am Ilsabet."

"Reichenbach."

He longed to ask her when she had come from. But of course that was taboo.

"Look," she said. "The archduke and duchess."

The royal car, inching forward, had reached them. Franz Ferdinand, red faced and tense in preposterous comic-opera uniform, waved halfheartedly to the bleakly staring crowd. Drab, plump Sophie beside him, absurdly overdressed, forced a smile. They were meaty-looking, florid people, rigid and nervous, all but clinging to each other in their nervousness.

"Now it starts," he said.

"Yes. The foreplay." She slipped her arm through his.

Not far away a tall, young, sallow-faced man appeared as if he had sprung from the pavement—wild hyperthyroid eyes, bobbing Adam's-apple, a sure desperado—and hurled something. It landed just behind the royal car. An odd popping sound—the detonator— and then Reichenbach heard a loud bang. There was a blurt of black smoke and the car behind the archduke's lurched and crumpled, dumping aides-de-camp into the street. The cortege halted abruptly. The imperial couple, unharmed, sat weirdly upright as if their survival depended on keeping their spines straight. A functionary riding with them said in a clear voice, "A bomb has gone off, your highness." And Franz Ferdinand, calm, disgusted: "I rather expected something like that. Look after the injured, will you?"

Ilsabet's hand tightened on Reichenbach's forearm as the bizarre comedy unfolded: the cars motionless, archduke and duchess still in plain view, the assassin wildly vaulting a parapet and plunging into the shallow river, police pursuing, pouncing, beating him with the flats of their swords, the crowd milling in confusion. At last the damaged car was pushed to the side of the road and the remaining vehicles rapidly drove off.

"End of act one," Ilsabet said, laughing.

"And forty minutes until act two. That drink, now?"

"I know a sidewalk cafe near here."

Under a broad turquoise umbrella Reichenbach had a slivovitz, Ilsabet a mug of dark beer. The stolid citizens at the surrounding tables talked more of hunting and fishing than of the bungled assassination. Reichenbach, pretending to be casual, studied Ilsabet hungrily. A cool, keen intelligence gleamed in her penetrating green eyes. Everything about her was sleek, self-possessed, sure. She was so much like him that he almost feared her, and that was a new feeling for him. What he feared most of all was that he would blunder here at the outset and lose her; but he knew, deep beneath all doubts, that he would not. They were meant for each other. He liked to believe that she came from this moment, and that there would be a chance to continue in realtime, when they had returned from displacement, whatever they began on this jaunt. Of course, one did not speak of such things.

Instead he said, "Where do you go next?"

"The burning of Rome. And you?"

"A drink with Shakespeare at the Mermaid Tavern."

"How splendid. I never thought of doing that."

He drew a deep breath and said, "We could do it together," and hesitated, watching her expression. She did not look displeased. "After we've heard Nero play his concerto. Eh?"

She seemed amused. "I like that idea."

He raised his glass. *"Prosit."*

"Zdravlje."

They snaked wrists, clinked glasses.

For a few minutes more they talked—lightly, playfully. He studied her gestures, her sentence structure, her use of idiom, seeking in the subtlest turns of her style some clue that might tell him that they were co-temporals, but she gave him nothing: a shrewd game player, this one. At length he said, "It's nearly time for the rest of the show."

Ilsabet nodded. He scattered some coins on the table and they returned to the embankment, walked up to the Latin Bridge, turned right into Franz Joseph Street. Shortly the royal motorcade, returning from a city-hall reception, came rolling along. There appeared to be some disagreement over the route: chauffeurs and aides-de-camp engaged in a noisy dispute and suddenly the royal car stopped. The chauffeur seemed to be trying to put the car into reverse. There was a clashing of gears. A gaunt boy emerged from a coffeehouse not three meters from the car, less than ten from Reichenbach and Ilsabet. He looked dazed, like a sleepwalker, as if astounded to find himself so close to the imperial heir. This is Gavrilo Princip, Reichenbach thought, the second and true assassin; but he felt little interest in what was about to happen. The gun was out, the boy was taking aim. But Reichenbach watched Ilsabet, more concerned with the quality of her reactions than with the deaths of two trivial people in fancy costumes. Thus he missed seeing the fatal shot through Franz Ferdinand's pouter-pigeon chest, though he observed Ilsabet's quick, frosty smile of satisfaction. When he glanced back at the royal car he saw the archduke sitting upright, stunned, tunic and lips stained with red, and the boy firing at the duchess. There was consternation among the aides-de-camp. The car sped away. It was 11:15.

"So," said Ilsabet. "Now the war begins, the dynasties topple, a civilization crumbles. Did you enjoy it?"

"Not as much as I enjoyed the way you smiled when the archduke was shot."

"Silly."

"The slaughter of a pair of overstaffed simpletons is ultimately less important to me than your smile."

It was risky: too strong too soon, maybe? But it got through to her the right way, producing a faint quirking of her lip that told him she was pleased.

"Come," she said, and took him by the hand.

Her hotel was an old gray stone building on the other side of the river. She had an elegant balconied room on the third floor, river view, ornate gas chandeliers, heavy damask draperies, capacious canopied bed. This era's style was certainly admirable, Reichenbach thought—lavish, slow, rich; even in a little provincial town like this, everything was deluxe. He shed his tight and heavy clothing with relief. She wore her timer high, a pale taut band just beneath her breasts. Her eyes glittered as she reached for him and drew him down beneath the canopy. At this moment at the other end of town, Franz Ferdinand and Sophie were dying. Soon there would be exchanges of stiff diplomatic notes, declarations of war by Austria-Hungary against Serbia, Germany against Russia and France, Europe engulfed in flames, the battle of the Marne, Ypres, Verdun, the Somme, the flight of the kaiser, the armistice, the transformation of the monarchies—he had studied it all with such keen intensity, and now, having seen the celebrated assassinations that triggered everything, he was unmoved. Ilsabet had eclipsed the Great War for him.

No matter. There would be other epochal events to savor. They had all history to wander.

"To Rome, now," he said huskily.

***

They rose, bathed, embraced, winked conspiratorially. They were off to a good start. Hastily they gathered their 1914 gear, waistcoats and petticoats and boots and all that, within the prescribed two-meter radius. They synchronized their timers and embraced again, naked, laughing, bodies pressed tight together, and went soaring across the centuries.

At the halfway house outside imperial Rome, they underwent their preparations, receiving their Roman hairstyles and clothing, their hypnocourses in Latin, their purses of denarii and sestertii, their plague inoculations, their new temporary names. He was Quintus Junius Veranius, she was Flavia Julia Lepida.

Nero's Rome was smaller and far less grand than he expected — the Colosseum was still in the future, there was no Arch of Titus, even the Forum seemed sparsely built. But the city was scarcely mean. The first day, they strolled vast gardens and dense, crowded markets, stared in awe at crazy Caligula's bridge from the Palatine to the Capitoline, went to the baths, gorged themselves at their inn on capon and truffled boar. On the next, they attended the gladiatorial games and afterward made love with frantic energy in a chamber they had hired near the Campus Martius. There was a wonderful frenzy about the city that Reichenbach found intoxicating, and Ilsabet, he knew, shared his fervor: her eyes were aglow, her face gleamed. They could hardly bear to sleep, but explored the narrow winding streets from dark to dawn.

They knew, of course, that the fire would break out in the Circus Maximus where it adjoined the Palatine and Caelian hills, and took care to situate themselves safely atop the Aventine, where they had a fine view. There they watched the fierce blaze sweeping through the Circus, climbing the hills, dipping to ravage the lower ground. No one seemed to be fighting the fire; indeed, Reichenbach thought he could detect subsidiary fires flaring up in outlying districts, as though arson were the sport of the hour, and soon those fires joined with the main one. The sky rained black soot; the stifling summer air was thick and almost impossible to breathe. For the first two days the destruction had a kind of fascinating beauty, as temples and mansions and arcades melted away, the Rome of centuries being unbuilt before their eyes. But then the discomfort, the danger, the monotony, began to pall on him. "Shall we go?" he said.

"Wait," Ilsabet replied. The conflagration seemed to have an almost sexual impact on her: she glistened with sweat, she trembled with some strange joy as the flames leaped from district to district. She could not get enough. And she clung to him in tight feverish embrace. "Not yet," she murmured, "not so soon. I want to see the emperor."

Yes. And here was Nero now, returning to town from holiday. In grand procession he crossed the charred city, descending from his litter now and then to inspect some ruined shrine or palace. They caught a glimpse of him as he entered the Gardens of Maecenas—thick-necked, paunchy, spindle-shanked, foul of complexion. "Oh, look," Ilsabet whispered. "He's *beautiful!* But where's the fiddle?" The emperor carried no fiddle, but he was grotesquely garbed in some kind of theatrical costume and his cheeks were daubed with paint. He waved and flung coins to the crowd and ascended the garden tower. For a better view, no doubt. Ilsabet pressed herself close to Reichenbach. "My throat is on fire," she said. "My lungs are choked with ashes. Take me to London. Show me Shakespeare."

***

There was smoke in the dark Cheapside alehouse too, thick sweet smoke curling up from sputtering logs on a dank February day. They sat in a cobwebbed corner playing word games while waiting for the actors to arrive. She was quick and clever, just as clever as he. Reichenbach took joy in that. He loved her for her agility and strength of soul. "Not many could be carrying off this tour," he told her. "Only special ones like us."

She grinned. "We who occupy the far side of the bell-shaped curve."

"Yes. Yes. It's horrible of us to have such good opinions of ourselves, isn't it?"

"Probably. But they're well earned, my dear."

He covered her hand with his, and squeezed, and she squeezed back. Reichenbach had never known anyone like her. Deeper and deeper was she drawing him, and his delight was tempered only by the knowledge that when they returned to realtime, to that iron world beyond the terminator where all paradoxes canceled out and the delicious freedoms of the jaunter did not apply, he must of necessity lose her. But there was no hurry about returning.

Voices, now: laughter, shouts, a company of men entering the tavern, actors, poets perhaps, Burbage, maybe, Heminges, Allen, Condell, Kemp, Ben Jonson possibly, and who was that, slender, high forehead, those eyes like lamps in the dark? Who else could it be? Plainly Shagspere, Chaxper, Shackspire, however they spelled it, surely Sweet Will here among these men calling for sack and malmsey, and behind that broad forehead Hamlet and Mercutio must be teeming, Othello, Hotspur, Prospero, Macbeth. The sight of him excited Reichenbach as Nero had Ilsabet. He inclined his head, hoping to hear scraps of dazzling table-talk, some bit of newborn verse, some talk of a play taking form; but at this distance everything blurred. "I have to go to him," Reichenbach muttered.

"The regulations?"

"Je m'en fous the regulations. I'll be quick. People of our kind don't need to worry about the regulations. I promise you, I'll be quick."

She winked and blew him a kiss. She looked gorgeously sluttish in her low-fronted gown.

Reichenbach felt a strange quivering in his calves as he crossed the straw-strewn floor to the far-off crowded table.

"Master Shakespeare!" he cried.

Heads turned. Cold eyes glared out of silent faces. Reichenbach forced himself to be bold. From his purse he took two slender, crude shilling-pieces and put them in front of Shakespeare. "I would stand you a flagon or two of the best sack," he said loudly, "in the name of good Sir John."

"Sir John?" said Shakespeare, blank-faced. He frowned and shook his head. "Sir John Woodcocke, d'ye mean? Sir John Holcombe? I know not your Sir John, fellow."

Reichenbach's cheeks blazed. He felt like a fool.

A burly man beside Shakespeare said, with a rough nudge, "Methinks he speaks of Falstaff, Will. Eh? You recall your Falstaff?"

"Yes," Reichenbach said. "In truth I mean no other."

"Falstaff," Shakespeare said in a distant way. He looked displeased, uncomfortable. "I recall the name, yes. Friend, I thank you, but take back your shillings. It is bad custom for me to drink of strangers' sack."

Reichenbach protested, but only fitfully, and quickly he withdrew lest the moment grow ugly: plainly these folk had no use for his wine or for him, and to be wounded in a tavern brawl here in A.D. 1604 would bring monstrous consequences in realtime. He made a courtly bow and retreated. Ilsabet, watching, wore a cat-grin. He went slinking back to her, upset, bitterly aware he had bungled his cherished meeting with Shakespeare and, worse, had looked bumptious in front of her.

"We should go," he said. "We're unwelcome here."

"Poor dear one. You look so miserable."

"The contempt in his eyes—"

"No," she said. "The man is probably bothered by strangers all the time. And he was, you know, with his friends in the sanctuary of his own tavern. He meant no personal rebuke."

"I expected him to be different—to be one of *us,* to reach out toward me and draw me to him, to—to—"

"No," said Ilsabet gently. "He has his life, his wife, his pains, his problems. Don't confuse him with your fantasy of him. Come, now. You look so glum, my dear. Find yourself again!"

"Somewhen else."

"Yes. Somewhen else."

***

Under her deft consolations the sting of his oafishness at the Mermaid Tavern eased, and his mood brightened as they went onward. Few words passed between them: a look, a smile, the merest of contacts, and they communicated. Attending the trial of Socrates, they touched fingertips lightly, secretly, and it was the deepest of communions. Afterward they made love under the clear, bright winter sky of Athens on a gray-green hillside rich with lavender and myrtle, and emerged from shivering ecstasies to find themselves with an audience of mournful scruffy goats — a perfect leap of context and metaphor, and for days thereafter they made one another laugh with only the most delicate pantomimed reminder of the scene. Onward they went to see grim, limping, austere old Magellan sail off around the world with his five little ships from the mouth of the Guadalquivir, and at a whim they leaped to India, staining their skins and playing at Hindus as they viewed the expedition of Vasco da Gama come sailing into harbor at Calicut, and then it seemed proper to go on to Spain in dry, hot summer to drink sour white wine and watch ruddy freckled-faced Columbus get his pitiful little fleet out to sea.

Of course, they took other lovers from time to time. That was part of the game, too tasty a treat to forswear. In Byzantium, on the eve of the Frankish conquest, he passed a night with a dark-eyed voluptuous Greek who oiled her breasts with musky mysterious unguents, and Ilsabet with a towering garlicky Swede of the imperial guard, and when they found each other the next day, just as the Venetian armada burst into the Bosporus, they described to one another in the most flamboyant of detail the strangenesses of their night's sport—the tireless Norseman's toneless bellowing of sagas in his hottest moments: the Byzantine's startling, convulsive, climactic fit, almost epileptic in style, and, as she had admitted playfully at dawn, mostly a counterfeit. In Cleopatra's Egypt, while waiting for glimpses of the queen and Antony, they diverted themselves with a dark-eyed Coptic pair, brother and sister, no more than children and blithely interchangeable in bed. At the crowning of Charlemagne she found herself a Frankish merchant who offered her an estate along the Rhine, and he a mysteriously elliptical dusky woman who claimed to be a Catalonian Moor, but who—Reichenbach suddenly realized a few days later—must almost certainly have been a jaunter like himself, playing elegant games with him.

All this lent spice to their love and did no harm. These separate but shared adventures only enhanced the intensity of the relationship they were welding. He prayed the jaunt would never end, for Ilsabet was the perfect companion, his utter match, and so long as they sprinted together through the aeons, she was his, though he knew that would end when realtime reclaimed him. Nevertheless, that sad moment still was far away, and he hoped before then to find some way around the inexorable rules, some scheme for locating her and continuing with her in his own true time. Small chance of that, he knew. In the world beyond the terminator there was no time-jaunting; jaunting could be done only in the fluid realm of "history," and history was arbitrarily defined as everything that had happened before the terminator year of 2187. The rest was realtime, rigid and immutable, and what if her realtime were fifty years ahead of his, or fifty behind? There was no bridging that by jaunting. He did not know her realtime locus, and he did not dare ask. Deep as the love between them had come to be, Reichenbach still feared offending her through some unpardonable breach of their special etiquette.

With all the world to choose from, they sometimes took brief solo jaunts. That was Ilsabet's idea, holidays within their holiday, so that they would not grow stale with one another. It made sense to him. Thereupon he vaulted to the Paris of the 1920s to sip Pernod on the Boulevard Saint-Germain and peer at Picasso and Hemingway and Joyce, she in epicanthic mask to old Cathay to see Kublai Khan ride in triumph through the Great Wall, he to Cape Kennedy to watch the great Apollo rocket roaring moonward, she to London for King Charles's beheading. But these were brief adventures, and they reunited quickly, gladly, and went on hand in hand to their next together, to the fall of Troy and the diamond jubilee of Queen Victoria and the assassination of Lincoln and the sack of Carthage. Always when they returned from separate exploits, they regaled each other with extensive narratives of what had befallen them, the sights, the tastes, the ironies and perceptions, and, of course, the amorous interludes. By now Reichenbach and Ilsabet had accumulated an elaborate fabric of shared experience, a richness of joint history that gave them virtually a private language of evocative recollection, so that the slightest of cues — a goat on a hill, the taste of burned toast, the sight of a lop-eared beggar — sprang them into an intimate realm that no one else could ever penetrate: their unique place, furnished with their own things, the artifacts of love, the treasures of memory. And even that which they did separately became interwoven in that fabric, as if the telling of events as they lay in each other's arms had transformed those events into communal possessions.

Yet gradually Reichenbach realized that something was beginning to go wrong.

From a solo jaunt to Paris of 1794, where she toured the Reign of Terror, Ilsabet returned strangely evasive. She spoke in brilliant detail of the death of Robespierre and the sad despoliation of Notre Dame, but what she reported was mere journalism, with no inner meaning. He had to fish for information. Where had she lodged? Had she feared for her safety? Had she had interesting conversations with the Parisians? Shrugs, deflections. Had she taken a lover? Yes, yes, a fleeting liaison, nothing worth talking about; and then it was back to an account of the mobs, the tumbrils, the sound of the guillotine. At first Reichenbach accepted that without demur, though her vaguenesses violated their custom. But she remained moody and oblique while they were visiting the Crucifixion, and as they were about to depart for the Black Death she begged off, saying she needed another day to herself, and would go to Prague for the premiere of *Don Giovanni*. That too failed to trouble him — he was not musical — and he spent the day observing Waterloo from the hills behind Wellington's troops. When Ilsabet rejoined him in the late spring of 1349 for the Black Death in London, though, she seemed even more preoccupied and remote, and told him little of her night at the opera. He began to feel dismay, for they had been marvelously close and now she was obviously voyaging on some other plane. The plague-smitten city seemed to bore her. Her only flicker of animation came toward evening, in a Southwark hostelry, when as they dined on gristly lamb, a stranger entered, a tall, gaunt, sharp-bearded man with the obvious aura of a jaunter. Reichenbach did not fail to notice the rebirth of light in Ilsabet's eyes, and the barely perceptible inclining-forward of her body as the stranger approached their table was amply perceptible to him. The newcomer knew them for what they were, naturally, and invited himself to join them. His name was Stavanger; he had been on his jaunt just a few days; he meant to see everything, *everything*, before his time was up. Not for many years had Reichenbach felt such jealousy. He was wise in these things, and it was not difficult to detect the current flowing from Ilsabet to Stavanger even as he sat there between them. Now he understood why she had no casual amours to report of her jaunts to Paris and Prague. This one was far from casual and would bear no retelling.

In the morning she said, "I still feel operatic. I'll go to Bayreuth tonight — the premiere of *Gotterdammerung.*"

Despising himself, he said. "A capital idea. I'll accompany you."

She looked disconcerted. "But music bores you!"

"A flaw in my character. Time I began to remedy it."

The fitful panic in Ilsabet's eyes gave way to cool and chilling calmness. "Another time, dear love. I prize my solitude. I'll make this little trip without you."

It was all plain to him. Gone now the open sharing; now there were secret rendezvous and an unwanted third player of their game. He could not bear it. In anguish he made his own arrangements and jaunted to Bayreuth in thick red wig and curling beard, and there she was, seated beside Stavanger in the Festspielhaus as the subterranean orchestra launched into the first notes. Reichenbach did not remain for the performance.

Stavanger now crossed their path openly and with great frequency. They met him at the siege of Constantinople, at the San Francisco earthquake, and at a fete at Versailles. This was more than coincidence, and Reichenbach said so to Ilsabet. "I suggested he follow some of our itinerary," she admitted. "He's a lonely man, jaunting alone. And quite charming. But of course if you dislike him, we can simply vanish without telling him where we're going, and he'll never find us again."

A disarming tactic, Reichenbach thought. It was impossible for her to admit to him that she and Stavanger were lovers, for there was too much substance to their affair; so instead she pretended he was a pitiful forlorn wanderer in need of company. Reichenbach was outraged. Fidelity was not part of his unspoken compact with her, and she was free to slip off to any era she chose for a tryst with Stavanger. But that she chose to conceal what was going on was deplorable, and that she was finding pretexts to drag Stavanger along on their travels, puncturing the privacy of their own rapport for the sake of a few smug stolen glances, was impermissible. Reichenbach was convinced now that Ilsabet and Stavanger were co-temporals, though he knew he had no rational basis for that idea; it simply seemed right to him, a final torment, the two of them now laying the groundwork for a realtime relationship that excluded him. Whether or not that was true, it was unbearable. Reichenbach was astounded by the intensity of his jealous fury. Yet it was a true emotion and one he would not attempt to repress. The joy he had known with Ilsabet had been unique, and Stavanger had tainted it.

He found himself searching for ways to dispose of his rival.

Merely whirling Ilsabet off elsewhen would achieve nothing. She would find ways of catching up with her paramour somewhen along the line. And if Ilsabet and Stavanger were co-temporal, and she and Reichenbach were not—no, no, Stavanger had to be expunged. Reichenbach, a stable and temperate man, had never imagined himself capable of such criminality; a bit of elitist regulation-bending was all he had ever allowed himself. But he had never been faced with the loss of an Ilsabet before, either.

In Borgia, Italy, Reichenbach hired a Florentine poisoner to do Stavanger in with a dram of nightshade. But the villain pocketed Reichenbach's down payment and disappeared without a care for the ducats due him on completion of the job. In the chaotic aftermath of the Ides of March, Reichenbach attempted to finger Stavanger as one of Caesar's murderers, but no one paid attention. Nor did he have luck denouncing him to the Inquisition one afternoon in 1485 in Torquemada's Castile, though even the most perfunctory questioning would have given sufficient proof of Stavanger's alliance with diabolical powers. Perhaps it would be necessary, Reichenbach concluded morosely, to deal with Stavanger with his own hands, repellent though that alternative was.

Not only was it repellent, it could be dangerous. He was without experience at serious crime, and Stavanger, cold-eyed and suave, promised to be a formidable adversary. Reichenbach needed an ally, an adviser, a collaborator. But who? While he and Ilsabet were making the circuit of the Seven Wonders, he puzzled over it, from Ephesus to Halicarnassus to Gizeh, and as they stood in the shadow of the Colossus of Rhodes, the answer came to him. There was only one person he could trust sufficiently, and that person was himself.

To Ilsabet he said, "Do you know where I want to go next?"

"We still have the Hanging Gardens of Babylon, the Lighthouse of Alexandria, the Statue of Zeus at—"

"No, I'm not talking about the Seven Wonders tour. I want to go back to Sarajevo, Ilsabet."

"Sarajevo? Whatever for?"

"A sentimental pilgrimage, love, to the place of our first meeting."

"But Sarajevo was a bore. And—"

"We could make it exciting. Consider: our earlier selves would already be there. We would watch them meet, find each other well matched, become lovers. Here for months we've been touring the great events of history, when we're neglecting a chance to witness our own personal greatest event." He smiled wickedly. "And there are other possibilities. We could introduce ourselves to them. Hint at the joys that lie ahead of them. Perhaps even seduce them, eh? A nice kinky quirky business that would be. And—"

"No," she said. "I don't like it."

"You find the idea improper? Morally offensive?"

"Don't be an idiot. I find it dangerous."

"How so?"

"We aren't supposed to reenter a time-span where we're already present. There must be some good reason for that. The rules—"

"The rules," he said, "are made by timid old sods who've never moved beyond the terminator in their lives. The rules are meant to guide us, not to control us. The rules are meant to be broken by those who are smart enough to avoid the consequences."

She stared somberly at him a long while. "And you are?"

"I think I am."

"Yes. A shrewd man, a superior man, a member of the elite corps that lives on the far side of society's bell-shaped curve. Eh? Doing as you please throughout life. Holding yourself above all restraints. Rich enough and lucky enough to be able to jaunt anywhere you like and behave like a little god."

"You live the same way, I believe."

"In general, yes. But I still won't go with you to Sarajevo."

"Why not?"

"Because I don't know what will happen to me if I do. Kinky and quirky it may be to pile into bed with our other selves, but something about the idea troubles me, and I dislike needless risk. Do you believe you understand paradox theory fully?"

"Does anybody?"

"Exactly. It isn't smart to—"

"Paradoxes are much overrated, don't you think? We're in the fluid zone, Ilsabet. Anything goes, this side of the terminator. If I were you I wouldn't worry about—"

"*I* am me. I worry. If I were you, I'd worry more. Take your Sarajevo trip without me."

He saw she was adamant, and dropped the issue. Indeed, he saw it would be much simpler to make the journey alone. They went on from Rhodes to the Babylon of Nebuchadnezzar, where they spent four happy days untroubled by the shadow of Stavanger; it was the finest time they had had together since Carthage. Then Ilsabet announced she felt the need for another brief solo musicological jaunt—to Mantua in 1607 for Monteverdi's *Orfeo*. Reichenbach offered no objection. The instant she was gone, he set his timer for the twenty-eighth of June, 1914, Sarajevo in Bosnia, 10:27 A.M.

In his Babylonian costume he knew he looked ridiculous or even insane, but it was too chancy to have gone to the halfway house for proper preparation, and he planned to stay here only a few minutes. Moments after he materialized in the narrow cobble-paved alleyway, his younger self appeared, decked out elegantly in natty Edwardian finery. He registered only the most brief quiver of amazement at the sight of another Reichenbach already there.

Reichenbach said, "I have to speak quickly. You will go out there and near the Bank of Austria-Hungary you'll meet the most wonderful woman you've ever known, and you'll share with her the greatest joys you've ever tasted. And just as your love for her reaches its deepest strength, you'll lose her to a rival—unless you cooperate with me to rid us of him before they can ever meet."

The eyes of the other Reichenbach narrowed. "Murder?"

"Removal. We'll put him in the way of harm, and harm will come to him."

"Is the woman such a marvel that the risks are worth it?"

"I swear it. I tell you, you'll suffer pain beyond belief if he isn't eliminated. Trust me. My welfare is your welfare, is this not so?"

"Of course." But the other Reichenbach looked unconvinced. "Still, why must there be two of us in this? It's not yet my affair, after all."

"It will be. He's too slippery to tackle without help. I need you. And ultimately you'll be grateful to me for this. Take it on faith."

"And what if this is some elaborate game, and I the victim?"

"Damn it, *this is no game!* Our happiness is at stake—yours, mine. We're both in this together. We're closer than any twins could ever be, don't you realize? You and me, different phases of the same person's timeline, following the same path? Our destinies are linked. Help me now or live forever with the torment of the consequences. Please help. *Please.*"

The other was wavering. "You ask a great deal."

"I offer a great deal," Reichenbach said. "Look, there's no more time for talking now. You have to get out there and meet Ilsabet before the archduke's assassination. Meet me in Paris, noon on the twenty-fifth of June, 1794, in the rue de Rivoli outside the Hotel de Ville." He grasped the other's arm and stared at him with all the intensity and conviction at his command. "Agreed?"

A last moment of hesitation.

"Agreed."

Reichenbach touched his timer and disappeared.

In Babylon again he gathered his possessions and jaunted to the halfway house for the French Revolution. Momentarily he dreaded running into his other self there, a malfeasance that would be hard to justify, but the place was too big for that; the Revolution and Terror spanned five years and an immense service facility was needed to handle the tourist demand. Outfitted in the simple countryfolk clothes appropriate to the revolutionary period, equipped with freshly implanted linguistic skills and proper revolutionary rhetoric, altogether disguised to blend with the citizenry, Reichenbach descended into the terrible heat of that bloody Parisian summer and quickly effected his rendezvous with himself.

The face he beheld was clearly his, and yet unfamiliar, for he was accustomed to his mirror image; but a mirror image is a reversed one, and now he saw himself as others saw him and nothing looked quite right. This is what it must be like to have a twin, he thought. In a low, hoarse voice he said, "She's coming tomorrow to hear Robespierre's final speech and then to see his execution. Our enemy is in Paris already, with rooms at the Hotel Brittanique in the rue Guenegaud. I'll track him down while you make contact with the Committee of Public Safety. I'll bring him here; you arrange the trap and the denunciation; with any luck he'll be hauled away in the same tumbril that takes Robespierre to the guillotine. *D'accord?*"

"*D'accord.*" A radiance came into the other's eyes. Softly he said, "You were right about Ilsabet. For such a woman even this is justifiable."

Reichenbach felt an unexpected pang. But to be jealous of himself was an absurdity. "Where have you been with her?"

"After Sarajevo, Nero's Rome. She's asleep there now, our third night: I intend to be gone only an instant. We go next to Shakespeare's time, and then—"

"Yes. I know. Socrates, Magellan, Vasco da Gama. All the best still lies ahead for you. But first there's work to do."

Without great difficulty he found his way to the Hotel Brittanique, a modest place not far from the Pont Neuf. The concierge, a palsied woman with a thin-lipped mouth fixed in an unchanging scowl, offered little aid until Reichenbach spoke of the committee, the Law of Suspects, the dangers of refusing to cooperate with the revolutionary tribunal; then she was quick enough to admit that a dark man of great height with a beard of just the sort that M'sieu described was living on the fifth floor, a certain M. Stavanger. Reichenbach rented the adjoining room. He waited there an hour, until he heard the footsteps in the hallway, sounds next door.

He went out and knocked.

Stavanger peered blankly at him. "Yes?"

He has not yet met her, Reichenbach thought. He has not yet spoken with her, he has not yet touched her body, they have not yet gone to their damned operas together. And never will.

He said, "This is a wonderful place for a jaunt, isn't it?"

"Who are you?"

"Reichenbach is my name. My friend and I saw you in the street and she sent me up to speak with you." He made a little self-deprecating gesture. "I often act as her — ah — go-between. She wishes to know if you'll meet her this afternoon and perhaps enjoy a day or two of French history with her. Her name is Ilsabet, and I can testify that you'll find her charming. Her particular interests are assassinations, architecture, and the first performances of great operas."

Stavanger showed sudden alertness. "Opera is a great passion of mine," he said. "Ordinarily I keep to myself when jaunting, but in this case — the possibilities — is she downstairs? Can you bring her to me?"

"Ah, no. She's waiting in front of the Hotel de Ville."

"And wants me to come to her?"

Reichenbach nodded. "Certain protocols are important to her."

Stavanger, after a moment's consideration, said, "Take me to your Ilsabet, then. But I make no promises. Is that understood?"

"Of course," said Reichenbach.

The streets were almost empty at this hour. The miasma of the atmosphere in this heavy heat must be a factor in that, Reichenbach thought, and also that it was midday and the Parisians were at their *dejeuner*; but beyond that it seemed that the city was suffering a desolation of the spirit, a paralysis of energy under the impact of the monstrous bloodletting of recent months. He walked quickly, struggling to keep up with Stavanger's long strides. As they approached the Hotel de Ville, Reichenbach caught sight of his other self, and with him two or three men in revolutionary costume. Good. Good. The other Reichenbach nodded. Everything was arranged. The challenge now was to keep Stavanger from going for his timer the moment he sensed he was in jeopardy.

"Where is she?" Stavanger asked.

"I left her speaking with that group of men," said Reichenbach. The other Reichenbach stood with his face turned aside—a wise move. Now, though they had not rehearsed it, they moved as if parts of a single organism, the other Reichenbach pivoting, pointing, crying out, "I accuse that man of crimes against liberty," while in the same instant Reichenbach stepped behind Stavanger, thrust his arms up past those of the taller man, reached into Stavanger's loose tunic to wrench his timer into ruin with one quick twist, and held him firmly. Stavanger bellowed and tried to break free, but in a moment the street was full of men who seized and overpowered him and dragged him away. Reichenbach, panting, sweating, looked in triumph toward his other self.

"That one, too," said the other Reichenbach.

Reichenbach blinked. "What?"

Too late. They had his arms; the other Reichenbach was groping for his timer, seizing, tearing. Reichenbach fought ferociously, but they bore him to the ground and knelt on his chest.

Through a haze of fear and pain he heard the other saying, "This man is the proscribed aristocrat Charles Evremonde, called Darnay, enemy of the Republic, member of a family of tyrants. I denounce him for having used his privileges in the oppression of the people."

"He will face the tribunal tonight," said the one kneeling on Reichenbach.

Reichenbach said in a shocked voice, "What are you doing?"

The other crouched close to him and replied in English. "We have been duplicated, you see. Why do you think there are rules against entering a time where one is already present? There's room for only one of us back in realtime, is that not so? So, then, how can we both return?"

Reichenbach said, with a gasp, "But that isn't true!"

"Isn't it? Are you sure? Do you really comprehend all the paradoxes?"

"Do *you*? How can you do this to me, when I—when I'm—"

"You disappoint me, not seeing these intricacies. I would have expected more from one of us. But you must have been too muddled by jealousy to think straight. Do you imagine I dare run the risk of letting you jaunt around on the loose? Which of us is to have Ilsabet, after all?"

Already Reichenbach felt the blade hurtling toward his neck.

"Wait—wait—" he cried. "Look at him! His face is mine! We are brothers, twins! If I'm an aristocrat, what is he? I denounce him too! Seize him and try him with me!"

"There is indeed a strange resemblance between you two," said one of those holding Reichenbach.

The other smiled. "We have often been taken for brothers. But there is no kinship between us. He is the aristocrat Evremond, citizens. And I, I am only poor Sydney Carton, a person of no consequence or significance whatever, happy to have been of service to the people." He bowed and walked away, and in a moment was gone.

Safe beside Ilsabet in Nero's Rome, Reichenbach thought bitterly.

"Come. Up with him and bring him to trial," someone called. "The tribunal has no time to waste these days."

THE POPE OF THE CHIMPS (1981)

INTRODUCTION

What's this, another Silverberg story about Popes? First he gives us a robot Pope, and now a chimpanzee?

No, not really. This one has no Vatican connections whatever. The Pope of the title is a purely metaphorical one. As for the story itself, I find I have relatively little to say about it, except that it is a personal favorite of mine. I wrote it in June of 1981, quickly, with great passion and conviction, in response to an invitation from the writer Alan Ryan to do a story for an anthology of science-fiction stories on religious themes called *Perpetual Light*, which came out the following year. The anthology appeared the following year and the story, which I think digs as deeply into human (and nonhuman) emotions as I've ever been able to do in short-story form, was nominated for a Nebula award. It probably would have won if it had appeared in one of the widely distributed science-fiction magazines instead of an anthology that relatively few of the voters had read. But it has frequently appeared in anthologies ever since.

The Pope of the Chimps

Early last month Vendelmans and I were alone with the chimps in the compound when suddenly he said, "I'm going to faint." It was a sizzling May morning, but Vendelmans had never shown any sign of noticing unusual heat, let alone suffering from it. I was busy talking to Leo and Mimsy and Mimsy's daughter Muffin, and I registered Vendelmans's remark without doing anything about it. When you're intensely into talking by sign language, as we are in the project, you sometimes tend not to pay a lot of attention to spoken words.

But then Leo began to sign the trouble sign at me, and I turned around and saw Vendelmans down on his knees in the grass, white-faced, gasping, covered with sweat. A few of the chimpanzees who aren't as sensitive to humans as Leo is thought it was a game and began to pantomime him, knuckles to the ground and bodies going limp. "Sick —" Vendelmans said. "Feel — terrible —"

I called for help, and Gonzo took his left arm and Kong took his right and somehow, big as he was, we managed to get him out of the compound and up the hill to headquarters. By then he was complaining about sharp pains in his back and under his arms, and I realized that it wasn't just heat prostration. Within a week the diagnosis was in.

Leukemia.

They put him on chemotherapy and hormones, and after ten days he was back with the project, looking cocky. "They've stabilized it," he told everyone. "It's in remission and I might have ten or twenty years left, or even more. I'm going to carry on with my work."

But he was gaunt and pale, with a tremor in his hands, and it was a frightful thing to have him among us. He might have been fooling himself, though I doubted it, but he wasn't fooling any of us: to us he was a memento mori, a walking death's-head-and-crossbones. That laymen think scientists are any more casual about such things than anyone else is something I blame Hollywood for. It is not easy to go about your daily work with a dying man at your side — or a dying man's wife, for Judy Vendelmans showed in her frightened eyes all the grief that Hal Vendelmans himself was repressing. She was going to lose a beloved husband unexpectedly soon and she hadn't had time to adjust to it and her pain was impossible to ignore. Besides, the nature of Vendelmans's dyingness was particularly unsettling because he had been so big and robust and outgoing, a true Rabelaisian figure, and somehow between one moment and the next he was transformed into a wraith. "The finger of God," Dave Yost said. "A quick flick of Zeus's pinkie and Hal shrivels like cellophane in a fireplace." Vendelmans was not yet forty.

The chimps suspected something, too.

Some of them, such as Leo and Ramona, are fifth-generation signers, bred for alpha intelligence, and they pick up subtleties and nuances very well. "Almost human," visitors like to say of them. We dislike that tag, because the important thing about chimpanzees is that they *aren't* human, that they are an alien intelligent species; but yet I know what people mean. The brightest of the chimps saw right away that something was amiss with Vendelmans, and started making odd remarks. "Big one rotten banana," said Ramona to Mimsy while I was nearby. "He getting empty," Leo said to me as Vendelmans stumbled past us. Chimp metaphors never cease to amaze me. And Gonzo asked him outright: "You go away soon?"

***

"Go away" is not the chimp euphemism for death. So far as our animals know, no human being has ever died. Chimps die. Human beings go away. We have kept things on that basis from the beginning, not intentionally at first, but such arrangements have a way of institutionalizing themselves. The first member of the group to die was Roger Nixon, in an automobile accident in the early years of the project long before my time here, and apparently no one wanted to confuse or disturb the animals by explaining what had happened to him, so no explanations were offered. My second or third year here, Tim Lippinger was killed in a ski-lift failure, and again it seemed easier not to go into details with them. And by the time of Will Bechstein's death in that helicopter crack-up four years ago the policy was explicit: we chose not to regard his disappearance from the group as death, but mere going away, as if he had only retired. The chimps do understand death, of course. They may even equate it with going away, as Gonzo's question suggests. But if they do, they surely see human death as something quite different from chimpanzee death — a translation to another state of being, an ascent on a chariot of fire. Yost believes that they have no comprehension of human death at all, that they think we are immortal, that they think we are gods.

***

Vendelmans now no longer pretends that he isn't dying. The leukemia is plainly acute, and he deteriorates physically from day to day. His original this-isn't-actually-happening attitude has been replaced by a kind of sullen, angry acceptance. It is only the fourth week since the onset of the ailment and soon he'll have to enter the hospital.

And he wants to tell the chimps that he's going to die.

"They don't know that human beings can die," Yost said.

"Then it's time they found out," Vendelmans snapped. "Why perpetuate a load of mythological bullshit about us? Why let them think we're gods? Tell them outright that I'm going to die, the way old Egbert died and Salami and Mortimer."

"But they all died naturally," Jan Morton said.

"And I'm not dying naturally?"

She became terribly flustered. "Of old age, I mean. Their life cycles clearly and understandably came to an end and they died and the chimps understood it. Whereas you—" She faltered.

"—am dying a monstrous and terrible death midway through my life," Vendelmans said, and started to break down and recovered with a fierce effort, and Jan began to cry, and it was generally a bad scene from which Vendelmans saved us by going on, "It should be of philosophical importance to the project to discover how the chimps react to a revaluation of the human metaphysic. We've ducked every chance we've had to help them understand the nature of mortality. Now I propose we use me to teach them that humans are subject to the same laws they are. That we are not gods."

"And that gods exist," said Yost, "who are capricious and unfathomable and to whom we ourselves are as less than chimps."

Vendelmans shrugged. "They don't need to hear all that now. But it's time they understood what we are. Or rather, it's time that we learned how much they already understand. Use my death as a way of finding out. It's the first time they've been in the presence of a human who's actually in the process of dying. The other times one of us has died, it's always been in some sort of accident."

Burt Christensen said, "Hal, have you already told them anything about—"

"No," Vendelmans said. "Of course not. Not a word. But I see them talking to each other. They know."

***

We discussed it far into the night. The question needed careful examination because of the far-reaching consequences of any change we might make in the metaphysical givens of our animals. These chimps have lived in a closed environment here for decades, and the culture they have evolved is a product of what we have chosen to teach them, compounded by their own innate chimpness plus whatever we have unknowingly transmitted to them about ourselves or them. Any radical conceptual material we offer them must be weighed thoughtfully, because its effects will be irreversible, and those who succeed us in this community will be unforgiving if we do anything stupidly premature. If the plan is to observe a community of intelligent primates over a period of many human generations, studying the changes in their intellectual capacity as their linguistic skills increase, then we must at all times take care to let them find things out for themselves, rather than skewing our data by giving the chimps more than their current concept-processing abilities may be able to handle.

On the other hand, Vendelmans was dying right now, allowing us a dramatic opportunity to convey the concept of human mortality. We had at best a week or two to make use of that opportunity: then it might be years before the next chance.

"What are you worried about?" Vendelmans demanded.

Yost said, "Do you fear dying, Hal?"

"Dying makes me angry. I don't fear it; but I still have things to do, and I won't be able to do them. Why do you ask?"

"Because so far as we know the chimps see death—chimp death—as simply part of the great cycle of events, like the darkness that comes after the daylight. But human death is going to come as a revelation to them, a shock. And if they pick up from you any sense of fear or even anger over your dying, who knows what impact that will have on their way of thought?"

"Exactly. *Who knows?* I offer you a chance to find out!" By a narrow margin, finally we voted to let Hal Vendelmans share his death with the chimpanzees. Nearly all of us had reservations about that. But plainly Vendelmans was determined to have a useful death, a meaningful death; the only way he could face his fate at all was by contributing it like this to the project. And in the end I think most of us cast our votes his way purely out of our love for him.

***

We rearranged the schedules to give Vendelmans more contact with the animals. There are ten of us, fifty of them; each of us has a special field of inquiry—number theory, syntactical innovation, metaphysical exploration, semiotics, tool use, and so on—and we work with chimps of our own choice, subject, naturally, to the shifting patterns of subtribal bonding within the chimp community. But we agreed that Vendelmans would have to offer his revelations to the alpha intelligences — Leo, Ramona, Grimsky, Alice, and Attila — regardless of the current structure of the chimp-human dialogues. Leo, for instance, was involved in an ongoing interchange with Beth Rankin on the notion of the change of seasons. Beth more or less willingly gave up her time with Leo to Vendelmans, for Leo was essential in this. We learned long ago that anything important had to be imparted to the alphas first, and they will impart it to the others. A bright chimp knows more about teaching things to his duller cousins than the brightest human being.

The next morning Hal and Judy Vendelmans took Leo, Ramona, and Attila aside and held a long conversation with them. I was busy in a different part of the compound with Gonzo, Mimsy, Muffin, and Chump, but I glanced over occasionally to see what was going on. Hal looked radiant — like Moses just down from the mountain after talking with God. Judy was trying to look radiant too, working at it, but her grief kept breaking through: once I saw her turn away from the chimps and press her knuckles to her teeth to hold it back.

Afterward Leo and Grimsky had a conference out by the oak grove. Yost and Charley Damiano watched it with binoculars, but they couldn't make much sense out of it. The chimps, when they sign to each other, use modified gestures much less precise than the ones they use with us; whether this marks the evolution of a special chimp-to-chimp argot designed not to be understood by us, or is simply a factor of chimp reliance on supplementary nonverbal ways of communicating, is something we still don't know, but the fact remains that we have trouble comprehending the sign language they use with each other, particularly the form the alphas use. Then, too, Leo and Grimsky kept wandering in and out of the trees, as if perhaps they knew we were watching them and didn't want us to eavesdrop. A little later in the day, Ramona and Alice had the same sort of meeting. Now all five of our alphas must have been in on the revelation.

Somehow the news began to filter down to the rest of them.

We weren't able to observe actual concept transmission. We did notice that Vendelmans, the next day, began to get rather more attention than normal. Little troops of chimpanzees formed about him as he moved — slowly, and in obvious difficulty — about the compound. Gonzo and Chump, who had been bickering for months, suddenly were standing side by side staring intently at Vendelmans. Chicory, normally shy, went out of her way to engage him in a conversation — about the ripeness of the apples on the tree, Vendelmans reported. Anna Livia's young twins, Shem and Shaun, climbed up and sat on Vendelmans's shoulders.

"They want to find out what a dying god is really like," Yost said quietly.

"But look there," Jan Morton said.

Judy Vendelmans had an entourage too: Mimsy, Muffin, Claudius, Buster, and Kong. Staring in fascination, eyes wide, lips extended, some of them blowing little bubbles of saliva.

"Do they think she's dying too?" Beth wondered.

Yost shook his head. "Probably not. They can see there's nothing physically wrong with her. But they're picking up the sorrow vibes, the death vibes."

"Is there any reason to think they're aware that Hal is Judy's mate?" Christensen asked.

"It doesn't matter," Yost said. "They can see that she's upset. That interests them, even if they have no way of knowing why Judy would be more upset than any of the rest of us."

"More mysteries out yonder," I said, pointing into the meadow. Grimsky was standing by himself out there, contemplating something. He is the oldest of the chimps, gray-haired, going bald, a deep thinker. He has been here almost from the beginning, more than thirty years, and very little has escaped his attention in that time.

Far off to the left, in the shade of the big beech tree, Leo stood similarly in solitary meditation. He is twenty, the alpha male of the community, the strongest and by far the most intelligent. It was eerie to see the two of them in their individual zones of isolation, like distant sentinels, like Easter Island statues, lost in private reveries.

"Philosophers," Yost murmured.

***

Yesterday Vendelmans returned to the hospital for good. Before he went, he made his farewells to each of the fifty chimpanzees, even the infants. In the past week he has altered markedly: he is only a shadow of himself, feeble, wasted. Judy says he'll live only another few weeks.

She has gone on leave and probably won't come back until after Hal's death. I wonder what the chimps will make of her "going away," and of her eventual return.

She said that Leo had asked her if she was dying, too.

Perhaps things will get back to normal here now.

***

Christensen asked me this morning, "Have you noticed the way they seem to drag the notion of death into whatever conversation you're having with them these days?"

I nodded. "Mimsy asked me the other day if the moon dies when the sun comes up and the sun dies when the moon is out. It seemed like such a standard primitive metaphor that I didn't pick up on it at first. But Mimsy's too young for using metaphor that easily and she isn't particularly clever. The older ones must be talking about dying a lot, and it's filtering down."

"Chicory was doing subtraction with me," Christensen said. "She signed, *'You take five, two die, you have three.'* Later she turned it into a verb: *'Three die one equals two.'"*

Others reported similar things. Yet none of the animals were talking about Vendelmans and what was about to happen to him, nor were they asking any overt questions about death or dying. So far as we were able to perceive, they had displaced the whole thing into metaphorical diversions. That in itself indicated a powerful obsession. Like most obsessives, they were trying to hide the thing that most concerned them, and they probably thought they were doing a good job of it. It isn't their fault that we're able to guess what's going on in their minds. They are, after all — and we sometimes have to keep reminding ourselves of this — only chimpanzees.

***

They are holding meetings on the far side of the oak grove, where the little stream runs. Leo and Grimsky seem to do most of the talking, and the others gather around and sit very quietly as the speeches are made. The groups run from ten to thirty chimps at a time. We are unable to discover what they're discussing, though of course we have an idea. Whenever one of us approaches such a gathering, the chimps very casually drift off into three or four separate groups and look exceedingly innocent — "We just out for some fresh air, boss."

Charley Damiano wants to plant a bug in the grove. But how do you spy on a group that converses only in sign language? Cameras aren't as easily hidden as microphones.

We do our best with binoculars. But what little we've been able to observe has been mystifying. The chimp-to-chimp signs they use at these meetings are even more oblique and confusing than the ones we had seen earlier. It's as if they're holding their meetings in pig-Latin, or double-talk or in some entirely new and private language.

Two technicians will come tomorrow to help us mount cameras in the grove.

***

Hal Vendelmans died last night. According to Judy, who phoned Dave Yost, it was very peaceful right at the end, an easy release. Yost and I broke the news to the alpha chimps just after breakfast. No euphemisms, just the straight news. Ramona made a few hooting sounds and looked as if she might cry, but she was the only one who seemed emotionally upset. Leo gave me a long deep look of what was almost certainly compassion, and then he hugged me very hard. Grimsky wandered away and seemed to be signing to himself in the new system. Now a meeting seems to be assembling in the oak grove, the first one in more than a week.

The cameras are in place. Even if we can't decipher the new signs, we can at least tape them and subject them to computer analysis until we begin to understand.

***

Now we've watched the first tapes of a grove meeting, but I can't say we know a lot more than we did before.

For one thing, they disabled two of the cameras right at the outset. Attila spotted them and sent Gonzo and Claudius up into the trees to yank them out. I suppose the remaining cameras went unnoticed; but by accident or deliberate diabolical craftiness, the chimps positioned themselves in such a way that none of the cameras had a clear angle. We did record a few statements from Leo and some give-and-take between Alice and Anna Livia. They spoke in a mixture of standard signs and the new ones, but, without a sense of the context, we've found it impossible to generate any sequence of meanings. Stray signs such as "shirt," "hat," "human," "change," and "banana fly," interspersed with undecipherable stuff, *seem* to be adding up to something, but no one is sure what. We observed no mention of Hal Vendelmans nor any direct references to death. We may be misleading ourselves entirely about the significance of all this.

Or perhaps not. We codified some of the new signs, and this afternoon I asked Ramona what one of them meant. She fidgeted and hooted and looked uncomfortable — and not simply because I was asking her to do a tough abstract thing like giving a definition. She was worried. She looked around for Leo, and when she saw him she made that sign at him. He came bounding over and shoved Ramona away. Then he began to tell me how wise and good and gentle I am. He may be a genius, but even a genius chimp is still a chimp, and I told him I wasn't fooled by his flattery. Then I asked *him* what the new sign meant.

"Jump high come again," Leo signed.

A simple chimpy phrase referring to fun and frolic? So I thought at first, and so did many of my colleagues. But Dave Yost said, "Then why was Ramona so evasive about defining it?"

"Defining isn't easy for them," Beth Rankin said.

"Ramona's one of the five brightest. She's capable of it. Especially since the sign can be defined by use of four other established signs, as Leo proceeded to do."

"What are you getting at, Dave?" I asked.

Yost said, *"'Jump high come again'* might be about a game they like to play, but it could also be an eschatological reference, sacred talk, a concise metaphorical way to speak of death and resurrection, no?"

Mick Falkenburg snorted. "Jesus, Dave, of all the nutty Jesuitical bullshit—"

"Is it?"

"It's possible sometimes to be too subtle in your analysis," Falkenburg said. "You're suggesting that these chimpanzees have a theology?"

"I'm suggesting that they may be in the process of evolving a religion," Yost replied.

Can it be?

Sometimes we lose our perspective with these animals, as Mick indicated, and we overestimate their intelligence; but just as often, I think, we underestimate them.

Jump high come again.

I wonder. Secret sacred talk? A chimpanzee theology? Belief in life after death? A religion?

***

They know that human beings have a body of ritual and belief that they call religion, though how much they really comprehend about it is hard to tell. Dave Yost, in his metaphysical discussions with Leo and some of the other alphas, introduced the concept long ago. He drew a hierarchy that began with God and ran downward through human beings and chimpanzees to dogs and cats and onward to insects and frogs, by way of giving the chimps some sense of the great chain of life. They had seen bugs and frogs and cats and dogs, but they wanted Dave to show them God, and he was forced to tell them that God is not actually tangible and accessible, but lives high overhead although His essence penetrates all things. I doubt that they grasped much of that. Leo, whose nimble and probing intelligence is a constant illumination to us, wanted Yost to explain how we talked to God and how God talked to us if He wasn't around to make signs, and Yost said that we had a thing called religion, which was a system of communicating with God. And that was where he left it, a long while back.

Now we are on guard for any indications of a developing religious consciousness among our troop. Even the scoffers—Mick Falkenburg, Beth, to some degree, Charley Damiano—are paying close heed. After all, one of the underlying purposes of this project is to reach an understanding of how the first hominids managed to cross the intellectual boundary that we like to think separates the animals from humanity. We can't reconstruct a bunch of Australopithecines and study them; but we *can* watch chimpanzees who have been given the gift of language build a quasi-protohuman society, and it is the closest thing to traveling back in time that we are apt to achieve. Yost thinks, I think, Burt Christensen is beginning to think, that we have inadvertently kindled an awareness of the divine, of the numinous force that must be worshipped, by allowing them to see that their gods—us—can be struck down and slain by an even higher power.

The evidence so far is slim. The attention given Vendelmans and Judy; the solitary meditations of Leo and Grimsky; the large gatherings in the grove; the greatly accelerated use of modified sign language in chimp-to-chimp talk at those gatherings; the potentially eschatological reference we think we see in the sign that Leo translated as "jump high come again." That's it. To those of us who want to interpret that as the foundations of religion, it seems indicative of what we want to see; to the rest, it all looks like coincidence and fantasy. The problem is that we are dealing with nonhuman intelligence and we must take care not to impose our own thought-constructs. We can never be certain if we are operating from a value system anything like that of the chimps. The built-in ambiguities of the sign-language grammar we must use with them complicate the issue. Consider the phrase "banana fly" that Leo used in a speech— a sermon?— in the oak grove, and remember Ramona's reference to the sick Vendelmans as "rotten banana." If we take *fly* to be a verb, "banana fly" might be considered a metaphorical description of Vendelmans's ascent to heaven. If we take it to be a noun, Leo might have been talking about the *Drosophila* flies that feed on decaying fruit, a metaphor for the corruption of the flesh after death. On the other hand, he may simply have been making a comment about the current state of our garbage dump.

We have agreed for the moment not to engage the chimpanzees in any direct interrogation about any of this. The Heisenberg principle is eternally our rule here: the observer can too easily perturb the thing observed, so we must make only the most delicate of measurements. Even so, of course, our presence among the chimps is bound to have its impact, but we do what we can to minimize it by avoiding leading questions and watching in silence.

***

Two unusual things today. Taken each by each, they would be interesting without being significant; but if we use each to illuminate the other, we begin to see things in a strange new light, perhaps.

One thing is an increase in vocalizing, noticed by nearly everyone, among the chimps. We know that chimpanzees in the wild have a kind of rudimentary spoken language—a greeting call, a defiance call, the grunts that mean "I like the taste of this," the male chimp's territorial hoot, and such—nothing very complex, really not qualitatively much beyond the language of birds or dogs. They also have a fairly rich nonverbal language, a vocabulary of gestures and facial expressions. But it was not until the first experiments decades ago in teaching chimpanzees human sign-language that any important linguistic capacity became apparent in them. Here at the research station the chimps communicate almost wholly in signs, as they have been trained to do for generations and as they have taught their young ones to do; they revert to hoots and grunts only in the most elemental situations. We ourselves communicate mainly in signs when we are talking to each other while working with the chimps, and even in our humans-only conferences, we use signs as much as speech, from long habit. But suddenly the chimps are making sounds at each other. Odd sounds, unfamiliar sounds, weird, clumsy imitations, one might say, of human speech. Nothing that we can understand, naturally: the chimpanzee larynx is simply incapable of duplicating the phonemes humans use. But these new grunts, these tortured blurts of sound, seem intended to mimic our speech. It was Damiano who showed us, as we were watching a tape of a grove session, how Attila was twisting his lips with his hands in what appeared unmistakably to be an attempt to make human sounds come out.

Why?

The second thing is that Leo has started wearing a shirt and a hat. There is nothing remarkable about a chimp in clothing; although we have never encouraged such anthropomorphization here, various animals have taken a fancy from time to time to some item of clothing, have begged it from its owner and have worn it for a few days or even weeks. The novelty here is that the shirt and the hat belonged to Hal Vendelmans, and that Leo wears them only when the chimps are gathered in the oak grove, which Dave Yost has lately begun calling the "holy grove." Leo found them in the toolshed beyond the vegetable garden. The shirt is ten sizes too big, Vendelmans having been so brawny, but Leo ties the sleeves across his chest and lets the rest dangle down over his back almost like a cloak.

What shall we make of this?

Jan is the specialist in chimp verbal processes. At the meeting tonight she said, "It sounds to me as if they're trying to duplicate the rhythms of human speech even though they can't reproduce the actual sounds. They're playing at being human."

"Talking the god-talk," said Dave Yost.

"What do you mean?" Jan asked.

"Chimps talk with their hands. Humans do, too, when speaking with chimps, but when humans talk to humans, they use their voices. Humans are gods to chimps, remember. Talking in the way the gods talk is one way of remaking yourself in the image of the gods, of putting on divine attributes."

"But that's nonsense," Jan said. "I can't possibly—"

"Wearing human clothing," I broke in excitedly, "would also be a kind of putting on divine attributes, in the most literal sense of the phrase. Especially if the clothes—"

"—had belonged to Hal Vendelmans," said Christensen.

"The dead god," Yost said.

We looked at each other in amazement.

Charley Damiano said, not in his usual skeptical way, but in a kind of wonder, "Dave, are you hypothesizing that Leo functions as some sort of priest, that those are his sacred garments?"

"More than just a priest," Yost said. "A high priest, I think. A pope. The pope of the chimps."

***

Grimsky is suddenly looking very feeble. Yesterday we saw him moving slowly through the meadow by himself, making a long circuit of the grounds as far out as the pond and the little waterfall, then solemnly and ponderously staggering back to the meeting place at the far side of the grove. Today he has been sitting quietly by the stream, occasionally rocking slowly back and forth, now and then dipping his feet in. I checked the records: he is forty-three years old, well along for a chimp, although some have been known to live fifty years and more. Mick wanted to take him to the infirmary, but we decided against it; if he is dying, and by all appearances he is, we ought to let him do it with dignity in his own way. Jan went down to the grove to visit him and reported that he shows no apparent signs of disease. His eyes are clear; his face feels cool. Age has withered him and his time is at hand. I feel an enormous sense of loss, for he has a keen intelligence, a long memory, a shrewd and thoughtful nature. He was the alpha male of the troop for many years, but a decade ago, when Leo came of age, Grimsky abdicated in his favor with no sign of a struggle. Behind Grimsky's grizzled forehead there must lie a wealth of subtle and mysterious perceptions, concepts and insights about which we know practically nothing, and very soon all that will be lost. Let us hope he's managed to teach his wisdom to Leo and Attila and Alice and Ramona.

***

Today's oddity: a ritual distribution of meat.

Meat is not very important in the diet of chimps, but they do like to have some, and as far back as I can remember, Wednesday has been meat-day here, when we give them a side of beef or some slabs of mutton or something of that sort. The procedure for dividing up the meat betrays the chimps' wild heritage, for the alpha males eat their fill first while the others watch, and then the weaker males beg for a share and are allowed to move in to grab, and finally the females and young ones get the scraps. Today was meat-day. Leo, as usual, helped himself first, but what happened after that was astounding. He let Attila feed, and then told Attila to offer some meat to Grimsky, who is even weaker today and brushed it aside. *Then Leo put on Vendelmans's hat* and began to parcel out scraps of meat to the others. One by one they came up to him in the current order of ranking and went through the standard begging maneuver, hand beneath chin, palm upward, and Leo gave each one a strip of meat.

"Like taking communion," Charley Damiano muttered. "With Leo the celebrant at the Mass."

Unless our assumptions are totally off base, there is a real religion going on here, perhaps created by Grimsky and under Leo's governance. And Hal Vendelmans's faded old blue work hat is the tiara of the pope.

***

Beth Rankin woke me at dawn and said, "Come fast. They're doing something strange with old Grimsky."

I was up and dressed and awake in a hurry. We have a closed-circuit system now that pipes the events in the grove back to us, and we paused at the screen so that I could see what was going on. Grimsky sat on his knees at the edge of the stream, eyes closed, barely moving. Leo, wearing the hat, was beside him, elaborately tying Vendelmans's shirt over Grimsky's shoulders. A dozen or more of the other adult chimps were squatting in a semicircle in front of them.

Burt Christensen said, "What's going on? Is Leo making Grimsky the assistant pope?"

"I think Leo is giving Grimsky the last rites," I said.

What else could it have been? Leo wore the sacred headdress. He spoke at length using the new signs — the ecclesiastical language, the chimpanzee equivalent of Latin or Hebrew or Sanskrit — and as his oration went on and on, the congregation replied periodically with outbursts of — I suppose — response and approval, some in signs, some with grunting garbled pseudohuman sounds that Dave Yost thought was their version of god-talk. Throughout it all Grimsky was silent and remote, though occasionally he nodded or murmured or tapped both his shoulders in a gesture whose meaning was unknown to us. The ceremony went on for more than an hour. Then Grimsky leaned forward, and Kong and Chump took him by the arms and eased him down until he was lying with his cheek against the ground.

For two, three, five minutes all the chimpanzees were still. At last Leo came forward and removed his hat, setting it on the ground beside Grimsky, and with great delicacy he untied the shirt Grimsky wore. Grimsky did not move. Leo draped the shirt over his own shoulders and donned the hat again.

He turned to the watching chimps and signed, using the old signs that were completely intelligible to us, "Grimsky now be human being."

We stared at each other in awe and astonishment. A couple of us were sobbing. No one could speak.

The funeral ceremony seemed to be over. The chimps were dispersing. We saw Leo sauntering away, hat casually dangling from one hand, the shirt in the other, trailing over the ground. Grimsky alone remained by the stream. We waited ten minutes and went down to the grove. Grimsky seemed to be sleeping very peacefully, but he was dead, and we gathered him up—Burt and I carried him; he seemed to weigh almost nothing—and took him back to the lab for the autopsy.

In midmorning the sky darkened and lightning leaped across the hills to the north. There was a tremendous crack of thunder almost instantly and sudden tempestuous rain. Jan pointed to the meadow. The male chimps were doing a bizarre dance, roaring, swaying, slapping their feet against the ground, hammering their hands against the trunks of the trees, ripping off branches and flailing the earth with them. Grief? Terror? Joy at the translation of Grimsky to a divine state? Who could tell? I had never been frightened by our animals before—I knew them too well, I regarded them as little hairy cousins—but now they were terrifying creatures and this was a scene out of time's dawn, as Gonzo and Kong and Attila and Chump and Buster and Claudius and even Pope Leo himself went thrashing about in that horrendous rain, pounding out the steps of some unfathomable rite.

The lightning ceased and the rain moved southward as quickly as it had come, and the dancers went slinking away, each to his favorite tree. By noon the day was bright and warm and it was as though nothing out of the ordinary had happened.

***

Two days after Grimsky's death I was awakened again at dawn, this time by Mick Falkenburg. He shook my shoulder and yelled at me to wake up, and as I sat there blinking he said, "Chicory's dead! I was out for an early walk and I found her near the place where Grimsky died."

"Chicory? But she's only—"

"Eleven, twelve, something like that. I know."

I put my clothes on while Mick woke the others, and we went down to the stream. Chicory was sprawled out, but not peacefully—there was a dribble of blood at the corner of her mouth, her eyes were wide and horrified, her hands were curled into frozen talons. All about her in the moist soil of the stream bank were footprints. I searched my memory for an instance of murder in the chimp community and could find nothing remotely like it—quarrels, yes, and lengthy feuds and some ugly ambushes and battles, fairly violent, serious injuries now and then. But this had no precedent.

"Ritual murder," Yost murmured.

"Or a sacrifice, perhaps?" suggested Beth Rankin.

"Whatever it is," I said, "they're learning too fast. Recapitulating the whole evolution of religion, including the worst parts of it. We'll have to talk to Leo."

"Is that wise?" Yost asked.

"Why not?"

"We've kept hands off so far. If we want to see how this thing unfolds—"

"During the night," I said, "the pope and the college of cardinals ganged up on a gentle young female chimp and killed her. Right now they may be off somewhere sending Alice or Ramona or Anna Livia's twins to chimp heaven. I think we have to weigh the value of observing the evolution of chimp religion against the cost of losing irreplaceable members of a unique community. I say we call in Leo and tell him that it's wrong to kill."

"He knows that," said Yost. "He must. Chimps aren't murderous animals."

"Chicory's dead."

"And if they see it as a holy deed?" Yost demanded.

"Then one by one we'll lose our animals, and at the end we'll just have a couple of very saintly survivors. Do you want that?"

***

We spoke with Leo. Chimps can be sly and they can be manipulative, but even the best of them, and Leo is the Einstein of chimpanzees, does not seem to know how to lie. We asked him where Chicory was and Leo told us that Chicory was now a human being. I felt a chill at that. Grimsky was also a human being, said Leo. We asked him how he knew that they had become human and he said, "They go where Vendelmans go. When human go away, he become god. When chimpanzee go away, he become human. Right?"

"No," we said.

The logic of the ape is not easy to refute. We told him that death comes to all living creatures, that it is natural and holy, but that only God could decide when it was going to happen. God, we said, calls His creatures to Himself one at a time. God had called Hal Vendelmans, God had called Grimsky, God would someday call Leo and all the rest here. But God had not yet called Chicory. Leo wanted to know what was wrong with sending Chicory to Him ahead of time. Did that not improve Chicory's condition? No, we replied. No, it only did harm to Chicory. Chicory would have been much happier living here with us than going to God so soon. Leo did not seem convinced. Chicory, he said, now could talk words with her mouth and wore shoes on her feet. He envied Chicory very much.

We told him that God would be angry if any more chimpanzees died. We told him that *we* would be angry. Killing chimpanzees was wrong, we said. It was not what God wanted Leo to be doing.

"Me talk to God, find out what God wants," Leo said.

***

We found Buster dead by the edge of the pond this morning, with indications of another ritual murder. Leo coolly stared us down and explained that God had given orders that all chimpanzees were to become human beings as quickly as possible, and this could only be achieved by the means employed on Chicory and Buster.

Leo is confined now in the punishment tank and we have suspended this week's meat distribution. Yost voted against both of those decisions, saying we ran the risk of giving Leo the aura of a religious martyr, which would enhance his already considerable power. But these killings have to stop. Leo knows, of course, that we are upset about them. But if he believes his path is the path of righteousness, nothing we say or do is going to change his mind.

***

Judy Vendelmans called today. She has put Hal's death fairly well behind her, misses the project, misses the chimps. As gently as I could, I told her what has been going on here. She was silent a very long time — Chicory was one of her favorites, and Judy has had enough grief already to handle for one summer — but finally she said, "I think I know what can be done. I'll be on the noon flight tomorrow."

We found Mimsy dead in the usual way late this afternoon. Leo is still in the punishment tank — the third day. The congregation has found a way to carry out its rites without its leader. Mimsy's death has left me stunned, but we are all deeply affected, virtually unable to proceed with our work.

It may be necessary to break up the community entirely to save the animals. Perhaps we can send them to other research centers for a few months, three of them here, five there, until this thing subsides. But what if it doesn't subside? What if the dispersed animals convert others elsewhere to the creed of Leo?

The first thing Judy said when she arrived was, "Let Leo out. I want to talk with him."

We opened the tank. Leo stepped forth, uneasy, abashed, shading his eyes against the strong light. He glanced at me, at Yost, at Jan, as if wondering which one of us was going to scold him; and then he saw Judy and it was as though he had seen a ghost. He made a hollow rasping sound deep in his throat and backed away. Judy signed hello and stretched out her arms to him. Leo trembled. He was terrified. There was nothing unusual about one of us going on leave and returning after a month or two, but Leo must not have expected Judy ever to return, must in fact have imagined her gone to the same place her husband had gone, and the sight of her shook him. Judy understood all that, obviously, for she quickly made powerful use of it, signing to Leo, "I bring you message from Vendelmans."

"Tell tell tell!"

"Come walk with me," said Judy.

She took him by the hand and led him gently out of the punishment area and into the compound and down the hill toward the meadow. I watched from the top of the hill, the tall, slender woman and the compact, muscular chimpanzee close together, side by side, hand in hand, pausing now to talk, Judy signing and Leo replying in a flurry of gestures, then Judy again for a long time, a brief response from Leo, another cascade of signs from Judy, then Leo squatting, tugging at blades of grass, shaking his head, clapping hand to elbow in his expression of confusion, then to his chin, then taking Judy's hand. They were gone for nearly an hour. The other chimps did not dare approach them. Finally Judy and Leo, hand in hand, came quietly up the hill to headquarters again. Leo's eyes were shining and so were Judy's.

She said, "Everything will be all right now. That's so, isn't it, Leo?"

Leo said, "God is always right."

She made a dismissal sign and Leo went slowly down the hill. The moment he was out of sight, Judy turned away from us and cried a little, just a little; then she asked for a drink; and then she said, "It isn't easy, being God's messenger."

"What did you tell him?" I asked.

"That I had been in heaven visiting Hal. That Hal was looking down all the time and he was very proud of Leo, except for one thing, that Leo was sending too many chimpanzees to God too soon. I told him that God was not yet ready to receive Chicory and Buster and Mimsy, that they would have to be kept in storage cells for a long time until their true time came, and that was not good for them. I told him that Hal wanted Leo to know that God hoped he would stop sending him chimpanzees. Then I gave Leo Hal's old wristwatch to wear when he conducts services, and Leo promised he would obey Hal's wishes. That was all. I suspect I've added a whole new layer of mythology to what's developing here, and I trust you won't be angry with me for doing it. I don't believe any more chimps will be killed. And I think I'd like another drink."

Later in the day we saw the chimps assembled by the stream. Leo held his arm aloft and sunlight blazed from the band of gold on his slim hairy wrist, and a great outcry of grunts in god-talk went up from the congregation and they danced before him, and then he donned the sacred hat and the sacred shirt and moved his arms eloquently in the secret sacred gestures of the holy sign language.

There have been no more killings. I think no more will occur. Perhaps after a time our chimps will lose interest in being religious, and go on to other pastimes. But not yet, not yet. The ceremonies continue, and grow ever more elaborate, and we are compiling volumes of extraordinary observations, and God looks down and is pleased. And Leo proudly wears the emblems of his papacy as he bestows his blessing on the worshipers in the holy grove.

NEEDLE IN A TIMESTACK (1982)

INTRODUCTION

I was back in the swing of things, now, after getting my "retirement" out of my system, and although I still had no plans for undertaking any novels, short stories were emanating from me all through 1981 with a swiftness that I had not experienced in a decade and a half. I had begun to do the cycle of tales that would be collected in the book called *Majipoor Chronicles*; I sold more stories to *Omni*, and to other such high-paying magazines as *Playboy* and *Penthouse*.

The *Playboy* relationship was particularly stimulating. *Playboy*'s fiction editor, Alice K. Turner, was bright, irreverent, funny, and as knowledgeable about the craft of the short story as any editor I've ever known. Over the course of nearly two decades she bought perhaps fifteen stories from me, and just about every one involved a battle royal down to the last semicolon — a series of good-humored author/editor confrontations from which both of us drew tremendous pleasure. (Most of the time I ultimately came to see the wisdom and logic of her objections to a story. Her big secret was that she knew when to let me win in cases where I didn't.)

Alice accepted a story from me ("Gianni") in February of 1981 and another ("The Conglomeroid Cocktail Party") in October of that year. Since she could publish only one story a month and every writer in America was sending her material, that should have been enough out of me for a while. But I was on a roll, writing with an ease and freedom I had not known since the prolific days of 1967, and when another *Playboy*-quality story idea came to me in January, 1982, I sent it to her unhesitatingly.

I had heard Bill Rotsler, a friend of mine, say to a young man who was bothering him at a science-fiction convention, "Go away, kid, or I'll change your future." Upon hearing that I said, "No, tell him that you'll change his PAST," and suddenly I realized that I had handed myself a very nice story idea. I wrote it in January, 1982 — its intricate time-travel plot unfolded for me with marvelous clarity as I worked — and Alice Turner bought it immediately for *Playboy*'s July, 1983 issue.

A few years ago a major American movie company bought it also. They gave me quite a lot of money, which was very pleasant, but so far they haven't done anything about actually making the movie. I hope they do, sooner or later. It's one science-fiction movie I'd actually like to see.

I played a nasty trick on bibliographers with this one, incidentally. In 1966 Ballantine Books published a short-story collection of mine called *Needle in a Timestack* — a delicious title dreamed up by Betty Ballantine, my editor there (and one of the two owners of the company.) In the fullness of time the book went out of print, and when I sold it to a British publisher in 1979 I dropped all but four of the original group of stories and replaced them with others, to avoid duplicating a different British collection of my stories. So there were two books of mine with the same name, one American, one British, made up of substantially different groups of stories!

Neither book, of course, contained the story called "Needle in a Timestack," because as of 1979 I hadn't written it yet. Three years later, though, when I wrote the story you are about to read, "Needle in a Timestack" seemed a perfectly fitting title for it, and I reached for it unhesitatingly, only too aware of the havoc I was creating for scholars of my work.

The final twist came a few years later, when the British *Needle in a Timestack,* almost entirely different in contents from the original American one, was published in the United States. I suppose it might have seemed logical to add the *Playboy* story to the group, thus uniting story title and book title for the first time, but I didn't, because I had already collected it in a different book, 1984's *The Conglomeroid Cocktail Party.*

Still with me? If you are, then you should be tuned up and ready for the story that follows.

Between one moment and the next the taste of cotton came into his mouth, and Mikkelsen knew that Tommy Hambleton had been tinkering with his past again. The cotton-in-the-mouth sensation was the standard tip-off for Mikkelsen. For other people it might be a ringing in the ears, a tremor of the little finger, a tightness in the shoulders. Whatever the symptom, it always meant the same thing: your time-track has been meddled with, your life has been retroactively transformed. It happened all the time. One of the little annoyances of modern life, everyone always said. Generally, the changes didn't amount to much.

But Tommy Hambleton was out to destroy Mikkelsen's marriage, or, more accurately, he was determined to unhappen it altogether, and that went beyond Mikkelsen's limits of tolerance. In something close to panic he phoned home to find out if he still had Janine.

Her lovely features blossomed on the screen — glossy dark hair, elegant cheekbones, cool sardonic eyes. She looked tense and strained, and Mikkelsen knew she had felt the backlash of this latest attempt too.

"Nick?" she said. "Is it a phasing?"

"I think so. Tommy's taken another whack at us, and Christ only knows how much chaos he's caused this time."

"Let's run through everything."

"All right," Mikkelsen said. "What's your name?"

"Janine."

"And mine?"

"Nick. Nicholas Perry Mikkelsen. You see? Nothing important has changed."

"Are you married?"

"Yes, of course, darling. To you."

"Keep going. What's our address?"

"11 Lantana Crescent."

"Do we have children?"

"Dana and Elise. Dana's five, Elise is three. Our cat's name is Minibelle, and—"

"Okay," Mikkelsen said, relieved. "That much checks out. But I tasted the cotton, Janine. Where has he done it to us this time? What's been changed?"

"It can't be anything major, love. We'll find it if we keep checking. Just stay calm."

"Calm. Yes." He closed his eyes. He took a deep breath. The little annoyances of modern life, he thought. In the old days, when time was just a linear flow from *then* to *now*, did anyone get bored with all that stability? For better or for worse it was different now. You go to bed a Dartmouth man and wake up Columbia, never the wiser. You board a plane that blows up over Cyprus, but then your insurance agent goes back and gets you to miss the flight. In the new fluid way of life there was always a second chance, a third, a fourth, now that the past was open to anyone with the price of a ticket. But what good is any of that, Mikkelsen wondered, if Tommy Hambleton can use it to disappear me and marry Janine again himself?

They punched for readouts and checked all their vital data against what they remembered. When your past is altered through time-phasing, all records of your life are automatically altered too, of course, but there's a period of two or three hours when memories of your previous existence still linger in your brain, like the phantom twitches of an amputated limb. They checked the date of Mikkelsen's birth, parents' names, his nine genetic coordinates, his educational record. Everything seemed right. But when they got to their wedding date the readout said 8 Feb 2017, and Mikkelsen heard warning chimes in his mind. "I remember a summer wedding," he said. "Outdoors in Dan Levy's garden, the hills all dry and brown, the 24th of August."

"So do I, Nick. The hills wouldn't have been brown in February. But I can see it—that hot dusty day—"

"Then five months of our marriage are gone, Janine. He couldn't unmarry us altogether, but he managed to hold us up from summer to winter." Rage made his head spin, and he had to ask his desk for a quick buzz of tranks. Etiquette called for one to be cool about a phasing. But he couldn't be cool when the phasing was a deliberate and malevolent blow at the center of his life. He wanted to shout to break things, to kick Tommy Hambleton's ass. He wanted his marriage left alone. He said, "You know what I'm going to do one of these days? I'm going to go back about fifty years and eradicate Tommy completely. Just arrange things so his parents never get to meet, and—"

"No, Nick. You mustn't."

"I know. But I'd love to." He knew he couldn't, and not just because it would be murder. It was essential that Tommy Hambleton be born and grow up and meet Janine and marry her, so that when the marriage came apart she would meet and marry Mikkelsen. If he changed Hambleton's past, he would change hers too, and if he changed hers, he would change his own, and anything might happen. Anything. But all the same he was furious. "Five months of our past, Janine—"

"We don't need them, love. Keeping the present and the future safe is the main priority. By tomorrow we'll always think we were married in February of 2017, and it won't matter. Promise me you won't try to phase him."

"I hate the idea that he can simply—"

"So do I. But I want you to promise you'll leave things as they are."

"Well—"

"Promise."

"All right," he said. "I promise."

***

Little phasings happened all the time. Someone in Illinois makes a trip to eleventh-century Arizona and sets up tiny ripple currents in time that have a tangential and peripheral effect on a lot of lives, and someone in California finds himself driving a silver BMW instead of a gray Toyota. No one minded trifling changes like that. But this was the third time in the last twelve months, so far as Mikkelsen was able to tell, that Tommy Hambleton had committed a deliberate phasing intended to break the chain of events that had brought about Mikkelsen's marriage to Janine.

The first phasing happened on a splendid spring day—coming home from work, sudden taste of cotton in mouth, sense of mysterious disorientation. Mikkelsen walked down the steps looking for his old ginger tomcat, Gus, who always ran out to greet him as though he thought he was a dog. No Gus. Instead a calico female, very pregnant, sitting placidly in the front hall.

"Where's Gus?" Mikkelsen asked Janine.

"Gus? Gus who?"

"Our cat."

"You mean Max?"

"Gus," he said. "Sort of orange, crooked tail—"

"That's right. But Max is his name. I'm sure it's Max. He must be around somewhere. Look, here's Minibelle." Janine knelt and stroked the fat calico. "Minibelle, where's Max?"

"Gus," Mikkelsen said. "Not Max. And who's this Minibelle?"

"She's our cat, Nick," Janine said, sounding surprised.

They stared at each other.

"Something's happened, Nick."

"I think we've been time-phased," he said.

Sensation as of dropping through a trapdoor — shock, confusion, terror. Followed by hasty and scary inventory of basic life-data to see what had changed. Everything appeared in order except for the switch of cats. He didn't remember having a female calico. Neither did Janine, although she had accepted the presence of the cat without surprise. As for Gus — Max — he was getting foggier about his name, and Janine couldn't even remember what he looked like. But she did recall that he had been a wedding gift from some close friend, and Mikkelsen remembered that the friend was Gus Stark, for whom they had named him, and Janine was then able to dredge up the dimming fact that Gus was a close friend of Mikkelsen's and also of Hambleton and Janine in the days when they were married, and that Gus had introduced Janine to Mikkelsen ten years ago when they were all on holiday in Hawaii.

Mikkelsen accessed the household callmaster and found no Gus Stark listed. So the phasing had erased him from their roster of friends. The general phone directory turned up a Gus Stark in Costa Mesa. Mikkelsen called him and got a freckle-faced man with fading red hair, who looked more or less familiar. But he didn't know Mikkelsen at all, and only after some puzzling around in his memory did he decide that they had been distantly acquainted way back when, but had had some kind of trifling quarrel and had lost touch with each other years ago.

"That's not how I think I remember it," Mikkelsen said. "I remember us as friends for years, really close. You and Donna and Janine and I were out to dinner only last week, is what I remember, over in Newport Beach."

"Donna?"

"Your wife."

"My wife's name is Karen. Jesus, this has been one hell of a phasing, hasn't it?" He didn't sound upset.

"I'll say. Blew away your marriage, our friendship, and who knows what-all else."

"Well, these things happen. Listen, if I can help you in any way, fella, just call. But right now Karen and I were on our way out, and — "

"Yeah. Sure. Sorry to have bothered you," Mikkelsen told him.

He blanked the screen.

Donna. Karen. Gus. Max. He looked at Janine.

"Tommy did it," she said.

She had it all figured out. Tommy, she said, had never forgiven Mikkelsen for marrying her. He wanted her back. He still sent her birthday cards, coy little gifts, postcards from exotic ports.

"You never mentioned them," Mikkelsen said.

She shrugged. "I thought you'd only get annoyed. You've always disliked Tommy."

"No," Mikkelsen said, "I think he's interesting in his oddball way, flamboyant, unusual. What I dislike is his unwillingness to accept the notion that you stopped being his wife a dozen years ago."

"You'd dislike him more if you knew how hard he's been trying to get me back."

"Oh?"

"When we broke up," she said, "he phased me four times. This was before I met you. He kept jaunting back to our final quarrel, trying to patch it up so that the separation wouldn't have happened. I began feeling the phasings and I knew what must be going on, and I told him to quit it or I'd report him and get his jaunt-license revoked. That scared him, I guess, because he's been pretty well behaved ever since, except for all the little hints and innuendoes and invitations to leave you and marry him again."

"Christ," Mikkelsen said. "How long were you and he married? Six months?"

"Seven. But he's an obsessive personality. He never lets go."

"And now he's started phasing again?"

"That's my guess. He's probably decided that you're the obstacle, that I really do still love you, that I want to spend the rest of my life with you. So he needs to make us unmeet. He's taken his first shot by somehow engineering a breach between you and your friend Gus a dozen years back, a breach so severe that you never really became friends and Gus never fixed you up with me. Only it didn't work out the way Tommy hoped. We went to that party at Dave Cushman's place and I got pushed into the pool on top of you and you introduced yourself and one thing led to another and here we still are."

"Not all of us are," Mikkelsen said. "My friend Gus is married to somebody else now."

"That didn't seem to trouble him much."

"Maybe not. But he isn't my friend any more, either, and that troubles *me*. My whole past is at Tommy Hambleton's mercy, Janine! And Gus the cat is gone too. Gus was a damned good cat. I miss him."

"Five minutes ago you weren't sure whether his name was Gus or Max. Two hours from now you won't know you ever had any such cat, and it won't matter at all."

"But suppose the same thing had happened to you and me as happened to Gus and Donna?"

"It didn't, though."

"It might the next time," Mikkelsen said.

***

But it didn't. The next time, which was about six months later, they came out of it still married to each other. What they lost was their collection of twentieth-century artifacts — the black-and-white television set and the funny old dial telephone and the transistor radio and the little computer with the typewriter keyboard. All those treasures vanished between one instant and the next, leaving Mikkelsen with the telltale cottony taste in his mouth, Janine with a short-lived tic below her left eye, and both of them with the nagging awareness that a phasing had occurred.

At once they did what they could to see where the alteration had been made. For the moment they both remembered the artifacts they once had owned, and how eagerly they had collected them in '21 and '22, when the craze for such things was just beginning. But there were no sales receipts in their files and already their memories of what they had bought were becoming blurry and contradictory. There was a grouping of glittery sonic sculptures in the corner, now, where the artifacts had been. What change had been effected in the pattern of their past to put those things in the place of the others?

They never really were sure — there was no certain way of knowing — but Mikkelsen had a theory. The big expense he remembered for 2021 was the time-jaunt that he and Janine had taken to Aztec Mexico, just before she got pregnant with Dana. Things had been a little wobbly between the Mikkelsens back then, and the time-jaunt was supposed to be a second honeymoon. But their guide on the jaunt had been a hot little item named Elena Schmidt, who had made a very determined play for Mikkelsen and who had had him considering, for at least half an hour of lively fantasy, leaving Janine for her.

"Suppose," he said, "that on our original time-track we never went back to the Aztecs at all, but put the money into the artifact collection. But then Tommy went back and maneuvered things to get us interested in time-jaunting, and at the same time persuaded that Schmidt cookie to show an interest in me. We couldn't afford both the antiques and the trip; we opted for the trip, Elena did her little number on me, it didn't cause the split that Tommy was hoping for, and now we have some gaudy memories of Moctezuma's empire and no collection of early electronic devices. What do you think?"

"Makes sense," Janine said.

"Will you report him, or should I?"

"But we have no proof, Nick!"

He frowned. Proving a charge of time-crime, he knew, was almost impossible, and risky besides. The very act of investigating the alleged crime could cause an even worse phase-shift and scramble their pasts beyond repair. To enter the past is like poking a baseball bat into a spiderweb: it can't be done subtly or delicately.

"Do we just sit and wait for Tommy to figure out a way to get rid of me that really works?" Mikkelsen asked.

"We can't just confront him with suspicions, Nick."

"You did it once."

"Long ago. The risks are greater now. We have more past to lose. What if he's not responsible? What if he gets scared of being blamed for something that's just coincidence, and *really* sets out to phase us? He's so damned volatile, so unstable—if he feels threatened, he's likely to do anything. He could wreck our lives entirely."

"If *he* feels threatened? What about—"

"Please, Nick. I've got a hunch Tommy won't try it again. He's had two shots and they've both failed. He'll quit it now. I'm sure he will."

Grudgingly Mikkelsen yielded, and after a time he stopped worrying about a third phasing. Over the next few weeks, other effects of the second phasing kept turning up, the way losses gradually make themselves known after a burglary. The same thing had happened after the first one. A serious attempt at altering the past could never have just one consequence; there was always a host of trivial—or not so trivial—secondary shifts, a ramifying web of transformations reaching out into any number of other lives. New chains of associations were formed in the Mikkelsens' lives as a result of the erasure of their plan to collect electronic artifacts and the substitution of a trip to pre-Columbian Mexico. People they had met on that trip now were good friends, with whom they exchanged gifts, spent other holidays, shared the burdens and joys of parenthood. A certain hollowness at first marked all those newly ingrafted old friendships, making them seem curiously insubstantial and marked by odd inconsistencies. But after a time everything felt real again, everything appeared to fit.

Then the third phasing happened, the one that pushed the beginning of their marriage from August to the following February, and did six or seven other troublesome little things, as they shortly discovered, to the contours of their existence.

"I'm going to talk to him," Mikkelsen said.

"Nick, don't do anything foolish."

"I don't intend to. But he's got to be made to see that this can't go on."

"Remember that he can be dangerous if he's forced into a corner," Janine said. "Don't threaten him. Don't push him."

"I'll tickle him," Mikkelsen said.

***

He met Hambleton for drinks at the Top of the Marina, Hambleton's favorite pub, swiveling at the end of a jointed stalk a thousand feet long rising from the harbor at Balboa Lagoon. Hambleton was there when Mikkelsen came in — a small sleek man, six inches shorter than Mikkelsen, with a slick confident manner. He was the richest man Mikkelsen knew, gliding through life on one of the big microprocessor fortunes of two generations back, and that in itself made him faintly menacing, as though he might try simply to *buy* back, one of these days, the wife he had loved and lost a dozen years ago when all of them had been so very young.

Hambleton's overriding passion, Mikkelsen knew, was time-travel. He was an inveterate jaunter — a compulsive jaunter, in fact, with that faintly hyperthyroid goggle-eyed look that frequent travelers get. He was always either just back from a jaunt or getting his affairs in order for his next one. It was as though the only use he had for the humdrum real-time event horizon was to serve as his springboard into the past. That was odd. What was odder still was where he jaunted. Mikkelsen could understand people who went zooming off to watch the battle of Waterloo, or shot a bundle on a firsthand view of the sack of Rome. If he had anything like Hambleton's money, that was what he would do. But according to Janine, Hambleton was forever going back seven weeks in time, or maybe to last Christmas, or occasionally to his eleventh birthday party. Time-travel as tourism held no interest for him. Let others roam the ferny glades of the Mesozoic: he spent fortunes doubling back along his own time-track, and never went anywhen other. The purpose of Tommy Hambleton's time-travel, it seemed, was to edit his past to make his life more perfect. He went back to eliminate every little contretemps and faux pas, to recover fumbles, to take advantage of the new opportunities that hindsight provides — to retouch, to correct, to emend. To Mikkelsen that was crazy, but also somehow charming. Hambleton was nothing if not charming. And Mikkelsen admired anyone who could invent his own new species of obsessive behavior, instead of going in for the standard hand-washing routines, or stamp-collecting or sitting with your back to the wall in restaurants.

The moment Mikkelsen arrived, Hambleton punched the autobar for cocktails and said, "Splendid to see you, Mikkelsen. How's the elegant Janine?"

"Elegant."

"What a lucky man you are. The one great mistake of my life was letting that woman slip through my grasp."

"For which I remain forever grateful, Tommy. I've been working hard lately to hang on to her, too."

Hambleton's eyes widened. "Yes? Are you two having problems?"

"Not with each other. Time-track troubles. You know, we were caught in a couple of phasings last year. Pretty serious ones. Now there's been another one. We lost five months of our marriage."

"Ah, the little annoyances of —"

" —modern life," Mikkelsen said. "Yes. A very familiar phrase. But these are what I'd call frightening annoyances. I don't need to tell you, of all people, what a splendid woman Janine is, how terrifying it is to me to think of losing her in some random twitch of the time-track."

"Of course. I quite understand."

"I wish I understood these phasings. They're driving us crazy. And that's what I wanted to talk to you about."

He studied Hambleton closely, searching for some trace of guilt or at least uneasiness. But Hambleton remained serene.

"How can I be of help?"

Mikkelsen said, "I thought that perhaps you, with all your vast experience in the theory and practice of time-jaunting, could give me some clue to what's causing them, so that I can head the next one off."

Hambleton shrugged elaborately. "My dear Nick, it could be anything! There's no way of tracing phasing effects back to their cause reliably. All our lives are interconnected in ways we never suspect. You say this last phasing delayed your marriage by a few months? Well, then, suppose that as a result of the phasing you decided to take a last bachelor fling and went off for a weekend in Banff, say, and met some lovely person with whom you spent three absolutely casual and nonsignificant but delightful days, thereby preventing her from meeting someone else that weekend with whom in the original time-track she had fallen in love and married. You then went home and married Janine, a little later than originally scheduled, and lived happily ever after; but the Banff woman's life was totally switched around, all as a consequence of the phasing that delayed your wedding. Do you see? There's never any telling how a shift in one chain of events can cause interlocking upheavals in the lives of utter strangers."

"So I realize. But why should we be hit with three phasings in a year, each one jeopardizing the whole structure of our marriage?"

"I'm sure I don't know," said Hambleton. "I suppose it's just bad luck, and bad luck always changes, don't you think? Probably you've been at the edge of some nexus of negative phases that has just about run its course." He smiled dazzlingly. "Let's hope so, anyway. Would you care for another filtered rum?"

He was smooth, Mikkelsen thought. And impervious. There was no way to slip past his defenses, and even a direct attack—an outright accusation that he was the one causing the phasings—would most likely bring into play a whole new line of defense. Mikkelsen did not intend to risk that. A man who used time-jaunting so ruthlessly to tidy up his past was too slippery to confront. Pressed, Hambleton would simply deny everything and hasten backward to clear away any traces of his crime that might remain. In any case, making an accusation of time-crime stick was exceedingly difficult, because the crime by definition had to have taken place on a track that no longer existed. Mikkelsen chose to retreat. He accepted another drink from Hambleton; they talked in a desultory way for a while about phasing theory, the weather, the stock market, the excellences of the woman they both had married, and the good old days of 2014 or so when they all used to hang out down in dear old La Jolla, living golden lives of wondrous irresponsibility. Then he extricated himself from the conversation and headed for home in a dark and brooding mood. He had no doubt that Hambleton would strike again, perhaps quite soon. How could he be held at bay? Some sort of preemptive strike, Mikkelsen wondered? Some bold leap into the past that would neutralize the menace of Tommy Hambleton forever? Chancy, Mikkelsen thought. You could lose as much as you gained, sometimes, in that sort of maneuver. But perhaps it was the only hope.

He spent the next few days trying to work out a strategy. Something that would get rid of Hambleton without disrupting the frail chain of circumstance that bound his own life to that of Janine—was it possible? Mikkelsen sketched out ideas, rejected them, tried again. He began to think he saw a way.

Then came a new phasing on a warm and brilliantly sunny morning that struck him like a thunderbolt and left him dazed and numbed. When he finally shook away the grogginess, he found himself in a bachelor flat ninety stories above Mission Bay, a thick taste of cotton in his mouth, and bewildering memories already growing thin of a lovely wife and two kids and a cat and a sweet home in mellow old Corona del Mar.

Janine? Dana? Elise? Minibelle?

Gone. All gone. He knew that he had been living in this condo since '22, after the breakup with Yvonne, and that Melanie was supposed to be dropping in about six. That much was reality. And yet another reality still lingered in his mind, fading, vanishing.

So it had happened. Hambleton had really done it, this time.

***

There was no time for panic or even for pain. He spent the first half hour desperately scribbling down notes, every detail of his lost life that he still remembered, phone numbers, addresses, names, descriptions. He set down whatever he could recall of his life with Janine and of the series of phasings that had led up to this one. Just as he was running dry the telephone rang. Janine, he prayed.

But it was Gus Stark. "Listen," he began, "Donna and I got to cancel for tonight, on account of she's got a bad headache, but I hope you and

Melanie aren't too disappointed, and—" He paused. "Hey, guy, are you okay?"

"There's been a bad phasing," Mikkelsen said.

"Uh-oh."

"I've got to find Janine."

"Janine?"

"Janine—Carter," Mikkelsen said. "Slender, high cheekbones, dark hair—you know."

"Janine," said Stark. "Do I know a Janine? Hey, you and Melanie on the outs? I thought—"

"This has nothing to do with Melanie," said Mikkelsen.

"Janine Carter." Gus grinned. "You mean Tommy Hambleton's girl? The little rich guy who was part of the La Jolla crowd ten-twelve years back when—"

"That's the one. Where do you think I'd find her now?"

"Married Hambleton, I think. Moved to the Riviera, unless I'm mistaken. Look, about tonight, Nick—"

"Screw tonight," Mikkelsen said. "Get off the phone. I'll talk to you later."

He broke the circuit and put the phone into search mode, all directories worldwide, Thomas and Janine Hambleton. While he waited, the shock and anguish of loss began at last to get to him, and he started to sweat, his hands shook, his heart raced in double time. I won't find her, he thought. He's got her hidden behind seven layers of privacy networks and it's crazy to think the phone number is listed, for Christ's sake, and—

The telephone. He hit the button. Janine calling, this time.

She looked stunned and disoriented, as though she were working hard to keep her eyes in focus. "Nick?" she said faintly. "Oh, God, Nick, it's you, isn't it?"

"Where are you?"

"A villa outside Nice. In Cap d'Antibes, actually. Oh, Nick—the kids—they're gone, aren't they? Dana. Elise. They never were born, isn't that so?"

"I'm afraid it is. He really nailed us, this time."

"I can still remember—just as though they were real—as though we spent ten years together—oh, Nick—"

"Tell me how to find you. I'll be on the next plane out of San Diego."

She was silent a moment.

"No. No, Nick. What's the use? We aren't the same people we were when we were married. An hour or two more and we'll forget we ever were together."

"Janine—"

"We've got no past left, Nick. And no future."

"Let me come to you!"

"I'm Tommy's wife. My past's with him. Oh, Nick, I'm so sorry, so awfully sorry—I can still remember, a little, how it was with us, the fun, the running along the beach, the kids, the little fat calico cat—but it's all gone, isn't it? I've got my life here, you've got yours. I just wanted to tell you—"

"We can try to put it back together. You don't love Tommy. You and I belong with each other. We—"

"He's a lot different, Nick. He's not the man you remember from the La Jolla days. Kinder, more considerate, more of a human being, you know? It's been ten years, after all."

Mikkelsen closed his eyes and gripped the edge of the couch to keep from falling. "It's been two hours," he said. "Tommy phased us. He just tore up our life, and we can't ever have that part of it back, but still we can salvage something, Janine, we can rebuild, if you'll just get the hell out of that villa and—"

"I'm sorry, Nick." Her voice was tender, throaty, distant, almost unfamiliar. "Oh, God, Nick, it's such a mess. I loved you so. I'm sorry, Nick. I'm so sorry."

The screen went blank.

***

Mikkelsen had not time-jaunted in years, not since the Aztec trip, and he was amazed at what it cost now. But he was carrying the usual credit cards and evidently his credit lines were okay, because they approved his application in five minutes. He told them where he wanted to go and how he wanted to look, and for another few hundred the makeup man worked him over, taking that dusting of early gray out of his hair and smoothing the lines from his face and spraying him with the good old Southern California tan that you tend to lose when you're in your late thirties and spending more time in your office than on the beach. He looked at least eight years younger, close enough to pass. As long as he took care to keep from running into his own younger self while he was back there, there should be no problems.

He stepped into the cubicle and sweet-scented fog enshrouded him and when he stepped out again it was a mild December day in the year 2012, with a faint hint of rain in the northern sky. Only fourteen years back, and yet the world looked prehistoric to him, the clothing and the haircuts and the cars all wrong, the buildings heavy and clumsy, the advertisements floating overhead offering archaic and absurd products in blaring gaudy colors. Odd that the world of 2012 had not looked so crude to him the first time he had lived through it; but then the present never looks crude, he thought, except through the eyes of the future. He enjoyed the strangeness of it: it told him that he had really gone backward in time. It was like walking into an old movie. He felt very calm. All the pain was behind him now; he remembered nothing of the life that he had lost, only that it was important for him to take certain countermeasures against the man who had stolen something precious from him. He rented a car and drove quickly up to La Jolla. As he expected, everybody was at the beach club except for young Nick Mikkelsen, who was back in Palm Beach with his parents. Mikkelsen had put this jaunt together quickly but not without careful planning.

They were all amazed to see him—Gus, Dan, Leo, Christie, Sal, the whole crowd. How young they looked! Kids, just kids, barely into their twenties, all that hair, all that baby fat—he had never before realized how *young* you were when you were young. "Hey," Gus said, "I thought you were in Florida!" Someone handed him a popper. Someone slipped a capsule to his ear and raucous overload music began to pound against his cheekbone. He made the rounds, grinning, hugging, explaining that Palm Beach had been a bore, that he had come back early to be with the gang. "Where's Yvonne?" he asked.

"She'll be here in a little while," Christie said.

Tommy Hambleton walked in five minutes after Mikkelsen. For one jarring instant Mikkelsen thought that the man he saw was the Hambleton of his own time, thirty-five years old, but no: there were little signs, a certain lack of tension in this man's face, a certain callowness about the lips, that marked him as younger. The truth, Mikkelsen realized, is that Hambleton had *never* looked really young, that he was ageless, timeless, sleek and plump and unchanging. It would have been very satisfying to Mikkelsen to plunge a knife into that impeccably shaven throat, but murder was not his style, nor was it an ideal solution to his problem. Instead, he called Hambleton aside, bought him a drink and said quietly, "I just thought you'd like to know that Yvonne and I are breaking up."

"Really, Nick? Oh, that's so sad! I thought you two were the most solid couple here!"

"We were. We were. But it's all over, man. I'll be with someone else New Year's Eve. Don't know who, but it won't be Yvonne."

Hambleton looked solemn. "That's so sad, Nick."

"No. Not for me and not for you." Mikkelsen smiled and nudged Hambleton amiably. "Look, Tommy, it's no secret to me that you've had your eye on Yvonne for months. She knows it too. I just wanted to let you know that I'm stepping out of the picture, I'm very gracefully withdrawing, no hard feelings at all. And if she asks my advice, I'll tell her that you're absolutely the best man she could find. I mean it, Tommy."

"That's very decent of you, old fellow. That's extraordinary!"

"I want her to be happy," Mikkelsen said.

Yvonne showed up just as night was falling. Mikkelsen had not seen her for years, and he was startled at how uninteresting she seemed, how bland, how unformed, almost adolescent. Of course, she was very pretty, close-cropped blonde hair, merry greenish blue eyes, pert little nose, but she seemed girlish and alien to him, and he wondered how he could ever have become so involved with her. But of course all that was before Janine. Mikkelsen's unscheduled return from Palm Beach surprised her, but not very much, and when he took her down to the beach to tell her that he had come to realize that she was really in love with Hambleton and he was not going to make a fuss about it, she blinked and said sweetly, "In love with Tommy? Well, I suppose I *could* be—though I never actually saw it like that. But I could give it a try, couldn't I? That is, if you truly are tired of me, Nick." She didn't seem offended. She didn't seem heartbroken. She didn't seem to care much at all.

He left the club soon afterward and got an express-fax message off to his younger self in Palm Beach: *Yvonne has fallen for Tommy Hambleton. However upset you are, for God's sake get over it fast, and if you happen to meet a young woman named Janine Carter, give her a close look. You won't regret it, believe me. I'm in a position to know.*

He signed it *A Friend,* but added a little squiggle in the corner that had always been his own special signature-glyph. He didn't dare go further than that. He hoped young Nick would be smart enough to figure out the score.

Not a bad hour's work, he decided. He drove back to the jaunt-shop in downtown San Diego and hopped back to his proper point in time.

***

There was the taste of cotton in his mouth when he emerged. So it feels that way even when you phase *yourself,* he thought. He wondered what changes he had brought about by his jaunt. As he remembered it, he had made the hop in order to phase himself back into a marriage with a woman named Janine, who apparently he had loved quite considerably until she had been snatched away from him in a phasing. Evidently the unphasing had not happened, because he knew he was still unmarried, with three or four regular companions—Cindy, Melanie, Elena and someone else—and none of them was named Janine. Paula, yes, that was the other one. Yet he was carrying a note, already starting to fade, that said: *You won't remember any of this, but you were married in 2016 or 17 to the former Janine Carter, Tommy Hambleton's ex-wife, and however much you may like your present life, you were a lot better off when you were with her.* Maybe so, Mikkelsen thought. God knows he was getting weary of the bachelor life, and now that Gus and Donna were making it legal, he was the only singleton left in the whole crowd. That was a little awkward. But he hadn't ever met anyone he genuinely wanted to spend the rest of his life with, or even as much as a year with. So he had been married, had he, before the phasing? Janine? How strange, how unlike him.

He was home before dark. Showered, shaved, dressed, headed over to the Top of the Marina. Tommy Hambleton and Yvonne were in town, and he had agreed to meet them for drinks. Hadn't seen them for years, not since Tommy had taken over his brother's villa on the Riviera. Good old Tommy, Mikkelsen thought. Great to see him again. And Yvonne. He recalled her clearly, little snub-nosed blonde, good game of tennis, trim compact body. He'd been pretty hot for her himself, eleven or twelve years ago, back before Adrienne, before Charlene, before Georgiana, before Nedra, before Cindy, Melanie, Elena, Paula. Good to see them both again. He stepped into the skylift and went shooting blithely up the long swivel-stalk to the gilded little cupola high above the lagoon. Hambleton and Yvonne were already there.

Tommy hadn't changed much—same old smooth slickly dressed little guy—but Mikkelsen was astonished at how time and money had altered Yvonne. She was poised, chic, sinuous, all that baby-fat burned away, and when she spoke there was the smallest hint of a French accent in her voice. Mikkelsen embraced them both and let himself be swept off to the bar.

"So glad I was able to find you," Hambleton said. "It's been years! Years, Nick!"

"Practically forever."

"Still going great with the women, are you?"

"More or less," Mikkelsen said. "And you? Still running back in time to wipe your nose three days ago, Tommy?"

Hambleton chuckled. "Oh, I don't do much of that any more. Yvonne and I were to the Fall of Troy last winter, but the short-hop stuff doesn't interest me these days. I—oh. How amazing!"

"What is it?" Mikkelsen asked, seeing Hambleton's gaze go past him into the darker corners of the room.

"An old friend," Hambleton said. "I'm sure it's she! Someone I once knew—briefly, glancingly—" He looked toward Yvonne and said, "I met her a few months after you and I began seeing each other, love. Of course, there was nothing to it, but there could have been—there could have been—" A distant wistful look swiftly crossed Hambleton's features and was gone. His smile returned. He said, "You should meet her, Nick. If it's really she, I know she'll be just your type. How amazing! After all these years! Come with me, man!"

He seized Mikkelsen by the wrist and drew him, astounded, across the room.

"Janine?" Hambleton cried. "Janine Carter?"

She was a dark-haired woman, elegant, perhaps a year or two younger than Mikkelsen, with cool perceptive eyes. She looked up, surprised. "Tommy? Is that you?"

"Of course, of course. That's my wife, Yvonne, over there. And this— this is one of my oldest and dearest friends, Nick Mikkelsen. Nick— Janine—"

She stared up at him. "This sounds absurd," she said, "but don't I know you from somewhere?"

Mikkelsen felt a warm flood of mysterious energy surging through him as their eyes met. "It's a long story," he said. "Let's have a drink and I'll tell you all about it."

SAILING TO BYZANTIUM (1984)

INTRODUCTION

It was the spring of 1984. I was back on track as a writer after the self-inflicted derailment of a decade earlier. I had just completed my historical/fantasy novel *Gilgamesh the King,* set in ancient Sumer, and antiquity was very much on my mind when Shawna McCarthy, who had just begun her brief and brilliant career as editor of *Isaac Asimov's Science Fiction Magazine,* came to the San Francisco area, where I live, on holiday. I ran into her at a party and she asked me if I'd write a story for her. "I'd like to, yes." And, since the novella is my favorite form, I added, "a long one."

"How long?"

"Long," I told her. "A novella."

"Good," she said. We did a little haggling over the price, and that was that. She went back to New York and I got going on "Sailing to Byzantium" and by late summer it was done.

It wasn't originally going to be called "Sailing to Byzantium." The used manila envelope on which I had jotted the kernel of the idea out of which "Sailing to Byzantium" grew — I always jot down my story ideas on the backs of old envelopes — bears the title, "The Hundred-Gated City." That's a reference to ancient Thebes, in Egypt, and this was my original note:

"Ancient Egypt has been recreated at the end of time, along with various other highlights of history — a sort of Disneyland. A twentieth century man, through error, has been regenerated in Thebes, though he belongs in the replica of Los Angeles. The misplaced Egyptian has been sent to Troy, or maybe Knossos, and a Cretan has been displaced into a Brasilia-equivalent of the twenty-ninth century. They move about, attempting to return to their proper places."

It's a nice idea, but it's not quite the story I ultimately wrote, perhaps because I decided that it might turn out to be nothing more than an updating of Murray Leinster's classic novella "Sidewise in Time," a story that was first published before I was born but which is still well remembered in certain quarters. I *did* use the "Hundred-Gated" tag in an entirely different story many years later — "Thebes of the Hundred Gates." (I'm thrifty with titles as well as old envelopes.) But what emerged in the summer of 1984 is the story you are about to read, which quickly acquired the title it now bears as I came to understand the direction my original idea had begun to take.

From the earliest pages I knew I was on to something special, and "Sailing to Byzantium" remains one of my favorite stories, out of all the millions and millions of words of science fiction I've published in the past fifty years. Shawna had one or two small editorial suggestions for clarifying the ending, which I accepted gladly, and a friend, Shay Barsabe, who read the story in manuscript, pointed out one subtle logical blunder in the plot that I hastily corrected; but otherwise the story came forth virtually in its final form as I wrote it.

It was published first as an elegant limited-edition book, now very hard to find, by the house of Underwood-Miller, and soon afterward it appeared in *Asimov's* for February, 1985. It met with immediate acclaim, and that year it was chosen with wonderful editorial unanimity for all three of the best-science-fiction-of-the-year anthologies, those edited by Donald A. Wollheim, Terry Carr, and Gardner Dozois. "A possible classic," is what Wollheim called it, praise that gave me great delight, because the crusty, sardonic Wollheim had been reading science fiction almost since the stuff was invented, and he was not one to throw such words around lightly. "Sailing to Byzantium" won me a Nebula award in 1986, and was nominated for a Hugo, but finished in second place, losing by four votes out of 800. Since then the story has been reprinted many times and translated into a dozen languages or more. Whenever I have one of those bleak four-in-the-morning moments when I ask myself whether I actually did ever accomplish anything worthwhile as a science-fiction writer, "Sailng to Byzantium" is one of the first pieces of evidence I offer myself to prove that I did.

At dawn he arose and stepped out onto the patio for his first look at Alexandria, the one city he had not yet seen. That year the five cities were Chang-an, Asgard, New Chicago, Timbuctoo, Alexandria: the usual mix of eras, cultures, realities. He and Gioia, making the long flight from Asgard in the distant north the night before, had arrived late, well after sundown, and had gone straight to bed. Now, by the gentle apricot-hued morning light, the fierce spires and battlements of Asgard seemed merely something he had dreamed.

The rumor was that Asgard's moment was finished anyway. In a little while, he had heard, they were going to tear it down and replace it, elsewhere, with Mohenjo-daro. Though there were never more than five cities, they changed constantly. He could remember a time when they had had Rome of the Caesars instead of Chang-an, and Rio de Janeiro rather than Alexandria. These people saw no point in keeping anything very long.

It was not easy for him to adjust to the sultry intensity of Alexandria after the frozen splendors of Asgard. The wind, coming off the water, was brisk and torrid both at once. Soft turquoise wavelets lapped at the jetties. Strong presences assailed his senses: the hot heavy sky, the stinging scent of the red lowland sand borne on the breeze, the sullen swampy aroma of the nearby sea. Everything trembled and glimmered in the early light. Their hotel was beautifully situated, high on the northern slope of the huge artificial mound known as the Paneium that was sacred to the goat-footed god. From here they had a total view of the city: the wide noble boulevards, the soaring obelisks and monuments, the palace of Hadrian just below the hill, the stately and awesome Library, the temple of Poseidon, the teeming marketplace, the royal lodge that Marc Antony had built after his defeat at Actium. And of course the Lighthouse, the wondrous many-windowed Lighthouse, the seventh wonder of the world, that immense pile of marble and limestone and reddish-purple Aswan granite rising in majesty at the end of its mile-long causeway. Black smoke from the beacon fire at its summit curled lazily into the sky. The city was awakening. Some temporaries in short white kilts appeared and began to trim the dense dark hedges that bordered the great public buildings. A few citizens wearing loose robes of vaguely Grecian style were strolling in the streets.

There were ghosts and chimeras and phantasies everywhere about. Two slim elegant centaurs, a male and a female, grazed on the hillside. A burly thick-thighed swordsman appeared on the porch of the temple of Poseidon holding a Gorgon's severed head and waved it in a wide arc, grinning broadly. In the street below the hotel gate three small pink sphinxes, no bigger than housecats, stretched and yawned and began to prowl the curbside. A larger one, lion-sized, watched warily from an alleyway: their mother, surely. Even at this distance he could hear her loud purring.

Shading his eyes, he peered far out past the Lighthouse and across the water. He hoped to see the dim shores of Crete or Cyprus to the north, or perhaps the great dark curve of Anatolia. *Carry me toward that great Byzantium,* he thought. *Where all is ancient, singing at the oars.* But he beheld only the endless empty sea, sun-bright and blinding though the morning was just beginning. Nothing was ever where he expected it to be. The continents did not seem to be in their proper places any longer. Gioia, taking him aloft long ago in her little flitterflitter, had shown him that. The tip of South America was canted far out into the Pacific, Africa was weirdly foreshortened; a broad tongue of ocean separated Europe and Asia. Australia did not appear to exist at all. Perhaps they had dug it up and used it for other things. There was no trace of the world he once had known. This was the fiftieth century. "The fiftieth century after *what?*" he had asked several times, but no one seemed to know, or else they did not care to say.

"Is Alexandria very beautiful?" Gioia called from within.

"Come out and see."

Naked and sleepy-looking, she padded out onto the white-tiled patio and nestled up beside him. She fit neatly under his arm. "Oh, yes, yes!" she said softly. "So very beautiful, isn't it? Look, there, the palaces, the Library, the Lighthouse! Where will we go first? The Lighthouse, I think. Yes? And then the marketplace — I want to see the Egyptian magicians — and the stadium, the races — will they be having races today, do you think? Oh, Charles, I want to see everything!"

"Everything? All on the first day?"

"All on the first day, yes," she said. "Everything."

"But we have plenty of time, Gioia."

"Do we?"

He smiled and drew her tight against his side.

"Time enough," he said gently.

He loved her for her impatience, for her bright bubbling eagerness. Gioia was not much like the rest in that regard, though she seemed identical in all other ways. She was short, supple, slender, dark-eyed, olive-skinned, narrow-hipped, with wide shoulders and flat muscles. They were all like that, each one indistinguishable from the rest, like a horde of millions of brothers and sisters—a world of small lithe childlike Mediterraneans, built for juggling, for bull-dancing, for sweet white wine at midday and rough red wine at night. They had the same slim bodies, the same broad mouths, the same great glossy eyes. He had never seen anyone who appeared to be younger than twelve or older than twenty. Gioia was somehow a little different, although he did not quite know how; but he knew that it was for that imperceptible but significant difference that he loved her. And probably that was why she loved him also.

He let his gaze drift from west to east, from the Gate of the Moon down broad Canopus Street and out to the harbor, and off to the tomb of Cleopatra at the tip of long slender Cape Lochias. Everything was here and all of it perfect, the obelisks, the statues and marble colonnades, the courtyards and shrines and groves, great Alexander himself in his coffin of crystal and gold: a splendid gleaming pagan city. But there were oddities—an unmistakable mosque near the public gardens, and what seemed to be a Christian church not far from the Library. And those ships in the harbor, with all those red sails and bristling masts—surely they were medieval, and late medieval at that. He had seen such anachronisms in other places before. Doubtless these people found them amusing. Life was a game for them. They played at it unceasingly. Rome, Alexandria, Timbuctoo—why not? Create an Asgard of translucent bridges and shimmering ice-girt palaces, then grow weary of it and take it away? Replace it with Mohenjo-daro? Why not? It seemed to him a great pity to destroy those lofty Nordic feasting halls for the sake of building a squat brutal sun-baked city of brown brick; but these people did not look at things the way he did. Their cities were only temporary. Someone in Asgard had said that Timbuctoo would be the next to go, with Byzantium rising in its place. Well, why not? Why not? They could have anything they liked. This was the fiftieth century, after all. The only rule was that there could be no more than five cities at once. "Limits," Gioia had informed him solemnly when they first began to travel together, "are very important." But she did not know why, or did not care to say.

He stared out once more toward the sea.

He imagined a newborn city congealing suddenly out of mists, far across the water: shining towers, great domed palaces, golden mosaics. That would be no great effort for them. They could just summon it forth whole out of time, the Emperor on his throne and the Emperor's drunken soldiery roistering in the streets, the brazen clangor of the cathedral gong rolling through the Grand Bazaar, dolphins leaping beyond the shoreside pavilions. Why not? They had Timbuctoo. They had Alexandria. Do you crave

Constantinople? Then behold Constantinople! Or Avalon, or Lyonesse, or Atlantis. They could have anything they liked. It is pure Schopenhauer here: the world as will and imagination. Yes! These slender dark-eyed people journeying tirelessly from miracle to miracle. Why not Byzantium next? Yes! Why not? *That is no country for old men,* he thought. *The young in one another's arms, the birds in the trees* – yes! Yes! Anything they liked. They even had him. Suddenly he felt frightened. Questions he had not asked for a long time burst through into his consciousness. *Who am I? Why am I here? Who is this woman beside me?*

"You're so quiet all of a sudden, Charles," said Gioia, who could not abide silence for very long. "Will you talk to me? I want you to talk to me. Tell me what you're looking for out there."

He shrugged. "Nothing."

"Nothing?"

"Nothing in particular."

"I could see you seeing something."

"Byzantium," he said. "I was imagining that I could look straight across the water to Byzantium. I was trying to get a glimpse of the walls of Constantinople."

"Oh, but you wouldn't be able to see as far as that from here. Not really."

"I know."

"And anyway Byzantium doesn't exist."

"Not yet. But it will. Its time comes later on."

"Does it?" she said. "Do you know that for a fact?"

"On good authority. I heard it in Asgard," he told her. "But even if I hadn't, Byzantium would be inevitable, don't you think? Its time would have to come. How could we not do Byzantium, Gioia? We certainly will do Byzantium, sooner or later. I know we will. It's only a matter of time. And we have all the time in the world."

A shadow crossed her face. "Do we? Do we?"

***

He knew very little about himself, but he knew that he was not one of them. That he knew. He knew that his name was Charles Phillips and that before he had come to live among these people he had lived in the year 1984, when there had been such things as computers and television sets and baseball and jet planes, and the world was full of cities, not merely five but thousands of them, New York and London and Johannesburg and Paris and Liverpool and Bangkok and San Francisco and Buenos Aires and a multitude of others, all at the same time. There had been four and a half billion people in the world then; now he doubted that there were as many as four and a half million. Nearly everything had changed beyond comprehension. The moon still seemed the same, and the sun; but at night he searched in vain for familiar constellations. He had no idea how they had brought him from then to now, or why. It did no good to ask. No one had any answers for him; no one so much as appeared to understand what it was that he was trying to learn. After a time he had stopped asking; after a time he had almost entirely ceased wanting to know.

He and Gioia were climbing the Lighthouse. She scampered ahead, in a hurry as always, and he came along behind her in his more stolid fashion. Scores of other tourists, mostly in groups of two or three, were making their way up the wide flagstone ramps, laughing, calling to one another. Some of them, seeing him, stopped a moment, stared, pointed. He was used to that. He was so much taller than any of them; he was plainly not one of them. When they pointed at him he smiled. Sometimes he nodded a little acknowledgment.

He could not find much of interest in the lowest level, a massive square structure two hundred feet high built of huge marble blocks: within its cool musty arcades were hundreds of small dark rooms, the offices of the Lighthouse's keepers and mechanics, the barracks of the garrison, the stables for the three hundred donkeys that carried the fuel to the lantern far above. None of that appeared inviting to him. He forged onward without halting until he emerged on the balcony that led to the next level. Here the Lighthouse grew narrower and became octagonal: its face, granite now and handsomely fluted, rose in a stunning sweep above him.

Gioia was waiting for him there. "This is for you," she said, holding out a nugget of meat on a wooden skewer. "Roast lamb. Absolutely delicious. I had one while I was waiting for you." She gave him a cup of some cool green sherbet also, and darted off to buy a pomegranate. Dozens of temporaries were roaming the balcony, selling refreshments of all kinds.

He nibbled at the meat. It was charred outside, nicely pink and moist within. While he ate, one of the temporaries came up to him and peered blandly into his face. It was a stocky swarthy male wearing nothing but a strip of red and yellow cloth about its waist. "I sell meat," it said. "Very fine roast lamb, only five drachmas."

Phillips indicated the piece he was eating. "I already have some," he said.

"It is excellent meat, very tender. It has been soaked for three days in the juices of—"

"Please," Phillips said. "I don't want to buy any meat. Do you mind moving along?"

The temporaries had confused and baffled him at first, and there was still much about them that was unclear to him. They were not machines—they looked like creatures of flesh and blood—but they did not seem to be

human beings, either, and no one treated them as if they were. He supposed
they were artificial constructs, products of a technology so consummate
that it was invisible. Some appeared to be more intelligent than others,
but all of them behaved as if they had no more autonomy than characters
in a play, which was essentially what they were. There were untold
numbers of them in each of the five cities, playing all manner of roles:
shepherds and swineherds, street-sweepers, merchants, boatmen, vendors
of grilled meats and cool drinks, hagglers in the marketplace,
schoolchildren, charioteers, policemen, grooms, gladiators, monks,
artisans, whores and cutpurses, sailors—whatever was needed to sustain
the illusion of a thriving, populous urban center. The darkeyed people,
Gioia's people, never performed work. There were not enough of them to
keep a city's functions going, and in any case they were strictly tourists,
wandering with the wind, moving from city to city as the whim took them,
Chang-an to New Chicago, New Chicago to Timbuctoo, Timbuctoo to
Asgard, Asgard to Alexandria, onward, ever onward.

The temporary would not leave him alone. Phillips walked away and
it followed him, cornering him against the balcony wall. When Gioia
returned a few minutes later, lips prettily stained with pomegranate juice,
the temporary was still hovering about him, trying with lunatic persistence
to sell him a skewer of lamb. It stood much too close to him, almost nose
to nose, great sad cowlike eyes peering intently into his as it extolled with
mournful mooing urgency the quality of its wares. It seemed to him that
he had had trouble like this with temporaries on one or two earlier
occasions. Gioia touched the creature's elbow lightly and said, in a short
sharp tone Phillips had never heard her use before, "He isn't interested.
Get away from him." It went at once. To Phillips she said, "You have to be
firm with them."

"I was trying. It wouldn't listen to me."

"You ordered it to go away, and it refused?"

"I asked it to go away. Politely. Too politely, maybe."

"Even so," she said. "It should have obeyed a human, regardless."

"Maybe it didn't think I was human," Phillips suggested. "Because of
the way I look. My height, the color of my eyes. It might have thought I
was some kind of temporary myself."

"No," Gioia said, frowning. "A temporary won't solicit another
temporary. But it won't ever disobey a citizen, either. There's a very clear
boundary. There isn't ever any confusion. I can't understand why it went
on bothering you." He was surprised at how troubled she seemed: far
more so, he thought, than the incident warranted. A stupid device, perhaps
miscalibrated in some way, over-enthusiastically pushing its wares—what
of it? What of it? Gioia, after a moment, appeared to come to the same
conclusion. Shrugging, she said, "It's defective, I suppose. Probably such

things are more common than we suspect, don't you think?" There was something forced about her tone that bothered him. She smiled and handed him her pomegranate. "Here. Have a bite, Charles. It's wonderfully sweet. They used to be extinct, you know. Shall we go on upward?"

***

The octagonal midsection of the Lighthouse must have been several hundred feet in height, a grim claustrophobic tube almost entirely filled by the two broad spiraling ramps that wound around the huge building's central well. The ascent was slow: a donkey team was a little way ahead of them on the ramp, plodding along laden with bundles of kindling for the lantern. But at last, just as Phillips was growing winded and dizzy, he and Gioia came out onto the second balcony, the one marking the transition between the octagonal section and the Lighthouse's uppermost story, which was cylindrical and very slender.

She leaned far out over the balustrade. "Oh, Charles, look at the view! Look at it!"

It was amazing. From one side they could see the entire city, and swampy Lake Mareotis and the dusty Egyptian plain beyond it, and from the other they peered far out into the gray and choppy Mediterranean. He gestured toward the innumerable reefs and shallows that infested the waters leading to the harbor entrance. "No wonder they needed a lighthouse here," he said. "Without some kind of gigantic landmark they'd never have found their way in from the open sea."

A blast of sound, a ferocious snort, erupted just above him. He looked up, startled. Immense statues of trumpet-wielding Tritons jutted from the corners of the Lighthouse at this level; that great blurting sound had come from the nearest of them. A signal, he thought. A warning to the ships negotiating that troubled passage. The sound was produced by some kind of steam-powered mechanism, he realized, operated by teams of sweating temporaries clustered about bonfires at the base of each Triton.

Once again he found himself swept by admiration for the clever way these people carried out their reproductions of antiquity. Or *were* they reproductions, he wondered? He still did not understand how they brought their cities into being. For all he knew, this place was the authentic Alexandria itself, pulled forward out of its proper time just as he himself had been. Perhaps this was the true and original Lighthouse, and not a copy. He had no idea which was the case, nor which would be the greater miracle.

"How do we get to the top?" Gioia asked.

"Over there, I think. That doorway."

The spiraling donkey-ramps ended here. The loads of lantern fuel went higher via a dumbwaiter in the central shaft. Visitors continued by way of a cramped staircase, so narrow at its upper end that it was impossible to turn around while climbing. Gioia, tireless, sprinted ahead. He clung to the rail and labored up and up, keeping count of the tiny window slits to ease the boredom of the ascent. The count was nearing a hundred when finally he stumbled into the vestibule of the beacon chamber. A dozen or so visitors were crowded into it. Gioia was at the far side, by the wall that was open to the sea.

It seemed to him he could feel the building swaying in the winds up here. How high were they? Five hundred feet, six hundred, seven? The beacon chamber was tall and narrow, divided by a catwalk into upper and lower sections. Down below, relays of temporaries carried wood from the dumbwaiter and tossed it on the blazing fire. He felt its intense heat from where he stood, at the rim of the platform on which the giant mirror of polished metal was hung. Tongues of flame leaped upward and danced before the mirror, which hurled its dazzling beam far out to sea. Smoke rose through a vent. At the very top was a colossal statue of Poseidon, austere, ferocious, looming above the lantern.

Gioia sidled along the catwalk until she was at his side. "The guide was talking before you came," she said, pointing. "Do you see that place over there, under the mirror? Someone standing there and looking into the mirror gets a view of ships at sea that can't be seen from here by the naked eye. The mirror magnifies things."

"Do you believe that?"

She nodded toward the guide. "It said so. And it also told us that if you look in a certain way, you can see right across the water into the city of Constantinople."

She is like a child, he thought. They all are. He said, "You told me yourself this very morning that it isn't possible to see that far. Besides, Constantinople doesn't exist right now."

"It will," she replied. "You said that to me, this very morning. And when it does, it'll be reflected in the Lighthouse mirror. That's the truth. I'm absolutely certain of it." She swung about abruptly toward the entrance of the beacon chamber. "Oh, look, Charles! Here come Nissandra and Aramayne! And there's Hawk! There's Stengard!" Gioia laughed and waved and called out names. "Oh, everyone's here! *Everyone!*"

They came jostling into the room, so many newcomers that some of those who had been there were forced to scramble down the steps on the far side. Gioia moved among them, hugging, kissing. Phillips could scarcely tell one from another—it was hard for him even to tell which were the men and which the women, dressed as they all were in the same sort of loose robes—but he recognized some of the names. These were her special friends, her set, with whom she had journeyed from city to city on an endless round of gaiety in the old days before he had come into her life. He had met a few of them before, in Asgard, in Rio, in Rome. The beacon-chamber guide, a squat wide-shouldered old temporary wearing a laurel wreath on its bald head, reappeared and began its potted speech, but no one listened to it; they were all too busy greeting one another, embracing, giggling. Some of them edged their way over to Phillips and reached up, standing on tiptoes, to touch their fingertips to his cheek in that odd hello of theirs. "Charles," they said gravely, making two syllables out of the name, as these people often did. "So good to see you again. Such a pleasure. You and Gioia—such a handsome couple. So well suited to each other."

Was that so? He supposed it was.

The chamber hummed with chatter. The guide could not be heard at all. Stengard and Nissandra had visited New Chicago for the water-dancing—Aramayne bore tales of a feast in Chang-an that had gone on for *days*—Hawk and Hekna had been to Timbuctoo to see the arrival of the salt caravan, and were going back there soon—a final party soon to celebrate the end of Asgard that absolutely should not be missed—the plans for the new city, Mohenjo-daro—we have reservations for the opening, we wouldn't pass it up for anything—and, yes, they were definitely going to do Constantinople after that, the planners were already deep into their Byzantium research—so good to see you, you look so beautiful all the time—have you been to the Library yet? The zoo? To the temple of Serapis?—

To Phillips they said, "What do you think of our Alexandria, Charles? Of course, you must have known it well in your day. Does it look the way you remember it?" They were always asking things like that. They did not seem to comprehend that the Alexandria of the Lighthouse and the Library was long lost and legendary by the time his twentieth century had been. To them, he suspected, all the places they had brought back into existence were more or less contemporary. Rome of the Caesars, Alexandria of the Ptolemies, Venice of the Doges, Chang-an of the T'angs, Asgard of the Aesir, none any less real than the next nor any less unreal, each one simply a facet of the distant past, the fantastic immemorial past, a plum plucked from that dark backward abysm of time. They had no contexts for separating one era from another. To them all the past was one borderless timeless realm. Why, then, should he not have seen the Lighthouse before, he who had leaped into this era from the New York of 1984? He had never been able to explain it to them. Julius Caesar and Hannibal, Helen of Troy and Charlemagne, Rome of the gladiators and New York of the Yankees and Mets, Gilgamesh and Tristan and Othello and Robin Hood and George Washington and Queen Victoria—to them, all equally real and unreal, none of them any more than bright figures moving about on a painted canvas.

The past, the past, the elusive and fluid past — to them it was a single place
of infinite accessibility and infinite connectivity. Of course, they would
think he had seen the Lighthouse before. He knew better than to try again
to explain things. "No," he said simply. "This is my first time in
Alexandria."

***

They stayed there all winter long, and possibly some of the spring.
Alexandria was not a place where one was sharply aware of the change of
seasons, nor did the passage of time itself make itself very evident when
one was living one's entire life as a tourist.

During the day there was always something new to see. The zoological
garden, for instance: a wondrous park, miraculously green and lush in
this hot dry climate, where astounding animals roamed in enclosures so
generous that they did not seem like enclosures at all. Here were camels,
rhinoceroses, gazelles, ostriches, lions, wild asses; and here, too, casually
adjacent to those familiar African beasts, were hippogriffs, unicorns,
basilisks, and fire-snorting dragons with rainbow scales. Had the original
zoo of Alexandria had dragons and unicorns? Phillips doubted it. But this
one did; evidently it was no harder for the backstage craftsmen to
manufacture mythic beasts than it was for them to turn out camels and
gazelles. To Gioia and her friends all of them were equally mythical,
anyway. They were just as awed by the rhinoceros as by the hippogriff.
One was no more strange — or any less — than the other. So far as Phillips
had been able to discover, none of the mammals or birds of his era had
survived into this one except for a few cats and dogs, though many had
been reconstructed.

And then the Library! All those lost treasures, reclaimed from the jaws
of time! Stupendous columned marble walls, airy high-vaulted reading
rooms, dark coiling stacks stretching away to infinity. The ivory handles
of seven hundred thousand papyrus scrolls bristling on the shelves.
Scholars and librarians gliding quietly about, smiling faint scholarly smiles
but plainly preoccupied with serious matters of the mind. They were all
temporaries, Phillips realized. Mere props, part of the illusion. But were
the scrolls illusions, too? "Here we have the complete dramas of
Sophocles," said the guide with a blithe wave of its hand, indicating shelf
upon shelf of texts. Only seven of his hundred twenty-three plays had
survived the successive burnings of the library in ancient times by Romans,
Christians, Arabs: were the lost ones here, the *Triptolemus,* the *Nausicaa,*
the *Jason,* and all the rest? And would he find here, too, miraculously
restored to being, the other vanished treasures of ancient literature — the
memoirs of Odysseus, Cato's history of Rome, Thucidydes' life of Pericles,

the missing volumes of Livy? But when he asked if he might explore the stacks, the guide smiled apologetically and said that all the librarians were busy just now. Another time, perhaps? Perhaps, said the guide. It made no difference, Phillips decided. Even if these people somehow had brought back those lost masterpieces of antiquity, how would he read them? He knew no Greek.

The life of the city buzzed and throbbed about him. It was a dazzlingly beautiful place: the vast bay thick with sails, the great avenues running rigidly east-west, north-south, the sunlight rebounding almost audibly from the bright walls of the palaces of kings and gods. They have done this very well, Phillips thought: very well indeed. In the marketplace hard-eyed traders squabbled in half a dozen mysterious languages over the price of ebony, Arabian incense, jade, panther skins. Gioia bought a dram of pale musky Egyptian perfume in a delicate tapering glass flask. Magicians and jugglers and scribes called out stridently to passersby, begging for a few moments of attention and a handful of coins for their labor. Strapping slaves, black and tawny and some that might have been Chinese, were put up for auction, made to flex their muscles, to bare their teeth, to bare their breasts and thighs to prospective buyers. In the gymnasium naked athletes hurled javelins and discuses, and wrestled with terrifying zeal. Gioia's friend Stengard came rushing up with a gift for her, a golden necklace that would not have embarrassed Cleopatra. An hour later she had lost it, or perhaps had given it away while Phillips was looking elsewhere. She bought another, even finer, the next day. Anyone could have all the money he wanted, simply by asking: it was as easy to come by as air for these people.

Being here was much like going to the movies, Phillips told himself. A different show every day: not much plot, but the special effects were magnificent and the detail work could hardly have been surpassed. A megamovie, a vast entertainment that went on all the time and was being played out by the whole population of Earth. And it was all so effortless, so spontaneous: just as when he had gone to a movie he had never troubled to think about the myriad technicians behind the scenes, the cameramen and the costume designers and the set builders and the electricians and the model makers and the boom operators, so, too, here he chose not to question the means by which Alexandria had been set before him. It felt real. It *was* real. When he drank the strong red wine it gave him a pleasant buzz. If he leaped from the beacon chamber of the Lighthouse he suspected he would die, though perhaps he would not stay dead for long: doubtless they had some way of restoring him as often as was necessary. Death did not seem to be a factor in these people's lives.

By day they saw sights. By night he and Gioia went to parties, in their hotel, in seaside villas, in the palaces of the high nobility. The usual people were there all the time, Hawk and Hekna, Aramayne, Stengard and Shelimir, Nissandra, Asoka, Afonso, Protay. At the parties there were five or ten temporaries for every citizen, some as mere servants, others as entertainers or even surrogate guests, mingling freely and a little daringly. But everyone knew, all the time, who was a citizen and who just a temporary. Phillips began to think his own status lay somewhere between. Certainly they treated him with a courtesy that no one ever would give a temporary, and yet there was a condescension to their manner that told him not simply that he was not one of them but that he was someone or something of an altogether different order of existence. That he was Gioia's lover gave him some standing in their eyes, but not a great deal: obviously he was always going to be an outsider, a primitive, ancient and quaint. For that matter he noticed that Gioia herself, though unquestionably a member of the set, seemed to be regarded as something of an outsider, like a tradesman's great-granddaughter in a gathering of Plantagenets. She did not always find out about the best parties in time to attend; her friends did not always reciprocate her effusive greetings with the same degree of warmth; sometimes he noticed her straining to hear some bit of gossip that was not quite being shared with her. Was it because she had taken him for her lover? Or was it the other way around: that she had chosen to be his lover precisely because she was *not* a full member of their caste?

Being a primitive gave him, at least, something to talk about at their parties. "Tell us about war," they said. "Tell us about elections. About money. About disease." They wanted to know everything, though they did not seem to pay close attention: their eyes were quick to glaze. Still, they asked. He described traffic jams to them, and politics, and deodorants, and vitamin pills. He told them about cigarettes, newspapers, subways, telephone directories, credit cards, and basketball. "Which was your city?" they asked. New York, he told them. "And when was it? The seventh century, did you say?" The twentieth, he told them. They exchanged glances and nodded. "We will have to do it," they said. "The World Trade Center, the Empire State Building, the Citicorp Center, the Cathedral of St. John the Divine: how fascinating! Yankee Stadium. The Verrazano Bridge. We will do it all. But first must come Mohenjo-daro. And then, I think, Constantinople. Did your city have many people?" Seven million, he said. Just in the five boroughs alone. They nodded, smiling amiably, unfazed by the number. Seven million, seventy million — it was all the same to them, he sensed. They would just bring forth the temporaries in whatever quantity was required. He wondered how well they would carry the job off. He was no real judge of Alexandrias and Asgards, after all. Here they could have unicorns and hippogriffs in the zoo, and live sphinxes prowling in the gutters, and it did not trouble him. Their fanciful Alexandria was as good as history's, or better. But how sad, how disillusioning it would be, if the New York that they conjured up had Greenwich Village uptown and Times Square in the Bronx, and the New Yorkers, gentle and polite, spoke with the honeyed accents of Savannah or New Orleans. Well, that was nothing he needed to brood about just now. Very likely they were only being courteous when they spoke of doing his New York. They had all the vastness of the past to choose from: Nineveh, Memphis of the Pharaohs, the London of Victoria or Shakespeare or Richard the Third, Florence of the Medici, the Paris of Abelard and Heloise or the Paris of Louis XIV, Moctezuma's Tenochtitlan and Atahuallpa's Cuzco; Damascus, St. Petersburg, Babylon, Troy. And then there were all the cities like New Chicago, out of time that was time yet unborn to him but ancient history to them. In such richness, such an infinity of choices, even mighty New York might have to wait a long while for its turn. Would he still be among them by the time they got around to it? By then, perhaps, they might have become bored with him and returned him to his own proper era. Or possibly he would simply have grown old and died. Even here, he supposed, he would eventually die, though no one else ever seemed to. He did not know. He realized that in fact he did not know anything.

***

The north wind blew all day long. Vast flocks of ibises appeared over the city, fleeing the heat of the interior, and screeched across the sky with their black necks and scrawny legs extended. The sacred birds, descending by the thousands, scuttered about in every crossroad, pouncing on spiders and beetles, on mice, on the debris of the meat shops and the bakeries. They were beautiful but annoyingly ubiquitous, and they splashed their dung over the marble buildings; each morning squadrons of temporaries carefully washed it off. Gioia said little to him now. She seemed cool, withdrawn, depressed; and there was something almost intangible about her, as though she were gradually becoming transparent. He felt it would be an intrusion upon her privacy to ask her what was wrong. Perhaps it was only restlessness. She became religious, and presented costly offerings at the temples of Serapis, Isis, Poseidon, Pan. She went to the necropolis west of the city to lay wreaths on the tombs in the catacombs. In a single day she climbed the Lighthouse three times without any sign of fatigue. One afternoon he returned from a visit to the Library and found her naked on the patio; she had anointed herself all over with some aromatic green salve. Abruptly she said, "I think it's time to leave Alexandria, don't you?"

***

She wanted to go to Mohenjo-daro, but Mohenjo-daro was not yet ready for visitors. Instead they flew eastward to Chang-an, which they had not seen in years. It was Phillips's suggestion: he hoped that the cosmopolitan gaudiness of the old T'ang capital would lift her mood.

They were to be guests of the Emperor this time: an unusual privilege, which ordinarily had to be applied for far in advance, but Phillips had told some of Gioia's highly placed friends that she was unhappy, and they had quickly arranged everything. Three endlessly bowing functionaries in flowing yellow robes and purple sashes met them at the Gate of Brilliant Virtue in the city's south wall and conducted them to their pavilion, close by the imperial palace and the Forbidden Garden. It was a light, airy place, thin walls of plastered brick braced by graceful columns of some dark, aromatic wood. Fountains played on the roof of green and yellow tiles, creating an unending cool rainfall of recirculating water. The balustrades were of carved marble, the door fittings were of gold.

There was a suite of private rooms for him, and another for her, though they would share the handsome damask-draped bedroom at the heart of the pavilion. As soon as they arrived, Gioia announced that she must go to her rooms to bathe and dress. "There will be a formal reception for us at the palace tonight," she said. "They say the imperial receptions are splendid beyond anything you could imagine. I want to be at my best." The Emperor and all his ministers, she told him, would receive them in the Hall of the Supreme Ultimate; there would be a banquet for a thousand people; Persian dancers would perform, and the celebrated jugglers of Chung-nan. Afterward everyone would be conducted into the fantastic landscape of the Forbidden Garden to view the dragon races and the fireworks.

He went to his own rooms. Two delicate little maidservants undressed him and bathed him with fragrant sponges. The pavilion came equipped with eleven temporaries who were to be their servants: soft-voiced unobtrusive catlike Chinese, done with perfect verisimilitude, straight black hair, glowing skin, epicanthic folds. Phillips often wondered what happened to a city's temporaries when the city's time was over. Were the towering Norse heroes of Asgard being recycled at this moment into wiry dark-skinned Dravidians for Mohenjo-daro? When Timbuctoo's day was done, would its brightly robed black warriors be converted into supple Byzantines to stock the arcades of Constantinople? Or did they simply discard the old temporaries like so many excess props, stash them in warehouses somewhere, and turn out the appropriate quantities of the new model? He did not know; and once when he had asked Gioia about it she had grown uncomfortable and vague. She did not like him to probe for information, and he suspected it was because she had very little to give. These people did not seem to question the workings of their own world; his curiosities were very twentieth-century of him, he was frequently told, in that gently patronizing way of theirs. As his two little maids patted him with their sponges he thought of asking them where they had served before Chang-an. Rio? Rome? Haroun al-Raschid's Baghdad? But these fragile girls, he knew, would only giggle and retreat if he tried to question them. Interrogating temporaries was not only improper but pointless: it was like interrogating one's luggage.

When he was bathed and robed in rich red silks he wandered the pavilion for a little while, admiring the tinkling pendants of green jade dangling on the portico, the lustrous auburn pillars, the rainbow hues of the intricately interwoven girders and brackets that supported the roof. Then, wearying of his solitude, he approached the bamboo curtain at the entrance to Gioia's suite. A porter and one of the maids stood just within. They indicated that he should not enter; but he scowled at them and they melted from him like snowflakes. A trail of incense led him through the pavilion to Gioia's innermost dressing room. There he halted, just outside the door.

Gioia sat naked with her back to him at an ornate dressing table of some rare flame-colored wood inlaid with bands of orange and green porcelain. She was studying herself intently in a mirror of polished bronze held by one of her maids: picking through her scalp with her fingernails, as a woman might do who was searching out her gray hairs.

But that seemed strange. Gray hair, on Gioia? On a citizen? A temporary might display some appearance of aging, perhaps, but surely not a citizen. Citizens remained forever young. Gioia looked like a girl. Her face was smooth and unlined, her flesh was firm, her hair was dark: that was true of all of them, every citizen he had ever seen. And yet there was no mistaking what Gioia was doing. She found a hair, frowned, drew it taut, nodded, plucked it. Another. Another. She pressed the tip of her finger to her cheek as if testing it for resilience. She tugged at the skin below her eyes, pulling it downward. Such familiar little gestures of vanity; but so odd here, he thought, in this world of the perpetually young. Gioia, worried about growing old? Had he simply failed to notice the signs of age on her? Or was it that she worked hard behind his back at concealing them? Perhaps that was it. Was he wrong about the citizens, then? Did they age even as the people of less blessed eras had always done, but simply have better ways of hiding it? How old was she, anyway? Thirty? Sixty? Three hundred?

Gioia appeared satisfied now. She waved the mirror away; she rose; she beckoned for her banquet robes. Phillips, still standing unnoticed by the door, studied her with admiration: the small round buttocks, almost but not quite boyish, the elegant line of her spine, the surprising breadth of her shoulders. No, he thought, she is not aging at all. Her body is still like a girl's. She looks as young as on the day they first had met, however long ago that was—he could not say; it was hard to keep track of time here; but he was sure some years had passed since they had come together. Those gray hairs, those wrinkles and sags for which she had searched just now with such desperate intensity, must all be imaginary, mere artifacts of vanity. Even in this remote future epoch, then, vanity was not extinct. He wondered why she was so concerned with the fear of aging. An affectation? Did all these timeless people take some perverse pleasure in fretting over the possibility that they might be growing old? Or was it some private fear of Gioia's, another symptom of the mysterious depression that had come over her in Alexandria?

Not wanting her to think that he had been spying on her, when all he had really intended was to pay her a visit, he slipped silently away to dress for the evening. She came to him an hour later, gorgeously robed, swaddled from chin to ankles in a brocade of brilliant colors shot through with threads of gold, face painted, hair drawn up tightly and fastened with ivory combs: very much the lady of the court. His servants had made him splendid also, a lustrous black surplice embroidered with golden dragons over a sweeping floor-length gown of shining white silk, a necklace and pendant of red coral, a five-cornered gray felt hat that rose in tower upon tower like a ziggurat. Gioia, grinning, touched her fingertips to his cheek. "You look marvelous!" she told him. "Like a grand mandarin!"

"And you like an empress," he said. "Of some distant land: Persia, India. Here to pay a ceremonial visit on the Son of Heaven." An excess of love suffused his spirit, and, catching her lightly by the wrist, he drew her toward him, as close as he could manage it considering how elaborate their costumes were. But as he bent forward and downward, meaning to brush his lips lightly and affectionately against the tip of her nose, he perceived an unexpected strangeness, an anomaly: the coating of white paint that was her makeup seemed oddly to magnify rather than mask the contours of her skin, highlighting and revealing details he had never observed before. He saw a pattern of fine lines radiating from the corners of her eyes, and the unmistakable beginning of a quirk mark in her cheek just to the left of her mouth, and perhaps the faint indentation of frown lines in her flawless forehead. A shiver traveled along the nape of his neck. So it was not affectation, then, that had had her studying her mirror so fiercely. Age was in truth beginning to stake its claim on her, despite all that he had come to believe about these people's agelessness. But a moment later he was not so sure. Gioia turned and slid gently half a step back from him—she must have found his stare disturbing—and the lines he had thought he had seen were gone. He searched for them and saw only girlish smoothness once again. A trick of the light? A figment of an overwrought imagination? He was baffled.

"Come," she said. "We mustn't keep the Emperor waiting."

Five mustachioed warriors in armor of white quilting and seven musicians playing cymbals and pipes escorted them to the Hall of the Supreme Ultimate. There they found the full court arrayed: princes and ministers, high officials, yellow-robed monks, a swarm of imperial concubines. In a place of honor to the right of the royal thrones, which rose like gilded scaffolds high above all else, was a little group of stern-faced men in foreign costumes, the ambassadors of Rome and Byzantium, of Arabia and Syria, of Korea, Japan, Tibet, Turkestan. Incense smoldered in enameled braziers. A poet sang a delicate twanging melody, accompanying himself on a small harp. Then the Emperor and Empress entered: two tiny aged people, like waxen images, moving with infinite slowness, taking steps no greater than a child's. There was the sound of trumpets as they ascended their thrones. When the little Emperor was seated—he looked like a doll up there, ancient, faded, shrunken, yet still somehow a figure of extraordinary power—he stretched forth both his hands, and enormous gongs began to sound. It was a scene of astonishing splendor, grand and overpowering.

These are all temporaries, Phillips realized suddenly. He saw only a handful of citizens—eight, ten, possibly as many as a dozen—scattered here and there about the vast room. He knew them by their eyes, dark, liquid, knowing. They were watching not only the imperial spectacle but also Gioia and him; and Gioia, smiling secretly, nodding almost imperceptibly to them, was acknowledging their presence and their interest. But those few were the only ones in here who were autonomous living beings. All the rest—the entire splendid court, the great mandarins and paladins, the officials, the giggling concubines, the haughty and resplendent ambassadors, the aged Emperor and Empress themselves, were simply part of the scenery. Had the world ever seen entertainment on so grand a scale before? All this pomp, all this pageantry, conjured up each night for the amusement of a dozen or so viewers?

At the banquet the little group of citizens sat together at a table apart, a round onyx slab draped with translucent green silk. There turned out to be seventeen of them in all, including Gioia; Gioia appeared to know all of them, though none, so far as he could tell, was a member of her set that he had met before. She did not attempt introductions. Nor was conversation at all possible during the meal: there was a constant astounding roaring din in the room. Three orchestras played at once and there were troupes of strolling musicians also, and a steady stream of monks and their attendants marched back and forth between the tables loudly chanting sutras and waving censers to the deafening accompaniment of drums and gongs. The Emperor did not descend from his throne to join the banquet; he seemed to be asleep, though now and then he waved his hand in time to the music. Gigantic half-naked brown slaves with broad cheekbones and mouths like gaping pockets brought forth the food, peacock tongues and breast of phoenix heaped on mounds of glowing saffron-colored rice, served on frail alabaster plates. For chopsticks they were given slender rods of dark jade. The wine, served in glistening crystal beakers, was thick and sweet, with an aftertaste of raisins, and no beaker was allowed to remain empty for more than a moment. Phillips felt himself growing dizzy: when the Persian dancers emerged he could not tell whether there were five of them or fifty, and as they performed their intricate whirling routines it seemed to him that their slender muslin-veiled forms were blurring and merging one into another. He felt frightened by their proficiency, and wanted to look away, but he could not. The Chung-nan jugglers that followed them were equally skillful, equally alarming, filling the air with scythes, flaming torches, live animals, rare porcelain vases, pink jade hatchets, silver bells, gilded cups, wagon wheels, bronze vessels, and never missing a catch. The citizens applauded politely but did not seem impressed. After the jugglers, the dancers returned, performing this time on stilts; the waiters brought platters of steaming meat of a pale lavender color, unfamiliar in taste and texture: filet of camel, perhaps, or haunch of hippopotamus, or possibly some choice chop from a young dragon. There was more wine. Feebly Phillips tried to wave it away, but the servitors were implacable. This was a dryer sort, greenish-gold, austere, sharp on the tongue. With it came a silver dish, chilled to a polar coldness, that held shaved ice flavored with some potent smoky-flavored brandy. The jugglers were doing a second turn, he noticed. He thought he was going to be ill. He looked helplessly toward Gioia, who seemed sober but fiercely animated, almost manic, her eyes blazing like rubies. She touched his cheek fondly. A cool draft blew through the hall: they had opened one entire wall, revealing the garden, the night, the stars. Just outside was a colossal wheel of oiled paper stretched on wooden struts. They must have erected it in the past hour: it stood a hundred fifty feet high or even more, and on it hung lanterns by the thousands, glimmering like giant fireflies. The guests began to leave the hall. Phillips let himself be swept along into the garden, where under a yellow moon strange crook-armed trees with dense black needles loomed ominously. Gioia slipped her arm through his. They went down to a lake of bubbling crimson fluid and watched scarlet flamingolike birds ten feet tall fastidiously spearing angry-eyed turquoise eels. They stood in awe before a fat-bellied Buddha of gleaming blue tilework, seventy feet high. A horse with a golden mane came prancing by, striking showers of brilliant red sparks wherever its hooves touched the ground. In a grove of lemon trees that seemed to have the power to wave their slender limbs about, Phillips came upon the Emperor, standing by himself and rocking gently back and forth. The old man seized Phillips by the hand and pressed something into his palm, closing his fingers tight about it; when he opened his fist a few moments later he found his palm full of gray irregular pearls. Gioia took them from him and cast them into the air, and they burst like exploding firecrackers, giving off splashes of colored light. A little later, Phillips realized that he was no longer wearing his surplice or his white silken undergown. Gioia was naked, too, and she drew him gently down into a carpet of moist blue moss, where they made love until dawn, fiercely at first, then slowly, languidly, dreamily. At sunrise he looked at her tenderly and saw that something was wrong.

"Gioia?" he said doubtfully.

She smiled. "Ah, no. Gioia is with Fenimon tonight. I am Belilala."

"With—Fenimon?"

"They are old friends. She had not seen him in years."

"Ah. I see. And you are—?"

"Belilala," she said again, touching her fingertips to his cheek.

***

It was not unusual, Belilala said. It happened all the time; the only unusual thing was that it had not happened to him before now. Couples formed, traveled together for a while, drifted apart, eventually reunited. It did not mean that Gioia had left him forever. It meant only that just now she chose to be with Fenimon. Gioia would return. In the meanwhile he would not be alone. "You and I met in New Chicago," Belilala told him. "And then we saw each other again in Timbuctoo. Have you forgotten? Oh, yes, I see that you have forgotten!" She laughed prettily; she did not seem at all offended.

She looked enough like Gioia to be her sister. But, then, all the citizens looked more or less alike to him. And apart from their physical resemblance, so he quickly came to realize, Belilala and Gioia were not really very similar. There was a calmness, a deep reservoir of serenity, in Belilala, that Gioia, eager and volatile and ever impatient, did not seem to have. Strolling the swarming streets of Chang-an with Belilala, he did not perceive in her any of Gioia's restless feverish need always to know what lay beyond, and beyond, and beyond even that. When they toured the Hsing-ch'ing Palace, Belilala did not after five minutes begin—as Gioia surely would have done—to seek directions to the Fountain of Hsuan-tsung or the Wild Goose Pagoda. Curiosity did not consume Belilala as it did Gioia. Plainly she believed that there would always be enough time for her to see everything she cared to see. There were some days when Belilala chose not to go out at all, but was content merely to remain at their pavilion playing a solitary game with flat porcelain counters, or viewing the flowers of the garden.

He found, oddly, that he enjoyed the respite from Gioia's intense world-swallowing appetites; and yet he longed for her to return. Belilala — beautiful, gentle, tranquil, patient — was too perfect for him. She seemed unreal in her gleaming impeccability, much like one of those Sung celadon vases that appear too flawless to have been thrown and glazed by human hands. There was something a little soulless about her: an immaculate finish outside, emptiness within. Belilala might almost have been a temporary, he thought, though he knew she was not. He could explore the pavilions and palaces of Chang-an with her, he could make graceful conversation with her while they dined, he could certainly enjoy coupling with her; but he could not love her or even contemplate the possibility. It was hard to imagine Belilala worriedly studying herself in a mirror for wrinkles and gray hairs. Belilala would never be any older than she was at this moment; nor could Belilala ever have been any younger. Perfection does not move along an axis of time. But the perfection of Belilala's glossy surface made her inner being impenetrable to him. Gioia was more vulnerable, more obviously flawed — her restlessness, her moodiness, her vanity, her fears — and therefore she was more accessible to his own highly imperfect twentieth-century sensibility.

Occasionally he saw Gioia as he roamed the city, or thought he did. He had a glimpse of her among the miracle-vendors in the Persian Bazaar, and outside the Zoroastrian temple, and again by the goldfish pond in the Serpentine Park. But he was never quite sure that the woman he saw was really Gioia, and he never could get close enough to her to be certain: she had a way of vanishing as he approached, like some mysterious Lorelei luring him onward and onward in a hopeless chase. After a while he came to realize that he was not going to find her until she was ready to be found.

He lost track of time. Weeks, months, years? He had no idea. In this city of exotic luxury, mystery, and magic all was in constant flux and transition and the days had a fitful, unstable quality. Buildings and even whole streets were torn down of an afternoon and reerected, within days, far away. Grand new pagodas sprouted like toadstools in the night. Citizens came in from Asgard, Alexandria, Timbuctoo, New Chicago, stayed for a time, disappeared, returned. There was a constant round of court receptions, banquets, theatrical events, each one much like the one before. The festivals in honor of past emperors and empresses might have given some form to the year, but they seemed to occur in a random way, the ceremony marking the death of T'ai Tsung coming around twice the same year, so it seemed to him, once in a season of snow and again in high summer, and the one honoring the ascension of the Empress Wu being held twice in a single season. Perhaps he had misunderstood something. But he knew it was no use asking anyone.

***

One day Belilala said unexpectedly, "Shall we go to Mohenjo-daro?"

"I didn't know it was ready for visitors," he replied.

"Oh, yes. For quite some time now."

He hesitated. This had caught him unprepared. Cautiously he said, "Gioia and I were going to go there together, you know."

Belilala smiled amiably, as though the topic under discussion were nothing more than the choice of that evening's restaurant.

"Were you?" she asked.

"It was all arranged while we were still in Alexandria. To go with you instead — I don't know what to tell you, Belilala." Phillips sensed that he was growing terribly flustered. "You know that I'd like to go. With you. But on the other hand I can't help feeling that I shouldn't go there until I'm back with Gioia again. If I ever am." How foolish this sounds, he thought. How clumsy, how adolescent. He found that he was having trouble looking straight at her. Uneasily he said, with a kind of desperation in his voice, "I did promise her — there was a commitment, you understand — a firm agreement that we would go to Mohenjo-daro together —"

"Oh, but Gioia's already there!" said Belilala in the most casual way.

He gaped as though she had punched him.

"What?"

"She was one of the first to go, after it opened. Months and months ago. You didn't know?" she asked, sounding surprised, but not very. "You really didn't know?"

That astonished him. He felt bewildered, betrayed, furious. His cheeks grew hot, his mouth gaped. He shook his head again and again, trying to clear it of confusion. It was a moment before he could speak. "Already there?" he said at last. "Without waiting for me? After we had talked about going there together — after we had agreed —"

Belilala laughed. "But how could she resist seeing the newest city? You know how impatient Gioia is!"

"Yes. Yes."

He was stunned. He could barely think.

"Just like all short-timers," Belilala said. "She rushes here, she rushes there. She must have it all, now, now, right away, at once, instantly. You ought never expect her to wait for you for anything for very long: the fit seizes her, and off she goes. Surely you must know that about her by now."

"A short-timer?" He had not heard that term before.

"Yes. You knew that. You must have known that." Belilala flashed her sweetest smile. She showed no sign of comprehending his distress. With a brisk wave of her hand she said, "Well, then, shall we go, you and I? To Mohenjo-daro?"

"Of course," Phillips said bleakly.

"When would you like to leave?"

"Tonight," he said. He paused a moment. "What's a short-timer, Belilala?"

Color came to her cheeks. "Isn't it obvious?" she asked.

***

Had there ever been a more hideous place on the face of the earth than the city of Mohenjo-daro? Phillips found it difficult to imagine one. Nor could he understand why, out of all the cities that had ever been, these people had chosen to restore this one to existence. More than ever they seemed alien to him, unfathomable, incomprehensible.

From the terrace atop the many-towered citadel he peered down into grim claustrophobic Mohenjo-daro and shivered. The stark, bleak city looked like nothing so much as some prehistoric prison colony. In the manner of an uneasy tortoise it huddled, squat and compact, against the gray monotonous Indus River plain: miles of dark burnt-brick walls enclosing miles of terrifyingly orderly streets, laid out in an awesome, monstrous gridiron pattern of maniacal rigidity. The houses themselves were dismal and forbidding too, clusters of brick cells gathered about small airless courtyards. There were no windows, only small doors that opened not onto the main boulevards but onto the tiny mysterious lanes that ran between the buildings. Who had designed this horrifying metropolis? What harsh sour souls they must have had, these frightening and frightened folk, creating for themselves in the lush fertile plains of India such a Supreme Soviet of a city!

"How lovely it is," Belilala murmured. "How fascinating!"

He stared at her in amazement.

"Fascinating? Yes," he said. "I suppose so. The same way that the smile of a cobra is fascinating."

"What's a cobra?"

"Poisonous predatory serpent," Phillips told her. "Probably extinct. Or formerly extinct, more likely. It wouldn't surprise me if you people had recreated a few and turned them loose in Mohenjo to make things livelier."

"You sound angry, Charles."

"Do I? That's not how I feel."

"How do you feel, then?"

"I don't know," he said after a long moment's pause. He shrugged. "Lost, I suppose. Very far from home."

"Poor Charles."

"Standing here in this ghastly barracks of a city, listening to you tell me how beautiful it is, I've never felt more alone in my life."

"You miss Gioia very much, don't you?"

He gave her another startled look.

"Gioia has nothing to do with it. She's probably been having ecstasies over the loveliness of Mohenjo just like you. Just like all of you. I suppose I'm the only one who can't find the beauty, the charm. I'm the only one who looks out there and sees only horror, and then wonders why nobody else sees it, why in fact people would set up a place like this for *entertainment, for pleasure—*"

Her eyes were gleaming. "Oh, you are angry! You really are!"

"Does that fascinate you, too?" he snapped. "A demonstration of genuine primitive emotion? A typical quaint twentieth-century outburst?" He paced the rampart in short quick anguished steps. "Ah. Ah. I think I understand it now, Belilala. Of course: I'm part of your circus, the star of the sideshow. I'm the first experiment in setting up the next stage of it, in fact." Her eyes were wide. The sudden harshness and violence in his voice seemed to be alarming and exciting her at the same time. That angered him even more. Fiercely he went on, "Bringing whole cities back out of time was fun for a while, but it lacks a certain authenticity, eh? For some reason you couldn't bring the inhabitants, too; you couldn't just grab a few million prehistorics out of Egypt or Greece or India and dump them down in this era, I suppose because you might have too much trouble controlling them, or because you'd have the problem of disposing of them once you were bored with them. So you had to settle for creating temporaries to populate your ancient cities. But now you've got me. I'm something more real than a temporary, and that's a terrific novelty for you, and novelty is the thing you people crave more than anything else: maybe the *only* thing you crave. And here I am, complicated, unpredictable, edgy, capable of anger, fear, sadness, love, and all those other formerly extinct things. Why settle for picturesque architecture when you can observe picturesque emotion, too? What fun I must be for all of you! And if you decide that I was really interesting, maybe you'll ship me back where I came from and check out a few other ancient types—a Roman gladiator, maybe, or a Renaissance pope, or even a Neanderthal or two—"

"Charles," she said tenderly. "Oh, Charles, Charles, Charles, how lonely you must be, how lost, how troubled! Will you ever forgive me? Will you ever forgive us all?"

Once more he was astounded by her. She sounded entirely sincere, altogether sympathetic. Was she? Was she, really? He was not sure he had ever had a sign of genuine caring from any of them before, not even Gioia. Nor could he bring himself to trust Belilala now. He was afraid of her, afraid of all of them, of their brittleness, their slyness, their elegance. He wished he could go to her and have her take him in her arms; but he felt too much the shaggy prehistoric just now to be able to risk asking that comfort of her.

He turned away and began to walk around the rim of the citadel's massive wall.

"Charles?"

"Let me alone for a little while," he said.

He walked on. His forehead throbbed and there was a pounding in his chest. All stress systems going full blast, he thought: secret glands dumping gallons of inflammatory substances into his bloodstream. The heat, the inner confusion, the repellent look of this place—

Try to understand, he thought. Relax. Look about you. Try to enjoy your holiday in Mohenjo-daro.

He leaned warily outward, over the edge of the wall. He had never seen a wall like this; it must be forty feet thick at the base, he guessed, perhaps even more, and every brick perfectly shaped, meticulously set. Beyond the great rampart, marshes ran almost to the edge of the city, although close by the wall the swamps had been dammed and drained for agriculture. He saw lithe brown farmers down there, busy with their wheat and barley and peas. Cattle and buffaloes grazed a little farther out. The air was heavy, dank, humid. All was still. From somewhere close at hand came the sound of a droning, whining stringed instrument and a steady insistent chanting.

Gradually a sort of peace pervaded him. His anger subsided. He felt himself beginning to grow calm again. He looked back at the city, the rigid interlocking streets, the maze of inner lanes, the millions of courses of precise brickwork.

It is a miracle, he told himself, that this city is here in this place and at this time. And it is a miracle that I am here to see it.

Caught for a moment by the magic within the bleakness, he thought he began to understand Belilala's awe and delight, and he wished now that he had not spoken to her so sharply. The city was alive. Whether it was the actual Mohenjo-daro of thousands upon thousands of years ago, ripped from the past by some wondrous hook, or simply a cunning reproduction, did not matter at all. Real or not, this was the true Mohenjo-daro. It had been dead, and now, for the moment, it was alive again. These people, these *citizens*, might be trivial, but reconstructing Mohenjo-daro was no trivial achievement. And that the city that had been reconstructed was oppressive and sinister-looking was unimportant. No one was compelled to live in Mohenjo-daro any more. Its time had come and gone, long ago; those little dark-skinned peasants and craftsmen and merchants down there were mere temporaries, mere inanimate things, conjured up like zombies to enhance the illusion. They did not need his pity. Nor did he need to pity himself. He knew that he should be grateful for the chance to behold these things. Someday, when this dream had ended and his hosts had returned him to the world of subways and computers and income tax and television networks, he would think of Mohenjo-daro as he had once beheld it, lofty walls of tightly woven dark brick under a heavy sky, and he would remember only its beauty.

Glancing back, he searched for Belilala and could not for a moment find her. Then he caught sight of her carefully descending a narrow staircase that angled down the inner face of the citadel wall.

"Belilala!" he called.

She paused and looked his way, shading her eyes from the sun with her hand. "Are you all right?"

"Where are you going?"

"To the baths," she said. "Do you want to come?"

He nodded. "Yes. Wait for me, will you? I'll be right there." He began to run toward her along the top of the wall.

***

The baths were attached to the citadel: a great open tank the size of a large swimming pool, lined with bricks set on edge in gypsum mortar and waterproofed with asphalt, and eight smaller tanks just north of it in a kind of covered arcade. He supposed that in ancient times the whole complex had had some ritual purpose, the large tank used by common folk and the small chambers set aside for the private ablutions of priests or nobles. Now the baths were maintained, it seemed, entirely for the pleasure of visiting citizens. As Phillips came up the passageway that led to the main bath he saw fifteen or twenty of them lolling in the water or padding languidly about, while temporaries of the dark-skinned Mohenjo-daro type served them drinks and pungent little morsels of spiced meat as though this were some sort of luxury resort. Which was, he realized, exactly what it was. The temporaries wore white cotton loincloths; the citizens were naked. In his former life he had encountered that sort of casual public nudity a few times on visits to California and the south of France, and it had made him mildly uneasy. But he was growing accustomed to it here.

The changing rooms were tiny brick cubicles connected by rows of closely placed steps to the courtyard that surrounded the central tank. They entered one and Belilala swiftly slipped out of the loose cotton robe that she had worn since their arrival that morning. With arms folded she stood leaning against the wall, waiting for him. After a moment he dropped his own robe and followed her outside. He felt a little giddy, sauntering around naked in the open like this.

On the way to the main bathing area they passed the private baths. None of them seemed to be occupied. They were elegantly constructed chambers, with finely jointed brick floors and carefully designed runnels to drain excess water into the passageway that led to the primary drain. Phillips was struck with admiration for the cleverness of the prehistoric engineers. He peered into this chamber and that to see how the conduits and ventilating ducts were arranged, and when he came to the last room in the sequence he was surprised and embarrassed to discover that it was in use. A brawny grinning man, big-muscled, deep-chested, with exuberantly flowing shoulder-length red hair and a flamboyant, sharply tapering beard, was thrashing about merrily with two women in the small tank. Phillips had a quick glimpse of a lively tangle of arms, legs, breasts, buttocks.

"Sorry," he muttered. His cheeks reddened. Quickly he ducked out, blurting apologies as he went. "Didn't realize the room was occupied — no wish to intrude —"

Belilala had proceeded on down the passageway. Phillips hurried after her. From behind him came peals of cheerful raucous booming laughter and high-pitched giggling and the sound of splashing water. Probably they had not even noticed him.

He paused a moment, puzzled, playing back in his mind that one startling glimpse. Something was not right. Those women, he was fairly sure, were citizens: little slender elfin dark-haired girlish creatures, the standard model. But the man? That great curling sweep of red hair? Not a citizen. Citizens did not affect shoulder-length hair. And *red*? Nor had he ever seen a citizen so burly, so powerfully muscular. Or one with a beard. But he could hardly be a temporary, either. Phillips could conceive no reason why there would be so Anglo-Saxon-looking a temporary at Mohenjo-daro; and it was unthinkable for a temporary to be frolicking like that with citizens, anyway. "Charles?"

He looked up ahead. Belilala stood at the end of the passageway, outlined in a nimbus of brilliant sunlight. "Charles?" she said again. "Did you lose your way?"

"I'm right here behind you," he said. "I'm coming."

"Who did you meet in there?"

"A man with a beard."

"With a what?"

"A beard," he said. "Red hair growing on his face. I wonder who he is."

"Nobody I know," said Belilala. "The only one I know with hair on his face is you. And yours is black, and you shave it off every day." She laughed. "Come along, now! I see some friends by the pool!"

He caught up with her, and they went hand in hand out into the courtyard. Immediately a waiter glided up to them, an obsequious little temporary with a tray of drinks. Phillips waved it away and headed for the pool. He felt terribly exposed: he imagined that the citizens disporting themselves here were staring intently at him, studying his hairy primitive body as though he were some mythical creature, a Minotaur, a werewolf, summoned up for their amusement. Belilala drifted off to talk to someone and he slipped into the water, grateful for the concealment it offered. It was deep, warm, comforting. With swift powerful strokes he breaststroked from one end to the other.

A citizen perched elegantly on the pool's rim smiled at him. "Ah, so you've come at last, Charles!" *Char-less.* Two syllables. Someone from Gioia's set: Stengard, Hawk, Aramayne? He could not remember which one. They were all so much alike.

Phillips returned the man's smile in a halfhearted, tentative way. He searched for something to say and finally asked, "Have you been here long?"

"Weeks. Perhaps months. What a splendid achievement this city is, eh, Charles? Such utter unity of mood — such a total statement of a uniquely single-minded aesthetic —"

"Yes. Single-minded is the word," Phillips said dryly.

"Gioia's word, actually. Gioia's phrase. I was merely quoting."

Gioia. He felt as if he had been stabbed.

"You've spoken to Gioia lately?" he said.

"Actually, no. It was Hekna who saw her. You do remember Hekna, eh?" He nodded toward two naked women standing on the brick platform that bordered the pool, chatting, delicately nibbling morsels of meat. They could have been twins. "There is Hekna, with your Belilala." Hekna, yes. So this must be Hawk, Phillips thought, unless there has been some recent shift of couples. "How sweet she is, your Belilala," Hawk said. "Gioia chose very wisely when she picked her for you."

Another stab: a much deeper one. "Is that how it was?" he said. "Gioia *picked* Belilala for me?"

"Why, of course!" Hawk seemed surprised. It went without saying, evidently. "What did you think? That Gioia would merely go off and leave you to fend for yourself?"

"Hardly. Not Gioia."

"She's very tender, very gentle, isn't she?"

"You mean Belilala? Yes, very," said Phillips carefully. "A dear woman, a wonderful woman. But of course I hope to get together with Gioia again soon." He paused. "They say she's been in Mohenjo-daro almost since it opened."

"She was here, yes."

"Was?"

"Oh, you know Gioia," Hawk said lightly. "She's moved along by now, naturally."

Phillips leaned forward. "Naturally," he said. Tension thickened his voice. "Where has she gone this time?"

"Timbuctoo, I think. Or New Chicago. I forget which one it was. She was telling us that she hoped to be in Timbuctoo for the closing-down party. But then Fenimon had some pressing reason for going to New Chicago. I can't remember what they decided to do." Hawk gestured sadly. "Either way, a pity that she left Mohenjo before the new visitor came. She had such a rewarding time with you, after all: I'm sure she'd have found much to learn from him also."

The unfamiliar term twanged an alarm deep in Phillips's consciousness. *"Visitor?"* he said, angling his head sharply toward Hawk. "What visitor do you mean?"

"You haven't met him yet? Oh, of course, you've only just arrived."

Phillips moistened his lips. "I think I may have seen him. Long red hair? Beard like this?"

"That's the one! Willoughby, he's called. He's—what?—a Viking, a pirate, something like that. Tremendous vigor and force. Remarkable person. We should have many more visitors, I think. They're far superior to temporaries, everyone agrees. Talking with a temporary is a little like talking to one's self, wouldn't you say? They give you no significant illumination. But a visitor—someone like this Willoughby—or like you, Charles—a visitor can be truly enlightening, a visitor can transform one's view of reality—"

"Excuse me," Phillips said. A throbbing began behind his forehead. "Perhaps we can continue this conversation later, yes?" He put the flats of his hands against the hot brick of the platform and hoisted himself swiftly from the pool. "At dinner, maybe—or afterward—yes? All right?" He set off at a quick half-trot back toward the passageway that led to the private baths.

***

As he entered the roofed part of the structure his throat grew dry, his breath suddenly came short. He padded quickly up the hall and peered into the little bath chamber. The bearded man was still there, sitting up in the tank, breast-high above the water, with one arm around each of the women. His eyes gleamed with fiery intensity in the dimness. He was grinning in marvelous self-satisfaction; he seemed to brim with intensity, confidence, gusto.

Let him be what I think he is, Phillips prayed. I have been alone among these people long enough.

"May I come in?" he asked.

"Aye, fellow!" cried the man in the tub thunderously. "By my troth, come ye in, and bring your lass as well! God's teeth, I wot there's room aplenty for more folk in this tub than we!"

At that great uproarious outcry Phillips felt a powerful surge of joy. What a joyous rowdy voice! How rich, how lusty, how totally uncitizenlike!

And those oddly archaic words! *God's teeth? By my troth?* What sort of talk was that? What else but the good pure sonorous Elizabethan diction! Certainly it had something of the roll and fervor of Shakespeare about it. And spoken with—an Irish brogue, was it? No, not quite: it was English, but English spoken in no manner Phillips had ever heard. Citizens did not speak that way. But a *visitor* might. So it was true. Relief flooded Phillips's soul. Not alone, then! Another relic of a former age—another wanderer— a companion in chaos, a brother in adversity—a fellow voyager, tossed even farther than he had been by the tempests of time—

The bearded man grinned heartily and beckoned to Phillips with a toss of his head. "Well, join us, join us, man! Tis good to see an English face again, amidst all these Moors and rogue Portugals! But what have ye done with thy lass? One can never have enough wenches, d'ye not agree?"

The force and vigor of him were extraordinary: almost too much so. He roared, he bellowed, he boomed. He was so very much what he ought to be that he seemed more a character out of some old pirate movie than anything else, so blustering, so real, that he seemed unreal. A stage Elizabethan, larger than life, a boisterous young Falstaff without the belly.

Hoarsely Phillips said, "Who are you?"

"Why, Ned Willoughby's son Francis am I, of Plymouth. Late of the service of Her Most Protestant Majesty, but most foully abducted by the powers of darkness and cast away among these blackamoor Hindus, or whatever they be. And thyself?"

"Charles Phillips." After a moment's uncertainty he added, "I'm from New York."

"*New* York? What place is that? In faith, man, I know it not!"

"A city in America."

"A city in America, forsooth! What a fine fancy that is! In America, you say, and not on the Moon, or perchance underneath the sea?" To the women Willoughby said, "D'ye hear him? He comes from a city in America! With the face of an Englishman, though not the manner of one, and not quite the proper sort of speech. A city in America! A city. God's blood, what will I hear next?"

Phillips trembled. Awe was beginning to take hold of him. This man had walked the streets of Shakespeare's London, perhaps. He had clinked canisters with Marlowe or Essex or Walter Raleigh; he had watched the ships of the Armada wallowing in the Channel. It strained Phillips's spirit to think of it. This strange dream in which he found himself was compounding its strangeness now. He felt like a weary swimmer assailed by heavy surf, winded, dazed. The hot close atmosphere of the baths was driving him toward vertigo. There could be no doubt of it any longer. He was not the only primitive — the only visitor — who was wandering loose in this fiftieth century. They were conducting other experiments as well. He gripped the sides of the door to steady himself and said, "When you speak of Her Most Protestant Majesty, it's Elizabeth the First you mean, is that not so?"

"Elizabeth, aye! As to the First, that is true enough, but why trouble to name her thus? There is but one. First and Last, I do trow, and God save her, there is no other!"

Phillips studied the other man warily. He knew that he must proceed with care. A misstep at this point and he would forfeit any chance that Willoughby would take him seriously. How much metaphysical bewilderment, after all, could this man absorb? What did he know, what had anyone of his time known, of past and present and future and the notion that one might somehow move from one to the other as readily as one would go from Surrey to Kent? That was a twentieth-century idea, late nineteenth at best, a fantastical speculation that very likely no one had even considered before Wells had sent his time traveler off to stare at the reddened sun of the earth's last twilight. Willoughby's world was a world of Protestants and Catholics, of kings and queens, of tiny sailing vessels, of swords at the hip and oxcarts on the road: that world seemed to Phillips far more alien and distant than was this world of citizens and temporaries. The risk that Willoughby would not begin to understand him was great. But this man and he were natural allies against a world they had never made. Phillips chose to take the risk.

"Elizabeth the First is the queen you serve," he said. "There will be another of her name in England, in due time. Has already been, in fact."

Willoughby shook his head like a puzzled lion. "Another Elizabeth, d'ye say?"

"A second one, and not much like the first. Long after your Virgin Queen, this one. She will reign in what you think of as the days to come. That I know without doubt."

The Englishman peered at him and frowned. "You see the future? Are you a soothsayer, then? A necromancer, mayhap? Or one of the very demons that brought me to this place?"

"Not at all," Phillips said gently. "Only a lost soul, like yourself." He stepped into the little room and crouched by the side of the tank. The two citizen-women were staring at him in bland fascination. He ignored them. To Willoughby he said, "Do you have any idea where you are?"

***

The Englishman had guessed, rightly enough, that he was in India: "I do believe these little brown Moorish folk are of the Hindu sort," he said. But that was as far as his comprehension of what had befallen him could go.

It had not occurred to him that he was no longer living in the sixteenth century. And of course he did not begin to suspect that this strange and somber brick city in which he found himself was a wanderer out of an era even more remote than his own. Was there any way, Phillips wondered, of explaining that to him?

He had been here only three days. He thought it was devils that had carried him off. "While I slept did they come for me," he said. "Mephistophilis Sathanas his henchmen seized me—God alone can say why—and swept me in a moment out to this torrid realm from England, where I had reposed among friends and family. For I was between one voyage and the next, you must understand, awaiting Drake and his ship— you know Drake, the glorious Francis? God's blood, there's a mariner for ye! We were to go to the Main again, he and I, but instead here I be in this other place—" Willoughby leaned close and said, "I ask you, soothsayer, how can it be, that a man go to sleep in Plymouth and wake up in India? It is passing strange, is it not?"

"That it is," Phillips said.

"But he that is in the dance must needs dance on, though he do but hop, eh? So do I believe." He gestured toward the two citizen-women. "And therefore to console myself in this pagan land I have found me some sport among these little Portugal women—"

"Portugal?" said Phillips.

"Why, what else can they be, but Portugals? Is it not the Portugals who control all these coasts of India? See, the people are of two sorts here, the blackamoors and the others, the fair-skinned ones, the lords and masters who lie here in these baths. If they be not Hindus, and I think they are not, then Portugals is what they must be." He laughed and pulled the women against himself and rubbed his hands over their breasts as though they were fruits on a vine. "Is that not what you are, you little naked shameless Papist wenches? A pair of Portugals, eh?"

They giggled, but did not answer.

"No," Phillips said. "This is India, but not the India you think you know. And these women are not Portuguese."

"Not Portuguese?" Willoughby said, baffled.

"No more so than you. I'm quite certain of that."

Willoughby stroked his beard. "I do admit I found them very odd, for Portugals. I have heard not a syllable of their Portugee speech on their lips. And it is strange also that they run naked as Adam and Eve in these baths, and allow me free plunder of their women, which is not the way of Portugals at home, God wot. But I thought me, this is India, they choose to live in another fashion here—"

"No," Phillips said. "I tell you, these are not Portuguese, nor any other people of Europe who are known to you."

"Prithee, who are they, then?"

Do it delicately, now, Phillips warned himself. *Delicately.*

He said, "It is not far wrong to think of them as spirits of some kind— demons, even. Or sorcerers who have magicked us out of our proper places in the world." He paused, groping for some means to share with Willoughby, in a way that Willoughby might grasp, this mystery that had enfolded them. He drew a deep breath. "They've taken us not only across the sea," he said, "but across the years as well. We have both been hauled, you and I, far into the days that are to come."

Willoughby gave him a look of blank bewilderment.

"Days that are to come? Times yet unborn, d'ye mean? Why, I comprehend none of that!"

"Try to understand. We're both castaways in the same boat, man! But there's no way we can help each other if I can't make you see—"

Shaking his head, Willoughby muttered, "In faith, good friend, I find your words the merest folly. Today is today, and tomorrow is tomorrow, and how can a man step from one to t'other until tomorrow be turned into today?"

"I have no idea," said Phillips. Struggle was apparent on Willoughby's face; but plainly he could perceive no more than the haziest outline of what Phillips was driving at, if that much. "But this I know," he went on. "That your world and all that was in it is dead and gone. And so is mine, though I was born four hundred years after you, in the time of the second Elizabeth."

Willoughby snorted scornfully. "Four hundred—"

"You must believe me!"

"Nay! Nay!"

"It's the truth. Your time is only history to me. And mine and yours are history to *them*—ancient history. They call us visitors, but what we are is captives." Phillips felt himself quivering in the intensity of his effort. He was aware how insane this must sound to Willoughby. It was beginning to sound insane to him. "They've stolen us out of our proper times — seizing us like gypsies in the night — "

"Fie, man! You rave with lunacy!"

Phillips shook his head. He reached out and seized Willoughby tightly by the wrist. "I beg you, listen to me!" The citizen-women were watching closely, whispering to one another behind their hands, laughing. "Ask them!" Phillips cried. "Make them tell you what century this is! The sixteenth, do you think? Ask them!"

"What century could it be, but the sixteenth of our Lord?"

"They will tell you it is the fiftieth."

Willoughby looked at him pityingly. "Man, man, what a sorry thing thou art! The fiftieth, indeed!" He laughed. "Fellow, listen to me, now. There is but one Elizabeth, safe upon her throne in Westminster. This is India. The year is Anno 1591. Come, let us you and I steal a ship from these Portugals, and make our way back to England, and peradventure you may get from there to your America — "

"There is no England."

"Ah, can you say that and not be mad?"

"The cities and nations we knew are gone. These people live like magicians, Francis." There was no use holding anything back now, Phillips thought leadenly. He knew that he had lost. "They conjure up places of long ago, and build them here and there to suit their fancy, and when they are bored with them they destroy them, and start anew. There is no England. Europe is empty, featureless, void. Do you know what cities there are? There are only five in all the world. There is Alexandria of Egypt. There is Timbuctoo in Africa. There is New Chicago in America. There is a great city in China — in Cathay, I suppose you would say. And there is this place, which they call Mohenjo-daro, and which is far more ancient than Greece, than Rome, than Babylon."

Quietly Willoughby said, "Nay. This is mere absurdity. You say we are in some far tomorrow, and then you tell me we are dwelling in some city of long ago."

"A conjuration, only," Phillips said in desperation. "A likeness of that city. Which these folk have fashioned somehow for their own amusement. Just as we are here, you and I: to amuse them. Only to amuse them."

"You are completely mad."

"Come with me, then. Talk with the citizens by the great pool. Ask them what year this is; ask them about England; ask them how you come to be here." Once again Phillips grasped Willoughby's wrist. "We should be allies. If we work together, perhaps we can discover some way to get ourselves out of this place, and — "

"Let me be, fellow."

"Please — "

"Let me be!" roared Willoughby, and pulled his arm free. His eyes were stark with rage. Rising in the tank, he looked about furiously as though searching for a weapon. The citizen-women shrank back away from him, though at the same time they seemed captivated by the big man's fierce outburst. "Go to, get you to Bedlam! Let me be, madman! Let me be!"

**

Dismally Phillips roamed the dusty unpaved streets of Mohenjo-daro alone for hours. His failure with Willoughby had left him bleak-spirited and somber: he had hoped to stand back to back with the Elizabethan against the citizens, but he saw now that that was not to be. He had bungled things; or, more likely, it had been impossible ever to bring Willoughby to see the truth of their predicament.

In the stifling heat he went at random through the confusing congested lanes of flat-roofed windowless houses and blank featureless walls until he emerged into a broad marketplace. The life of the city swirled madly around him: the pseudo-life, rather, the intricate interactions of the thousands of temporaries who were nothing more than wind-up dolls set in motion to provide the illusion that pre-Vedic India was still a going concern. Here vendors sold beautiful little carved stone seals portraying tigers and monkeys and strange humped cattle, and women bargained vociferously with craftsmen for ornaments of ivory, gold, copper, and bronze. Weary-looking women squatted behind immense mounds of newly made pottery, pinkish red with black designs. No one paid any attention to him. He was the outsider here, neither citizen nor temporary. They belonged.

He went on, passing the huge granaries where workmen ceaselessly unloaded carts of wheat and others pounded grain on great circular brick platforms. He drifted into a public restaurant thronging with joyless silent people standing elbow to elbow at small brick counters, and was given a flat round piece of bread, a sort of tortilla or chapatti, in which was stuffed some spiced mincemeat that stung his lips like fire. Then he moved onward down a wide shallow timbered staircase into the lower part of the city, where the peasantry lived in cell-like rooms packed together as though in hives.

It was an oppressive city, but not a squalid one. The intensity of the concern with sanitation amazed him: wells and fountains and public privies everywhere, and brick drains running from each building, leading to covered cesspools. There was none of the open sewage and pestilent gutters that he knew still could be found in the India of his own time. He wondered whether ancient Mohenjo-daro had in truth been so fastidious. Perhaps the citizens had redesigned the city to suit their own ideals of cleanliness. No: most likely what he saw was authentic, he decided, a function of the same obsessive discipline that had given the city its rigidity of form. If Mohenjo-daro had been a verminous filthy hole, the citizens probably would have re-created it in just that way, and loved it for its fascinating reeking filth. Not that he had ever noticed an excessive concern with authenticity on the part of the citizens; and Mohenjo-daro, like all the other restored cities he had visited, was full of the usual casual anachronisms. Phillips saw images of Shiva and Krishna here and there on the walls of buildings he took to be temples, and the benign face of the mother-goddess Kali loomed in the plazas. Surely those deities had arisen in India long after the collapse of the Mohenjo-daro civilization. Were the citizens indifferent to such matters of chronology? Or did they take a certain naughty pleasure in mixing the eras—a mosque and a church in Greek Alexandria, Hindu gods in prehistoric Mohenjo-daro? Perhaps their records of the past had become contaminated with errors over the thousands of years. He would not have been surprised to see banners bearing portraits of Gandhi and Nehru being carried in procession through the streets. And there were phantasms and chimeras at large here again, too, as if the citizens were untroubled by the boundary between history and myth: little fat elephant-headed Ganeshas blithely plunging their trunks into water fountains, a six-armed three-headed woman sunning herself on a brick terrace. Why not? Surely that was the motto of these people: *Why not, why not, why not?* They could do as they pleased, and they did. Yet Gioia had said to him, long ago, "Limits are very important." In what, Phillips wondered, did they limit themselves, other than the number of their cities? Was there a quota, perhaps, on the number of "visitors" they allowed themselves to kidnap from the past? Until today he had thought he was the only one; now he knew there was at least one other; possibly there were more elsewhere, a step or two ahead or behind him, making the circuit with the citizens who traveled endlessly from New Chicago to Chang-an to Alexandria. We should join forces, he thought, and compel them to send us back to our rightful eras. *Compel?* How? File a class-action suit, maybe? Demonstrate in the streets? Sadly he thought of his failure to make common cause with Willoughby. We are natural allies, he thought. Together perhaps we might have won some compassion from these people. But to Willoughby it must be literally unthinkable that Good Queen Bess and her subjects were sealed away on the far side of a barrier hundreds of centuries thick. He would prefer to believe that England was just a few months' voyage away around the Cape of Good Hope, and that all he need do was commandeer a ship and set sail for home. Poor Willoughby: probably he would never see his home again.

The thought came to Phillips suddenly:

Neither will you.

And then, after it:

If you could go home, would you really want to?

One of the first things he had realized here was that he knew almost nothing substantial about his former existence. His mind was well stocked with details on life in twentieth-century New York, to be sure; but of himself he could say not much more than that he was Charles Phillips and had come from 1984. Profession? Age? Parents' names? Did he have a wife? Children? A cat, a dog, hobbies? No data: none. Possibly the citizens had stripped such things from him when they brought him here, to spare him from the pain of separation. They might be capable of that kindness. Knowing so little of what he had lost, could he truly say that he yearned for it? Willoughby seemed to remember much more of his former life, somehow, and longed for it all the more intensely. He was spared that. Why not stay here, and go on and on from city to city, sightseeing all of time past as the citizens conjured it back into being? Why not? Why not? The chances were that he had no choice about it, anyway.

He made his way back up toward the citadel and to the baths once more. He felt a little like a ghost, haunting a city of ghosts.

Belilala seemed unaware that he had been gone for most of the day. She sat by herself on the terrace of the baths, placidly sipping some thick milky beverage that had been sprinkled with a dark spice. He shook his head when she offered him some.

"Do you remember I mentioned that I saw a man with red hair and a beard this morning?" Phillips said. "He's a visitor. Hawk told me that."

"Is he?" Belilala asked.

"From a time about four hundred years before mine. I talked with him. He thinks he was brought here by demons." Phillips gave her a searching look. "I'm a visitor, too, isn't that so?"

"Of course, love."

"And how was I brought here? By demons also?"

Belilala smiled indifferently. "You'd have to ask someone else. Hawk, perhaps. I haven't looked into these things very deeply."

"I see. Are there many visitors here, do you know?"

A languid shrug. "Not many, no, not really. I've only heard of three or four besides you. There may be others by now, I suppose." She rested her hand lightly on his. "Are you having a good time in Mohenjo, Charles?"

He let her question pass as though he had not heard it.

"I asked Hawk about Gioia," he said.

"Oh?"

"He told me that she's no longer here, that she's gone on to Timbuctoo or New Chicago, he wasn't sure which."

"That's quite likely. As everybody knows, Gioia rarely stays in the same place very long."

Phillips nodded. "You said the other day that Gioia is a short-timer. That means she's going to grow old and die, doesn't it?"

"I thought you understood that, Charles."

"Whereas you will not age? Nor Hawk, nor Stengard, nor any of the rest of your set?"

"We will live as long as we wish," she said. "But we will not age, no."

"What makes a person a short-timer?"

"They're born that way, I think. Some missing gene, some extra gene — I don't actually know. It's extremely uncommon. Nothing can be done to help them. It's very slow, the aging. But it can't be halted."

Phillips nodded. "That must be very disagreeable," he said. "To find yourself one of the few people growing old in a world where everyone stays young. No wonder Gioia is so impatient. No wonder she runs around from place to place. No wonder she attached herself so quickly to the barbaric hairy visitor from the twentieth century, who comes from a time when *everybody* was a short-timer. She and I have something in common, wouldn't you say?"

"In a manner of speaking, yes."

"We understand aging. We understand death. Tell me: is Gioia likely to die very soon, Belilala?"

"Soon? Soon?" She gave him a wide-eyed childlike stare. "What is soon? How can I say? What you think of as soon and what I think of as soon are not the same things, Charles." Then her manner changed: she seemed to be hearing what he was saying for the first time. Softly she said, "No, no, Charles. I don't think she will die very soon."

"When she left me in Chang-an, was it because she had become bored with me?"

Belilala shook her head. "She was simply restless. It had nothing to do with you. She was never bored with you."

"Then I'm going to go looking for her. Wherever she may be, Timbuctoo, New Chicago, I'll find her. Gioia and I belong together."

"Perhaps you do," said Belilala. "Yes. Yes, I think you really do." She sounded altogether unperturbed, unrejected, unbereft. "By all means, Charles. Go to her. Follow her. Find her. Wherever she may be."

***

They had already begun dismantling Timbuctoo when Phillips got there. While he was still high overhead, his flitterflitter hovering above the dusty tawny plain where the River Niger met the sands of the Sahara, a surge of keen excitement rose in him as he looked down at the square gray flat-roofed mud brick buildings of the great desert capital. But when he landed he found gleaming metal-skinned robots swarming everywhere, a horde of them scuttling about like giant shining insects, pulling the place apart.

He had not known about the robots before. So that was how all these miracles were carried out, Phillips realized: an army of obliging machines. He imagined them bustling up out of the earth whenever their services were needed, emerging from some sterile subterranean storehouse to put together Venice or Thebes or Knossos or Houston or whatever place was required, down to the finest detail, and then at some later time returning to undo everything that they had fashioned. He watched them now, diligently pulling down the adobe walls, demolishing the heavy metal-studded gates, bulldozing the amazing labyrinth of alleyways and thoroughfares, sweeping away the market. On his last visit to Timbuctoo that market had been crowded with a horde of veiled Tuaregs and swaggering Moors, black Sudanese, shrewd-faced Syrian traders, all of them busily dickering for camels, horses, donkeys, slabs of salt, huge green melons, silver bracelets, splendid vellum Korans. They were all gone now, that picturesque crowd of swarthy temporaries. Nor were there any citizens to be seen. The dust of destruction choked the air. One of the robots came up to Phillips and said in a dry crackling insect-voice, "You ought not to be here. This city is closed."

He stared at the flashing, buzzing band of scanners and sensors across the creature's glittering tapered snout. "I'm trying to find someone, a citizen who may have been here recently. Her name is—"

"This city is closed," the robot repeated inexorably.

They would not let him stay as much as an hour. There is no food here, the robot said, no water, no shelter. This is not a place any longer. You may not stay. You may not stay. You may not stay.

This is not a place any longer.

Perhaps he could find her in New Chicago, then. He took to the air again, soaring northward and westward over the vast emptiness. The land below him curved away into the hazy horizon, bare, sterile. What had they done with the vestiges of the world that had gone before? Had they turned their gleaming metal beetles loose to clean everything away? Were there no ruins of genuine antiquity anywhere? No scrap of Rome, no shard of Jerusalem, no stump of Fifth Avenue? It was all so barren down there: an empty stage, waiting for its next set to be built. He flew on a great arc across the jutting hump of Africa and on into what he supposed was southern Europe: the little vehicle did all the work, leaving him to doze or stare as he wished. Now and again he saw another flitterflitter pass by, far away, a dark distant winged teardrop outlined against the hard clarity of the sky. He wished there was some way of making radio contact with them, but he had no idea how to go about it. Not that he had anything he wanted to say; he wanted only to hear a human voice. He was utterly isolated.

He might just as well have been the last living man on Earth. He closed his eyes and thought of Gioia.

***

"Like this?" Phillips asked. In an ivory-paneled oval room sixty stories above the softly glowing streets of New Chicago he touched a small cool plastic canister to his upper lip and pressed the stud at its base. He heard a foaming sound; and then blue vapor rose to his nostrils.

"Yes," Cantilena said. "That's right."

He detected a faint aroma of cinnamon, cloves, and something that might almost have been broiled lobster. Then a spasm of dizziness hit him and visions rushed through his head: Gothic cathedrals, the Pyramids, Central Park under fresh snow, the harsh brick warrens of Mohenjo-daro, and fifty thousand other places all at once, a wild roller-coaster ride through space and time. It seemed to go on for centuries. But finally his head cleared and he looked about, blinking, realizing that the whole thing had taken only a moment. Cantilena still stood at his elbow. The other citizens in the room—fifteen, twenty of them—had scarcely moved. The strange little man with the celadon skin over by the far wall continued to stare at him.

"Well?" Cantilena asked. "What did you think?"

"Incredible."

"And very authentic. It's an actual New Chicagoan drug. The exact formula. Would you like another?"

"Not just yet," Phillips said uneasily. He swayed and had to struggle for his balance. Sniffing that stuff might not have been such a wise idea, he thought.

He had been in New Chicago a week, or perhaps it was two, and he was still suffering from the peculiar disorientation that that city always aroused in him. This was the fourth time that he had come here, and it had been the same every time. New Chicago was the only one of the reconstructed cities of this world that in its original incarnation had existed *after* his own era. To him it was an outpost of the incomprehensible future; to the citizens it was a quaint simulacrum of the archaeological past. That paradox left him aswirl with impossible confusions and tensions.

What had happened to *old* Chicago was of course impossible for him to discover. Vanished without a trace, that was clear: no Water Tower, no Marina City, no Hancock Center, no Tribune building, not a fragment, not an atom. But it was hopeless to ask any of the million-plus inhabitants of New Chicago about their city's predecessor. They were only temporaries; they knew no more than they had to know, and all that they had to know was how to go through the motions of whatever it was that they did by way of creating the illusion that this was a real city. They had no need of knowing ancient history.

Nor was he likely to find out anything from a citizen, of course. Citizens did not seem to bother much about scholarly matters. Phillips had no reason to think that the world was anything other than an amusement park to them. Somewhere, certainly, there had to be those who specialized in the serious study of the lost civilizations of the past—for how, otherwise, would these uncanny reconstructed cities be brought into being? "The planners," he had once heard Nissandra or Aramayne say, "are already deep into their Byzantium research." But who were the planners? He had no idea. For all he knew, they were the robots. Perhaps the robots were the real masters of this whole era, who created the cities not primarily for the sake of amusing the citizens but in their own diligent attempt to comprehend the life of the world that had passed away. A wild speculation, yes; but not without some plausibility, he thought.

He felt oppressed by the party gaiety all about him. "I need some air," he said to Cantilena, and headed toward the window. It was the merest crescent, but a breeze came through. He looked out at the strange city below.

New Chicago had nothing in common with the old one but its name. They had built it, at least, along the western shore of a large inland lake that might even be Lake Michigan, although when he had flown over it had seemed broader and less elongated than the lake he remembered. The city itself was a lacy fantasy of slender pastel-hued buildings rising at odd angles and linked by a webwork of gently undulating aerial bridges. The streets were long parentheses that touched the lake at their northern and southern ends and arched gracefully westward in the middle. Between each of the great boulevards ran a track for public transportation—sleek aquamarine bubble-vehicles gliding on soundless wheels—and flanking each of the tracks were lush strips of park. It was beautiful, astonishingly so, but insubstantial. The whole thing seemed to have been contrived from sunbeams and silk.

A soft voice beside him said, "Are you becoming ill?"

Phillips glanced around. The celadon man stood beside him: a compact, precise person, vaguely Oriental in appearance. His skin was of a curious gray-green hue like no skin Phillips had ever seen, and it was extraordinarily smooth in texture, as though he were made of fine porcelain.

He shook his head. "Just a little queasy," he said. "This city always scrambles me."

"I suppose it can be disconcerting," the little man replied. His tone was furry and veiled, the inflection strange. There was something feline about him. He seemed sinewy, unyielding, almost menacing. "Visitor, are you?"

Phillips studied him a moment. "Yes," he said.

"So am I, of course."

"Are you?"

"Indeed." The little man smiled. "What's your locus? Twentieth century? Twenty-first at the latest, I'd say."

"I'm from 1984. A.D. 1984."

Another smile, a self-satisfied one. "Not a bad guess, then." A brisk tilt of the head. "Y'ang-Yeovil."

"Pardon me?" Phillips said.

"Y'ang-Yeovil. It is my name. Formerly Colonel Y'ang-Yeovil of the Third Septentriad."

"Is that on some other planet?" asked Phillips, feeling a bit dazed.

"Oh, no, not at all," Y'ang-Yeovil said pleasantly. "This very world, I assure you. I am quite of human origin. Citizen of the Republic of Upper Han, native of the city of Port Ssu. And you — forgive me — your name — ?"

"I'm sorry. Phillips. Charles Phillips. From New York City, once upon a time."

"Ah, New York!" Y'ang-Yeovil's face lit with a glimmer of recognition that quickly faded. "New York — New York — it was very famous, that I know — "

This is very strange, Phillips thought. He felt greater compassion for poor bewildered Francis Willoughby now. This man comes from a time so far beyond my own that he barely knows of New York — he must be a contemporary of the real New Chicago, in fact; I wonder whether he finds this version authentic — and yet to the citizens this Y'ang-Yeovil too is just a primitive, a curio out of antiquity —

"New York was the largest city of the United States of America," Phillips said.

"Of course. Yes. Very famous."

"But virtually forgotten by the time the Republic of Upper Han came into existence, I gather."

Y'ang-Yeovil said, looking uncomfortable, "There were disturbances between your time and mine. But by no means should you take from my words the impression that your city was — "

Sudden laughter resounded across the room. Five or six newcomers had arrived at the party. Phillips stared, gasped, gaped. Surely that was Stengard — and Aramayne beside him — and that other woman, half hidden behind them —

"If you'll pardon me a moment — " Phillips said, turning abruptly away from Y'ang-Yeovil. "Please excuse me. Someone just coming in — a person I've been trying to find ever since — "

He hurried toward her.

***

"Gioia?" he called. "Gioia, it's me! Wait! Wait!"

Stengard was in the way. Aramayne, turning to take a handful of the little vapor-sniffers from Cantilena, blocked him also. Phillips pushed through them as though they were not there. Gioia, halfway out the door, halted and looked toward him like a frightened deer.

"Don't go," he said. He took her hand in his. He was startled by her appearance. How long had it been since their strange parting on that night of mysteries in Chang-an? A year? A year and a half? So he believed. Or had he lost all track of time? Were his perceptions of the passing of the months in this world that unreliable? She seemed at least ten or fifteen years older. Maybe she really was; maybe the years had been passing for him here as in a dream, and he had never known it. She looked strained, faded, worn. Out of a thinner and strangely altered face her eyes blazed at him almost defiantly, as though saying, *See? See how ugly I have become?*

He said, "I've been hunting for you for—I don't know how long it's been, Gioia. In Mohenjo, in Timbuctoo, now here. I want to be with you again."

"It isn't possible."

"Belilala explained everything to me in Mohenjo. I know that you're a short-timer—I know what that means, Gioia. But what of it? So you're beginning to age a little. So what? So you'll only have three or four hundred years, instead of forever. Don't you think I know what it means to be a short-timer? I'm just a simple ancient man of the twentieth century, remember? Sixty, seventy, eighty years is all we would get. You and I suffer from the same malady, Gioia. That's what drew you to me in the first place. I'm certain of that. That's why we belong with each other now. However much time we have, we can spend the rest of it together, don't you see?"

"You're the one who doesn't see, Charles," she said softly.

"Maybe. Maybe I still don't understand a damned thing about this place. Except that you and I—that I love you—that I think you love me—"

"I love you, yes. But you don't understand. It's precisely because I love you that you and I—you and I can't—"

With a despairing sigh she slid her hand free of his grasp. He reached for her again, but she shook him off and backed up quickly into the corridor.

"Gioia?"

"Please," she said. "No. I would never have come here if I knew you were here. Don't come after me. Please. Please."

She turned and fled.

He stood looking after her for a long moment. Cantilena and Aramayne appeared, and smiled at him as if nothing at all had happened. Cantilena offered him a vial of some sparkling amber fluid. He refused with a brusque gesture. Where do I go now, he wondered? What do I do? He wandered back into the party.

Y'ang-Yeovil glided to his side. "You are in great distress," the little man murmured.

Phillips glared. "Let me be."

"Perhaps I could be of some help."

"There's no help possible," said Phillips. He swung about and plucked one of the vials from a tray and gulped its contents. It made him feel as if there were two of him, standing on either side of Y'ang-Yeovil. He gulped another. Now there were four of him. "I'm in love with a citizen," he blurted. It seemed to him that he was speaking in chorus.

"Love. Ah. And does she love you?"

"So I thought. So I think. But she's a short-timer. Do you know what that means? She's not immortal like the others. She ages. She's beginning to look old. And so she's been running away from me. She doesn't want me to see her changing. She thinks it'll disgust me, I suppose. I tried to remind her just now that I'm not immortal either, that she and I could grow old together, but she—"

"Oh, no," Y'ang-Yeovil said quietly. "Why do you think you will age? Have you grown any older in all the time that you've been here?"

Phillips was nonplussed. "Of course I have. I—I—"

"Have you?" Y'ang-Yeovil smiled. "Here. Look at yourself." He did something intricate with his fingers and a shimmering zone of mirrorlike light appeared between them.

Phillips stared at his reflection. A youthful face stared back at him. It was true, then. He had simply not thought about it. How many years had he spent in this world? The time had simply slipped by: a great deal of time, though he could not calculate how much. They did not seem to keep close count of it here, nor had he. But it must have been many years, he thought. All that endless travel up and down the globe—so many cities had come and gone—Rio, Rome, Asgard, those were the first three that came to mind—and there were others; he could hardly remember every one. Years. His face had not changed at all. Time had worked its harshness on Gioia, yes, but not on him.

"I don't understand," he said. "Why am I not aging?"

"Because you are not real," said Y'ang-Yeovil. "Are you unaware of that?"

Phillips blinked. "Not—real?"

"Did you think you were lifted bodily out of your own time?" the little man asked. "Ah, no, no, there is no way for them to do such a thing. We are not actual time travelers: not you, not I, not any of the visitors. I thought you were aware of that. But perhaps your era is too early for a proper understanding of these things. We are very cleverly done, my friend. We are ingenious constructs, marvelously stuffed with the thoughts and attitudes and events of our own times. We are their finest achievement, you know: far more complex even than one of these cities. We are a step beyond the temporaries—more than a step, a great deal more. They do only what they are instructed to do, and their range is very narrow. They are nothing but machines, really. Whereas we are autonomous. We move about by our own will; we think, we talk, we even, so it seems, fall in love. But we will not age. How could we age? We are not real. We are mere artificial webworks of mental responses. We are mere illusions, done so well that we deceive even ourselves. You did not know that? Indeed, you did not know?"

***

He was airborne, touching destination buttons at random. Somehow he found himself heading back toward Timbuctoo. *This city is closed. This is not a place any longer.* It did not matter to him. Why should anything matter?

Fury and a choking sense of despair rose within him. I am software, Phillips thought. I am nothing but software.

Not real. Very cleverly done. An ingenious construct. A mere illusion.

No trace of Timbuctoo was visible from the air. He landed anyway. The gray sandy earth was smooth, unturned, as though there had never been anything there. A few robots were still about, handling whatever final chores were required in the shutting-down of a city. Two of them scuttled up to him. Huge bland gleaming silver-skinned insects, not friendly.

"There is no city here," they said. "This is not a permissible place."

"Permissible by whom?"

"There is no reason for you to be here."

"There's no reason for me to be anywhere," Phillips said. The robots stirred, made uneasy humming sounds and ominous clicks, waved their antennae about. They seemed troubled, he thought. They seem to dislike my attitude. Perhaps I run some risk of being taken off to the home for unruly software for debugging. "I'm leaving now," he told them. "Thank you. Thank you very much." He backed away from them and climbed into his flitterflitter. He touched more destination buttons.

We move about by our own will. We think, we talk, we even fall in love.

He landed in Chang-an. This time there was no reception committee waiting for him at the Gate of Brilliant Virtue. The city seemed larger and more resplendent: new pagodas, new palaces. It felt like winter: a chilly cutting wind was blowing. The sky was cloudless and dazzlingly bright. At the steps of the Silver Terrace he encountered Francis Willoughby, a great hulking figure in magnificent brocaded robes, with two dainty little temporaries, pretty as jade statuettes, engulfed in his arms. "Miracles and wonders! The silly lunatic fellow is here, too!" Willoughby roared. "Look, look, we are come to far Cathay, you and I!"

We are nowhere, Phillips thought. *We are mere illusions, done so well that we deceive even ourselves.*

To Willoughby he said, "You look like an emperor in those robes, Francis."

"Aye, like Prester John!" Willoughby cried. "Like Tamburlaine himself! Aye, am I not majestic?" He slapped Phillips gaily on the shoulder, a rough playful poke that spun him halfway about, coughing and wheezing. "We flew in the air, as the eagles do, as the demons do, as the angels do! Soared like angels! Like angels!" He came close, looming over Phillips. "I would have gone to England, but the wench Belilala said there was an enchantment on me that would keep me from England just now; and so we voyaged to Cathay. Tell me this, fellow, will you go witness for me when we see England again? Swear that all that has befallen us did in truth befall? For I fear they will say I am as mad as Marco Polo, when I tell them of flying to Cathay."

"One madman backing another?" Phillips asked. "What can I tell you? You still think you'll reach England, do you?" Rage rose to the surface in him, bubbling hot. "Ah, Francis, Francis, do you know your Shakespeare? Did you go to the plays? We aren't real. *We aren't real.* We are such stuff as dreams are made on, the two of us. That's all we are. O brave new world! What England? Where? There's no England. There's no Francis Willoughby. There's no Charles Phillips. What we are is —"

"Let him be, Charles," a cool voice cut in.

He turned. Belilala, in the robes of an empress, coming down the steps of the Silver Terrace.

"I know the truth," he said bitterly. "Y'ang-Yeovil told me. The visitor from the twenty-fifth century. I saw him in New Chicago."

"Did you see Gioia there, too?" Belilala asked.

"Briefly. She looks much older."

"Yes. I know. She was here recently."

"And has gone on, I suppose?"

"To Mohenjo again, yes. Go after her, Charles. Leave poor Francis alone. I told her to wait for you. I told her that she needs you, and you need her."

"Very kind of you. But what good is it, Belilala? I don't even exist. And she's going to die."

"You exist. How can you doubt that you exist? You feel, don't you? You suffer. You love. You love Gioia: is that not so? And you are loved by Gioia. Would Gioia love what is not real?"

"You think she loves me?"

"I know she does. Go to her, Charles. Go. I told her to wait for you in Mohenjo."

Phillips nodded numbly. What was there to lose?

"Go to her," said Belilala again. "Now."

"Yes," Phillips said. "I'll go now." He turned to Willoughby. "If ever we meet in London, friend, I'll testify for you. Fear nothing. All will be well, Francis."

He left them and set his course for Mohenjo-daro, half expecting to find the robots already tearing it down. Mohenjo-daro was still there, no lovelier than before. He went to the baths, thinking he might find Gioia there. She was not; but he came upon Nissandra, Stengard, Fenimon.

"She has gone to Alexandria," Fenimon told him. "She wants to see it one last time, before they close it."

"They're almost ready to open Constantinople," Stengard explained. "The capital of Byzantium, you know, the great city by the Golden Horn. They'll take Alexandria away, you understand, when Byzantium opens. They say it's going to be marvelous. We'll see you there for the opening, naturally?"

"Naturally," Phillips said.

He flew to Alexandria. He felt lost and weary. All this is hopeless folly, he told himself. I am nothing but a puppet jerking about on its strings. But somewhere above the shining breast of the Arabian Sea the deeper implications of something that Belilala had said to him started to sink in, and he felt his bitterness, his rage, his despair, all suddenly beginning to leave him. *You exist. How can you doubt that you exist? Would Gioia love what is not real?* Of course. Of course. Y'ang-Yeovil had been wrong: visitors were something more than mere illusions. Indeed, Y'ang-Yeovil had voiced the truth of their condition without understanding what he was really saying: *We think, we talk, we fall in love.* Yes. That was the heart of the situation. The visitors might be artificial, but they were not unreal. Belilala had been trying to tell him that just the other night. *You suffer. You love. You love Gioia. Would Gioia love what is not real?* Surely he was real, or at any rate real enough. What he was was something strange, something that would probably have been all but incomprehensible to the twentieth-century people whom he had been designed to simulate. But that did not mean that he was unreal. Did one have to be of woman born to be real? No. No. No. His kind of reality was a sufficient reality. He had no need to be ashamed of it. And, understanding that, he understood that Gioia did not need to grow old and die. There was a way by which she could be saved, if only she would embrace it. If only she would.

When he landed in Alexandria he went immediately to the hotel on the slopes of the Paneium where they had stayed on their first visit, so very long ago; and there she was, sitting quietly on a patio with a view of the harbor and the Lighthouse. There was something calm and resigned about the way she sat. She had given up. She did not even have the strength to flee from him any longer.

***

"Gioia," he said gently.

She looked older than she had in New Chicago. Her face was drawn and sallow and her eyes seemed sunken; and she was not even bothering these days to deal with the white strands that stood out in stark contrast against the darkness of her hair. He sat down beside her and put his hand over hers and looked out toward the obelisks, the palaces, the temples, the Lighthouse. At length he said, "I know what I really am now."

"Do you, Charles?" She sounded very far away.

"In my age we called it software. All I am is a set of commands, responses, cross-references, operating some sort of artificial body. It's infinitely better software then we could have imagined. But we were only just beginning to learn how, after all. They pumped me full of twentieth-century reflexes. The right moods, the right appetites, the right irrationalities, the right sort of combativeness. Somebody knows a lot about what it was like to be a twentieth-century man. They did a good job with Willoughby, too, all that Elizabethan rhetoric and swagger. And I suppose they got Y'ang-Yeovil right. *He* seems to think so: who better to judge? The twenty-fifth century, the Republic of Upper Han, people with gray-green skin, half Chinese and half Martian for all I know. *Somebody* knows. Somebody here is very good at programming, Gioia."

She was not looking at him.

"I feel frightened, Charles," she said in that same distant way.

"Of me? Of the things I'm saying?"

"No, not of you. Don't you see what has happened to me?"

"I see you. There are changes."

"I lived a long time wondering when the changes would begin. I thought maybe they wouldn't, not really. Who wants to believe they'll get old? But it started when we were in Alexandria that first time. In Chang-an it got much worse. And now — now — "

He said abruptly, "Stengard tells me they'll be opening Constantinople very soon."

"So?"

"Don't you want to be there when it opens?"

"I'm becoming old and ugly, Charles."

"We'll go to Constantinople together. We'll leave tomorrow, eh? What do you say? We'll charter a boat. It's a quick little hop, right across the Mediterranean. Sailing to Byzantium! There was a poem, you know, in my time. Not forgotten, I guess, because they've programmed it into me. All these thousands of years, and someone still remembers old Yeats. *The young in one another's arms, birds in the trees.* Come with me to Byzantium, Gioia."

She shrugged. "Looking like this? Getting more hideous every hour? While *they* stay young forever? While *you* – " She faltered; her voice cracked; she fell silent.

"Finish the sentence, Gioia."

"Please. Let me alone."

"You were going to say, 'While *you* stay young forever, too, Charles,' isn't that it? You knew all along that I was never going to change. I didn't know that, but you did."

"Yes. I knew. I pretended that it wasn't true – that as I aged, you'd age, too. It was very foolish of me. In Chang-an, when I first began to see the real signs of it – that was when I realized I couldn't stay with you any longer. Because I'd look at you, always young, always remaining the same age, and I'd look at myself, and – " She gestured, palms upward. "So I gave you to Belilala and ran away."

"All so unnecessary, Gioia."

"I didn't think it was."

"But you don't have to grow old. Not if you don't want to!"

"Don't be cruel, Charles," she said tonelessly. "There's no way of escaping what I have."

"But there is," he said.

"You know nothing about these things."

"Not very much, no," he said. "But I see how it can be done. Maybe it's a primitive simpleminded twentieth-century sort of solution, but I think it ought to work. I've been playing with the idea ever since I left Mohenjo. Tell me this, Gioia: Why can't you go to them, to the programmers, to the artificers, the planners, whoever they are, the ones who create the cities and the temporaries and the visitors. And have yourself made into something like me!"

She looked up, startled. "What are you saying?"

"They can cobble up a twentieth-century man out of nothing more than fragmentary records and make him plausible, can't they? Or an Elizabethan, or anyone else of any era at all, and he's authentic, he's convincing. So why couldn't they do an even better job with you? Produce a Gioia so real that even Gioia can't tell the difference? But a Gioia that will never age — a Gioia-construct, a Gioia-program, a visitor-Gioia! Why not? Tell me why not, Gioia."

She was trembling. "I've never heard of doing any such thing!"

"But don't you think it's possible?"

"How would I know?"

"Of course it's possible. If they can create visitors, they can take a citizen and duplicate her in such a way that—"

"It's never been done. I'm sure of it. I can't imagine any citizen agreeing to any such thing. To give up the body — to let yourself be turned into — into—"

She shook her head, but it seemed to be a gesture of astonishment as much as of negation.

He said, "Sure. To give up the body. Your natural body, your aging, shrinking, deteriorating short-timer body. What's so awful about that?"

She was very pale. "This is craziness, Charles. I don't want to talk about it any more."

"It doesn't sound crazy to me."

"You can't possibly understand."

"Can't I? I can certainly understand being afraid to die. I don't have a lot of trouble understanding what it's like to be one of the few aging people in a world where nobody grows old. What I can't understand is why you aren't even willing to consider the possibility that—"

"No," she said. "I tell you, it's crazy. They'd laugh at me."

"Who?"

"All of my friends. Hawk, Stengard, Aramayne—" Once again she would not look at him. "They can be very cruel, without even realizing it. They despise anything that seems ungraceful to them, anything sweaty and desperate and cowardly. Citizens don't do sweaty things, Charles. And that's how this will seem. Assuming it can be done at all. They'll be terribly patronizing. Oh, they'll be sweet to me, yes, dear Gioia, how wonderful for you, Gioia, but when I turn my back they'll laugh. They'll say the most wicked things about me. I couldn't bear that."

"They can afford to laugh," Phillips said. "It's easy to be brave and cool about dying when you know you're going to live forever. How very fine for them: but why should you be the only one to grow old and die? And they won't laugh, anyway. They're not as cruel as you think. Shallow, maybe, but not cruel. They'll be glad that you've found a way to save yourself. At the very least, they won't have to feel guilty about you any longer, and that's bound to please them. You can—"

"Stop it," she said.

She rose, walked to the railing of the patio, stared out toward the sea. He came up behind her. Red sails in the harbor, sunlight glittering along the sides of the Lighthouse, the palaces of the Ptolemies stark white against the sky. Lightly he rested his hand on her shoulder. She twitched as if to pull away from him, but remained where she was.

"Then I have another idea," he said quietly. "If you won't go to the planners, *I* will. Reprogram me, I'll say. Fix things so that I start to age at the same rate you do. It'll be more authentic, anyway, if I'm supposed to be playing the part of a twentieth-century man. Over the years I'll very gradually get some lines in my face, my hair will turn gray, I'll walk a little more slowly — we'll grow old together, Gioia. To hell with your lovely immortal friends. We'll have each other. We won't need them."

She swung around. Her eyes were wide with horror.

"Are you serious, Charles?"

"Of course."

"No," she murmured. "No. Everything you've said to me today is monstrous nonsense. Don't you realize that?"

He reached for her hand and enclosed her fingertips in his. "All I'm trying to do is find some way for you and me to —"

"Don't say any more," she said. "Please." Quickly, as though drawing back from a suddenly flaring flame, she tugged her fingers free of his and put her hand behind her. Though his face was just inches from hers he felt an immense chasm opening between them. They stared at one another for a moment; then she moved deftly to his left, darted around him, and ran from the patio.

Stunned, he watched her go, down the long marble corridor and out of sight. It was folly to give pursuit, he thought. She was lost to him: that was clear, that was beyond any question. She was terrified of him. Why cause her even more anguish? But somehow he found himself running through the halls of the hotel, along the winding garden path, into the cool green groves of the Paneium. He thought he saw her on the portico of Hadrian's palace, but when he got there the echoing stone halls were empty. To a temporary that was sweeping the steps he said, "Did you see a woman come this way?" A blank sullen stare was his only answer.

Phillips cursed and turned away.

"Gioia?" he called. "Wait! Come back!"

Was that her, going into the Library? He rushed past the startled mumbling librarians and sped through the stacks, peering beyond the mounds of double-handled scrolls into the shadowy corridors. "Gioia? *Gioia!*" It was a desecration, bellowing like that in this quiet place. He scarcely cared.

Emerging by a side door, he loped down to the harbor. The Lighthouse! Terror enfolded him. She might already be a hundred steps up that ramp, heading for the parapet from which she meant to fling herself into the sea. Scattering citizens and temporaries as if they were straws, he ran within.

Up he went, never pausing for breath, though his synthetic lungs were screaming for respite, his ingeniously designed heart was desperately pounding. On the first balcony he imagined he caught a glimpse of her, but he circled it without finding her. Onward, upward. He went to the top, to the beacon chamber itself: no Gioia. Had she jumped? Had she gone down one ramp while he was ascending the other? He clung to the rim and looked out, down, searching the base of the Lighthouse, the rocks offshore, the causeway. No Gioia. I will find her somewhere, he thought. I will keep going until I find her. He went running down the ramp, calling her name. He reached ground level and sprinted back toward the center of town. Where next? The temple of Poseidon? The tomb of Cleopatra?

He paused in the middle of Canopus Street, groggy and dazed.

"Charles?" she said.

"Where are you?"

"Right here. Beside you." She seemed to materialize from the air. Her face was unflushed, her robe bore no trace of perspiration. Had he been chasing a phantom through the city? She came to him and took his hand, and said, softly, tenderly, "Were you really serious, about having them make you age?"

"If there's no other way, yes."

"The other way is so frightening, Charles."

"Is it?"

"You can't understand how much."

"More frightening than growing old? Than dying?"

"I don't know," she said. "I suppose not. The only thing I'm sure of is that I don't want you to get old, Charles."

"But I won't have to. Will I?"

He stared at her.

"No," she said. "You won't have to. Neither of us will."

Phillips smiled. "We should get away from here," he said after a while. "Let's go across to Byzantium, yes, Gioia? We'll show up in Constantinople for the opening. Your friends will be there. We'll tell them what you've decided to do. They'll know how to arrange it. Someone will."

"It sounds so strange," said Gioia. "To turn myself into — into a visitor? A visitor in my own world?"

"That's what you've always been, though."

"I suppose. In a way. But at least I've been *real* up to now."

"Whereas I'm not?"

"Are you, Charles?"

"Yes. Just as real as you. I was angry at first, when I found out the truth about myself. But I came to accept it. Somewhere between Mohenjo and here, I came to see that it was all right to be what I am: that I perceive things, I form ideas, I draw conclusions. I am very well designed, Gioia. I can't tell the difference between being what I am and being completely alive, and to me that's being real enough. I think, I feel, I experience joy and pain. I'm as real as I need to be. And you will be, too. You'll never stop being Gioia, you know. It's only your body that you'll cast away, the body that played such a terrible joke on you anyway." He brushed her cheek with his hand. "It was all said for us before, long ago:

"Once out of nature I shall never take
My bodily form from any natural thing,
But such a form as Grecian goldsmiths make
Of hammered gold and gold enameling
To keep a drowsy Emperor awake—'"

"Is that the same poem?" she asked.
"The same poem, yes. The ancient poem that isn't quite forgotten yet."
"Finish it, Charles."

"'—Or set upon a golden bough to sing
To lords and ladies of Byzantium
Of what is past, or passing, or to come.'"

"How beautiful. What does it mean?"
"That it isn't necessary to be mortal. That we can allow ourselves to be gathered into the artifice of eternity, that we can be transformed, that we can move on beyond the flesh. Yeats didn't mean it in quite the way I do—he wouldn't have begun to comprehend what we're talking about, not a word of it—and yet, and yet—the underlying truth is the same. Live, Gioia! With me!" He turned to her and saw color coming into her pallid cheeks. "It does make sense, what I'm suggesting, doesn't it? You'll attempt it, won't you? Whoever makes the visitors can be induced to remake you. Right? What do you think: can they, Gioia?"

She nodded in a barely perceptible way. "I think so," she said faintly. "It's very strange. But I think it ought to be possible. Why not, Charles? Why not?"

"Yes," he said. "Why not?"

***

In the morning they hired a vessel in the harbor, a low sleek pirogue with a blood-red sail, skippered by a rascally-looking temporary whose smile was irresistible. Phillips shaded his eyes and peered northward across the sea. He thought he could almost make out the shape of the great city sprawling on its seven hills, Constantine's New Rome beside the Golden

Horn, the mighty dome of Hagia Sophia, the somber walls of the citadel, the palaces and churches, the Hippodrome, Christ in glory rising above all else in brilliant mosaic streaming with light.

"Byzantium," Phillips said. "Take us there the shortest and quickest way."

"It is my pleasure," said the boatman with unexpected grace.

Gioia smiled. He had not seen her looking so vibrantly alive since the night of the imperial feast in Chang-an. He reached for her hand—her slender fingers were quivering lightly—and helped her into the boat.

ENTER A SOLDIER. LATER: ENTER ANOTHER (1987)

INTRODUCTION

A curious phenomenon of American science-fiction publishing in the late 1980s, one which will probably not be dealt with in a kindly way by future historians of the field, was the "shared world" anthology. I use the past tense for it because the notion of assembling a group of writers to produce stories set in a common background defined by someone else has largely gone out of fashion today. But for a time in 1987 and thereabouts it began to seem as though everything in science fiction was becoming part of some shared-world project.

I will concede that some excellent fiction came out of the various shared-world enterprises, as well as a mountain of junk. The idea itself was far from new in the 1980s; it goes back at least to 1952 and *The Petrified Planet*, a book in which the scientist John D. Clark devised specifications for an unusual planet and the writers Fletcher Pratt, H. Beam Piper, and Judith Merril produced superb novellas set on that world. Several similar books followed in the next few years.

In the late 1960s I revived the idea with a book called *Three for Tomorrow* — fiction by James Blish, Roger Zelazny, and myself, based on a theme proposed by Arthur C. Clarke — and I did three or four others later on. In 1975 came Harlan Ellison's *Medea*, an elaborate and brilliantly conceived colossus of a book that made use of the talents of Frank Herbert, Theodore Sturgeon, Frederik Pohl, and a whole galaxy of other writers of that stature. But the real deluge of shared-world projects began a few years afterward, in the wake of the vast commercial success of Robert Asprin's fantasy series, *Thieves' World*. Suddenly, every publisher in the business wanted to duplicate the *Thieves' World* bonanza, and from all sides appeared platoons of hastily conceived imitators.

I dabbled in a couple of these books myself — a story that I wrote for one of them won a Hugo, in fact — but my enthusiasm for the shared-world whirl cooled quickly once I perceived how shapeless and incoherent most of the books were. The writers tended not to pay much attention to the specifications, and simply went off in their own directions; the editors, generally, were too lazy or too cynical or simply too incompetent to do anything about it; and the books became formless jumbles of incompatible work.

Before I became fully aware of that, though, I let myself be seduced into editing one shared-world series myself. The initiator of this was Jim Baen, the publisher of Baen Books, whose idea centered around pitting computer-generated simulacra of historical figures against each other in intellectual conflict. That appealed to me considerably, and I agreed to work out the concept in detail and serve as the series' general editor.

I produced an elaborate prospectus outlining the historical background of the near-future world in which these simulacra would hold forth; I rounded up a group of capable writers; and to ensure that the book would unfold with consistency to my underlying vision, I wrote the first story myself in October of 1987, a 15,000-word opus for which I chose Socrates and Francisco Pizarro as my protagonists.

The whole thing was, I have to admit, a matter of commerce rather than art: just a job of work, to fill somebody's current publishing need. But a writer's intention and the ultimate result of his work don't bear any necessary relationship. In this case I was surprised and delighted to find the story taking on unanticipated life as I wrote, and what might have been a routine job of word-spinning turned out, unexpectedly, to be rather more than that when I was done with it.

Gardner Dozois published it in *Isaac Asimov's Science Fiction Magazine*, and then I used it as the lead story in the shared-world anthology, *Time Gate*. Dozois picked it for his 1989 Year's Best Science Fiction Collection, and in 1990 it was a finalist on both the Nebula and Hugo ballots — one of my most widely liked stories in a long time. The Nebula eluded me, but at the World Science Fiction Convention in Holland in August, 1990, "Enter a Soldier" brought me a Hugo award, my fourth, as the year's best novelet.

Even so, I decided soon after to avoid further involvement in the shared-world milieu, and have done no work of that sort in many years. Perhaps it was always unrealistic to think that any team of gifted, independent-minded writers could produce what is in essence a successful collaborative novel that has been designed by someone else. But my brief sojourn as editor of *Time Gate* did, at least, produce a story that I now see was one of the major achievements of my career.

Enter a Soldier. Later: Enter Another

AD 2130

It might be heaven. Certainly it wasn't Spain and he doubted it could be Peru. He seemed to be floating, suspended midway between nothing and nothing. There was a shimmering golden sky far above him and a misty, turbulent sea of white clouds boiling far below. When he looked down he saw his legs and his feet dangling like child's toys above an unfathomable abyss, and the sight of it made him want to puke, but there was nothing in him for the puking. He was hollow. He was made of air. Even the old ache in his knee was gone, and so was the everlasting dull burning in the fleshy part of his arm where the Indian's little arrow had taken him, long ago on the shore of that island of pearls, up by Panama.

It was as if he had been born again, sixty years old but freed of all the harm that his body had experienced and all its myriad accumulated injuries: freed, one might almost say, of his body itself.

"Gonzalo?" he called. "Hernando?"

Blurred dreamy echoes answered him. And then silence.

"Mother of God, am I dead?"

No. No. He had never been able to imagine death. An end to all striving? A place where nothing moved? A great emptiness, a pit without a bottom? Was this place the place of death, then? He had no way of knowing. He needed to ask the holy fathers about this.

"Boy, where are my priests? Boy?"

He looked about for his page. But all he saw was blinding whorls of light coiling off to infinity on all sides. The sight was beautiful but troublesome. It was hard for him to deny that he had died, seeing himself afloat like this in a realm of air and light. Died and gone to heaven. This is heaven, yes, surely, surely. What else could it be?

So it was true, that if you took the Mass and took the Christ faithfully into yourself and served Him well you would be saved from your sins, you would be forgiven, you would be cleansed. He had wondered about that. But he wasn't ready yet to be dead, all the same. The thought of it was sickening and infuriating. There was so much yet to be done. And he had no memory even of being ill. He searched his body for wounds. No, no wounds. Not anywhere. Strange. Again he looked around. He was alone here. No one to be seen, not his page, nor his brother, nor de Soto, nor the priests, nor anyone. "Fray Marcos! Fray Vicente! Can't you hear me? Damn you, where are you? Mother of God! Holy Mother, blessed among women! Damn you, Fray Vicente, tell me — tell me —"

His voice sounded all wrong: too thick, too deep, a stranger's voice. The words fought with his tongue and came from his lips malformed and lame, not the good crisp Spanish of Estremadura but something shameful and odd. What he heard was like the spluttering foppishness of Madrid or even the furry babble that they spoke in Barcelona; why, he might almost be a Portuguese, so coarse and clownish was his way of shaping his speech.

He said carefully and slowly, "I am the Governor and Captain-General of New Castile."

That came out no better, a laughable noise.

"Adelantado — Alguacil Mayor — Marques de la Conquista —"

The strangeness of his new way of speech made insults of his own titles. It was like being tongue-tied. He felt streams of hot sweat breaking out on his skin from the effort of trying to frame his words properly; but when he put his hand to his forehead to brush the sweat away before it could run into his eyes he seemed dry to the touch, and he was not entirely sure he could feel himself at all.

He took a deep breath. "I am Francisco Pizarro!" he roared, letting the name burst desperately from him like water breaching a rotten dam.

The echo came back, deep, rumbling, mocking. *Frantheethco. Peetharro.*

That too. Even his own name, idiotically garbled.

"O great God!" he cried. "Saints and angels!"

More garbled noises. Nothing would come out as it should. He had never known the arts of reading or writing; now it seemed that true speech itself was being taken from him. He began to wonder whether he had been right about this being heaven, supernal radiance or no. There was a curse on his tongue; a demon, perhaps, held it pinched in his claws. Was this hell, then? A very beautiful place, but hell nevertheless?

He shrugged. Heaven or hell, it made no difference. He was beginning to grow more calm, beginning to accept and take stock. He knew — had learned, long ago — that there was nothing to gain from raging against that which could not be helped, even less from panic in the face of the unknown. He was here, that was all there was to it — wherever *here* was — and he must find a place for himself, and not this place, floating here between nothing and nothing. He had been in hells before, small hells, hells on Earth. That barren isle called Gallo, where the sun cooked you in your own skin and there was nothing to eat but crabs that had the taste of dog-dung. And that dismal swamp at the mouth of the Rio Biru, where the rain fell in rivers and the trees reached down to cut you like swords.

And the mountains he had crossed with his army, where the snow was so cold that it burned, and the air went into your throat like a dagger at every breath. He had come forth from those, and they had been worse than this. Here there was no pain and no danger; here there was only soothing light and a strange absence of all discomfort. He began to move forward. He was walking on air. Look, look, he thought, I am walking on air! Then he said it out loud. "I am walking on air," he announced, and laughed at the way the words emerged from him. "Santiago! Walking on air! But why not? I am Pizarro!" He shouted it with all his might, "Pizarro! Pizarro!" and waited for it to come back to him.

Peetharro. Peetharro.

He laughed. He kept on walking.

                              ***

Tanner sat hunched forward in the vast sparkling sphere that was the ninth-floor imaging lab, watching the little figure at the distant center of the holotank strut and preen. Lew Richardson, crouching beside him with both hands thrust into the data gloves so that he could feed instructions to the permutation network, seemed almost not to be breathing — seemed to be just one more part of the network, in fact.

But that was Richardson's way, Tanner thought: total absorption in the task at hand. Tanner envied him that. They were very different sorts of men. Richardson lived for his programming and nothing but his programming. It was his grand passion. Tanner had never quite been able to understand people who were driven by grand passions. Richardson was like some throwback to an earlier age, an age when things had really mattered, an age when you were able to have some faith in the significance of your own endeavors.

"How do you like the armor?" Richardson asked.

"The armor's very fine, I think. We got it from old engravings. It has real flair."

"Just the thing for tropical climates," said Tanner. "A nice tin suit with matching helmet."

He coughed and shifted about irritably in his seat. The demonstration had been going on for half an hour without anything that seemed to be of any importance happening — just the minuscule image of the bearded man in Spanish armor tramping back and forth across the glowing field — and he was beginning to get impatient.

Richardson didn't seem to notice the harshness in Tanner's voice or the restlessness of his movements. He went on making small adjustments. He was a small man himself, neat and precise in dress and appearance, with faded blonde hair and pale blue eyes and a thin, straight mouth.

Tanner felt huge and shambling beside him. In theory Tanner had authority over Richardson's research projects, but in fact he always had simply permitted Richardson to do as he pleased. This time, though, it might be necessary finally to rein him in a little.

This was the twelfth or thirteenth demonstration that Richardson had subjected him to since he had begun fooling around with this historical-simulation business. The others all had been disasters of one kind or another, and Tanner expected that this one would finish the same way. And basically Tanner was growing uneasy about the project that he once had given his stamp of approval to, so long ago. It was getting harder and harder to go on believing that all this work served any useful purpose. Why had it been allowed to absorb so much of Richardson's group's time and so much of the lab's research budget for so many months? What possible value was it going to have for anybody? What possible use?

It's just a game, Tanner thought. One more desperate meaningless technological stunt, one more pointless pirouette in a meaningless ballet. The expenditure of vast resources on a display of ingenuity for ingenuity's sake and nothing else: now *there's* decadence for you.

The tiny image in the holotank suddenly began to lose color and definition.

"Uh-oh," Tanner said. "There it goes. Like all the others."

But Richardson shook his head. "This time it's different, Harry."

"You think?"

"We aren't losing him. He's simply moving around in there of his own volition, getting beyond our tracking parameters. Which means that we've achieved the high level of autonomy that we were shooting for."

"Volition, Lew? Autonomy?"

"You know that those are our goals."

"Yes, I know what our goals are supposed to be," said Tanner, with some annoyance. "I'm simply not convinced that a loss of focus is a proof that you've got volition."

"Here," Richardson said. "I'll cut in the stochastic tracking program. He moves freely, we freely follow him." Into the computer ear in his lapel he said. "Give me a gain boost, will you?" He made a quick flicking gesture with his left middle finger to indicate the quantitative level.

The little figure in ornate armor and pointed boots grew sharp again. Tanner could see fine details on the armor, the plumed helmet, the tapering shoulder-pieces, the joints at the elbows, the intricate pommel of his sword. He was marching from left to right in a steady hip-rolling way, like a man who was climbing the tallest mountain in the world and didn't mean to break his stride until he was across the summit. The fact that he was walking in what appeared to be midair seemed not to trouble him at all.

"There he is," Richardson said grandly. "We've got him back, all right?
The conqueror of Peru, before your very eyes, in the flesh. So to speak."

Tanner nodded. Pizarro, yes, before his very eyes. And he had to admit
that what he saw was impressive and even, somehow, moving. Something
about the dogged way with which that small armored figure was moving
across the gleaming pearly field of the holotank aroused a kind of sympathy
in him. That little man was entirely imaginary, but *he* didn't seem to know
that, or if he did he wasn't letting it stop him for a moment: he went
plugging on, and on and on, as if he intended actually to get somewhere.
Watching that, Tanner was oddly captivated by it, and found himself
surprised suddenly to discover that his interest in the entire project was
beginning to rekindle.

"Can you make him any bigger?" he asked. "I want to see his face."

"I can make him big as life," Richardson said. "Bigger. Any size you
like. Here."

He flicked a finger and the hologram of Pizarro expanded
instantaneously to a height of about two meters. The Spaniard halted in
midstride as though he might actually be aware of the imaging change.

That can't be possible, Tanner thought. That isn't a living consciousness
out there. Or is it?

Pizarro stood poised easily in midair, glowering, shading his eyes as
if staring into a dazzling glow. There were brilliant streaks of color in the
air all around him, like an aurora. He was a tall, lean man in late middle
age with a grizzled beard and a hard, angular face. His lips were thin, his
nose was sharp, his eyes were cold, shrewd, keen. It seemed to Tanner
that those eyes had come to rest on him, and he felt a chill.

My God, Tanner thought, he's *real*.

***

It had been a French program to begin with, something developed at
the Centre Mondiale de la Computation in Lyons about the year 2119. The
French had some truly splendid minds working in software in those days.
They worked up astounding programs, and then nobody did anything
with them. That was *their* version of Century Twenty-Two Malaise.

The French programmers' idea was to use holograms of actual
historical personages to dress up the *son et lumiere* tourist events at the
great monuments of their national history. Not just preprogrammed robot
mockups of the old Disneyland kind, which would stand around in front
of Notre Dame or the Arc de Triomphe or the Eiffel Tower and deliver
canned spiels, but apparent reincarnations of the genuine great ones, who
could freely walk and talk and answer questions and make little quips.
Imagine Louis XIV demonstrating the fountains of Versailles, they said,

or Picasso leading a tour of Paris museums, or Sartre sitting in his Left Bank cafe exchanging existential *bons mots* with passersby! Napoleon! Joan of Arc! Alexandre Dumas! Perhaps the simulations could do even more than that: perhaps they could be designed so well that they would be able to extend and embellish the achievements of their original lifetimes with new accomplishments, a fresh spate of paintings and novels and works of philosophy and great architectural visions by vanished masters.

The concept was simple enough in essence. Write an intelligencing program that could absorb data, digest it, correlate it, and generate further programs based on what you had given it. No real difficulty there. Then start feeding your program with the collected written works — if any — of the person to be simulated: that would provide not only a general sense of his ideas and positions but also of his underlying pattern of approach to situations, his style of thinking — for *le style,* after all, *est l'homme meme.* If no collected works happened to be available, why, find works *about* the subject by his contemporaries, and use those. Next, toss in the totality of the historical record of the subject's deeds, including all significant subsequent scholarly analyses, making appropriate allowances for conflicts in interpretation — indeed, taking advantages of such conflicts to generate a richer portrait, full of the ambiguities and contradictions that are the inescapable hallmarks of any human being. Now build in substrata of general cultural data of the proper period so that the subject has a loam of references and vocabulary out of which to create thoughts that are appropriate to his place in time and space. Stir. *Et voila!* Apply a little sophisticated imaging technology and you had a simulation capable of thinking and conversing and behaving as though it is the actual self after which it was patterned.

Of course, this would require a significant chunk of computer power. But that was no problem in a world where 150-gigaflops networks were standard laboratory items and ten-year-olds carried pencil-sized computers with capacities far beyond the ponderous mainframes of their great-great-grandparents' day. No, there was no theoretical reason why the French project could not have succeeded. Once the Lyons programmers had worked out the basic intelligencing scheme that was needed to write the rest of the programs, it all should have followed smoothly enough.

Two things went wrong: one rooted in an excess of ambition that may have been a product of the peculiarly French personalities of the original programmers, and the other having to do with an abhorrence of failure typical of the major nations of the mid-twenty-second century, of which France was one.

The first was a fatal change of direction that the project underwent in its early phases. The King of Spain was coming to Paris on a visit of state; and the programmers decided that in his honor they would synthesize

Don Quixote for him as their initial project. Though the intelligencing program had been designed to simulate only individuals who had actually existed, there seemed no inherent reason why a fictional character as well documented as Don Quixote could not be produced instead. There was Cervantes' lengthy novel; there was amply background data available on the milieu in which Don Quixote supposedly had lived; there was a vast library of critical analysis of the book and of the Don's distinctive and flamboyant personality. Why should bringing Don Quixote to life out of a computer be any different from simulating Louis XIV, say, or Moliere, or Cardinal Richelieu? True, they had all existed once, and the knight of La Mancha was a mere figment; but had Cervantes not provided far more detail about Don Quixote's mind and soul than was known of Richelieu, or Moliere, or Louis XIV?

Indeed he had. The Don—like Oedipus, like Odysseus, like Othello, like David Copperfield—had come to have a reality far more profound and tangible than that of most people who had indeed actually lived. Such characters as those had transcended their fictional origins. But not so far as the computer was concerned. It was able to produce a convincing fabrication of Don Quixote, all right—a gaunt bizarre holographic figure that had all the right mannerisms, that ranted and raved in the expectable way, that referred knowledgeably to Dulcinea and Rosinante and Mambrino's helmet. The Spanish king was amused and impressed. But to the French the experiment was a failure. They had produced a Don Quixote who was hopelessly locked to the Spain of the late sixteenth century and to the book from which he had sprung. He had no capacity for independent life and thought—no way to perceive the world that had brought him into being, or to comment on it, or to interact with it. There was nothing new or interesting about that. Any actor could dress up in armor and put on a scraggly beard and recite snatches of Cervantes. What had come forth from the computer, after three years of work, was no more than a predictable reprocessing of what had gone into it, sterile, stale.

Which led the Centre Mondiale de la Computation to its next fatal step: abandoning the whole thing. *Zut!* and the project was cancelled without any further attempts. No simulated Picassos, no simulated Napoleons, no Joans of Arc. The Quixote event had soured everyone and no one had the heart to proceed with the work from there. Suddenly it had the taint of failure about it, and France—like Germany, like Australia, like the Han Commercial Sphere, like Brazil, like any of the dynamic centers of the modern world, had a horror of failure. Failure was something to be left to the backward nations or the decadent ones—to the Islamic Socialist Union, say, or the Soviet People's Republic, or to that slumbering giant, the United States of America. So the historic-personage simulation scheme was put aside.

The French thought so little of it, as a matter of fact, that after letting it lie fallow for a few years they licensed it to a bunch of Americans, who had heard about it somehow and felt it might be amusing to play with.

***

"You may really have done it this time," Tanner said.

"Yes. I think we have. After all those false starts."

Tanner nodded. How often had he come into this room with hopes high, only to see some botch, some inanity, some depressing bungle? Richardson had always had an explanation. Sherlock Holmes hadn't worked because he was fictional: that was a necessary recheck of the French Quixote project, demonstrating that fictional characters didn't have the right sort of reality texture to take proper advantage of the program, not enough ambiguity, not enough contradiction. King Arthur had failed for the same reason. Julius Caesar? Too far in the past, maybe: unreliable data, bordering on fiction. Moses? Ditto. Einstein? Too complex, perhaps, for the project in its present level of development: they needed more experience first. Queen Elizabeth I? George Washington? Mozart? We're learning more each time, Richardson insisted after each failure. This isn't black magic we're doing, you know. We aren't necromancers, we're programmers, and we have to figure out how to give the program what it needs.

And now Pizarro?

"Why do you want to work with *him?*" Tanner had asked, five or six months earlier. "A ruthless medieval Spanish imperialist, is what I remember from school. A bloodthirsty despoiler of a great culture. A man without morals, honor, faith—"

"You may be doing him an injustice," said Richardson. "He's had a bad press for centuries. And there are things about him that fascinate me."

"Such as?"

"His drive. His courage. His absolute confidence. The other side of ruthlessness, the good side of it, is a total concentration on your task, an utter unwillingness to be stopped by any obstacle. Whether or not you approve of the things he accomplished, you have to admire a man who—"

"All right," Tanner said, abruptly growing weary of the whole enterprise. "Do Pizarro. Whatever you want."

The months had passed. Richardson gave him vague progress reports, nothing to arouse much hope. But now Tanner stared at the tiny strutting figure in the holotank and the conviction began to grow in him that Richardson finally had figured out how to use the simulation program as it was meant to be used.

"So you've actually recreated him, you think? Someone who lived— what, five hundred years ago?"

"He died in 1541," said Richardson.

"Almost six hundred, then."

"And he's not like the others—not simply a re-creation of a great figure out of the past who can run through a set of preprogrammed speeches. What we've got here, if I'm right, is an artificially generated intelligence which can think for itself in modes other than the ones its programmers think in. Which has more information available to itself, in other words, than we've provided it with. That would be the real accomplishment. That's the fundamental philosophical leap that we were going for when we first got involved with this project. To use the program to give us new programs that are capable of true autonomous thought—a program that can think like Pizarro, instead of like Lew Richardson's idea of some historian's idea of how Pizarro might have thought."

"Yes," Tanner said.

"Which means we won't just get back the expectable, the predictable. There'll be surprises. There's no way to learn anything, you know, except through surprises. The sudden combination of known components into something brand new. And that's what I think we've managed to bring off here, at long last. Harry, it may be the biggest artificial-intelligence breakthrough ever achieved."

Tanner pondered that. Was it so? Had they truly done it?

And if they had—

Something new and troubling was beginning to occur to him, much later in the game than it should have. Tanner stared at the holographic figure floating in the center of the tank, that fierce old man with the harsh face and the cold, cruel eyes. He thought about what sort of man he must have been—the man after whom this image had been modeled. A man who was willing to land in South America at age fifty or sixty or whatever he had been, an ignorant illiterate Spanish peasant wearing a suit of ill-fitting armor and waving a rusty sword, and set out to conquer a great empire of millions of people spreading over thousands of miles. Tanner wondered what sort of man would be capable of carrying out a thing like that. Now that man's eyes were staring into his own and it was a struggle to meet so implacable a gaze.

After a moment he looked away. His left leg began to quiver. He glanced uneasily at Richardson.

"Look at those eyes, Lew. Christ, they're scary!"

"I know. I designed them myself, from the old prints."

"Do you think he's seeing us right now? Can he do that?"

"All he is is software, Harry."

"He seemed to know it when you expanded the image."

Richardson shrugged. "He's very good software. I tell you, he's got autonomy, he's got volition. He's got an electronic *mind,* is what I'm saying.

He may have perceived a transient voltage kick. But there are limits to his perceptions, all the same. I don't think there's any way that he can see anything that's outside the holotank unless it's fed to him in the form of data he can process, which hasn't been done."

"You don't *think?* You aren't sure?"

"Harry. Please."

"This man conquered the entire enormous Incan empire with fifty soldiers, didn't he?"

"In fact I believe it was more like a hundred and fifty."

"Fifty, a hundred fifty, what's the difference? Who knows what you've actually got here? What if you did an even better job than you suspect?"

"What are you saying?"

"What I'm saying is, I'm uneasy all of a sudden. For a long time I didn't think this project was going to produce anything at all. Suddenly I'm starting to think that maybe it's going to produce more than we can handle. I don't want any of your goddamned simulations walking out of the tank and conquering *us.*"

Richardson turned to him. His face was flushed, but he was grinning. "Harry, Harry! For God's sake! Five minutes ago you didn't think we had anything at all here except a tiny picture that wasn't even in focus. Now you've gone so far the other way that you're imagining the worst kind of—"

"I see his eyes, Lew. I'm worried that his eyes see me."

"Those aren't real eyes you're looking at. What you see is nothing but a graphics program projected into a holotank. There's no visual capacity there as you understand the concept. His eyes will see you only if I want them to. Right now they don't."

"But you can make them see me?"

"I can make them see anything I want them to see. I created him, Harry."

"With volition. With autonomy."

"After all this time you start worrying *now* about these things?"

"It's my neck on the line if something that you guys on the technical side make runs amok. This autonomy thing suddenly troubles me."

"I'm still the one with the data gloves," Richardson said. "I twitch my fingers and he dances. That's not really Pizarro down there, remember. And that's no Frankenstein monster either. It's just a simulation. It's just so much data, just a bunch of electromagnetic impulses that I can shut off with one movement of my pinkie."

"Do it, then."

"Shut him off? But I haven't begun to show you—"

"Shut him off, and then hum him on," Tanner said.

Richardson looked bothered. "If you say so, Harry."

He moved a finger. The image of Pizarro vanished from the holotank. Swirling gray mists moved in it for a moment, and then all was white wool. Tanner felt a quick jolt of guilt, as though he had just ordered the execution of the man in the medieval armor. Richardson gestured again, and color flashed across the tank, and then Pizarro reappeared.

"I just wanted to see how much autonomy your little guy really has," said Tanner. "Whether he was quick enough to head you off and escape into some other channel before you could cut his power."

"You really don't understand how this works at all, do you, Harry?"

"I just wanted to see," said Tanner again, sullenly. After a moment's silence he said, "Do you ever feel like God?"

"Like God?"

"You breathed life in. Life of a sort, anyway. But you breathed free will in, too. That's what this experiment is all about, isn't it? All your talk about volition and autonomy? You're trying to recreate a human mind — which means to create it all over again — a mind that can think in its own special way, and come up with its own unique responses to situations, which will not necessarily be the responses that its programmers might anticipate, in fact almost certainly will not be, and which might not be all that desirable or beneficial, either, and you simply have to allow for that risk, just as God, once he gave free will to mankind, knew that He was likely to see all manner of evil deeds being performed by His creations as they exercised that free will —"

"Please, Harry —"

"Listen, is it possible for me to talk with your Pizarro?"

"Why?"

"By way of finding out what you've got there. To get some firsthand knowledge of what the project has accomplished. Or you could say I just want to test the quality of the simulation. Whatever. I'd feel more a part of this thing, more aware of what it's all about in here, if I could have some direct contact with him. Would it be all right if I did that?"

"Yes. Of course."

"Do I have to talk to him in Spanish?"

"In any language you like. There's an interface, after all. He'll think it's his own language coming in, no matter what, sixteenth-century Spanish. And he'll answer you in what seems like Spanish to him, but you'll hear it in English."

"Are you sure?"

"Of course."

"And you don't mind if I make contact with him?"

"Whatever you like."

"It won't upset his calibration, or anything?"

"It won't do any harm at all, Harry."

"Fine. Let me talk to him, then."

***

There was a disturbance in the air ahead, a shifting, a swirling, like a little whirlwind. Pizarro halted and watched it for a moment, wondering what was coming next. A demon arriving to torment him, maybe. Or an angel. Whatever it was, he was ready for it.

Then a voice out of the whirlwind said, in that same comically exaggerated Castilian Spanish that Pizarro himself had found himself speaking a little while before, "Can you hear me?"

"I hear you, yes. I don't see you. Where are you?"

"Right in front of you. Wait a second. I'll show you." Out of the whirlwind came a strange face that hovered in the middle of nowhere, a face without a body, a lean face, close-shaven, no beard at all, no moustache, the hair cut very short, dark eyes set close together. He had never seen a face like that before.

"What are you?" Pizarro asked. "A demon or an angel?"

"Neither one." Indeed he didn't sound very demonic. "A man, just like you."

"Not much like me, I think. Is a face all there is to you, or do you have a body, too?"

"All you see of me is a face?"

"Yes."

"Wait a second."

"I will wait as long as I have to. I have plenty of time."

The face disappeared. Then it returned, attached to the body of a big, wide-shouldered man who was wearing a long loose gray robe, something like a priest's cassock, but much more ornate, with points of glowing light gleaming on it everywhere. Then the body vanished and Pizarro could see only the face again. He could make no sense out of any of this. He began to understand how the Indians must have felt when the first Spaniards came over the horizon, riding horses, carrying guns, wearing armor.

"You are very strange. Are you an Englishman, maybe?"

"American."

"Ah," Pizarro said, as though that made things better. "An American. And what is that?"

The face wavered and blurred for a moment. There was mysterious new agitation in the thick white clouds surrounding it. Then the face grew steady and said, "America is a country north of Peru. A very large country, where many people live."

"You mean New Spain, which was Mexico, where my kinsman Cortes is Captain-General?"

"North of Mexico. Far to the north of it."

Pizarro shrugged. "I know nothing of those places. Or not very much. There is an island called Florida, yes? And stories of cities of gold, but I think they are only stories. I found the gold, in Peru. Enough to choke on, I found. Tell me this, am I in heaven now?"

"No."

"Then this is hell?"

"Not that, either. Where you are—it's very difficult to explain, actually—"

"I am in America."

"Yes. In America, yes."

"And am I dead?"

There was silence for a moment.

"No, not dead," the voice said uneasily.

"You are lying to me, I think."

"How could we be speaking with each other, if you were dead?"

Pizarro laughed hoarsely. "Are you asking *me*? I understand nothing of what is happening to me in this place. Where are my priests? Where is my page? Send me my brother!" He glared. "Well? Why don't you get them for me?"

"They aren't here. You're here all by yourself, Don Francisco."

"In America. All by myself in your America. Show me your America, then. Is there such a place? Is America all clouds and whorls of light? Where is America? Let me see America. Prove to me that I am in America."

There was another silence, longer than the last. Then the face disappeared and the wall of white cloud began to boil and churn more fiercely than before. Pizarro stared into the midst of it, feeling a mingled sense of curiosity and annoyance. The face did not reappear. He saw nothing at all. He was being toyed with. He was a prisoner in some strange place and they were treating him like a child, like a dog, like—like an Indian. Perhaps this was the retribution for what he had done to King Atahuallpa, then, that fine noble foolish man who had given himself up to him in all innocence, and whom he had put to death so that he might have the gold of Atahuallpa's kingdom.

Well, so be it, Pizarro thought. Atahuallpa accepted all that befell him without complaint and without fear, and so will I. Christ will be my guardian, and if there is no Christ, well, then I will have no guardian, and so be it. So be it.

The voice out of the whirlwind said suddenly, "Look, Don Francisco. This is America."

A picture appeared on the wall of cloud. It was a kind of picture Pizarro had never before encountered or even imagined, one that seemed to open before him like a gate and sweep him in and carry him along through a vista of changing scenes depicted in brilliant, vivid bursts of color. It was like flying high above the land, looking down on an infinite scroll of miracles. He saw vast cities without walls, roadways that unrolled like endless skeins of white ribbon, huge lakes, mighty rivers, gigantic mountains, everything speeding past him so swiftly that he could scarcely absorb any of it. In moments it all became chaotic in his mind: the buildings taller than the highest cathedral spire, the swarming masses of people, the shining metal chariots without beasts to draw them, the stupendous landscapes, the close-packed complexity of it all. Watching all this, he felt the fine old hunger taking possession of him again: he wanted to grasp this strange vast place, and seize it, and clutch it close, and ransack it for all it was worth. But the thought of that was overwhelming. His eyes grew glassy and his heart began to pound so terrifyingly that he supposed he would be able to feel it thumping if he put his hand to the front of his armor. He turned away, muttering, "Enough. Enough."

The terrifying picture vanished. Gradually the clamor of his heart subsided.

Then he began to laugh.

"Peru!" he cried. "Peru was nothing, next to your America! Peru was a hole! Peru was mud! How ignorant I was! I went to Peru, when there was America, ten thousand times as grand! I wonder what I could find, in America." He smacked his lips and winked. Then, chuckling, he said, "But don't be afraid. I won't try to conquer your America. I'm too old for that now. And perhaps America would have been too much for *me*, even before. Perhaps." He grinned savagely at the troubled staring face of the short-haired beardless man, the American. "I really am dead, is this not so? I feel no hunger, I feel no pain, no thirst, when I put my hand to my body I do not feel even my body. I am like one who lies dreaming. But this is no dream. Am I a ghost?"

"Not—exactly."

"Not exactly a ghost! Not exactly! No one with half the brains of a pig would talk like that. What is that supposed to mean?"

"It's not easy explaining it in words you would understand, Don Francisco."

"No, of course not. I am very stupid, as everyone knows, and that is why I conquered Peru, because I was so very stupid. But let it pass. I am not exactly a ghost, but I am dead all the same, right?"

"Well—"

"I am dead, yes. But somehow I have not gone to hell or even to purgatory but I am still in the world, only it is much later now. I have slept as the dead sleep, and now I have awakened in some year that is far beyond my time, and it is the time of America. Is this not so? Who is king now? Who is pope? What year is this? 1750? 1800?"

"The year 2130," the face said, after some hesitation.

"Ah." Pizarro tugged thoughtfully at his lower lip. "And the king? Who is the king?"

A long pause. "Alfonso is his name," said the face.

"Alfonso? The kings of Aragon were called Alfonso. The father of Ferdinand, he was Alfonso. Alfonso V, he was."

"Alfonso XIX is King of Spain now."

"Ah. Ah. And the pope? Who is the pope?"

A pause again. Not to know the name of the pope, immediately upon being asked? How strange. Demon or no, this was a fool.

"Pius," said the voice, when some time had passed. "Pius XVI."

"The sixteenth Pius," said Pizarro somberly. "Jesus and Mary, the sixteenth Pius! What has become of me? Long dead, is what I am. Still unwashed of all my sins. I can feel them clinging to my skin like mud, still. And you are a sorcerer, you American, and you have brought me to life again. Eh? Eh? Is that not so?"

"It is something like that, Don Francisco," the face admitted.

"So you speak your Spanish strangely because you no longer understand the right way of speaking it. Eh? Even I speak Spanish in a strange way, and I speak it in a voice that does not sound like my own. No one speaks Spanish any more, eh? Eh? Only American, they speak. Eh? But you try to speak Spanish, only it comes out stupidly. And you have caused me to speak the same way, thinking it is the way I spoke, though you are wrong. Well, you can do miracles, but I suppose you can't do everything perfectly, even in this land of miracles of the year 2130. Eh? Eh?" Pizarro leaned forward intently. "What do you say? You thought I was a fool, because I don't have reading and writing? I am not so ignorant, eh? I understand things quickly."

"You understand very quickly indeed."

"But you have knowledge of many things that are unknown to me. You must know the manner of my death, for example. How strange that is, talking to you of the manner of my death, but you must know it, eh? When did it come to me? And how? Did it come in my sleep? No, no, how could that be? They die in their sleep in Spain, but not in Peru. How was it, then? I was set upon by cowards, was I? Some brother of Atahuallpa, falling upon me as I stepped out of my house? A slave sent by the Inca Manco, or one of those others? No. No. The Indians would not harm me, for all that I did to them. It was the young Almagro who took me down, was it not, in vengeance for his father, or Juan de Herrada, eh? Or perhaps even Picado, my own secretary — no, not Picado, he was my man, always —

but maybe Alvarado, the young one, Diego—well, one of those, and it would have been sudden, very sudden or I would have been able to stop them—am I right, am I speaking the truth? Tell me. You know these things. Tell me of the manner of my dying." There was no answer. Pizarro shaded his eyes and peered into the dazzling pearly whiteness. He was no longer able to see the face of the American. "Are you there?" Pizarro said. "Where have you gone? Were you only a dream? American! American! Where have you gone?"

***

The break in contact was jolting. Tanner sat rigid, hands trembling, lips tightly clamped. Pizarro, in the holotank, was no more than a distant little streak of color now, no larger than his thumb, gesticulating amid the swirling clouds. The vitality of him, the arrogance, the fierce probing curiosity, the powerful hatreds and jealousies, the strength that had come from vast ventures recklessly conceived and desperately seen through to triumph, all the things that were Francisco Pizarro, all that Tanner had felt an instant before—all that had vanished at the flick of a finger.

After a moment or two Tanner felt the shock beginning to ease. He turned toward Richardson.

"What happened?"

"I had to pull you out of there. I didn't want you telling him anything about how he died."

"I don't know how he died."

"Well, neither does he, and I didn't want to chance it that you did. There's no predicting what sort of psychological impact that kind of knowledge might have on him."

"You talk about him as though he's alive."

"Isn't he?" Richardson said.

"If I said a thing like that, you'd tell me that I was being ignorant and unscientific."

Richardson smiled faintly. "You're right. But somehow I trust myself to know what I'm saying when I say that he's alive. I know I don't mean it literally and I'm not sure about you. What did you think of him, anyway?"

"He's amazing," Tanner said. "Really amazing. The strength of him— I could feel it pouring out at me in waves. And his mind! So quick, the way he picked up on everything. Guessing that he must be in the future. Wanting to know what number pope was in office. Wanting to see what America looked like. And the cockiness of him! Telling me that he's not up to the conquest of America, that he might have tried for it instead of Peru a few years earlier, but not now, now he's a little too old for that. Incredible! Nothing could faze him for long, even when he realized that he must have been dead for a long time. Wanting to know how he died, even!" Tanner frowned. "What age did you make him, anyway, when you put this program together?"

"About sixty. Five or six years after the conquest, and a year or two before he died. At the height of his power, that is."

"I suppose you couldn't have let him have any knowledge of his actual death. That way he'd be too much like some kind of a ghost."

"That's what we thought. We set the cutoff at a time when he had done everything that he had set out to do, when he was the complete Pizarro. But before the end. He didn't need to know about that. Nobody does. That's why I had to yank you, you see? In case you knew. And started to tell him."

Tanner shook his head. "If I ever knew, I've forgotten it. How did it happen?"

"Exactly as he guessed: at the hands of his own comrades."

"So he saw it coming."

"At the age we made him, he already knew that a civil war had started in South America, that the conquistadores were quarreling over the division of the spoils. We built that much into him. He knows that his partner Almagro has turned against him and been beaten in battle, and that they've executed him. What he doesn't know, but obviously can expect, is that Almagro's friends are going to break into his house and try to kill him. He's got it all figured out pretty much as it's going to happen. As it *did* happen, I should say."

"Incredible. To be that shrewd."

"He was a son of a bitch, yes. But he was a genius, too."

"Was he, really? Or is it that you made him one when you set up the program for him?"

"All we put in were the objective details of his life, patterns of event and response. Plus an overlay of commentary by others, his contemporaries and later historians familiar with the record, providing an extra dimension of character density. Put in enough of that kind of stuff and apparently they add up to the whole personality. It isn't *my* personality or that of anybody else who worked on this project, Harry. When you put in Pizarro's set of events and responses you wind up getting Pizarro. You get the ruthlessness and you get the brilliance. Put in a different set, you get someone else. And what we've finally seen, this time, is that when we do our work right we get something out of the computer that's bigger than the sum of what we put in."

"Are you sure?"

Richardson said, "Did you notice that he complained about the Spanish that he thought you were speaking?"

"Yes. He said that it sounded strange, that nobody seemed to know how to speak proper Spanish any more. I didn't quite follow that. Does the interface you built speak lousy Spanish?"

"Evidently it speaks lousy sixteenth-century Spanish," Richardson said. "Nobody knows what sixteenth-century Spanish actually sounded like. We can only guess. Apparently we didn't guess very well."

"But how would *he* know? You synthesized him in the first place! If you don't know how Spanish sounded in his time, how would he? All he should know about Spanish, or about anything, is what you put into him."

"Exactly," Richardson said.

"But that doesn't make any sense, Lew!"

"He also said that the Spanish he heard himself speaking was no good, and that his own voice didn't sound right to him either. That we had *caused* him to speak this way, thinking that was how he actually spoke, but we were wrong."

"How could he possibly know what his voice really sounded like, if all he is is a simulation put together by people who don't have the slightest notion of what his voice really—"

"I don't have any idea," said Richardson quietly. "But he *does* know."

"Does he? Or is this just some diabolical Pizarro-like game that he's playing to unsettle us, because *that's* in his character as you devised it?"

"I think he does know," Richardson said.

"Where's he finding it out, then?"

"It's there. We don't know where, but he does. It's somewhere in the data that we put through the permutation network, even if we don't know it and even though we couldn't find it now if we set out to look for it. *He* can find it. He can't manufacture that kind of knowledge by magic, but he can assemble what looks to us like seemingly irrelevant bits and come up with new information leading to a conclusion which is meaningful to him. That's what we mean by artificial intelligence, Harry.

"We've finally got a program that works something like the human brain: by leaps of intuition so sudden and broad that they seem inexplicable and nonquantifiable, even if they really aren't. We've fed in enough stuff so that he can assimilate a whole stew of ostensibly unrelated data and come up with new information. We don't just have a ventriloquist's dummy in that tank. We've got something that thinks it's Pizarro and thinks like Pizarro and knows things that Pizarro knew and we don't. Which means we've accomplished the qualitative jump in artificial intelligence capacity that we set out to achieve with this project. It's awesome. I get shivers down my back when I think about it."

"I do, too," Tanner said. "But not so much from awe as fear."

"Fear?"

"Knowing now that he has capabilities beyond those he was programmed for, how can you be so absolutely certain that he can't commandeer your network somehow and get himself loose?"

"It's technically impossible. All he is is electromagnetic impulses. I can pull the plug on him any time I like. There's nothing to panic over here. Believe me, Harry."

"I'm trying to."

"I can show you the schematics. We've got a phenomenal simulation in that computer, yes. But it's still only a simulation. It isn't a vampire, it isn't a werewolf, it isn't anything supernatural. It's just the best damned computer simulation anyone's ever made."

"It makes me uneasy. *He* makes me uneasy."

"He should. The power of the man, the indomitable nature of him — why do you think I summoned him up, Harry? He's got something that we don't understand in this country any more. I want us to study him. I want us to try to learn what that kind of drive and determination is really like. Now that you've talked to him, now that you've touched his spirit, of course you're shaken up by him. He radiates tremendous confidence. He radiates fantastic faith in himself. That kind of man can achieve anything he wants — even conquer the whole Inca empire with a hundred fifty men, or however many it was. But I'm not frightened of what we've put together here. And you shouldn't be either. We should all be damned proud of it. You as well as the people on the technical side. And you will be, too."

"I hope you're right," Tanner said.

"You'll see."

For a long moment Tanner stared in silence at the holotank, where the image of Pizarro had been.

"Okay," said Tanner finally. "Maybe I'm overreacting. Maybe I'm sounding like the ignoramus layman that I am. I'll take it on faith that you'll be able to keep your phantoms in their boxes."

"We will," Richardson said.

"Let's hope so. All right," said Tanner. "So what's your next move?"

Richardson looked puzzled. "My next move?"

"With this project? Where does it go from here?"

Hesitantly Richardson said, "There's no formal proposal yet. We thought we'd wait until we had approval from you on the initial phase of the work, and then—"

"How does this sound?" Tanner asked. "I'd like to see you start in on another simulation right away."

"Well—yes, yes, of course—"

"And when you've got him worked up, Lew, would it be feasible for you to put him right there in the tank with Pizarro?"

Richardson looked startled. "To have a sort of dialog with him, you mean?"

"Yes."

"I suppose we could do that," Richardson said cautiously. "*Should* do that. Yes. Yes. A very interesting suggestion, as a matter of fact." He ventured an uneasy smile. Up till now Tanner had kept in the background of this project, a mere management functionary, an observer, virtually an outsider. This was something new, his interjecting himself into the planning process, and plainly Richardson didn't know what to make of it. Tanner watched him fidget. After a little pause Richardson said, "Was there anyone particular you had in mind for us to try next?"

"Is that new parallax thing of yours ready to try?" Tanner asked. "The one that's supposed to compensate for time distortion and myth contamination?"

"Just about. But we haven't tested—"

"Good," Tanner said. "Here's your chance. What about trying for Socrates?"

***

There was billowing whiteness below him, and on every side, as though all the world were made of fleece. He wondered if it might be snow. That was not something he was really familiar with. It snowed once in a great while in Athens, yes, but usually only a light dusting that melted in the morning sun. Of course he had seen snow aplenty when he had been up north in the war, at Potidaea, in the time of Pericles. But that had been long ago; and that stuff, as best he remembered it, had not been much like this. There was no quality of coldness about the whiteness that surrounded him now. It could just as readily be great banks of clouds.

But what would clouds be doing *below* him? Clouds, he thought, are mere vapor, air and water, no substance to them at all. Their natural place was overhead. Clouds that gathered at one's feet had no true quality of cloudness about them.

Snow that had no coldness? Clouds that had no buoyancy? Nothing in this place seemed to possess any quality that was proper to itself in this place, including himself. He seemed to be walking, but his feet touched nothing at all. It was more like moving through air. But how could one move in the air? Aristophanes, in that mercilessly mocking play of his, had sent him floating through the clouds suspended in a basket, and made him say things like, "I am traversing the air and contemplating the sun." That was Aristophanes' way of playing with him, and he had not been seriously upset, though his friends had been very hurt on his behalf. Still, that was only a play.

This felt real, insofar as it felt like anything at all.

Perhaps he was dreaming, and the nature of his dream was that he thought he was really doing the things he had done in Aristophanes' play. What was that lovely line? "I have to suspend my brain and mingle the subtle essence of my mind with this air, which is of the same nature, in order clearly to penetrate the things of heaven." Good old Aristophanes! Nothing was sacred to him! Except, of course, those things that were truly sacred, such as wisdom, truth, virtue. "I would have discovered nothing if I had remained on the ground and pondered from below the things that are above: for the earth by its force attracts the sap of the mind to itself. It's the same way with watercress." And Socrates began to laugh.

He held his hands before him and studied them, the short sturdy fingers, the thick powerful wrists. His hands, yes. His old plain hands that had stood him in good stead all his life, when he had worked as a stonemason as his father had, when he had fought in his city's wars, when he had trained at the gymnasium. But now when he touched them to his face he felt nothing. There should be a chin here, a forehead, yes, a blunt stubby nose, thick lips; but there was nothing. He was touching air. He could put his hand right through the place where his face should be. He could put one hand against the other, and press with all his might, and feel nothing.

This is a very strange place indeed, he thought.

Perhaps it is that place of pure forms that young Plato liked to speculate about, where everything is perfect and nothing is quite real. Those are ideal clouds all around me, not real ones. This is ideal air upon which I walk. I myself am the ideal Socrates, liberated from my coarse ordinary body. Could it be? Well, maybe so. He stood for a while, considering that possibility. The thought came to him that this might be the life after life, in which case he might meet some of the gods, if there were any gods in the first place, and if he could manage to find them. I would like that, he thought. Perhaps they would be willing to speak with me. Athena would discourse with me on wisdom, or Hermes on speed, or Ares on the nature of courage, or Zeus on — well, whatever Zeus cared to speak on. Of course, I would seem to be the merest fool to them, but that would be all right: anyone who expects to hold discourse with the gods as though he were their equal *is* a fool. I have no such illusion. If there are gods at all, surely they are far superior to me in all respects, for otherwise, why would men regard them as gods?

Of course he had serious doubts that the gods existed at all. But if they did, it was reasonable to think that they might be found in a place such as this.

He looked up. The sky was radiant with brilliant golden light. He took a deep breath and smiled and set out across the fleecy nothingness of this airy world to see if he could find the gods.

***

Tanner said, "What do you think now? Still so pessimistic?"

"It's too early to say," said Richardson, looking glum.

"He *looks* like Socrates, doesn't he?"

"That was the easy part. We've got plenty of descriptions of Socrates that came down from people who knew him, the flat wide nose, the bald head, the thick lips, the short neck. A standard Socrates face that everybody recognizes, just as they do Sherlock Holmes, or Don Quixote. So that's how we made him look. It doesn't signify anything important. It's what's going on inside his head that'll determine whether we really have Socrates."

"He seems calm and good-humored as he wanders around in there. The way a philosopher should."

"Pizarro seemed just as much of a philosopher when we turned him loose in the tank."

"Pizarro may *be* just as much of a philosopher," Tanner said. "Neither man's the sort who'd be likely to panic if he found himself in some mysterious place." Richardson's negativism was beginning to bother him. It was as if the two men had exchanged places: Richardson now uncertain of the range and power of his own program, Tanner pushing the way on and on toward bigger and better things.

Bleakly Richardson said, "I'm still pretty skeptical. We've tried the new parallax filters, yes. But I'm afraid we're going to run into the same problem the French did with Don Quixote, and that we did with Holmes and Moses and Caesar. There's too much contamination of the data by myth and fantasy. The Socrates who has come down to us is as much fictional as real, or maybe *all* fictional.

"For all we know, Plato made up everything we think we know about him, the same way Conan Doyle made up Holmes. And what we're going to get, I'm afraid, will be something secondhand, something lifeless, something lacking in the spark of self-directed intelligence that we're after."

"But the new filters—"

"Perhaps. Perhaps."

Tanner shook his head stubbornly. "Holmes and Don Quixote are fiction through and through. They exist in only one dimension, constructed for us by their authors. You cut through the distortions and fantasies of later readers and commentators and all you find underneath is a made-up character. A lot of Socrates may have been invented by Plato for his own purposes, but a lot wasn't. He really existed. He took an actual part in civic activities in fifth-century Athens. He figures in books by a lot of other contemporaries of his besides Plato's dialogues. That gives us the parallax you're looking for, doesn't it—the view of him from more than one viewpoint?"

"Maybe it does. Maybe not. We got nowhere with Moses. Was *he* fictional?"

"Who can say? All you had to go by was the Bible. And a ton of Biblical commentary, for whatever that was worth. Not much, apparently."

"And Caesar? You're not going to tell me that Caesar wasn't real," said Richardson.

"But what we have of him is evidently contaminated with myth. When we synthesized him we got nothing but a caricature, and I don't have to remind you how fast even that broke down into sheer gibberish."

"Not relevant," Tanner said. "Caesar was early in the project. You know much more about what you're doing now. I think this is going to work."

Richardson's dogged pessimism, Tanner decided, must be a defense mechanism, designed to insulate himself against the possibility of a new failure. Socrates, after all, hadn't been Richardson's own choice. And this was the first time he had used these new enhancement methods, the parallax program that was the latest refinement of the process.

Tanner looked at him. Richardson remained silent.

"Go on," Tanner said. "Bring up Pizarro and let the two of them talk to each other. Then we'll find out what sort of Socrates you've conjured up here."

***

Once again there was a disturbance in the distance, a little dark blur on the pearly horizon, a blotch, a flaw in the gleaming whiteness. Another demon is arriving, Pizarro thought. Or perhaps it is the same one as before, the American, the one who liked to show himself only as a face, with short hair and no beard.

But as this one drew closer Pizarro saw that he was different from the last, short and stocky, with broad shoulders and a deep chest. He was nearly bald and his thick beard was coarse and unkempt. He looked old, at least sixty, maybe sixty-five. He looked very ugly, too, with bulging eyes and a flat nose that had wide, flaring nostrils, and a neck so short that his oversized head seemed to sprout straight from his trunk. All he wore was a thin, ragged brown robe. His feet were bare.

"You, there," Pizarro called out. "You! Demon! Are you also an American, demon?"

"Your pardon. An Athenian, did you say?"

"*American* is what I said. That's what the last one was. Is that where you come from, too, demon? America?"

A shrug. "No, I think not. I am of Athens." There was a curious mocking twinkle in the demon's eyes.

"A Greek? This demon is a Greek?"

"I am of Athens," the ugly one said again. "My name is Socrates, the son of Sophroniscus. I could not tell you what a Greek is, so perhaps I may be one, but I think not, unless a Greek is what you call a man of Athens." He spoke in a slow, plodding way, like one who was exceedingly stupid. Pizarro had sometimes met men like this before, and in his experience they were generally not as stupid as they wanted to be taken for. He felt caution rising in him. "And I am no demon, but just a plain man: very plain, as you can easily see."

Pizarro snorted. "You like to chop words, do you?"

"It is not the worst of amusements, my friend," said the other, and put his hands together behind his back in the most casual way, and stood there calmly, smiling, looking off into the distance, rocking back and forth on the balls of his feet.

"Well?" Tanner said. "Do we have Socrates or not? I say that's the genuine article there."

Richardson looked up and nodded. He seemed relieved and quizzical both at once. "So far so good, I have to say. He's coming through real and true."

"Yes."

"We may actually have worked past the problem of information contamination that ruined some of the earlier simulations. We're not getting any of the signal degradation we encountered then."

"He's some character, isn't he?" Tanner said. "I liked the way he just walked right up to Pizarro without the slightest sign of uneasiness. He's not at all afraid of him."

"Why should he be?" Richardson asked.

"Wouldn't you? If you were walking along through God knows what kind of unearthly place, not knowing where you were or how you got there, and suddenly you saw a ferocious-looking bastard like Pizarro standing in front of you wearing full armor and carrying a sword—" Tanner shook his head. "Well, maybe not. He's Socrates, after all, and Socrates wasn't afraid of anything except boredom."

"And Pizarro's just a simulation. Nothing but software."

"So you've been telling me all along. But Socrates doesn't know that."

"True," Richardson said. He seemed lost in thought a moment. "Perhaps there is some risk."

"Huh?"

"If our Socrates is anything like the one in Plato, and he surely ought to be, then he's capable of making a considerable pest of himself. Pizarro may not care for Socrates' little verbal games. If he doesn't feel like playing, I suppose there's a theoretical possibility that he'll engage in some sort of aggressive response."

That took Tanner by surprise. He swung around and said, "Are you telling me that there's some way he can *harm* Socrates?"

"Who knows?" said Richardson. "In the real world one program can certainly crash another one. Maybe one simulation can be dangerous to another one. This is all new territory for all of us, Harry. Including the people in the tank."

***

The tall grizzled-looking man, said, scowling, "You tell me you're an Athenian, but not a Greek. What sense am I supposed to make of that? I could ask Pedro de Candia, I guess, who is a Greek but not an Athenian. But he's not here. Perhaps you're just a fool, eh? Or you think I am."

"I have no idea what you are. Could it be that you are a god?"

"A *god?*"

"Yes," Socrates said. He studied the other impassively. His face was harsh, his gaze was cold. "Perhaps you are Ares. You have a fierce warlike look about you, and you wear armor, but not such armor as I have ever seen. This place is so strange that it might well be the abode of the gods, and that could be a god's armor you wear, I suppose. If you are Ares, then I salute you with the respect that is due you. I am Socrates of Athens, the stonemason's son."

"You talk a lot of nonsense. I don't know your Ares."

"Why, the god of war, of course! Everyone knows that. Except barbarians, that is. Are you a barbarian, then? You sound like one, I must say — but then, I seem to sound like a barbarian myself, and I've spoken the tongue of Hellas all my life. There are many mysteries here, indeed."

***

"Your language problem again," Tanner said. "Couldn't you even get classical Greek to come out right? Or are they both speaking Spanish to each other?"

"Pizarro thinks they're speaking Spanish. Socrates thinks they're speaking Greek. And of course the Greek is off. We don't know how *anything* that was spoken before the age of recordings sounded. All we can do is guess."

"But can't you —"

"Shh," Richardson said.

***

Pizarro said, "I may be a bastard, but I'm no barbarian, fellow, so curb your tongue. And let's have no more blasphemy out of you either."

"If I blaspheme, forgive me. It is in innocence. Tell me where I trespass, and I will not do it again."

"This crazy talk of gods. Of my being a god. I'd expect a heathen to talk like that, but not a Greek. But maybe you're a heathen kind of Greek, and not to be blamed. It's heathens who see gods everywhere. Do I look like a god to you? I am Francisco Pizarro, of Trujillo in Estremadura, the son of the famous soldier Gonzalo Pizarro, colonel of infantry, who served in the wars of Gonzalo de Cordova whom men call the Great Captain. I have fought some wars myself."

"Then you are not a god but simply a soldier? Good. I have been a soldier myself. I am more at ease with soldiers than with gods, as most people are, I would think."

"A soldier? You?" Pizarro smiled. This shabby ordinary little man, more bedraggled-looking than any self-respecting groom would be, a soldier? "In which wars?"

"The wars of Athens. I fought at Potidaea, where the Corinthians were making trouble, and withholding the tribute that was due us. It was very cold there, and the siege was long and bleak, but we did our duty. I fought again some years later at Delium against the Boeotians. Laches was our general then, but it went badly for us,, and we did our best fighting in retreat. And then," Socrates said, "when Brasidas was in Amphipolis, and they sent Cleon to drive him out, I—"

"Enough," said Pizarro with an impatient wave of his hand. "These wars are unknown to me." A private soldier, a man of the ranks, no doubt. "Well, then this is the place where they send dead soldiers, I suppose."

"Are we dead, then?"

"Long ago. There's an Alfonso who's king, and a Pius who's pope, and you wouldn't believe their numbers. Pius the Sixteenth, I think the demon said. And the American said also that it is the year 2130. The last year that I can remember was 1539. What about you?"

The one who called himself Socrates shrugged again. "In Athens we use a different reckoning. But let us say, for argument's sake, that we are dead. I think that is very likely, considering what sort of place this seems to be, and how airy I find my body to be. So we have died, and this is the life after life. I wonder: is this a place where virtuous men are sent, or those who were not virtuous? Or do all men go to the same place after death, whether they were virtuous or not? What would you say?"

"I haven't figured that out yet," said Pizarro.

"Well, were you virtuous in your life, or not?"

"Did I sin, you mean?"

"Yes, we could use that word."

"Did I sin, he wants to know," said Pizarro, amazed. "He asks, Was I a sinner? Did I live a virtuous life? What business is that of his?"

"Humor me," said Socrates. "For the sake of the argument, if you will, allow me a few small questions—"

***

"So it's starting," Tanner said. "You see? You really *did* do it! Socrates is drawing him into a dialog!"

Richardson's eyes were glowing. "He is, yes. How marvelous this is, Harry!"

"Socrates is going to talk rings around him."

"I'm not so sure of that," Richardson said.

***

"I gave as good as I got," said Pizarro. "If I was injured, I gave injury back. There's no sin in that. It's only common sense. A man does what is necessary to survive and to protect his place in the world. Sometimes I might forget a fast day, yes, or use the Lord's name in vain—those are sins, I suppose, Fray Vicente was always after me for things like that—but does that make me a sinner? I did my penances as soon as I could find time for them. It's a sinful world and I'm no different from anyone else, so why be harsh on me? Eh? God made me as I am. I'm done in His image. And I have faith in His son."

"So you are a virtuous man, then."

"I'm not a sinner, at any rate. As I told you, if ever I sinned I did my contrition, which made it the same as if the sin hadn't ever happened."

"Indeed," said Socrates. "Then you are a virtuous man and I have come to a good place. But I want to be absolutely sure. Tell me again: is your conscience completely clear?"

"What are you, a confessor?"

"Only an ignorant man seeking understanding. Which you can provide, by taking part with me in the exploration. If I have come to the place of virtuous men, then I must have been virtuous myself when I lived. Ease my mind, therefore, and let me know whether there is anything on your soul that you regret having done."

Pizarro stirred uneasily. "Well," he said, "I killed a king."

"A wicked one? An enemy of your city?"

"No. He was wise and kind."

"Then you have reason for regret indeed. For surely that is a sin, to kill a wise king."

"But he was a heathen."

"A what?"

"He denied God."

"He denied his own god?" said Socrates. "Then perhaps it was not so wrong to kill him."

"No. He denied mine. He *preferred* his own. And so he was a heathen. And all his people were heathens, since they followed his way. That could not be. They were at risk of eternal damnation because they followed him. I killed him for the sake of his people's souls. I killed him out of the love of God."

"But would you not say that all gods are the reflection of the one God?"

Pizarro considered that. "In a way, that's true, I suppose."

"And is the service of God not itself godly?"

"How could it be anything but godly, Socrates?"

"And would you say that one who serves his god faithfully according to the teachings of his god is behaving in a godly way?"

Frowning, Pizarro said, "Well—if you look at it that way, yes—"

"Then I think the king you killed was a godly man, and by killing him you sinned against God."

"Wait a minute!"

"But think of it: by serving his god he must also have served yours, for any servant of a god is a servant of the true god who encompasses all our imagined gods."

"No," said Pizarro sullenly. "How could he have been a servant of God? He knew nothing of Jesus. He had no understanding of the Trinity. When the priest offered him the Bible, he threw it to the ground in scorn. He was a heathen, Socrates. And so are you. You don't know anything of these matters at all, if you think that Atahuallpa was godly. Or if you think you're going to get me to think so."

"Indeed I have very little knowledge of anything. But you say he was a wise man, and kind?"

"In his heathen way."

"And a good king to his people?"

"So it seemed. They were a thriving people when I found them."

"Yet he was not godly."

"I told you. He had never had the sacraments, and in fact he spurned them right up until the moment of his death, when he accepted baptism. *Then* he came to be godly. But by then the sentence of death was upon him and it was too late for anything to save him."

"Baptism? Tell me what that is, Pizarro."

"A sacrament."

"And that is?"

"A holy rite. Done with holy water, by a priest. It admits one to Holy Mother Church, and brings forgiveness from sin both original and actual, and gives the gift of the Holy Spirit."

"You must tell me more about these things another time. So you made this good king godly by this baptism? And then you killed him?"

"Yes."

"But he was godly when you killed him. Surely, then, to kill him was a sin."

"He had to die, Socrates!"

"And why was that?" asked the Athenian.

***

"Socrates is closing in for the kill," Tanner said. "Watch this!"

"I'm watching. But there isn't going to be any kill," said Richardson. "Their basic assumptions are too far apart."

"You'll see."

"Will I?"

***

Pizarro said, "I've already told you why he had to die. It was because his people followed him in all things. And so they worshipped the sun, because he said the sun was God. Their souls would have gone to hell if we had allowed them to continue that way."

"But if they followed him in all things," said Socrates, "then surely they would have followed him into baptism, and become godly, and thus done that which was pleasing to you and to your god! Is that not so?"

"No," said Pizarro, twisting his fingers in his beard.

"Why do you think that?"

"Because the king agreed to be baptized only after we had sentenced him to death. He was in the way, don't you see? He was an obstacle to our power! So we had to get rid of him. He would never have led his people to the truth of his own free will. That was why we had to kill him. But we didn't want to kill his soul as well as his body, so we said to him, Look, Atahuallpa, we're going to put you to death, but if you let us baptize you we'll strangle you quickly, and if you don't we'll burn you alive and it'll be very slow. So of course he agreed to be baptized, and we strangled him. What choice was there for anybody? He had to die. He still didn't believe the true faith, as we all well knew. Inside his head he was as big a heathen as ever. But he died a Christian all the same."

"A what?"

"A Christian! A Christian! One who believes in Jesus Christ the Son of God."

"The *son* of God," Socrates said, sounding puzzled. "And do Christians believe in God, too, or only his son?"

"What a fool you are!"

"I would not deny that."

"There is God the Father, and God the Son, and then there is the Holy Spirit."

"Ah," said Socrates. "And which did your Atahuallpa believe in, then, when the strangler came for him?"

"None of them."

"And yet he died a Christian? Without believing in any of your three gods? How is that?"

"Because of the baptism," said Pizarro in rising annoyance. "What does it matter what he believed? The priest sprinkled the water on him! The priest said the words! If the rite is properly performed, the soul is saved regardless of what the man understands or believes! How else could you baptize an infant? An infant understands nothing and believes nothing — but he becomes a Christian when the water touches him!"

"Much of this is mysterious to me," said Socrates. "But I see that you regard the king you killed as godly as well as wise, because he was washed by the water your gods require, and so you killed a good king who now lived in the embrace of your gods because of the baptism. Which seems wicked to me; and so this cannot be the place where the virtuous are sent after death, so it must be that I too was not virtuous, or else that I have misunderstood everything about this place and why we are in it."

"Damn you, are you trying to drive me crazy?" Pizarro roared, fumbling at the hilt of his sword. He drew it and waved it around in fury. "If you don't shut your mouth I'll cut you in thirds!"

***

"Uh-oh," Tanner said. "So much for the dialectical method."

***

Socrates said mildly, "It isn't my intention to cause you any annoyance, my friend. I'm only trying to learn a few things."

"You are a fool!"

"That is certainly true, as I have already acknowledged several times. Well, if you mean to strike me with your sword, go ahead. But I don't think it'll accomplish very much."

"Damn you," Pizarro muttered. He stared at his sword and shook his head. "No. No, it won't do any good, will it? It would go through you like air. But you'd just stand there and let me try to cut you down, and not even blink, right? Right?" He shook his head. "And yet you aren't stupid. You argue like the shrewdest priest I've ever known."

"In truth I am stupid," said Socrates. "I know very little at all. But I strive constantly to attain some understanding of the world, or at least to understand something of myself."

Pizarro glared at him. "No," he said. "I won't buy this false pride of yours. I have a little understanding of people myself, old man. I'm on to your game."

"What game is that, Pizarro?"

"I can see your arrogance. I see that you believe you're the wisest man in the world, and that it's your mission to go around educating poor sword-waving fools like me. And you pose as a fool to disarm your adversaries before you humiliate them."

***

"Score one for Pizarro," Richardson said. "He's wise to Socrates' little tricks, all right."

"Maybe he's read some Plato," Tanner suggested.

"He was illiterate."

"That was then. This is now."

"Not guilty," said Richardson. "He's operating on peasant shrewdness alone, and you damned well know it."

"I wasn't being serious," Tanner said. He leaned forward, peering toward the holotank. "God, what an astonishing thing this is, listening to them going at it. They seem absolutely real."

"They are," said Richardson.

***

"No, Pizarro, I am not wise at all," Socrates said. "But, stupid as I am, it may be that I am not the least wise man who ever lived."

"You think you're wiser than I am, don't you?"

"How can I say? First tell me how wise you are."

"Wise enough to begin my life as a bastard tending pigs and finish it as Captain-General of Peru."

"Ah, then you must be very wise."

"I think so, yes."

"Yet you killed a wise king because he wasn't wise enough to worship God the way you wished him to. Was that so wise of you, Pizarro? How did his people take it, when they found out that their king had been killed?"

"They rose in rebellion against us. They destroyed their own temples and palaces, and hid their gold and silver from us, and burned their bridges, and fought us bitterly."

"Perhaps you could have made some better use of him by *not* killing him, do you think?"

"In the long run we conquered them and made them Christians. It was what we intended to accomplish."

"But the same thing might have been accomplished in a wiser way?"

"Perhaps," said Pizarro grudgingly. "Still, we accomplished it. That's the main thing, isn't it? We did what we set out to do. If there was a better way, so be it. Angels do things perfectly. We were no angels, but we achieved what we came for, and so be it, Socrates. So be it."

***

"I'd call that one a draw," said Tanner.

"Agreed."

"It's a terrific game they're playing."

"I wonder who we can use to play it next," said Richardson.

"I wonder what we can do with this besides using it to play games," said Tanner.

***

"Let me tell you a story," said Socrates. "The oracle at Delphi once said to a friend of mine, 'There is no man wiser than Socrates,' but I doubted that very much, and it troubled me to hear the oracle saying something that I knew was so far from the truth. So I decided to look for a man who was obviously wiser than I was. There was a politician in Athens who was famous for his wisdom, and I went to him and questioned him about many things. After I had listened to him for a time, I came to see that though many people, and most of all he himself, thought that he was wise, yet he was not wise. He only imagined that he was wise. So I realized that I must be wiser than he. Neither of us knew anything that was really worthwhile, but he knew nothing and thought that he knew, whereas I neither knew anything nor thought that I did. At least on one point, then, I was wiser than he: I didn't think that I knew what I didn't know."

"Is this intended to mock me, Socrates?"

"I feel only the deepest respect for you, friend Pizarro. But let me continue. I went to other wise men, and they, too, though sure of their wisdom, could never give me a clear answer to anything. Those whose reputations for wisdom were the highest seemed to have the least of it. I went to the great poets and playwrights. There was wisdom in their works, for the gods had inspired them, but that did not make *them* wise, though they thought that it had. I went to the stonemasons and pioneers and other craftsmen. They were wise in their own skills, but most of them seemed to think that that made them wise in everything, which did not appear to be the case. And so it went. I was unable to find anyone who showed true wisdom. So perhaps the oracle was right: that although I am an ignorant man, there is no man wiser than I am. But oracles often are right without their being much value in it, for I think that all she was saying was that no man is wise at all, that wisdom is reserved for the gods. What do you say, Pizarro?"

"I say that you are a great fool, and very ugly besides."

"You speak the truth. So, then, you are wise after all. And honest."

"Honest, you say? I won't lay claim to that. Honesty's a game for fools. I lied whenever I needed to. I cheated. I went back on my word. I'm not proud of that, mind you. It's simply what you have to do to get on in the world. You think I wanted to tend pigs all my life? I wanted gold, Socrates! I wanted power over men! I wanted fame!"

"And did you get those things?"

"I got them all."

"And were they gratifying, Pizarro?"

Pizarro gave Socrates a long look. Then he pursed his lips and spat.

"They were worthless."

"Were they, do you think?"

"Worthless, yes. I have no illusions about that. But still it was better to have had them than not. In the long run nothing has any meaning, old man. In the long run we're all dead, the honest man and the villain, the king and the fool. Life's a cheat. They tell us to strive, to conquer, to gain — and for what? What? For a few years of strutting around. Then it's taken away, as if it had never been. A cheat, I say." Pizarro paused. He stared at his hands as though he had never seen them before. "Did I say all that just now? Did I mean it?" He laughed. "Well, I suppose I did. Still, life is all there is, so you want as much of it as you can. Which means getting gold, and power, and fame."

"Which you had. And apparently have no longer. Friend Pizarro, where are we now?"

"I wish I knew."

"So do I," said Socrates soberly.

***

"He's real," Richardson said. "They both are. The bugs are out of the system and we've got something spectacular here. Not only is this going to be of value to scholars, I think it's also going to be a tremendous entertainment gimmick, Harry."

"It's going to be much more than that," said Tanner in a strange voice.

"What do you mean by that?"

"I'm not sure yet," Tanner said. "But I'm definitely on to something big. It just began to hit me a couple of minutes ago, and it hasn't really taken shape yet. But it's something that might change the whole goddamned world."

Richardson looked amazed and bewildered.

"What the hell are you talking about, Harry?"

Tanner said, "A new way of settling political disputes, maybe. What would you say to a kind of combat-at-arms between one nation and another? Like a medieval tournament, so to speak. With each side using champions that we simulate for them—the greatest minds of all the past, brought back and placed in competition—" He shook his head. "Something like that. It needs a lot of working out, I know. But it's got possibilities."

"A medieval tournament—combat-at-arms, using simulations? Is that what you're saying?"

"Verbal combat. Not actual jousts, for Christ's sake."

"I don't see how—" Richardson began.

"Neither do I, not yet. I wish I hadn't even spoken of it."

"But—"

"Later, Lew. Later. Let me think about it a little while more."

***

"You don't have any idea what this place is?" Pizarro said.

"Not at all. But I certainly think this is no longer the world where we once dwelled. Are we dead, then? How can we say? You look alive to me."

"And you to me."

"Yet I think we are living some other kind of life. Here, give me your hand. Can you feel mine against yours?"

"No. I can't feel anything."

"Nor I. Yet I see two hands clasping. Two old men standing on a cloud, clasping hands." Socrates laughed. "What a great rogue you are, Pizarro!"

"Yes, of course. But do you know something, Socrates? You are, too. A windy old rogue. I like you. There were moments when you were driving me crazy with all your chatter, but you amused me, too. Were you really a soldier?"

"When my city asked me, yes."

"For a soldier, you're damned innocent about the way the world works, I have to say. But I guess I can teach you a thing or two."

"Will you?"

"Gladly," said Pizarro.

"I would be in your debt," Socrates said.

"Take Atahuallpa," Pizarro said. "How can I make you understand why I had to kill him? There weren't even two hundred of us, and twenty-four millions of them, and his word was law, and once he was gone they'd have no one to command them. So of *course* we had to get rid of him if we wanted to conquer them. And so we did, and then they fell."

"How simple you make it seem."

"Simple is what it was. Listen, old man, he would have died sooner or later anyway, wouldn't he? This way I made his death useful: to God, to the Church, to Spain. And to Francisco Pizarro. Can you understand that?"

"I think so," said Socrates. "But do you think King Atahuallpa did?"

"Any king would understand such things."

"Then he should have killed you the moment you set foot in his land."

"Unless God meant us to conquer him, and allowed him to understand that. Yes. Yes, that must have been what happened."

"Perhaps he is in this place, too, and we could ask him," said Socrates.

Pizarro's eyes brightened. "Mother of God, yes! A good idea! And if he didn't understand, why, I'll try to explain it to him. Maybe you'll help me. You know how to talk, how to move words around and around. What do you say? Would you help me?"

"If we meet him, I would like to talk with him," Socrates said. "I would indeed like to know if he agrees with you on the subject of the usefulness of his being killed by you."

Grinning, Pizarro said, "Slippery, you are! But I like you. I like you very much. Come. Let's go look for Atahuallpa."

FIVE
The 1990s

THE 1990s

And so, the 1990s, an era still fresh in most memories. The post-modern, post-Soviet, post-inflationary, pre-terrorist world, when life was pretty good for nearly everybody, and about the worst thing we needed to worry about was our President's definition of the verb "is." My sixtieth birthday came and went during the nineties: one of the most precocious writers in science-fiction history, the youngest ever to win a Hugo, was now an official senior citizen. I made a reasonably good adaptation to that momentous change. My health was good, my imagination still served up story ideas whenever one was needed, my narrative skills had not yet faded. But something unquestionably had changed within me. I would no longer have a sense of building a career, merely of sustaining one at the level that I had attained: very few artists set out to reshape and transform the field within which they work at that age, and most consider themselves lucky to be able to go on functioning at all. I went on functioning. I think I functioned pretty well, all things considered. More awards would come to me in the new decade; books of mine that had been out of print went into new editions; publishers still sought my work. If my books and stories of the 1990s broke no new paths, they were, at least, no disgrace to the reputation that I had steadily been building over the long span of my writing life, and some of them, I like to think, added a touch of autumnal distinction to my earlier accomplishments.

HUNTERS IN THE FOREST (1990)

INTRODUCTION

This story, like the one just preceding it, is one that I wrote for a book that I was editing myself. That's one of the pleasant secondary aspects of being a writer who dabbles in editing, as I have done: every once in a while you get to sell a story to yourself. Of course, I have to sell *every* story I write to myself before I can sell it to anyone else — if I don't think much of it, after all, how can I offer it to someone for publication with a straight face? — but when I'm simultaneously both writer and editor I don't have to worry, at least, about all those silly little editorial quibbles that other editors have been known to insist on inflicting on me before they'll publish something of mine.

In this case, my good friend, the well-known book packager and publisher Byron Preiss, with whom I have been involved in all sorts of projects over the years, and who is, in fact, the publisher of the U.S. paperback edition of this very book, was assembling a majestic coffee-table volume called *The Ultimate Dinosaur,* which was going to offer a mixture of scientific essays, short stories, and color plates. I was serving as fiction editor for the book. Like Byron, I have been fascinated by dinosaurs ever since I was a small boy. (Perhaps all small boys are, and a good many small girls too, but it is easiest to catch dinosaur mania if you grow up, as Byron and I did, in New York City, where the world's finest collection of dinosaur fossils is on display at the American Museum of Natural History.)

Science-fiction writers who love to write about dinosaurs are not very difficult to find. I assembled a top-level team (Poul Anderson, L. Sprague de Camp, Gregory Benford, Connie Willis, Harry Turtledove, etc.) to write the stories, each of whom was matched in theme to one of the essays. And I grabbed the theme of "Dinosaur Predators" for myself and illustrated it with this nasty little item, in which, as often happens in my fiction, the most dangerous beast turns out to be something other than the obvious one.

I wrote the story in November, 1990. Ellen Datlow, who had succeeded Robert Sheckley as fiction editor of *Omni,* bought magazine rights to it and published it in her October, 1991 issue, and *The Ultimate Dinosaur* appeared the following year.

Hunters in the Forest

Twenty minutes into the voyage nothing more startling than a dragonfly the size of a hawk has come into view, fluttering for an eyeblink moment in front of the timemobile window and darting away, and Mallory decides it's time to exercise Option Two: abandon the secure cozy comforts of the time mobile capsule, take his chances on foot out there in the steamy mists, a futuristic pygmy roaming virtually unprotected among the dinosaurs of this fragrant Late Cretaceous forest. That has been his plan all along — to offer himself up to the available dangers of this place, to experience the thrill of the hunt without ever quite being sure whether he was the hunter or the hunted.

Option One is to sit tight inside the timemobile capsule for the full duration of the trip — he has signed up for twelve hours — and watch the passing show, if any, through the invulnerable window. Very safe, yes. But self-defeating, also, if you have come here for the sake of tasting a little excitement for once in your life. Option Three, the one nobody ever talks about except in whispers and which perhaps despite all rumors to the contrary no one has actually ever elected, is self-defeating in a different way: simply walk off into the forest and never look back. After a prearranged period, usually twelve hours, never more than twenty-four, the capsule will return to its starting point in the twenty-third century whether or not you're aboard. But Mallory isn't out to do himself in, not really. All he wants is a little endocrine action, a hit of adrenaline to rev things up, the unfamiliar sensation of honest fear contracting his auricles and chilling his bowels: all that good old chancy stuff, damned well unattainable down the line in the modern era where risk is just about extinct. Back here in the Mesozoic, risk aplenty is available enough for those who can put up the price of admission. All he has to do is go outside and look for it. And so it's Option Two for him, then, a lively little walk about, and then back to the capsule in plenty of time for the return trip.

With him he carries a laser rifle, a backpack medical kit, and lunch. He jacks a thinko into his waistband and clips a drinko to his shoulder. But no helmet, no potted air supply. He'll boldly expose his naked nostrils to the Cretaceous atmosphere. Nor does he avail himself of the one-size-fits-all body armor that the capsule is willing to provide. That's the true spirit of Option Two, all right: go forth unshielded into the Mesozoic dawn.

Open the hatch, now. Down the steps, hop skip jump. Booted feet bouncing on the spongy primordial forest floor.

There's a hovering dankness but a surprisingly pleasant breeze is blowing. Things feel tropical but not uncomfortably torrid. The air has an unusual smell. The mix of nitrogen and carbon dioxide is different from what he's accustomed to, he suspects, and certainly none of the impurities that six centuries of industrial development have poured into the atmosphere are present. There's something else, too, a strange subtext of an odor that seems both sweet and pungent: it must be the aroma of dinosaur farts, Mallory decides. Uncountable hordes of stupendous beasts simultaneously releasing vast roaring boomers for a hundred million years surely will have filled the prehistoric air with complex hydrocarbons that won't break down until the Oligocene at the earliest.

Scaly tree trunks thick as the columns of the Parthenon shoot heavenward all around him. At their summits, far overhead, whorls of stiff long leaves jut tensely outward. Smaller trees that look like palms, but probably aren't, fill in the spaces between them, and at ground level there are dense growths of awkward angular bushes. Some of them are in bloom, small furry pale-yellowish blossoms, very diffident-looking, as though they were so newly evolved that they were embarrassed to find themselves on display like this. All the vegetation big and little has a battered, shopworn look, trunks leaning this way and that, huge leafstalks bent and dangling, gnawed boughs hanging like broken arms. It is as though an army of enormous tanks passes through this forest every few days. In fact that isn't far from the truth, Mallory realizes.

But where are they? Twenty-five minutes gone already and he still hasn't seen a single dinosaur, and he's ready for some.

"All right," Mallory calls out. "Where are you, you big dopes?"

As though on cue the forest hurls a symphony of sounds back at him: strident honks and rumbling snorts and a myriad blatting snuffling wheezing skreeing noises. It's like a chorus of crocodiles getting warmed up for Handel's Messiah.

Mallory laughs. "Yes, I hear you, I hear you!"

He cocks his laser rifle. Steps forward, looking eagerly to right and left. This period is supposed to be the golden age of dinosaurs, the grand tumultuous climactic epoch just before the end, when bizarre new species popped out constantly with glorious evolutionary profligacy, and all manner of grotesque goliaths roamed the earth. The thinko has shown him pictures of them, spectacularly decadent in size and appearance, long-snouted duckbilled monsters as big as a house and huge lumbering ceratopsians with frilly baroque bony crests and toothy things with knobby horns on their elongated skulls and others with rows of bristling spikes along their high-ridged backs. He aches to see them. He wants them to scare him practically to death. Let them loom; let them glower; let their great jaws yawn. Through all his untroubled days in the orderly and carefully regulated world of the twenty-third century Mallory has never shivered with fear as much as once, never known a moment of terror or even real uneasiness, is not even sure he understands the concept; and he has paid a small fortune for the privilege of experiencing it now.

Forward. Forward.

Come on, you oversized bastards, get your asses out of the swamp and show yourselves!

There. Oh, yes, yes, there!

He sees the little spheroid of a head first, rising above the treetops like a grinning football attached to a long thick hose. Behind it is an enormous humped back, unthinkably high. He hears the pile driver sound of the behemoth's footfall and the crackle of huge tree trunks breaking as it smashes its way serenely toward him.

He doesn't need the murmured prompting of his thinko to know that this is a giant sauropod making its majestic passage through the forest — "one of the titanosaurs or perhaps an ultrasaur," the quiet voice says, admitting with just a hint of chagrin in its tone that it can't identify the particular species — but Mallory isn't really concerned with detail on that level. He is after the thrill of size. And he's getting size, all right. The thing is implausibly colossal. It emerges into the clearing where he stands and he is given the full view, and gasps. He can't even guess how big it is. Twenty meters high? Thirty? Its ponderous corrugated legs are thick as sequoias. Giraffes on tiptoe could go skittering between them without grazing the underside of its massive belly. Elephants would look like house cats beside it. Its tail, held out stiffly to the rear, decapitates sturdy trees with its slow steady lashing. A hundred million years of saurian evolution have produced this thing, Darwinianism gone crazy, excess building remorselessly on excess, irrepressible chromosomes gleefully reprogramming themselves through the millennia to engender thicker bones, longer legs, ever bulkier bodies, and the end result is this walking mountain, this absurdly overstated monument to reptilian hyperbole.

"Hey!" Mallory cries. "Look here! Can you see this far down? There's a human down here. Homo sapiens. I'm a mammal. Do you know what a mammal is? Do you know what my ancestors are going to do to your descendants?" He is practically alongside it, no more than a hundred meters away. Its musky stink makes him choke and cough. Its ancient leathery brown hide, as rigid as cast iron, is pocked with parasitic growths, scarlet and yellow and ultramarine, and crisscrossed with the gulleys and ravines of century-old wounds deep enough for him to hide in. With each step it takes Mallory feels an earthquake. He is nothing next to it, a flea, a gnat. It could crush him with a casual stride and never even know.

And yet he feels no fear. The sauropod is so big he can't make sense out of it, let alone be threatened by it.

Can you fear the Amazon River? The planet Jupiter? The pyramid of Cheops?

No, what he feels is anger, not terror. The sheer preposterous bulk of the monster infuriates him. The pointless superabundance of it inspires him with wrath.

"My name is Mallory," he yells. "I've come from the twenty-third century to bring you your doom, you great stupid mass of meat. I'm personally going to make you extinct, do you hear me?"

He raises the laser rifle and centers its sight on the distant tiny head. The rifle hums its computations and modifications and the rainbow beam jumps skyward. For an instant the sauropod's head is engulfed in a dazzling fluorescent nimbus. Then the light dies away, and the animal moves on as though nothing has happened.

No brain up there? Mallory wonders.

Too dumb to die?

He moves up closer and fires again, carving a bright track along one hypertrophied haunch. Again, no effect. The sauropod moves along untroubled, munching on treetops as it goes. A third shot, too hasty, goes astray and cuts off the crown of a tree in the forest canopy. A fourth zings into the sauropod's gut but the dinosaur doesn't seem to care. Mallory is furious now at the unkillability of the thing. His thinko quietly reminds him that these giants supposedly had had their main nerve-centers at the base of their spines. Mallory runs around behind the creature and stares up at the galactic expanse of its rump, wondering where best to place his shot. Just then the great tail swings upward and to the left and a torrent of immense steaming green turds as big as boulders comes cascading down, striking the ground all around Mallory with thunderous impact. He leaps out of the way barely in time to keep from being entombed, and goes scrambling frantically away to avoid the choking fetor that rises from the sauropod's vast mound of excreta. In his haste he stumbles over a vine, loses his footing in the slippery mud, falls to hands and knees. Something that looks like a small blue dog with a scaly skin and a ring of sharp spines around its neck jumps up out of the muck, bouncing up and down and hissing and screeching and snapping at him. Its teeth are deadly-looking yellow fangs. There isn't room to fire the laser rifle. Mallory desperately rolls to one side and bashes the thing with the butt instead, hard, and it runs away growling. When he has a chance finally to catch his breath and look up again, he sees the great sauropod vanishing in the distance.

He gets up and takes a few limping steps further away from the reeking pile of ordure.

He has learned at last what it's like to have a brush with death. Two brushes, in fact, within the span of ten seconds. But where's the vaunted thrill of danger narrowly averted, the hot satisfaction of the frisson? He feels no pleasure, none of the hoped-for rush of keen endocrine delight.

Of course not. A pile of falling turds, a yapping little lizard with big teeth: what humiliating perils! During the frantic moments when he was defending himself against them he was too busy to notice what he was feeling, and now, muddy all over, his knee aching, his dignity dented, he is left merely with a residue of annoyance, frustration, and perhaps a little ironic self-deprecation, when what he had wanted was the white ecstasy of genuine terror followed by the postorgasmic delight of successful escape recollected in tranquility.

Well, he still has plenty of time. He goes onward, deeper into the forest.

Now he is no longer able to see the timemobile capsule. That feels good, that sudden new sense of being cut off from the one zone of safety he has in this fierce environment. He tries to divert himself with fantasies of jeopardy. It isn't easy. His mind doesn't work that way; nobody's does, really, in the nice, tidy, menace-free society he lives in. But he works at it. Suppose, he thinks, I lose my way in the forest and can't get back to — no, no hope of that, the capsule sends out constant directional pulses that his thinko picks up by microwave transmission. What if the thinko breaks down, then? But they never do. If I take it off and toss it into a swamp? That's Option Three, though, self-damaging behavior designed to maroon him here. He doesn't do such things. He can barely even fantasize them.

Well, then, the sauropod comes back and steps on the capsule, crushing it beyond use —

Impossible. The capsule is strong enough to withstand submersion to 30-atmosphere pressures.

The sauropod pushes it into quicksand, and it sinks out of sight?

Mallory is pleased with himself for coming up with that one. It's good for a moment or two of interesting uneasiness. He imagines himself standing at the edge of some swamp, staring down forlornly as the final minutes tick away and the timemobile, functional as ever even though it's fifty fathoms down in gunk, sets out for home without him. But no, no good: the capsule moves just as effectively through space as through time, and it would simply activate its powerful engine and climb up onto terra firma again in plenty of time for his return trip.

What if, he thinks, a band of malevolent intelligent dinosaurs appears on the scene and forcibly prevents me from getting back into the capsule?

That's more like it. A little shiver that time. Good! Cut off, stranded in the Mesozoic! Living by his wits, eating God knows what, exposing himself to extinct bacteria. Getting sick, blazing with fever, groaning in unfamiliar pain. Yes! Yes! He piles it on. It becomes easier as he gets into the swing of it. He will lead a life of constant menace. He imagines himself taking out his own appendix. Setting a broken leg. And the unending hazards, day and night. Toothy enemies lurking behind every bush. Baleful eyes glowing in the darkness. A life spent forever on the run, never a moment's ease. Cowering under fern-fronds as the giant carnivores go lalloping by. Scorpions, snakes, gigantic venomous toads. Insects that sting. Everything that has been eliminated from life in the civilized world pursuing him here: and he flitting from one transitory hiding place to another, haggard, unshaven, bloodshot, brow shining with sweat, struggling unceasingly to survive, living a gallant life of desperate heroism in this nightmare world—

"Hello," he says suddenly. "Who the hell are you?"

In the midst of his imaginings a genuine horror has presented itself, emerging suddenly out of a grove of tree ferns. It is a towering bipedal creature with the powerful thighs and small dangling forearms of the familiar tyrannosaurus, but this one has an enormous bony crest like a warrior's helmet rising from its skull, with five diabolical horns radiating outward behind it and two horrendous incisors as long as tusks jutting from its cavernous mouth, and its huge lashing tail is equipped with a set of great spikes at the tip. Its mottled and furrowed skin is a bilious yellow and the huge crest on its head is fiery scarlet. It is everybody's bad dream of the reptilian killer-monster of the primeval dawn, the ghastly overspecialized end-product of the long saurian reign, shouting its own lethality from every bony excrescence, every razor-keen weapon on its long body.

The thinko scans it and tells him that it is a representative of an unknown species belonging to the saurischian order and it is almost certainly predatory.

"Thank you very much," Mallory replies.

He is astonished to discover that even now, facing this embodiment of death, he is not at all afraid. Fascinated, yes, by the sheer deadliness of the creature, by its excessive horrificality. Amused, almost, by its grotesqueries of form. And coolly aware that in three bounds and a swipe of its little dangling paw it could end his life, depriving him of the sure century of minimum expectancy that remains to him. Despite that threat he remains calm. If he dies, he dies; but he can't actually bring himself to believe that he will. He is beginning to see that the capacity for fear, for any sort of significant psychological distress, has been bred out of him. He is simply too stable. It is an unexpected drawback of the perfection of human society.

The saurischian predator of unknown species slavers and roars and glares. Its narrow yellow eyes are like beacons. Mallory unslings his laser rifle and gets into firing position. Perhaps this one will be easier to kill than the colossal sauropod.

Then a woman walks out of the jungle behind it and says, "You aren't going to try to shoot it, are you?"

Mallory stares at her. She is young, only fifty or so unless she's on her second or third retread, attractive, smiling. Long sleek legs, a fluffy burst of golden hair. She wears a stylish hunting outfit of black spray-on and carries no rifle, only a tiny laser pistol. A space of no more than a dozen meters separates her from the dinosaur's spiked tail, but that doesn't seem to trouble her.

He gestures with the rifle. "Step out of the way, will you?"

She doesn't move. "Shooting it isn't a smart idea."

"We're here to do a little hunting, aren't we?"

"Be sensible," she says. "This one's a real son of a bitch. You'll only annoy it if you try anything, and then we'll both be in a mess." She walks casually around the monster, which is standing quite still, studying them both in an odd perplexed way as though it actually wonders what they might be. Mallory has aimed the rifle now at the thing's left eye, but the woman coolly puts her hand to the barrel and pushes it aside.

"Let it be," she says. "It's just had its meal and now it's sleepy. I watched it gobble up something the size of a hippopotamus and then eat half of another one for dessert. You start sticking it with your little laser and you'll wake it up, and then it'll get nasty again. Mean-looking bastard, isn't it?" she says admiringly.

"Who are you?" Mallory asks in wonder. "What are you doing here?"

"Same thing as you, I figure. Cretaceous Tours?"

"Yes. They said I wouldn't run into any other —"

"They told me that too. Well, it sometimes happens. Jayne Hyland. New Chicago, 2281."

"Tom Mallory. New Chicago also. And also 2281."

"Small geological epoch, isn't it? What month did you leave from?"

"August."

"I'm September."

"Imagine that."

The dinosaur, far above them, utters a soft snorting sound and begins to drift away.

"We're boring it," she says.

"And it's boring us, too. Isn't that the truth? These enormous terrifying monsters crashing through the forest all around us and we're as blase as if we're home watching the whole thing on the polyvid." Mallory raises his rifle again. The scarlet-frilled killer is almost out of sight. "I'm tempted to take a shot at it just to get some excitement going."

"Don't," she says. "Unless you're feeling suicidal. Are you?"

"Not at all."

"Then don't annoy it, okay?—I know where there's a bunch of ankylosaurs wallowing around. That's one really weird critter, believe me. Are you interested in having a peek?"

"Sure," says Mallory.

He finds himself very much taken by her brisk no-nonsense manner, her confident air. When we get back to New Chicago, he thinks, maybe I'll look her up. The September tour, she said. So he'll have to wait a while after his own return. I'll give her a call around the end of the month, he tells himself.

She leads the way unhesitatingly, through the tree-fern grove and around a stand of giant horsetails and across a swampy meadow of small plastic-looking plants with ugly little mud-colored daisyish flowers. On the far side they zig around a great pile of bloodied bones and zag around a treacherous bog with a sinisterly quivering surface. A couple of giant dragonflies whiz by, droning like airborne missiles. A crimson frog as big as a rabbit grins at them from a pond. They have been walking for close to an hour now and Mallory no longer has any idea where he is in relation to his timemobile capsule. But the thinko will find the way back for him eventually, he assumes.

"The ankylosaurs are only about a hundred meters further on," she says, as if reading his mind. She looks back and gives him a bright smile. "I saw a pack of troodons the day before yesterday out this way. You know what they are? Little agile guys, no bigger than you or me, smart as whips. Teeth like sawblades, funny knobs on their heads. I thought for a minute they were going to attack, but I stood my ground and finally they backed off. You want to shoot something, shoot one of those."

"The day before yesterday?" Mallory asks, after a moment. "How long have you been here?"

"About a week. Maybe two. I've lost count, really. Look, there are those ankylosaurs I was telling you about."

He ignores her pointing hand. "Wait a second. The longest available time tour lasts only—"

"I'm Option Three," she says.

He gapes at her as though she has just sprouted a scarlet bony crest with five spikes behind it.

"Are you serious?" he asks.

"As serious as anybody you ever met in the middle of the Cretaceous forest. I'm here for keeps, friend. I stood right next to my capsule when the twelve hours were up and watched it go sailing off into the ineffable future. And I've been having the time of my life ever since."

A tingle of awe spreads through him. It is the strongest emotion he has ever felt, he realizes.

She is actually living that gallant life of desperate heroism that he had fantasized. Avoiding the myriad menaces of this incomprehensible place for a whole week or possibly even two, managing to stay fed and healthy, in fact looking as trim and elegant as if she had just stepped out of her capsule a couple of hours ago. And never to go back to the nice safe orderly world of 2281. Never. Never. She will remain here until she dies — a month from now, a year, five years, whenever. Must remain. Must. By her own choice. An incredible adventure.

Her face is very close to his. Her breath is sweet and warm. Her eyes are bright, penetrating, ferocious. "I was sick of it all," she tells him. "Weren't you? The perfection of everything. The absolute predictability. You can't even stub your toe because there's some clever sensor watching out for you. The biomonitors. The automedics. The guides and proctors. I hated it."

"Yes. Of course."

Her intensity is frightening. For one foolish moment, Mallory realizes, he was actually thinking of offering to rescue her from the consequences of her rashness. Inviting her to come back with him in his own capsule when his twelve hours are up. They could probably both fit inside, if they stand very close to each other. A reprieve from Option Three, a new lease on life for her. But that isn't really possible, he knows. The mass has to balance in both directions of the trip within a very narrow tolerance; they are warned not to bring back even a twig, even a pebble, nothing aboard the capsule that wasn't aboard it before. And in any case being rescued is surely the last thing she wants. She'll simply laugh at him. Nothing could make her go back. She loves it here. She feels truly alive for the first time in her life. In a universe of security-craving dullards she's a woman running wild. And her wildness is contagious. Mallory trembles with sudden new excitement at the sheer proximity of her.

She sees it, too. Her glowing eyes flash with invitation.

"Stay here with me!" she says. "Let your capsule go home without you, the way I did."

"But the dangers —" he hears himself blurting inanely.

"Don't worry about them. I'm doing all right so far, aren't I? We can manage. We'll build a cabin. Plant fruits and vegetables. Catch lizards in traps. Hunt the dinos. They're so dumb they just stand there and let you shoot them. The laser charges won't ever run out. You and me, me and you, all alone in the Mesozoic! Like Adam and Eve, we'll be. The Adam and Eve of the Late Cretaceous. And they can all go to hell back there in 2281."

His fingers are tingling. His throat is dry. His cheeks blaze with savage adrenal fires. His breath is coming in ragged gasps. He has never felt anything like this before in his life.

He moistens his lips.

"Well—"

She smiles gently. The pressure eases. "It's a big decision, I know. Think about it," she says. Her voice is soft now. The wild zeal of a moment before is gone from it. "How soon before your capsule leaves?"

He glances at his wrist. "Eight, nine more hours."

"Plenty of time to make up your mind."

"Yes. Yes."

Relief washes over him. She has dizzied him with the overpowering force of her revelation and the passionate frenzy of her invitation to join her in her escape from the world they have left behind. He isn't used to such things. He needs time now, time to absorb, to digest, to ponder. To decide. That he would even consider such a thing astonishes him. He has known her how long—an hour, an hour and a half?—and here he is thinking of giving up everything for her. Unbelievable. Unbelievable.

Shakily he turns away from her and stares at the ankylosaurs wallowing in the mudhole just in front of them.

Strange, strange, strange. Gigantic low-slung tubby things, squat as tanks, covered everywhere by armor. Vaguely triangular, expanding vastly toward the rear, terminating in armored tails with massive bony excrescences at the tips, like deadly clubs. Slowly snuffling forward in the muck, tiny heads down, busily grubbing away at soft green weeds. Jayne jumps down among them and dances across their armored backs, leaping from one to another. They don't even seem to notice. She laughs and calls to him. "Come on," she says, prancing like a she-devil.

They dance among the ankylosaurs until the game grows stale. Then she takes him by the hand and they run onward, through a field of scarlet mosses, down to a small clear lake fed by a swift-flowing stream. They strip and plunge in, heedless of risk. Afterward they embrace on the grassy bank. Some vast creature passes by, momentarily darkening the sky. Mallory doesn't bother even to look up.

Then it is on, on to spy on something with a long neck and a comic knobby head, and then to watch a pair of angry ceratopsians butting heads in slow motion, and then to applaud the elegant migration of a herd of towering duckbills across the horizon. There are dinosaurs everywhere, everywhere, everywhere, an astounding zoo of them. And the time ticks away.

It's fantastic beyond all comprehension. But even so—

Give up everything for this? he wonders.

The chalet in Gstaad, the weekend retreat aboard the L-5 satellite, the hunting lodge in the veldt? The island home in the Seychelles, the plantation in New Caledonia, the pied-a-terre in the shadow of the Eiffel Tower?

For this? For a forest full of nightmare monsters, and a life of daily peril? Yes. Yes. Yes. Yes.

He glances toward her. She knows what's on his mind, and she gives him a sizzling look. Come live with me and be my love, and we will all the pleasures prove. Yes. Yes. Yes. Yes.

A beeper goes off on his wrist and his thinko says, "It is time to return to the capsule. Shall I guide you?"

And suddenly it all collapses into a pile of ashes, the whole shimmering fantasy perishing in an instant.

"Where are you going?" she calls.

"Back," he says. He whispers the word hoarsely — croaks it, in fact.

"Tom!"

"Please. Please."

He can't bear to look at her. His defeat is total; his shame is cosmic. But he isn't going to stay here. He isn't. He isn't. He simply isn't. He slinks away, feeling her burning contemptuous glare drilling holes in his shoulder blades. The quiet voice of the thinko steadily instructs him, leading him around pitfalls and obstacles. After a time he looks back and can no longer see her.

On the way back to the capsule he passes a pair of sauropods mating, a tyrannosaur in full slather, another thing with talons like scythes, and half a dozen others. The thinko obligingly provides him with their names, but Mallory doesn't even give them a glance. The brutal fact of his own inescapable cowardice is the only thing that occupies his mind. She has had the courage to turn her back on the stagnant over-perfect world where they live, regardless of all danger, whereas he — he —

"There is the capsule, sir," the thinko says triumphantly.

Last chance, Mallory.

No. No. No. He can't do it.

He climbs in. Waits. Something ghastly appears outside, all teeth and claws, and peers balefully at him through the window. Mallory peers back at it, nose to nose, hardly caring what happens to him now. The creature takes an experimental nibble at the capsule. The impervious metal resists. The dinosaur shrugs and waddles away.

A chime goes off. The Late Cretaceous turns blurry and disappears.

***

In mid-October, seven weeks after his return, he is telling the somewhat edited version of his adventure at a party for the fifteenth time that month when a woman to his left says, "There's someone in the other room who's just came back from the dinosaur tour too."

"Really," says Mallory, without enthusiasm.

"You and she would love to compare notes, I'll bet. Wait, and I'll get her. Jayne! Jayne, come in here for a moment!"

Mallory gasps. Color floods his face. His mind swirls in bewilderment and chagrin. Her eyes are as sparkling and alert as ever, her hair is a golden cloud.

"But you told me—"

"Yes," she says. "I did, didn't I?"

"Your capsule—you said it had gone back—"

"It was just on the far side of the ankylosaurs, behind the horsetails. I got to the Cretaceous about eight hours before you did. I had signed up for a 24-hour tour."

"And you let me believe—"

"Yes. So I did." She grins at him and says softly, "It was a lovely fantasy, don't you think?"

He comes close to her and gives her a cold, hard stare. "What would you have done if I had let my capsule go back without me and stranded myself there for the sake of your lovely fantasy? Or didn't you stop to think about that?"

"I don't know," she tells him. "I just don't know." And she laughs.

DEATH DO US PART (1994)

INTRODUCTION

Through most of the 1980s and 1990s my writing rhythm involved beginning a novel when the California rainy season starts in November, finishing it about March, and following it with several short stories before the coming of summer called a halt to all work during the dry, sunny months that commence here in April. If the novel ran long, short-story production got shorter shrift: some years none get written at all.

My book for 1993-94 was the relatively short novel *The Mountains of Majipoor,* which I finished so early in the rainy season that there was time to do several shorter pieces afterward, before shutting the fiction factory down for its traditional summer recess. So I wrote this one in February, 1994, tacking a couple of new twists on the old notion of the quasi-immortal who falls in love with someone of normal lifespan, and thereby once again coming to grips with some virtually obsessive themes of my fiction.

Ellen Datlow bought it for *Omni,* but it never saw print there, because *Omni,* once so successful, had run into hard times and was beginning a Cheshire-Cat routine of vanishing into the mysterious on-line world of the Internet. The idea was to distribute both a conventional print version of *Omni* and an on-line version, but the printed magazine gradually disappeared, leaving only the electronic edition. Though I have, like almost everyone else, become a daily user of the Internet, I still have not come to feel comfortable about reading fiction on a computer, and I tend to believe that anything published on the Internet might just as well have been published on Mars, at least so far as I'm concerned. The on-line version of *Omni* did indeed make the story available to its cyberspace following, finally, in December of 1996, and technically that's its first publication. But to my outmoded way of thinking "Death Do Us Part" made its publishing debut in the August, 1997 issue of *Asimov's Science Fiction,* an actual paper-and-ink operation. As a concession to the realities of the twenty-first century I've given the *Omni* use of the story priority in the copyright acknowledgments at the back of this book, though.

Death Do Us Part

It was her first, his seventh. She was 32, he was 363: the good old April/ September number. They honeymooned in Venice, Nairobi, the Malaysia Pleasure Dome, and one of the posh L-5 resorts, a shimmering glassy sphere with round-the-clock sunlight and waterfalls that tumbled like cascades of diamonds, and then they came home to his lovely sky-house suspended on tremulous guy-wires a thousand meters above the Pacific to begin the everyday part of their life together.

Her friends couldn't get over it. "He's ten times your age!" they would exclaim. "How could you possibly want anybody that old?" Marilisa admitted that marrying Leo was more of a lark for her than anything else. An impulsive thing; a sudden impetuous leap. Marriages weren't forever, after all—just thirty or forty years and then you moved along. But Leo was sweet and kind and actually quite sexy. And he had wanted her so much. He genuinely did seem to love her. Why should his age be an issue? He didn't appear to be any older than 35 or so. These days you could look as young as you liked. Leo did his Process faithfully and punctually, twice each decade, and it kept him as dashing and vigorous as a boy.

There were little drawbacks, of course. Once upon a time, long long ago, he had been a friend of Marilisa's great-grandmother: they might even have been lovers. She wasn't going to ask. Such things sometimes happened and you simply had to work your way around them. And then also he had an ex-wife on the scene, Number Three, Katrin, 247 years old and not looking a day over 30. She was constantly hovering about. Leo still had warm feelings for her. "A wonderfully dear woman, a good and loyal friend," he would say. "When you get to know her you'll be as fond of her as I am." That one was hard, all right. What was almost as bad, he had children three times Marilisa's age and more. One of them—the next-to-youngest, Fyodor—had an insufferable and presumptuous way of winking and sniggering at her, that hundred-year-old son of a bitch. "I want you to meet our father's newest toy," Fyodor said of her, once, when yet another of Leo's centenarian sons, previously unsuspected by Marilisa, turned up. "We get to play with her when he's tired of her." Someday Marilisa was going to pay him back for that.

Still and all, she had no serious complaints. Leo was an ideal first husband: wise, warm, loving, attentive, generous. She felt nothing but the greatest tenderness for him. And then too he was so immeasurably experienced in the ways of the world. If being married to him was a little like being married to Abraham Lincoln or Augustus Caesar, well, so be it: they had been great men, and so was Leo. He was endlessly fascinating. He was like seven husbands rolled into one. She had no regrets, none at all, not really.

***

In the spring of '87 they go to Capri for their first anniversary. Their hotel is a reconstructed Roman villa on the southern slope of Monte Tiberio: alabaster walls frescoed in black and red, a brilliantly colored mosaic of sea creatures in the marble bathtub, a broad travertine terrace that looks out over the sea. They stand together in the darkness, staring at the awesome sparkle of the stars. A crescent moon slashes across the night. His arm is around her; her head rests against his breast. Though she is a tall woman, Marilisa is barely heart-high to him.

"Tomorrow at sunrise," he says, "we'll see the Blue Grotto. And then in the afternoon we'll hike down below here to the Cave of the Mater Magna. I always get a shiver when I'm there. Thinking about the ancient islanders who worshipped their goddess under that cliff, somewhere back in the Pleistocene. Their rites and rituals, the offerings they made to her."

"Is that when you first came here?" she asks, keeping it light and sly. "Somewhere back in the Pleistocene?"

"A little later than that, really. The Renaissance, I think it was. Leonardo and I traveled down together from Florence—"

"You and Leonardo, you were just like that."

"Like that, yes. But not like that, if you take my meaning."

"And Cosimo di' Medici. Another one from the good old days. Cosimo gave such great parties, right?"

"That was Lorenzo," he says. "Lorenzo the Magnificent, Cosimo's grandson. Much more fun than the old man. You would have adored him."

"I almost think you're serious when you talk like that."

"I'm always serious. Even when I'm not." His arm tightens around her. He leans forward and down, and buries a kiss in her thick dark hair. "I love you," he whispers.

"I love you," she says. "You're the best first husband a girl could want."

"You're the finest last wife a man could ever desire."

The words skewer her. Last wife? Is he expecting to die in the next ten or twenty or thirty years? He is old—ancient—but nobody has any idea yet where the limits of Process lie. Five hundred years? A thousand? Who can say? No one able to afford the treatments has died a natural death yet, in the four hundred years since Process was invented. Why, then, does he speak so knowingly of her as his last wife? He may live long enough to have seven, ten, fifty wives after her.

Marilisa is silent a long while.

Then she asks him, quietly, uncertainly, "I don't understand why you said that."

"Said what?"

"The thing about my being your last wife."

He hesitates just a moment. "But why would I ever want another, now that I have you?"

"Am I so utterly perfect?"

"I love you."

"You loved Tedesca and Thane and Iavilda too," she says. "And Miaule and Katrin." She is counting on her fingers in the darkness. One wife missing from the list. "And—Syantha. See, I know all their names. You must have loved them but the marriages ended anyway. They have to end. No matter how much you love a person, you can't keep a marriage going forever."

"How do you know that?"

"I just do. Everybody knows it."

"I would like this marriage never to end," he tells her. "I'd like it to go on and on and on. To continue to the end of time. Is that all right? Is such a sentiment permissible, do you think?"

"What a romantic you are, Leo!"

"What else can I be but romantic, tonight? This place; the spring night; the moon, the stars, the sea; the fragrance of the flowers in the air. Our anniversary. I love you. Nothing will ever end for us. Nothing."

"Can that really be so?" she asks.

"Of course. Forever and ever, as it is this moment."

***

She thinks from time to time of the men she will marry after she and Leo have gone their separate ways. For she knows that she will. Perhaps she'll stay with Leo for ten years, perhaps for fifty; but ultimately, despite all his assurances to the contrary, one or the other of them will want to move on. No one stays married forever. Fifteen, twenty years, that's the usual. Sixty or seventy, tops.

She'll marry a great athlete next, she decides. And then a philosopher; and then a political leader; and then stay single for a few decades, just to clear her palate, so to speak, an intermezzo in her life, and when she wearies of that she'll find someone entirely different, a simple rugged man who likes to hunt, to work in the fields with his hands, and then a yachtsman with whom she'll sail the world, and then maybe when she's about 300 she'll marry a boy, an innocent of 18 or 19 who hasn't even had his first Prep yet, and then — then —

A childish game. It always brings her to tears, eventually. The unknown husbands that wait for her in the misty future are vague chilly phantoms, fantasies, frightening, inimical. They are like swords that will inevitably fall between her and Leo, and she hates them for that.

The thought of having the same husband for all the vast expanse of time that is the rest of her life is a little disturbing — it gives her a sense of walls closing in, and closing and closing and closing — but the thought of leaving Leo is even worse. Or of his leaving her. Maybe she isn't truly in love with him, at any rate not as she imagines love at its deepest to be, but she is happy with him. She wants to stay with him. She can't really envision parting from him and moving on to someone else.

But of course she knows that she will. Everybody does, in the fullness of time.

Everybody.

***

Leo is a sand-painter. Sand-painting is his fifteenth or twentieth career. He has been an architect, an archaeologist, a space-habitats developer, a professional gambler, an astronomer, and a number of other disparate and dazzling things. He reinvents himself every decade or two. That's as necessary to him as Process itself. Making money is never an issue, since he lives on the compounding interest of investments set aside centuries ago. But the fresh challenge — ah, yes, always the fresh challenge —!

Marilisa hasn't entered on any career path yet. It's much too soon. She is, after all, still in her first life, too young for Process, merely in the Prep stage yet. Just a child, really. She has dabbled in ceramics, written some poetry, composed a little music. Lately she has begun to think about studying economics or perhaps Spanish literature. No doubt her actual choice of a path to follow will be very far from any of these. But there's time to decide. Oh, is there ever time!

Just after the turn of the year she and Leo go to Antibes to attend the unveiling of Leo's newest work, commissioned by Lucien Nicolas, a French industrialist. Leo and Lucien Nicolas were schoolmates, eons ago. At the airport they embrace warmly, almost endlessly, like brothers long separated. They even look a little alike, two full-faced square-jawed dark-haired men with wide-flanged noses and strong, prominent lips.

"My wife Marilisa," Leo says finally.

"How marvelous," says Lucien Nicolas. "How superb." He kisses the tips of his fingers to her.

Nicolas lives in a lofty villa overlooking the Mediterranean, surrounded by a lush garden in which the red spikes of aloes and the yellow blooms of acacias stand out dazzlingly against a palisade of towering palms. The weather, this January day, is mild and pleasant, with a light drizzle falling. The industrialist has invited a splendid international roster of guests to attend the unveiling of the painting; diplomats and jurists, poets and playwrights, dancers and opera singers, physicists and astronauts and mentalists and sculptors and seers. Leo introduces Marilisa to them all. In the antechamber to the agate dining hall she listens, bemused, to the swirl of conversations in half a dozen languages. The talk ranges across continents, decades, generations. It seems to her that she hears from a distance the names of several of Leo's former wives invoked—Syantha, Tedesca, Katrin?—but possibly she is mistaken.

Dinner is an overindulgent feast of delicacies. Squat animated servitors bring the food on glistening covered trays of some exotic metal that shimmers diffractively. After every third course a cool ray of blue light descends from a ceiling aperture and a secondary red radiance rises from the floor: they meet in the vicinity of the great slab of black diamond that is the table, and a faint whiff of burning carbon trickles into the air, and then the diners are hungry all over again, ready for the next delight.

The meal is a symphony of flavors and textures. The balance is perfect between sweet and tart, warm and cool, spicy and bland. A pink meat is followed by a white one, and then by fruit, then cheese, and meat again, a different kind, and finer cheeses. A dozen wines or more are served. An occasional course is still alive, moving slowly about its plate; Marilisa takes her cue from Leo, conquers any squeamishness, traps and consumes her little wriggling victims with pleasure. Now and then the underlying dish is meant to be eaten along with its contents, as she discovers by lagging just a moment behind the other guests and imitating their behavior.

After dinner comes the unveiling of the painting, in the atrium below the dining hall. The guests gather along the balcony of the dining hall and the atrium roof is retracted.

Leo's paintings are huge rectangular constructions made of fine sparkling sand of many colors, laid out within a high border of molten copper. The surfaces of each work are two-dimensional, but the cloudy hint of a third dimension is always visible, and even that is only the tip of an underlying multidimensional manifold that vanishes at mysterious angles into the fabric of the piece. Down in those churning sandy depths lie wells of color with their roots embedded in the hidden mechanisms that control the piece. These wells constantly contribute streams of minute glittering particles to the patterns at the surface, in accordance with the changing signals from below. There is unending alteration; none of Leo's pieces is ever the same two hours running.

A ripple of astonishment breaks forth as the painting is revealed, and then a rising burst of applause. The pattern is one of interlaced spirals in gentle pastels, curvilinear traceries in pink and blue and pale green, with thin black circles surrounding them and frail white lines radiating outward in groups of three to the vivid turquoise borders of the sand. Leo's friends swarm around him to congratulate him. They even congratulate Marilisa. "He is a master—an absolute master!" She basks in his triumph.

Later in the evening she returns to the balcony to see if she can detect the first changes in the pattern. The changes, usually, are minute and subtle ones, requiring a discriminating eye, but even in her short while with Leo she has learned to discern the tiniest of alterations.

This time, though, no expertise is required. In little more than an hour the lovely surface has been significantly transformed. A thick, jagged black line has abruptly sprung into being, descending like a dark scar from upper right to lower left. Marilisa has never seen such a thing happen before. It is like a wound in the painting: a mutilation. It draws a little involuntary cry of shock from her.

Others gather. "What does it mean?" they ask. "What is he saying?"

From someone in African tribal dress, someone who nevertheless is plainly not African, comes an interpretation: "We see the foretelling of schism, the evocation of a transformation of the era. The dark line moves in brutal strokes through the center of our stability-point. There, do you see, the pink lines and the blue? And then it drops down into the unknown dominion beyond the painting's eastern border, the realm of the mythic, the grand apocalyptic."

Leo is summoned. He is calm. But Leo is always calm. He shrugs away the urgent questions: the painting, he says, is its own meaning, not subject to literal analysis. It is what it is, nothing more. A stochastic formula governs the changes in his works. All is random. The jagged black line is simply a jagged black line.

Music comes from another room. New servitors appear, creatures with three metal legs and one telescoping arm, offering brandies and liqueurs. The guests murmur and laugh. "A master," they tell Marilisa once again. "An absolute master!"

***

She likes to ask him about the faraway past—the quaint and remote twenty-third century, the brusque and dynamic twenty-fourth. He is like some great heroic statue rising up out of the mists of time, embodying in himself firsthand knowledge of eras that are mere legends to her.

"Tell me how people dressed, back then," she begs him. "What sorts of things they said, the games they played, where they liked to go on their holidays. And the buildings, the architecture: how did things look? Make me feel what it was like: the sounds, the smells, the whole flavor of the long-ago times."

He laughs. "It gets pretty jumbled, you know. The longer you live, the more muddled-up your mind becomes."

"Oh, I don't believe that at all! I think you remember every bit of it. Tell me about your father and mother."

"My father and my mother —" He pronounces the words musingly, as though they are newly minted concepts for him. "My father — he was tall, even taller than I am — a mathematician, he was, or maybe a composer, something abstruse like that —"

"And his eyes? What kind of eyes did he have?"

"His eyes — I don't know, his eyes were unusual, but I can't tell you how — an odd color, or very penetrating, maybe — there was something about his eyes —" His voice trails off.

"And your mother?"

"My mother. Yes." He is staring into the past and it seems as if he sees nothing but haze and smoke there. "My mother. I just don't know what to tell you. She's dead, you realize. A long time, now. Hundreds of years. They both died before Process. It was all such a long time ago, Marilisa."

His discomfort is only too apparent.

"All right," she says. "We don't have to talk about them. But tell me about the clothing, at least. What you wore when you were a young man. Whether people liked darker colors then. Or the food, the favorite dishes. Anything. The shape of ordinary things. How they were different."

Obligingly he tries to bring the distant past to life for her. Images come through, though, however blurry, however indistinct. The strangeness, the alien textures of the long ago. Whoever said the past is another country was right; and Leo is a native of that country. He speaks of obsolete vehicles, styles, ideas, flavors. She works hard at comprehending his words, she eagerly snatches concrete meanings from his clusters of hazy impressions. Somehow the past seems as important to her as the future, or even more so. The past is where Leo has lived so very much of his life. His gigantic past stretches before her like an endless pathless plain. She needs to learn her way across it; she needs to find her bearings, the points of her compass, or she will be lost.

***

It is time for Leo to undergo Process once more. He goes every five years and remains at the clinic for eleven days. She would like to accompany him, but guests are not allowed, not even spouses. The procedures are difficult and delicate. The patients are in a vulnerable state while undergoing treatment.

So off he goes without her to be made young again. Elegant homeostatic techniques of automatic bioenergetic correction will extend his exemption from sagging flesh and spreading waistline and blurry eyesight and graying hair and hardening arteries for another term.

Marilisa has no idea what Process is actually like. She imagines him sitting patiently upright day after day in some bizarre womblike tank, his body entirely covered in a thick mass of some sort of warm, quivering purplish gel, only his head protruding, while the age-poisons are extracted from him by an elaborate array of intricate pipettes and tubes, and the glorious fluids of new youthfulness are pumped into him. But of course she is only imagining. For all she knows, the whole thing is done with a single injection, like the Prep that she undergoes every couple of years to keep her in good trim until she is old enough for Process.

While Leo is away, his son Fyodor pays her an uninvited visit. Fyodor is the child of Miaule, the fifth wife. The marriage to Miaule was Leo's briefest one, only eight years. Marilisa has never asked why. She knows nothing substantial about Leo's previous marriages and prefers to keep it that way.

"Your father's not here," she says immediately, when she finds Fyodor's flitter docked to the harbor of their sky-house.

"I'm not here to visit him. I'm here to see you." He is a compact, blockily built man with a low center of gravity, nothing at all in appearance like his rangy father. His sly sidewise smile is insinuating, possessive, maddening. "We don't know each other as well as we should, Marilisa. You're my stepmother, after all."

"What does that have to do with anything? You have half a dozen stepmothers." Was that true? Could the wives before Miaule be regarded as his stepmothers, strictly speaking?

"You're the newest one. The most mysterious one."

"There's nothing mysterious about me at all. I'm terribly uninteresting."

"Not to my father, apparently." A vicious sparkle enters Fyodor's eyes. "Are you and he going to have children?"

The suggestion startles her. She and Leo have never talked about that; she has never so much as given it a thought.

Angrily she says, "I don't think that that's any of your—"

"He'll want to. He always does."

"Then we will. Twenty years from now, maybe. Or fifty. Whenever it seems appropriate. Right now we're quite content just with each other."
He has found an entirely new level on which to unsettle her, and Marilisa

is infuriated even more with him for that. She turns away from him. "If you'll excuse me, Fyodor, I have things to—"

"Wait." His hand darts out, encircles her wrist, seizes it a little too tightly, then relaxes to a gentler, almost affectionate grip. "You shouldn't be alone at a time like this. Come stay with me for a few days while he's at the clinic."

She glowers at him. "Don't be absurd."

"I'm simply being hospitable, Mother."

"I'm sure he'd be very amused to hear that."

"He's always found what I do highly amusing. Come. Pack your things and let's go. Don't you think you owe yourself a little amusement too?"

Not bothering to conceal her anger and loathing, Marilisa says, "What exactly are you up to, Fyodor? Are you looking for vengeance? Trying to get even with him for something?"

"Vengeance? Vengeance?" Fyodor seems genuinely puzzled. "Why would I want that? I mean, after all, what is he to me?"

"Your father, for one thing."

"Well, yes. I'll grant you that much. But what of it? All of that happened such a long time ago." He laughs. He sounds almost jolly. "You're such an old-fashioned kind of girl, Marilisa!"

***

A couple of hours after she succeeds in getting rid of Fyodor, she has another unexpected and unwanted visitor: Katrin. At least Katrin has the grace to call while she is still over Nevada to say that she would like to drop in. Marilisa is afraid to refuse. She knows that Leo wants some sort of relationship to develop between them. Quite likely he has instigated this very visit. If she turns Katrin away, Leo will find out, and he will be hurt. The last thing Marilisa would want to do is to hurt Leo.

It is impossible for her to get used to Katrin's beauty: that sublime agelessness, which looks so unreal precisely because it is real. She genuinely seems to be only 30, golden-haired and shining in the first dewy bloom of youth. Katrin was Leo's wife for forty years. Estil and Liss, the two children they had together, are almost 200 years old. The immensity of Katrin's history with Leo looms over her like some great monolithic slab.

"I talked to Leo this morning at the clinic," Katrin announces. "He's doing very well."

"You talked to him? But I thought that nobody was allowed—"

"Oh, my dear, I've taken forty turns through that place! I know everybody there only too well. When I call, they put me right through. Leo sends his warmest love."

"Thank you."

"He loves you terribly, you know. Perhaps more than is really good for him. You're the great love of his life, Marilisa."

Marilisa feels a surge of irritation, and allows it to reach the surface. "Oh, Katrin, be serious with me! How could I ever believe something like that?" And what does she mean, Perhaps more than is really good for him?

"You should believe it. You must, in fact. I've had many long talks with him about you. He adores you. He'd do anything for you. It's never been like this for him before. I have absolute proof of that. Not with me, not with Tedesca, not with Thane, not with—"

She recites the whole rest of the list. Syantha, Miaule, Iavilda, while Marilisa ticks each one off in her mind. They could do it together in a kind of choral speaking, the litany of wives' names, but Marilisa remains grimly silent. She is weary of that list of names. She hates the idea that Katrin talks with Leo about her; she hates the idea that Katrin still talks with Leo at all. But she must accept it, apparently. Katrin bustles about the house, admiring this, exclaiming rapturously over that. To celebrate Leo's imminent return she has brought a gift, a tiny artifact, a greenish little bronze sculpture recovered from the sea off Greece, so encrusted by marine growths that it is hard to make out what it represents. A figurine of some sort, an archer, perhaps, holding a bow that has lost its string. Leo is a collector of small antiquities. Tiny fragments of the past are arrayed in elegant cases in every room of their house. Marilisa offers proper appreciation. "Leo will love it," she tells Katrin. "It's perfect for him."

"Yes. I know."

Yes. You do.

Marilisa offers drinks. They nibble at sweet dainty cakes and chat. Two pretty young well-to-do women idling away a pleasant afternoon, but one is 200 years older than the other. For Marilisa it is like playing hostess to Cleopatra, or Helen of Troy.

Inevitably the conversation keeps circling back to Leo.

"The kindest man I've ever known," says Katrin. "If he has a fault, I think, it's that he's too kind. Time and again, he's let himself endure great pain for the sake of avoiding being unkind to some other person. He's utterly incapable of disappointing other people, of letting anyone down in any way, of hurting anyone, regardless of the distress to himself, the damage, the pain. I'm speaking of emotional pain, of course."

Marilisa doesn't want to hear Katrin talk about Leo's faults, or his virtues, or anything else. But she is a dutiful wife; she sees the visit through to its end, and embraces Katrin with something indistinguishable from warmth, and stands by the port watching Katrin's flitter undock and go zipping off into the northern sky. Then, only then, she permits herself to cry. The conversation, following so soon upon Fyodor's visit, has unnerved her. She sifts through it, seeking clues to the hidden truths that everyone but she seems to know. Leo's alleged vast love for her. Leo's unwillingness to injure others, heedless of the costs to himself. He loves you terribly, you know. Perhaps more than is really good for him. And suddenly she has the answer. Leo does love her, yes. Leo always loves his wives. But the marriage was fundamentally a mistake; she is much too young for him, callow, unformed; what he really needs is a woman like Katrin, ancient behind her beauty and infinitely, diabolically wise. The reality, she sees, is that he has grown bored already with his new young wife, he is in fact unhappy in the marriage, but he is far too kindhearted to break the truth to her, and so he inverts it, he talks of a marriage that will endure forever and ever. And confides in Katrin, unburdening himself of his misery to her.

If any of this is true, Marilisa thinks, then I should leave him. I can't ask him to suffer on and on indefinitely with a wife who can't give him what he needs.

She wonders what effect all this crying has had on her face, and activates a mirror in front of her. Her eyes are red and puffy, yes. But what's this? A line, in the corner of her eye? The beginning of age-wrinkles? These doubts and conflicts are suddenly aging her: can it be? And this? A gray hair? She tugs it out and stares at it; but as she holds it at one angle or another it seems just as dark as all the rest. Illusions. An overactive imagination, nothing more. Damn Katrin! Damn her!

***

Even so, she goes for a quick gerontological exam two days before Leo is due to come home from the clinic. It is still six months until the scheduled date of her next Prep injection, but perhaps a few signs of age are beginning to crop up prematurely. Prep will arrest the onset of aging but it won't halt it altogether, the way Process will do; and it is occasionally the case, so she has heard, for people in the immediate pre-Process age group to sprout a few lines on their faces, a few gray hairs, while they are waiting to receive the full treatment that will render them ageless forever.

The doctor is unwilling to accelerate her Prep schedule, but he does confirm that a few little changes are cropping up, and sends her downstairs for some fast cosmetic repairs. "It won't get any worse, will it?" she asks him, and he laughs and assures her that everything can be fixed, everything, all evidence that she is in fact closer now to her 40th birthday than she is to her 30th swiftly and painlessly and confidentially eradicated. But she hates the idea that she is actually aging, ever so slightly, while all about her are people much older than she — her husband, his many former wives, his swarm of children—whose appearance is frozen forever in perfect unassailable youthfulness. If only she could start Process now and be done with it! But she is still too young. Her somatotype report is unanswerable; the treatment will not only be ineffective at this stage in her cellular development, it might actually be injurious. She will have to wait. And wait and wait and wait.

***

Then Leo comes back, refreshed, invigorated, revitalized. Marilisa's been around people fresh from Process many times before—her parents, her grandparents, her great-grandparents—and knows what to expect; but even so she finds it hard to keep up with him. He's exhaustingly cheerful, almost frighteningly ardent, full of high talk and ambitious plans. He shows her the schematics for six new paintings, a decade's worth of work conceived all at once. He proposes that they give a party for three hundred people. He suggests that they take a grand tour for their next anniversary—it will be their fifth—to see the wonders of the world, the Pyramids, the Taj Mahal, the floor of the Mindanao Trench. Or a tour of the moon—the asteroid belt—

"Stop!" she cries, feeling breathless. "You're going too fast!"

"A weekend in Paris, at least," he says.

"Paris. All right. Paris."

They will leave next week. Just before they go, she has lunch with a friend from her single days, Loisa, a pre-Process woman like herself who is married to Ted, who is also pre-Process by just a few years. Loisa has had affairs with a couple of older men, men in their nineties and early hundreds, so perhaps she understands the other side of things as well.

"I don't understand why he married me," Marilisa says. "I must seem like a child to him. He's forgotten more things than I've ever known, and he still knows plenty. What can he possibly see in me?"

"You give him back his youth," Loisa says. "That's what all of them want. They're like vampires, sucking the vitality out of the young."

"That's nonsense and you know it. Process gives him back his youth. He doesn't need a young wife to do that for him. I can provide him with the illusion of being young, maybe, but Process gives him the real thing."

"Process jazzes them up, and then they need confirmation that it's genuine. Which only someone like you can give. They don't want to go to bed with some old hag a thousand years old. She may look gorgeous on the outside but she's corroded within, full of a million memories, loaded with all the hate and poison and vindictiveness that you store up over a life that long, and he can feel it all ticking away inside her and he doesn't want it. Whereas you—all fresh and new—"

"No. No. It isn't like that at all. The older women are the interesting ones. We just seem empty."

"All right. If that's what you want to believe."

"And yet he wants me. He tells me he loves me. He tells one of his old ex-wives that I'm the great love of his life. I don't understand it."

"Well, neither do I," says Loisa, and they leave it at that.

In the bathroom mirror, after lunch, Marilisa finds new lines in her forehead, new wisps of gray at her temples. She has them taken care of before Paris. Paris is no city to look old in.

***

In Paris they visit the Louvre and take the boat ride along the Seine and eat at little Latin Quarter bistros and buy ancient objets d'art in the galleries of St.-Germain-des-Pres. She has never been to Paris before, though of course he has, so often that he has lost count. It is very beautiful but strikes her as somehow fossilized, a museum exhibit rather than a living city, despite all the life she sees going on around her, the animated discussions in the cafes, the bustling restaurants, the crowds in the Metro. Nothing must have changed here in five hundred years. It is all static — frozen — lifeless. As though the entire place has been through Process.

Leo seems to sense her gathering restlessness, and she sees a darkening in his own mood in response. On the third day, in front of one of the rows of ancient bookstalls along the river, he says, "It's me, isn't it?"

"What is?"

"The reason why you're so glum. It can't be the city, so it has to be me. Us. Do you want to leave, Marilisa?"

"Leave Paris? So soon?"

"Leave me, I mean. Perhaps the whole thing has been just a big mistake. I don't want to hold you against your will. If you've started to feel that I'm too old for you, that what you really need is a much younger man, I wouldn't for a moment stand in your way."

Is this how it happens? Is this how his marriages end, with him sadly, lovingly, putting words in your mouth?

"No," she says. "I love you, Leo. Younger men don't interest me. The thought of leaving you has never crossed my mind."

"I'll survive, you know, if you tell me that you want out."

"I don't want out."

"I wish I felt completely sure of that."

She is getting annoyed with him, now. "I wish you did too. You're being silly, Leo. Leaving you is the last thing in the world I want to do. And Paris is the last place in the world where I would want my marriage to break up. I love you. I want to be your wife forever and ever."

"Well, then." He smiles and draws her to him; they embrace; they kiss. She hears a patter of light applause. People are watching them. People have been listening to them and are pleased at the outcome of their negotiations. Paris! Ah, Paris!

***

When they return home, though, he is called away almost immediately to Barcelona to repair one of his paintings, which has developed some technical problem and is undergoing rapid disagreeable metamorphosis. The work will take three or four days; and Marilisa, unwilling to put herself through the fatigue of a second European trip so soon, tells him to go without her. That seems to be some sort of cue for Fyodor to show up, scarcely hours after Leo's departure. How does he know so unerringly when to find her alone?

His pretense is that he has brought an artifact for Leo's collection, an ugly little idol, squat and frog-faced, covered with lumps of brown oxidation. She takes it from him brusquely and sets it on a randomly chosen shelf, and says, mechanically, "Thank you very much. Leo will be pleased. I'll tell him you were here."

"Such charm. Such hospitality."

"I'm being as polite as I can. I didn't invite you."

"Come on, Marilisa. Let's get going."

"Going? Where? What for?"

"We can have plenty of fun together and you damned well know it. Aren't you tired of being such a loyal little wife? Politely sliding through the motions of your preposterous little marriage with your incredibly ancient husband?"

His eyes are shining strangely. His face is flushed.

She says softly, "You're crazy, aren't you?"

"Oh, no, not crazy at all. Not as nice as my father, maybe, but perfectly sane. I see you rusting away here like one of the artifacts in his collection and I want to give you a little excitement in your life before it's too late. A touch of the wild side, do you know what I mean, Marilisa? Places and things he can't show you, that he can't even imagine. He's old. He doesn't know anything about the world we live in today. Jesus, why do I have to spell it out for you? Just drop everything and come away with me. You won't regret it." He leans forward, smiling into her face, utterly sure of himself, plainly confident now that his blunt unceasing campaign of bald invitation will at last be crowned with success.

His audacity astounds her. But she is mystified, too.

"Before it's too late, you said. Too late for what?"

"You know."

"Do I?"

Fyodor seems exasperated by what he takes to be her willful obtuseness. His mouth opens and closes like a shutting trap; a muscle quivers in his cheek; something seems to be cracking within him, some carefully guarded bastion of self-control. He stares at her in a new way — angrily? Contemptuously? — and says, "Before it's too late for anybody to want you. Before you get old and saggy and shriveled. Before you get so withered and ancient-looking that nobody would touch you."

Surely he is out of his mind. Surely. "Nobody has to get that way any more, Fyodor."

"Not if they undergo Process, no. But you — you, Marilisa — " He smiles sadly, shakes his head, turns his hands palms upward in a gesture of hopeless regret.

She peers at him, bewildered. "What can you possibly be talking about?"

For the first time in her memory Fyodor's cool cocky aplomb vanishes. He blinks and gapes. "So you still haven't found out. He actually did keep you in the dark all this time. You're a null, Marilisa! A short-timer! Process won't work for you! The one-in-ten-thousand shot, that's you, the inherent somatic unreceptivity. Christ, what a bastard he is, to hide it from you like this! You've got eighty, maybe ninety years and that's it. Getting older and older, wrinkled and bent and ugly, and then you'll die, the way everybody in the world used to. So you don't have forever and a day to get your fun, like the rest of us. You have to grab it right now, fast, while you're still young. He made us all swear never to say a word to you, that he was going to be the one to tell you the truth in his own good time, but why should I give a damn about that? We aren't children. You have a right to know what you really are. Fuck him, is what I say. Fuck him!" Fyodor's face is crimson now. His eyes are rigid and eerily bright with a weird fervor. "You think I'm making this up? Why would I make up something like this?"

It is like being in an earthquake. The floor seems to heave. She has never been so close to the presence of pure evil before. With the tightest control she can manage she says, "You'd make it up because you're a lying miserable bastard, Fyodor, full of hatred and anger and pus. And if you think — But I don't need to listen to you any more. Just get out of here!"

"It's true. Everybody knows it, the whole family! Ask Katrin! She's the one I heard it from first. Christ, ask Leo! Ask Leo!"

"Out," she says, flicking her hand at him as though he is vermin. "Now. Get the hell out. Out."

***

She promises herself that she will say nothing to Leo about the monstrous fantastic tale that has come pouring out of his horrid son, or even about his clumsy idiotic attempt at seduction—it's all too shameful, too disgusting, too repulsive, and she wants to spare him the knowledge of Fyodor's various perfidies—but of course it all comes blurting from her within an hour after Leo is back from Barcelona. Fyodor is intolerable, she says. Fyodor's behavior has been too bizarre and outrageous to conceal. Fyodor has come here unasked and spewed a torrent of cruel fantastic nonsense in a grotesque attempt at bludgeoning her into bed.

Leo says gravely, "What kind of nonsense?" and she tells him in a quick unpunctuated burst and watches his smooth taut face collapse into weary jowls, watches him seem to age a thousand years in the course of half a minute. He stands there looking at her, aghast; and then she understands that it has to be true, every terrible word of what Fyodor has said. She is one of those, the miserable statistical few of whom everybody has heard, but only at second or third hand. The treatments will not work on her. She will grow old and then she will die. They have tested her and they know the truth, but the whole bunch of them have conspired to keep it from her, the doctors at the clinic, Leo's sons and daughters and wives, her own family, everyone. All of it Leo's doing. Using his influence all over the place, his enormous accrued power, to shelter her in her ignorance.

"You knew from the start?" she asks, finally. "All along?"

"Almost. I knew very early. The clinic called me and told me, not long after we got engaged."

"My God. Why did you marry me, then?"

"Because I loved you."

"Because you loved me."

"Yes. Yes. Yes. Yes."

"I wish I knew what that meant," she says. "If you loved me, how could you hide a thing like this from me? How could you let me build my life around a lie?"

Leo says, after a moment, "I wanted you to have the good years, untainted by what would come later. There was time for you to discover the truth later. But for now—while you were still young—the clothes, the jewelry, the traveling, all the joy of being beautiful and young—why ruin it for you? Why darken it with the knowledge of what would be coming?"

"So you made everybody go along with the lie? The people at the clinic. Even my own family, for God's sake!"

"Yes."

"And all the Prep treatments I've been taking—just a stupid pointless charade, right? Accomplishing nothing. Leading nowhere."

"Yes. Yes."

She begins to tremble. She understands the true depths of his compassion now, and she is appalled. He has married her out of charity. No man her own age would have wanted her, because the developing signs of bodily deterioration in the years just ahead would surely horrify him; but Leo is beyond all that, he is willing to overlook her unfortunate little somatic defect and give her a few decades of happiness before she has to die. And then he will proceed with the rest of his life, the hundreds or thousands of years yet to come, serene in the knowledge of having allowed the tragically doomed Marilisa the happy illusion of having been a member of the ageless elite for a little while. It is stunning. It is horrifying. There is no way that she can bear it.

"Marilisa —"

He reaches for her, but she turns away. Runs. Flees.

***

It was three years before he found her. She was living in London, then, a little flat in the Bayswater Road, and in just those three years her face had changed so much, the little erosions of the transition between youth and middle age, that it was impossible for him entirely to conceal his instant reaction. He, of course, had not changed in the slightest way. He stood in the doorway, practically filling it, trying to plaster some sort of facade over his all too visible dismay, trying to show her the familiar Leo smile, trying to make the old Leo-like warmth glow in his eyes. Then after a moment he extended his arms toward her. She stayed where she was.

"You shouldn't have tracked me down," she says.

"I love you," he tells her. "Come home with me."

"It wouldn't be right. It wouldn't be fair to you. My getting old, and you always so young."

"To hell with that. I want you back, Marilisa. I love you and I always will."

"You love me?" she says. "Even though —?"

"Even though. For better, for worse."

She knows the rest of the passage —for richer for poorer, in sickness and in health—and where it goes from there. But there is nothing more she can say. She wants to smile gently and thank him for all his kindness and close the door, but instead she stands there and stands there and stands there, neither inviting him in nor shutting him out, with a roaring sound in her ears as all the million years of mortal history rise up around her like mountains.

BEAUTY IN THE NIGHT (1997)

INTRODUCTION

The Alien Years, which I look upon as one of the most successful novels I wrote in my post-"retirement" period, had a curious composite history. Between 1983 and 1986 I had written a number of stories in which the Earth is invaded by virtually omnipotent alien beings. The first of these was "Against Babylon," which I wrote late in 1983 for *Omni* (which took two years to publish it). Then came 1985's "Hannibal's Elephants," also for *Omni* (published in 1988), and 1986's "The Pardoner's Tale," written for *Playboy* and published in 1987. These stories were in no way intended as a series, and in fact were contradictory and incompatible in most details beyond the basic concept of an invaded Earth. But over time it dawned on me that the seeds of a major novel lay in these relatively lighthearted tales of interplanetary conquest.

In 1995 I offered the book to Harper Collins, my publisher at that time, and wrote it in the winter of 1996-97. "Against Babylon," virtually in its entirety, became the opening chapter. A small piece of "Hannibal's Elephants" was incorporated into one of the early sequences. Then I used nearly all of "The Pardoner's Tale" in the latter part of the book. In each case I altered the names of characters to make them fit the overall story I had devised for the novel.

It was all done so smoothly that very few people—not even my own bibliographer—noticed that I had tucked two and a half decade-old short stories into the lengthy new novel. And to make life even more difficult for bibliographers, I then proceeded to carve three *new* stories out of the text of the book and sell them as individual items to the glossy, high-paying new science-fiction magazine *Science Fiction Age,* which Scott Edelman was editing.

They needed a little bending and polishing around the edges to turn into properly rounded short stories, of course. But the process of extraction and revision turned out to be a success. Especially the first of the three, "Beauty in the Night." Scott used it in his September, 1997 issue, and it was chosen the following year not only for Gardner Dozois's annual *Year's Best Science Fiction* anthology but also for David Hartwell's similar collection, *Year's Best SF.* It has gone on to various other sorts of publication, both in the United States and abroad, since then.

The other two—"On the Inside" (*Science Fiction Age*, November, 1997) and the novella "The Colonel in Autumn" (*Science Fiction Age*, March, 1998)—have had successful independent afterlives as well. But "Beauty in the Night" strikes me as the strongest of the extracted segments of *The Alien Years*, and a fitting representative of my work in the second half of the 1990s.

ONE:
NINE YEARS FROM NOW

He was a Christmas child, was Khalid — Khalid the Entity-Killer, the first to raise his hand against the alien invaders who had conquered Earth in a single day, sweeping aside all resistance as though we were no more than ants to them. Khalid Haleem Burke, that was his name, English on his father's side, Pakistani on his mother's, born on Christmas Day amidst his mother's pain and shame and his family's grief. Christmas child though he was, nevertheless he was not going to be the new Savior of mankind, however neat a coincidence that might have been. But he would live, though his mother had not, and in the fullness of time he would do his little part, strike his little blow, against the awesome beings who had with such contemptuous ease taken possession of the world into which he had been born.

***

To be born at Christmastime can be an awkward thing for mother and child, who even at the best of times must contend with the risks inherent in the general overcrowding and understaffing of hospitals at that time of year. But prevailing hospital conditions were not an issue for the mother of the child of uncertain parentage and dim prospects who was about to come into the world in unhappy and disagreeable circumstances in an unheated upstairs storeroom of a modest Pakistani restaurant grandly named Khan's Mogul Palace in Salisbury, England, very early in the morning of this third Christmas since the advent of the conquering Entities from the stars.

Salisbury is a pleasant little city that lies to the south and west of London and is the principal town of the county of Wiltshire. It is noted particularly for its relatively unspoiled medieval charm, for its graceful and imposing thirteenth-century cathedral, and for the presence, eight miles away, of the celebrated prehistoric megalithic monument known as Stonehenge.

Which, in the darkness before the dawn of that Christmas Day, was undergoing one of the most remarkable events in its long history; and, despite the earliness (or lateness) of the hour, a goodly number of Salisbury's inhabitants had turned out to witness the spectacular goings-on.

But not Haleem Khan, the owner of Khan's Mogul Palace, nor his wife Aissha, both of them asleep in their beds. Neither of them had any interest in the pagan monument that was Stonehenge, let alone the strange thing that was happening to it now. And certainly not Haleem's daughter Yasmeena Khan, who was seventeen years old and cold and frightened, and who was lying half naked on the bare floor of the upstairs storeroom of her father's restaurant, hidden between a huge sack of raw lentils and an even larger sack of flour, writhing in terrible pain as shame and illicit motherhood came sweeping down on her like the avenging sword of angry Allah.

She had sinned. She knew that. Her father, her plump, reticent, overworked, mortally weary, and in fact already dying father, had several times in the past year warned her of sin and its consequences, speaking with as much force as she had ever seen him muster; and yet she had chosen to take the risk. Just three times, three different boys, only one time each, all three of them English and white.

Andy. Eddie. Richie.

Names that blazed like bonfires in the neural pathways of her soul.

Her mother—no, not really her mother; her true mother had died when Yasmeena was three; this was Aissha, her father's second wife, the robust and stolid woman who had raised her, had held the family and the restaurant together all these years—had given her warnings too, but they had been couched in entirely different terms. "You are a woman now, Yasmeena, and a woman is permitted to allow herself some pleasure in life," Aissha had told her. "But you must be careful." Not a word about sin, just taking care not to get into trouble.

Well, Yasmeena had been careful, or thought she had, but evidently not careful enough. Therefore she had failed Aissha. And failed her sad quiet father too, because she had certainly sinned despite all his warnings to remain virtuous, and Allah now would punish her for that. Was punishing her already. Punishing her terribly.

She had been very late discovering she was pregnant. She had not expected to be. Yasmeena wanted to believe that she was still too young for bearing babies, because her breasts were so small and her hips were so narrow, almost like a boy's. And each of those three times when she had done It with a boy—impulsively, furtively, half reluctantly, once in a musty cellar and once in a ruined omnibus and once right here in this very storeroom—she had taken precautions afterward, diligently swallowing the pills she had secretly bought from the smirking Hindu woman at the shop in Winchester, two tiny green pills in the morning and the big yellow one at night, five days in a row.

The pills were so nauseating that they had to work. But they hadn't. She should never have trusted pills provided by a Hindu, Yasmeena would tell herself a thousand times over; but by then it was too late.

The first sign had come only about four months before. Her breasts suddenly began to fill out. That had pleased her, at first. She had always been so scrawny; but now it seemed that her body was developing at last. Boys liked breasts. You could see their eyes quickly flicking down to check out your chest, though they seemed to think you didn't notice it when they did. All three of her lovers had put their hands into her blouse to feel hers, such as they were; and at least one — Eddie, the second — had actually been disappointed at what he found there. He had said so, just like that: "Is that all?"

But now her breasts were growing fuller and heavier every week, and they started to ache a little, and the dark nipples began to stand out oddly from the smooth little circles in which they were set. So Yasmeena began to feel fear; and when her bleeding did not come on time, she feared even more. But her bleeding had never come on time. Once last year it had been almost a whole month late, and she an absolute pure virgin then.

Still, there were the breasts; and then her hips seemed to be getting wider. Yasmeena said nothing, went about her business, chatted pleasantly with the customers, who liked her because she was slender and pretty and polite, and pretended all was well. Again and again at night her hand would slide down her flat boyish belly, anxiously searching for hidden life lurking beneath the taut skin. She felt nothing.

But something was there, all right, and by early October it was making the faintest of bulges, only a tiny knot pushing upward below her navel, but a little bigger every day. Yasmeena began wearing her blouses untucked, to hide the new fullness of her breasts and the burgeoning rondure of her belly. She opened the seams of her trousers and punched two new holes in her belt. It became harder for her to do her work, to carry the heavy trays of food all evening long and to put in the hours afterward washing the dishes, but she forced herself to be strong. There was no one else to do the job. Her father took the orders and Aissha did the cooking and Yasmeena served the meals and cleaned up after the restaurant closed. Her brother Khalid was gone, killed defending Aissha from a mob of white men during the riots that had broken out after the Entities came, and her sister Leila was too small, only five, no use in the restaurant.

No one at home commented on the new way Yasmeena was dressing. Perhaps they thought it was the current fashion. Life was very strange, in these early years of the Conquest.

Her father scarcely glanced at anyone these days; preoccupied with his failing restaurant and his failing health, he went about bowed over, coughing all the time, murmuring prayers endlessly under his breath. He was forty years old and looked sixty. Khan's Mogul Palace was nearly empty, night after night, even on the weekends. People did not travel any more, now that the Entities were here. No rich foreigners came from distant parts of the world to spend the night at Salisbury before going on to visit Stonehenge. The inns and hotels closed; so did most of the restaurants, though a few, like Khan's, struggled on because their proprietors had no other way of earning a living. But the last thing on Haleem Khan's mind was his daughter's changing figure.

As for her stepmother, Yasmeena imagined that she saw her giving her sidewise looks now and again, and worried over that. But Aissha said nothing. So there was probably no suspicion. Aissha was not the sort to keep silent, if she suspected something.

The Christmas season drew near. Now Yasmeena's swollen legs were as heavy as dead logs and her breasts were hard as boulders and she felt sick all the time. It was not going to be long, now. She could no longer hide from the truth. But she had no plan. If her brother Khalid were here, he would know what to do. Khalid was gone, though. She would simply have to let things happen and trust that Allah, when He was through punishing her, would forgive her and be merciful.

Christmas Eve, there were four tables of customers. That was a surprise, to be so busy on a night when most English people had dinner at home. Midway through the evening Yasmeena thought she would fall down in the middle of the room and send her tray, laden with chicken biriani and mutton vindaloo and boti kebabs and schooners of lager, spewing across the floor. She steadied herself then; but an hour later she did fall; or, rather, sagged to her knees, in the hallway between the kitchen and the garbage bin where no one could see her. She crouched there, dizzy, sweating, gasping, nauseated, feeling her bowels quaking and strange spasms running down the front of her body and into her thighs; and after a time she rose and continued on with her tray toward the bin.

It will be this very night, she thought.

And for the thousandth time that week she ran through the little calculation in her mind: December 24 minus nine months is March 24, Therefore it is Richie Burke, the father. At least he was the one who gave me pleasure also.

Andy, he had been the first. Yasmeena couldn't remember his last name. Pale and freckled and very thin, with a beguiling smile, and on a humid summer night just after her sixteenth birthday when the restaurant was closed because her father was in hospital for a few days with the beginning of his trouble, Andy invited her dancing and treated her to a couple of

pints of brown ale and then, late in the evening, told her of a special party at
a friend's house that he was invited to, only there turned out to be no party,
just a shabby stale-smelling cellar room and an old spavined couch, and
Andy's busy hands roaming the front of her blouse and then going between
her legs and her trousers coming off and then, quick, quick!, the long hard
narrow reddened thing emerging from him and sliding into her, done and
done and done in just a couple of moments, a gasp from him and a shudder
and his head buried against her cheek and that was that, all over and done
with. She had thought it was supposed to hurt, the first time, but she had felt
almost nothing at all, neither pain nor anything that might have been delight.
The next time Yasmeena saw him in the street Andy grinned and turned
crimson and winked at her, but said nothing to her, and they had never
exchanged a word since.

Then Eddie Glossop, in the autumn, the one who had found her breasts
insufficient and told her so. Big broad-shouldered Eddie, who worked for
the meat merchant and who had an air of great worldliness about him. He
was old, almost twenty-five. Yasmeena went with him because she knew
there was supposed to be pleasure in it and she had not had it from Andy.
But there was none from Eddie either, just a lot of huffing and puffing as
he lay sprawled on top of her in the aisle of that burned-out omnibus by
the side of the road that went toward Shaftesbury. He was much bigger
down there than Andy, and it hurt when he went in, and she was glad that
this had not been her first time. But she wished she had not done it at all.

And then Richie Burke, in this very storeroom on an oddly warm night
in March, with everyone asleep in the family apartments downstairs at
the back of the restaurant. She tiptoeing up the stairs, and Richie clambering
up the drainpipe and through the window, tall, lithe, graceful Richie who
played the guitar so well and sang and told everyone that some day he
was going to be a general in the war against the Entities and wipe them
from the face of the Earth. A wonderful lover, Richie. Yasmeena kept her
blouse on because Eddie had made her uneasy about her breasts. Richie
caressed her and stroked her for what seemed like hours, though she was
terrified that they would be discovered and wanted him to get on with it;
and when he entered her, it was like an oiled shaft of smooth metal gliding
into her, moving so easily, easily, easily, one gentle thrust after another, on
and on and on until marvelous palpitations began to happen inside her
and then she erupted with pleasure, moaning so loud that Richie had to
put his hand over her mouth to keep her from waking everyone up.

That was the time the baby had been made. There could be no doubt
of that. All the next day she dreamed of marrying Richie and spending the
rest of the nights of her life in his arms. But at the end of that week Richie
disappeared from Salisbury — some said he had gone off to join a secret

underground army that was going to launch guerrilla warfare against the
Entities — and no one had heard from him again.

Andy. Eddie. Richie.

***

And here she was on the floor of the storeroom again, with her trousers
off and the shiny swollen hump of her belly sending messages of agony
and shame through her body. Her only covering was a threadbare blanket
that reeked of spilled cooking oil. Her water had burst about midnight.
That was when she had crept up the stairs to wait in terror for the great
disaster of her life to finish happening. The contractions were coming closer
and closer together, like little earthquakes within her. Now the time had
to be two, three, maybe four in the morning. How long would it be?
Another hour? Six? Twelve?

Relent and call Aissha to help her?

No. No. She didn't dare.

Earlier in the night voices had drifted up from the streets to her. The
sound of footsteps. That was strange, shouting and running in the street,
this late. The Christmas revelry didn't usually go on through the night
like this. It was hard to understand what they were saying; but then out of
the confusion there came, with sudden clarity:

"The aliens! They're pulling down Stonehenge, taking it apart!"

"Get your wagon, Charlie, we'll go and see!"

Pulling down Stonehenge. Strange. Strange. Why would they do that?
Yasmeena wondered. But the pain was becoming too great for her to be
able to give much thought to Stonehenge just now, or to the Entities who
had somehow overthrown the invincible white men in the twinkling of an
eye and now ruled the world, or to anything else except what was
happening within her, the flames dancing through her brain, the ripplings
of her belly, the implacable downward movement of — of —

Something.

"Praise be to Allah, Lord of the Universe, the Compassionate, the
Merciful," she murmured timidly. "There is no god but Allah, and
Mohammed is His prophet."

And again: "Praise be to Allah, Lord of the Universe."

And again.

And again.

The pain was terrible. She was splitting wide open.

"Abraham, Isaac, Ishmael!" That something had begun to move in a
spiral through her now, like a corkscrew driving a hot track in her flesh.
"Mohammed! Mohammed! Mohammed! There is no god but Allah!" The
words burst from her with no timidity at all, now. Let Mohammed and

Allah save her, if they really existed. What good were they, if they would not save her, she so innocent and ignorant, her life barely begun? And then, as a spear of fire gutted her and her pelvic bones seemed to crack apart, she let loose a torrent of other names, Moses, Solomon, Jesus, Mary, and even the forbidden Hindu names, Shiva, Krishna, Shakti, Kali, anyone at all who would help her through this, anyone, anyone, anyone, anyone—

She screamed three times, short, sharp, piercing screams.

She felt a terrible inner wrenching and the baby came spurting out of her with astonishing swiftness. A gushing Ganges of blood followed it, a red river that spilled out over her thighs and would not stop flowing.

Yasmeena knew at once that she was going to die.

Something wrong had happened. Everything would come out of her insides and she would die. That was absolutely clear to her. Already, just moments after the birth, an eerie new calmness was enfolding her. She had no energy left now for further screaming, or even to look after the baby. It was somewhere down between her spread thighs, that was all she knew. She lay back, drowning in a rising pool of blood and sweat. She raised her arms toward the ceiling and brought them down again to clutch her throbbing breasts, stiff now with milk. She called now upon no more holy names. She could hardly remember her own.

She sobbed quietly. She trembled. She tried not to move, because that would surely make the bleeding even worse.

An hour went by, or a week, or a year.

Then an anguished voice high above her in the dark:

"What? Yasmeena? Oh, my god, my god, my god! Your father will perish!"

Aissha, it was. Bending to her, engulfing her. The strong arm raising her head, lifting it against the warm motherly bosom, holding her tight.

"Can you hear me, Yasmeena? Oh, Yasmeena! My god, my god!" And then an ululation of grief rising from her stepmother's throat like some hot volcanic geyser bursting from the ground. "Yasmeena! Yasmeena!"

"The baby?" Yasmeena said, in the tiniest of voices.

"Yes! Here! Here! Can you see?"

Yasmeena saw nothing but a red haze.

"A boy?" she asked, very faintly.

"A boy, yes."

In the blur of her dimming vision she thought she saw something small and pinkish-brown, smeared with scarlet, resting in her stepmother's hands. Thought she could hear him crying, even.

"Do you want to hold him?"

"No. No." Yasmeena understood clearly that she was going. The last of her strength had left her. She was moored now to the world by a mere thread.

"He is strong and beautiful," said Aissha. "A splendid boy."

"Then I am very happy." Yasmeena fought for one last fragment of energy. "His name—is—Khalid. Khalid Haleem Burke."

"Burke?"

"Yes. Khalid Haleem Burke."

"Is that the father's name, Yasmeena? Burke?"

"Burke. Richie Burke." With her final sliver of strength she spelled the name.

"Tell me where he lives, this Richie Burke. I will get him. This is shameful, giving birth by yourself, alone in the dark, in this awful room! Why did you never say anything? Why did you hide it from me? I would have helped. I would—"

***

But Yasmeena Khan was already dead. The first shaft of morning light now came through the grimy window of the upstairs storeroom. Christmas Day had begun.

Eight miles away, at Stonehenge, the Entities had finished their night's work. Three of the towering alien creatures had supervised while a human work crew, using handheld pistol-like devices that emitted a bright violet glow, had uprooted every single one of the ancient stone slabs of the celebrated megalithic monument on windswept Salisbury Plain as though they were so many jackstraws. And had rearranged them so that what had been the outer circle of immense sandstone blocks now had become two parallel rows running from north to south; the lesser inner ring of blue slabs had been moved about to form an equilateral triangle; and the sixteen-foot-long block of sandstone at the center of the formation that people called the Altar Stone had been raised to an upright position at the center.

A crowd of perhaps two thousand people from the adjacent towns had watched through the night from a judicious distance as this inexplicable project was being carried out. Some were infuriated; some were saddened; some were indifferent; some were fascinated. Many had theories about what was going on, and one theory was as good as another, no better, no worse.

TWO:
SIXTEEN YEARS FROM NOW

You could still see the ghostly lettering over the front door of the former restaurant, if you knew what to look for, the pale greenish outlines of the words that once had been painted there in bright gold: KHAN'S MOGUL PALACE. The old swinging sign that had dangled above the door was still lying out back, too, in a clutter of cracked basins and discarded stewpots and broken crockery.

But the restaurant itself was gone, long gone, a victim of the Great Plague that the Entities had casually loosed upon the world as a warning to its conquered people, after an attempt had been made at an attack on an Entity encampment. Half the population of Earth had died so that the Entities could teach the other half not to harbor further rebellious thoughts. Poor sad Haleem Khan himself was gone too, the ever-weary little brown-skinned man who in ten years had somehow saved five thousand pounds from his salary as a dishwasher at the Lion and Unicorn Hotel and had used that, back when England had a queen and Elizabeth was her name, as the seed money for the unpretentious little restaurant that was going to rescue him and his family from utter hopeless poverty. Four days after the Plague had hit Salisbury, Haleem was dead. But if the Plague hadn't killed him, the tuberculosis that he was already harboring probably would have done the job soon enough. Or else simply the shock and disgrace and grief of his daughter Yasmeena's ghastly death in childbirth two weeks earlier, at Christmastime, in an upstairs room of the restaurant, while bringing into the world the bastard child of the long-legged English boy, Richie Burke, the future traitor, the future quisling.

Haleem's other daughter, the little girl Leila, had died in the Plague also, three months after her father and two days before what would have been her sixth birthday. As for Yasmeena's older brother, Khalid, he was already two years gone by then. That was during the time that now was known as the Troubles. A gang of long-haired yobs had set forth late one Saturday afternoon in fine English wrath, determined to vent their resentment over the conquest of the Earth by doing a lively spot of Paki-bashing in the town streets, and they had encountered Khalid escorting Aissha home from the market. They had made remarks; he had replied hotly; and they beat him to death.

Which left, of all the family, only Aissha, Haleem's hardy and tireless second wife. She came down with the Plague, too, but she was one of the lucky ones, one of those who managed to fend the affliction off and survive — for whatever that was worth — into the new and transformed and diminished world. But she could hardly run the restaurant alone, and in any case, with three quarters of the population of Salisbury dead in the Plague, there was no longer much need for a Pakistani restaurant there.

Aissha found other things to do. She went on living in a couple of rooms of the now gradually decaying building that had housed the restaurant, and supported herself, in this era when national currencies had ceased to mean much and strange new sorts of money circulated in the land, by a variety of improvised means. She did housecleaning and laundry for those people who still had need of such services. She cooked meals for elderly folks too feeble to cook for themselves. Now and then, when her number came up in the labor lottery, she put in time at a factory that the Entities had established just outside town, weaving little strands of colored wire together to make incomprehensibly complex mechanisms whose nature and purpose were never disclosed to her.

And when there was no such work of any of those kinds available, Aissha would make herself available to the lorry-drivers who passed through Salisbury, spreading her powerful muscular thighs in return for meal certificates or corporate scrip or barter units or whichever other of the new versions of money they would pay her in. That was not something she would have chosen to do, if she had had her choices. But she would not have chosen to have the invasion of the Entities, for that matter, nor her husband's early death and Leila's and Khalid's, nor Yasmeena's miserable lonely ordeal in the upstairs room, but she had not been consulted about any of those things, either. Aissha needed to eat in order to survive; and so she sold herself, when she had to, to the lorry-drivers, and that was that.

As for why survival mattered, why she bothered at all to care about surviving in a world that had lost all meaning and just about all hope, it was in part because survival for the sake of survival was in her genes, and — mostly — because she wasn't alone in the world. Out of the wreckage of her family she had been left with a child to look after — her grandchild, her dead stepdaughter's baby, Khalid Haleem Burke, the child of shame. Khalid Haleem Burke had survived the Plague too. It was one of the ugly little ironies of the epidemic that the Entities had released upon the world that children who were less than six months old generally did not contract it. Which created a huge population of healthy but parentless babes.

He was healthy, all right, was Khalid Haleem Burke. Through every deprivation of those dreary years, the food shortages and the fuel shortages and the little outbreaks of diseases that once had been thought to be nearly extinct, he grew taller and straighter and stronger all the time. He had his mother's wiry strength and his father's long legs and dancer's grace. And he was lovely to behold. His skin was tawny golden-brown, his eyes were a glittering blue-green, and his hair, glossy and thick and curly, was a wonderful bronze color, a magnificent Eurasian hue. Amidst all the sadness and loss of Aissha's life, he was the one glorious beacon that lit the darkness for her.

There were no real schools, not any more. Aissha taught little Khalid herself, as best she could. She hadn't had much schooling herself, but she could read and write, and showed him how, and begged or borrowed books for him wherever she might. She found a woman who understood arithmetic, and scrubbed her floors for her in return for Khalid's lessons. There was an old man at the south end of town who had the Koran by heart, and Aissha, though she was not a strongly religious woman herself, sent Khalid to him once a week for instruction in Islam. The boy was, after all, half Moslem. Aissha felt no responsibility for the Christian part of him, but she did not want to let him go into the world unaware that there was — somewhere, somewhere! — a god known as Allah, a god of justice and compassion and mercy, to whom obedience was owed, and that he would, like all people, ultimately come to stand before that god upon the Day of Judgment.

***

"And the Entities?" Khalid asked her. He was six, then. "Will they be judged by Allah too?"

"The Entities are not people. They are jinn."

"Did Allah make them?"

"Allah made all things in heaven and on Earth. He made us out of potter's clay and the jinn out of smokeless fire."

"But the Entities have brought evil upon us. Why would Allah make evil things, if He is a merciful god?"

"The Entities," Aissha said uncomfortably, aware that wiser heads than hers had grappled in vain with that question, "do evil. But they are not evil themselves. They are merely the instruments of Allah."

"Who has sent them to us to do evil," said Khalid. "What kind of god is that, who sends evil among His own people, Aissha?"

She was getting beyond her depth in this conversation, but she was patient with him. "No one understands Allah's ways, Khalid. He is the One God and we are nothing before him. If He had reason to send the Entities to us, they were good reasons, and we have no right to question them." And also to send sickness, she thought, and hunger, and death, and the English boys who killed your uncle Khalid in the street, and even the English boy who put you into your mother's belly and then ran away. Allah sent all of those into the world, too. But then she reminded herself that if Richie Burke had not crept secretly into this house to sleep with Yasmeena, this beautiful child would not be standing here before her at this moment. And so good sometimes could come forth from evil. Who were we to demand reasons from Allah? Perhaps even the Entities had been sent here, ultimately, for our own good.

Perhaps.

***

Of Khalid's father, there was no news all this while. He was supposed to have run off to join the army that was fighting the Entities; but Aissha had never heard that there was any such army, anywhere in the world.

Then, not long after Khalid's seventh birthday, when he returned in mid-afternoon from his Thursday Koran lesson at the house of old Iskander Mustafa Ali, he found an unknown white man sitting in the room with his grandmother, a man with a great untidy mass of light-colored curling hair and a lean, angular, almost fleshless face with two cold, harsh blue-green eyes looking out from it as though out of a mask. His skin was so white that Khalid wondered whether he had any blood in his body. It was almost like chalk. The strange white man was sitting in his grandmother's own armchair, and his grandmother was looking very edgy and strange, a way Khalid had never seen her look before, with glistening beads of sweat along her forehead and her lips clamped together in a tight thin line.

The white man said, leaning back in the chair and crossing his legs, which were the longest legs Khalid had ever seen, "Do you know who I am, boy?"

"How would he know?" his grandmother said.

The white man looked toward Aissha and said, "Let me do this, if you don't mind." And then, to Khalid: "Come over here, boy. Stand in front of me. Well, now, aren't we the little beauty? What's your name, boy?"

"Khalid."

"Khalid. Who named you that?"

"My mother. She's dead now. It was my uncle's name. He's dead too."

"Devil of a lot of people are dead who used to be alive, all right. Well, Khalid, my name is Richie."

"Richie," Khalid said, in a very small voice, because he had already begun to understand this conversation.

"Richie, yes. Have you ever heard of a person named Richie? Richie Burke."

"My—father." In an even smaller voice.

"Right you are! The grand prize for that lad! Not only handsome but smart, too! Well, what would one expect, eh?—Here I be, boy, your long-lost father! Come here and give your long-lost father a kiss."

Khalid glanced uncertainly toward Aissha. Her face was still shiny with sweat, and very pale. She looked sick. After a moment she nodded, a tiny nod.

He took half a step forward and the man who was his father caught him by the wrist and gathered him roughly in, pulling him inward and pressing him up against him, not for an actual kiss but for what was only a rubbing of cheeks. The grinding contact with that hard, stubbly cheek was painful for Khalid.

"There, boy. I've come back, do you see? I've been away seven worm-eaten miserable years, but now I'm back, and I'm going to live with you and be your father. You can call me 'Dad.'"

Khalid stared, stunned.

"Go on. Do it. Say, 'I'm so very glad that you've come back, Dad.'"

"Dad," Khalid said uneasily.

"The rest of it too, if you please."

"I'm so very glad—" He halted.

"That I've come back."

"That you've come back—"

"Dad."

Khalid hesitated. "Dad," he said.

"There's a good boy! It'll come easier to you after a while. Tell me, did you ever think about me while you were growing up, boy?"

Khalid glanced toward Aissha again. She nodded surreptitiously.

Huskily he said, "Now and then, yes."

"Only now and then? That's all?"

"Well, hardly anybody has a father. But sometimes I met someone who did, and then I thought of you. I wondered where you were. Aissha said you were off fighting the Entities. Is that where you were, Dad? Did you fight them? Did you kill any of them?"

"Don't ask stupid questions. Tell me, boy: do you go by the name of Burke or Khan?"

"Burke. Khalid Haleem Burke."

"Call me 'sir' when you're not calling me 'Dad.' Say, 'Khalid Haleem Burke, sir.'"

"Khalid Haleem Burke, sir. Dad."

"One or the other. Not both." Richie Burke rose from the chair, unfolding himself as though in sections, up and up and up. He was enormously tall, very thin. His slenderness accentuated his great height. Khalid, though tall for his age, felt dwarfed beside him. The thought came to him that this man was not his father at all, not even a man, but some sort of demon, rather, a jinni, a jinni that had been let out of its bottle, as in the story that Iskander Mustafa Ali had told him. He kept that thought to himself. "Good," Richie Burke said. "Khalid Haleem Burke. I like that. Son should have his father's name. But not the Khalid Haleem part. From now on your name is—ah—Kendall. Ken for short."

"Khalid was my—"

"—uncle's name, yes. Well, your uncle is dead. Practically everybody is dead, Kenny. Kendall Burke, good English name. Kendall Hamilton Burke, same initials, even, only English. Is that all right, boy? What a pretty one you are, Kenny! I'll teach you a thing or two, I will. I'll make a man out of you."

***

Here I be, boy, your long-lost father!

Khalid had never known what it meant to have a father, nor ever given the idea much examination. He had never known hatred before, either, because Aissha was a fundamentally calm, stable, accepting person, too steady in her soul to waste time or valuable energy hating anything, and Khalid had taken after her in that. But Richie Burke, who taught Khalid what it meant to have a father, made him aware of what it was like to hate, also.

Richie moved into the bedroom that had been Aissha's, sending Aissha off to sleep in what had once had been Yasmeena's room. It had long since gone to rack and ruin, but they cleaned it up, some, chasing the spiders out and taping oilcloth over the missing windowpanes and nailing down a couple of floorboards that had popped up out of their proper places. She carried her clothes-cabinet in there by herself, and set up on it the framed photographs of her dead family that she had kept in her former bedroom, and draped two of her old saris that she never wore any more over the bleak places on the wall where the paint had flaked away.

It was stranger than strange, having Richie living with them. It was a total upheaval, a dismaying invasion by an alien life-form, in some ways as shocking in its impact as the arrival of the Entities had been.

He was gone most of the day. He worked in the nearby town of Winchester, driving back and forth in a small brown pre-Conquest automobile. Winchester was a place where Khalid had never been, though his mother had, to purchase the pills that were meant to abort him. Khalid had never been far from Salisbury, not even to Stonehenge, which now was a center of Entity activity anyway, and not a tourist sight. Few people in Salisbury traveled anywhere these days. Not many had automobiles, because of the difficulty of obtaining petrol, but Richie never seemed to have any problem about that.

Sometimes Khalid wondered what sort of work his father did in Winchester; but he asked about it only once. The words were barely out of his mouth when his father's long arm came snaking around and struck him across the face, splitting his lower lip and sending a dribble of blood down his chin.

Khalid staggered back, astounded. No one had ever hit him before. It had not occurred to him that anyone would.

"You must never ask that again!" his father said, looming mountain-high above him. His cold eyes were even colder, now, in his fury. "What I do in Winchester is no business of yours, nor anyone else's, do you hear me, boy? It is my own private affair. My own — private — affair."

Khalid rubbed his cut lip and peered at his father in bewilderment. The pain of the slap had not been so great; but the surprise of it, the shock—that was still reverberating through his consciousness. And went on reverberating for a long while thereafter.

He never asked about his father's work again, no. But he was hit again, more than once, indeed with fair regularity. Hitting was Richie's way of expressing irritation. And it was difficult to predict what sort of thing might irritate him. Any sort of intrusion on his father's privacy, though, seemed to do it. Once, while talking with his father in his bedroom, telling him about a bloody fight between two boys that he had witnessed in town, Khalid unthinkingly put his hand on the guitar that Richie always kept leaning against his wall beside his bed, giving it only a single strum, something that he had occasionally wanted to do for months; and instantly, hardly before the twanging note had died away, Richie unleashed his arm and knocked Khalid back against the wall. "You keep your filthy fingers off that instrument, boy!" Richie said; and after that Khalid did. Another time Richie struck him for leafing through a book he had left on the kitchen table, that had pictures of naked women in it; and another time, it was for staring too long at Richie as he stood before the mirror in the morning, shaving. So Khalid learned to keep his distance from his father; but still he found himself getting slapped for this reason and that, and sometimes for no reason at all. The blows were rarely as hard as the first one had been, and never ever created in him that same sense of shock. But they were blows, all the same. He stored them all up in some secret receptacle of his soul.

Occasionally Richie hit Aissha, too—when dinner was late, or when she put mutton curry on the table too often, or when it seemed to him that she had contradicted him about something. That was more of a shock to Khalid than getting slapped himself, that anyone should dare to lift his hand to Aissha.

The first time it happened, which occurred while they were eating dinner, a big carving knife was lying on the table near Khalid, and he might well have reached for it had Aissha not, in the midst of her own fury and humiliation and pain, sent Khalid a message with her furious blazing eyes that he absolutely was not to do any such thing. And so he controlled himself, then and any time afterward when Richie hit her. It was a skill that Khalid had, controlling himself—one that in some circuitous way he must have inherited from the ever-patient, all-enduring grandparents whom he had never known and the long line of oppressed Asian peasants from whom they descended. Living with Richie in the house gave Khalid daily opportunity to develop that skill to a fine art.

Richie did not seem to have many friends, at least not friends who visited the house. Khalid knew of only three.

There was a man named Arch who sometimes came, an older man with greasy ringlets of hair that fell from a big bald spot on the top of his head. He always brought a bottle of whiskey, and he and Richie would sit in Richie's room with the door closed, talking in low tones or singing raucous songs. Khalid would find the empty whiskey bottle the following morning, lying on the hallway floor. He kept them, setting them up in a row amidst the restaurant debris behind the house, though he did not know why.

The only other man who came was Syd, who had a flat nose and amazingly thick fingers, and gave off such a bad smell that Khalid was able to detect it in the house the next day. Once, when Syd was there, Richie emerged from his room and called to Aissha, and she went in there and shut the door behind her and was still in there when Khalid went to sleep. He never asked her about that, what had gone on while she was in Richie's room. Some instinct told him that he would rather not know.

There was also a woman: Wendy, her name was, tall and gaunt and very plain, with a long face like a horse's and very bad skin, and stringy tangles of reddish hair. She came once in a while for dinner, and Richie always specified that Aissha was to prepare an English dinner that night, lamb or roast beef, none of your spicy Paki curries tonight, if you please. After they ate, Richie and Wendy would go into Richie's room and not emerge again that evening, and the sounds of the guitar would be heard, and laughter, and then low cries and moans and grunts.

One time in the middle of the night when Wendy was there, Khalid got up to go to the bathroom just at the time she did, and encountered her in the hallway, stark naked in the moonlight, a long white ghostly figure. He had never seen a woman naked until this moment, not a real one, only the pictures in Richie's magazine; but he looked up at her calmly, with that deep abiding steadiness in the face of any sort of surprise that he had mastered so well since the advent of Richie. Coolly he surveyed her, his eyes rising from the long thin legs that went up and up and up from the floor and halting for a moment at the curious triangular thatch of woolly hair at the base of her flat belly, and from there his gaze mounted to the round little breasts set high and far apart on her chest, and at last came to her face, which, in the moonlight had unexpectedly taken on a sort of handsomeness if not actual comeliness, though before this Wendy had always seemed to him to be tremendously ugly. She didn't seem displeased at being seen like this. She smiled and winked at him, and ran her hand almost coquettishly through her straggly hair, and blew him a kiss as she drifted on past him toward the bathroom. It was the only time that anyone associated with Richie had ever been nice to him: had even appeared to notice him at all.

But life with Richie was not entirely horrid. There were some good aspects.

One of them was simply being close to so much strength and energy: what Khalid might have called virility, if he had known there was any such word. He had spent all his short life thus far among people who kept their heads down and went soldiering along obediently, people like patient plodding Aissha, who took what came to her and never complained, and shriveled old Iskander Mustafa Ali, who understood that Allah determined all things and one had no choice but to comply, and the quiet, tight-lipped English people of Salisbury, who had lived through the Conquest, and the Great Silence when the aliens had turned off all the electrical power in the world, and the Troubles, and the Plague, and who were prepared to be very, very English about whatever horror was coming next.

Richie was different, though. Richie hadn't a shred of passivity in him. "We shape our lives the way we want them to be, boy," Richie would say again and again. "We write our own scripts. It's all nothing but a bloody television show, don't you see that, Kenny-boy?"

That was a startling novelty to Khalid: that you might actually have any control over your own destiny, that you could say "no" to this and "yes" to that and "not right now" to this other thing, and that if there was something you wanted, you could simply reach out and take it. There was nothing Khalid wanted. But the idea that he might even have it, if only he could figure out what it was, was fascinating to him.

Then, too, for all of Richie's roughness of manner, his quickness to curse you or kick out at you or slap you when he had had a little too much to drink, he did have an affectionate side, even a charming one. He often sat with them and played his guitar, and taught them the words of songs, and encouraged them to sing along with them, though Khalid had no idea what the songs were about and Aissha did not seem to know either. It was fun, all the same, the singing; and Khalid had known very little fun. Richie was immensely proud of Khalid's good looks and agile, athletic grace, also, and would praise him for them, something which no one had ever done before, not even Aissha. Even though Khalid understood in some way that Richie was only praising himself, really, he was grateful even so.

Richie took him out behind the building and showed him how to throw and catch a ball. How to kick one, too, a different kind of ball. And sometimes there were cricket matches in a field at the edge of town; and when Richie played in these, which he occasionally did, he brought Khalid along to watch. Later, at home, he showed Khalid how to hold the bat, how to guard a wicket.

Then there were the drives in the car. These were rare, a great privilege. But sometimes, of a sunny Sunday, Richie would say, "Let's take the old flivver for a spin, eh, Kenny, lad?" And off they would go into the green countryside, usually no special destination in mind, only driving up and down the quiet lanes, Khalid gawking in wonder at this new world beyond the town. It made his head whirl in a good way, as he came to understand that the world actually did go on and on past the boundaries of Salisbury, and was full of marvels and splendors.

So, though at no point did he stop hating Richie, he could see at least some mitigating benefits that had come from his presence in their home. Not many. Some.

THREE:
NINETEEN YEARS FROM NOW

Once Richie took him to Stonehenge. Or as near to it as it was possible now for humans to go. It was the year Khalid turned ten: a special birthday treat.

"Do you see it out there in the plain, boy? Those big stones? Built by a bunch of ignorant prehistoric buggers who painted themselves blue and danced widdershins in the night. Do you know what 'widdershins' means, boy? No, neither do I. But they did it, whatever it was. Danced around naked with their thingummies jiggling around, and then at midnight they'd sacrifice a virgin on the big altar stone. Long, long ago. Thousands of years—come on, let's get out and have a look."

Khalid stared. Huge gray slabs, set out in two facing rows flanking smaller slabs of blue stone set in a three-cornered pattern, and a big stone standing upright in the middle. And some other stones lying sideways on top of a few of the gray ones. A transparent curtain of flickering reddish-green light surrounded the whole thing, rising from hidden vents in the ground to nearly twice the height of a man. Why would anyone have wanted to build such a thing? It all seemed like a tremendous waste of time.

"Of course, you understand this isn't what it looked like back then. When the Entities came, they changed the whole business around from what it always was, buggered it all up. Got laborers out here to move every single stone. And they put in the gaudy lighting effects, too. Never used to be lights, certainly not that kind. You walk through those lights, you die, just like a mosquito flying through a candle flame. Those stones there, they were set in a circle originally, and those blue ones there—hey, now, lad, look what we have! You ever see an Entity before, Ken?"

Actually, Khalid had: twice. But never this close. The first one had been right in the middle of the town at noontime. It had been standing outside the entrance of the cathedral cool as you please, as though it happened to be in the mood to go to church: a giant purple thing with orange spots and big yellow eyes. But Aissha had put her hand over his face before he could get a good look, and had pulled him quickly down the street that led away from the cathedral, dragging him along as fast as he was able to go. Khalid had been about five then. He dreamed of the Entity for months thereafter.

The second time, a year later, he had been with friends, playing within sight of the main highway, when a strange vehicle came down the road, an Entity car that floated on air instead of riding on wheels, and two Entities were standing in it, looking right out at them for a moment as they went floating by. Khalid saw only the tops of their heads that time: their great eyes again, and a sort of a curving beak below, and a great V-shaped slash of a mouth, like a frog's. He was fascinated by them. Repelled, too, because they were so bizarre, these strange alien beings, these enemies of mankind, and he knew he was supposed to loathe and disdain them. But fascinated. Fascinated. He wished he had been able to see them better.

Now, though, he had a clear view of the creatures, three of them. They had emerged from what looked like a door that was set right in the ground, out on the far side of the ancient monument, and were strolling casually among the great stones like lords or ladies inspecting their estate, paying no heed whatever to the tall man and the small boy standing beside the car parked just outside the fiery barrier. It amazed Khalid, watching them teeter around on the little ropy legs that supported their immense tubular bodies, that they were able to keep their balance, that they didn't simply topple forward and fall with a crash.

It amazed him, too, how beautiful they were. He had suspected that from his earlier glances, but now their glory fell upon him with full impact.

The luminous golden-orange spots on the glassy, gleaming purple skin—like fire, those spots were. And the huge eyes, so bright, so keen: you could read the strength of their minds in them, the power of their souls. Their gaze engulfed you in a flood of light. Even the air about the Entities partook of their beauty, glowing with a liquid turquoise radiance.

"There they be, boy. Our lords and masters. You ever see anything so bloody hideous?"

"Hideous?"

"They ain't pretty, isn't that right?"

Khalid made a noncommittal noise. Richie was in a good mood; he always was, on these Sunday excursions. But Khalid knew only too well the penalty for contradicting him in anything. So he looked upon the Entities in silence, lost in wonder, awed by the glory of these strange gigantic creatures, never voicing a syllable of his admiration for their elegance and majesty.

Expansively Richie said, "You heard correctly, you know, when they told you that when I left Salisbury just before you were born, it was to go off and join an army that meant to fight them. There was nothing I wanted more than to kill Entities, nothing. Christ Eternal, boy, did I ever hate those creepy bastards! Coming in like they did, taking our world away quick as you please. But I got to my senses pretty fast, let me tell you. I listened to the plans the underground army people had for throwing off the Entity yoke, and I had to laugh. I had to laugh! I could see right away that there wasn't a hope in hell of it. This was even before they put the Great Plague upon us, you understand. I knew. I damn well knew, I did. They're as powerful as gods. You want to fight against a bunch of gods, lots of luck to you. So I quit the underground then and there. I still hate the bastards, mind you, make no mistake about that, but I know it's foolish even to dream about overthrowing them. You just have to fashion your accommodation with them, that's all there is. You just have to make your peace within yourself and let them have their way. Because anything else is a fool's own folly."

Khalid listened. What Richie was saying made sense. Khalid understood about not wanting to fight against gods. He understood also how it was possible to hate someone and yet go on unprotestingly living with him.

"Is it all right, letting them see us like this?" he asked. "Aissha says that sometimes when they see you, they reach out from their chests with the tongues that they have there and snatch you up, and they take you inside their buildings and do horrible things to you there."

Richie laughed harshly. "It's been known to happen. But they won't touch Richie Burke, lad, and they won't touch the son of Richie Burke at Richie Burke's side. I guarantee you that. We're absolutely safe."

Khalid did not ask why that should be. He hoped it was true, that was all.

Two days afterward, while he was coming back from the market with a packet of lamb for dinner, he was set upon by two boys and a girl, all of them about his age or a year or two older, whom he knew only in the vaguest way. They formed themselves into a loose ring just beyond his reach and began to chant in a high-pitched, nasal way: "Quisling, quisling, your father is a quisling!"

"What's that you call him?"

"Quisling."

"He is not."

"He is! He is! Quisling, quisling, your father is a quisling!"

Khalid had no idea what a quisling was. But no one was going to call his father names. Much as he hated Richie, he knew he could not allow that. It was something Richie had taught him: Defend yourself against scorn, boy, at all times. He meant against those who might be rude to Khalid because he was part Pakistani; but Khalid had experienced very little of that. Was a quisling someone who was English but had had a child with a Pakistani woman? Perhaps that was it. Why would these children care, though? Why would anyone?

"Quisling, quisling—"

Khalid threw down his package and lunged at the closest boy, who darted away. He caught the girl by the arm, but he would not hit a girl, and so he simply shoved her into the other boy, who went spinning up against the side of the market building. Khalid pounced on him there, holding him close to the wall with one hand and furiously hitting him with the other.

His two companions seemed unwilling to intervene. But they went on chanting, from a safe distance, more nasally than ever.

"Quis-ling, quis-ling, your fa-ther is a quis-ling!"

"Stop that!" Khalid cried. "You have no right!" He punctuated his words with blows. The boy he was holding was bleeding, now, his nose, the side of his mouth. He looked terrified.

"Quis-ling, quis-ling—"

They would not stop, and neither would Khalid. But then he felt a hand seizing him by the back of his neck, a big adult hand, and he was yanked backward and thrust against the market wall himself. A vast meaty man, a navvy, from the looks of him, loomed over Khalid. "What do you think you're doing, you dirty Paki garbage? You'll kill the boy!"

"He said my father was a quisling!"

"Well, then, he probably is. Get on with you, now, boy! Get on with you!"

He gave Khalid one last hard shove, and spat and walked away. Khalid looked sullenly around for his three tormentors, but they had run off already. They had taken the packet of lamb with them, too.

That night, while Aissha was improvising something for dinner out of yesterday's rice and some elderly chicken, Khalid asked her what a quisling was. She spun around on him as though he had cursed Allah to her ears. Her face all ablaze with a ferocity he had not seen in it before, she said, "Never use that word in this house, Khalid. Never! Never!" And that was all the explanation she would give. Khalid had to learn, on his own, what a quisling was; and when he did, which was soon thereafter, he understood why his father had been unafraid, that day at Stonehenge when they stood outside that curtain of light and looked upon the Entities who were strolling among the giant stones. And also why those three children had mocked him in the street. You just have to fashion your accommodation with them, that's all there is. Yes. Yes. Yes. To fashion your accommodation.

FOUR:
TWENTY YEARS FROM NOW

It was after the time that Richie beat Aissha so severely, and then did worse than that—violated her, raped her—that Khalid definitely decided that he was going to kill an Entity.

Not kill Richie. Kill an Entity.

It was a turning point in Khalid's relationship with his father, and indeed in Khalid's whole life, and in the life of any number of other citizens of Salisbury, Wiltshire, England, that time when Richie hurt Aissha so. Richie had been treating Aissha badly all along, of course. He treated everyone badly. He had moved into her house and had taken possession of it as though it were his own. He regarded her as a servant, there purely to do his bidding, and woe betide her if she failed to meet his expectations. She cooked; she cleaned the house; Khalid understood now that sometimes, at his whim, Richie would make her come into his bedroom to amuse him or his friend Syd or both of them together. And there was never a word of complaint out of her. She did as he wished; she showed no sign of anger or even resentment; she had given herself over entirely to the will of Allah. Khalid, who had not yet managed to find any convincing evidence of Allah's existence, had not. But he had learned the art of accepting the unacceptable from Aissha. He knew better than to try to change what was unchangeable. So he lived with his hatred of Richie, and that was merely a fact of daily existence, like the fact that rain did not fall upward.

Now, though, Richie had gone too far.

Coming home plainly drunk, red-faced, enraged over something, muttering to himself. Greeting Aissha with a growling curse, Khalid with a stinging slap. No apparent reason for either. Demanding his dinner early. Getting it, not liking what he got. Aissha offering mild explanations of why beef had not been available today. Richie shouting that beef bloody well should have been available to the household of Richie Burke.

So far, just normal Richie behavior when Richie was having a bad day. Even sweeping the serving-bowl of curried mutton off the table, sending it shattering, thick oily brown sauce splattering everywhere, fell within the normal Richie range.

But then, Aissha saying softly, despondently, looking down at what had been her prettiest remaining sari now spotted in twenty places, "You have stained my clothing." And Richie going over the top. Erupting. Berserk. Wrath out of all measure to the offense, if offense there had been.

Leaping at her, bellowing, shaking her, slapping her. Punching her, even. In the face. In the chest. Seizing the sari at her midriff, ripping it away, tearing it in shreds, crumpling them and hurling them at her. Aissha backing away from him, trembling, eyes bright with fear, dabbing at the blood that seeped from her cut lower lip with one hand, spreading the other one out to cover herself at the thighs.

Khalid staring, not knowing what to do, horrified, furious.

Richie yelling. "I'll stain you, I will! I'll give you a sodding stain!" Grabbing her by the wrist, pulling away what remained of her clothing, stripping her all but naked right there in the dining room. Khalid covering his face. His own grandmother, forty years old, decent, respectable, naked before him: how could he look? And yet how could he tolerate what was happening? Richie dragging her out of the room, now, toward his bedroom, not troubling even to close the door. Hurling her down on his bed, falling on top of her. Grunting like a pig, a pig, a pig, a pig.

I must not permit this.

Khalid's breast surged with hatred: a cold hatred, almost dispassionate. The man was inhuman, a jinni. Some jinn were harmless, some were evil; but Richie was surely of the evil kind, a demon.

His father. An evil jinni.

But what did that make him? What? What? What? What?

Khalid found himself going into the room after them, against all prohibitions, despite all risks. Seeing Richie plunked between Aissha's legs, his shirt pulled up, his trousers pulled down, his bare buttocks pumping in the air. And Aissha staring upward past Richie's shoulder at the frozen Khalid in the doorway, her face a rigid mask of horror and shame: gesturing to him, making a repeated brushing movement of her hand through the air, wordlessly telling him to go away, to get out of the room, not to watch, not to intervene in any way.

He ran from the house and crouched cowering amid the rubble in the rear yard, the old stewpots and broken jugs and his own collection of Arch's empty whiskey bottles. When he returned, an hour later, Richie was in his room, chopping malevolently at the strings of his guitar, singing some droning tune in a low, boozy voice. Aissha was dressed again, moving about in a slow, downcast way, cleaning up the mess in the dining room. Sobbing softly. Saying nothing, not even looking at Khalid as he entered. A sticking-plaster on her lip. Her cheeks looked puffy and bruised. There seemed to be a wall around her. She was sealed away inside herself, sealed from all the world, even from him.

"I will kill him," Khalid said quietly to her.

"No. That you will not do." Aissha's voice was deep and remote, a voice from the bottom of the sea.

She gave him a little to eat, a cold chapati and some of yesterday's rice, and sent him to his room. He lay awake for hours, listening to the sounds of the house, Richie's endless drunken droning song, Aissha's barely audible sobs. In the morning nobody said anything about anything.

***

Khalid understood that it was impossible for him to kill his own father, however much he hated him. But Richie had to be punished for what he had done. And so, to punish him, Khalid was going to kill an Entity.

The Entities were a different matter. They were fair game.

For some time now, on his better days, Richie had been taking Khalid along with him as he drove through the countryside, doing his quisling tasks, gathering information that the Entities wanted to know and turning it over to them by some process that Khalid could not even begin to understand, and by this time Khalid had seen Entities on so many different occasions that he had grown quite accustomed to being in their presence.

And had no fear of them. To most people, apparently, Entities were scary things, ghastly alien monsters, evil, strange; but to Khalid they still were, as they always had been, creatures of enormous beauty. Beautiful the way a god would be beautiful. How could you be frightened by anything so beautiful? How could you be frightened of a god?

They didn't ever appear to notice him at all. Richie would go up to one of them and stand before it, and some kind of transaction would take place. While that was going on, Khalid simply stood to one side, looking at the Entity, studying it, lost in admiration of its beauty. Richie offered no explanations of these meetings and Khalid never asked.

The Entities grew more beautiful in his eyes every time he saw one. They were beautiful beyond belief. He could almost have worshipped them. It seemed to him that Richie felt the same way about them: that he was caught in their spell, that he would gladly fall down before them and bow his forehead to the ground.

And so.

I will kill one of them, Khalid thought.

Because they are so beautiful. Because my father, who works for them, must love them almost as much as he loves himself, and I will kill the thing he loves. He says he hates them, but I think it is not so: I think he loves them, and that is why he works for them. Or else he loves them and hates them both. He may feel the same way about himself. But I see the light that comes into his eyes when he looks upon them.

So I will kill one, yes. Because by killing one of them I will be killing some part of him. And maybe there will be some other value in my doing it, besides.

FIVE:
TWENTY-TWO YEARS FROM NOW

Richie Burke said, "Look at this goddamned thing, will you, Ken? Isn't it the goddamnedest fantastic piece of shit anyone ever imagined?"

They were in what had once been the main dining room of the old defunct restaurant. It was early afternoon. Aissha was elsewhere, Khalid had no idea where. His father was holding something that seemed something like a rifle, or perhaps a highly streamlined shotgun, but it was like no rifle or shotgun he had ever seen. It was a long, slender tube of greenish-blue metal with a broad flaring muzzle and what might have been some type of gunsight mounted midway down the barrel and a curious sort of computerized trigger arrangement on the stock. A one-of-a-kind sort of thing, custom made, a home inventor's pride and joy.

"Is it a weapon, would you say?"

"A weapon? A weapon? What the bloody hell do you think it is, boy? It's a fucking Entity-killing gun! Which I confiscated this very day from a nest of conspirators over Warminster way. The whole batch of them are under lock and key this very minute, thank you very much, and I've brought Exhibit A home for safekeeping. Have a good look, lad. Ever seen anything so diabolical?"

Khalid realized that Richie was actually going to let him handle it. He took it with enormous care, letting it rest on both his outstretched palms. The barrel was cool and very smooth, the gun lighter than he had expected it to be.

"How does it work, then?"

"Pick it up. Sight along it. You know how it's done. Just like an ordinary gunsight."

Khalid put it to his shoulder, right there in the room. Aimed at the fireplace. Peered along the barrel.

A few inches of the fireplace were visible in the crosshairs, in the most minute detail. Keen magnification, wonderful optics. Touch the right stud, now, and the whole side of the house would be blown out, was that it? Khalid ran his hand along the butt.

"There's a safety on it," Richie said. "The little red button. There. That. Mind you don't hit it by accident. What we have here, boy, is nothing less than a rocket-powered grenade gun. A bomb-throwing machine, virtually. You wouldn't believe it, because it's so skinny, but what it hurls is a very graceful little projectile that will explode with almost incredible force and cause an extraordinary amount of damage, altogether extraordinary. I know because I tried it. It was amazing, seeing what that thing could do."

"Is it loaded now?"

"Oh, yes, yes, you bet your little brown rump it is! Loaded and ready! An absolutely diabolical Entity-killing machine, the product of months and months of loving work by a little band of desperados with marvelous

mechanical skills. As stupid as they come, though, for all their skills. —
Here, boy, let me have that thing before you set it off somehow."

Khalid handed it over.

"Why stupid?" he asked. "It seems very well made."

"I said they were skillful. This is a goddamned triumph of
miniaturization, this little cannon. But what makes them think they could
kill an Entity at all? Don't they imagine anyone's ever tried? Can't be done,
Ken, boy. Nobody ever has, nobody ever will."

Unable to take his eyes from the gun, Khalid said obligingly, "And
why is that, sir?"

"Because they're bloody unkillable!"

"Even with something like this? Almost incredible force, you said, sir.
An extraordinary amount of damage."

"It would fucking well blow an Entity to smithereens, it would, if you
could ever hit one with it. Ah, but the trick is to succeed in firing your
shot, boy! Which cannot be done. Even as you're taking your aim, they're
reading your bloody mind, that's what they do. They know exactly what
you're up to, because they look into our minds the way we would look
into a book. They pick up all your nasty little unfriendly thoughts about
them. And then — bam! — they give you the bloody Push, the thing they do
to people with their minds, you know, and you're done for, piff paff poof.
We've heard of four cases, at least. Attempted Entity assassination. Trying
to take a shot as an Entity went by. Found the bodies, the weapons, just so
much trash by the roadside." Richie ran his hands up and down the gun,
fondling it almost lovingly. " — This gun here, it's got an unusually great
range, terrific sight, will fire upon the target from an enormous distance.
Still wouldn't work, I wager you. They can do their telepathy on you from
three hundred yards away. Maybe five hundred. Who knows, maybe a
thousand. Still, a damned good thing that we broke this ring up in time.
Just in case they could have pulled it off somehow."

"It would be bad if an Entity was killed, is that it?" Khalid asked.

Richie guffawed. "Bad? Bad? It would be a bloody catastrophe. You
know what they did, the one time anybody managed to damage them in
any way? No, how in hell would you know? It was right around the
moment you were getting born. Some buggerly American idiots launched
a laser attack from space on an Entity building. Maybe killed a few, maybe
didn't, but the Entities paid us back by letting loose a plague on us that
wiped out damn near every other person there was in the world. Right
here in Salisbury they were keeling over like flies. Had it myself. Thought
I'd die. Damned well hoped I would, I felt so bad. Then I arose from my bed
of pain and threw it off. But we don't want to risk bringing down another
plague, do we, now? Or any other sort of miserable punishment that they
might choose to inflict. Because they certainly will inflict one. One thing

that has been clear from the beginning is that our masters will take no shit from us, no, lad, not one solitary molecule of shit."

He crossed the room and unfastened the door of the cabinet that had held Khan's Mogul Palace's meager stock of wine in the long-gone era when this building had been a licensed restaurant. Thrusting the weapon inside, Richie said, "This is where it's going to spend the night. You will make no reference to its presence when Aissha gets back. I'm expecting Arch to come here tonight, and you will make no reference to it to him, either. It is a top secret item, do you hear me? I show it to you because I love you, boy, and because I want you to know that your father has saved the world this day from a terrible disaster, but I don't want a shred of what I have shared with you just now to reach the ears of another human being. Or another inhuman being for that matter. Is that clear, boy? Is it?"

"I will not say a word," said Khalid.

***

And said none. But thought quite a few.

All during the evening, as Arch and Richie made their methodical way through Arch's latest bottle of rare pre-Conquest whiskey, salvaged from some vast horde found by the greatest of good luck in a Southampton storehouse, Khalid clutched to his own bosom the knowledge that there was, right there in that cabinet, a device that was capable of blowing the head off an Entity, if only one could manage to get within firing range without announcing one's lethal intentions.

Was there a way of achieving that? Khalid had no idea.

But perhaps the range of this device was greater than the range of the Entities' mind-reading capacities. Or perhaps not. Was it worth the gamble? Perhaps it was. Or perhaps not.

Aissha went to her room soon after dinner, once she and Khalid had cleared away the dinner dishes. She said little these days, kept mainly to herself, drifted through her life like a sleepwalker. Richie had not laid a violent hand on her again, since that savage evening several years back, but Khalid understood that she still harbored the pain of his humiliation of her, that in some ways she had never really recovered from what Richie had done to her that night. Nor had Khalid.

He hovered in the hall, listening to the sounds from his father's room until he felt certain that Arch and Richie had succeeded in drinking themselves into their customary stupor. Ear to the door: silence. A faint snore or two, maybe.

He forced himself to wait another ten minutes. Still quiet in there. Delicately he pushed the door, already slightly ajar, another few inches open. Peered cautiously within.

Richie slumped head down at the table, clutching in one hand a glass that still had a little whiskey in it, cradling his guitar between his chest and knee with the other. Arch on the floor opposite him, head dangling to one side, eyes closed, limbs sprawled every which way. Snoring, both of them. Snoring. Snoring. Snoring.

Good. Let them sleep very soundly.

Khalid took the Entity-killing gun now from the cabinet. Caressed its satiny barrel. It was an elegant thing, this weapon. He admired its design. He had an artist's eye for form and texture and color, did Khalid: some fugitive gene out of forgotten antiquity miraculously surfacing in him after a dormancy of centuries, the eye of a Gandharan sculptor, of a Rajput architect, a Gujerati miniaturist coming to the fore in him after passing through all those generations of the peasantry. Lately he had begun doing little sketches, making some carvings. Hiding everything away so that Richie would not find it. That was the sort of thing that might offend Richie, his taking up such piffling pastimes. Sports, drinking, driving around: those were proper amusements for a man.

On one of his good days last year Richie had brought a bicycle home for him: a startling gift, for bicycles were rarities nowadays, none having been available, let alone manufactured, in England in ages. Where Richie had obtained it, from whom, with what brutality, Khalid did not like to think. But he loved his bike. Rode long hours through the countryside on it, every chance he had. It was his freedom; it was his wings. He went outside now, carrying the grenade gun, and carefully strapped it to the bicycle's basket.

He had waited nearly three years for this moment to make itself possible.

Nearly every night nowadays, Khalid knew, one could usually see Entities traveling about on the road between Salisbury and Stonehenge, one or two of them at a time, riding in those cars of theirs that floated a little way above the ground on cushions of air. Stonehenge was a major center of Entity activities nowadays and there were more and more of them in the vicinity all the time. Perhaps there would be one out there this night, he thought. It was worth the chance: he would not get a second opportunity with this captured gun that his father had brought home.

About halfway out to Stonehenge there was a place on the plain where he could have a good view of the road from a little copse several hundred yards away. Khalid had no illusion that hiding in the copse would protect him from the mind-searching capacities the Entities were said to have. If they could detect him at all, the fact that he was standing in the shadow of a leafy tree would not make the slightest difference. But it was a place to wait, on this bright moonlit night. It was a place where he could feel alone, unwatched.

He went to it. He waited there.

He listened to night-noises. An owl; the rustling of the breeze through the trees; some small nocturnal animal scrabbling in the underbrush.

He was utterly calm.

Khalid had studied calmness all his life, with his grandmother Aissha as his tutor. From his earliest days he had watched her stolid acceptance of poverty, of shame, of hunger, of loss, of all kinds of pain. He had seen her handling the intrusion of Richie Burke into her household and her life with philosophical detachment, with stoic patience. To her it was all the will of Allah, not to be questioned. Allah was less real to Khalid than He was to Aissha, but Khalid had drawn from her her infinite patience and tranquility, at least, if not her faith in God. Perhaps he might find his way to God later on. At any rate, he had long ago learned from Aissha that yielding to anguish was useless, that inner peace was the only key to endurance, that everything must be done calmly, unemotionally, because the alternative was a life of unending chaos and suffering. And so he had come to understand from her that it was possible even to hate someone in a calm, unemotional way. And had contrived thus to live calmly, day by day, with the father whom he loathed.

For the Entities he felt no loathing at all. Far from it. He had never known a world without them, the vanished world where humans had been masters of their own destinies. The Entities, for him, were an innate aspect of life, simply there, as were hills and trees, the moon, or the owl who roved the night above him now, cruising for squirrels or rabbits. And they were very beautiful to behold, like the moon, like an owl moving silently overhead, like a massive chestnut tree.

He waited, and the hours passed, and in his calm way he began to realize that he might not get his chance tonight, for he knew he needed to be home and in his bed before Richie awakened and could find him and the weapon gone. Another hour, two at most, that was all he could risk out here.

Then he saw turquoise light on the highway, and knew that an Entity vehicle was approaching, coming from the direction of Salisbury. It pulled into view a moment later, carrying two of the creatures standing serenely upright, side by side, in their strange wagon that floated on a cushion of air.

Khalid beheld it in wonder and awe. And once again marveled, as ever, at their elegance of these Entities, their grace, their luminescent splendor.

How beautiful you are! Oh, yes. Yes.

They moved past him on their curious cart as though traveling on a river of light, and it seemed to him, dispassionately studying the one on the side closer to him, that what he beheld here was surely a jinni of the jinn: Allah's creature, a thing made of smokeless fire, a separate creation.

Which none the less must in the end stand before Allah in judgment, even as we.

How beautiful. How beautiful.

I love you.

He loved it, yes. For its crystalline beauty. A jinni? No, it was a higher sort of being than that; it was an angel. It was a being of pure light—of cool clear fire, without smoke. He was lost in rapt admiration of its angelic perfection.

Loving it, admiring it, even worshipping it, Khalid calmly lifted the grenade gun to his shoulder, calmly aimed, calmly stared through the gun-sight. Saw the Entity, distant as it was, transfixed perfectly in the crosshairs. Calmly he released the safety, as Richie had inadvertently showed him how to do. Calmly put his finger to the firing stud.

His soul was filled all the while with love for the beautiful creature before him as—calmly, calmly, calmly—he pressed the stud. He heard a whooshing sound and felt the weapon kicking back against his shoulder with astonishing force, sending him thudding into a tree behind him and for a moment knocking the breath from him; and an instant later the left side of the beautiful creature's head exploded into a cascading fountain of flame, a shower of radiant fragments. A greenish-red mist of what must be alien blood appeared and went spreading outward into the air.

The stricken Entity swayed and fell backward, dropping out of sight on the floor of the wagon.

In that same moment the second Entity, the one that was riding on the far side, underwent so tremendous a convulsion that Khalid wondered if he had managed to kill it, too, with that single shot. It stumbled forward, then back, and crashed against the railing of the wagon with such violence that Khalid imagined he could hear the thump. Its great tubular body writhed and shook, and seemed even to change color, the purple hue deepening almost to black for an instant and the orange spots becoming a fiery red. At so great a distance it was hard to be sure, but Khalid thought, also, that its leathery hide was rippling and puckering as if in a demonstration of almost unendurable pain.

It must be feeling the agony of its companion's death, he realized. Watching the Entity lurch around blindly on the platform of the wagon in what had to be terrible pain, Khalid's soul flooded with compassion for the creature, and sorrow, and love. It was unthinkable to fire again. He had never had any intention of killing more than one; but in any case he knew that he was no more capable of firing a shot at this stricken survivor now than he would be of firing at Aissha.

During all this time the wagon had been moving silently onward as though nothing had happened; and in a moment more it turned the bend in the road and was gone from Khalid's sight, down the road that led toward Stonehenge.

He stood for a while watching the place where the vehicle had been when he had fired the fatal shot. There was nothing there now, no sign that anything had occurred. Had anything occurred? Khalid felt neither satisfaction nor grief nor fear nor, really, any emotion of any other sort. His mind was all but blank. He made a point of keeping it that way, knowing he was as good as dead if he relaxed his control even for a fraction of a second.

Strapping the gun to the bicycle basket again, he pedaled quietly back toward home. It was well past midnight; there was no one at all on the road. At the house, all was as it had been; Arch's car parked in front, the front lights still on, Richie and Arch snoring away in Richie's room.

Only now, safely home, did Khalid at last allow himself the luxury of letting the jubilant thought cross his mind, just for a moment, that had been flickering at the threshold of his consciousness for an hour:

Got you, Richie! Got you, you bastard!

He returned the grenade gun to the cabinet and went to bed, and was asleep almost instantly, and slept soundly until the first birdsong of dawn.

***

In the tremendous uproar that swept Salisbury the next day, with Entity vehicles everywhere and platoons of the glossy balloon-like aliens that everybody called Spooks going from house to house, it was Khalid himself who provided the key clue to the mystery of the assassination that had occurred in the night.

"You know, I think it might have been my father who did it," he said almost casually, in town, outside the market, to a boy named Thomas whom he knew in a glancing sort of way. "He came home yesterday with a strange sort of big gun. Said it was for killing Entities with, and put it away in a cabinet in our front room."

Thomas would not believe that Khalid's father was capable of such a gigantic act of heroism as assassinating an Entity. No, no, no, Khalid argued eagerly, in a tone of utter and sublime disingenuousness: he did it, I know he did it, he's always talked of wanting to kill one of them one of these days, and now he has.

He has?

Always his greatest dream, yes, indeed.

Well, then—

Yes. Khalid moved along. So did Thomas. Khalid took care to go nowhere near the house all that morning. The last person he wanted to see was Richie. But he was safe in that regard. By noon Thomas evidently had spread the tale of Khalid Burke's wild boast about the town with great effectiveness, because word came traveling through the streets around that time that a detachment of Spooks had gone to Khalid's house and had taken Richie Burke away.

"What about my grandmother?" Khalid asked. "She wasn't arrested too, was she?"

"No, it was just him," he was told. "Billy Cavendish saw them taking him, and he was all by himself. Yelling and screaming, he was, the whole time, like a man being hauled away to be hanged."

Khalid never saw his father again.

During the course of the general reprisals that followed the killing, the entire population of Salisbury and five adjacent towns was rounded up and transported to walled detention camps near Portsmouth. A good many of the deportees were executed within the next few days, seemingly by random selection, no pattern being evident in the choosing of those who were put to death. At the beginning of the following week the survivors were sent on from Portsmouth to other places, some of them quite remote, in various parts of the world.

Khalid was not among those executed. He was merely sent very far away.

He felt no guilt over having survived the death-lottery while others around him were being slain for his murderous act. He had trained himself since childhood to feel very little indeed, even while aiming a rifle at one of Earth's beautiful and magnificent masters. Besides, what affair was it of his, that some of these people were dying and he was allowed to live? Everyone died, some sooner, some later. Aissha would have said that what was happening was the will of Allah. Khalid more simply put it that the Entities did as they pleased, always, and knew that it was folly to ponder their motives.

Aissha was not available to discuss these matters with. He was separated from her before reaching Portsmouth and Khalid never saw her again, either. From that day on it was necessary for him to make his way in the world on his own.

He was not quite thirteen years old. Often, in the years ahead, he would look back at the time when he had slain the Entity; but he would think of it only as the time when he had rid himself of Richie Burke, for whom he had had such hatred. For the Entities he had no hatred at all, and when his mind returned to that event by the roadside on the way to Stonehenge, to the alien being centered in the crosshairs of his weapon, he would think only of the marvelous color and form of the two starborn creatures in the floating wagon, of that passing moment of beauty in the night.

SIX

The 2000s

THE 2000s

INTRODUCTION

How strange that looks, and how ugly it sounds — the 2000s! But what are we supposed to call them? We all were agreed on the standard nicknames for the passing decades of the previous century, and knew what we meant when we referred to them — the Twenties, the Thirties, the Forties, the Fifties, the Sixties, they all fell easily on the ear and each period so labeled had a strongly defined character. And of course there was the Gay Nineties in the century before that, an appellation that in our time has taken on an entirely different semantic charge. But I'm not at all sure what the people of the early twentieth century did about their decade-naming problem when they were at the same point of their century that we are now. "The 1900s" has an unobjectionable sound, but it could apply to the entire century as well as to its first decade. Here I am using the unsatisfying "the 2000s" for our decade, for lack of anything better. And what will we follow it with? The Teens? That has semantic problems too that didn't exist a hundred years ago. I guess we are stuck with an anomalous labeling problem until the Twenties come round once more in the current century.

In any case I see no great need to give the present decade any characterizing label right now, since, as I write this, we are only a couple of years into that decade anyway. Its history has yet to be created, and, even though speculation on future events is my specialty, I would not at the moment want to try to assign any special characterological distinction to it. It has already been marred by a ghastly terrorist event, and I have little doubt that there will be more of those to come, but I would not want to have to think of the decade I lamely call "the 2000s" as the decade of terrorism, and I know not what else its remaining years will bring.

For me, at any rate, it has brought a sixth decade of my career in science fiction: a decade of greatly decreased productivity, at least when measured against earlier ones. But it ill befits my present status as a venerable senior writer to be pounding out the stories at the jackrabbit pace of forty years ago. I am supposed to be calm, measured, reflective, unhurried, now. That may or may not be the case; but at least I'm still doing some writing — a twentieth century science fiction writer doing his best to make sense out of the twenty-first century world — as the two stories that follow will demonstrate.

543

THE MILLENNIUM EXPRESS (2000)

INTRODUCTION

So a new century, indeed a new millennium, began to glimmer on the horizon. I had been reading and writing about the twenty-first century for more than fifty years, and now here it was, turning up right on schedule.

A little ahead of schedule, actually. Pedants like me think that new centuries begin in years that end with the digit 1 — 1701, 1801, 1901, 2001 — and that new millennia begin with the first year of the new century. But our modern civilization is not kind to pedants and their pedantry, and it was easy to see, well in advance of the actual event, that almost everybody else was going to hail January 1, 2000, as the first day of the third millennium.

I decided not to fight it. I would celebrate the dawning of Y2K with the rest of the populace that day, reserving to myself a private conviction that it wasn't *really* going to arrive for another year. And when Alice Turner of *Playboy* told me that the January, 2000 issue of that magazine was going to be the special Millennium issue, for which she would like me to write a short story with an appropriate theme, I offered no resistance at all. I did tell her, though, that I wasn't going to write a story about the beginning of the *third* millennium, because I was, after all, a science-fiction writer, and my specialty was writing about the future. The third millennium was on the verge of becoming the present. So I told her I'd be looking a thousand years ahead, setting my story in 2999 with the fourth millennium on the verge. She had no objections, and I sent her "The Millennium Express," which duly appeared in *Playboy's* millennium issue.

Really sharp-eyed purists are going to object, at this point, that I have grouped the stories in this book by decades, and "The Millennium Express," since I wrote it in 1999 and the magazine containing it, although dated 2000, was indeed on sale in the waning days of 1999, really belongs in the 1990s section, and not this one. To which I reply with a pooh! and a bah! When the whole world decided that the twenty-first century was going to begin on January 1, 2000, I decided, wisely enough, to let the whole world have its way, and kept quiet about my own arithmetical reservations. But I can play that game too. Here's a story that I wrote in January, 1999, but since it was published in a magazine bearing a Year 2000 date, I tell you now with a straight face that it is my first story of the twenty-first century, and has every right to be included in the 2000s segment of this collection. Those who object may ask the publisher for a refund.

In a quiet moment late in the tranquil year of 2999 four men are struggling to reach an agreement over the details of their plan to blow up the Louvre. They have been wrangling for the last two days over the merits of implosion versus explosion. Their names are Albert Einstein (1879-1955), Pablo Picasso (1881-1973), Ernest Hemingway (1899-1961), and Vjong Cleversmith (2683-2804).

Why, you may wonder, do these men want to destroy the world's greatest repository of ancient art? And how does it come to pass that a man of the twenty eighth century, more or less, is conspiring with three celebrities of a much earlier time?

Strettin Vulpius (2953-), who has been tracking this impish crew across the face of the peaceful world for many months now, knows much more about these people than you do, but he too has yet to fathom their fondness for destruction and is greatly curious about it. For him it is a professional curiosity, or as close to professional as anything can be, here in this happy time at the end of the Third Millennium, when work of any sort is essentially a voluntary activity.

At the moment Vulpius is watching them from a distance of several thousand meters. He has established himself in a hotel room in the charming little Swiss village of Zermatt and they are making their headquarters presently in a lovely villa of baroque style that nestles far above the town in a bower of tropical palms and brightly blossoming orchids on the lush green slopes of the Matterhorn. Vulpius has succeeded in affixing a minute spy-eye to the fleshy inner surface of the room where the troublesome four are gathered. It provides him with a clear image of all that is taking place in there.

Cleversmith, who is the ringleader, says, "We need to make up our minds." He is slender, agile, a vibrant long-limbed whip of a man. "The clock keeps on pulsing, you know. The Millennium Express is roaring toward us minute by minute."

"I tell you, implosion is the way for us to go," says Einstein. He looks to be about forty, smallish of stature, with a great mop of curling hair and soft thoughtful eyes, incongruous above his deep chest and sturdy athletic shoulders. "An elegant symbolic statement. The earth opens; the museum and everything it contains quietly disappears into the chasm."

"Symbolic of what?" asks Picasso scornfully. He too is short and stocky, but he is almost completely bald, and his eyes, ferociously bright and piercing, are the antithesis of Einstein's gentle ones. "Blow the damn thing up, I say. Let the stuff spew all around the town and come down like snow. A snowfall of paintings, the first snow anywhere in a thousand years."

Cleversmith nods. "A very pretty image, yes. Thank you, Pablo...Ernest?"

"Implode," says the biggest of the men. "The quiet way, the subtle way." He lounges against the wall closest to the great curving window with his back to the others, a massive burly figure, holding himself braced on one huge hand that is splayed out no more than five centimeters from the spy-eye as he stares down into the distant valley. He carries himself like a big cat, graceful, loose-jointed, subtly menacing. "The pretty way, eh? — Your turn, Vjong."

But Picasso says, before Cleversmith can reply, "Why be quiet or subtle about welcoming the new millennium? What we want to do is make a splash."

"My position precisely," Cleversmith says. "My vote goes with you, Pablo. And so we are still deadlocked, it seems."

Hemingway says, still facing away from them, "Implosion reduces the chance that innocent passersby will get killed."

"Killed?" cries Picasso, and claps his hands in amusement. "Killed? Who worries about getting killed, in the year 2999? It isn't as though dying is forever."

"It can be a great inconvenience," says Einstein quietly.

"When has that ever concerned us?" Cleversmith says. Frowning, he glances around the room. "Ideally we ought to be unanimous on this, but at the very least we need a majority. It was my hope today that one of you would be willing to switch his vote."

"Why don't you switch yours, then?" Einstein says. "Or you, Pablo: you of all people ought to prefer to have all those paintings and sculptures sink unharmed into the ground rather than having them be blown sky-high."

Picasso grins malevolently. "What fallacy is this, Albert? Why should I give a damn about paintings and sculptures? Do you care about — what was it called, physics? Does our Ernest write little stories?"

"Is the Pope Catholic?" Hemingway says.

"Gentlemen — gentlemen — "

The dispute quickly gets out of hand. There is much shouting and gesticulation. Picasso yells at Einstein, who shrugs and jabs a finger at Cleversmith, who ignores what Einstein says to him and turns to

Hemingway with an appeal that is met with scorn. They are all speaking Anglic, of course. Anything else would have been very strange. These men are not scholars of obsolete tongues.

What they are, thinks the watching Vulpius, is monsters and madmen. Something must be done about them, and soon. As Cleversmith says, the clock is pulsing ceaselessly, the millennium is coming ever nearer.

***

It was on a grassy hilltop overlooking the ruins of sunken Istanbul that he first had encountered them, about a year and a half earlier. A broad parapet placed here centuries ago for the benefit of tourists provided a splendid view of the drowned city's ancient wonders, gleaming valiantly through the crystalline waters of the Bosporus: the great upjutting spears that were the minarets of Haghia Sophia and the Mosque of Suleyman the Magnificent and the other great buildings of that sort, the myriad domes of the covered bazaar, the immense walls of Topkapi Palace.

Of all the submerged and partly submerged cities Vulpius had visited — New York, San Francisco, Tokyo, London, and the rest — this one was one of the loveliest. The shallow emerald waters that covered it could not fully conceal the intermingling layers upon layers of antiquity here, white marble and colored tile and granite slabs, Constantinople of the Byzantine Emperors, Stamboul of the Sultans, Istanbul of the Industrial Age: toppled columns, fallen friezes, ponderous indestructible fortifications, the vague chaotic outlines of the hilly city's winding streets, the shadowy hints of archaic foundations and walls, the slumping mud-engulfed ruins of the sprawling hotels and office buildings of a much later era that itself was also long gone. What a density of history! Standing there on that flower-bedecked hillside he felt himself becoming one with yesterday's seven thousand years.

A mild humid breeze was blowing out of the hinterland to the east, bearing the pungent scent of exotic blooms and unidentifiable spices. Vulpius shivered with pleasure. It was a lovely moment, one of a great many he had known in a lifetime of travel. The world had gone through long periods of travail over the centuries, but now it was wholly a garden of delight, and Vulpius had spent twenty years savoring its multitude of marvels, with ever so much still ahead for him.

He was carrying, as he always did, a pocket mnemone, a small quasi-organic device, somewhat octopoid in form, in whose innumerable nodes and bumps were stored all manner of data that could be massaged forth by one who was adept in the technique. Vulpius aimed the instrument now at the shimmering sea below him and squeezed it gently, and in its soft, sighing, semi-sentient voice it provided him with the names of the half-visible structures and something of their functions in the days of the former world: this had been the Galata Bridge, this the Castle of Roumeli Hissar, this the Mosque of Mehmet the Conqueror, these were the scattered remnants of the great Byzantine imperial palace.

"It tells you everything, does it?" said a deep voice behind him. Vulpius turned. A small bald-headed man, broad-shouldered and cocky-looking, grinning at him in a powerfully insinuating way. His obsidian eyes were like augers. Vulpius had never seen eyes like those. A second man, much taller, darkly handsome, smiling lazily, stood behind him. The little bald one pointed toward the place in the water where six graceful minarets came thrusting upward into the air from a single vast building just below the surface. "What's that one, for instance?"

Vulpius, who was of an obliging nature, massaged the mnemone. "The famous Blue Mosque," he was told. "Built by the architect Mehmet Aga by order of Sultan Ahmet I in the seventeenth century. It was one of the largest mosques in the city and perhaps the most beautiful. It is the only one with six minarets."

"Ah," said the small man. "A famous mosque. Six minarets. What, I wonder, could a mosque have been? Would you know, Ernest?" He looked over his shoulder at his hulking companion, who merely shrugged. Then, quickly, to Vulpius: " — But no, no, don't bother to find out. It's not important. Those things are the minarets, I take it?" He pointed again. Vulpius followed the line of the pointing hand. It seemed to him, just then, that the slender towers were gently swaying, as though they were mere wands moving in the breeze. The effect was quite weird. An earthquake, perhaps? No: the hillside here was altogether steady. Some hallucination, then? He doubted that. His mind was as lucid as ever.

The towers were definitely moving from side to side, though, whipping back and forth now as if jostled by a giant hand. The waters covering the flooded city began to grow agitated. Wavelets appeared where all had been calm. A huge stretch of the surface appeared almost to be boiling. The disturbance was spreading outward from a central vortex of churning turmoil. What strange kind of upheaval was going on down there?

Two minarets of the Blue Mosque tottered and fell into the water, and three more went down a moment later. And the effect was still expanding. Vulpius, stunned, appalled, scanned the sunken metropolis from one side to the other, watching the fabled ruins crumble and collapse and disappear into the suddenly beclouded Bosporus.

He became aware then of two more men clambering up to the observation parapet, where they were exuberantly greeted by the first pair. The newcomers — one of them short, bushy-haired, soft-eyed, the other long and lean and fiercely energetic — seemed flushed, excited, oddly exhilarated.

Much later, it was determined that vandalous parties unknown had placed a turbulence bomb just offshore, the sort of device that once had been used to demolish the useless and ugly remains of the half-drowned urban settlements that had been left behind in every lowland coastal area by the teeming populace of Industrial times. A thing that had once been employed to pulverize the concrete walls and patios of hideous tract housing and the squat squalid bulks of repellent cinderblock factory buildings had been utilized to shake to flinders the fantastic fairy-tale towers of the great imperial capital by the Golden Horn.

Vulpius had no reason to connect the calamity that had befallen sunken Istanbul with the presence of the four men on the hillside across the way. Not until much later did that thought enter his mind. But the event would not leave him: he went over and over it, replaying its every detail in a kind of chilled fascination. He was deeply unsettled, of course, by what he had witnessed; but at the same time he could not deny having felt a certain perverse thrill at having been present at the moment of such a bizarre event. The shattering of the age-old city was the final paragraph of its long history, and he, Strettin Vulpius, had been on the scene to see it written. It was a distinction of a sort.

Other equally mysterious disasters followed in subsequent months.

The outer wall of the Park of Extinct Animals was breached and many of the inner enclosures were opened, releasing into the wilderness nearly the entire extraordinary collection of carefully cloned beasts of yesteryear: moas, quaggas, giant ground sloths, dodos, passenger pigeons, aurochses, oryxes, saber-toothed cats, great auks, wisents, cahows, and many another lost species that had been called back from oblivion by the most painstaking manipulation of fossil genetic material. Though the world into which they now had been so brusquely set loose was as close to a paradise as its human population could imagine, it was no place for most of these coddled and cherished creatures, for in their resuscitated existences at the Park they never had had to learn the knack of fending for themselves. All but the strongest met swift death in one fashion or another, some set upon by domestic cats and dogs, others drowned or lost in quagmires, a few killed inadvertently during attempts at recapturing them, many perishing quickly of starvation even amidst the plenty of the garden that was the world, and still others expiring from sheer bewilderment at finding themselves on their own in unfamiliar freedom. The loss was incalculable; the best estimate was that it would take a hundred years of intense work to restock the collection.

The Museum of Industrial Culture was attacked next. This treasury of medieval technological artifacts was only perfunctorily guarded, for who would care to steal from a place that was everyone's common storehouse of quaint and delightful objects? Society had long since evolved past such pathetic barbarism. All the same, a band of masked men broke into the building and ransacked it thoroughly, carrying off a mountain of booty, the curious relics of the harsh and bustling age that had preceded the present one: devices that had been used as crude computers, terrifying medical implements, machines that once had disseminated aural and visual images, weaponry of various sorts, simple vision-enhancing things worn on hooks that went around one's ears, instruments used in long-distance communication, glass and ceramic cooking vessels, and all manner of other strange and oddly moving detritus of that vanished day. None of these items was ever recovered. The suspicion arose that they had all gone into the hands of private holders who had hidden them from sight, which would be an odd and troublesome revival of the seeking and secret hoarding of possessions that had caused so much difficulty in ancient times.

Then came the undermining of the Washington Monument; the nearly simultaneous aerial explosion that ruptured the thousands of gleaming windows that still were intact in the gigantic abandoned buildings marking the watery site where Manhattan Island had been in the days before the Great Warming; the destruction through instantaneous metal fatigue of the Great Singapore Tower; and the wholly unexpected and highly suspicious eruption of Mount Vesuvius that sent new lava spilling down over the excavations at Pompeii and Herculaneum.

By this time Vulpius, like a great many other concerned citizens all over the world, had grown profoundly distressed by these wanton acts of desecration. They were so primitive, so crass, so horrifyingly atavistic. They negated all the great achievements of the Third Millennium.

After all those prior centuries of war and greed and unthinkable human suffering, mankind had attained true civilization at last. There was an abundance of natural resources and a benevolent climate from pole to pole. Though much of the planet had been covered by water during the time of the Great Warming, humanity had moved to higher ground and lived there happily in a world without winter. A stable population enjoyed long life and freedom from want of any kind. One respected all things living and dead; one did no harm; one went about one's days quietly and benignly. The traumas of previous epochs seemed unreal, almost mythical, now. Why would anyone want to disrupt the universal harmony and tranquility that had come to enfold the world here in the days just before the dawning of the thirty-first century?

It happened that Vulpius was in Rome, standing in the huge plaza in front of St. Peter's, when a great column of flame sprang into the sky before him. At first he thought it was the mighty basilica that was on fire. But no, the blaze seemed to be located to the right of the building, in the Vatican complex itself. Sirens now began to shriek; people were running to and fro in the plaza. Vulpius caught at the arm of a portly man with the florid jowly face of a Roman Caesar. "What's going on? Where's the fire?"

"A bomb," the man gasped. "In the Sistine Chapel!"

"No," cried Vulpius. "Impossible! Unthinkable!"

"The church will go next. Run!" He broke free of Vulpius's grasp and went sprinting away.

Vulpius, though, found himself unable to flee. He took a couple of wobbly steps toward the obelisk at the center of the plaza. The pillar of fire above the Vatican roof was growing broader. The air was stiflingly hot. It will all be destroyed, he thought, the Chapel, the Rooms of Raphael, the Vatican library, the entire dazzling horde of treasures that he had visited only a few hours before. They have struck again, it seems. They. They.

He reached the steps at the base of the obelisk and paused there, panting in the heat. An oddly familiar face swam up out of the smoky haze: bald head, prominent nose, intensely penetrating eyes. Unforgettable eyes.

The little man from Istanbul, the day when the ruins had been destroyed.

Beside him was the other little man, the one with the thick bushy hair and the moody, poetic gaze. Leaning against the obelisk itself was the very big one, the handsome man with the immense shoulders. And, next to him, the wiry, long-legged one.

The same four men that Vulpius had seen at Istanbul. Staring wide-eyed, transfixed by the sight of the burning building. Their faces, red with the reflection of the fiery glow overhead, displayed a kind of grim joy, an almost ecstatic delight.

Another catastrophe, and the same four men present at it? That went beyond the possibilities of coincidence.

No. No.

Not a coincidence at all.

***

He has been pursuing them around the world ever since, traveling now not as a tourist but as a secret agent of the informal governmental police that maintains such order as is still necessary to be enforced in the world. He has seen them at their filthy work, again and again, one monstrous cataclysm after another. The trashing of the Taj Mahal; the attack on Tibet's lofty Potala; the tumbling of the Parthenon, high on its acropolis above the lake that once was Athens. They are always present at these acts of pre-millennial vandalism. So is he, now. He has taken care, though, not to let them see him.

By this time he knows their names.

The little one with the terrifying staring eyes is called Pablo Picasso. He had been cloned from the remains of some famous artist of a thousand years before. Vulpius has taken the trouble to look up some of the original Picasso's work: there is plenty of it in every museum, wild, stark, garish, utterly incomprehensible paintings, women shown in profile with both eyes visible at once, humanoid monsters with the heads of bulls, jumbled gaudy landscapes showing scenes not to be found anywhere in the real world. But of course this Picasso is only a clone, fabricated from a scrap of the genetic material of his ancient namesake; whatever other sins he may have committed, he cannot be blamed for the paintings. Nor does he commit new ones of the same disagreeable sort, or of any sort at all. No one paints pictures any more.

The other little man is Albert Einstein, another clone fashioned from a man of the previous millennium—a thinker, a scientist, responsible for something called the theory of relativity. Vulpius has been unable to discover precisely what that theory was, but it hardly matters, since the present Einstein probably has no idea of its meaning either. Science itself is as obsolete as painting. All that was in need of discovering has long since been discovered.

The big husky man's name is Ernest Hemingway. He too owes his existence to a shred of DNA retrieved from the thousand-years-gone corpse of a celebrated figure, this one a writer. Vulpius has retrieved some of the first Hemingway's work from the archives. It means very little to him, but perhaps it has lost something in translation into modern Anglic. And in any case the writing and reading of stories are diversions that are no longer widely practiced. The twentieth-century historical context that Vulpius consults indicates that in his own time, at least, Hemingway was considered an important man of letters.

Vjong Cleversmith, the fourth of the vandals, has been cloned from a man dead a little less than two hundred years, which means that no grave-robbing was necessary in order to obtain the cells from which he was grown. The ancestral Cleversmith, like nearly everyone else in recent centuries, had left samples of his genetic material on deposit in the cloning vaults. The record indicates that he was an architect: the Great Singapore Tower, brought now to ruination by his own posthumous gene-bearer, was regarded as his masterwork.

The very concept of cloning makes Vulpius queasy. There is a ghoulishness about it, an eeriness, that he dislikes.

There is no way to replicate in clones the special qualities, good or bad, that distinguished the people from whom they were drawn. The resemblance is purely a physical one. Those who specify that they are to be cloned after death may believe that they are attaining immortality of a sort, but to Vulpius it has always seemed that what is achieved is a facsimile of the original, a kind of animated statue, a mere external simulation. Yet the practice is all but universal. In the past five hundred years the people of the Third Millennium have come to dislike the risks and burdens of actual childbearing and childrearing. Even though a lifetime of two centuries is no longer unusual, the increasing refusal to reproduce and the slow but steady emigration to the various artificial satellite planetoids have brought the number of Earth's inhabitants to its lowest level since prehistoric times. Cloning is practiced not only as an amusement but as a necessary means of fending off depopulation.

Vulpius himself has occasionally played with the notion that he too is a clone. He has only vague memories of his parents, who are mere blurred elongated shadows in his mind, faceless and unknowable, and sometimes he thinks he has imagined even those. There is no evidence to support this: his progenitors' names are set down in the archives, though the last contact he had with either of them was at the age of four. But again and again he finds himself toying with the thought that he could not have been conceived of man and woman in the ancient sweaty way, but instead was assembled and decanted under laboratory conditions. Many people he knows have this fantasy.

But for this quartet, these men whom Vulpius has followed across the world all this year, clonehood is no fantasy. They are genuine replicas of men who lived long ago. And now they spend their days taking a terrible revenge against the world's surviving antiquities. Why was that? What pleasure did this rampage of destruction give them? Could it be that clones were different from naturally conceived folk, that they lacked all reverence for the artifacts of other times?

Vulpius wants very much to know what drives them. More than that: they must be stopped from doing further mischief. The time has come to confront them directly, straightforwardly, and command them in the name of civilization to halt.

To do that, he supposes, he will have to hike up the flank of the Matterhorn to their secluded lodge close to the summit. He has been there once already to plant the spy-eye, and found it a long and arduous walk that he is not eager to make a second time. But luck is with him. They have chosen to descend into the town of Zermatt this bright warm afternoon. Vulpius encounters Hemingway and Einstein in the cobbled, swaybacked main street, outside a pretty little shop whose dark half-timbered facade gives it a look of incalculable age: a survivor, no doubt, of that long-ago era when there were no palm trees here, when this highland valley and the mighty Alpine peak just beyond it were part of winter's bleak realm, a land eternally imprisoned in ice and snow, a playground for those who thrived on chilly pleasures.

"Excuse me," Vulpius says, approaching them boldly.

They look at him uneasily. Perhaps they realize that they have seen him more than once before.

But he intends to be nothing if not forthright with them. "Yes, you know me," he tells them. "My name is Strettin Vulpius. I was there the day Istanbul was destroyed. I was in the plaza outside St. Peter's when the Vatican burned."

"Were you, now?" says Hemingway. His eyes narrow like a sleepy cat's. "Yes, come to think of it, you do look familiar."

"Agra," Vulpius says. "Lhasa. Athens."

"He gets around," says Einstein.

"A world traveler," says Hemingway, nodding.

Picasso now has joined the group, with Cleversmith just behind him. Vulpius says, "You'll be departing for Paris soon, won't you?"

"What's that?" Cleversmith asks, looking startled.

Hemingway leans over and whispers something in his ear. Cleversmith's expression darkens.

"Let there be no pretense," says Vulpius stonily. "I know what you have in mind. The Louvre must not be touched."

Picasso says, "There's nothing in it but a lot of dusty junk, you know."

Vulpius shakes his head. "Junk to you, perhaps. To the rest of us the things you've been destroying are precious. I say, enough is enough. You've had your fun. Now it has to stop."

Cleversmith indicates the colossal mass of the Matterhorn above the town. "You've been eavesdropping on us, have you?"

"For the past five or six days."

"That isn't polite, you know."

"And blowing up museums is?"

"Everyone's entitled to some sort of pastime," says Cleversmith. "Why do you want to interfere with ours?"

"You actually expect me to answer that?"

"It seems like a reasonable question to me."

Vulpius does not quite know, for the moment, how to reply to that. Into his silence Picasso says, "Do we really need to stand here discussing all this in the public street? We've got some excellent brandy in our lodge."

***

It does not occur to Vulpius except in the most theoretical way that he might be in danger. Touching off an eruption of Mount Vesuvius, causing the foundation of the Washington Monument to give way, dropping a turbulence bomb amidst the ruins of Byzantium, all these are activities of one certain sort; actually taking human life is a different kind of thing entirely. It is not done. There has not been an instance of it in centuries.

The possibility exists, of course, that these four might well be capable of it. No one has destroyed any museums in a long time either, perhaps not since the savage and brutal twentieth century in which the originals of three of these four men lived their lives. But these are not actual men of the twentieth century, and, in any case, from what Vulpius knows of their originals he doubts that they themselves would have been capable of murder. He will take his chances up above.

The brandy is, in fact, superb. Picasso pours with a free hand, filling and refilling the sparkling bowl-shaped glasses. Only Hemingway refuses to partake. He is not, he explains, fond of drinking.

Vulpius is astonished by the mountaintop villa's elegance and comfort. He had visited it surreptitiously the week before, entering in the absence of the conspirators to plant his spy-eye, but stayed only long enough then to do the job. Now he has the opportunity to view it detail. It is a magnificent eyrie, a chain of seven spherical rooms clinging to a craggy outthrust fang of the Matterhorn. Great gleaming windows everywhere provide views of the surrounding peaks and spires and the huge breathtaking chasm that separates the mountain from the town below. The air outside is moist and mild. Tropical vines and blossoming shrubs grow all about. It is hard even to imagine that this once was a place of glittering glaciers and killing cold.

"Tell us," Cleversmith says, after a while, "why it is you believe that the artifacts of the former world are worthy of continued preservation. Eh, Vulpius? What do you say?"

"You have it upside down," Vulpius says. "I don't need to do any defending. You do."

"Do I? We do as we please. For us it is pleasant sport. No lives are lost. Mere useless objects are swept into nonexistence, which they deserve. What possible objection can you have to that?"

"They are the world's heritage. They are all we have to show for ten thousand years of civilization."

"Listen to him," says Einstein, laughing. "Civilization!"

"Civilization," says Hemingway, "gave us the Great Warming. There was ice up here once, you know. There were huge ice packs at both poles. They melted and flooded half the planet. The ancients caused that to happen. Is that something to be proud of, what they did?"

"I think it is," Vulpius says, with a defiant glare. "It brought us our wonderful gentle climate. We have parks and gardens everywhere, even in these mountains. Would you prefer ice and snow?"

"Then there's war," Cleversmith says. "Battle, bloodshed, bombs. People dying by tens of millions. We barely have tens of millions of people any more, and they would kill off that many in no time at all in their wars. That's what the civilization you love so much accomplished. That's what all these fancy temples and museums commemorate, you know. Terror and destruction."

"The Taj Mahal—the Sistine Chapel—"

"Pretty in themselves," says Einstein. "But you get behind the prettiness and you find that they're just symbols of oppression, conquest, tyranny. Wherever you look in the ancient world, that's what you find: oppression, conquest, tyranny. Better that all of that is swept away, wouldn't you think?"

Vulpius is speechless.

"Have another brandy," Picasso says, and fills everyone's glass unasked.

Vulpius sips. He's already had a little too much, and perhaps there's some risk in having more just now, because he feels it already affecting his ability to respond to what they are saying. But it is awfully good.

He shakes his head to clear it and says, "Even if I were to accept what you claim, that everything beautiful left to us from the ancient world is linked in some way to the terrible crimes of the ancients, the fact is that those crimes are no longer being committed. No matter what their origin, the beautiful objects that the people of the past left behind ought to be protected and admired for their great beauty, which perhaps we're incapable of duplicating today. Whereas if you're allowed to have your way, we'll soon be left without anything that represents—"

"What did you say?" Cleversmith interrupts. "'Which perhaps we're incapable of duplicating today,' wasn't it? Yes. That's what you said. And I quite agree. It's an issue we need to consider, my friend, because it has bearing on our dispute. Where's today's great art? Or great science, for that matter? Picasso, Einstein, Hemingway—the original ones—who today can match their work?"

Vulpius says, "And don't forget your own ancestor, Cleversmith, who built the Great Singapore Tower, which you yourself turned to so much rubble."

"My point exactly. He lived two hundred years ago. We still had a little creativity left, then. Now we function on the accumulated intellectual capital of the past."

"What are you talking about?" Vulpius says, bewildered.

"Come. Here. Look out this window. What do you see?"

"The mountainside. Your villa's garden, and the forest beyond."

"A garden, yes. A glorious one. And on and on right to the horizon, garden after garden. It's Eden out there, Vulpius. That's an ancient name for paradise. Eden. We live in paradise."

"Is there anything wrong with that?"

"Nothing much gets accomplished in paradise," Hemingway says. "Look at the four of us: Picasso, Hemingway, Einstein, Cleversmith. What have we created in our lives, we four, that compares with the work of the earlier men who had those names?"

"But you aren't those men. You're nothing but clones."

They seem stung by that for an instant. Then Cleversmith, recovering quickly, says, "Precisely so. We carry the genes of great ancient overachievers, but we do nothing to fulfill our own potential. We're superfluous men, mere genetic reservoirs. Where are our great works? It's as though our famous forebears have done it all and nothing's left for us to attempt."

"What would be the point of writing Hemingway's books all over again, or painting Picasso's paintings, or—"

"I don't mean that. There's no need for us to do their work again, obviously, but why haven't we even done our own? I'll tell you why. Life's too easy nowadays. I mean that without strife, without challenge—"

"No," Vulpius says. "Ten minutes ago Einstein here was arguing that the Taj Mahal and the Sistine Chapel had to be destroyed because they're symbols of a bloody age of tyranny and war. That thesis made very little sense to me, but let it pass, because now you seem to be telling me that what we need most in the world is a revival of war—"

"Of challenge," says Cleversmith. He leans forward. His entire body is taut. His eyes now have taken on some of the intensity of Picasso's. In a low voice he says, "We are slaves to the past, do you know that? Out of that grisly brutal world that lies a thousand years behind us came the soft life that we all lead today, which is killing us with laziness and boredom. It's antiquity's final joke. We have to sweep it all away, Vulpius. We have to make the world risky again...Give him another drink, Pablo."

"No. I've had enough."

But Picasso pours. Vulpius drinks.

"Let me see if I understand what you're trying to say—"

***

Somewhere during the long boozy night the truth finds him like an arrow coursing through darkness: these men are fiercely resentful of being clones, and want to destroy the world's past so that their own lives can at last be decoupled from it. They may be striking at the Blue Mosque and the Sistine Chapel, but their real targets are Picasso, Hemingway, Cleversmith, and Einstein. And, somewhere much later in that sleepless night, just as a jade-hued dawn streaked with broad swirling swaths of scarlet and topaz is breaking over the Alps, Vulpius's own resistance to their misdeeds breaks down. He is more tipsy than he has ever been before, and weary almost to tears besides. And when Picasso suddenly says, "By the way, Vulpius, what are the great accomplishments of your life?" he collapses inwardly before the thrust.

"Mine?" he says dully, blinking in confusion.

"Yes. We're mere clones, and nothing much is to be expected from us, but what have you managed to do with your time?"

"Well—I travel—I observe—I study phenomena—"

"And then what?"

He pauses a moment. "Why, nothing. I take the next trip."

"Ah. I see."

Picasso's cold smile is diabolical, a wedge that goes through Vulpius with shattering force. In a single frightful moment he sees that all is over, that the many months of his quest have been pointless. He has no power to thwart this kind of passionate intensity. That much is clear to him now. They are making an art-form out of destruction, it seems. Very well. Let them do as they please. Let them. Let them. If this is what they need to do, he thinks, what business is it of his? There's no way that his logic can be any match for their lunacy.

Cleversmith is saying, "Do you know what a train is, Vulpius?

"A train. Yes."

"We're at the station. The train is coming, the Millennium Express. It'll take us from the toxic past to the radiant future. We don't want to miss the train, do we, Vulpius?"

"The train is coming," says Vulpius. "Yes." Picasso, irrepressible, waves yet another flask of brandy at him. Vulpius shakes him off. Outside, the first shafts of golden sunlight are cutting through the dense atmospheric vapors. Jagged Alpine peaks, mantled in jungle greenery reddened by the new day, glow in the distance, Mont Blanc to the west, the Jungfrau in the north, Monte Rosa to the east. The gray-green plains of Italy unroll southward.

"This is our last chance to save ourselves," says Cleversmith urgently. "We have to act now, before the new era can get a grasp on us and throttle us into obedience." He looms up before Vulpius, weaving in the dimness of the room like a serpent. "I ask you to help us."

"Surely you can't expect me to take part in—"

"Decide for us, at least. The Louvre has to go. That's a given. Well, then: implosion or explosion, which is it to be?"

"Implosion," says Einstein, swaying from side to side in front of Vulpius. The soft eyes beg for his support. Behind him, Hemingway makes vociferous gestures of agreement.

"No," Picasso says. "Blow it up!" He flings his arms grandly outward. "Boom! Boom!"

"Boom, yes," says Cleversmith, very quietly. "I agree. So, Vulpius: you will cast the deciding vote."

"No. I absolutely refuse to —"

"Which? Which? One or the other?"

They march around and around him, demanding that he decide the issue for them. They will keep him here, he sees, until he yields. Well, what difference does it make, explode, implode? Destruction is destruction.

"Suppose we toss a coin for it," Cleversmith says finally, and the others nod eager agreement. Vulpius is not sure what that means, tossing a coin, but sighs in relief: apparently he is off the hook. But then Cleversmith produces a sleek bright disk of silvery metal from his pocket and presses it into Vulpius's palm. "Here," he says. "You do it."

Coinage is long obsolete. This is an artifact, hundreds of years old, probably stolen from some museum. It bears a surging three-tailed comet on one face and the solar-system symbol on the other. "Heads we explode, tails we implode," Einstein declares. "Go on, dear friend. Toss it and catch it and tell us which side is up." They crowd in, close up against him. Vulpius tosses the coin aloft, catches it with a desperate lunge, claps it down against the back of his left hand. Holds it covered for a moment. Reveals it. The comet is showing. But is that side heads or tails? He has no idea.

Cleversmith says sternly, "Well? Heads or tails?"

Vulpius, at the last extremity of fatigue, smiles benignly up at him. Heads or tails, what does it matter? What concern of his is any of this?

"Heads," he announces randomly. "Explosion."

"Boom!" cries jubilant Picasso. "Boom! Boom! Boom!"

"My friend, you have our deepest thanks," Cleversmith says. "We are all agreed, then, that the decision is final? Ernest? Albert?"

"May I go back to my hotel now?" Vulpius asks.

They accompany him down the mountainside, see him home, wish him a fond farewell. But they are not quite done with him. He is still asleep, late that afternoon, when they come down into Zermatt to fetch him. They are leaving for Paris at once, Cleversmith informs him, and he is invited to accompany them. He must witness their deed once more; he must give it his benediction. Helplessly he watches as they pack his bag. A car is waiting outside.

"Paris," Cleversmith tells it, and off they go.

Picasso sits beside him. "Brandy?" he asks.

"Thank you, no."

"Don't mind if I do?"

Vulpius shrugs. His head is pounding. Cleversmith and Hemingway, in the front seat, are singing raucously. Picasso, a moment later, joins in, and then Einstein. Each one of them seems to be singing in a different key. Vulpius takes the flask from Picasso and pours some brandy for himself with an unsteady hand.

In Paris, Vulpius rests at their hotel, a venerable gray heap just south of the Seine, while they go about their tasks. This is the moment to report them to the authorities, he knows. Briefly he struggles to find the will to do what is necesary. But it is not there. Somehow all desire to intervene has been burned out of him. Perhaps, he thinks, the all-too-placid world actually needs the goad of strife that these exasperating men so gleefully provide. In any case the train is nearing the station: it's too late to halt it now.

"Come with us," Hemingway says, beckoning from the hallway.

He follows them, willy-nilly. They lead him to the highest floor of the building and through a narrow doorway that leads onto the roof. The sky is a wondrous black star-speckled vault overhead. Heavy tropic warmth hangs over Paris this December night. Just before them lies the river, glinting by the light of a crescent moon. The row of ancient bookstalls along its rim is visible, and the gray bulk of the Louvre across the way, and the spires of Notre Dame far off to the right.

"What time is it?" Einstein asks.

"Almost midnight," says Picasso. "Shall we do it, Vjong?"

"As good a time as any," says Cleversmith, and touches two tiny contacts together.

For a moment nothing happens. Then there is a deafening sound and a fiery lance spurts up out of the glass pyramid in the courtyard of the museum on the far side of the river. Two straight fissures appear in the courtyard's pavement, crossing at ninety-degree angles, and very quickly the entire surface of the courtyard peels upward and outward along the lines of the subterranean incision, hurling two quadrants toward the river and flipping the other two backward into the streets of the Right Bank. As the explosion gathers force, the thick-walled medieval buildings of the surrounding quadrangle of the Louvre are carried high into the air, the inner walls giving way first, then the dark line of the roof. Into the air go the hoarded treasures of the ages, Mona Lisa and the Winged Victory of Samothrace, Venus de Milo and the Codex of Hammurabi, Rembrandt and Botticelli, Michelangelo and Rubens, Titian and Brueghel and Bosch, all soaring grandly overhead. The citizenry of Paris, having heard that great boom, rush into the streets to watch the spectacle. The midnight sky is raining the billion fragments of a million masterpieces. The crowd is cheering.

And then an even greater cry goes up, wrung spontaneously from ten thousand throats. The hour of the new millennium has come. It is, very suddenly, the year 3000. Fireworks erupt everywhere, a dazzling sky-splitting display, brilliant reds and purples and greens forming sphere within sphere within sphere. Hemingway and Picasso are dancing together about the rooftop, the big man and the small. Einstein does a wild solo, flinging his arms about. Cleversmith stands statue-still, head thrown back, face a mask of ecstasy. Vulpius, who has begun to tremble with strange excitement, is surprised to find himself cheering with all the rest. Unexpected tears of joy stream from his eyes. He is no longer able to deny the logic of these men's madness. The iron hand of the past has been flung aside. The new era will begin with a clean slate.

WITH CAESAR IN THE UNDERWORLD (2001)

INTRODUCTION

Even if the previous story earns its place in the final section of this book under slightly fishy circumstances, I still am writing, here in the real twenty-first century, and to prove it, I close this collection with one that unquestionably came forth from the word processor in November of 2001, a genuine twenty-first-century year, and was published in *Asimov's Science Fiction* in the authentically twenty-first-century issue dated October-November 2002. It was one of the major segments of my *Roma Eterna* sequence, a ten-part project that occupied me through three different decades.

In the autumn of 1987 I wrote a story for Ellen Datlow of *Omni* called "To the Promised Land," postulating that the Hebrew exodus from Egypt under Moses had failed and thus there had never been a Jewish presence in Palestine out of which the prophet we know as Jesus had emerged. Rome, therefore, undistracted by the problems that the rise of Christianity had caused for it, was able in its continuing pagan state to fend off the various barbarian tribes that (in our timeline) caused its downfall, renewing itself constantly during the period we call the Dark Ages and continuing to rule most of Europe and much of Asia on into our own day. "To the Promised Land," which I set in what would have been the late twentieth century of the Christian era but was the year 2723 of the Roman calendar, depicted the Jews still in Egypt — a province of the Second Roman Republic — working now on the development of a starship that would take them to some new destiny on another world.

It was a clever idea, I thought. Too clever, perhaps, to toss away on a single short story. In odd moments I began sketching out a chronology for my imaginary Rome — the true Roma Eterna, invincible and unending — covering some fifteen centuries. My history of this alternate world was more or less identical (aside from a somewhat different sequence of third-century Emperors) to that of *our* Rome as it developed through the fourth century A.D., when Constantine the Great first divided the Empire into eastern and western domains, but then things began to diverge, since the historical western half of the Roman Empire collapsed in the fifth century A.D., and mine did not. I allowed for periods of decadence and revival, and for the conquest of the Western Empire by its Byzantine counterpart and its eventual liberation, leading to a reunification of the whole vast dominion. I planned for equivalents of the Renaissance and the industrial revolution, and even for a Roman version of the French revolution, complete with its own reign of terror.

And then, bit by bit, as occasions arose, I wrote the stories that illustrated the events on my chart.

The first of them was written in April of 1989 for the 40th anniversary issue of *Fantasy & Science Fiction*. I still remembered my delight, as a barely adolescent young reader of science fiction in 1949, at the birth of that elegant magazine, and I had always taken special pleasure in writing stories for it. My "Sundance" of 1968 had been reprinted in *F&SF's* huge 30th anniversary issue, October, 1979, which assembled landmark stories from the magazine's first three decades. Now Ed Ferman, *F&SF's* editor and publisher, wanted a new story from me for the 40th anniversary, and I provided the second Roma Eterna piece, "Tales from the Venia Woods," which duly appeared in the October, 1989 issue.

Gardner Dozois picked it for his *Year's Best Science fiction* anthology the following year, and, indeed, expressed great enthusiasm for the whole Roma Eterna concept — so much so that in 1991 I wrote a third Roma story, "An Outpost of the Empire," for Dozois's own magazine, *Asimov's Science Fiction*. By this time I saw that I could ultimately assemble the entire series of stories into a book, and I went on writing Roma stories now and then through the 1990s — "Via Roma" and "Waiting for the End" for Gardner, "Getting to Know the Dragon" for my own anthology, *Far Horizons*, and "A Hero of the Empire" for *Fantasy & Science Fiction*, published in yet another anniversary issue of that magazine — its 50th. Having had stories in the 30th and 40th anniversary editions, it seemed only proper to contribute to this one, too, and Gordon van Gelder, who had succeeded Ferman as the magazine's editor and publisher, agreed.

Then I put the series away for a while. But in the winter of 2001-2002 I decided to complete the group for book publication, and wrote three final Roma Eterna stories to deal with various untold segments of my original chronology. The complete version was published in 2003 as *Roma Eterna*. So, after some fifteen years, I was finished with my alternate-Rome project.

"With Caesar in the Underworld" was the longest and, I think, the richest of the three. It was designed to be the opening story of the book — how fitting that after I had done the last story in the sequence first, the first one chronologically would be among the last ones written, fourteen years later!

The timeline of the Roma Eterna stories runs from 753 B.C., the traditional date of the founding of the city; our year 2004 is 2757 by Roman reckoning. "With Caesar in the Underworld" is set in the Roman year 1282 — that is, 529 A.D., when my imaginary history had only begun to diverge from Rome's real one. My intention was to portray the dazzling strangeness, the potent *alienness,* of the actual Rome of history, against my own invented background. When I had done with "With Caesar" I went on to write the other two, and the complete group of stories, linked now to form a kind of chronicle-novel, was published in 2003 as *Roma Eterna.* So, after some fifteen years, I was finished with my alternate-Rome project.

But lately it has occurred to me that *Fantasy & Science Fiction* is due for its 60th anniversary in the autumn of 2009. That date, which once sounded so futuristic, is now just a few years away. If Gordon van Gelder, his magazine, and I all hold out until then, he will no doubt ask me to contribute something to the issue, since I've had material in the previous three of these once-in-a-decade events.

My parallel-world Roman history spans fifteen hundred years. The ten stories of *Roma Eterna* deal fairly comprehensively with most of the dramatic moments of those fifteen centuries, but there were a couple of major crises that I mentioned only indirectly in the ten existing stories. So there is room to continue the saga. Will I return to eternal Rome once more, even though the book is finished? We'll all find out, I guess, in 2009.

With Caesar in the Underworld

The newly arrived ambassador from the Eastern Emperor was rather younger than Faustus had expected him to be: a smallish sort, finely built, quite handsome in what was almost a girlish kind of way, though obviously very capable and sharp, a man who would bear close watching. There was something a bit frightening about him, though not at first glance. He gleamed with the imperviousness of fine armor. His air of sophisticated and fastidious languor coupled with hidden strength made Faustus, a tall, robust, florid-faced man going thick through the waist and thin about the scalp, feel positively plebeian and coarse despite his own lofty and significant ancestry.

That morning Faustus, whose task as an official of the Chancellery it was to greet all such important visitors to the capital city, had gone out to Ostia to meet him at the Imperial pier — the Greek envoy, coming west by way of Sicillia, had sailed up the coast from Neapolis in the south — and had escorted him to the rooms in the old Severan Palace where the occasional ambassadors from the Eastern half of the Empire were housed. Now it was the time to begin establishing a little rapport. They faced each other across an onyx-slab table in the Lesser Hall of Columns, which several reigns ago had been transformed into a somewhat oversized sitting-room. A certain amount of preliminary social chatter was required at this point. Faustus called for some wine, one of the big, elegant wines from the great vineyards of Gallia Transalpina.

After they had had a chance to savor it for a little while he said, wanting to get the ticklish part of the situation out in the open right away, "The prince Heraclius himself, unfortunately, has been called without warning to the northern frontier. Therefore tonight's dinner has been canceled. This will be a free evening for you, then, an evening for resting after your long journey. I trust that that'll be acceptable to you."

"Ah," said the Greek, and his lips tightened for an instant. Plainly he was a little bewildered at being left on his own like this, his first evening in Roma. He studied his perfectly manicured fingers. When he glanced up again, there was a gleam of concern in the dark eyes. "I won't be seeing the Emperor either, then?"

"The Emperor is in very poor health. He will not be able to see you tonight and perhaps not for several days. The prince Heraclius has taken over many of his responsibilities. But in the prince's unexpected and unavoidable absence your host and companion for your first few days in Roma will be his younger brother Maximilianus. You will, I know, find him amusing and very charming, my lord Menandros."

"Unlike his brother, I gather," said the Greek ambassador coolly.

Only too true, Faustus thought. But it was a remarkably blunt thing to say. Faustus searched for the motive behind the little man's words. Menandros had come here, after all, to negotiate a marriage between his royal master's sister and the very prince of whom he had just spoken so slightingly. When a diplomat as polished as this finely oiled Greek says something as egregiously undiplomatic as that, there was usually a good reason for it. Perhaps, Faustus supposed, Menandros was simply showing annoyance at the fact that Prince Heraclius had tactlessly managed not to be on hand to welcome him upon his entry into Roma.

Faustus was not going to let himself be drawn any deeper into comparisons, though. He allowed himself only an oblique smile, that faint sidewise smile he had learned from his young friend the Caesar Maximilianus. "The two brothers are quite different in personality, that I do concede...Will you have more wine, your excellence?"

That brought yet another shift of tone. "Ah, no formalities, no formalities, I pray you. Let us be friends, you and I." And then, leaning forward cozily and shifting from the formal to the intimate form of speech: "You must call me Menandros. I will call you Faustus. Eh, my friend?— And yes, more wine, by all means. What excellent stuff! We have nothing that can match it in Constantinopolis. What sort is it, actually?"

Faustus flicked a glance at one of the waiting servitors, who quickly refilled the bowls. "A wine from Gallia," he said. "I forget the name." A swift flash of unmistakable displeasure, quickly concealed but not quickly enough, crossed the Greek's face. To be caught praising a provincial wine so highly must have embarrassed him. But embarrassing him had not been Faustus's intention. There was nothing to be gained by creating discomfort for so powerful and potentially valuable a personage as the lord of the East's ambassador to the Western court.

This was all getting worse and worse. Hastily Faustus set about smoothing the awkwardness over. "The heart of our production lies in Gallia, now. The Emperor's cellars contain scarcely any Italian wines at all, they tell me. Scarcely any! These Gallian reds are His Imperial Majesty's preference by far, I assure you."

"While I am here I must acquire some, then, for the cellars of His Majesty Justinianus," said Menandros.

They drank a moment in silence. Faustus felt as though he were dancing on swords.

"This is, I understand, your first visit to Urbs Roma?" Faustus asked, when the silence had gone on just a trifle too long. He took care to use the familiar form too, now that Menandros had started it.

"My first, yes. Most of my career has been spent in Aegyptus and Syria."

Faustus wondered how extensive that career could have been. This Menandros seemed to be no more than twenty-five or so, thirty at the utmost. Of course, all these smooth-skinned dark-eyed Greeks, buffed and oiled and pomaded in their Oriental fashion, tended to look younger than they really were. And now that Faustus had passed fifty, he was finding it harder and harder to make distinctions of age in any precise way: everybody around him at the court seemed terribly young to him now, a congregation of mere boys and girls. Of those who had ruled the Empire when Faustus himself was young, there was no one left except the weary, lonely old Emperor himself, and hardly anyone had laid eyes on the Emperor in recent times. Of Faustus's own generation of courtiers, some had died off, the others had gone into cozy retirement far away. Faustus was a dozen years older than his own superior minister in the Chancellery. His closest friend here now was Maximilianus Caesar, who was considerably less than half his age. From the beginning Faustus had always regarded himself as a relic of some earlier era, because that was, in truth, what he was, considering that he was a member of a family that had held the throne three dynasties ago; but the phrase had taken on a harsh new meaning for him in these latter days, now that he had survived not just his family's greatness but even his own contemporaries.

It was a little disconcerting that Justinianus had sent so youthful and apparently inexperienced an ambassador on so delicate a mission. But Faustus suspected it would be a mistake to underestimate this man; and at least Menandros's lack of familiarity with the capital city would provide him with a convenient way to glide past whatever difficulties Prince Heraclius's untimely absence might cause in the next few days.

Stagily Faustus clapped his hands. "How I envy you, friend Menandros! To see Urbs Roma in all its splendor for the first time! What an overwhelming experience it will be for you! We who were born here, who take it all for granted, can never appreciate it as you will. The grandeur. The magnificence." Yes, yes, he thought, let Maximilianus march him from one end of the city to the other until Heraclius gets back. We will dazzle him with our wonders and after a time he'll forget how discourteously Heraclius has treated him. "While you're waiting for the Caesar to return, we'll arrange the most extensive tours for you. All the great temples — the amphitheater—the baths—the Forum—the Capitol—the palaces—the wonderful gardens—"

"The grottos of Titus Gallius," Menandros said, unexpectedly. "The underground temples and shrines. The marketplace of the sorcerers. The catacomb of the holy Chaldean prostitutes. The pool of the Baptai. The labyrinth of the Maenads. The caverns of the witches."

"Ah? So you know of those places too?"

"Who doesn't know about the Underworld of Urbs Roma? It's the talk of the whole Empire." In an instant that bright metallic facade of his seemed to melt away, and all his menacing poise. Something quite different was visible in Menandros's eyes now, a wholly uncalculated eagerness, an undisguised boyish enthusiasm. And a certain roguishness, too, a hint of rough, coarse appetites that belied his urbane gloss. In a soft, confiding tone he said, "May I confess something, Faustus? Magnificence bores me. I've got a bit of a taste for the low life. All that dodgy stuff that Roma's so famous for, the dark, seamy underbelly of the city, the whores and the magicians, the freak shows and the orgies and the thieves' markets, the strange shrines of your weird cults—do I shock you, Faustus? Is this dreadfully undiplomatic of me to admit? I don't need a tour of the temples. But as long as we have a few days before I have to get down to serious business, it's the other side of Roma I want to see, the mysterious side, the dark side. We have temples and palaces enough in Constantinopolis, and baths, and all the rest of that. Miles and miles of glorious shining marble, until you want to cry out for mercy. But the true subterranean mysteries, the earthy, dirty, smelly, underground things, ah, no, Faustus, those are what really interest me. We've rooted all that stuff out, at Constantinopolis. It's considered dangerous decadent nonsense."

"It is here, too," said Faustus quietly.

"Yes, but you permit it! You revel in it, even! Or so I'm told, on pretty good authority...You heard me say I was formerly stationed in Aegyptus and Syria. The ancient East, that is to say, thousands of years older than Roma or Constantinopolis. Most of the strange cults originated there, you know. That was where I developed my interest in them. And the things I've seen and heard and done in places like Damascus and Alexandria and Antioch, well—but nowadays Urbs Roma is the center of everything of that sort, is it not, the capital of marvels! And I tell you, Faustus, what I truly crave experiencing is—"

He halted in midsentence, looking flushed and a little stunned.

"This wine," he said, with a little shake of his head. "I've been drinking it too quickly. It must be stronger than I thought."

Faustus reached across the table and laid his hand gently on the younger man's wrist. "Have no fear, my friend. These revelations of yours cause me no dismay. I am no stranger to the Underworld, nor is the prince

Maximilianus. And while we await the return of Prince Heraclius he and I will show you everything you desire." He rose, stepping back a couple of paces so that he would not seem, in his bulky way, to be looming in an intimidating manner over the reclining ambassador. After a bad start he had regained some advantage; he didn't want to push it too far. "I'll leave you now. You've had a lengthy journey, and you'll want your rest. I'll send in your servants. In addition to those who accompanied you from Constantinopolis, these men and women" — he indicated the slaves who stood arrayed in the shadows around the room—"are at your command day and night. They are yours. Ask them for anything. *Anything*, my lord Menandros."

***

His palanquin and bearers were waiting outside. "Take me to the apartments of the Caesar," Faustus said crisply, and clambered inside.

They knew which Caesar he meant. In Roma the name could be applied to a great many persons of high birth, from the Emperor on down—Faustus himself had some claim to using it—but as a rule, these days, it was an appellation employed only in reference to the two sons of the Emperor Maximilianus II. And, whether or not Faustus's bearers happened to be aware that the elder son was out of town, they were clever enough to understand that their master would in all probability not be asking them to take him to the chambers of the austere and dreary Prince Heraclius. No, no, it was the younger son, the pleasantly dissolute Maximilianus Caesar, whose rooms would surely be his chosen destination: Prince Maximilianus, the friend, the companion, the dearest and most special friend and companion, for all intents and purposes at the present time the *only* true friend and companion, of that aging and ever lonelier minor official of the Imperial court, Faustus Flavius Constantinus Caesar.

Maximilianus lived over at the far side of the Palatine, in a handsome pink-marble palace of relatively modest size that had been occupied by younger sons of the Emperor for the past half dozen reigns or so. The prince, a red-haired, blue-eyed, long-limbed man who was a match for Faustus in height but lean and rangy where Faustus was burly and ponderous, peeled himself upward from a divan as Faustus entered and greeted him with a warm embrace and a tall beaker of chilled white wine. That Faustus had been drinking red with the Greek ambassador for the past hour and a half did not matter now. Maximilianus, in his capacity as prince of the royal blood, had access to the best caves of the Imperial cellars, and what was most pleasing to the prince's palate was the rare white wines of the Alban Hills, the older and sweeter and colder the better. When

Faustus was with him, the white wines of the Alban Hills were what Faustus drank.

"Look at these," Maximilianus said, before Faustus had had a chance to say anything whatever beyond a word of appreciation for the wine. The prince drew forth a long, fat pouch of purple velvet and with a great sweeping gesture sent a blazing hoard of jewelry spilling out on the table: a tangled mass of necklaces, earrings, rings, pendants, all of them evidently fashioned from opals set in filigree of gold, opals of every hue and type, pink ones, milky ones, opals of shimmering green, midnight black, fiery scarlet. Maximilianus exultantly scooped them up in both hands and let them dribble through his fingers. His eyes were glowing. He appeared enthralled by the brilliant display.

Faustus stared puzzledly at the sprawling scatter of bright trinkets. These were extremely beautiful baubles, yes: but the degree of Maximilianus's excitement over them seemed excessive. Why was the prince so fascinated by them? "Very pretty," Faustus said. "Are they something you won at the gambling tables? Or did you buy these trinkets as a gift for one of your ladies?"

"Trinkets!" Maximilianus cried. "The jewels of Cybele is what they are! The treasure of the high priestess of the Great Mother! Aren't they lovely, Faustus? The Hebrew brought them just now. They're stolen, of course. From the goddess's most sacred sanctuary. I'm going to give them to my new sister-in-law as a wedding present."

"Stolen? From the sanctuary? Which sanctuary? Which Hebrew? What are you talking about, Maximilianus?"

The prince grinned and pressed one of the biggest of the pendants into the fleshy palm of Faustus's left hand, closing Faustus's fingers tightly over it. He gave Faustus a broad wink. "Hold it. Squeeze it. Feel the throbbing magic of the goddess pouring into you. Is your cock getting stiff yet? That's what should be happening, Faustus. Amulets of fertility are what we have here. Of enormous efficacy. In the sanctuary, the priestess wears them and anyone she touches with the stone becomes an absolute seething mass of procreative energy. Heraclius's princess will conceive an heir for him the first time he gets inside her. It's virtually guaranteed. The dynasty continues. My little favor for my chilly and sexless brother. I'll explain it all to his beloved, and she'll know what to do. Eh? Eh?" Maximilianus amiably patted Faustus's belly. "What are you feeling down there, old man?"

Faustus handed the pendant back. "What I feel is that you may have gone a little too far, this time. Who did you get these things from? Danielus bar-Heap?"

"Bar-Heap, yes, of course. Who else?"

"And where did he get them? Stole them from the Temple of the Great Mother, did he? Strolled through the grotto one dark night and slipped into the sanctuary when the priestesses weren't looking?" Faustus closed his eyes, put his hand across them, blew his breath outward through closed lips in a noisy, rumbling burst of astonishment and disapproval. He was even shocked, a little. That was something of an unusual emotion for him. Maximilianus was the only man in the realm capable of making him feel stodgy and priggish. "In the name of Jove Almighty, Maximilianus, tell me how you think you can give stolen goods as a wedding gift! For a royal wedding, no less. Don't you think there'll be an outcry raised from here to India and back when the high priestess finds out that this stuff is missing?"

Maximilianus, offering Faustus his sly, inward sort of smile, gathered the jewelry back into the pouch. "You grow silly in your dotage, old man. Is it your idea that these jewels were stolen from the sanctuary yesterday? As a matter of fact, it happened during the reign of Marcus Anastasius, which was — what? Two hundred fifty years ago? — and the sanctuary they were stolen from wasn't here at all, it was somewhere in Phrygia, wherever that may be, and they've had at least five legitimate owners since then, which is certainly enough to disqualify them as stolen goods by this time. It happens also that I paid good hard cash for them. I told the Hebrew that I needed a fancy wedding present for the elder Caesar's bride, and he said that this little collection was on the market, and I said, fine, get them for me, and I gave him enough gold pieces to outweigh *two* fat Faustuses, and he went down into the Jewelers' Grotto this very night past and closed the deal, and here they are. I want to see the look on my dear brother's face when I present these treasures to his lovely bride Sabbatia, gifts truly worthy of a queen. And then when I tell him about the special powers they're supposed to have. 'Beloved brother,'" Maximilianus said, in a high, piping tone of savage derision, "'I thought you might need some aid in consummating your marriage, and therefore I advise you to have your bride wear this ring on the wedding night, and to put this bracelet upon her wrist, and also to invite your lady to drape this pendant between her breasts—'"

Faustus felt the beginnings of a headache. There were times when the Caesar's madcap exuberance was too much even for him. In silence he helped himself to more wine, and drank it down in deep, slow, deliberate drafts. Then he walked toward the window and stood with his back toward the prince.

Could he trust what Maximilianus was telling him about the provenance of these jewels? Had they in fact been taken from the sanctuary in antiquity, or had some thief snatched them just the other day? That would be all we need, he thought. Right in the middle of the negotiations for a desperately needed military alliance that were scheduled to follow the marriage of the Western prince and the Eastern princess, the pious and exceedingly virtuous Justinianus discovers that his new brother-in-law's brother has blithely given the sister of the Eastern Emperor a stolen and sacrilegious wedding gift. A gift that even now might be the object of an intensive police search.

Maximilianus was still going on about the jewels. Faustus paid little attention. A soothing drift of cool air floated toward him out of the twilight, carrying with it a delightfully complex mingling of odors, cinnamon, pepper, nutmeg, roasted meat, rich wine, pungent perfume, the tang of sliced lemons, all the wondrous aromas of some nearby lavish banquet. It was quite refreshing.

Under the benign mellowing influence of the fragrant breeze from outside Faustus felt his little fit of scrupulosity beginning to pass. There was nothing to worry about here, really. Very likely the transaction had been legitimate. But even if the opals *had* just been stolen from the Great Mother's sanctuary, there would be little that the outraged priestesses could do about it, since the police investigation was in no way likely to reach into the household of the Imperial family. And that Maximilianus's gift was reputed to have aphrodisiac powers would be a fine joke on his prissy, tight-lipped brother.

Faustus felt a great sudden surge of love for his friend Maximilianus pass through him. Once again the prince had shown him that although he was only half his age, he was more than his equal in all-around deviltry; and that was saying quite a lot.

"Did the ambassador show you a picture of her, by the way?" Maximilianus asked.

Faustus glanced around. "Why should he? I'm not the one who's marrying her."

"I was just curious. I was wondering if she's as ugly as they say. The word is that she looks just like her brother, you know. And Justinianus has the face of a horse. She's a lot older than Heraclius, too."

"Is she? I hadn't heard."

"Justinianus is forty-five or so, right? Is it likely that he would have a sister of eighteen or twenty?"

"She could be twenty-five, perhaps."

"Thirty-five, more likely. Or even older. Heraclius is twenty-nine. My brother is going to marry an ugly old woman. Who may not even still be of childbearing age—has anyone considered that?"

"An ugly old woman, if that's indeed the case, who happens to be the sister of the Eastern Emperor," Faustus pointed out, "and who therefore will create a blood bond between the two halves of the realm that will be very useful to us when we ask Justinianus to lend us a few legions to help us fend off the barbarians in the north, now that our friends the Goths and the Vandals are chewing on our toes up there again. Whether she's of childbearing age is incidental. Heirs to the throne can always be adopted, you know."

"Yes. Of course they can. But the main thing, the grand alliance—is that so important, Faustus? If the smelly barbarians have come back for another round, why can't we fend them off ourselves? My father managed a pretty good job of that when they came sniffing around our frontiers in '42, didn't he? Not to mention what his grandfather did to Attila and his Huns some fifty years before that."

"'42 was a long time ago," Faustus said. "Your father's old and sick, now. And we're currently a little short on great generals."

"What about Heraclius? He might amaze us all."

"Heraclius?" said Faustus. That was a startling thought—the aloof, waspish, ascetic Heraclius Caesar leading an army in the field. Even Maximilianus, frivolous and undisciplined and rowdy as he was, would make a more plausible candidate for the role of military hero than the pallid Heraclius.

With a mock-haughty sniff Maximilianus said, "I remind you, my lord Faustus, that we're a fighting dynasty. We have the blood of mighty warriors in our veins, my brother and I."

"Yes, the mighty warrior Heraclius," Faustus said acidly, and they both laughed.

"All right, then. I yield the point. We do need Justinianus's help, I suppose. So my brother marries the ugly princess, *her* brother helps us smash the savage hairy men of the north for once and all, and the whole Empire embarks upon a future of eternal peace, except perhaps for a squabble or two with the Persians, who are Justinianus's problem, not ours. Well, so be it. In any case, why should I care what Heraclius's wife looks like? *He* probably won't."

"True." The heir to the throne was not notorious for his interest in women.

"The Great Mother's jewels, if their reputation has any substance to it, will help him quickly engender a new little Caesar, let us hope. After which, he'll probably never lay a finger on her again, to her great relief and his, eh?" Maximilianus bounded up from his divan to pour more wine for Faustus, and for himself. "Has he really gone up north to inspect the troops, by the way? That's the tale I've heard, anyway."

"And I," said Faustus. "It's the official story, but I have my doubts. More likely he's headed off to his forests for a few days of hunting, by way of ducking the marriage issue as long as he can." That was the Caesar Heraclius's only known amusement, the tireless, joyless pursuit of stag and boar and fox and hare. "Let me tell you, the Greek ambassador was more than a little miffed when he found out that the prince had chosen the very week of his arrival to leave town. He let it be known very clearly, how annoyed he was. Which brings me to the main reason for this visit, in fact. I have work for you. It becomes your job and mine to keep the ambassador amused until Heraclius deigns to get back here."

Maximilianus responded with a lazy shrug. "Your job, perhaps. But why is it mine, old friend?"

"Because I think you'll enjoy it, once you know what I have in mind. And I've already committed you to it, besides, and you don't dare let me down. The ambassador wants to go on a tour of Roma—but not to the usual tourist attractions. He's interested in getting a look at the Underworld."

The Caesar's eyes widened. "He is? An ambassador, going *there?*"

"He's young. He's Greek. He may be pretty kinky, or else he'd simply like to be. I said that you and I would show him temples and palaces, and he said to show him the grottos and the whorehouses. The marketplace of the sorcerers, the caverns of the witches, that sort of thing. 'I've got a bit of a taste for the low life' is what he told me," Faustus said, in passable imitation of the drawling tones of Menandros's Eastern-accented Latin. "'The dark, seamy underbelly of the city,' is the very phrase he used. "'All that dodgy stuff that Roma's so famous for.'"

"A tourist," Maximilianus said, with scorn. "He just wants to take a tour that's slightly different from the standard one."

"Whatever. At any rate, I have to keep him entertained, and with your brother hiding out in the woods and your father ill I need to trot forth some other member of the Imperial family to play host for him, and who else is there but you? It's no more than half a day since he arrived in town and Heraclius has succeeded in offending him already, without even being here. The more annoyed he gets, the harder a bargain he's going to drive once your brother shows up. He's tougher than he looks and it's dangerous to underestimate him. If I leave him stewing in his own irritation for the next few days, there may be big trouble."

"Trouble? Of what sort? He can't call off the marriage just because he feels snubbed."

"No, I suppose he can't. But if he gets his jaw set the wrong way, he may report back to Justinianus that the next Emperor of the West is a bumbling fool not worth wasting soldiers on, let alone a sister. The princess Sabbatia quietly goes back to Constantinopolis a few months after the wedding and we get left to deal with the barbarians on our own. I like to think I'll be able to head all that off if I can distract the ambassador for a week or two by showing him a little dirty fun in the catacombs. You can help me with that. We've had some good times down there, you and I, eh, my friend? Now we can take him to some of our favorite places. Yes? Agreed?"

"May I bring along the Hebrew?" Maximilianus asked. "To be our guide. He knows the Underworld even better than we do."

"Danielus bar-Heap, you mean."

"Yes. Bar-Heap."

"By all means," said Faustus. "The more the merrier."

***

It was too late in the evening by the time he left Maximilianus's to go to the baths. Faustus returned to his own quarters instead and called for a hot bath, a massage, and, afterward, the slave-girl Oalathea, that dusky, lithe little sixteen-year-old Numidian with whom the only language Faustus had in common was that of Eros.

A long day it had been, and a hard, wearying one. He hadn't expected to find Heraclius gone when he came back from Ostia with the Eastern ambassador. Since the old Emperor Maximilianus was in such poor shape, the plan had been for the Greek ambassador to dine with Prince Heraclius on his first evening at the capital; but right after Faustus had set off for Ostia Heraclius had abruptly skipped out of the city, leaving behind the flimsy inspecting-the-northern-troops excuse. With the Emperor unwell and Heraclius away, there was no one of appropriate rank available to serve as official host at a state dinner except Heraclius's rapscallion brother Maximilianus, and none of the officials of the royal household had felt sufficiently audacious to propose *that* without getting Faustus's approval first. So the state dinner had simply been scrubbed that afternoon, a fact that Faustus had not discovered until his return from the port. By then it was too late to do anything about that, other than to send a frantic message after the vanished prince imploring him to head back to Urbs Roma as quickly as possible. If Heraclius had indeed gone hunting, the message would reach him at his forest lodge in the woods out beyond Lake Nemorensis, and perhaps, perhaps, he would pay heed to it. If he had, against all probability, really gone to the military frontier, he was unlikely to return very soon. And that left only the Caesar Maximilianus, willy-nilly, to do the job. A risky business, that could be.

Well, the ambassador's little confession of a bit of a taste for the low life had taken care of the issue of keeping him entertained, at least for the next couple of days. If slumming in the Underworld was what Menandros was truly after, then Maximilianus would become the solution instead of the problem.

Faustus leaned back in the bath, savoring the warmth of the water, enjoying the sweet smell of the oils floating on the surface. It was while in the bath that proper Romans of the olden days—Seneca, say, or the poet Lucan, or that fierce old harridan Antonia, the mother of the Emperor

Claudius—would take the opportunity to slit their wrists rather than continue to endure the inadequacies and iniquities of the society in which they lived. But these were not the olden days, and Faustus was not as offended by the inadequacies and iniquities of society as those grand old Romans had been, and, in any event, suicide as a general concept was not something that held great appeal for him.

Still, it certainly was a sad time for Roma, he thought. The old Emperor as good as dead, the heir to the throne a ninny and a prude, the Emperor's other son a wastrel, and the barbarians, who were supposed to have been crushed years ago, once again knocking at the gates. Faustus knew that he was no model of the ancient Roman virtues himself—who was, five centuries after Augustus's time?—but, for all his own weaknesses and foibles, he could not help crying out within himself, sometimes, at the tawdriness of the epoch. We call ourselves Romans, he thought, and we know how to imitate, up to a point, the attitudes and poses of our great Roman forebears. But that's all we do: strike attitudes and imitate poses. We merely play at being Romans, and deceive ourselves, sometimes, into accepting the imitation for the reality.

It is a sorry era, Faustus told himself.

He was of royal blood himself, more or less. His very name proclaimed that: Faustus Flavius Constantinus Caesar. Embedded within it was the cognomen of his famous imperial ancestor, Constantinus the Great, and along with it the name of Constantinus's wife Fausta, herself the daughter of the Emperor Maximianus. The dynasty of Constantinus had long vanished from the scene, of course, but by various genealogical zigs and zags Faustus could trace his descent back to it, and that entitled him to add the illustrious name "Caesar" to his array. Even so he was merely a secondary official in the chancellery of Maximilianus II Augustus, and his father before him had been an officer of trifling rank in the Army of the North, and his father before him—well, Faustus thought, best not to think of *him*. The family had had some reverses in the course of the two centuries since Constantinus the Great had occupied the throne. But no one could deny his lineage, and there were times when he found himself secretly looking upon the current royal family as mere newcomers to power, jumped up out of nowhere. Of course, the early Emperors, Augustus and Tiberius and Claudius and such, would have looked even upon Constantinus the Great as a jumped-up newcomer; and the great men of the old Republic, Camillus, for instance, or Claudius Marcellus, would probably have thought the same of Augustus and Tiberius. Ancestry was a foolish game to play, Faustus thought. The past existed here in Roma in layer upon layer, a past that was nearly thirteen hundred years deep, and everyone had been a jumped-up newcomer once upon a time, even the founder Romulus himself.

So the era of the great Constantinus had come and gone, and here was his distant descendant Faustus Flavius Constantinus Caesar, growing old, growing plump, growing bald, spending his days toiling in the middle echelons of the Imperial Chancellery. And the Empire itself seemed to be aging badly too. Everything had gone soft, here in the final years of the long reign of Maximilianus II. The great days of Titus Gallius and his dynasty, of Constantinus and his, of the first Maximilianus and his son and grandson, seemed already like something out of the legends of antiquity, even if the second Maximilianus still did hold the throne. Things had changed, in the past decade or two. The Empire no longer seemed as secure as it had been. And all this year there had been talk, all up and down the shadowy corridors of the sorcerers' marketplace, of mystic oracular prophecies, lately found in a newly discovered manuscript of the Sybilline Books, that indicated that Roma had entered into its last century, after which would come fire, apocalyptic chaos, the collapse of everything.

If that is so, Faustus thought, let it wait another twenty or thirty years. Then the world can come to an end, for all that I will care.

But it was something new, this talk of the end of eternal Roma. For hundreds of years, now, there had always been some great man available to step in and save things in time of crisis. Three hundred and some years ago, Septimius Severus had been there to rescue the Empire from crazy Commodus. A generation later, after Severus's even crazier son Caracalla had worked all sorts of harm, it was the superb Titus Gallius who took charge and repaired the damage. The barbarians were beginning to make serious trouble at the Empire's edges by then, but, again and again, strong Emperors beat them back: first Titus Gallius, then his nephew Gaius Martius, and Marcus Anastasius after him, and then Diocletianus, the first Emperor to divide the realm among jointly ruling Emperors, and Constantinus, who founded the second capital in the East, and on and on, down to the present time. But now the throne was to all intents and purposes vacant, and everyone could see that the heir-in-waiting was worthless, and where, Faustus wondered, was the next great savior of the realm to come from?

Prince Maximilianus was right that his own dynasty had been a line of mighty warriors. Maximilianus I, a northerner, not a Roman of Roma at all but a man who could trace his roots back to the long-ago Etruscan race, had founded that line when he made himself the successor to the great Emperor Theodosius on the Imperial throne. As a vigorous young general he drove back the Goths who were threatening Italia's northern border, and then in the autumn of his years joined with Theodosius II of the Eastern Empire to smash the Hunnish invaders under Attila. Then came Maximilianus's son Heraclius I, who held the line on all frontiers, and when the next wave of Goths and their kinsmen the Vandals began rampaging through Gallia and the Germanic lands, Heraclius's son, the young Emperor Maximilianus II, cut them to pieces with a fierce counterattack that seemed to have ended their threat for all time.

But no: there seemed to be no end of Goths and Vandals and similar nomadic tribes. Here, forty years after Maximilianus II had marched with twenty legions across the Rhenus into Gallia and inflicted a decisive defeat on them, they were massing for what looked like the biggest attack since the days of Theodosius. Now, though, Maximilianus II was old and feeble, very likely dying. The best anyone could say was that the Emperor was dwelling in seclusion somewhere, seen only by his doctors, but there were a great many unreliable stories circulating about his location: perhaps he was here in Roma, perhaps on the isle of Capraeae down in the south, or maybe even in Carthago or Volubilis or some other sun-blessed African city. For all Faustus knew, he was already dead, and his panicky ministers were afraid to release the news. It would not be the first time in Roma's history that that had happened.

And after Maximilianus II, what? Prince Heraclius would take the throne, yes. But there was no reason to be optimistic about the sort of Emperor that he would be. Faustus could imagine the course of events only too easily: the Goths, unstoppable, break through in the north and invade Italia, sack the city, slaughter the aristocracy, proclaim one of their kings as monarch of Roma. While off in the west the Vandals or some other tribe of that ilk lay claim to the rich provinces of Gallia and Hispania, which now become independent kingdoms, and the Empire is dissolved.

"The best and in fact only hope," Faustus had heard the Imperial Chancellor Licinius Obsequens say a month before, "is the royal marriage. Justinianus, for the sake of saving his brother-in-law's throne but also not wanting a pack of unruly barbarian kingdoms springing up along his own borders where the Western Empire used to be, sends an army to back up ours, and with the help of a few competent Greek generals the Goths finally get taken care of. But even that solution solves nothing for us. One can easily see one of Justinianus's generals offering to stay around as an 'adviser' to our young Emperor Heraclius, and next thing you know Heraclius turns up poisoned and the general lets it be known that he will graciously accept the Senate's invitation to take the throne, and from that point on the Western Empire comes completely under the dominance of the East, all our tax money starts to flow toward Constantinopolis, and Justinianus rules the world."

Our best and in fact only hope. I really should slash my wrists, Faustus thought. Make a rational exit in the face of insuperable circumstances, as many a Roman hero has done before me. Certainly there is ample precedent. He thought of Lucan, who calmly recited his own poetry as he died. Petronius Arbiter, who did the same. Cocceius Nerva, who starved himself to death to show his distaste for the doings of Tiberius. "The foulest death," said Seneca, "is preferable to the fairest slavery." Very true; but perhaps I am not a true Roman hero.

He rose from the bath. Two slaves rushed to cover him with soft towels. "Send in the Numidian girl," he said, heading for the bedchamber.

***

"We will enter," Danielus bar-Heap explained, "by way of the gateway of Titus Gallius, which is the most famous opening into the Underworld. There are many other entrances, but this is the most impressive."

It was mid-morning: early in the day, perhaps, for going down below, certainly early in the day for the hard-living Prince Maximilianus to be up and about at all. But Faustus wanted to embark on the excursion as early as possible. Keeping the ambassador amused was his highest priority now.

The Hebrew had very quickly taken charge of the enterprise, doing all of the planning and most of the talking. He was one of the prince's most cherished companions. Faustus had met him more than once before: a big deep-voiced square-shouldered man, with jutting cheekbones and a great triangular beak of a nose, who wore his dark, almost blue-black hair in closely braided ringlets. Though it had been for many years the fashion for men to go clean-shaven in Roma, bar-Heap sported a conspicuous beard, thick and dense, that clung in tight coils to his jaws and chin. Instead of a toga he was clad in a knee-length tunic of rough white linen that was inscribed along its margins with bold lightning-bolt patterns done in bright green thread.

Ambassador Menandros, Easterner though he was, had apparently never met a Hebrew before, and needed to have bar-Heap explained to him. "They are a small tribe of desert folk who settled in Aegyptus long ago," Faustus told him. "Scatterings of them live all over the Empire by now. I dare say you would find a few in Constantinopolis. They are shrewd, determined, rather argumentative people, who don't always have the highest respect for the law, except for the laws of their own tribe, by which they abide under all circumstances in the most fanatic way. I understand they have no belief in the gods, for instance, and only the most grudging allegiance to the Emperor."

"No belief in the gods?" said Menandros. "None at all?"

"Not that I can see," said Faustus.

"Well, they do have some god of their own," Maximilianus put in. "But no one may ever see him, and they make no statues of him, and he has laid down a whole lot of absurd laws about what they can eat, and so forth. Bar-Heap will probably tell you all the details, if you ask him. Or perhaps he won't. Like all his kind, he's a prickly, unpredictable sort."

Faustus had advised the ambassador that it would be best if they dressed simply for the outing, nothing that might indicate their rank. Menandros's wardrobe, of course, ran largely to luxurious silken robes and other such Eastern splendiferousness, but Faustus had provided a plain woolen toga for him that had no stripes of rank on it. Menandros appeared to know how to drape the garment properly around himself. Maximilianus Caesar, who as the son of the reigning Emperor was entitled to wear a toga bedecked with a purple stripe and strands of golden thread, wore an unmarked one also. So did Faustus, although, since he too was the descendant of an Emperor, he was permitted the purple stripe as well. Even so, no one down below was likely to mistake them for anything other than what they were, Romans of the highest class. But it was never a good idea to flaunt aristocratic airs too ostentatiously in the subterranean world of Roma.

The entrance that the Hebrew had chosen for them was at the edge of the teeming quarter known as the Subura, which lay east of the Forum in the valley between the Viminal and Esquiline Hills. Here, in a district marked by stench and squalor and deafening hubbub, where the common folk of Roma lived jammed elbow to elbow in shoddy buildings four and five stories high and screeching carts proceeded with much difficulty through narrow, winding streets, the Emperor Titus Gallius had begun carving, about the year 980, an underground refuge in which the citizens of Roma could take shelter if the unruly Goths, then massing in the north, should break through Roma's defenses and enter the city.

The Goths, as it happened, were routed long before they got anywhere near the capital. But by then Titus Gallius had built a complex network of passageways under the Subura, and he and his successors went on enlarging it for decades, sending tentacles out in all directions, creating linkages to the existing labyrinthine chain of underground galleries and tunnels and chambers that Romans had been constructing here and there about the city for a thousand years.

And by now that Underworld was a city beneath the city, an entity unto itself down there in the dank and humid darkness. The portals of Titus Gallius lay before them, two ornate stone arches like the gaping jaws of a giant mouth, rising in the middle of the street where Imperial forces centuries ago had cleared away a block of ancient hovels on both sides to make room for the entrance plaza. The opening into the Underground was wide enough to allow three wagons to pass at the same time. A ramp of well-worn brown brick led downward into the depths.

"Here are your lanterns," bar-Heap said, lighting them and handing them around. "Remember to hold them high, to keep them from going out. The air is heavier down by your knees and will smother the flame."

As they embarked on the ramp the Caesar took the position at the front of the group; Faustus positioned himself next to the Greek; bar-Heap brought up the rear. Menandros had been taken aback to learn that they would be traveling by foot, but Faustus had explained that using porter-borne litters would be inconvenient in the crowded world below. They would not even be accompanied by servants. The Greek seemed delighted to hear that. He was truly slumming today, that was clear. He wanted to travel through the Underworld as an ordinary Roman would, to get right down into all its muck and filth and danger.

Even this early in the day the ramp was crowded, both in the upward and downward directions, a quick, jostling throng. Ahead, all was cloaked in a palpable gloom. Going into the Underworld had always seemed to Faustus like entering the lair of some enormous creature. He was enveloped once again now by the thick, fierce darkness, cool, spicy. He savored its embrace. How often had he and Caesar entered here in search of a night's strange entertainment, and how many times they had found it!

Quickly his eyes began to adapt to the dim murky gleam of the lanterns. By the dull light of distant torches he could see the long ranges of far-off vaults running off on every side. The descent had quickly leveled out into the broad vestibule. Gusts of fetid underground air blew toward them, bearing a host of odors: smoke, sweat, mildew, the smell of animal bodies. It was very busy here, long lines of people and beasts of burden coming and going out of a dozen directions. The wide avenue known as the Via Subterranea stretched before them, and a myriad narrower subsidiary passages branched off to right and left. Faustus saw once more the familiar piers and arches and bays, the curving walls of warm golden brick, the heavy rock-hewn pillars and the innumerable alcoves behind them. At once the darkness of this shadowy world seemed less oppressive.

He glanced down at the Greek. Menandros's soft features were alive with excitement. His nostrils were quivering, his lips were drawn back. His expression was like that of a small child who was being taken to the gladiatorial games for the first time. He almost seemed like a child among the three tall men, too, a flimsy, diminutive figure alongside long-limbed Maximilianus and sturdy, deep-chested bar-Heap and fleshy, bulky Faustus.

"What is that?" Menandros asked, pointing to the enormous marble relief of a bearded head, cemented into the wall just ahead of them. From above came a spike of light from one of the openings that pierced the vaulted roof, admitting a white beam that lit up the carved features with an eerie nimbus.

"He is a god," said bar-Heap from behind, with a tincture of contempt in his voice. "An Emperor put him up there, many years ago. Perhaps he is one of yours, or perhaps one from Syria. We call him Jupiter of the Caverns." The Hebrew raised his lantern far over his head to provide an additional burst of illumination for that powerful profile, the great staring eye, the huge all-hearing ear, the ominously parted lips, the massive coiling stone beard thicker even than his own. Everything above the eye was gone, and below the beard there was nothing also: it was a single colossal fragment that looked unthinkably ancient, a brooding relic of some great former age. "Hail, Jupiter!" bar-Heap said in a resonant tone, and laughed. But Menandros paused to examine the immense somber face, and to take note of the marble altar, worn smooth by adoring hands and luminous in the reflected light of candles mounted along its rim, just below it. The charred bones of sacrifices, recent ones, lay in a niche in its side.

Maximilianus beckoned him impatiently onward with quick imperious gestures. "This is only the beginning," the Caesar said. "We have many miles ahead of us."

"Yes. Yes, of course," said the Greek. "But still — it is so new to me, it is so strange —"

After they had gone some two hundred paces down the Via Subterranea Maximilianus made a sharp left turn into a curving passage where cold damp came stealing down the walls in a steady drip, forming pools beneath their feet. The air had a moist, choking mustiness to it.

It seemed less crowded here. At least there was less foot traffic than in the main avenue. The overhead light-shafts were spaced much farther apart. Fewer torches could be seen ahead. But out of the darkness came unsettling sounds, harsh laughter and blurred incomprehensible whispers and giddy murmurs in unknown tongues and the occasional high, sharp shriek. There were strong odors, too, those of meat roasting over smoky fires, cauliflower stew, tubs of hot peppery broth, fried fish. This was no city of the dead, however dark and grim it might look: it was bursting with secret life, roaring with it, this hidden frenetic underground world. Everywhere around, in chambers and vaults cut from the living rock, an abundance of events was going forward, Faustus knew: the sale of enchantments and the casting of spells, business deals both licit and illicit, the performance of the religious rites of a hundred cults, carnal acts of every kind.

"Where are we now?" Menandros asked.

"These are the grottos of Titus Gallius," said Caesar. "One of the busiest sectors — a place of general activities, very hard to characterize. One may see anything here, and rarely the same thing twice."

They went from chamber to chamber, following the low-ceilinged winding path that threaded everything together. It was Maximilianus, still, who led the way, hot-eyed now, almost frenzied, pulling them all behind him in his wake, often faster than Menandros wanted to go. Faustus and the Hebrew went along obligingly. This behavior of Caesar's was nothing new to them. It was almost as if some fit came over him when he was here in these tangled grottos, driving him on from one sight to the next. Faustus had seen this happen many times before down here, the bursting forth of this restless furious hunger of the Caesar's for novelty, this raging inexhaustible curiosity of his.

It was the curse of an idle life, Faustus thought, the poignant anguish of an Emperor's superfluous younger son, vexed by the endless torment of his own uselessness, the mocking powerlessness within great power that was the only thing that his high birth had brought him. It was as if the greatest challenge that Maximilianus faced was the boredom of his own gilded existence, and in the Underworld he warded off that challenge through this quest for the ultimate and the impossible. The Hebrew was a necessary facilitator for this: more often than not it took a quick word from bar-Heap, not always speaking Latin, to gain admittance for them to some sector of the caverns normally closed to the uninvited.

Here, under an array of blazing sconces that filled the air with black smoke, lights that were never extinguished in this place where no distinction was made between night and day, was a marketplace where strange delicacies were being sold — the tongues of nightingales and flamingos, lamprey spleen, camel heels, bright yellow cockscombs, parrot heads, the livers of pikes, the brains of pheasants and peacocks, the ears of dormice, the eggs of pelicans, bizarre things from every corner of the Empire, everything heaped in big meaty mounds on silver trays. Menandros, that cosmopolitan Greek, stared in wonder like any provincial bumpkin. "Do Romans dine on such things every day?" he asked, and Caesar, smiling that opaque Etruscan smile of his, assured him that they constantly did, not only at the Imperial table but everywhere in Roma, even in the humblest houses, and promised him a meal of nightingales' tongues and peacock brains at the earliest opportunity.

And here was a noisy plaza filled with clowns, jugglers, acrobats, sword-swallowers, fire-eaters, tightrope-walkers, and performers of a dozen other kinds, with snarling barkers loudly calling out the praises of the acts that employed them. Maximilianus tossed silver coins freely to them, and at his urging Menandros did the same. Beyond it was a colonnaded hallway in which a freak show was being offered: hunchbacks and dwarfs, three simpering pinheads in elaborate scarlet livery, a man who looked like a living skeleton, another who must have been nearly ten feet high. "The one with the ostrich head is no longer here," said bar-Heap, obviously disappointed. "And also the girl with three eyes, and the twins joined at the waist." Here, too, they distributed coins liberally, all but bar-Heap, who kept the strings of his purse drawn tight.

"Do you know, Faustus, who is the greatest freak and monster of them all?" asked Maximilianus, under his breath, as they walked along. And when Faustus remained silent the prince offered an answer to his own question that Faustus had not anticipated: "It is the Emperor, my friend, for he stands apart from all other men, distinct, unique, forever isolated from all honesty and love, from normal feeling of any sort. He is a grotesque thing, an Emperor is. There is no monster so pitiable on this earth as an Emperor, Faustus." The Caesar, gripping the fleshiest part of Faustus's arm with iron force, gave him such a queer look of fury and anguish that Faustus was astounded by its intensity. This was a side of his friend he had never seen before. But then Maximilianus grinned and jabbed him lightheartedly in the ribs, and winked as if to take the sting out of his words.

Farther on was a row of apothecary stalls cluttered one upon the next in a series of narrow alcoves that were part of what looked like an abandoned temple. Lamps were burning before each one. These dealers in medicines offered such things as the bile of bulls and hyenas, the sloughed-off skins of snakes, the webs of spiders, the dung of elephants. "What is this?" the Greek asked, pointing into a glass vial that contained some fine gray powder, and bar-Heap, after making inquiry, reported that it was the excrement of Sicilian doves, much valued in treating tumors of the leg and many other maladies. Another booth sold only rare aromatic barks from the trees of India; another, small disks made of rare red clay from the isle of Lemnos, stamped with the sacred seal of Diana and reputed to cure the bite of mad dogs and the effects of the most lethal poisons. "And this man here," said Maximilianus grandly at the next stall, "purveys nothing but theriac, the universal antidote, potent even for leprosy. It is made mainly from the flesh of vipers steeped in wine, I think, but there are other ingredients, secret ones, and even if we put him to the torture he would not reveal them." And, with a wink to the drug's purveyor, a one-eyed hawk-faced old Aegyptian, "Eh, Ptolemaios, is that not so? Not even if we put you to the torture?"

"It will not come to that, I hope, Caesar," the man replied.

"So they know you here?" Menandros asked, when they had moved onward.

"Some do. This one has several times brought his wares to the palace to treat my ailing father."

"Ah," the Greek said. "Your ailing father, yes. All the world prays for his swift recovery."

Maximilianus nodded casually, as though Menandros had expressed nothing more than a wish for fair weather on the next day.

Faustus felt troubled by the strangeness of the Caesar's mood. He knew Maximilianus to be an unpredictable man who veered constantly between taut control and wild abandon, but it was mere courtesy to offer a grateful word for such an expression of sympathy, and yet he had been unable to bring himself to do it. What, he wondered, does the ambassador think of this strange prince? Or does he think nothing at all, except that this is what one can expect the younger son of a Roman Emperor to be like?

There were no clocks in this subterranean world, nor was there any clue in this sunless place to the hour available from from the skies, but Faustus's belly was telling him the time quite unmistakably, now. "Shall we go above to eat," he asked Menandros, "or would you prefer to dine down here?"

"Oh, down here, by all means," said the Greek. "I'm not at all ready to go above!"

***

They ate at a torchlit tavern two galleries over from the arcade of the apothecaries, sitting cheek by jowl with scores of garlicky commoners on rough wooden benches: a meal of meat stewed in a spicy sauce made from fermented fish, fruits steeped in honey and vinegar, harsh acrid wine not much unlike vinegar itself. Menandros seemed to love it. He must never have encountered such indelicate delicacies before, and he ate and drank with ravenous appetite. The effects of this indulgence showed quickly on him: the sweat-shiny brow, the ruddy cheeks, the glazing eyes. Maximilianus, too, allowed himself course after course, washing his food down with awesome quantities of the dreadful wine; but, then, Maximilianus adored this stuff and never knew when to stop when wine of any kind was within reach. Faustus, not a man of great moderation himself, who loved drinking to excess, loved the dizzy float upward that too much wine brought on, the severing of his soaring mind from his ever more gross and leaden flesh, had to force himself to swallow it. But eventually he took to drinking most of each new pitcher as fast as he could, regardless of the taste, in order to keep the Caesar from overindulging. He gave much of the rest to the stolid, evidently bottomless bar-Heap, for he knew what perils were possible if the prince, far gone in drunkenness, should get himself into some foolish brawl down here. He could easily imagine bringing Maximilianus back on a board from the caverns some day, with his royal gut slashed from one side to the other and his body already stiffening. If that happened the best he could hope for himself would be to spend the remainder of his own life in brutal exile in some dismal Teutonic outpost.

When they went onward finally, somewhere late in the afternoon, a subtle change of balance had taken place in the group. Maximilianus, either because he had suddenly grown bored or because he had eaten too much, seemed to lose interest in the expedition. No longer did he sprint ahead, beckoning them on along from corridor to corridor as though racing some unseen opponent from one place to the next. Now it was Menandros, fueled by his heavy input of wine, who seized command, displaying now a hunger to see it all even more powerful than the prince's had been, and rushing them along through the subterranean city. Not knowing any of the routes, he made random turns, taking them now into pitch-black cul-de-sacs, now to the edges of dizzying abysses where long many-runged ladders led to spiraling successions of lower levels, now to chambers with painted walls where rows of cackling madwomen sat in throne-like niches demanding alms.

Most of the time Maximilianus did not seem to be able to identify the places into which Menandros had led them, or did not care to say. It became the task of bar-Heap, whose mastery of the underground city seemed total, to explain what they were seeing. "This place is the underground arena," the Hebrew said, as they peered into a black hole that seemed to stretch for many leagues. "The games are held here at the midnight hour, and all contests are to the death." They came soon afterward to a gleaming marble facade and a grand doorway leading to some interior chamber: the Temple of Jupiter Imperator, bar-Heap explained. That was the cult established by the Emperor Gaius Martius in the hope, not entirely realized, of identifying the father of the gods with the head of the state in the eyes of the common people, who otherwise might wander off into some kind of alien religious belief that could weaken their loyalty to the state. "And this," said bar-Heap at an adjacent temple flush against the side of Jupiter's, "is the House of Cybele, where they worship the Great Mother."

"We have that cult in the East as well," said Menandros, and halted to examine with a connoisseur's eye the fanciful mosaic ornamentation, row upon row of patterned tiles, red and blue and orange and green and gold, that proclaimed this place the dwelling of the full-breasted goddess. "How fine this is," the Greek said, "to build such a wonder underground, where it can barely be seen except by this dirty torchlight, and not well even then. How bold! How extravagant!"

"It is a very wealthy creed, Cybele's," said Maximilianus, nudging Faustus broadly as though to remind him of the stolen opals of the goddess that would be his gift to his brother's Constantinopolitan bride.

Menandros drew them tirelessly on through the dark labyrinth—past bubbling fountains and silent burial-chambers and frescoed cult-halls and bustling marketplaces, and then through a slit-like opening in the wall that took them into a huge, empty space from which a multitude of dusty unmarked corridors radiated, and down one and then another of those, until, in a place of awkwardly narrow passages, even bar-Heap seemed uncertain of where they were. A frown furrowed the Hebrew's forehead. Faustus, who by this time was feeling about ready to drop from fatigue, began to worry too. Suddenly there was no one else around. The only sounds here were the sounds of their own echoing footsteps. Everyone had heard tales of people roaming the subterranean world who had taken injudicious turns and found themselves irretrievably lost in mazes built in ancient days to delude possible invaders, bewilderingly intricate webworks of anarchic design whose outlets were essentially unfindable and from which the only escape was through starvation. A sad fate for the little Greek emissary and the dashing, venturesome royal prince, Faustus thought. A sad fate for Faustus, too.

But this was not a maze of that sort. Four sharp bends, a brief climb by ladder, a left turn, and they were back on the Via Subterranea, somehow, though no doubt very far from the point where they had entered the underground metropolis that morning. The vaulted ceiling was pointed, here, and inlaid with rows of coral-colored breccia. A procession of chanting priests was coming toward them, gaunt men whose faces were smeared with rouge and whose eyesockets were painted brightly in rings of yellow and green. They wore white tunics crisscrossed with narrow purple stripes and towering saffron-colored caps that bore the emblem of a single glaring eye at their summits. Energetically they flogged one another with whips of knotted woolen yarn studded with the knucklebones of sheep as they danced along, and cried out in harsh, jabbering rhythmic tones, uttering prayers in some foreign tongue.

"Eunuchs, all of them," said bar-Heap in disgust. "Worshippers of Dionysus. Step aside, or they'll bowl you over, for they yield place to no one when they march like this."

Close behind the priests came a procession of deformed clowns, squinting hunchbacked men who also were carrying whips, but only pretending to use them on each other. Maximilianus flung them a handful of coins, and Menandros did the same, and they broke formation at once, scrabbling enthusiastically in the dimness to scoop them up. On the far side of them the Hebrew pointed out a chamber that he identified as a chapel of Priapus, and Menandros was all for investigating it; but this time Maximilianus said swiftly, "I think that is for another day, your excellence. One should be in fresh condition for such amusements, and you must be tired, now, after this long first journey through the netherworld."

The ambassador looked unhappy. Faustus wondered whose will would prevail: that of the visiting diplomat, whose whims ought to be respected, or of the Emperor's son, who did not expect to be gainsaid. But after a moment's hesitation Menandros agreed that it was time to go back above. Perhaps he saw the wisdom of checking his voracious curiosity for a little while, or else simply that of yielding to the prince's request.

"There is an exit ramp over there," bar-Heap said, pointing to his right. With surprising speed they emerged into the open. Night had fallen. The sweet cool air seemed, as ever upon emerging, a thousand times fresher and more nourishing than that of the world below. Faustus was amused to see that they were not far from the Baths of Constantinus, only a few hundred yards from where they had gone in, although his legs were aching fiercely, as though he had covered many leagues that day. They must have traveled in an enormous circle, he decided.

He yearned for his own bath, and a decent dinner, and a massage afterward and the Numidian girl.

Maximilianus, with an Imperial prince's casual arrogance, hailed a passing litter that bore Senatorial markings, and requisitioned its use for his own purposes. Its occupant, a balding man whom Faustus recognized by face but could not name, hastened to comply, scuttling away into the night without protest. Faustus and Menandros and the Caesar clambered aboard, while the Hebrew, with no more farewell than an irreverent offhand wave, vanished into the darkness of the streets.

There was no message waiting at home for Faustus to tell him that Prince Heraclius was heading back to the city. He had been hoping for such news. Tomorrow would be another exhausting day spent underground, then.

He slept badly, though the little Numidian did her best to soothe his nerves.

***

This time they entered the Underworld farther to the west, between the column of Marcus Aurelius and the Temple of Isis and Sarapis. That was, bar-Heap said, the quickest way to reach the marketplace of the sorcerers, which Menandros had some particular interest in seeing.

Diligent guide that he was, the Hebrew showed them all the notable landmarks along the way: the Whispering Gallery, where even the faintest of sounds traveled enormous distances, and the Baths of Pluto, a series of steaming thermal pools that gave off a foul sulphurous reek but which nevertheless abounded in patrons even here at midday, and the River Styx nearby it, the black subterranean stream that followed a rambling course through the underground city until it emerged into the Tiber just upstream from the great sewer of the Cloaca Maxima.

"Truly, the Styx?" Menandros asked, with a credulity Faustus had not expected of him.

"We call it that," said bar-Heap. "Because it is the river of our Underworld, you see. But the true one is somewhere in your own eastern realm, I think. Here—we must turn—"

A jagged, irregularly oval aperture in the passageway wall proved to be the entrance to the great hall that served as the sorcerers' marketplace. Originally, so they said, it had been intended as a storage vault for the

Imperial chariots, to keep them from being seized by invading barbarians. When such precautions had turned out to be unnecessary, the big room had been taken over by a swarm of sorcerers, who divided it by rows of pumice-clad arches into a collection of small low-walled chambers. An octagonal light-well, high overhead in the very center of the roof of the hall, allowed pale streams of sunlight to filter down from the street above, but most of the marketplace's illumination came from the smoky braziers in front of each stall. These, whether by some enchantment or mere technical skill, all burned with gaudy many-hued flames, and dancing strands of violet and pale crimson and cobalt blue and brilliant emerald mingled with the more usual reds and yellows of a charcoal fire.

The roar of commerce rose up on every side. Each of the sorcerers' stalls had its barker, crying the merits of his master's wares. Scarcely had the ambassador Menandros entered the room than one of these, a fat, sweaty-faced man wearing a brocaded robe of Syrian style, spied him as a likely mark, beckoning him inward with both arms while calling out, "Eh, there, you dear little fellow: what about a love spell today, an excellent inflamer, the finest of its kind?"

Menandros indicated interest. The barker said, "Come, then, let me show you this splendid wizardry! It attracts men to women, women to men, and makes virgins rush out of their homes to find lovers!" He reached behind him, snatched up a rolled parchment scroll, and waved it in front of Menandros's nose. "Here, friend, here! You take a pure papyrus and write on it, with the blood of an ass, the magical words contained on this. Then you put in a hair of the woman you desire, or a snip of her clothing, or a bit of her bedsheet—acquire it however you may. And then you smear the papyrus with a bit of vinegar gum, and stick it to the wall of her house, and you will marvel! But watch that you are not struck yourself, or you may find yourself bound by the chains of love to some passing drover, or to his donkey, perhaps, or even worse! Three sestertii! Three!"

"If infallible love is to be had so cheaply," Maximilianus said to the man, "why is it that languishing lovers hurl themselves into the river every day of the week?"

"And also why is it that the whorehouses are kept so busy," added Faustus, "when for three brass coins anyone can have the woman of his dreams?"

"Or the man," said Menandros. "For this charm will work both ways, so he tells us."

"Or on a donkey," put in Danielus bar-Heap, and they laughed and passed onward.

Nearby, a spell of invisibility was for sale, at a price of two silver denarii. "It is the simplest thing," insisted the barker, a small lean man tight as a coiled spring, whose swarthy sharp-chinned face was marked by the scars of some ancient knife-fight. "Take a night-owl's eye and a ball of the dung of the beetles of Aegyptus and the oil of an unripe olive and grind them all together until smooth, and smear your whole body with it, and then go to the nearest shrine of the lord Apollo by dawn's first light and utter the prayer that this parchment will give you. And you will be invisible to all eyes until sunset, and can go unnoticed among the ladies at their baths, or slip into the palace of the Emperor and help yourself to delicacies from his table, or fill your purse with gold from the moneychangers' tables. Two silver denarii, only!"

"Quite reasonable, for a day's invisibility," Menandros said. "I'll have it, for my master's delight." And reached for his purse; but the Caesar, catching him by the wrist, warned him never to accept the quoted first price in a place like this. Menandros shrugged, as though to point out that the price asked was only a trifle, after all. But to the Caesar Maximilianus there was an issue of principle here. He invoked the aid of bar-Heap, who quickly bargained the fee down to four copper dupondii, and, since Menandros did not have coins as small as that in his purse, it was Faustus who handed over the price.

"You have done well," the barker said, giving the Greek his bit of parchment. Menandros, turning away, opened it. "The letters are Greek," he said.

Maximilianus nodded. "Yes. Most of this trash is set out in Greek. It is the language of magic, here."

"The letters are Greek," said Menandros, "but not the words. Listen. And he read out in a rolling resonant tone: 'BORKE PHOIOUR IO ZIZIA APARXEOUCH THYTHE LAILAM AAAAAA IIII OOOO IEO IEO IEO.'" Then he looked up from the scroll. "And there are three more lines, of much the same sort. What do you make of that, my friends?"

"I think it is well that you didn't read the rest," said Faustus, "or you might have disappeared right before our noses."

"Not without employing the beetle-dung and the owl's eye and the rest," bar-Heap observed. "Nor is that dawn's first light coming down that shaft, even if you would pretend that this is Apollo's temple."

"'IO IO O PHRIXRIZO EOA,'" Menandros read, and giggled in pleasure, and rolled the scroll and put it in his purse.

It did not appear likely to Faustus that the Greek was a believer in this nonsense, as his earlier eagerness to visit this marketplace had led him to suspect. No. Doubtless he was merely looking for quaint souvenirs to bring back to his Emperor in Constantinopolis, entertaining examples of modern-day Roman gullibility; for Menandros must surely have noticed by this time an important truth about this room, which was that nearly all the sorcerers and their salesmen were citizens of the Eastern half of the empire, which had a reputation for magic going back to the distant days of the

Pharaohs and the kings of Babylon, while the customers — and there were plenty of them — all were Romans of the West. It was an oily place, the Eastern Empire. All the mercantile skills had been invented there. The East's roots went deep down into antiquity, into a time long before Roma itself ever was, and one needed to keep a wary eye out in any dealings with its citizens.

Menandros was an enthusiastic buyer. Was stuff like this no longer available in the other Empire? Surely it must be, at least in the provinces. He was just trying to collect evidence of Roman silliness, yes. Using bar-Heap to beat the prices down for him, he went from booth to booth, gathering up the merchandise. He acquired instructions for fashioning a ring of power that would permit one to get whatever one asks from anybody, or to calm the anger of masters and kings. He bought a charm to induce wakefulness, and another to bring on sleep. He got a lengthy scroll that offered a whole catalog of mighty mysteries, and gleefully read from it to them: "'You will see the doors thrown open, and seven virgins coming from deep within, dressed in linen garments, and with the faces of asps. They are called the Fates of Heaven, and wield golden wands. When you see them, greet them in this manner — " He found a spell that necromancers could use to keep skulls from speaking out of turn while their owners were using them in the casting of spells; he found one that would summon the Headless One who had created earth and heaven, the mighty Osoronnophris, and conjure Him to expel demons from a sufferer's body; he found one that would bring back lost or stolen property; he went back to the first booth and bought the infallible love potion, for a fraction of the original asking price; and, finally, picked up one that would cause one's fellow drinkers at a drinking party to think that they had grown the snouts of apes.

At last, well satisfied with his purchases, Menandros said he was willing to move on. At the far end of the hall, beyond the territory of the peddlers of spells, they paused at the domain of the soothsayers and augurs. "For a copper or two," Faustus told the Greek, "they will look at the palm of your hand, or the pattern of lines on your forehead, and tell you your future. For a higher price they will examine the entrails of chickens or the liver of a sheep, and tell you your *true* future. Or even the future of the Empire itself."

Menandros looked astonished. "The future of the Empire? Common diviners in a public marketplace offer prophecies of a sort like that? I'd think only the Imperial augurs would deal in such news, and only for the Emperor's ear."

"The Imperial augurs provide more reliable information, I suppose," said Faustus. "But this is Roma, where everything is for sale to anyone." He looked down the row, and saw the one who had claimed new

knowledge of the Sybilline prophecies and foretold the imminent end of the
Empire—an old man, unmistakably Roman, not a Greek or any other kind
of foreigner, with faded blue eyes and a lengthy, wispy white beard. "Over
there is one of the most audacious of our seers, for instance," Faustus said,
pointing. "For a fee he will tell you that our time of Empire is nearly over,
that a year is coming soon when the seven planets will meet at Capricorn
and the entire universe will be consumed by fire."

"The great *ekpyrosis*," Menandros said. "We have the same prophecy.
What does he base his calculations on, I wonder?"

"What does it matter?" cried Maximilianus, in a burst of sudden
unconcealed rage. "It is all foolishness!"

"Perhaps so," Faustus said gently. And, to Menandros, whose curiosity
about the old man and his apocalyptic predictions still was apparent: "It
has something to do with the old tale of King Romulus and the twelve
eagles that passed overhead on the day he and his brother Remus fought
over the proper location for the city of Roma."

"They were twelve vultures, I thought," said bar-Heap.

Faustus shook his head. "No. Eagles, they were. And the prophecy of
the Sibyl is that Roma will endure for twelve Great Years of a hundred
years each, one for each of Romulus's eagles, and one century more beyond
that. This is the year 1282 since the founding. So we have eighteen years
left, says the long-bearded one over there."

"This is all atrocious foolishness," said Maximilianus again, his eyes
blazing.

"May we speak with this man a moment, even so?" Menandros asked.

The Caesar most plainly did not want to go near him. But his guest's
mild request could hardly be refused. Faustus saw Maximilianus
struggling with his anger as they walked toward the soothsayer's booth,
and with some effort putting it aside. "Here is a visitor to our city," said
Maximilianus to the old man in a clenched voice, "who wants to hear
what you've to say concerning the impending fiery end of Roma. Name
your price and tell him your fables."

But the soothsayer shrank back, trembling in fear. "No, Caesar. I pray
you, let me be!"

"You recognize me, do you?"

"Who would not recognize the Emperor's son? Especially one whose
profession it is to pierce all veils."

"You've pierced mine, certainly. But why do I frighten you so? I mean
you no harm. Come, man, my friend here is a Greek from Justianianus's
court, full of questions for you about the terrible doom that shortly will be
heading our way. Speak your piece, will you?" Maximilianus pulled out
his purse and drew a shining gold piece from it. "A fine newly minted
aureus, is that enough to unseal your lips? Two? Three?"

It was a fortune. But the man seemed paralyzed with terror. He moved back in his booth, shivering, now, almost on the verge of collapse. The blood had drained from his face and his pale blue eyes were bulging and rigid. It was asking too much of him, Faustus supposed, to be compelled to speak of the approaching destruction of the world to the Emperor's actual son.

"Enough," Faustus murmured. "You'll scare the poor creature to death, Maximilianus."

But the Caesar was bubbling with fury. "No! Here's gold for him! Let him speak! Let him speak!"

"Caesar, *I* will speak to you, if you like," said a high-pitched, sharp-edged voice from behind them. "And will tell you such things as are sure to please your ears."

It was another soothsayer, a ratty little squint-faced man in a tattered yellow tunic, who now made so bold as to pluck at the edge of Maximilianus's toga. He had cast an augury for Maximilianus just now upon seeing the Caesar's entry into the marketplace, he said, and would not even ask a fee for it. No, not so much as two coppers for the news he had to impart. Not even one.

"Not interested," Maximilianus said brusquely, and turned away.

But the little diviner would not accept the rebuff. With frantic squirrelly energy he ran around Maximilianus's side to face him again and said, with the reckless daring of the utterly insignificant confronting the extremely grand, "I threw the bones, Caesar, and they showed me your future. It is a glorious one. You will be one of Roma's greatest heroes! Men will sing your praises for centuries to come."

Instantly a bright blaze of fury lit Maximilianus's entire countenance. Faustus had never seen the prince so incensed. "Do you dare to mock me to my face?" the Caesar demanded, his voice so thick with wrath that he could barely get the words out. His right arm quivered and jerked as though he were struggling to keep it from lashing out in rage. "A hero, you say! A hero! A *hero!*" If the little man had spat in his face it could not have maddened him more.

But the soothsayer persisted. "Yes, my lord, a great general, who will shatter the barbarian armies like so many empty husks! You will march against them at the head of a mighty force not long after you become Emperor, and —"

That was too much for the prince. "Emperor, too!" Maximilianus bellowed, and in that same moment struck out wildly at the man, a fierce backhanded blow that sent him reeling against the bench where the other soothsayer, the old bearded one, still was cowering. Then, stepping forward, Maximilianus caught the little man by the shoulder and slapped him again and again, back, forth, back, forth, knocking his head from side to side until blood poured from his mouth and nose and his eyes began to glaze over. Faustus, frozen at first in sheer amazement, moved in after a time to intervene. "Maximilianus!" he said, trying to catch the Caesar's flailing arm. "My lord—I beg you—it is not right, my lord—"

He signaled to bar-Heap, and the Hebrew caught Maximilianus's other arm. Together they pulled him back.

There was sudden silence in the hall. The sorcerers and their employees had ceased their work and were staring in astonishment and horror, as was Menandros.

The ragged little soothsayer, sprawling now in a kind of daze against the bench, spat out a tooth and said, in a kind of desperate defiance, "Even so, your majesty, it is the truth: Emperor."

It was all that Faustus and the Hebrew could manage to get the prince away from there without his doing further damage.

This capacity for wild rage was an aspect of Maximilianus that Faustus had never seen. The Caesar took nothing seriously. The world was a great joke to him. He had always let it be known that he cared for nothing and no one, not even himself. He was too cynical and wanton of spirit, too flighty, too indifferent to anything of any real importance, ever to muster the kind of involvement with events that true anger required. Then why had the soothsayer's words upset him so? His fury had been out of all proportion to the offense, if offense there had been. The man was merely trying to flatter. Here is a royal prince come among us: very well, tell him he will be a great hero, tell him even that he will be Emperor some day. The second of those, at least, was not impossible. Heraclius, who soon would have the throne, might well die childless, and they would have no choice but to ask his brother to ascend to power, however little Maximilianus himself might care for the idea.

Saying that Maximilianus would become a great hero, though: that must have been what stung him so, Faustus thought. Doubtless he did not regard himself as having a single iota of the stuff of heroes in him, whatever a flattering soothsayer might choose to say. And must believe also that all Roma perceived him not as a handsome young prince who might yet achieve great things but only as the idle wencher and gambler and dissipated profligate rogue that he was in his own eyes. And so he was able to interpret the soothsayer's words not as flattery but merely as mockery of the most inflammatory kind.

"We should quickly find ourselves a wine-shop, I think," Faustus said. "Some wine will cool your overheated blood, my lord."

**

Indeed the wine, vile though it was, calmed Maximilianus rapidly, and soon he was laughing and shaking his head over the impudence of the ratty little man. "A hero of the realm! Me! And Emperor, too? Was there ever a soothsayer so far from the truth in his auguries?"

"If they are all like that one," said bar-Heap, "then I think there's no need to fear the coming fiery destruction of the universe, either. These men are clowns, or worse. All they provide is amusement for fools."

"A useful function in the world, I would say," Menandros observed. "There are so many fools, and should they not have amusement too?"

Faustus said very little. The episode among the sorcerers and soothsayers had left him in a mood of uncharacteristic bleakness. He had always been a good-humored man; the Caesar prized him for the jolly companionship he offered; but his frame of mind had grown steadily more sober since the coming to Roma of this Greek ambassador, and now he felt himself ringed round with an inchoate host of despondent thoughts. It was spending so much time in this underground realm of darkness and flickering shadows, he told himself, that had done this to him. He and the prince had found only pleasure here in days gone by, but their time these two days past in these ancient tunnels, this mysterious kingdom of inexplicable noises and visitations, of invisible beings, of lurking ghosts, had made him weary and uncomfortable. This dank sunless underground world, he thought, was the true Roma, a benighted kingdom of magic and terror, a place of omens and dread.

Would the world be destroyed by flame in eighteen years, as the old man said? Probably not. In any case he doubted that he would live to see it. The universe's end might not be approaching, but surely his own was: five years, ten, at best fifteen, and he would be gone, well before the promised catastrophe, the—what had the Greek called it?—the great *ekpyrosis*.

But even if no flaming apocalypse was really in store, the Empire did seem to be crumbling. There were symptoms of disease everywhere. That the man second in line for the throne would react with such fury at the possibility that he might be called upon to serve the realm was a sign of the extent of the illness. That the barbarians might soon be battering at the gates again, only a generation after they supposedly had been put to rout forever, was another. We seem to have lost our way.

Faustus filled his cup again. He knew he was drinking too much too fast: even his capacious paunch had its limits. But the wine eased the pain. Drink, then, old Faustus. Drink. If nothing else, you can allow your body a little comfort.

Yes, he was getting old. But Roma was even older. The immensity of the city's past pressed down on him from all sides. The narrow streets, choked with dunghill-rubbish, that gave way to the great plazas and their myriad fountains with their silvery jets, and the palaces of the rich and mighty, and the statues everywhere, the obelisks, the columns taken from far-off temples, the spoils of a hundred Imperial conquests, the shrines of a hundred foreign gods, and the clean old Roma of the early Republic somewhere beneath it all: level upon level of history here, twelve centuries of it, the present continually written over the past, the city an enormous palimpsest — yes, he told himself, it has been a good long run, and perhaps, now that we have created so much past for ourselves, we have very little future, and really are wandering toward the finish now, and will disappear into our own softness, our own confusion, our own fatal love of pleasure and ease.

That troubled him greatly. But why, he wondered, did he care? He was nothing but a licentious old idler himself, the companion to a licentious young one. It had been his lifelong pretense never to care about anything.

And yet, yet, he could not let himself forget that he had the blood of the prodigious Constantinus in his veins, one of the greatest Emperors of all. The fate of the Empire had mattered profoundly to Constantinus: he had toiled for decades at its helm, and ultimately he had saved it from collapse by creating a new capital for it in the East, a second foundation to help carry the weight that Urbs Roma itself was no longer capable of bearing alone. Here am I, two and a quarter centuries later, and I am to my great ancestor Constantinus as a plump, sleepy old cat is to a raging lion: but I must care at least a little about the fate of the Empire to which he pledged his life. For his sake, if not particularly for my own. Otherwise, Faustus asked himself fiercely, what is the point of having the blood of an Emperor in my veins?

"You've grown very quiet, old man," Maximilianus said. "Did I upset you, shouting and rioting like that back there?"

"A little. But that's over now."

"What is it, then?"

"Thinking. A pernicious pastime, which I regret." Faustus swirled his cup about and peered glumly into its depths. "Here we are," he said, "down in the bowels of the city, this weird dirty place. I have always thought that everything seems unreal here, that it is all a kind of stage-show. And yet right now it seems to me that it's far more real than anything up above. Down here, at least, there are no pretenses. It's every man for himself amidst the fantasies and grotesqueries, and no one has any illusions. We know why we are here and what we must do." Then, pointing toward the world above them: "Up there, though, folly reigns supreme. We delude ourself into thinking that it is the world of stern reality, the world of Imperial power and Roman commercial might, but no one actually behaves as though any of it has to be taken seriously. Our heads are in the sand, like that great African bird's. The barbarians are coming, but we're doing nothing to stop them. And this time the barbarians will swallow us. They'll go roaring at last through the marble city that's sitting up there above us, looting and torching, and afterward nothing will remain of Roma but this, this dark, dank, hidden, eternally mysterious Underworld of strange gods and ghastly monstrosities. Which I suppose is the true Roma, the eternal city of the shadows."

"You're drunk," Maximilianus said.

"Am I?"

"This place down here is a mere fantasy-world, Faustus, as you are well aware. It's a place without meaning." The prince pointed upward as Faustus just had done. "The true Roma that you speak of is up there. Always was, always will be. The palaces, the temples, the Capitol, the walls. Solid, indestructible, imperishable. The eternal city, yes. And the barbarians will never swallow it. Never. *Never.*"

That was a tone of voice Faustus had never heard the prince use before, either. The second unfamiliar one in less than an hour, this one hard, clear, passionate. There was, again, an odd new intensity in his eyes. Faustus had seen that strange intensity the day before, too, when the prince had spoken of Emperors as freaks and monsters. It was as though something new was trying to burst free inside the Caesar these two days past, Faustus realized. And it must be getting very close to the surface now. What will happen to us all, he wondered, when it breaks loose?

He closed his own eyes a moment, nodded, smiled. Let what will come come, he thought. Whatsoever it may be.

They ended their day in the Underworld soon afterward. Maximilianus's savage outburst in the hall of the soothsayers seemed to have placed a damper on everything, even Menandros's previously insatiable desire to explore the infinite crannies of the underground caverns.

It was near sundown when Faustus reached his chambers, having promised Menandros that he would dine with him later at the ambassador's lodgings in the Severan Palace. A surprise was waiting for him. Prince Heraclius had indeed gone to his hunting lodge, not to the frontier, and the message that Faustus had sent to him there had actually reached him. The prince was even now on his way back to Roma, arriving this very evening, and wished to meet with the emissary from Justinianus as soon as possible.

Hurriedly Faustus bathed and dressed in formal costume. The Numidian girl was ready and waiting, but Faustus dismissed her, and told his equerry that he would not require her services later in the evening, either.

"A curious day," Menandros said, when Faustus arrived.

"It was, yes," said Faustus.

"Your friend the Caesar was greatly distressed by that man's talk of his becoming Emperor some day. Is the idea so distasteful to him?"

"It's not something he gives any thought to at all, becoming Emperor. Heraclius will be Emperor. That's never been in doubt. He's the older by six years: he was well along in training for the throne when Maximilianus was born, and has always been treated by everyone as his father's successor. Maximilianus sees no future for himself in any way different from the life he leads now. He's never looked upon himself as a potential ruler."

"Yet the Senate could name either brother as Emperor, is that not so?"

"The Senate could name me as Emperor, if it chose. Or even you. In theory, as you surely know, there's nothing hereditary about it. In practice things are different. Heraclius's way to the throne is clear. Besides, Maximilianus doesn't *want* to be Emperor. Being Emperor is hard work, and Maximilianus has never worked at anything in his life. I think that's what upset him so much today, the mere thought that he somehow could be Emperor, some day."

Faustus knew Menandros well enough by now to be able to detect the barely masked disdain that these words of his produced. Menandros understood what an Emperor was supposed to be: a man like that severe and ruthless soldier Justinianus, who held sway from Dacia and Thrace to the borders of Persia, and from the frosty northern shores of the Pontic Sea to some point far down in torrid Africa, exerting command over everything and everyone, the whole complex crazyquilt that was the Eastern Empire, with the merest flick of an eye. Whereas here, in the ever flabbier West, which was about to ask Justinianus's help in fighting off its own long-time enemies, the reigning Emperor was currently ill and invisible, the heir to the throne was so odd that he was capable of slipping out of town just as Justinianus's ambassador was arriving to discuss the very alliance the West so urgently needed, and the man second in line to the Empire cared so little for the prospect of attaining the Imperial grandeur that he would thrash someone half his size for merely daring to suggest he might.

He sees us of the West as next to worthless, Faustus thought. And perhaps he is correct.

This was not a profitable discussion. Faustus cut it short by telling him that Prince Heraclius would return that very evening.

"Ah, then," said Menandros, "affairs must be settling down on your northern frontier. Good."

Faustus did not think it was his duty to explain that the Caesar couldn't possibly have made the round trip to the frontier and back in so few days, that in fact he had merely been away at his hunting lodge in the countryside. Heraclius would be quite capable of achieving his own trivialization without Faustus's assistance.

Instead Faustus gave orders for their dinner to be served. They had just reached the last course, the fruits and sherbets, when a messenger entered with word that Prince Heraclius was now in Roma, and awaited the presence of the ambassador from Constantinopolis in the Hall of Marcus Anastasius at the Imperial palace.

The closest part of the five-hundred-year-old string of buildings that was the Imperial compound was no more than ten minutes' walk from where they were now. But Heraclius, with his usual flair for the inappropriate gesture, had chosen for the place of audience not his own residential quarters, which were relatively nearby, but the huge, echoing chamber where the Great Council of State ordinarily met, far over on the palace's northern side at the very crest of the Palatine Hill. Faustus had two litters brought to take them up there.

The prince had boldly stationed himself on the thronelike seat at the upper end of the chamber that the Emperor used during meetings of the Council. He sat there now with Imperial haughtiness, waiting in silence while Menandros undertook the endless unavoidable ambassadorial plod across the enormous room, with Faustus hulking along irritatedly behind him. For one jarring instant Faustus wondered whether the old Emperor had actually, unbeknownst to him, died during the day, and the reason Heraclius was in Roma was that he had hurried back to take his father's place. But someone surely would have said something to him in that case, Faustus thought.

Menandros knew his job. He knelt before the prince and made the appropriate gesticulation. When he rose, Heraclius had risen also and was holding forth his hand, which bore an immense carnelian ring, to be kissed. Menandros kissed the prince's ring. The ambassador made a short, graceful speech expressing his greetings and the best wishes of the Emperor Justinianus for the good health of his royal colleague the Emperor Maximilianus, and for that of his royal son the Caesar Heraclius, and offered thanks for the hospitality that had been rendered him thus far. He gave credit warmly to Faustus but — quite shrewdly, Faustus thought — did not mention the role of Prince Maximilianus at all.

Heraclius listened impassively. He seemed jittery and remote, more so, even, than he ordinarily was.

Faustus had never felt any love for the Imperial heir. Heraclius was a stiff, tense person, ill at ease under the best of circumstances: a short, slight, inconsequential figure of a man with none of his younger brother's easy athleticism. He was cold-eyed, too, thin-lipped, humorless. It was hard to see him as his father's son. The Emperor Maximilianus, in earlier days, had looked much the way the prince his namesake did today: a tall, slender, handsome man with glinting russet hair and smiling blue eyes. Heraclius, though, was dark-haired, where he still had hair at all, and his eyes were dark as coals, glowering under heavy brows out of his pale, expressionless face.

The meeting was inconclusive. The prince and the ambassador both understood that this first encounter was not the time to begin any discussion of the royal marriage or the proposed East-West military alliance, but even so Faustus was impressed by the sheer vacuity of the conversation. Heraclius asked if Menandros cared to attend the gladiatorial games the following week, said a sketchy thing or two about his Etruscan ancestors and their religious beliefs, of which he claimed to be a student of sorts, and spoke briefly of some idiotic Greek play that had been presented at the Odeum of Agrippa Ligurinus the week before. Of the barbarians massing at the border he said nothing at all. Of his father's grave illness, nothing. Of his hope of close friendship with Justinianus, nothing. He might just as well have been discussing the weather. Menandros gravely met immateriality with immateriality. He could do nothing else, Faustus understood. The Caesar Heraclius must be allowed to lead, here.

And then, very quickly, Heraclius made an end of it. "I hope we have an opportunity to meet again very shortly," the prince said, arbitrarily terminating the visit with such suddenness that even the quick-witted Menandros was caught off guard by his blunt dismissal, and Faustus heard a tiny gasp from him. "To my regret, I will have to leave the city again tomorrow. But upon my return, at the earliest opportunity—" And he held forth his ringed hand to be kissed again.

Menandros said, when they were outside and waiting for their litters to be brought, "May we speak frankly, my friend?"

Faustus chuckled. "Let me guess. You found the Caesar to be less than engaging."

"I would use some such phrase, yes. Is he always like that?"

"Oh, no," Faustus said. "He's ordinarily much worse. He was on his best behavior for you, I'd say."

"Indeed. Very interesting. And this is to be the next Emperor of the West. Word had reached us in Constantinopolis, you know, that the Caesar Heraclius was, well, not altogether charming. But—even so—I was not fully prepared—"

"Did you mind very much kissing his ring?"

"Oh, no, not at all. One expects, as an ambassador, to have to show a certain deference, at least to the Emperor. And to his son as well, I suppose, if he requires it of one. No, Faustus, what I was struck by—how can I say this?—let me think a moment—" Menandros paused. He looked off into the night, at the Forum and the Capitol far across the valley. "You know," he said at last, "I'm a relatively young man, but I've made a considerable study of Imperial history, both Eastern and Western, and I think I know what is required to be a successful Emperor. We have a Greek word — *charisma*, do you know it? — it is something like your Latin word *virtus*, but not quite — that describes the quality that one must have. But there are many sorts of charisma. One can rule well through sheer force of personality, through the awe and fear and respect that one engenders — Justinianus is a good example of that, or Vespasianus of ancient times, or Titus Gallius. One can rule through a combination of great personal determination and guile, as Augustus did, and Diocletianus. One can be a man of grace and deep wisdom — Hadrianus, say, or Marcus Aurelius. One can win acclaim through great military valor: I think of Trajan here, and Gaius Martius, and your two Emperors who bore the name Maximilianus. But —" and again Menandros paused, and this time he drew in his breath deeply before continuing" — if one has neither grace, nor wisdom, nor valor, nor guile, nor the capability to engender fear and respect —"

"Heraclius will be able to engender fear, I think," said Faustus.

"Fear, yes. Any Emperor can do that, at least for a time. Caligula, eh? Nero. Domitianus. Commodus."

"The four that you name were all eventually assassinated, I think," Faustus said.

"Yes. That is so, isn't it?" The litters were arriving, now. Menandros turned to him and gave him a serene, almost unworldly smile. "How odd it is, Faustus, would you not say, that the two royal brothers are so far from being alike, and that the one who has charisma is so little interested in serving his Empire as its ruler, and the one who is destined to have the throne has so little charisma? What a pity that is: for them, for you, perhaps, even, for the world. It is one of the little jokes that the gods like to play, eh, my friend? But what the gods may find amusing is not so amusing for us, sometimes."

***

There was no visit to the Underworld the following day. From Menandros came a message declaring that he would remain in his quarters all that day, preparing despatches to be sent to Constantinopolis. The Caesar Maximilianus likewise sent word to Faustus that his company would not be required that day. Faustus spent it dealing with the copious outpouring of routine documents his own office endlessly generated, holding his regular midweek meeting with the other functionaries of the Chancellery, soaking for several hours at the public baths, and dining with the little bright-eyed Numidian, who watched him wordlessly across the table for an hour and a half, eating very little herself — she had the appetite of a bird, a very small bird—and following him obligingly to the couch when the meal was done. After she had gone he lay in bed reading, at random choice, one of the plays of Seneca, the gory *Thyestes,* until he came upon a passage he would just as soon not have seen that evening: "I live in mighty fear that all the universe will be broken into a thousand fragments in the general ruin, that formless chaos will return and vanquish the gods and men, that the earth and sea will be engulfed by the planets wandering in the heavens." Faustus stared at those words until they swam before his eyes. The next lines rose up before him, then: "Of all the generations, it is we who have been chosen to merit the bitter fate, to be crushed by the falling pieces of the broken sky." That was unappealing bedtime reading. He tossed the scroll aside and closed his eyes.

And so, he thought, passes another day in the life of Faustus Flavius Constantinus Caesar. The barbarians are massing at the gates, the Emperor is dying day by day, the heir apparent is out in the forest poking spears into hapless wild beasts, and old Faustus shuffles foolish official papers, lolls half a day in a great marble tub of warm water, amuses himself for a while with a dusky plaything of a girl, and stumbles upon evil omens as he tries to read himself to sleep.

The next day commenced with the arrival of one of Menandros's slaves, bearing a note telling him that it was the ambassador's pleasure to carry out a third exploration of the subterranean city in mid-afternoon. He had a special interest, Menandros said, in seeing the chapel of Priapus and the pool of the Baptai, and perhaps the catacomb of the sacred whores of Chaldea. The ambassador's mood, it seemed, had taken an erotic turn.

Quickly Faustus dashed off a note to the Caesar Maximilianus, telling him of the day's plans and requesting him to summon Danielus bar-Heap the Hebrew once more to be their guide. "Let me know by the sixth hour where you would like us to meet you," Faustus concluded. But midday came and went with no reply from the prince. A second message produced no response either. By now it was nearly time for Faustus to set out for the Severan Palace to pick up the ambassador. It was beginning to look as though he would be Menandros's sole escort on today's expedition. But Faustus realized then that he did not care for that idea: he felt too dour this morning, too cheerless and morose. He needed Maximilianus's high-spirited company to get him through the task.

"Take me to the Caesar," he told his bearers.

Maximilianus, unbathed, unshaven, red-eyed, wearing a coarse old robe with great rents in it, looked startled to see him. "What is this, Faustus? Why do you come to me unannounced?"

"I sent two notes this morning, Caesar. We are to take the Greek to the Underworld again."

The prince shrugged. Clearly he hadn't seen either one. "I've been awake only an hour. And had only three hours of sleep before that. It's been a difficult night. My father is dying."

"Yes. Of course. We have all been aware of that sad fact for some time, and are greatly grieved by it," said Faustus unctuously. "Perhaps it will come as a deliverance when His Majesty's long ordeal is—"

"I don't mean simply that he's sick. I mean that he's in his last hours, Faustus. I've been in attendance on him all night at the palace."

Faustus blinked in surprise. "Your father is in Roma?"

"Of course. Where do you think he'd be?"

"There were stories that he was in Capraea, or Sicilia, or perhaps even Africa—"

"All those stories are so much nitwit blather. He's been right here for months, since he came back from taking the waters at Baiae. Didn't you know that?—Visited by only a very few, of course, because he's become so feeble, and even the shortest of conversations drains his strength. But yesterday about noon he entered into some sort of crisis. Began vomiting black blood, and there were some tremendous convulsions. The whole corps of doctors was sent for. A whole army of them and every last one of them determined to be the one who saves his life, even if they kill him in the process." In an almost manic way Maximilianus began to list the remedies that had been employed in the last twenty-four hours: applications of lion's fat, potations of dog's milk, frogs boiled in vinegar, dried cicadas dissolved in wine, figs stuffed with mouse liver, dragon's tongue boiled in oil, the eyes of river crabs, and any number of other rare and costly medicines, virtually the whole potent pharmacopeia—enough medication, Faustus thought, to do even a healthy man in. And they had done even more. They had drawn his blood. They had bathed him in tubs of honey sprinkled with powdered gold. They had coated him in warm mud from the slopes of Vesuvius. "And the ultimate preposterous touch, just before dawn," said Maximilianus: "the naked virgin who touches her hand to him and invokes Apollo three times to restrain the progress of his disease. It's a wonder they could even *find* a virgin on such short order. Of course, they could always create one by retroactive decree, I guess." And the prince smiled a savage smile. But Faustus could see that it was mere bravado, a strenuously willed flash of the sort of cool cynicism Faustus was supposed to expect from him: the expression in the Caesar's red-rimmed, swollen eyes was that of a young man pained to the core by his beloved father's suffering.

"Will he die today, do you think?" Faustus asked.

"Probably not. The doctors told me that his strength is prodigious, even now. He'll last at least another day, even two or three, perhaps—but no more than that."

"And is your brother with him?"

"My brother?" Maximilians said, in a dumbfounded tone. "My brother's at his hunting lodge, you told me!"

"He came back, the night before last. Gave audience to the Greek at the Hall of Marcus Anastasius. I was there myself."

"No," Maximilianus muttered. "No. The bastard! The bastard!"

"The whole meeting lasted perhaps fifteen minutes, I suppose. And then he announced that he would be leaving town again the next morning, but surely, once he found out that your father was so gravely ill—" Faustus, comprehending suddenly, stared in disbelief. "You mean you never saw him at all, yesterday? He didn't go to visit your father at any time during the day?"

For a moment neither of them could speak.

Maximilianus said, finally, "Death frightens him. The sight of it, the smell of it, the thought of it. He can't bear to be near anyone who's ill. And so he's been careful to keep his distance from the Emperor since he took sick. In any case he's never cared a spoonful of spider's piss for my father. It's perfectly in character for him to come to Roma and sleep right under the same roof as the old man and not even take the trouble of making inquiries after his health, let alone going to see him, and then leave again the next day. So he would never have found out that the end was getting very close. As for me, I wouldn't have expected him to bother getting in touch with me while he was here."

"He should be summoned back to Roma again," Faustus said.

"Yes. I suppose he should be. He'll be Emperor in another day or two, you know." Maximilianus gave Faustus a bleary look. He seemed half addled with fatigue. "Will you do it, Faustus? Straightaway. Meanwhile I'll bathe and dress. The Greek is waiting for us to take him down below, isn't he?"

Thunderstruck, Faustus said, "You mean you want to go there now—today?—while—while your father—?"

"Why not? There's nothing I can do for the old man right now, is there? And his doctors solemnly assure me that he'll last the day." A kind of eerie iciness had come over the Caesar suddenly. Faustus wanted to back away from the chill that emanated from him. In a fierce, cold voice Maximilianus said, "Anyway, I'm not the one who's going to become Emperor. It's my brother's responsibility to stand around waiting to pick up the reins, not mine. Send a messenger off to Heraclius to tell him he had better get himself back here as fast as he can, and let's you and I and the Greek go off and have ourselves a little fun. It may be our last chance for a long time."

***

On such short notice there was no way of finding the Hebrew, so they would have to do without his invaluable assistance for today's outing. Faustus felt edgy about that, because spying on the chapel of Priapus was not without its risks, and he preferred to have the strong, fearless bar-Heap along in case they blundered into any trouble. Maximilianus, though, did not appear to be worried. The prince's mood seemed an unusually impetuous one, even for him, this day. His fury over his brother's absence and the strain of his father's illness had left him very tightly strung indeed, a man who gave every indication of being on the verge of some immense explosion.

But his demeanor was calm enough as he led the way down the winding ramp that entered the Underworld beside the Baths of Constantinus and guided them toward the grotto where the rites of Priapus were enacted. The passageway was low-roofed and moist-walled, with splotchy gray-green fungoid stains clinging to its sides. Menandros, as they neared their goal, displayed such signs of boyish anticipation that Faustus felt both amusement and contempt. Did they no longer have any such shady cults in Constantinopolis? Was Justinianus such a stern master that they had all been suppressed, when Justinianus's own wife Theodora was herself a former actress, said to be of the loosest morality imaginable?

"This way," Maximilianus whispered, indicating an opening in the cavern wall, the merest sliver of an entrance. "It takes us up and over the chapel, where we'll have a very good view. But be absolutely quiet in there. A single sneeze and we're done for, because this is the only way out, and they'll be waiting for us here with hatchets if they find out we've been spying on them."

The passage slanted sharply upward. It was impossible for men as tall as Maximilianus or Faustus to stand upright in it, though Menandros had no difficulty. The nimble young Maximilianus moved easily there, but Faustus, slow and bulky, found every step a challenge. Quickly he was sweating and panting. Once he banged his lantern against the wall and sent a reverberant thump down the length of the passage that drew an angry hiss and a glare from Maximilianus.

Before long came confirmation that a service was in progress: a clash of cymbals, the booming of drums, the hoarse screech of horns, the high jabbing of flutes. When they reached the place from which the scene below could best be viewed, Maximilianus gestured for the lanterns to be laid to one side where they would cast no gleam that could be spied from the shrine, and moved Menandros into position for the best view.

Faustus did not even try to look. He had seen it all too many times before: the wall covered with gaudy erotic murals, the great altar of the god of lust, and the seated figure of Priapus himself with his enormous phallus rising like a pillar of stone from his thighs. Half a dozen naked worshippers, all of them women, were dancing before that fearsome idol. Their bodies were oiled and painted; their eyes had a wild, frantic shine; their nostrils were distended, their lips were drawn back in toothy grimaces, and the dancers' swinging breasts bobbled freely about as they leaped and pranced.

Chanted words came up from below, harsh jabbing rhythms:

"Come to me, great Lord Priapus, as sunlight comes to the morning sky. Come to me, great Lord Priapus, and give me favor, sustenance, elegance, beauty, and delight. Your names in heaven are LAMPTHEN — OUOTH OUASTHEN — OUTHI OAMENOTH — ENTHOMOUCH. And I know your forms: in the east you are an ibis, in the west you are a wolf, in the north you have the form of a serpent, and in the south you are an eagle. Come to me, Lord Priapus — come to me, Lord Priapus, come — "

One by one the women danced up to the great statue, kissed the tip of that great phallus, caressed it lasciviously.

"I invoke you, Priapus! Give me favor, form, beauty! Give me delight. For you are I, and I am you. Your name is mine, and mine is yours."

There was a tremendous demoniacal clatter of drumming. Faustus knew what that meant: one of the worshippers was mounting the statue of the god. Menandros, avidly staring, leaned much too far forward. At this stage of the ceremony there was little risk that any of the impassioned celebrants would look upward and catch a glimpse of him, but there was some danger that he might go tumbling down into the cavern below and land amongst them. It had been known to happen. Death was the penalty for any man caught spying on the rites of the adherents of Priapus. Faustus reached for him; but Maximilianus had already caught him and was tugging him back.

Though covert surveillance of these rites was forbidden, men were not entirely excluded from the chapel. Faustus knew that five or six strapping slaves were lined up along the wall of the chapel in the shadows behind statue. Soon the priestess of Priapus would give the signal and the orgy would begin.

They practically needed to drag Menandros away. He crouched by the rim of the aperture like a small boy greedy to discover the intimate secrets of womankind, and even after the event had gone on and on long beyond the point where even the most curious of men should have been sated by the sight, Menandros wanted to see more. Faustus was baffled by this strange hunger of his. He could barely remember a time when any of what was taking place down there had been new and unfamiliar to him, and it was hard to understand Menandros's passionate curiosity over so ordinary a matter as orgiastic copulation. The court of the Emperor Justinianus, Faustus thought, must place an extraordinarily high value on chastity and propriety. But that was not what Faustus had been told.

At last they got the ambassador out of there and they went on to the next place on his list, the pool of the Baptai. "I'll wait for you here," said Faustus, as they arrived at the steep spiraling stairway that led down into the pit of utter blackness where the rites of this cult of immersion occurred. "I'm getting too fat and slow for that much clambering."

It was, he knew, an enchanting place: the smooth-walled rock-hewn chambers bedecked with iridescent glass mosaics in white and red and blue, brightened even further by splashes and touches of vivid golden paint, the scenes of Diana at the hunt, of cooing doves, of cupids swimming among swans, of voluptuous nymphs, of rampant satyrs. But the air was damp and heavy, the interminable downward spiral of the narrow, slippery stone steps would be hard on his aging legs, and the final taxing stage of the long descent, the one that went from the chamber of the mosaics to the fathomless black pool that lay at the lowest level, was beyond all doubt much too much for him. And of course the mere thought of the ascent afterward was utterly appalling.

So he waited. A tinkling trickle of laughter drifted up to him out of the darkness. The goddess Bendis of Thrace was the deity worshipped here, a coarse lank-haired demon whose devotees were utterly shameless, and at any hour of the day or night one generally could find a service in progress, a ritual that involved the usual sort of orgiastic stuff enlivened by a climactic baptismal plunge into the icy pool, where Bendis lurked to provide absolution for sins just committed and encouragement for those yet to come. This was no secret cult. All were welcome here. But the mysteries of the cult of Bendis were no longer mysterious to Faustus. He had had baptism in those freezing waters often enough for one lifetime; he did not seek it again. And the skillful ministrations of his Numidian playmate Oalathea were gratification enough for his diminishing lusts these days.

It was a very long time before Menandros and Maximilianus returned from the depths. They said little when they emerged, but it was clear from the flushed, triumphant look on the little Greek's face that he had found whatever ecstasies he had been seeking in the shrine of the Baptai.

Now it was time for the place of the Chaldean whores, far across the underground city near the welter of caverns below the Circus Maximus. Menandros seemed to have heard a great deal about these women, most of it incorrect. "You mustn't call them whores, you know," Faustus explained. "What they are is prostitutes—sacred prostitutes."

"This is a very subtle distinction," said the Greek wryly.

"What he means," said the Caesar, "is that they're all women of proper social standing, who belong to a cult that came to us out of Babylonia.

Some of them are of Babylonian descent themselves, most are not. Either way, the women of this cult are required at some point in their lives, between the ages of — what is it, Faustus, sixteen and thirty? — something like that — to go to the sanctuary of their goddess and sit there waiting for some stranger to come along and choose her for the night. He throws a small silver coin into her lap, and she must rise and go with him, however hideous he is, however repellent. And with that act she fulfills her obligation to her goddess, and returns therewith to a life of blameless purity."

"Some, I understand, are said to go back more than once to fulfill their obligations," Faustus said. "Out of an excess of piety, I suppose. Unless it is for the simple excitement of meeting strangers, of course,"

"I must see this," Menandros said. He was aglow with boyish eagerness again. "Virtuous women, you say, wives and daughters of substantial men? And they *must* give themselves? They can't refuse under any circumstances? Justinianus will find this hard to believe."

"It is an Eastern thing," said Faustus. "Out of Babylonian Chaldea. How strange that you have none of this at your own capital." It did not ring true. From all accounts Faustus had heard, Constantinopolis was at least as much a hotbed of Oriental cults as Roma itself. He began to wonder whether there was some reason of state behind Menandros's apparent desire to paint the Eastern Empire as a place of such rigorous piety and virtue. Perhaps it had something to do with the terms of the treaty that Menandros had come here to negotiate. But he could not immediately see what the connection might be.

Nor did they see the holy Chaldean prostitutes that day. They were less than halfway across the Underworld when they became aware of a muddled din of upraised voices coming to them out of the Via Subterranea ahead, and as they drew closer to that broad thoroughfare they began to distinguish some detail of individual words. The shouts still were blurred and confused, but what they seemed to be saying was:

"The Emperor is dead! The Emperor is dead!"

"Can it be?" Faustus asked. "Am I hearing rightly?"

But then it came again, a male voice with the force of the bellowings of a bull rising above all the others: "THE EMPEROR IS DEAD! THE EMPEROR IS DEAD!" There was no possible doubt of the meaning now.

"So soon," Maximilianus murmured, in a voice that could have been that of a dead man itself. "It wasn't supposed to happen today."

Faustus glanced toward the Caesar. His face was chalk-white, as though he had spent his whole life in these underground caverns, and his eyes had a hard, frightening glitter to them that gave them the look of brilliantly polished sapphires. Those stony eyes were terrifying to behold.

A man in the loose yellow robes of some Asian priesthood came running toward them, looking half unhinged by fear. He stumbled up against Maximilianus in the narrow hallway and tried to shoulder his way past, but the Caesar, seizing the man by both forearms and holding him immobilized, thrust his face into the other's and demanded to know the news. "His Majesty —" the man gasped, goggle-eyed. He had a thick Syrian lisp. "Dead. They have lit the great bonfire before the palace. The Praetorians have gone into the street to maintain order."

Muttering a curse, Maximilianus shoved the Syrian away from him so vehemently that the man went ricocheting off the wall, and turned his gaze toward Faustus. "I must go to the palace," the Caesar said, and without another word turned and ran, leaving Faustus and Menandros behind as he vanished in furious long-legged strides toward the Via Subterranea.

Menandros looked overwhelmed by the news. "We should not be here either," he said.

"No. We should not."

"Are we to go to the palace, then?"

"It could be dangerous. Anything can happen, when an Emperor dies and the heir apparent isn't on the scene." Faustus slipped his arm through the Greek's. Menandros appeared startled at that, but seemed quickly to understand that it was for the sake of keeping them from being separated in the growing chaos of the underground city. Thus linked, they set out together for the nearest exit ramp.

The news had spread everywhere by now, and hordes of people were running madly to and fro. Faustus, though his heart was pounding from the exertion, moved as quickly as he was able, virtually dragging Menandros along with him, using his bulk to shove anyone who blocked his path out of the way.

"The Emperor is dead!" the endless chorus cried. "The Emperor is dead!" As he came forth blinking into the daylight, Faustus saw the look of stunned shock on every face.

He felt a little stunned himself, though Emperor Maximilianus's passing had not exactly come as a bolt out of the blue to him. But the old man had held the throne for more than forty years, one of the longest reigns in Roman history, longer even than Augustus's, perhaps second only to that of his grandfather the first Maximilianus. These Etruscan Emperors were long-lived men. Faustus had been a slender stripling the last time the Imperial throne had changed hands, and that other time the succession had been handled well, the magnificent young prince who was to become Maximilianus II standing at the side of his dying father in his last moments, and going immediately thereafter to the temple of Jupiter Capitolinus to receive the homage of the Senate and to accept the badges and titles of office.

This was a different situation. There was no magnificent young heir waiting to take the throne, only the deplorable Prince Heraclius, and Heraclius had so contrived matters that he was not even at the capital on the day of his father's death. Great surprises sometimes happened when the throne became vacant and the expected heir was not on hand to claim it. That was how the stammering cripple Claudius had become Emperor when Caligula was assassinated. That was how Titus Gallius had risen to greatness after the murder of Caracalla. For that matter, that was the way the first of the Etruscans had come to power, when Theodosius, having outlived his own son Honorius, had finally died in 1168. Who could say what shifts in the balance of power might be accomplished in Roma before this day reached its end?

It was Faustus's duty now to get Justinianus's ambassador safely back to the Severan Palace, and then to make his own way to the Chancellery to await the developments of the moment. But Menandros did not quite seem to grasp the precariousness of the situation. He was fascinated by the tumult in the streets, and, feckless tourist that he was at heart, wanted to head for the Forum to watch the action at first hand. Faustus had to push the bounds of diplomatic courtesy a little to get him to abandon that foolhardy idea and head for the safety of his own quarters. Menandros agreed reluctantly, but only after seeing a phalanx of Praetorians moving through the street across from them, freely clubbing anyone who seemed to be behaving in a disorderly fashion.

Faustus was the last of the officials of the Chancellery to reach the administrative headquarters, just across the way from the royal palace. The Chancellor, Licinius Obsequens, greeted him sourly. "Where have you been all this while, Faustus?"

"With the ambassador Menandros, touring the Underworld," Faustus replied, just as sourly. He cared very little for Licinius Obsequens, a wealthy Neapolitan who had bribed his way to high office, and he suspected that under the new Emperor neither he nor Licinius Obsequens would continue to hold their posts at the Chancellery, anyway. "The ambassador was very eager to visit the chapel of Priapus, and other such places," Faustus added, with a bit of malice to his tone. "So we took him there. How was I to know that the Emperor was going to die today?"

"*We* took him, Faustus?"

"The Caesar Maximilianus and I."

Licinius's yellowish eyes narrowed to slits. "Of course. Your good friend the Caesar. And where is the Caesar now, may I ask?"

"He left us," said Faustus, "the moment news reached us underground of His Majesty's death. I have no information about where he might be at the present time. The Imperial palace, I would imagine." He paused a moment. "And the Caesar Heraclius, who is our Emperor now? Has anyone happened to hear from him?"

"He is at the northern frontier," Licinius said.

"No. No, he isn't. He's off at his hunting lodge behind Lake Nemorensis. He never went north at all."

Licinius was visibly rocked by that. "You know this for a fact, Faustus?"

"Absolutely. I sent a message to him there, just the other night, and he came back to the city that evening and met with the ambassador Menandros. I was there, as it happens." A look of sickly astonishment came over Licinius's jowly face. Faustus was beginning to enjoy this more than somewhat. "The Caesar then went back to his forest preserve yesterday morning. Early today, when I was informed of His Majesty's grave condition, I sent a second message to him at the lake, once more summoning him to Roma. Beyond that I can tell you nothing."

"You knew that the Caesar was hunting, and not at the frontier, and never reported this to me?" Licinius asked.

Loftily Faustus said, "Sir, I was wholly preoccupied with looking after the Greek ambassador. It is a complicated task. It never occurred to me that you were unaware of the movements of the Caesar Heraclius. I suppose I assumed that when he reached Roma the night before last he would take the trouble to meet with his father's Chancellor and ascertain the state of his father's health, but evidently it didn't occur to him to do that, and therefore—"

Abruptly he cut his words short. Asellius Proculus, the Prefect of the Praetorian Guard, had just shouldered his way into the room. For the Praetorian Prefect to set foot in the Chancellery at all was an unusual event; for him to be here on the day of the Emperor's death verged on the unthinkable. Licinius Obsequens, who was starting to look like a man besieged, gaped at him in consternation.

"Asellius? What—"

"A message," the Praetorian Prefect said hoarsely. "From Lake Nemorensis." He signaled with an upraised thumb and a man in the green uniform of the Imperial courier service came lurching in. He was glassy-eyed and rumpled and haggard, as though he had run all the way from the lake without pausing. Pulling a rolled-up despatch from his tunic, he thrust it with a trembling hand toward Licinius Obsequens, who snatched at it, opened it, read it through, read it again. When the Chancellor looked up at Faustus his plump face was sagging in shock.

"What does it say?" Faustus asked. Licinius seemed to be having difficulties forming words.

"The Caesar," Licinius said. "His Majesty the Emperor, that is. Wounded. A hunting accident, this morning. He remains at his lodge. The Imperial surgeons have been called."

"Wounded? How seriously?"

Licinius responded with a blank look. "Wounded, it says. That's all: wounded. The Caesar has been wounded, while hunting. The Emperor… He *is* our Emperor now, is he not?" The Chancellor seemed numb, as though he had had a stroke. To the courier he said, "Do you know any other details, man? How badly is he hurt? Did you see him yourself? Who's in charge at the lodge?" But the courier knew nothing. He had been given the message by a member of the Caesar's guard and told to get it immediately to the capital; that was all he was able to report.

***

Four hours later, dining with the ambassador Menandros in the ambassador's rooms at the Severan Palace, Faustus said, "The messages continued to come in from the lake all afternoon. Wounded, first. Then, wounded seriously. Then a description of the wound: speared in the gut by one of his own men, he was, some sort of confusion while they were closing in on a boar for the kill, somebody's horse rearing at the wrong moment. Then the next message, half an hour later: the Imperial surgeons are optimistic. Then, the Caesar Heraclius is dying. And then: the Caesar Heraclius is dead."

"The Emperor Heraclius, should you not call him?" Menandros asked.

"It's not certain who died first, the Emperor Maximilianus at Roma or the Caesar Heraclius at Lake Nemorensis. I suppose they can work all that out later. But what difference does it make, except to the historians? Dead is dead. Whether he died as Heraclius Caesar or as Heraclius Augustus, he's still dead, and his brother is our next Emperor. Can you believe it? Maximilianus going to be Emperor? One moment he's wallowing around with you in some orgy at the pool of the Baptai, and the next he's sitting on the throne. Maximilianus! The last thing he ever imagined, becoming Emperor."

"That soothsayer told him that he would," Menandros said.

A shiver of awe ran through Faustus. "Yes! Yes, by Isis, so he did! And Maximilianus was as furious as though the man had laid a curse on him. Which perhaps he had." Shakily he refilled his wine-bowl. "*Emperor!* Maximilianus!"

"Have you seen him yet?"

"No, not yet. It isn't seemly to rush to him so fast."

"You were his closest friend, weren't you?"

"Yes, yes, of course. And doubtless there'll be some benefit to that." Faustus allowed himself a little smirk of pleasure. "Under Heraclius, I'd have been finished, I suppose. Pensioned off, shipped to the country. But it'll be different for me with Maximilianus in charge. He'll need me. He will, won't he?" The thought had only then occurred to him in any coherent way. But the more he examined it, the more it pleased him. "He's never cultivated any of the court officials; he doesn't know them, really, won't know which ones to trust, which to get rid of. I'm the only one who can advise him properly. I might even become Chancellor, Menandros, do you realize that? — But that's exactly why I haven't gone speeding over to see him tonight. He's busy with the priests, anyway, doing whatever religious rites it is a new Emperor is supposed to perform, and then the Senators are calling on him one by one, and so on and so forth. It would be too blatant, wouldn't it, if I turned up there so soon, his bawdy and disreputable old drinking companion Faustus, who by coming around the very first night would be sending an all too obvious signal that he's showing up right away to claim his reward for these years of hearty good fellowship the two of us have shared. No, Menandros, I wouldn't do anything so crass. Maximilianus is not going to forget me. Tomorrow, I suppose, he'll be holding his first *salutatio,* and I can come around then and—"

"His what? I don't know the word."

"*Salutatio?* You must know what that means. In your language you'd say, 'a greeting.' But what it is in Imperial terms is a mass audience with the Roman populace: the Emperor sits enthroned in the Forum, and the people pass before him and salute him and hail him as Emperor. It'll be quite appropriate for me to go before him then, with all the rest. And have him smile at me, and wink, and say, 'Come to me after all this nonsense is over, Faustus, because we have important things to discuss.'"

"This is not a custom we have at Constantinopolis, the *salutatio,*" Menandros said.

"A Roman thing, it is."

"We are Romans also, you know."

"So you are. But you are Greekified Romans, you Easterners—in your particular case, a Romanized Greek, even—with customs that bear the tincture of the old Oriental despots who lie far back in your history, the Pharaohs, the Persian kings, Alexander the Great. Whereas we are Romans of Roma. We once had a Republic here that chose its leaders every year, do you know that?—two outstanding men whom the Senate picked to share power with each other, and at the end of their year they would step down and two others were brought forward. We lived like that for hundreds of years, ruled by our Consuls, until a few problems arose and it became necessary for Augustus Caesar to alter the arrangements somewhat. But we still maintain some traces of that staunch old Republic of the early days. The *salutatio* is one of them."

"I see," Menandros said. He did not sound impressed. He busied himself with his wine for a time. Then, breaking a long silence that had developed between them, he said, "You don't think Prince Maximilianus might have had his brother murdered, do you?"

"What?"

"Hunting accidents aren't all that hard to arrange. A scuffle among the horses in the morning fog, an unfortunate little collision, a spear thrust in the wrong place—"

"Are you serious, Menandros?"

"About half, I'd say. These things have been known to happen. Even I could see from the very first what contempt Maximilianus had for his brother. And now the old Emperor is on his last legs. The Empire will go to the unpopular and inadequate Heraclius. So your friend the Caesar, either for the good of the Empire or purely out of the love of power, decides to have Heraclius removed, just as the Emperor is plainly sinking toward his end. The assassin then is slain also, to keep him quiet in case there's an inquest and he's put to the torture, and there you are—Heraclius is gone and Maximilianus III Augustus is in charge. It's not impossible. What became of the man who put the spear into Prince Heraclius, do you by any chance know?"

"He killed himself within an hour of the event, as a matter of fact, out of sheer chagrin. Do you think Maximilianus bribed him to do that, too?"

Menandros smiled faintly and made no reply. This was all just a game for him, Faustus realized.

"The good of the Empire," Faustus said, "is not a concept upon which the Caesar Maximilianus has ever expended much thought. If you were listening closely to much of what he said when he was in our company, you might have perceived that. As for the love of power, here you will have to take my word for it, but I think he has not an atom of that within himself. You saw how enraged he became when that idiot of a soothsayer told him he was going to be a great hero of the Empire? 'You are mocking me to my face,' Maximilianus said, or words to that effect. And then, when the man went on to predict that Maximilianus was going to become Emperor, too—" Faustus laughed. "No, my friend, there was never any conspiracy here. Not even in his dreams did Maximilianus see himself as an Emperor. What happened to Prince Heraclius was mere accident, the gods making sport with us yet again, and my guess is that our new Emperor is having a hard time coming to terms with fate's little prank. I would go so far as to say that he is the unhappiest man in Roma tonight."

"Poor Roma," said Menandros.

***

A *salutatio*, yes, the very next day. Faustus was correct about that. The line was already forming when he got himself down to the Forum, bathed and shaven and clad in his finest toga, in the third hour after sunrise.

And there was Maximilianus, resplendent in the purple Imperial toga with the border of threads of gold, sitting enthroned in front of the Temple of Jupiter Imperator. A crown of laurel was on his head. He looked magnificent, as a new Emperor should: utterly upright of posture, a calm, graceful figure who displayed in every aspect an almost godlike look of the highest nobility far removed from any expression Faustus had seen him wear during his roistering days. Faustus's bosom swelled with pride at the sight of him sitting like that. What a superb actor the Caesar is, Faustus thought, what a glorious fraud!

But I must not think of him as the Caesar any more. Wonder of wonders, he is the Augustus now, Maximilianus III of Roma.

The Praetorians were keeping the line under careful control. The members of the Senate had already passed through, it seemed, because Faustus saw none of them in evidence. That was appropriate: they should be the first to hail a new Emperor. Faustus was pleased to note that he had arrived just in time to join the line of officials of the late Emperor's court. He caught sight of Chancellor Licinius up ahead, and the Minister of the Privy Purse, the Chamberlain of the Imperial Bedroom, the Master of the Treasury, the Master of the Horses, and most of the others, down to such mid-level people as the Prefect of Works, the Master of Greek Letters, the Secretary of the Council, the Master of Petitions. Faustus, joining the group, exchanged nods and smiles with a few of them, but said nothing to anyone. He knew that he was conspicuous among them, not only because of his height and bulk, but also because they must all be aware that he was the dearest friend the unexpected new Emperor had, and was likely to receive significant preferment in the administration that soon would be taking form. The golden aura of power, Faustus thought, must already be gathering about his shoulders as he stood here in the line.

The line moved forward at a very slow pace. Each man in turn, as he came before Maximilianus, made the proper gestures of respect and obeisance, and Maximilianus responded with a smile, a word or two, an amiable lifting of his hand. Faustus was amazed at the easy assurance of his manner. He seemed to be enjoying this, too. It might all be a wondrous pretense, but Maximilianus was making it seem as though it were he, and not the lamented Prince Heraclius, who had been schooled all his life for this moment of ascension to the summit of power.

And at last Faustus himself was standing before the Emperor.

"Your Majesty," Faustus murmured humbly, relishing the words. He bowed. He knelt. He closed his eyes a moment to savor the wonder of it all. *Rise, Faustus Flavius Constantinus Caesar, you who are to be Imperial*

Chancellor in the government of the third Maximilianus, is what he imagined the Emperor would say.

Faustus rose. The Emperor said nothing at all. His lean, youthful face was solemn. His blue eyes seemed cold and hard. It was the iciest look Faustus had ever seen.

"Your Majesty," Faustus said again, in a huskier, more rasping tone this time. And then, very softly, with a smile, a bit of the old twinkle: "What an ironic turn of fate this all is, Maximilianus! How playful destiny is with our lives!—Emperor! Emperor! And I know what pleasure you will get from it, my lord."

The icy gaze was unrelenting. A quiver of something like impatience, or perhaps it was irritation, was visible on Maximilianus's lips. "You speak as though you know me," the Emperor said. "Do you? And do I know you?"

That was all. He beckoned, the merest movement of the tips of the fingers of his left hand, and Faustus knew that he must move along. The Emperor's words resounded in his mind as he made his way across the front of the temple and up the path that led from the Forum to the Palatine Hill. *Do you know me? Do I know you?*

Yes. He knew Maximilianus, and Maximilianus knew him. It was all a joke, Maximilianus having a little amusement at his expense in this first meeting between them since everything had changed. But some things, Faustus knew, had not changed, and never could. They had seen in the dawn together too many times, the prince and he, for any transformation to come over their friendship now, however strangely and marvelously Maximilianus himself had been transformed by his brother's death.

But still—

Still—

It was a joke, yes, that Maximilianus had been playing on him, but it was a cruel one for all that, and although Faustus knew that the prince could be cruel, the prince had never been cruel to him. Until now. And perhaps even not even now. It had been mere playfulness just now, those words of his. Yes. Yes. Mere playfulness, nothing more, Maximilianus's style of humor making itself known even here on the day of his ascent to the throne.

Faustus returned to his lodgings.

For the three days following, he had little company but his own. The Chancellery, like all the offices of the government, would be closed all this week for the double funeral of the old Emperor Maximilianus and the prince his son, and then the ceremonies of installation of the new Emperor Maximilianus. Maximilianus himself was inaccessible to Faustus, as he was to virtually everyone but the highest officials of the realm. During the formal days of mourning the streets of the city were quiet, for once. Not even the Underworld would be stirring. Faustus remained at home, too dispirited to bother summoning his Numidian. When he wandered over to the Severan Palace to see Menandros, he was told that the ambassador, as the representative in Roma of the new Emperor's Imperial colleague of the East, the Basileus Justinianus, had been called into conference at the royal palace, and would be staying at the palace for the duration of the meetings.

On the fourth day Menandros returned. Faustus saw the litter bearing him crossing the Palatine, and unhesitatingly hurried across to the Severan to greet him. Perhaps Menandros would bear some word for him from Maximilianus.

Indeed he did. Menandros handed Faustus a bit of parchment sealed with the Imperial seal and said, "The Emperor gave me this for you."

Faustus yearned to open it at once, but that seemed unwise. He realized he was a little afraid of finding out what Maximilianus had to say to him, and preferred not to read the message in front of Menandros.

"And the Emperor?" Faustus asked. "You found him well?"

"Very well. Not at all troubled by the cares of office, thus far. He has made an excellent adaptation to the great change in his circumstances. You may have been wrong about him, my friend, when you said he had no interest in being Emperor. I think he rather likes being Emperor."

"He can be very surprising at times," said Faustus.

"I think that is true. Be that as it may, my task here is done. I thank you for your good company, friend Faustus, and for your having enabled me to gain the friendship of the former Caesar Maximilianus. A happy accident, that was. The days I spent with the Caesar in the Underworld greatly facilitated the negotiations I have now completed with him on the treaty of alliance."

"There is a treaty, is there?"

"Oh, yes, most definitely a treaty. His Majesty will marry the Emperor Justinianus's sister Sabbatia in the place of his late and much lamented brother. His Majesty has a gift of some wonderful jewelry to offer his bride: magnificent gems, opals, quite fine. He showed them to me himself. And there will be military assistance, of course. The Eastern Empire will send its finest legions to aid your Emperor in crushing the barbarians who trouble your borders." Menandros's cheeks were glowing with pleasure. "It has all gone very well, I think. I will leave tomorrow. You will send me, I hope, some of that noble wine of Gallia Transalpina that you shared with me on my first day in Roma? And I will have gifts for you as well, my friend. I am deeply grateful to you for everything. In particular," he said, "for the chapel of Priapus, and the pool of the Baptai, eh, friend Faustus?" And he winked.

Faustus lost no time unsealing the Emperor's message once he had escaped from Menandros.

> *You said you thought our time of greatness was ending, Faustus,*
> *that day in the marketplace of the sorcerers. But no, Faustus,*
> *you are wrong. We are not ended at all. We are only just begun.*
> *It is a new dawn and a new sun rises.*

M.

And there below that casually scrawled initial was the formal signature in all its majesty, Imperator Caesar Maximilianus Tiberius Antoninus Augustus Imperator.

***

Faustus's pension was a generous one, and when he and Maximilianus met, as occasionally they did in the early months of Maximilianus's reign, the Emperor was affable enough, with always the amicable word, though they never were intimates again. And in the second year of his reign Maximilianus went north to the frontier, where the legions of his royal colleague Justinianus were assembling to join him, and he remained there, doing battle against the barbarians, for the next seven years, which were the last years of Faustus's life.

The northern wars of Maximilianus III ended in complete triumph. Roma would have no further trouble with invading barbarians. It was a significant turning point in the history of the Empire, which now was free to enter into a time of prosperity and abundance such as it had not known since the great days of Trajan and Hadrianus and Antoninus Pius four centuries before. There had been two mighty Emperors named Maximilianus before him, but men would never speak of the third Maximilianus otherwise than as Maximilianus the Great.

ACKNOWLEDGMENTS

The Road to Nightfall, Copyright © 1958, 1986 by Agberg, Ltd. First published in FANTASTIC UNIVERSE.

The Macauley Circuit, Copyright © 1956, 1984 by Agberg, Ltd. First published in FANTASTIC UNIVERSE.

Sunrise on Mercury, Copyright © 1957, 1985 by Agberg, Ltd. First published in SCIENCE FICTION STORIES.

Warm Man, Copyright © 1957, 1985 by Agberg, Ltd. First published in FANTASY & SCIENCE FICTION.

To See the Invisible Man, Copyright © 1963, 1991 by Agberg, Ltd. First published in WORLDS OF TOMORROW.

Flies, Copyright © 1967, 1995 by Agberg, Ltd. First published in DANGEROUS VISIONS.

Nightwings, Copyright © 1968, 1996 by Agberg, Ltd. First published in GALAXY SCIENCE FICTION.

Passengers, Copyright © 1968, 1996 by Agberg, Ltd. First published in ORBIT.

Sundance, Copyright © 1969, 1997 by Agberg, Ltd. First published in FANTASY & SCIENCE FICTION.

Good News from the Vatican, Copyright © 1971, 1999 by Agberg, Ltd. First published in UNIVERSE.

Capricorn Games, Copyright © 1974 by Agberg, Ltd. First published in THE FAR SIDE OF TIME.

Born with the Dead, Copyright © 1974 by Agberg, Ltd. First published in FANTASY & SCIENCE FICTION.

Schwartz between the Galaxies, Copyright © 1974 by Agberg, Ltd. First published in STELLAR SCIENCE FICTION.

The Far Side of the Bell-Shaped Curve, Copyright © 1980 by Agberg, Ltd. First published in OMNI.

The Pope of the Chimps, Copyright © 1982 by Agberg, Ltd. First published in PERPETUAL LIGHT.

Needle in a Timestack, Copyright © 1983 by Agberg, Ltd. First published in PLAYBOY.

Sailing to Byzantium, Copyright © 1985 by Agberg, Ltd. First published in ISAAC ASIMOV'S SCIENCE FICTION MAGAZINE.

Enter a Soldier. Later: Enter Another, Copyright © 1989 by Agberg, Ltd. First published in ISAAC ASIMOV'S SCIENCE FICTION MAGAZINE.

Hunters in the Forest, Copyright © 1991 by Agberg, Ltd. First published in OMNI.

Death Do Us Part, Copyright © 1996 by Agberg, Ltd. First published in OMNI ON-LINE.

Beauty in the Night, Copyright © 1997 by Agberg, Ltd. First published in SCIENCE FICTION AGE.

The Millennium Express, Copyright © 1999 by Agberg, Ltd. First published in PLAYBOY.

With Caesar in the Underworld, Copyright © 2002 by Agberg, Ltd. First published in ASIMOV'S SCIENCE FICTION.

623

To order a copy of Robert Silverberg's *Phases of the Moon*
as a limited hardcover edition, or to order other
Subterranean Press titles, please contact us in one of
the following ways:

Subterranean Press
P. O. Box 190106
Burton, MI 48519

e-mail:
info@subterraneanpress.com

website:
www.subterraneanpress.com